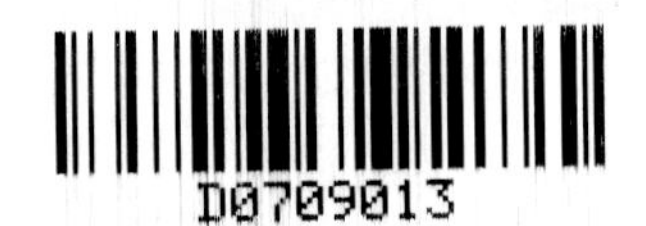

MAGGIE SHAYNE

★★★THE★★★ TEXAS BRAND:

In the Beginning

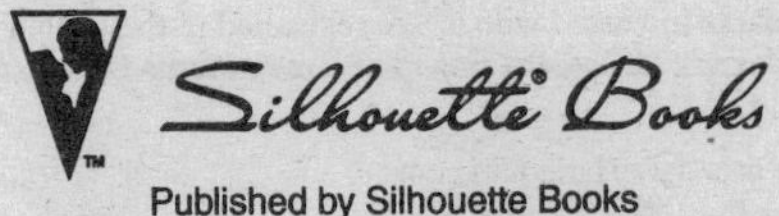

Published by Silhouette Books
America's Publisher of Contemporary Romance

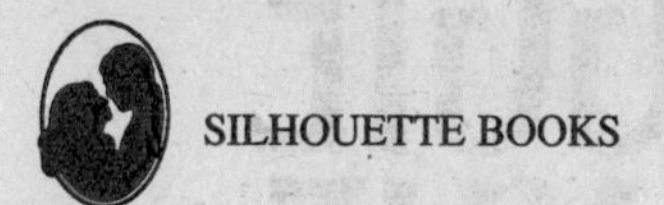

ISBN 0-373-18510-3

by Request

THE TEXAS BRAND: IN THE BEGINNING

This edition published by arrangement with Harlequin Books S.A.

Visit Silhouette at www.eHarlequin.com

Printed in U.S.A.

CONTENTS

Dear Reader,

Way back in the dawn of time, when I was a brand-new, starry-eyed writer, a very wise editor suggested that I might want to try writing a Western romance.

I did not want to. I wrote two things: paranormal and suspense. Period. But the editor kept nudging me, saying things like, "You can do paranormal or suspense. Just try setting one of them in, oh, say, Texas, and see what happens."

Meanwhile, my husband was asking what the heck I had against Westerns anyway? I loved to watch them on TV, and I adored reading Louis L'Amour and Zane Grey novels. So what was my problem?

Finally, reluctantly, I gave in, and agreed to write "one, and ONLY one," romance set in Texas. To gear up for the book, I read a pile of L'Amour's "Sackett" books, and I fell head over heels in love with that family. What I loved best about the Sacketts was that when one Sackett got into trouble, relatives would just come crawling out of the woodwork to get him out of it. I decided I wanted to create a family like that for my "just one book." I also watched *In the Heat of the Night* reruns (though I'm fully aware that's not a Western show) and found myself irrationally turned on by Bubba Skinner.

So my "one, and only one" Western romance was naturally about an oversize, shy-around-women sheriff, who was also the head of a huge and tightly knit family.

I became so enamored of the Brand family that I simply had to do a book for each member, and then of course there were the missing cousins, and then I discovered the single mom and five sisters who made up the Oklahoma branch of the family.

So far, my "one, and only one" has stretched into eleven. I've just completed the twelfth, and I have plans for at least two more. And who knows where I might find more Brands lurking?

Happy reading,

Maggie Shayne

THE LITTLEST COWBOY

To the Otselic Valley Lady Vikings soccer team of 1995.
You're #1 in my book!

Chapter 1

Garret Brand awoke in a cold sweat, some foreign kind of dread gnawing at his stomach. Heart pounding, he sat up fast and wide-eyed, his fists clenching defensively before he got hold of himself. Blinking the sleep haze from his eyes and taking a few deep breaths, he let his tense muscles relax and unclenched his fists. There was nothing wrong. There was no reason for that panicky feeling that had slipped through him like a ghost slipping through a wall. No reason at all.

And still he couldn't shake it. It hadn't been a bad dream. Far as Garrett could recall, he'd been sleeping like a bear in January until that odd feeling had jerked him awake.

Okay, he'd just take stock.

He sat in the middle of his king-size bed and scanned the room. Red sunlight spilled through the open window, but the curtains hung motionless. No breeze. Already the early-morning air grew heavier, hotter. He listened, but didn't hear anything he hadn't ought to. A horse blowing now and then. A handful of songbirds.

Still, the feeling that something was wrong remained. Garrett had never been much for ESP or any of that nonsense. But stories he'd heard about mothers knowing instinctively when something was wrong with their kids floated through his mind now. He was no mother to Wes, Elliot and Jessi. No father to them, either. But he was as close to a parent as they'd had in almost twenty years. He'd only been seventeen when Orrin and Maria Brand had been killed in that car accident, leaving him as sole caretaker to his five younger siblings. And when he thought about anything happening to any of them…

An odd sound reached him then, a sound that made the hairs on his nape prickle. Soft and faint, but out of place, whatever it was.

Garrett pulled on his jeans, socks and boots in the space of a couple of seconds. He didn't bother with a shirt. But he did yank the revolver out of his top dresser drawer and gave the cylinder a quick spin to be sure it was loaded. On the way out, he snatched the black Stetson from the bedpost and dropped it on his head. It was a gesture so automatic it was done without forethought. Like breathing.

Softly, Garrett moved along the hallway to the next bedroom. He was glad of the braided runner covering the hardwood floor. It cushioned and muffled his steps. He stopped outside the door. Elliot's room, though if you looked inside, you'd think it belonged to a ten-year-old boy, not a man of twenty-five. Lariats and spurs decorated the walls, along with a collection of hats and framed photos of champion cowboys. His closet was an explosion of fringed chaps and hand-tooled boots. Only the sizes had changed over the years. Elliot's dreams never had. He'd lived for the rodeo since he'd been old enough to say the word.

Garrett held his Colt, barrel up in his right hand, and pushed the door open with his left.

The hinges creaked loudly when Garrett stepped through, and Elliot's sleeping face twisted into a grimace. "Whaddaya want?" he muttered, still half-asleep.

Relieved, Garrett stifled his sigh. "I thought I heard something is all. Go back to sleep." He backed toward the door.

Elliot sat up, his rusty hair so tousled he looked like an angry rooster. "What the hell you doing with the gun, Garrett?"

"I told you, I thought I heard something."

"So you're gonna *shoot* it?" This as he climbed out of bed in a pair of baggy pajamas bottoms with rearing mustangs all over them.

Garrett shook his head, not ready to discuss the odd feeling that had awakened him. "I'm going to check on the others."

"I'm coming with you," Elliot said with a pointed look at Garrett's gun. "Just in case you've been so responsible and levelheaded for so long that it's finally driven you over the edge."

Garrett sent him a glare, but Elliot only returned a wink and a crooked grin as he grabbed his hat off the dresser and plunked it on top of his unruly red hair.

They slipped into the hall, and Garrett moved past the next two doors. Adam and Ben had gone their own way last year. Adam had hightailed it to New York City, ostensibly because of a job offer in some bigwig corporation. But everyone knew he'd really moved away because Kirsten Armstrong had left him at the altar to marry an older, richer man, and Adam couldn't stand being in the same town with her anymore. Ben, of course, was trying to find some peace. The hills of Tennessee, where he was living like a hermit, wouldn't heal him, though. Only time could do that, Garrett thought. Ben's young wife had died just about a year ago, and even though they'd both known she was terminal before they'd married, the blow of finally losing her had almost done Ben in.

Garrett and Elliot reached the next room. Wes's. If there were trouble, Wes was likely to be involved. Oh, he'd calmed down a lot since prison. But he still wasn't over the anger of being sent there unjustly. It was a rage Garrett supposed would eat at a man for a long time. And with Wes's temper...well, an explosion always seemed within shouting distance.

He tapped on the door, didn't walk in the way he'd done with Elliot. Wes was still pretty riled up over returning home to find his half brother wearing a badge. And he'd developed a real touchy attitude about privacy, too, while he'd been away. No sense pushing his buttons by walking in unannounced, gun in hand.

The door opened and Wes stood there looking more like a Comanche warrior than a Brand at that moment, despite the jeans and pale denim shirt. His dark hair hung to his shoulders—longer than a man of thirty ought to be wearing it, Garrett thought—and his eyes gleamed like onyx. His Comanche mother had named him Raven Eyes, and Garrett had always thought it incredibly appropriate.

"What is it?"

Garrett shrugged. "I'm not sure. Did you hear anything unusual just now?"

"No, but I was—"

A high, soft sound interrupted Wes, and he went rigid. It seemed to come from farther down the hall, and all three heads turned in that direction. Jessi's room. A second later, the three of them stampeded for their twenty-two-year-old baby sister's door. Garret saw Wes pull that damn bowie knife of his from his boot with a move so quick and smooth and practiced, it seemed to have just materialized in his hand.

They stopped outside Jessi's door, and the sound came again. Not a normal cry. But obviously one of distress. Garrett's blood ran cold when he tried the knob and found the door locked. He didn't even think about it first. He just stepped back and kicked it open. Three Brand men exploded into Jessi's bedroom at once, one holding a Colt, one wielding a bowie and the other poised with fists raised in a boxer's stance, though the effect was probably ruined by the horsey pajamas.

Jessi screeched as she whirled to face them. Then she just rolled her eyes and shook her head. "You idiots! You almost scared me right outta my slippers!"

"Sorry, Jes," Garrett told her, feeling more foolish by the minute. "I thought I heard—"

"Me, too," Jessi said. "But it's coming from outside." She jerked her head in the direction of her open bedroom window.

Garrett lowered his revolver, sighing in relief. "You okay, Jessi?"

She only smiled and shook her short-cropped head in vexation. "How could I not be with you three on duty?" Giving her bathrobe sash a tug for good measure, she shouldered past them, apparently on her way downstairs to investigate the noise.

It was Wes who gripped her shoulder and gently stepped in front of her without a word. She made a face at him, but stayed behind him as they headed through the hall to the wide staircase and started down it. Wes and Garrett in the lead, Jessi and Elliot behind them.

''I think you guys are overreacting. Sounds like a lost calf or something.''

''Shh,'' Elliot warned, but Jessi had never really known when to shut up.

''Garret, you haven't got the sense God gave a goat if you think anyone up to no-good would be lurking around the Texas Brand. Everyone knows you're sheriff of Quinn.''

''Be quiet, Jessi,'' Garrett ordered. They'd reached the bottom of the staircase. The parlor spread out before them, but there was nothing out of place. The huge fireplace they used only rarely. A wide picture window on the far left side that looked out over the lawn and the driveway, and the one on the back wall that faced the barns and unending, flat green fields beyond. They gave no clue. The knotty hardwood walls had nothing to say. The golden oak gun cabinet stood silent, its glass doors still locked up tight.

Blue wasn't in his usual spot in front of the window, though. That alone signaled something wrong. That dog barely moved enough to breathe.

They continued on through the wide archway into the dining room and through that to the kitchen.

The front door loomed at the far end, and there was ol' Blue, poised beside it. Not growling, though. His tail was wagging. *Wagging!* Hell, he was about twenty dog years past his wagging days. He stared at the door, tilting his big head from one side to another. His ears perked as ears that long and floppy could perk. The two black spots above his eyes rose in question as if they were eyebrows.

Garrett tried to swallow, but it felt as if his throat were full of sand. He knew his family—and apparently his dog—thought he was overreacting, but he couldn't shake this feeling, this ominous certainty that something *drastic* was about to happen. Something *horrible* must be awaiting him on the other side of that door.

"Stay here," he said. "Until I make sure it's safe."

"Always a hero," Jessi muttered.

Garrett ignored her and moved forward as his stomach tied itself up in knots. He unlocked the front door and opened it to step out onto the porch.

And then he just stood there, gaping.

A basket sat at his feet. A big basket. And inside the basket, rapidly kicking free of the thin blankets tucked around it, was a fat, smiling baby.

Garrett's gun clattered to the porch's floorboards. He stared down at the infant, too stunned to do much more than push his Stetson farther back on his head.

From behind him, he heard, "Well, I'll be..." and "Who do you suppose..." and "What in the world..."

The baby, though, only had eyes for Garrett. Blue eyes, so blue their whites seemed to have a slight blue tint. It stared at him hard, and then it smiled again, a small trickle of drool running from one corner of its mouth to its double—no, triple—chin.

Blue pushed past the crowd in the doorway and stood two feet from the baby. He looked from it, to Garrett and back again.

"Gaa!" the baby announced.

Blue jumped out of his skin and retreated a few steps.

"Ooohh," Jessi sang, and then she was passing Garrett, scooping that baby up into her arms and snuggling it close to her.

"Garrett, there's a bag over there, and it looks like a note's attached," Elliot said, pointing.

Garrett saw a little satchel with blue and yellow bunnies all over it. A thin red haze of anger clouded his vision, and with his hands on his hips, he turned to face his two brothers, ready to knock their teeth out. "So, which one of you is responsible for this?"

They just looked at him, then at each other.

"How many times have I talked to you about responsibility? Huh? How many times have I told you what it means to father a child? It means you take care of it, dammit. It means you marry the woman and you—"

"Um, Garrett?"

"Not now, Jes. But pay attention. You need to hear this, too. Don't ever let any sweet-talking cowboy with no sense of honor, like either one of these two fine examples right here, talk you into—"

"Garrett, you better read this."

Something in her voice made him clamp his jaw shut. Wes and Elliot, though, both looked decidedly uncomfortable, and he could tell they were mentally going through their list of one-night stands to determine which of them might have resulted in this mess! Garrett wanted to scream and rant and shake them. He'd tried so hard to instill some ethics into them, to be a good example. He never drank, never whored around town the way some did. Hell, he'd been working so hard at showing them how to be men, he'd become known as the most morally upright, impeccably mannered, responsible, reliable, stand-up guy in the state of Texas. To think that one of his own brothers…

"'You were more kind to me than anyone I'd ever known,'" Jessi began, and Garrett came to attention when he realized she was reading from the note. "'Though it was only for one night, I never forgot you. And I knew I could count on you to take care of our son when I realized I no longer could.'"

"You ought to be pretty damned proud of yourselves," Garrett muttered. Blue sat down close beside him, staring at Wes and Elliott, as well.

Jessi read on. "'He's six months old this week. He hates strained peas, but will eat most anything else.'"

"Well, now, that much is obvious," Elliot joked. But no one laughed.

"'I named him after his father. I only hope he'll grow up to be half the man you are.'"

Garrett felt his two brothers tense beside him when Jessi looked up, her eyes round and dark brown.

"Go on, Jessi," he urged. "Read the name."

She blinked at him, eyes wider than a startled doe's before she lowered them to the page once more. "'His name is Garrett Ethan. But I call him Ethan. Please, Garrett, love him. Just love him, and I'll be at peace.'"

He'd been poleaxed right between the eyes. For a second, he didn't move, and nobody else did, either, except that Wes and Elliot seemed to sag just a bit. Relief would do that to a man. Then Garrett shook his head at the absurdity of it all and snatched the letter from his little sister's hand. His eyes sped over the lines.

"Hell, this thing isn't even signed!"

"What's the matter, big brother?" Elliot chirped,

thumbs hooked in the waistband of his baggy pajama bottoms, a lopsided grin pulling at his lips. ''Been so many you can't remember her name?''

Garrett grated his teeth and drew a breath. Calm. He needed calm here. ''This is bull. I didn't father that kid any more than Sam Houston did. It's bull.''

''Sure it is, Garrett.'' Elliot shrugged and glanced at the squirming baby anchored on Jessi's slender hip. ''Well, I'll be damned....''

''What?''

''He has your nose!''

Jessi joined Elliot in laughing out loud.

''Dammit, Elliot—''

''Maybe the sainted Garrett Brand has more of his father's genes in him than we realized,'' Wes broke in, but there wasn't an ounce of humor in *his* voice.

Garrett flinched at the barb, and turned to his sloe-eyed brother. ''Wes, I didn't speak to Pa for six months after I found out about his affair with your mother, and that was *before* I realized he'd fathered you and left you behind to come back to us. I wouldn't do something like that.''

Wes didn't answer, only lifted his black brows and slanted a glance at the baby as if its very presence proved otherwise.

Garrett groaned. ''I can't believe you guys don't believe me.''

''Oh, sure, Garrett! The way you'd have believed us if the little lady had scrawled one of our names on that note, right?''

Elliot had a point, the little bastard.

''Stop all this caterwaulin'. You're scaring the baby!'' Jessi rocked the wide-eyed child in her arms and cooed at him. ''Doesn't matter who fathered him, does it? He's here now and we'll just have to deal with it. Wes, that old wooden cradle is still stored up overhead in the toolshed, isn't it? Go on out there and bring it in, get it cleaned up. And Elliot, the baby quilt Mamma made for me is upstairs in my cedar chest. Bring it out here and hang it over the railing so it can air out some. Garrett, bring the bag and follow me. This son of yours could use a fresh diaper, and you can bet the ranch I'm not doin' it."

Wes and Elliot turned in opposite directions to do her bidding. Jessi reached for the screen door.

"Hold up a second, all of you."

Three pairs of eyes turned to stare at him—no, four pairs. One pair of baby blues fixed on him like laser beams.

Garrett swallowed the bile in his throat, cleared it and said what he had to. "We're not keeping this baby."

Jessi blinked. Elliot shook his head. And Wes just stared at him, condemnation in those black eyes of his.

"Look, I don't know whose child he is, but I do know this. He ain't mine."

"But, Garrett—"

"No buts, Jessi. Somewhere, his real family is out there waiting for him. It wouldn't be fair for us to keep him here. Now, I'm going inside and calling Social Services, and then—"

"Not on a Saturday morning, you aren't," Elliot observed. He lifted his hat and replaced it at a more comfortable angle with just the right amount of smugness. The horsey pajamas ruined the effort, though.

Again, the little bastard had a point. Quinn, Texas was a speck-on-the-map town in a county that wasn't much bigger. There wasn't a thing Garrett could do about this until Monday. Ah, hell, make that Tuesday. Monday was Memorial Day.

"I'll just go get that quilt," Elliott said, and he let the screen door bang closed behind him.

"I'll change little Ethan," Jessi offered, "*this time.* But don't you start thinkin' this is gonna become a habit." She bent to pick up the bunny bag with her free hand.

Garrett held the door for her. "He won't be here long enough for it to become a habit, Jes."

Blue jumped up and trotted into the house beside Jessi. His sister shot Garrett a few daggers as she passed. But they were nothing compared to the glare of Wes's eyes on his back. He felt as if his skin were being seared. He stiffened his shoulders and turned to face his silent accuser.

Wes leaned against the porch railing, eyeing him.

"It's not my kid," Garrett said, and the fact that he sounded so defensive made him as angry as the look in his brother's eyes.

"At least our father owned up to his mistakes, Garrett. When my mother died and he found out about me—"

"When Stands Alone died, Wes, it was *my* mother who found out about you, not Pa. She was the one who went to the reservation to find out if her suspicions were true, and once she knew, there was no question about your coming to live with us. If our father hadn't done right by you, she'd have skinned him."

Wes straightened as Garrett spoke. "You saying Orrin wouldn't have acknowledged me if Maria hadn't forced him?"

"I'm saying who the hell knows *what* he would have done. He was no saint, Wes."

"And neither is his firstborn," Wes said in a dangerously soft voice.

"No, I'm no saint. I never claimed to be. But I didn't father that kid in there, and—"

"And you don't want him." Wes turned away suddenly, an act that made his careless shrug a second later seem false. "What the hell do I care? I don't even like kids." He banged down the three porch steps and started along the well-worn path to the barn.

Garrett would have gone after him, but changed his mind at Jessi's shrill squawk—at least he thought it was Jessi's. It might also have been a bald eagle caught in a blender, but he didn't think that very likely. Ah, hell.

He headed inside.

Jessi had one hand at her stomach and the other over her mouth. Behind her, the baby lay on the parlor floor, his diaper undone, his legs in the air. Garrett took another step forward before the aroma hit him full in the face and made his eyes water.

"I can't do it, Garrett," Jessi gasped, "and there's nothing you can say to make me. Gawd!" She headed up the stairs at light speed.

"Jessi!"

No use. She was long gone. He heard the bedroom door slam, then refocused his gaze on the kid. Damn shame Jessi hadn't laid some newspapers or something underneath him.

Grimacing, he squared his shoulders and strode the rest of the way into the parlor. Blue whimpered from his spot on the floor in front of the window, where he tended to bask in the morning sunlight. Then he lowered his head and put both paws over his nose.

"I know the feeling, Blue." Garrett snatched up the

bunny bag and dug into it. Clean diapers, that horrible disposable kind that lived for ten thousand years in the dump. If he ever had a kid, he'd use cloth. Good ol' cotton, and...

Taking another look at the condition of little Ethan's diaper, he frowned again, seriously rethinking that position. Who'd wanna try to clean something like that? Hell, he'd swabbed out drunk tanks that had been more appealing than...*that.*

He took a diaper from the bag, and a box of premoistened baby wipes, which made him raise his eyebrows.

"Baby wipes, hell," he muttered. "I think you need a high-pressure hose, kid."

"Dababa," Ethan chirped. He wasn't looking at Garrett. Instead, he held one foot in his hand and eyed his own toes with fascination.

Garrett caught himself smiling like an idiot, checked it and dived into the bag again. This time, he emerged with a half-dozen mysterious items. Oil, ointment, powder. He wasn't sure what to use, but figured he could safely rule out the teething lotion.

"Baa!"

"Yeah, I'm coming." He dumped his plunder on the floor, snagged himself about thirty or so baby wipes and wished to God he had a clothespin for his nose and a pair of rubber gloves for his hands. As he hunkered down beside the kid, he revised that wish. What he needed was a full-fledged space suit.

Despite the unpleasantness of it, though, the job didn't take all that long. Snatch the dirty diaper off, clean him up, dust him with powder, tape a fresh diaper firmly in place. Now the question was, what the hell did he do with the, uh, used one? The trash pail in the kitchen was out of the question. He finally decided on the big can out behind the house, though he'd rather incinerate the thing than can it. If this kid ended up sticking around the Texas Brand, they were going to have to invest in an asbestos tank and a flamethrower. Gathering up the diaper and the used baby wipes, he glanced down at Ethan. The baby had managed to pull his foot all the way up to his face and was gnawing on one of his own toes.

"Stunning good looks and talent, too," Garrett told him. "Will wonders never cease? Stay where you are, Ethan."

"Buhbuhbuh," the baby responded, a serious expression on his face.

"Okay. Bubba it is. I'll be right back, Bubba." And he turned to carry the toxic bundle down the hall and out the back door to the trash can. When he came back inside, he stopped in the downstairs bathroom and scrubbed his hands almost raw. Then he sauntered back into the parlor.

Only little Ethan wasn't where he'd been.

"Hey, Bubba," Garrett called. "Where'd you go?"

No answer. What did he expect, an announcement?

Then he spotted the little pudge. He'd crawled over to where ol' Blue lay in that pool of sunlight and was sitting close beside him. Ethan grinned, lifted the prize he'd captured in his little hands and prepared to take his very first bite of hound-dog ear.

"Ethan, *no!*" Garrett dived in a way he hadn't done since high school football and managed to pull a fat little hand away from a drippy little mouth just in time.

Ethan just stared at him, big eyes all innocence.

Blue lifted his head and laid it down again across the baby's legs. This was nothing less than amazing to

Garrett. This morning's activities added up to the most that lazy hound had moved in six months! And he was *never* this friendly. Meanwhile, little hands began smacking down on Blue's head as if it were a bongo drum. Ethan even tried to sing along.

"Gawgawgawgawgagaw..."

Blue's head lifted again. He gave Ethan's chubby cheek a big swipe of dog tongue, then sighed in contentment, closed his droopy eyes and laid his head down in the baby's lap once more.

Garrett swept his hat off with one hand and rumpled his hair with the other. "Well, I'll be..."

Chapter 2

Chelsea Brennan resisted the urge to hug herself against the chill of this room as much as she resisted the urge to grimace at the sickeningly sweet odor of it. The lights were too bright. It ought to be dim in a room like this. Bright lights didn't belong in here. Neither did all the chrome or the shiny white floor tiles.

The cold did, though. The cold was at home here.

The drawer squealed when he pulled it open. Chelsea grated her teeth at the sound. Beneath a stark white sheet, the body jiggled like gelatin when its bed came to a halt. And then an ash gray hand fell to one side and dangled there. Still. Perfect nails, painted pink.

Chelsea didn't move. Couldn't move. Her eyes fixed on the small hand. On every sharply delineated bone and a wrist so narrow it made her wince. Not Michele. Not like this.

"Are you ready, Ms. Brennan?"

She nodded to the white-coated medical examiner,

stiffened her spine and lifted her gaze from that limp hand. He pulled the sheet away from a lifeless face. A face as emaciated as the hand, with sharpened cheekbones and hollowed eyes.

A face she'd never seen before, and yet so dear…so familiar. *Michele.*

A great suction drew all the air from her lungs, and Chelsea couldn't seem to inhale any to replace it. Her jaw worked like the gaping gills of a fish when it's suffocating on dry land. For just an instant, Michele's features swam and re-formed again. Only this time, it was their mother's face Chelsea saw. The circles under Michele's eyes became bruises. Her lips swelled and split.

Chelsea tried harder to draw a breath, but the constriction in her chest wouldn't allow it. Her mouth gaped wider, and she blinked the image of her mother away. Michele. It was Michele lying on the table. Not Mom. Ironic that the resemblance Chelsea saw so clearly now hadn't been apparent before. In death, they could have been twins. And that's when the other similarity became blatantly clear.

The young Texas Ranger who'd been standing in the doorway, as if he couldn't bring himself to move further into the stench of death and disinfectant, came for war now. He stepped in front of her, blocking the body from her sight. And she breathed at last.

"I'm sorry you had to go through this, ma'am."

Sweet, the way he called her "ma'am" all the time. She wondered briefly what vices he kept hidden beneath his compassionate facade.

"Is it her?" he asked, fingers twisting the brim of the hat he held in his hands. "Is it your sister?"

She couldn't meet his eyes as she nodded. Instead,

she focused on the way his hands worked the hat, and she managed to find her voice again. "She's so thin," Chelsea whispered. "Gaunt."

"Drugs will do that to a person, ma'am."

Chelsea's head rose slowly, and she did meet those clear blue eyes this time. "Drugs didn't do this to my sister. A man did."

It was the ranger's turn to avert his eyes. "I'm sorry, ma'am, but she did this to herself. Injected herself with enough heroin to kill a horse."

Chelsea's knees wobbled just a little, but she snapped them into place again by sheer will. "You're saying…suicide?"

"You did say it had been nearly a year since you'd seen her," he reminded her.

"But I talked with her…just last week. We were making plans. I told her I'd fly down here at the end of the month and…"

And she asked if I could come sooner, right away. And there was something in her voice, even though she said she was all right. I should have known….

"No," Chelsea said at last. "No, my sister didn't kill herself."

"It could have been an accidental overdose, ma'am. Maybe she didn't realize how much—"

"She wasn't suicidal, Ranger. And she wasn't stupid, either."

He nodded to the medical examiner, who slid the noisy drawer closed again. Then he touched Chelsea's elbow as if to ease her out of the room, but she jerked away from the contact. She didn't want any man laying a finger on her. Not now. Not ever.

"You'll want these." When she looked his way

again, he was holding out a plastic zipper bag, with a few items inside. "Her personal effects, ma'am."

She blinked, not reaching for the bag. "Don't you need to hold on to them...until the case is closed or—"

"The case *is* closed."

For some reason, her gaze shifted to that drawer again. The one that held her sister on a cold metal table. God, how the hell had the Brennan women come to this? One left. Just one left.

"I want to make it perfectly clear," he said slowly, as if speaking to someone who barely understood the language. He pushed the plastic bag into her hand and turned to start up the stairway, leaving Chelsea no choice but to follow. "There is absolutely no evidence that anyone else stuck that hypodermic into your sister's belly."

Her steps faltered, but she forced herself to continue up the stairs and outside through heavy metal doors. The rain fell harder now, ricocheting of the black-topped parking lot and the shiny cars. The ranger's black umbrella popped open and tilted over her head. No colors here, she thought dully. She'd stepped into a world of black and white. Night, and rain, and heat, and mist hovering low as a result of the other three. She smelled rain and exhaust. Cars passed on the streets of El Paso, their white headlights illuminating the gray building, then leaving it in darkness once more.

She didn't have the strength to argue with the ranger. Not now. Not tonight. Seemed he wasn't open to her input anyway. For now...for now, she only wanted one thing.

She turned to him beneath the sheltering dome of

the umbrella, saw the rainwater streaming from its edges. ''Where is the baby?''

The ranger blinked, his eyes going wider.

''When my sister ran off with that oversize cowboy a year ago, she was pregnant. Last week, when we talked, she told me she had a son. A six-month-old son. Ethan.'' Her throat tightened a little when she said the name. But there were still no tears. There hadn't been tears for Chelsea Brennan in twenty years. ''Where is he?''

The ranger shook his head. ''Ma'am, she was found in an alley outside town. No purse, no ID, and no sign of any baby.''

Chelsea's heart pumped a little faster, a swell of panic rising from the pit of her stomach to engulf it.

''We only knew to call you because we found your name and address on a note in her pocket. We haven't even been able to find out where she was living before she...'' He lowered his head, shook it slowly.

''I don't know where she was living, either. She didn't say, when she called.'' Chelsea pushed her hair off her forehead, closed her eyes. ''I didn't even know she was in Texas before that.''

''Do you know the name of the man she left New York with?''

Chelsea frowned at the mention of the bastard. ''I saw him once, from the window of my apartment. A big guy in a cowboy hat. Michele never talked about him. I imagine she thought I'd disapprove.''

''Why would she think that?''

She lifted her chin, met the younger man's eyes. ''Because I probably would have. My sister had a habit of taking up with losers, Ranger. This one was just the last in a long line of men who treated her like dirt.''

"But you don't know that for sure."

"I'm as sure as I have to be."

For just a moment, he searched her face, then he sighed as if at a loss and started walking again toward her rental car. She kept pace.

"I imagine the child is with his father," he said after a moment.

"With his mother's killer, you mean."

"Ma'am, there's no—"

"Evidence. I know." Chelsea took the keys from her pocket, but then forgot what it was she was supposed to be doing with them and just stared at them in her open palm. "If he didn't have anything to do with this," she said softly, maybe more to herself than to the ranger beside her, "then where is he? Why hasn't he reported her missing? Why isn't *he* the one here identifying her body?"

He took the keys from her hand, unlocked the car and opened the door, all the while keeping that damned funereal umbrella over her head. "Could be they parted on bad terms," he said as he straightened away from the door to let her in. "Could be any number of things besides murder."

"Could be," she said. "But isn't."

"Why are you so sure?"

Chelsea slid behind the wheel and took the keys he held out to her. "Family tradition," she said, and closed the door. When she pulled away, the ranger still stood there in the rain, staring after her.

She didn't get far before the nausea hit her. Pulling into a dilapidated convenience store's parking lot, she managed to make it to a rest room before she lost control. But her heaving stomach couldn't produce anything anyway. She hadn't eaten since she'd had the call from the Texas Rangers, asking her if she had a sister, describing her, telling her to come down and identify the body.

She collapsed on the dirty tiled floor, her guts tied up in knots. If she could break down in rivers of tears, it might take the edge off. But she couldn't. She couldn't cry. Sometimes she thought she and Michele had used up all their tears that night when their father had finally hit their mother one too many times.

Years of abuse. Years of the two of them watching it, too young and afraid to do anything to stop it. Though Chelsea had wished a million times she had done something. She wished she'd murdered that bastard in his sleep. She wished she hadn't always cried when her father hit her because maybe then her mother wouldn't have always stepped in. Always deflected the bastard's anger—away from her daughters and onto herself. Chelsea should have killed him. Maybe Mom would still be alive. Maybe Michele wouldn't have grown up to repeat the same damned cycle.

To Chelsea, it seemed as if the men of this world had it in for the Brennan women. Which was why she'd long ago decided never to have anything to do with any of them. She'd die a virgin and of old age, not at an angry man's hand. And never again, no matter what else she might face, would she let another person take her place in battle. Any battle.

Like the battle she was facing right now.

Stiffening her resolve, Chelsea gripped the stall door and pulled herself to her feet. Her throat burned, and she reached into her coat pocket for a cough drop, only to encounter the plastic bag that was all she had left of her sister. Grating her teeth, she pulled it out, opened it and emptied its meager contents into her palm. There was her sister's high school ring. A pair of cheap metal earrings with gold-colored paint. And a locket on a thin silver chain.

Chelsea dropped the other items back into her pocket, letting the bag fall to the floor. She held the locket in trembling hands. It had belonged to her grandmother, Alice. Mamma had given it to Michele after one of their father's violent episodes. She'd given the matching earrings to Chelsea. She'd done that a lot. Given them gifts. As if she could ease their pain with baubles.

Chelsea opened the locket.

A red newborn face was framed inside the silver heart. Dark hair sticking up in odd angles, tiny hands clenched into fists, eyes squinting tightly.

"Ethan," she whispered, and she ran the pad of her thumb over that innocent face. "I'll find you, baby. I promise. I'll find you."

And then she turned the locket over. There was a tiny compartment in the back. You'd never know it was there unless someone showed it to you, the way their mother had shown it to Michele and Chelsea. And as she pried at it, Chelsea wondered if maybe she'd find a photo of the man who'd murdered her sister and taken her nephew. Maybe she'd have something to go on, some jumping-off point in her search for her sister's child.

Blinking rapidly, Chelsea succeeded in opening the tiny compartment, then gasped as a small, folded slip of paper fell to the floor. She dropped to her knees to retrieve it.

Her hands shook so badly she could barely unfold the thing without tearing it, but when she did, she almost sagged in relief at what she saw there. A name, and an address.

There was no doubt in Chelsea's mind that it was the name of the bastard who was responsible for her sister's death. And no doubt that when she found the scum, she'd find her nephew, as well.

Men had all but wiped out the Brennan women. First Mom, and then Michele. Chelsea stood straighter and lifted her chin. Well, it was high time one of the Brennan women fought back. And she was the only one left to do it. She'd taken all she could take. All those years of impotence against her father...well, it was over. She wasn't a helpless little girl anymore, and the rage she'd stored up back then would be all she'd need to keep her going now. Just long enough to unleash it on a worthless, abusive pig.

When she got through with the man whose name Michele had written here, he was going to wish he'd never been born. And if she had any doubts that this man had fathered her sister's child, they were erased as she reread the name.

Garrett *Ethan* Brand.

Someone tapped on the rest room door. "You all right in there, ma'am?"

"Fine. Just a minute." Chelsea took a moment to snap the locket closed again, then fastened the chain around her own neck. She dropped the note into her pocket and turned to open the door.

The young woman who'd pointed the rest room out to her lingered outside.

"Sorry I took so long," Chelsea said, stepping out of the rest room into the main part of the little store again.

The clerk looked worried as she surveyed Chelsea.

Only then did Chelsea wonder about her appearance. Glancing down at herself, she saw the dirt smudged on her skirt and the runs in her nylons. No doubt her hair was wild, too, with the humidity and the rain.

"I was just gettin' worried, is all," the woman said. "Is everything all right?"

"Yes. Fine. Listen, do you have road maps in here?"

"Sure," the clerk said, looking relieved, maybe because the need for a map indicated the wild-looking woman in her store was headed out of town. "Where you going?" As she asked, she went to the counter to thumb through a rack of road maps, her back to Chelsea.

"To a ranch called the Texas Brand in the town of Quinn," Chelsea replied. Silently, she added, *to make one Garrett Ethan Brand sorry he ever heard the name Brennan.*

Chapter 3

Insistent wails broke through the satin bonds of sleep like a randy bull crashing through a fence to get to an in-season heifer.

Garrett pulled his pillow over his head and groaned. It was only Ethan's second night in the house, and Garrett's second without more than ten straight minutes of shut-eye. But it seemed as if it had been a year.

The crying didn't stop. Ah, hell, no wonder. Poor kid was among strangers, in an unfamiliar place. Was probably missing his mamma. Garrett dragged himself out of bed and slogged into the hallway. He wore shorts and a T-shirt, having learned last night that getting undressed with Ethan only a beller away was as useless as teats on a bore-hog. His bare feet scuffed the braided runner as he headed to the bedroom across from his. Aside from Adam's and Ben's, this was the only empty bedroom in the house. It had been his parents' room. Now it was reserved strictly for guests. Garrett had never had the heart to use his brothers' bedrooms for visitors because he was always half-hoping they'd just show up, home to stay, one of these days.

Garrett crossed the hall, opened the door and scuffed inside. Ethan stopped crying the second Garrett leaned over the cradle. Not a single tear dampened the little demon's cheeks. Not one. All noise and no substance, his crying. His eyes were far from red and swollen. No, they were bright blue, sparkling and wide.

They focused on Garrett's face and fairly twinkled at him. His little arms flailed as if he were trying to fly, and he flashed Garrett a dimply grin. Anyone would think the kid was glad to see him.

Garrett's impatience melted like butter in a hot skillet as he bent to scoop the baby up, and was rewarded by an actual, audible laugh. "Just lonely, aren't you, Bubba? Yeah, well, I know all about that." He carried the baby out into the hall and down the stairs, hoping his siblings would appreciate the trouble he was taking to let them sleep in peace. The rocker seemed to be the key. Little Ethan hadn't conceded to sleep last night until Garrett had rocked him.

Hmm, looked like ol' Blue was one step ahead. The hound stood in front of the rocking chair, head cocked to one side, tail upright, as if awaiting their arrival. Garrett eased himself down, and Blue lay on his feet with a contented sigh. Damn dog seemed to think a baby was exactly what had been lacking in this house.

Garrett moved to shift Ethan onto his lap, but the baby's face nuzzled into the crook between Garrett's neck and shoulder, the little body cozying closer to his chest. Some very odd, kind of warm, fuzzy sensation washed over him at the feel of that tiny, clingy body, so relaxed and trusting in his big arms. He pulled the blanket up over Ethan's shoulders and patted the little back slowly and rhythmically with a hand that spanned its width. He pushed the rocker into motion with his feet.

If someone had told Garrett a week ago that he'd be sitting here cuddling a little baby in the middle of the night—and *enjoying it* he'd have had them tested for drugs or alcohol. So small. He'd never held onto anything so small and fragile before. He'd been awfully uncomfortable at first. Garrett was a big man, and people tended to take one look at him and just assume he was rough and dangerous. He went to extremes to be gentle, moving slowly and speaking softly to counteract the impressions made by his size. But he still felt big and clumsy around tiny, fragile things. He ran one hand over Ethan's downy hair, as dark as Wes's.

That woman who'd left this bundle on the front porch…what had she been thinking? Did she have any idea what she was giving up? At that moment, as that little child clung to him, Garrett knew there wasn't a more precious treasure in the whole world than the one in his arms right now. And more love had never come in a smaller package. 'Cause somewhere between yesterday and the moment Garrett had leaned over that crib tonight, this baby seemed to have decided to love *him.* He practically bubbled over every time Garrett went anywhere near him.

"Dababababa," Ethan sang, his voice soft and sleepy as he cuddled closer.

Garrett rubbed circles on Ethan's back and inhaled the sweet baby smells as he rocked. "You're just a little bird, aren't you, Bubba? All the time singing."

Ethan made a motor noise with his lips that resulted in Garrett's T-shirt getting wet.

"Yeah," Garrett said softly, rocking and patting in time. "Your mamma must have known what she was doing, huh? I got a feeling she wouldn't have left you without some pretty big reasons."

Ethan wiggled himself into a more comfortable position, snuggling close again as one tiny hand gripped a fold of Garrett's T-shirt.

"She's a smart lady, your mamma," Garrett went on, his voice just a little above a whisper. "She had to know I'd realize you weren't my flesh and blood. But she also must've known how it would look to the kids if I turned you away. What a bad example it would've set."

Garrett didn't know who the woman might be. He knew beyond a doubt *he* hadn't fathered the child. Though knowing it wasn't as pleasant a feeling as it ought to be. Hell, being a daddy to something this cuddly wouldn't be much of a chore. Garrett wished to God he knew who the mother was, why she'd brought Ethan here. Only one thing was obvious. Whoever she was, she hadn't left the child at just any old ranch house. She hadn't chosen at random. Her note called Garrett by name. Hell, it went so far as to claim the child was named for him. So this action she'd taken had to have been well thought out, planned. She'd deliberately left her child in Garrett's care.

He was having serious second thoughts about turning Ethan over to Social Services come Tuesday morning. After all, he was the town sheriff. There was no reason he couldn't make a few inquiries on his own, try to find the woman himself. If she'd wanted Ethan in the system, she'd have taken him there, wouldn't she? And suppose she came back for her baby in a week, or a month? Lord knows, once kids go into foster care, it's sheer hell for a parent to get them back. All that red tape could be avoided if Garrett could just keep little Ethan here with him. Just for a short while. Just to give the woman a chance.

A little palm patted Garrett's face.

Oh, yeah, he was changing his mind, all right. Hell, he was smitten by the little mite already, and he'd only had him a couple of days. What must it have done to Ethan's mamma to leave him alone on that porch? Torn her insides out, Garrett figured. But she'd done it, and in doing so, she'd put her trust in *him.* No way was Garrett going to let her down.

He lowered his head to the side, so his cheek brushed Ethan's silky hair. "Don't you worry, little Bubba. I'm gonna make things right for you." Ethan heaved a deep sigh, and Garrett closed his eyes.

It was still dark outside when he heard a vehicle and felt the touch of headlights on his eyelids. He'd fallen asleep! Sitting right here in the rocker, holding that baby! Of all the idiotic things to do. What if he'd dropped Ethan on his head?

But his arms were still firmly anchored around that little body, as if they'd been on guard duty even as he'd slept. He squinted at the antique pendulum clock that sat on the mantel. Three a.m. He'd been asleep almost three hours!

And who the hell was pulling into the driveway at this time of night? Could be an emergency in town, maybe. He *was* the sheriff. But wouldn't someone have called instead of driving clear out here?

Garrett got up real slow and turned to lay Ethan on the couch. Then he pulled the nearest armchair up beside it, back first, so there was no way the baby could roll onto the floor. He was just tucking the blanket over that sleeping angel when he heard the pounding on the front door. Not knocking. *Pounding.*

His stomach twisted a little as he thought about his gun, clear out of reach upstairs, and he tried to recall if he'd arrested any particularly ornery characters lately. But hell, aside from the occasional drunk and disorderly boys over at La Cucaracha, he rarely arrested *anyone.* Quinn was a quiet little town. Not much happened there.

Garrett hustled through the dining room, casting one last glance over his shoulder at Ethan as he went. Still asleep despite the racket at the door. Good. He paused in the kitchen only long enough to flick on the outdoor light so he could get a look at the rude S.O.B. who was trying to knock the door off its hinges. He parted the curtain and peered out.

Hostile eyes peered back at him. Hostile...and then some. The creature that stared back at him seemed, in that first instant, to be nothing *but* eyes. Huge, round, and wild. The impact when those eyes met his sent him two full steps backward before he'd even been aware of moving. Like he'd been kicked hard in the chest. Those eyes...they were hurting. Hurting like he'd never seen anyone hurt before, and it looked to him as if they intended to hurt back.

Garrett blinked and gave his head a shake. Hell, he'd best get a grip and look again. There had been more there than a pair of stricken eyes.

He leaned forward again, this time flicking the lock and twisting the knob. No use with the locks. It was a woman, even if she was all eyes. And he could handle a woman, no matter how crazed.

The door opened.

She shouldered inside before he stepped out of the way, then stood toe-to-toe with him. "Are you Garrett Ethan Brand?"

Her voice was like cherry-tree bark—stringy and coarse.

She had burnished bronze hair that seemed as riled up as she was. Her clothes were dirty and her stockings full of runs. Mud clung to her high-heeled shoes. She was a mess. He figured she must have had an accident or something. But unless she'd lost a limb—which she obviously hadn't—he couldn't see any explanation for the pain and rage in her eyes.

"Yeah, I'm Garrett," he told her. "Why don't you sit down and I'll—"

He reeled backward at the impact of her fist—not her hand, *her fist*—connecting with his left cheekbone and snapping his head sideways so hard and fast he thought he'd probably need a neckbrace.

"Damn, woman! What the hell was that—hold on a minute!" He caught her fist in his hands before she could land another blow. So she kicked him in the shins with those muddy, pointy-toed shoes of hers. He yelped in agony. Damned if he wanted to hurt any woman, but this one was pushing even *his* legendary patience. He dropped her hands just long enough to wrap his arms tight around her middle, pinning *her* arms to her sides. At the same instant, he pressed her up against the door and pushed his body tight to her considerably smaller one. So tight she couldn't swing those deadly feet again. But even as he did it, he took great pains not to hurt her. She was so small he got the feeling she'd break easily.

And then he just stood there, his body plastered to

hers, panting from the struggle and the surprise and, mostly to be honest, the pain. And he wondered what the hell to do next. Lord, her heart hammered like a scared jackrabbit's hind feet. Her lungs moved in and out too rapidly. She had cheeks as pink as a tea rose and eyes that damn near put him on his knees just with the force of the emotions he saw roiling in them as he stared down at her from a distance of well over a foot.

He caught his breath in short order, though she still breathed as if she'd just run a mile uphill. "You want to tell me why you're trying to cripple me now, ma'am, or on the way to jail?"

Her eyes narrowed and...they were green. Deep, forest green. Like pine needles in the sunlight. He'd never seen eyes like those.

"Where is he?"

Garrett blinked twice. "Where is who?"

"You know damn well who. Where is he?"

A bitter dread settled in the pit of his stomach. God wouldn't be so cruel, would he? This crazy woman couldn't possibly be little Ethan's mamma...*could she?*

He cleared his throat, trying to figure out a decent reason to lie to her, when Ethan made up his own mind. He let out a yelp. And an outright miracle happened. That wildcat in Garrett's arms went limp as a noodle. The fury left her eyes, and instead they softened, melted. A look of utter longing and bittersweet relief took over, and the tension left her so fast it felt as if her bones had turned to water. He wasn't sure she'd still be standing on her feet if he wasn't holding her.

"Ethan?" she whispered.

"Yes, ma'am, that's Ethan. But I'll tell you, I'm not

inclined to let anyone as violent as you within a hundred miles of him."

Her eyes flashed up at him, anger flickering to life once more. Tempered now, though.

"Are, uh, are you his mamma?"

Soft auburn brows drew together. "You know perfectly well where his mother is, mister."

"No, ma'am, I surely don't."

"Yes, *cowboy,*" she said, mocking his drawl and saying "cowboy" as if it were a cuss word. "You surely *do.*" Her voice lowered until it became a little more than a harsh, tortured whisper. "She's lying in a morgue in El Paso. And you put her there, you bastard."

She was shaking—*shaking*—like a road sign in a killing wind. Vibrating with the force of whatever emotions roiled inside her right now.

The kitchen light flashed on, and Wes appeared at Garrett's side. His open hand might look harmless to a stranger, but Garrett saw the way his fingers twitched just a little. He'd snatch the bowie from his boot at the drop of a hat.

"What's going on, Garrett?"

He didn't answer. His gaze remained fixed on the wild-eyed creature whose soul was crying, even if her eyes were not. "Ethan's mamma is dead?"

She didn't reply, only glared at him. He heard Jessi's soft gasp behind him and realized she'd come into the kitchen, too. And probably Elliot, as well. The scent of baby powder told him one of them was carrying Ethan. That and the way the woman trapped between his chest and the door suddenly stared at a point beyond him.

"Answer me. Is she dead?"

A single nod.

"Are you sure?"

Her eyes finally came back to his. "I just came from identifying my sister's body, you murdering slug. You're damned right I'm sure."

Wes stiffened, closed his eyes, shook his head. Elliot snorted, coming forward to stand at Garrett's other side. "Lady, you don't know my brother at all if you think he could hurt a woman."

His words had no impact on her. She merely lifted her chin and continued staring at Garrett. "I came for my nephew. Give him to me and I'll leave."

"Well, now, I'm real sorry, ma'am, but I can't do that."

"I'll kill you myself before I'll let you keep him." And Garrett believed she meant every word of it.

"You'll have to go through me," Wes told her, his eyes going cold. Wes's eyes, when they went cold like that, could make a rattler tremble. Two black marbles without a hint of feeling. "And going through me won't be an easy job, lady."

"Damn straight it won't," Elliot agreed. "And when you finish with Wes, you'll have to get by me."

"And then me," Jessi said.

Nothing fazed the woman. She didn't even blink. "If that's the way you want it." She faced Garrett again. "Let go of me, Brand. I'll leave, but when I come back it will be with the law."

"No need to leave for that, ma'am. I happen to *be* the law. 'Round here, leastwise."

For the first time, he saw fear tinge her eyes. She glanced down at his arms, imprisoning her, and it seemed to Garrett she was suddenly afraid of him. He eased his hold on her that very second. Let her go completely, and even stepped back away from her. It stunned him, that fear. Made him feel kind of queasy. He didn't like scaring people. Especially women or kids. Though he usually tried to be less intimidating because of his size, he knew only too well it wasn't always enough. Hell, nothing made Garrett more miserable than people being afraid of him.

Especially her.

She was very small, he realized. Smaller than Jessi, even. She'd been through some kind of hell tonight. And he figured she was probably telling the truth about having just identified her sister's body in El Paso. She certainly *looked* like someone who'd just lost a sister. And if she truly thought him responsible...well, hell, he'd have been just as angry in her shoes.

She didn't lash out at him again. Only stood there, looking like she'd fall down in a few more minutes. Looking like the stress was tearing her nerves right to shreds.

Garrett turned around and took little Ethan from Jessi's arms, though she protested. Ethan chirped and grinned and blew spit bubbles. He latched onto one of Garrett's fingers and held tight. Garrett turned back to the woman, who stood near the front door. "Come on into the parlor," he said to her, and he tried harder than he ever had to make his deep voice sound soft and gentle. We'll talk this out."

She blinked, licked her lips. "I just want to take him and go."

"I understand that. But you have to understand my position here. I'm a sheriff, ma'am. A woman left her child in my care. I can't just hand him over to the first stranger who comes along and claims him, now can I?"

She eyed him so skeptically he squirmed inside.

"I'll check out your story," he went on. It was more than her smallness that made her seem as fragile as bone china right now. And he felt big and awkward beside her. "If you are who you say you are, and Ethan really is your nephew, I'll let you take him. But, ma'am, even if I were sure right this minute, I wouldn't let you out of here now. You're in no shape to be driving tonight. Especially not with a baby in the car."

He had her there. She knew it. He saw the concession in her eyes. "I'm not leaving here without him."

"Then you're gonna have to stay a spell."

She looked at the baby he held and she put her arms out. Little Ethan looked back at her and smiled. Her white hands trembled as she took a step forward. Then she dropped like a sack of potatoes right at Garrett's feet. Garrett pushed little Ethan into the nearest set of arms, which turned out to be Wes's, and bent down to scoop the woman up off the floor. As he turned to carry her through the house and upstairs, he noticed that she smelled like violets.

Chapter 4

Chelsea awoke to hot sunlight burning over her eyelids and face, cool, crisp sheets against her skin, and the smell of coffee. Good, strong coffee.

The smell, she discovered after blinking the sleep haze from her eyes, originated from the carafe that sat on the round table beside the bed. A pink cloth with lacy white edging covered the table and draped halfway to the floor, leaving only the bottom portion of the broad, carved, totem pole-like pedestal visible. Chelsea wanted to reach for that coffee. And for the plate of the steaming, fragrant, omelet-type concoction beside it. But she couldn't summon the energy to move.

"Well, the beast lives," a feminine voice announced.

Chelsea jerked her gaze to where the young woman she remembered from last night stood near the window. The curtains were as pink as the tablecloth. In fact, so were the sheets. Pale pink fabric with lilac blossoms lined the two overstuffed chairs in the room, and the wallpaper matched. It was very loud, very flowery and *very* pink. A white vanity with more filigree trim than substance stood in one corner. It was laden with pretty bottles and jars of every size, shape and color.

"Looks like the inside of Jeannie's bottle, doesn't it?" The woman let the curtains fall closed. "My brothers think all the frilly stuff makes up for being the only female in a houseful of men. I let them indulge me."

She was young. Early twenties, Chelsea guessed. Her pixie-short hair gleamed a reddish brown like the coat of a deer. And those huge brown eyes of hers reinforced the image of a doe. She was taller than Chelsea, curvier, too.

"So, do I pass inspection, Your Majesty?"

Chelsea cleared her throat, trying to work up enough energy to put the spoiled brat in her place. All she managed was, "What do you want?"

"I don't *want* anything, least of all to wait on some lunatic in my own house. I wouldn't be in here at all if Garrett hadn't insisted I stay with you until you came around. He said he was afraid you'd be *scared waking up in a strange place.*" She said the last bit in a whiny, mocking tone, and Chelsea wished she could slap her. "So I suggested my room. At least here I can keep an eye on you."

"I wouldn't be here if I had a choice about it."

"You wouldn't be here if *I* had a choice about it, either, lady."

Chelsea closed her eyes at the look of hostility in the pretty face.

"You might as well eat." The girl pushed herself away from the wall she'd been leaning on and came to the bed to hand the tray of food to Chelsea.

"Thanks," Chelsea said.

"Don't thank me. I wouldn't cook for you if you were starving. Garrett brought this up."

Chelsea looked up from the plate of food on her lap to the glittering brown eyes. "Look, I don't have a problem with you. It's your brother—"

"You have a problem with one Brand, lady, you have a problem with all of them."

"He might have killed my sister." And why the hell was she suddenly qualifying her accusations with a "might have." Last night she'd been so sure. Chelsea sat up straighter, suddenly losing interest in the food. "You can't expect me to just—"

"He didn't even *know* your sister! And *you* don't know Garrett. Of all my brothers, he's the most gentle, the sweetest, the kindest, the—"

She broke off, turning away fast and blinking tears from her eyes. As if she didn't want Chelsea to see her crying.

"Garrett wouldn't hurt a fly. You can ask anyone who knows him. The boys in town, they have a joke. They call him the gentle giant." She turned again, with one angry swipe at her eyes. "But *I'm* not gentle. And neither is Wes. And I'll tell you right now, we're not gonna stand by and let you hurt Garrett this way. You can't go around accusing him of murder. You do and I'll—"

"That's enough, Jessi."

The command was spoken softly, but in a voice so big it didn't seem like anyone would disobey. The man Chelsea had believed to be a cold-blooded killer stood in the doorway, looking at his little sister with a frown, but adoringly all the same.

"But, Garrett—"

"No buts. Go on, now. Wes needs your help in the barn. That new calf got himself tangled in some wire and cut his hind leg up. He needs tending."

"Wes can handle a cut calf."

"Wes isn't the Brand one semester away from a degree in veterinary medicine, Jes. You are. Now get out there and see to the calf before he gets infected or something."

The girl—Jessi—blinked twice, and seemed to forget all about Chelsea. With budding concern in her eyes, she yanked open a closet door and snatched out a brown leather satchel. Then she headed out of the room, and Chelsea heard her feet taking the stairs at a trot a second later.

Garrett Brand came farther into the room, but he left the door open. He really *was* big. Not just tall, but as broad shouldered as a lumberjack. He had bodybuilder arms that bore the coppery kiss of the sun beneath a fine mist of dark hair. His eyes were as deeply brown as his sister's. Soft eyes, bottomless and kind.

Deceptively so.

"We ought to talk," he said in that slow, easy way of his. He moved slowly, too, as if giving her time to object with every step he took. When she didn't, he eased his big frame into one of Jessi's pink-and-lilac chairs, and Chelsea wondered if she were about to witness a scene from *Goldilocks and the Three Bears*. Nope, the fragile-looking chair legs held.

It was only when those deep brown eyes moved slowly down her sheet-draped body and then darkened that Chelsea became suddenly, acutely interested in what the hell she was wearing. She lifted the sheet, peeked down and gasped.

"I'm naked under here," she blurted, mainly because she was so surprised.

Garrett shifted in the chair, his face reddening all the way to his ears. "Well, I asked Jessi to get you out of your clothes last night. I mean...you were pretty well soaked from the rain and all, and..."

She scowled at him when he ran out of words.

"You want me to leave so you can get dressed?"

"In what? I don't see any of my things in here."

"Well, you must have luggage in your car, right? I can have Elliot go out and—"

"Just say what you have to say and get it over with, will you?"

He nodded fast, keeping his eyes carefully lowered, though whenever they did come up, they focused on certain strategic bits of the sheet and she wondered how much he could see through it.

"All right," he said. "For starters, ma'am, I'm not sure what—" he frowned, meeting her eyes "—what's your name?"

"My name?"

"I can't talk to you without even knowing your name. It feels too odd."

She closed her eyes, sighed. "Chelsea Brennan."

His lips curled upward just slightly at the corners. "I like it."

"I'm so glad it meets with your approval," she snapped, then saw a wounded look come and go in his eyes and almost regretted her words.

"I didn't hurt your sister, Chelsea Brennan," he said, and there was so much sincerity in his deep, steady voice that it made her wonder. "But I'd like to help you find out who did...if you'll let me."

Nothing he could have said would have shocked her more. Denials, she expected. Threats, even. But an offer of help? What was this? A trick?

"Why would you want to help me? You don't even know me."

"That's true, I don't. But I know Ethan." He licked his lips as if he were nervous or something, dipped his head. It might sound foolish to you, Chelsea, but I made that little fella a promise. I told him I'd make things right for him again, and that's what I intend to do."

She studied him, scanning the little worry lines—or were they laugh lines?—at the corners of his brown eyes. Telling herself that just because his appearance and demeanor were so damned gentle and approachable didn't mean that's the way he truly was. Inside. Where it counted.

Hell, her father hadn't looked like the monster he was, either.

"Why should I believe you? How do I know this isn't just an act? That you aren't just lying to throw me off track?"

"Why *shouldn't* you believe me?"

"You want me to list the reasons?"

He nodded, watching her with those soft eyes of his.

"Fine. I will, then. A year ago, my sister, Michele, got herself pregnant by the lowlife she'd been dating. She didn't tell me his name, but I saw him once from a distance. He was big...like you. And he wore a hat—" she pointed at the black hat he'd perched on the arm of the chair "—like that."

He glanced down at his hat with a frown, then

picked it up. His lips pursed in thought as he turned the brim slowly in his big hands and ran his fingers around the edge and then through the dip in the hat's center in what seemed uncomfortably like a caress. "Most of the men in Texas wear hats like this one," he replied, calm and quiet. "And I imagine a lot of them are big."

He stroked the black felt over and over. Chelsea's stomach tightened and twisted, and she jerked her gaze away from those slow-moving hands.

"A week ago Michele called me. She told me she had a son, Ethan, and she asked me to come down here right away to see him." Chelsea clenched her jaw, closing her eyes before rushing on. "If only I had, she might still be alive. But I knew I couldn't get time off work on such short notice. I promised to fly down in a couple of weeks, but..."

"There was no way you could have known," he said.

But she should have known. There'd been something in Michele's voice, something she should have picked up on. But she hadn't. Not until it had been too late. She'd live with that for the rest of her life.

"Then, yesterday, I got a call from the Texas Rangers, telling me they had a body they wanted me to look at."

"And it was her," Garrett finished softly.

Chelsea nodded. "Someone left her for dead, only she wasn't quite. But she didn't live long enough to make it to the hospital."

It surprised her when a warm hand slid over her cold one on the bed. And she stared at it for a long moment. A big, powerful hand, only it wasn't hurting. It wasn't controlling or cruel. She pushed her brows together at the unexpectedness of that. And then the hand moved away, and Garrett cleared his throat.

"They gave me her things," Chelsea went on. "There was a locket with Ethan's picture. Your name and address were in a compartment in the back."

"So you assumed I was the killer. And Ethan's daddy." Garrett shook his head.

"She named him after you."

"And I still haven't figured out why, or how she even knew me, or who she even was." He shook his head slowly, such sincere regret in his eyes that he had her almost believing him.

Chelsea sat up, clutching the pink sheet to her chest. She pointed at the floor, where someone had slung her mud-spattered purse. "Hand me my bag, would you?"

Garrett nodded and retrieved the bag for her, returning to his seat with those slow, careful movements of his.

Chelsea dug out her billfold and opened it to the photo of her sister. She handed the picture to the big man at the bedside. "This is Michele, Ethan's mother."

Garrett narrowed his eyes as he studied the snapshot. Then they widened in recognition, and Chelsea knew, whether he'd admit it or not, that he'd known Michele.

"I remember her," he said slowly.

"You do?" She hadn't expected him to admit it.

He nodded. "It was last summer. I saw her out on the River Road, middle of nowhere, alone, with a flat tire on her beat-up old car."

"And?"

"Well, I stopped and changed it for her, of course." He looked at her as if she should have known that much. "She seemed jittery, as I recall. Had a scared-rabbit look to her that worried me. I invited her back here for supper that night, and she came. Adam and Ben were here then, too, so it was a houseful.'' He shook his head, then his brows drew together again.

''Did she spend the night with you?'' Chelsea knew her meaning was clear in her tone.

His head came up and he gave her a sharp look. ''We invited her to stay over in the guest room. She refused. Said she had to be on her way. All told, she didn't spend more than two or three hours under this roof.''

''It only takes a few minutes to get a woman pregnant,'' Chelsea said.

Garrett sighed hard. ''She was already pregnant. Ma'am, do you think your sister was stupid?''

She blinked and sat up in the bed, holding the sheet to her chest. ''No. Michele was irresponsible and flighty and drawn to bad men, but she wasn't stupid.''

He nodded, handing the photo back to Chelsea. ''You said you heard from her for the first time in over a year, just before she was killed. Now, why do you think she called you then, after all that time? Hmm?''

Chelsea drew a breath, braced her shoulders, taking full blame, which she deserved. ''She knew...I think she was reaching out to me because she needed help.''

''You think she knew this S.O.B. was after her.''

Closing her eyes tight, Chelsea nodded.

''If it were you,'' Garrett said, his voice deep and smooth, ''and you had your own little baby boy in your arms and a man trying to kill you and no one to turn to, what would you do, Chelsea?''

Facing him without flinching, she said, ''I'd cut the bastard's heart out before he could do it to me.''

Garrett blinked, maybe in surprise. It had to be surprise in his eyes the way he stared at her for a full minute before he finally nodded and spoke again. ''I do believe you would,'' he said slowly, his gaze brushing her face from forehead to chin before focusing on her eyes again. ''Fair enough, then. But what about Michele? Is that what she would have done?''

Chelsea's lips trembled as she imagined Michele's fear and desperation. She stared down at her sister's image, then closed her eyes. ''She never fought back, never in her life. When things got tough for Michele, she'd run. She'd run right back home to me, and I'd take her in, find her a job, bail her out, whatever she needed. Until the next slug came along with a mouthful of promises. Then she'd take off again.''

''So you think if she were scared this time, if she knew someone was trying to kill her, she would've run?''

Chelsea nodded.

''And what about the baby, Chelsea? It's hard to run for your life with a baby.''

''She'd never have taken Ethan with her if she'd known she was in danger,'' Chelsea said quickly. ''She'd never risk him that way. I know my sister. She'd have found a safe place to hide him and then she'd have run as far and as fast as she could.''

She heard his sigh, his *relieved* sigh, and opened her eyes again to see him nodding in understanding. He held her gaze.

''Don't you see it, Chelsea? That's exactly what she did. We found little Ethan on our front porch day before yesterday. She left him here so he'd be safe.'' He must have seen the doubt in her eyes, because he went on. ''I live right here on the Texas Brand. Have all my life,'' he said. ''I run the ranch and I show up in a little bitty office in town every weekday with a star pinned to my shirt. Everybody in Quinn knows just about every move I make. I promise, I haven't had time to be terrorizing any woman. I haven't been to New York in years, either, and I can probably prove that if you'll just tell me the date this boyfriend of your sister's was there."

He meant it. She could tell he meant it, and her doubts about his guilt were stronger than ever.

"My sister ran away with that cowboy last year on April first," she said. "Bitter irony, isn't it?"

"April Fool's Day," Garrett observed. "Okay. I'll see if I can find some proof of my whereabouts that day for you."

She studied him, wondering why, if he really was innocent, he wasn't throwing her out on her backside. She'd stormed into his house in the middle of the night, accused him of murder and physically attacked him. He, in turn, had cooked her breakfast.

She looked down again at the omelet.

"It's getting cold," he told her.

"Doesn't matter. I'm not hungry anyway."

"When's the last time you had a meal, Chelsea Brennan?"

Every time she heard her name spoken in those slow, drawling tones, she felt a chill run up her spine. She tried to remember when her last meal had been, found she couldn't, then shrugged.

"You'll be skin and bone if you don't eat soon."

His words made her remember the way Michele had looked in the morgue, and she felt cold inside.

"Just a little," he urged. "I didn't put too much spice in 'em. If you want, though, I can run downstairs for the jalapeño sauce."

She almost smiled. Hot sauce on eggs? She forced herself to take a bite of the omelet, which melted on her tongue like butter. Garrett got up and poured coffee from the carafe, filling a fat clay mug with the steaming brew. He leaned close to hand it to her, and she caught his scent. It made her want to sniff more of it.

It scared her.

"I want my clothes," she said, feeling uneasy and suddenly wishing this man were far away from her. "I want to take Ethan and go back to New York this morning."

Garrett lowered his head. He looked truly sorry. "No. Not yet."

"What do you mean, not yet?"

"I'm sorry. No, listen, I mean it. I am sorry. But I can't just let you take off with Bubba until I know—"

"Bubba?"

"Er, Ethan. Look, you're stuck here for today. There's no two ways about that, so you may as well get used to the idea."

Her fork dropped onto the plate and she glared at him. "You *can't* keep me here against my will!"

"Sure I can. I'm the sheriff. And last night you assaulted me. I can toss you in jail and I will, Chelsea Brennan, if you try to take Bu—Ethan out of this house today."

"You son of a—"

"You insult my mamma, Chelsea, and you're gonna regret it."

She blinked and defiantly stuck out her chin. "What are you going to do, *Sheriff* Brand? You going to kill me the way you did my sister?"

He closed his eyes, shook his head slowly from side

to side. "Damn. I give up." He turned and left the room, closing the door behind him.

She knew it had been a cheap shot. Because she really didn't have a reason in the world to suspect that big man of murder.

Garrett stood in the hallway outside Jessi's room and took a long, deep breath. It had been a long time since anyone had tested his temper as sorely as that hellcat, Chelsea Brennan, was doing.

Worse than that, she was beautiful. All of her. And there hadn't been much hidden with nothing over her but that thin pink sheet of Jessi's. It had clung to her. There'd been a little indentation over her belly button, and her breasts might as well have been exposed.

They were small and firm and…

He clamped his jaw against the tide of reaction that tried, once again, to sweep him away. Tried not to think about the soft, pale color of her skin, or the satin texture of her neck and shoulders, or those pine-tree green eyes. Tried not to feel that small, china-doll hand, cool and trembling underneath his big callused one.

He couldn't afford to have tender feelings for her. Hell, she'd come here to take little Bubba away to Lord only knows what kind of life! She was accusing Garrett of murder, to boot!

Easy enough to solve the latter problem. The former one bothered him, though. If she turned out to be Ethan's aunt after all, then he'd have no right to keep that boy here.

Garrett sneaked into the guest bedroom where Ethan's cradle was, and saw the little pudge had decided to wake up at last. He was playing with his toes and drooling. A crooked smile tugged at Garrett's mouth, and he went to the cradle. "Morning, Bubba."

"Ga!"

He bent to pick up the baby, then thought better of it and removed the diaper first. Then the little T-shirt. He laid a fresh diaper under Ethan, but didn't tape it up. "You lie there and kick for a minute while I run a baby-size bath for you." Ethan's huge smile and gurgles of joy followed Garrett into the bathroom. "Never did know a fella who enjoyed being buck naked the way you do, Bubba."

He turned on the water.

Chelsea heard splashing. And the enthusiastic coos and chirps that went with it. Ethan! God, she'd come so far, waited so long to finally see him. That big lug of a sheriff might be able to keep her from taking him home, for the moment at least, but he couldn't keep her from seeing him.

She got out of the pink bed, holding the sheet around her in case anyone barged in, and went to the closet. She found a satin robe. Pink, of course, and a bit too long for her, but she belted it around her waist anyway, tying the sash nice and tight. Then she left the bedroom barefoot, and followed the sounds into the big bedroom down the hall. A cradle stood empty beside a made-up bed with a wagon-wheel headboard. And farther inside, another door stood open.

Chelsea moved toward it, then stood stock-still just beyond the doorway, staring in utter shock at what she saw. The fat, laughing baby slapping his hands against the water in the tub so that sprays of droplets exploded all over the place. And the big man kneeling on the floor beside the tub, one hand firmly around the baby for support, while the other ran a washcloth over a round little belly.

Garrett had stripped off his T-shirt. Not in time, by the looks of it. It lay on the floor in a wet ball. Water dripped from that brick-wall chest and from those bodybuilder arms. And from his hair. Its thick, dark waves hung in straggles, some clinging to his face.

And he was laughing as much as the baby. A deep, rich sound that made her shiver.

Ethan. Her little Ethan. He was staring up at Garrett Brand with adoration oozing from his deep blue eyes.

Damned if the big cowboy wasn't looking back at the baby with something very similar shining from his brown ones.

Garrett turned, but never released his hold on Ethan. He'd tell her to get out, she guessed. He'd tell her to go back to the bedroom and stay there until further notice. He'd tell her—

"You mind handin' me that towel over there, Chelsea? I think I'm wetter than Bubba."

She blinked, gave her head a shake, then followed his gaze to the stack of towels on the washstand. She reached for one, handed it to him.

"Thanks." One-handed, he wiped his face and chest dry, then scooped the baby out of the tub and wrapped him up in another big, fluffy towel. The way he held Ethan, the way he cuddled him close... "Do me a favor and take it from here, Chelsea? I need some dry clothes, and then I ought to head out to check on that calf."

Her eyes burned and her throat closed too tightly for words to emerge as Garrett gently placed her sister's child into her arms.

"All his things are in that bag next to the cradle.

You need anything, just step to the front door and holler.''

She nodded, but mutely. She couldn't take her eyes from the baby. Garrett turned and walked away, leaving her alone with Ethan. She came as close to crying as she had since her mother died. No tears spilled over, but she felt them burning her eyes. Felt that choking sensation, the spasms in her chest.

''Ethan,'' she murmured, and she hugged him close. Felt his little fingers twisting and tugging at her hair. Smelled him. The little angel. The only family she had left. The best thing Michele had ever done in her short, misery-ridden life. God, how Michele must have loved this baby! ''I'll take care of him,'' she whispered, praying somehow her sister could hear her and finally be at peace.

She carried the baby back into his room, walked to the wide, arching window and parted the curtains to stare out at the red-orange sky.

''It's all right now, Michele. I'll take care of him, I swear I will. I'll give him...I'll give him the things we didn't have.''

Her voice trembled as she spoke, but she went on, feeling she needed to. She had to reassure her sister as well as herself. She had to speak the promise aloud to make it real, make it solid and attainable.

''He'll have a house, Michele. With a yard and room to grow. And...and he'll have a family. I'll love him so much...you'll see. And I'll never, ever hit him, Michele. No one will, I promise you that. He won't have to hide his bruises before he goes off to school, the way we did. I swear it. I'll protect him with my life. His grandfather will never even know he exists. And if his father tries to take him from me, Michele,

I'll fight him to the death. I will. He's not going to grow up to be like them. He'll be...he'll be our son, Michele. Yours and mine. I'll tell him about you. I'll make sure he never forgets his mother."

Ethan's hand tugged at Chelsea's hair, and she smiled and hugged him again.

Jessi wiped the single tear from her cheek and tiptoed quietly back down the hall to her own room. Maybe...maybe she'd been a little hard on that strange city woman. She tried to imagine what her reaction would have been if their situations were reversed. If it had been one of her own precious brothers who'd been killed, and if she'd been convinced of who'd done it. Hell, she'd have been far rougher on the suspect than Chelsea Brennan had been on Garrett. She'd have probably shot first and asked questions later. And that would have been a crying shame, because Jessi never missed what she shot at.

Two things were for sure. Chelsea had loved her sister. And she loved little Ethan. And those were two things Jessi could fully understand.

That other stuff she'd overheard Chelsea talking about...about never hitting, and about hiding bruises...that stuff worried her. She decided to repeat the entire, one-sided conversation to Garrett just as soon as he came back inside.

Meanwhile, it was her turn to clean up the breakfast dishes.

Chapter 5

Garrett was more than a little put out to find that none of his normally well-mannered siblings had bothered to bring Chelsea Brennan's luggage in from her car. It was pushing 9:00 a.m. by the time he'd finished tending the wounded calf, returned it to its mamma and ridden the fence lines, checking on the cattle as he did every morning and again every night. The two hours it took to cover the entire ranch did him as much good as it did the cattle, he thought. It relaxed him.

This morning, he'd only found one minor problem. Some brush had blown into the wire, shorting out the electric fence and leaving a portion vulnerable. Fortunately, the cows hadn't figured it out yet. Fat, happy Herefords stood around chewing grass and eyeing him while he cut the brush away and tested the fence.

When he and Duke galloped toward the barns again, Garrett saw Chelsea. She sat in the porch swing, Bubba in her arms. And she was still wearing Jessi's pink robe.

The picture she made there struck him hard for some reason, and he drew Duke to a stop and just sat there, not quite sure why or what to do next. Duke needed some oats and a good rubdown. But his unwilling houseguest was obviously being neglected.

Good manners prevailed, as they generally did with Garrett. He touched his heels to Duke's flanks and turned the horse toward the house. He stopped at the front porch and slid easily to the ground. He took a second to loop the reins around the hitching rail even though it was unnecessary. Duke wouldn't stray. In truth, he needed a minute to shake off the odd feeling the sight of her and Ethan sitting there in that porch swing—almost as if they were waiting for him—had caused in his gut. Like indigestion, only worse. He glanced around, looking everywhere but at her. Wes crouched near the gate to the horse pasture, tinkering with that loose hinge. Elliot held the thing in place for him as he worked. Both, though, were watching Garrett and Chelsea. Garrett saw the sneaky glances, the narrowed eyes.

His brothers didn't like Miss Chelsea Brennan very much, he deduced. And they trusted her even less.

"So, how's the calf?" she asked.

Garrett brought his head around fast. Was that an attempt at civil conversation? Or was she just gearing up to make some nasty remark?

"Out in the pasture with his mamma. He'll be fine."

"Barbed wire is cruel," she observed, and though her voice was deep and soft, he heard the acid in her tone. "It ought to be illegal."

Garrett narrowed his eyes at her and tried not to

notice the swell of her breasts peeking out at him from where the robe's neckline took a swan dive. ''We've replaced it with smooth wire for that very reason. The piece that calf found was left over from days gone by. Grass had grown over it, so we must have missed it when we were clearing out the old fences.''

And just why the hell was he explaining himself to her?

''Electric shock therapy for cows,'' she decreed with all the pomposity of a haughty despot, ''is just as bad.''

''I have to disagree with you there, ma'am. The voltage is real low, and once they get bit on the nose, they tend to stay away from it.''

She sniffed and looked away from him.

''It's better than letting them wander off and get lost,'' Garrett persisted. ''Even a city girl ought to have sense enough to see that much.''

She slanted him a glance that stung worse than any electric fence he'd ever accidentally grabbed hold of.

Garrett shifted his stance, regretting his hostile response. If he wanted to help Bubba, he couldn't go making this woman his enemy. He had to try to cozy up to her, keep her here until he figured out what to do. Okay, time to start over again. He cleared his throat. ''I was thinking—''

''Did it hurt much?''

Garrett clenched his jaw. Cozying up to the hellcat wasn't going to be an easy task. ''I was thinking,'' he began again, ''you might want to drive into town with me.''

''And why would I want to do that?''

''April first was a weekday. I ought to have something at the office to prove I wasn't in New York City.''

"So make me a copy."

She was one ornery creature! "And have you accuse me of doctoring it up to cover my tracks?"

She met his eyes, and he felt heat. Only it wasn't from anger. And it had nothing to do with the sun already blazing down from the wide Texas sky. This heat was searing and electric. It sort of rushed up from his toes and made him a little bit dizzy. He had to look away first.

"What about Ethan?" she finally asked.

The screen door creaked, and Jessi stepped out onto the porch, wiping her hands on a checkered dish towel. "I'll take care of Ethan."

Garrett nodded, but Chelsea turned a wary gaze on his little sister.

"Don't do me any favors," Chelsea said.

Jessi had never had what Garrett would call tolerance. Her temper flared quicker than a sparkler on the Fourth of July. Hotter, too.

"Don't worry, I wasn't offering. I'll watch him for my brother. For you, I wouldn't cross the road, and if you think I—" Jessi stopped suddenly and bit her lower lip.

Garrett was perplexed. He'd never seen Jessi cut herself off in mid-tirade before.

Jessi shook her head, took a deep breath. "Sorry."

Sorry?

"Truth is, I just adore little Ethan. I'd love to take care of him this morning."

Garrett almost fell down in shock, and a quick glance at Chelsea's puckered brow told him she was as surprised as he.

Chelsea waited a moment and finally nodded. "All right, then. I'll need a few minutes."

Jessi came forward and took the baby from Chelsea's arms. She propped him on her slender hip. "You can use the shower in my room if you want."

Chelsea's eyes narrowed, but she nodded, got to her feet and walked into the house without another word.

Garrett tilted his head, fixing his baby sister with a questioning glance. "Why the change of heart, Jes?"

Jessi looked through the screen door into the house, and Garrett sensed she was waiting until Chelsea had moved out of earshot to answer him. When she finally turned back to him, she looked worried.

"Jes?"

She pressed her cheek to the baby's. "Garrett, I think somebody's hurt that woman. I think somebody's hurt her bad."

Garrett frowned. "Course she's hurt. She just lost her sister."

Jessi shook her head. "No, Garrett. I mean *really hurt* her. Physically."

Her meaning became clear, and Garrett felt a dark cloud settle right over his soul. A thundercloud. "Maybe you'd better tell me about it."

He kept looking at her. Not *just* looking, though. He kept searching her face as if trying to see something there, and it was making Chelsea damned uncomfortable.

She rode beside him in the oversize pickup truck, over dusty roads and finally paved ones, into the small town of Quinn. The truck was big. One of those kinds that needed two sets of wheels in the back just to push it along. Seemed everything about Garrett Brand was big. His home, his truck. Even his speckled horse had been huge. Then again, she supposed it would have to be to support a man of his size.

He pulled to a stop in front of an adobe-like structure with no curtains in the windows and a sign over the door that read Sheriff's Office.

"Here we are."

He got out and came around as if to open her door for her. She beat him to it. But then he took her arm to help her out, getting the best of her anyway.

Chelsea stepped out, stumbling a little because of her heels and the long reach to the ground. Garrett's big hands circled her waist surely and firmly, and he lifted her right up off her feet, setting her down again on the small stretch of sidewalk in front of the building.

But his hands remained for a second or two, even after her feet touched the ground. She felt every one of those fingers pressing into her flesh. The warmth of them seeped right through her silk suit.

His sigh made her look up to see him shaking his head slowly.

"What?"

His hands still hadn't moved away.

"I..." He looked down, took his hands away. "I'm just not used to handling tiny things," he said, and he looked embarrassed. "Like Ethan, and now you."

Her throat went dry. She didn't know how the hell to reply to a comment like that, so she said nothing. Garrett finally turned away and headed for the door. He used a set of keys she hadn't noticed to unlock it, then pushed it open and stood aside, waiting for her to go first.

The office consisted of only one sparsely furnished

room, and two cells at the far back. That was it. She looked at him in surprise.

"Not much happens around here," he explained, reading her expression. He left the door wide open after coming in behind her.

"Obviously."

He shrugged and moved past her to the file cabinet, which wasn't even locked. After riffling through a drawer, he pulled out a folder, tossed it onto his desk and took a seat in the big hardwood chair behind it. As he began flipping pages, Chelsea felt restless. She prowled the office, examining some photos on the wall, and paused at one that had been taken right in front of the ranch house. A huge family. Five boys and a little baby girl. Two proud parents standing behind the group of smiling kids.

The oldest of the boys, she knew without a doubt, was Garrett. He stood taller than his father, with shoulders that seemed too big for his body. He'd been a gangly teen, she thought a little smugly. Long limbed and awkward.

Her gaze stole to him as he sat behind that desk, dwarfing the big antique. He certainly had grown into his body. His proportions were perfect now. He ought to be a centerfold.

She drew a little gasp at her uncharacteristic thought.

He looked up, caught her staring at him. He held her gaze with his for a long moment, and finally he smiled. His smile was a killer.

"That's a pretty suit, by the way."

Confusion made her blink. She glanced down at the forest green silk skirt and the sleeveless blouse that matched it. "It's too hot here for silk. I should have known better."

"It's the same color as your eyes."

Her head came up fast.

A deep red color crept up his neck into his face, and he looked for all the world as if his blurted compliment had been as surprising to him as it had been to her. "I mean...you know. Green and all." He quickly lowered his gaze to the papers in front of him again, shuffling madly.

"Yeah," she said in a voice just above a whisper. "Green and all."

"*Muchacho,* what *are* you doing here on a holiday?"

Chelsea turned, surprised by the frail, heavily accented voice coming through the open door.

"Hey, Marisella," Garrett said, and he rose, went to the door and took both of the deeply tanned, wrinkled hands in his. "How's my best girl?"

"Oh, now, Garrett..." The elderly woman—who wore jeans and a Travis Tritt T-shirt of all things—gazed up into the big man's eyes much like little Ethan had done earlier. Her black eyes beamed adoration.

"How's the arthritis, Marisella?" His tone was more serious now.

"No worse than usual."

"And ol' Pedro?"

She shook her head slowly, her dark eyes going sad. "He doesn't eat, Garrett. Pedro, he is turning his nose up at everything I offer. Doc Ramone is away at that veterinary convention, and I am sick with worry." Marisella glanced over Garrett's shoulder at Chelsea, then smiled. "And who is the *chica?*"

Garrett turned to her. "Marisella, I'd like you to meet Chelsea Brennan. She's staying out at the ranch with us for a few days."

A few days?

"Chelsea, Marisella del Carmen Jalisco. Prettiest widow lady either side of the Rio Grande."

Marisella's sun-bronzed face crinkled when she smiled, and she waved a dismissive hand at Garrett's compliments, nodding to Chelsea. "Good to meet you, Señorita Brennan. You are from the east, yes?"

"New York."

Silvery brows went up. "And which of the Brands is it you've come to...see?"

Chelsea frowned. "I'm not sure what—"

"None of them, Marisella," Garrett interrupted. "She's a friend. That's all. Now listen, I'll come by this evening to have a look at that worthless ol' cat of yours, all right? Maybe Jessi and I can doctor him up for you."

"It will be a relief to me if you do! When Pedro is not well, I feel as bad as he does."

"We'll be there."

She reached up to pat Garrett's cheek. "You do your papa proud, *hombre*. Never a time anyone in Quinn has trouble, but that you offer a hand. I do believe the woman who captures your heart will have her hands on a diamond." After the last pointed statement, she aimed a wink in Chelsea's direction, then turned to go.

Garrett hurried to grip her elbow and ease her down the steps, his hands touching her as if she might break. He really did *seem* gentle.

As he stepped outside with Marisella, a breeze wafted in through the door, lifting the papers from the desk and scattering them. And then it died, leaving the air as still and muggy as before. Chelsea automatically went to pick the papers up, gathering them into a stack, one by one. But she paused with one sheet in hand because the date across the top caught her eye. April 1.

She froze, then hurriedly scanned the sheet, certain she was about to find a record of a return trip from N.Y. detailed there somewhere. But instead, she found the opposite.

Each sheet in the stack was a typewritten record of the day's events. Only they didn't read like dry, technical police reports. More like a journal or a diary. This particular page began with a single paragraph that took all the wind out of her sails.

> Nine a.m.—Career Day at Quinn Elementary. Talked until 10:00 and answered questions till 10:40. Lord, but we have some characters in this town! Almost made me wish I had my own little brood at home.

Below that, marked with two stars, a postscript: "Note—check in on Brian Muldoon's mamma."

"Those are personal notes you're reading, Chelsea, not official records."

She looked up with a start to see Garrett lounging in the doorway, arms folded across his chest, looking at her. She swallowed hard, shook her head, added the sheet to the top of the stack and crossed the room to hand it to him.

He took the papers, glancing down at what she'd been reading, and nodded. "Career Day," he said. "How could I have forgotten that one?"

Chelsea tried to drag her gaze away from him, but couldn't. Had she been all wrong about him? She cleared her throat, searching for something to say, before latching onto the first thing that came to mind. "What was wrong with Brian Muldoon's mother?"

Garrett frowned down at the paper, then lifted his head and focused his big, soft brown eyes on her face. His voice more gentle than she'd heard up to now, he said, "Brian's daddy liked to hit her."

The pain sparked to life, though she slammed the door on her emotions before they could show. She fixed her face into an iron mask, refusing to flinch. "And what did you do about it?"

"Oh, the usual. We arrested him a couple of times, tried to talk her into pressing charges. She was too afraid of him to do it, though. And we couldn't blame her. We all knew he wouldn't serve enough time to do him any good."

"So he's still here in Quinn, beating the hell out of his wife?"

Garrett shook his head slowly. "We don't take to that kind of thing around here, Chelsea."

"Right. But your hands are tied, isn't that it?"

"Not by a long shot. I warned the worthless fool to stop...or else. He hurt her again. So my brothers and I went over there and...had a little talk with him."

Chelsea tilted her head, staring at him in disbelief.

"We made him see that the best thing for all concerned would be for him to get out of Quinn and never set foot here again."

"And he did? Just like that?"

"Well, we can be pretty convincing when we set our minds to it."

"You...you beat him up, didn't you?"

He drew a breath that lifted his shoulders and slowly let it all out again. Then he came forward and placed both his hands on her shoulders. She automatically shrugged away from his touch. She didn't like men putting their hands on her.

He frowned, but let his hands fall to his sides. "Chelsea Brennan, I'd rather be shot than lift a violent hand to anyone…or anything, for that matter."

"Oh?" He was too close to her. She could feel his warm breath on her lips. "Thing is, I'd have rather been drawn and quartered than to stand by and do nothing. So I told him to leave her alone in the only language he could understand. The way I see it, I didn't have much of a choice."

"And he never came back?"

"Nope. He never did."

"You violated his civil rights," she observed, but it was a weak argument. "You could lose your job and go to prison for that."

He nodded slowly. "No man has the right to lift a hand to a woman, Chelsea. Nor to a child. If you'd been in my shoes, would you have done anything different?"

She met his gaze head-on, and for just a moment the pain got the best of her. "If I'd been in your shoes," she said softly, "I'd have shot the bastard."

He narrowed his eyes as he studied her. "You're one angry woman, Chelsea Brennan."

She nodded. "You might want to take back your offer to help me find the man who murdered my sister, Garrett Brand. Because when I do, I'll probably kill him."

He smiled a little, and for a second she wondered why.

"I take that to mean you're finally convinced it wasn't me," he explained when she frowned at him.

She lowered her head, remembering her accusations,

the way she'd hit him. If she'd been wrong... But it was pretty obvious she *had* been wrong, wasn't it?

"I probably owe you an apology."

"Probably."

He stood there, and his hands rose as if to touch her shoulders again. She stiffened, and he stopped himself, lowering them again with a thoughtful expression on his face. He was waiting.

"I apologize."

"I accept," he said with an abbreviated bow, really no more than a dip of his head and shoulders, but he never broke eye contact.

"Then you're more forgiving than I'd be." There was an invisible beam running between her eyes and his. Something that held her captive.

"Must be those green eyes of yours, making me feel generous." He moved a little closer.

Warmth curled in the pit of her stomach before she reminded herself he'd just given similarly effusive compliments to Marisella. "Then you won't object to my taking my nephew home anymore?"

Garrett stiffened and the smile left his face. "I'm afraid I have to."

Shock sent her backward. "Why?"

"I still have some unanswered questions, Chelsea."

"*Your* unanswered questions don't mean squat to me, Sheriff! We're talking about *my* nephew here. You can't keep him."

Garrett pushed a hand through his thick hair and turned to pace away from her. Then he came back again. "Will you just use your head for a minute, woman? Suppose you're right, and this no-account your sister was with *did* kill her. Don't you suppose he's looking for his son about now?"

"I'm sure of it, you big, dense *redneck!* That's why I want to get Ethan the hell out of here!"

"And you think this guy doesn't know about you? You think in a whole year with him your sister never once told him about you? Legally, he could still take his son from you, Chelsea. You wouldn't have a leg to stand on in court. Not unless you can prove your suspicions about him are true."

"He can't take Ethan from me if he can't find me," she argued, no longer sure why she was in such a hurry to get out of Texas and away from Garrett Brand. The man shook her in ways she'd never been shaken before.

"Hell, you said yourself you'd seen him from your apartment window. It kind of follows that he knows where you live!"

She opened her mouth, but lost the power of speech.

He knows where I live.

A gut-deep fear engulfed her—one she hadn't felt since she was a little girl lying in bed late at night, listening to the thudding sounds of fists against flesh and the guttural groans of her mother. A man like that one knew where she lived.

She'd sworn she'd never be afraid again. But she was afraid now.

Two hesitant backward steps put her up against a wall. One she needed, or she'd collapse. She was trembling. God, she hated this kind of fear.

"Chelsea?"

He was there in front of her, looking worried and scared.

"I'll kill him," she whispered, and for a second she wasn't even sure if she was talking about her father or Ethan's.

"Damn, your face is as white as a lily, woman." And a moment later, he lifted his hands, hesitated and awkwardly gathered her close to him. He held her to his chest and ran one hand up and down her back the way he might do with the baby. Trying to comfort her. "I didn't say that to scare you, Chelsea. I didn't mean to—"

"I'm not afraid of that bastard," she muttered.

"No. No, of course you're not. Hell, any woman who'd march right up to a fella my size and deliver a right hook isn't afraid of anything."

One of his hands ran over her hair, and she closed her eyes. Then, realizing how very safe she felt in his arms, she went stiff as a board. "I don't need any *man* to protect me."

He stilled. Then slowly, his hands fell away and he stepped back. "I didn't say you did. But let's just be practical. If you go home to New York, he'll know where to find you and Ethan. But right now, he has no idea where you are."

"Assuming he's even looking for us. He might not care any more about his son than he did Michele."

"Maybe not. But why risk it?"

She searched his face as the answer was there.

"Just stay for a day or two, Chelsea. Long enough for me to try to find out who this man is and what he's capable of. Please. Do it for Ethan."

She lifted her chin a little. It galled her to admit Ethan was safer here with Garrett than he would be back in New York with her, but dammit, the man had a point. And she couldn't very well risk the baby for the sake of her pride.

"All right," she said at last. "All right, we'll stay. But only for a day or two."

Garrett smiled fully, and just for an instant, Chelsea forgot how to breathe. Now that she knew he hadn't killed her sister, she noticed that this man was attractive. Incredibly attractive. And that was something Chelsea had stopped noticing about *any* man a very long time ago. Maybe Garrett Brand wasn't physically dangerous to her after all. But she was only now beginning to realize how emotionally dangerous it might be to spend much time around him.

Because he couldn't possibly be as kind and gentle as he was pretending. No man could.

Chapter 6

Vincent de Lorean downed his third shot of tequila and lifted his gaze from the sparkling water in the terrazzo-tiled pool to scan the faces of the three men who stood in front of him. He didn't like the expressions they wore. He didn't expect to like the news they were about to deliver, either. Setting the cut-crystal glass down on the umbrella-shaded table beside him, he sent a pointed glance at Monique.

"Go inside."

She gave him a playful pout, but obeyed. She knew better than to question him. Smarter than the last pretty woman he'd brought here. Maybe she'd turn out better. Monique rose with the sensuality she knew he liked, lowering her long legs slowly, running one hand over plump breasts and then slowly over her belly before turning to click her heels across the concrete and wiggle her butt through the stucco villa's glass doors. The three men turned to watch her bikini-clad body as she moved away from them. They wanted her. Vincent knew it, and it pleased him. He liked other people to crave what was his.

As long as they didn't try to take it from him.

"Have you found my son?" he asked, and all three heads snapped around to face him again.

Jonas had been with him for ten years, and Vincent knew the fear in his eyes was real when he shook his head slowly from side to side. William, too, had the good sense to be afraid. But the third one, the new man...something was wrong there. Lash, he called himself, though Vincent was unsure whether it was a first name or last. He stood there, by all appearances, respectful. But there was no fear in his face nor in his blue eyes. In fact, Vincent smelled the smallest hint of defiance in the man.

He needed a lesson, this one. Vincent knew how to keep his men loyal. Fear. Once they knew he held their lives in his hands, they would never betray him. He sat quietly while Jonas spoke, assessing the best way to deliver the lesson.

"It's only a matter of time, boss. You know that we will—"

"The sister?" Vincent interrupted, having come to a decision on today's teaching methods. "What about the sister?"

"She was in El Paso," Jonas said. "She identified Michele's body, asked about Ethan, then left. She hasn't checked into any hotels in the area and she hasn't returned to New York."

"Then where the hell is she?"

Jonas closed his eyes, swallowed hard. "We have men watching her apartment, Vince. We'll find her. I swear it."

Vincent pursed his lips and shifted his gaze to Lash. "You. You were supposed to be staking out the medical examiner's office. You were told to follow this Chelsea Brennan when she left there. What happened?"

He didn't flinch or look away. He shrugged instead. "I lost her. It was pouring rain and she was driving like a maniac."

Vincent didn't like this man. He usually never hired men larger than himself or better-looking. He'd made an exception this time, because his oldest employee, Jonas, had told him what an asset this one would be. Furthermore, this Lash's voice held the slightest hesitation. The way a man spoke when he was lying...or when he was nervous. Vincent's ego preferred the latter theory to the former. Nervousness wasn't fear, but it was a start. The lesson he had in mind should solidify the man's loyalty.

Vincent drew a breath and released it slowly. As he did, he dropped his right hand to the folded towel beside his lounge chair. They couldn't see that hand. And they couldn't see the gun he pulled from beneath the towel, either. Not until he quickly leveled it on Jonas and pulled the trigger.

Jonas didn't have time to blink. His head snapped back. His knees buckled. He thudded to the concrete. William staggered a few steps backward before he started to cry and snivel, probably expecting to be next. The other one just stood there, staring right into Vincent's eyes, his own as cold as ice. Those eyes registered disgust and a little surprise. Still no fear.

"Jonas told me you'd be an asset," Vincent said softly, and he examined the silvery weapon in his hands. "He was wrong. I don't tolerate mistakes in my employees. Do you understand that now?"

"Jonas was the smartest man you had working for you," Lash replied in a steady, controlled voice. "He might have found your son for you. Now...who knows?"

Vincent stood up, walked closer to Lash. "*I* know. You will find him. And if you fail..." He said nothing more. Just sent a glance down at the body. "Now get him out of here. And find that woman. If she thinks she can keep my son from me, she's going to be very sorry. As sorry as her pathetic sister."

Garrett took his time. He drove Chelsea around Quinn, pointing out the shops he thought might interest her. Then he took her over the River Road to show her the Rio Grande. The idea was to calm her down a little bit. Because she'd been damned scared back there in his office. Hell, he'd never seen that kind of fear come over a person so suddenly or so completely as it had come over her when he'd pointed out that a killer knew where she lived.

She might talk a big game and she might be so filled with anger she was ready to take on the world. But deep inside, Chelsea Brennan was a frightened woman.

And she didn't like to be touched. He'd discerned that, as well. Whenever he'd had call to put his hands on her—which, as a matter of fact, he'd done more often than was probably necessary—she reacted like a skittish colt. Got all stiff and nervous and always ended the contact just as quickly as possible.

He was thinking that Jessi had been right about her suspicions. That maybe Chelsea had been hurt, physically hurt, by someone in her past.

He didn't like thinking that because it made him angry, and he hated being angry. He was too big to allow himself the luxury of a short temper. All his life he'd struggled to be calm and relaxed, no matter what. Hell, he hadn't even lost his temper when he'd put the fear of God into Brian Muldoon's heavy-fisted father. And the truth was, he'd taken his brothers along, not for support, but just to be sure he didn't actually *hurt* the man, much as the bastard deserved to be hurt.

He didn't like the feeling that came over him now, though, when he thought about someone lifting a violent hand to the woman beside him. Because it went beyond anger. It made him sick. He almost didn't *want* to know if it were true. He almost didn't want to know who had hurt her.

Almost.

She seemed a little calmer when they arrived back at the ranch that afternoon. Not much, but a littlc.

Ethan sat in a high chair in the kitchen, and Elliot was making motor noises and driving a spoonful of green goo into his mouth.

Garrett frowned. ''Where'd that come from?''

''The baby food or the high chair?'' Jessi asked after taking a bite of her fajita. Then she grinned. ''Actually, it doesn't matter. Both of them were provided by our grouchy brother who claims to dislike babies.''

''Wes?'' Garrett shifted his gaze to Wes, who scowled back at him.

''Kid needed a place to sit, didn't he?''

Elliot grinned broadly at Wes's muttered reply. ''Hell, I think Wes here would make a great little mother. Don't you, Jessi?''

''Of course he would. He ought to have a whole

slew of babies crawling all over him, and maybe run a nursery school on the side.''

''Old Mother Goose,'' Elliot sang, ''when *he* wanted to wander, would fly through the air on a very fine, er, Paint. Gee, Wes, that doesn't fit. Any chance you can change Paint's name to Gander?''

Wes grimaced and attacked his fajita. Garrett just shook his head and went to the table. ''Did you leave us any crumbs or anything?''

Elliot pointed to the heaping platter in the table's center. ''I know it's not enough to fill *you* up, big brother, but it might make an appetizer.''

''Come on, Chelsea,'' Jessi said. ''There's plenty. Sit down and eat.''

Garrett noticed Chelsea's surprised expression. She covered it fast and came forward anyway. Wes grabbed the platter and set it down in front of her, while Elliot popped a bite into the baby's mouth, then got up to go to the fridge. He poured a glass of milk and set it down in front of Chelsea. Without a word, he just set it down, then returned to his baby-feeding duties.

Chelsea looked disconcerted. ''Th-thank you.''

Wes cleared his throat. ''We, uh, we were rough on you last night.''

He turned those black eyes of his on her. Garrett saw it and half-expected her to melt into a puddle at his devilishly handsome, half-Comanche brother's feet the way most women did if he so much as glanced their way.

''I wasn't exactly polite,'' Chelsea replied, remaining solid.

Jessi passed the tossed salad. ''We Brands are a tight bunch. We take care of our own. But we've been talking and…well, I guess you were just doing the same thing we'd have done in your shoes. So…"

"What my sister is trying to say, Chelsea," Elliot explained, "is that we're sorry about what happened to your sister, and we want to help you and little Ethan through this if we can."

Garrett felt his back straighten, and battled a smile. Maybe he'd taught them something after all. Chelsea sat at his right, and he thought he saw a lump come and go in her throat, but he wasn't sure. He thought he understood the change now. He was pretty certain Jessi had told the other two about what she'd heard and about her theory. He knew the thought of some bastard beating up on a little thing like Chelsea would turn their stomachs the same way it did his own.

"I, um…" Chelsea shook her head and pushed away from the table. "I have to go upstairs." She turned and quickly left.

"Garrett?" Jessi asked, staring after her.

"I don't know, Jes. Let's let her be for now. I'm going back to the office later to run a check on her and her sister, see what I can find out. Jes, I'll need you to come with me. Marisella's cat is off his feed again, and she's making herself sick worrying about him."

"Sure."

"Elliot and I can take care of things here tonight, Garrett. Leave whenever you need to."

Garrett nodded at Wes and, a few hours later, did just that.

But what he found out was not one bit pleasing to him, and it only made matters worse.

That evening, after he'd dropped Jessi at Marisella's, he'd spent a good hour sitting at his desk trying to get over the shock of it.

Chelsea Brennan's father, Calvin Brennan, had been arrested twenty-five times for spousal and/or child abuse. New York State Social Services had been called in when school officials reported the two girls often coming to school covered in bruises. But they hadn't taken action soon enough. Calvin was in Attica, serving the eighteenth year of a twenty-year sentence for beating his wife to death.

Garrett swore under his breath and thought again about the turmoil and the pain and the rage he saw every time he looked into Chelsea Brennan's eyes.

And he felt a burning moisture taking shape in his own.

Chelsea sat by the fireplace, imagining a cheerful fire burning in the grate. Anything cheerful would be a relief if it would dispel the grim mood that had settled over her.

Elliot and Wes bantered in the kitchen over whose turn it was to clean up the dinner dishes. From the wide window in the living room, Chelsea could see Jessi feeding carrots to a spotted horse. An ancient pickup truck with a driver Chelsea had recognized as Marisella del Carmen Whatever had dropped Jessi off twenty minutes ago, but Garrett still hadn't returned. She wondered what was keeping him in town. A woman, maybe? The idea gnawed at her a little more than it should have as she watched Jessi coax the beautiful animal closer and then stroke its muzzle as it snapped the carrots from her hands. Behind Jessi, the lush grass seemed to go on forever, a wide green blanket beneath a gigantic, sapphire sky as blue as little Ethan's eyes.

She remembered the photo she'd seen, the one of the Brand family taken years ago, and she thought this must have been a magical place for children. Room to run. Room to grow. This huge family surrounding them like a protective cocoon. A child would thrive here.

Ethan sat on the braided rug in the center of the polished hardwood floor, chewing on a worn-out old teddy bear's paw. Chelsea had no idea where the bear had come from. No doubt one of the Brands had dug it up from somewhere. They treated Ethan as if he were their own. Close beside Ethan—as always, she'd noticed—the big, gentle dog, eyes alert, watching the baby's every move and occasionally inching closer in hopes of a pat or a tug on the ear.

Chelsea battled the sense of unease that had settled on her like a shroud at the dinner table tonight. These people were good and kind. They had the type of happy, stable life she and her sister had always craved and dreamed about. And along comes Chelsea Brennan and her dead sister's baby, with maybe a killer on her trail. The thought that she might bring disaster raining down on this haven ate away at her. They wanted to help her but they'd only get hurt if they tried. The way her mother had. And she couldn't let that happen.

Yet, for the moment, Ethan was safer here than in any other place she could imagine. Chelsea was torn.

To battle her restlessness, she got up and headed into the kitchen, not the least bit worried about Ethan. She'd noticed the way the outlets in the living room had all been plugged and anything breakable had been moved out of Ethan's reach. Someone had placed an expandable gate across the bottom of the stairway. Ethan was safe here.

Safe.

She walked into the kitchen just in time to see Elliot

snap Wes with the twisted end of a dish towel. Both laughed out loud, then stopped when they saw her standing in the doorway.

"Why not let me do the dishes this time?" she offered. "I know you have stuff to do outside."

"Hey, that's—"

"No way," Wes interrupted his brother. "You're a guest. Garrett would have our hides nailed to the barn wall."

"At least let me help. I need something to do, you know?"

Wes's dark eyes held hers for a moment. They were powerful, his black eyes. He was obviously part Native American, and Chelsea wondered why he seemed so different from the other Brands. He also had a way of looking at a person that was piercing and knowing. He nodded, snatched the dish towel from his brother and tossed it to her. "Okay. You can dry."

"Okay," she said, catching the towel and moving forward to the sink where Elliot had resumed washing dishes. Wes went back to clearing the table.

Chelsea could see these people had decided to make her welcome here. And though she was uncomfortable with them, she was grateful, too. If it hadn't been for this family, God only knows what might have happened to the baby.

"It's nice to see men doing housework and a woman outside with the horses," she said in an attempt at normal conversation. "Is it always like this?"

"We share the work around here," Elliot told her. "Garrett says he doesn't want Jess raised to think all she's good for is cooking and cleaning for a bunch of males. So we divide up the duties equally, inside and out."

She nodded. It was something she would have expected Garrett to think about. "I saw a photo in his office, of the whole family, I think, only you were all kids. You know the one I mean?"

Elliot suddenly stilled with a plate in his hand. Frowning, Chelsea turned to see Wes had paused in what he'd been doing, as well.

"I'm sorry. Did I say something wrong?"

"No," Wes told her. He gave his head a shake and gathered up a few more plates, turned and brought them to the sink. "We all have copies of that photo. It was the last one we had taken before Orrin and Maria were killed."

She frowned. "Your parents?"

"Yeah," Elliot said softly. "Our parents."

"Orrin was my father, Maria my stepmother, but she treated me like her own son," Wes clarified.

"I'm so sorry. God, you were all so young. Jessi was just a baby in that photo. What did you do?"

"Garrett held things together." Elliot shook his head, plunging his hands back into the soapy water. "He'd only just finished high school when it happened and he'd already been accepted at Texas State, but he didn't go. He stayed home instead. Ran the ranch as well as any grown man could have done. And took care of this brood like a mother hen herding chicks."

"The state wanted to separate us," Wes said, picking up the story. "They wanted to send me to a family on the Comanche reservation, and the others into foster care elsewhere. If it hadn't been for Garret, they would have."

"No wonder you all love him so much."

"We'd kill for him," Wes said, his voice low, his

face expressionless, but Chelsea sensed the deep feeling underlying his words.

''We'd die for him,'' Elliot added with a firm nod and a slight crack in his voice.

It made her throat go tight to see such closeness in a family. It was the sort of thing she'd always fantasized about but had long since given up on finding for herself.

She dried the last cup and stacked it in the cupboard, swallowed hard and decided to change the subject. ''There were six children in the photo.''

''Yeah. Adam and Ben are the two you haven't met. Adam's in New York. Landed himself a job there last summer,'' Elliot explained.

''So far from home?'' It seemed uncharacteristic in such a tight family.

''His fiancée dumped him for another man the day of their wedding,'' Elliot went on. ''He couldn't stand being in the same town with her any—''

''Elliot.''

Wes's voice held a warning. Family secrets, Chelsea supposed. And she wasn't family.

''I didn't mean to pry.''

Elliot sent her a sheepish smile. Wes just sighed, shook his head and grabbed a sponge to begin wiping off the table.

''Hell, everyone in town knows about it anyway,'' Elliot added, unperturbed by his brother's censure. ''And Ben, he's off in the mountains somewhere in Tennessee. Took off after his wife, Penny, died nearly a year ago, and we haven't heard a word from him since.''

''Garrett has,'' Wes contradicted. ''If he didn't

know Ben was all right, he'd have hauled all of us over there to hunt him down."

"Yeah, but a postcard once a month telling us he's still breathing isn't what I call correspondence."

"He must be hurting," Chelsea said softly.

Elliot lowered his head in a sad, slow nod. "We Brand men haven't exactly been lucky in love."

"I just wish they'd both lick their wounds and get back here," Wes declared."It's tough running a ranch shorthanded."

"What we need," Elliot remarked, pulling the plug and watching the water swirl down the drain, "is one good crisis. If they thought we were in trouble, they'd be here so fast—"

"Careful what you wish for, boy," Wes warned him. He gave the oval oak table one last swipe and tossed the sponge into the sink. Then he snatched his hat off the back of a chair and dropped it on his head. "Come on. We're burning daylight, and those two heifers are due to freshen any day now."

Elliot took the towel from Chelsea, wiped his hands and sent her a wink as he followed his brother outside.

Chelsea decided maybe Garrett had been right after all. It was safe here. In fact, while she hated to admit it after the way she'd initially treated all of them, she felt safer here than she'd ever felt in her entire life. Maybe it *would* be better to stay...just for a couple of days. Just to be sure her sister's killer wasn't a threat to her or to Ethan.

She picked up the phone. If she was staying, she'd need more funds, and she knew her last week's paycheck would be in her mail by now. She called her apartment manager, who was also a friend who lived down the hall from her, and felt lucky to catch the party animal at home.

"Mindy?"

"Chelsea? Is that you?"

"Yes. I'm—"

"Where *are* you? What's going on? Did you find Michele?"

That was Mindy. She talked a mile a minute and barely took time to breathe in between. "Michele…" Chelsea swallowed past the lump in her throat. "She'd dead, Mindy."

"Oh, my God! What happened? Are you okay? Did you find the baby? Is he all right? What about—"

"He's all right. He's with me. We're both fine. But I'm going to be down here awhile."

"You need anything, Chels? Anything I can do on this end, you know? Water your plants, send you something. 'Cause if I can do anything, I—"

"Yes. I do need you to do something."

"Anything. You name it and I'll do it. You poor kid, are you sure you're all right?"

"Fine. I need you to forward my mail for a few days, okay?"

"Sure. You got it. Let me grab a pen… Okay, here we go. Give me the address."

"I'm at the Texas Brand, Quinn, Texas."

"Sounds like a dude ranch."

"I don't know the zip."

"I'll get it from the post office, Chelsea. Don't worry, I'll send your stuff out tomorrow morning first thing, okay?"

"Thanks. I appreciate it."

"Chelsea?"

"Yes?"

"Michele's...funeral. You'll let me know, won't you?"

Chelsea closed her eyes as a deep shudder worked up from her feet all the way to her shoulders. She had to bury her sister. If this didn't kill her, she didn't think anything ever would.

"Yeah. I'll let you know."

"Thanks, Chels. You take care, okay?"

Chelsea didn't answer. She just replaced the receiver and turned her head to see sweet little Ethan on the floor. He'd fallen asleep there, and that old dog had curled up close beside him.

The creak of the screen door brought her gaze around, and it locked with Garrett's. His eyes—deep brown and soft as velvet—scanned her face, narrowed and probed. "Chelsea?"

She lowered her head. "I don't think I can do this."

He took a step toward her, then stopped, stood still. "Chelsea Brennan, I think you can do just about anything you set your mind to."

She shook her head.

He sighed deeply, his eyes roaming her face for a long moment. Then he came a little closer. "Did I ever tell you how much you remind me of my mamma?"

She looked up at him then, brows raised.

"She was the prettiest woman in the state of Texas. Her eyes were brown, not green, but they flashed with that same fire I see in yours sometimes. I never thought I'd know another woman with the kind of strength she had in her. But I was wrong about that."

"I'm not strong."

"To survive what you have, lady, you must have bones of solid granite."

Chelsea's eyes widened as she searched his face.

And she saw the knowledge there, as plain as day. He didn't try to hide it. "You know, don't you?"

"About your father? Yeah, I know."

Chelsea closed her eyes, unable to look at him, knowing that her sordid past was an open book to him. She should have known that he'd find out. Her family history was largely a matter of public record after all, and he was a sheriff with access to all of it.

"I dream about him, you know," she whispered, not sure why her lips were moving, why she felt compelled to tell this man anything more horrible than he already knew. "I dream about the day he's released from prison. I'm there at the front gate, waiting for him. And as soon as he sees me, as soon as he looks straight into my eyes...I kill him." She looked at Garrett, half-expecting to see shock or disapproval in his eyes. But she only saw a reflection of her own pain. As if he felt it, too. "It scares me, Garrett. It scares the hell out of me because I think I could really do it."

"Then he'd win. Because you'd end up in prison, or dead, and every one of the Brennan women would be gone. And I think deep down, you know that, Chelsea. I think you're too smart to let him get the best of you that way. Even if you weren't, I don't think you'd kill him. Not when it came right down to it. Because deep down inside, you're not like him. Not at all."

"I wish I was as sure of that as you are," she whispered. "I hate him."

"I know." He took another step, this one bringing him close to her, but he didn't touch her. He just stood near enough so she could feel the heat from his body floating into hers. When she breathed, it was his scent and his breath she was inhaling. "I don't even know him, Chelsea, and I hate him, too."

"Why?" She looked up as she asked the question, saw him staring down at her.

"Because he hurt you."

"Why do you give a damn about that? You barely know me."

Garrett shrugged his big shoulders. "Damned if I know. Been asking myself the same thing all night. Doesn't matter, though, does it? Point is, I do give a damn. And right now, I'm fighting everything in me to keep from putting my arms around you, little Chelsea Brennan, and pulling you close to me and holding you until you stop shaking like a scared rabbit. Just the way I used to do with Jessi late at night when she'd had a bad dream. Or with Elliot when he'd wake up crying for Mamma. I'm fighting it because I know you don't like men putting their hands on you. And I can't say as I blame you for it."

He spoke slowly, his deep voice soft and steady and low. She realized he was trying to calm her, comfort her.

"M-maybe…it would be all right…."

He sighed, and his big hands slipped around her waist, their touch warm, but light as air. He didn't pull her to him. He just put his arms loosely around her and waited. Chelsea was the one who moved forward until her body was pressed to his. She turned her head to the side and rested it against his chest, right over the drumming of his heart. His arms tightened but only a little. One hand moved upward to stroke her hair slowly, soothingly, over and over.

"No one," she whispered, her words coming harder now, "has held me like this…since my mother…"

"It's okay," Garrett told her. "It's gonna be okay now, Chelsea."

"We heard him yelling at her. Heard the slaps. It was nothing we hadn't heard before. So many times before... She told us to stay in our room when he was like that, but I couldn't. It was different that time. There was something inside me, telling me...and I knew...I knew she was in trouble. I knew it when she stopped screaming. So I went...and she was just lying there...her face was so...it didn't even look like her."

His hand stilled in her hair, and she felt his muscles go taut. "And him?"

"Gone," she whispered. "Just gone. I bent over my mother. I touched her. I shook her. But she wouldn't wake up. She just wouldn't wake up."

His arms tightened around her convulsively. He held her hard now and rocked very gently from side to side. "Damn," he muttered.

"I was nine years old, Garrett. But it feels like yesterday."

He held her tighter.

"Mom," Chelsea cried softly, "Jesus, Mom, why?" Something warm trickled down her face, surprising her. Shocking her. Tears. She hadn't cried since that night. But she was crying now. And she couldn't seem to stop the tears. Garrett's shirt dampened with them, then became soaked with them, and still she cried. So many years' worth of teardrops and she wasn't sure she'd ever stop crying again.

Chapter 7

When she heard her brothers' booted feet coming up the steps, Jessi turned away from the screen door and put a finger to her lips.

Wes frowned at her. Elliot tilted his head.

She waved them closer, still shushing them, and when they were close enough, she pointed.

In the kitchen, Garrett held the mite of a woman in his great big arms. He held her very close and stroked her hair while she sobbed as if her heart were breaking into a million bits. And as they watched, Chelsea's hands rose slowly until they closed on Garrett's shoulders, and she clung to him as if she were holding on for dear life. The tears she shed were not pretty ones. She sobbed out loud with great heaving spasms that should have torn a woman her size right in half.

As tears brimmed in her own eyes, Jessi turned away and walked quietly off the big front porch. She didn't stop until she'd reached the gate to the east pasture, where horses grazed contentedly, and then she leaned against it, blinking her eyes dry.

She wasn't surprised when Wes's hand lowered to her shoulder. "What happened in there, Jessi?"

Jessi turned around and flung herself right into her brother's arms, and he hugged her tight. "Oh, Wes, it's more horrible than I thought! I know I shouldn't have been listening at the door, but I couldn't help myself when I heard what she was saying."

Wes eased her away from him and searched her face with those black eyes that seemed to see right inside a person.

Jessi wiped her eyes dry with the back of one hand, then shook her head. "We can't let her go back east. I'll tell you that much. That girl needs a family like nobody I've ever seen."

"She isn't a stray dog, Jessi," Wes said softly. "You can't just decide to keep her."

Jessi sniffed. "I've *already* decided. Now all I have to do is convince her she belongs here."

Elliot had joined them by this time and heard most of what they said. He stood very still, staring thoughtfully back toward the house.

Wes shook his head slowly. "We have enough trouble on our hands, Jessi. My gut tells me that this woman is only gonna bring more."

"I don't care," Jessi told him. "I want her to stay."

"Contrary to what you've been led to believe, little sister," Wes replied, "you can't have everything you want."

"Well, now, I wouldn't be too sure about *that.*" Elliot looked at them briefly, then right back at the house again. "When's the last time *you* saw Garrett hugging on a female the way he was hugging on that one?''

''Don't be stupid, Elliot. Garrett's never given a damn about women.''

''There's a first time for everything, Wes. And from what I saw in that kitchen, I'd say our big brother's perched himself right on the very brink of giving a damn.''

''Yeah,'' Jessi said slowly, drawing out the word as the solution became clear in her mind. ''All he needs is a little nudge.''

''No way.'' Wes's narrow eyes went from Jessi to Elliot and back again. ''*No.* You two stay the hell out of this. I mean it. We don't need any women cluttering things up around here, and...ah, hell, Jes, don't look like that. I didn't mean you. Just think about it for a minute. Look at Adam and Ben, both nursing broken hearts. You want to put Garrett through the same garbage?''

''Just because love didn't work out for Adam or Ben doesn't mean it won't for Garrett,'' Jessi argued. ''Come on, Wes! Garrett is different.''

''Chelsea Brennan is trouble.''

''Maybe she is,'' Jessi went on with a little pout. ''But she's *in* trouble, too. And since when has trouble been anything the Brands couldn't handle?''

Wes shook his head, turned on his heel and started to walk away.

''Wait, Wes.'' He stopped, but didn't turn to face her. ''Just listen. Let me tell you what I overheard in that kitchen. *Then* decide whether you want to help her or not.''

He turned slowly, grimacing. ''I didn't say we

shouldn't help her, kid, just that we shouldn't force-feed her to Garrett.''

''Didn't see nobody forcing him just now,'' Elliot said, earning a scowl. He grinned at Wes and nodded to Jessi. ''Go on, hon. Tell us what you know.''

Garrett had never felt more big and awkward and clumsy than he had when he'd held Chelsea's small body in his arms. But he'd also never felt weaker. Made his knees turn to jelly to think about the hell she'd been through. And the thought that she'd actually talked to him about it, that she'd let him comfort her even a little bit, filled him to brimming with something else altogether, something he didn't even try to put a name to, because he knew he couldn't.

Chores were finished, dinner over. And, as was their habit of an evening, the Brands gathered in the huge living room to rehash the day. Elliot and Jessi sat close together on the sofa, exchanging glances now and then that told Garrett they were sharing a secret. Wes had the settee to himself and looked pensive. Garrett had opted for the big easy chair, and Chelsea sat in the rocker close beside it, while Ethan crawled around the floor in a diaper and T-shirt, rushing from one pair of legs to another with all the energy of a frisky colt.

This time, he headed for Wes's legs and turned himself around to plop down onto his backside, staring up at Wes expectantly. Wes didn't notice.

''Ga!'' Ethan announced when Wes hadn't looked down at him quickly enough to suit him.

When Wes did look, Ethan put his hands up in the air. International baby code for ''Hey, pick me up, you big dummy.''

A panicked look came into Wes's eyes.

"Oh, go on, Wes. He won't bite you," Jessi teased.

When Wes still hesitated, Jessi jumped to her feet, scooped the baby up and deposited him gently on Wes's lap. Ethan grinned from ear to ear and reached up to grab Wes's slightly hawkish nose.

Elliot burst out laughing, and Wes scowled at him as he gently removed the baby's hand. Ethan snuggled into Wes's lap, resting, for the moment. Wes looked stunned.

"I still don't understand why his mamma left him here with us," Jessi mused, returning to the sofa. "And his name couldn't have been a coincidence. Garrett, are you sure you didn't—"

"Jessi, I've sworn on a stack of Bibles I didn't father this baby. You telling me you *still* don't believe me?" Being accused in front of Chelsea was somehow worse, though Garrett wasn't quite sure why.

"Of course I believe you! I was gonna say, are you sure you didn't meet Chelsea's sister somewhere, maybe a long time ago? I mean, she must have known you sometime."

Garrett looked at Chelsea, saw the silent question in her eyes. "No, I didn't tell them," he said. "Why don't you get that photo and show it to Jessi. See if she remembers." He hoped she would. Because he'd felt better if he were sure Chelsea believed what he'd told her, and having Jessi confirm his recollection would go a long ways toward convincing her.

"I don't know why I didn't show you all right at the beginning. Instead, I stormed in here like a..." She shook her head.

"Like a wet hen?" Jessi offered.

"No," Elliot said. "No, I'd say she was more like a wounded bear."

"She can't be a bear, Elliot. She's way too small," Wes countered. "She came in here like a Texas wildfire."

They were all grinning at Chelsea, treating her just the way they treated each other, and at first Garrett thought she'd be offended. But she shook her head again in self-deprecation and smiled back at them as she got up from the rocker.

She headed upstairs and Garrett watched her go, wondering how anything as delicate-looking as she was could have such a steel core. She came back seconds later and handed the photograph to Jessi, who waited at the bottom of the stairs.

Jessi studied it, tilting her head. "She looks familiar." Jessi passed the photo to Elliot, who passed it to Wes. "I know!" Jessi shouted, startling both Ethan and ol' Blue. "Remember, Garrett, it was about a year ago? That girl you found out on the River Road with the flat tire."

"That's right," Elliot said. "You changed her tire and then had her follow you back here and stay to dinner. I remember now! Hell, she was out to here!" He held his hands out in front of his belly in an exaggerated account of her size.

Wes shook his head. "She was *not* out to there, Elliot. She was only showing a little. But I do remember her. She seemed scared or something. Remember? We offered her a room for a night or two, but she was in a hurry to move on."

"Didn't she tell us her name was Ann or something? Anna Smith, wasn't it?" Jessi said softly as if thinking aloud. "Why would she have given us a false name?"

Chelsea came close to where Garrett sat, taking the photo from Wes as she passed, and stared down at it.

"Maybe she was running from him even then. God, why didn't she just come back to me?"

"If she knew she was in trouble, Chelsea, she might not have wanted to get you involved. Or maybe... maybe she never got the chance to get that far," Garrett said gently.

Chelsea nodded.

"I still don't know why she'd name the baby after Garrett and then bring him back here," Jessi said.

"I do," Chelsea replied, her voice raw. She looked around the room at each of them. "Garrett told me about her visit here, and I've had some time to think about this. And I think I know exactly why she did what she did."

Garrett tilted his head, eager to hear Chelsea's theory.

"She was here even if it was just for a short time. And she knew...she saw what you have."

Garrett frowned, but Chelsea went on.

"When Michele and I were little, we used to pretend a lot. Our favorite make-believe game was the one where we had a big family. Lots of brothers and sisters. A nice big house, with a yard." She looked down at ol' Blue. He cocked his ears and whined, then hauled himself to his feet and came to her for a pat, which she gave. "Even a dog," she said, stroking his head and smiling. But it was a sad smile. "We'd get out all our dolls and stuffed animals and they'd all play a part in the fantasy." She drew a breath, swallowed hard. "When my sister walked through your front door, she must have seen our childhood make-believe world come true, in everything you have right here. And not just because of the big house, or the dog, or the number of people here. Because of her love that fills this old place. She must have thought this would be the happiest home in the world for a child. So later, when she had to find a safe place for her baby, she thought of this place."

"So, she brought little Ethan here and left him on our doorstep," Jessi said. "And it was probably the highest compliment anyone's ever paid us, Chelsea. Sometimes I forget how lucky I am to have these big lugs. Thanks for reminding me."

Elliot cleared his throat, averting his gaze monetarily. Wes just stared down at that baby in his lap as if he was seeing him for the first time.

"Chelsea, we haven't talked about this before," Garrett said as she took her seat in the rocker once more. "You don't have to now, if it's too much. But I checked with the Texas Rangers in El Paso today. They said Michele died of a drug overdose and that they had no reason to suspect foul play."

Chelsea's eyes widened and she looked up at him fast. "You didn't tell them about Ethan—"

"No. Of course not. I don't want his father coming for him any more than you do. But that's going to have to be dealt with sooner or later. The man has a legal claim—"

Chelsea reached across the short distance between his chair and hers, clasping one of Garrett's hands with two of her own. "Garrett, no. You can't let him take Ethan. Not ever. He killed my sister. I know he did."

Her eyes were enough to send his heart slamming against his rib cage. But he was a sheriff after all. He needed facts. "Don't you think your…past experiences…might be clouding your judgment, though?"

She shook her head, squeezing his hand more tightly. "The heroin was injected. My sister never did drugs in her life. She was running scared and she left her baby. She wouldn't have done that just so she could go shoot herself up with drugs. She wouldn't have left Ethan unless she knew she was in danger. Those things alone would convince me, Garrett. But she also had a phobia about needles. She never would have injected anything into her own body. She'd have passed out at the sight of a hypodermic."

Garrett frowned. "Did you tell the Rangers that?"

"No. I wasn't even thinking clearly, and then I came here and..." She released his hand, closed her eyes. "I just left her there. I shouldn't have done that. I shouldn't have left my sister there alone."

"There's a family plot, Chelsea," Jessi said softly, and Garrett thought she sounded close to tears. "And, well, you and little Ethan, you're just like family now."

Chelsea opened her eyes with something like awe flooding their green depths. She stared at Jessi, then turned her gaze to each of the others in the room, one by one. And one by one, Elliot, Wes and finally Garrett nodded in agreement.

"You'd...you'd let me bring Michele here? Let me..."

"It's a beautiful plot," Jessi said.

"Mamma would approve," Elliot added. "She'd have said it was right."

Chelsea just shook her head, staring at them as if in disbelief.

"I'll take care of things," Garrett told her. "We'll do it quietly. No one besides us need know where Michele is laid to rest. For now, at least."

Chelsea's eyes grew moist as she scanned the faces in the room. "There is no way to tell you what this means to me...what it would have meant to my sister.'' Her gaze settled on Jessi. ''Thank you, Jessi. I wish...I wish I could accept. But I can't.''

Jessi frowned, tilting her head.

''Michele would want to be near our mother. I'm going to make arrangements to take her back home to New York.'' She lifted her gaze to Garrett's. ''I'd like to do it soon. The idea of her spending even one more night in that horrible room...'' Her eyes fell closed and she shook her head slowly.

Garrett bit his lip to keep his objections to himself. This was no time for Chelsea to be hightailing it back to New York. Deep in his gut, he had a feeling that told him not to let her go. Not now. Maybe not for quite a while.

''I think the littlest cowboy on the Texas Brand has fallen asleep,'' Wes observed, his voice a bit gruff. He rose awkwardly, moving slow so he wouldn't disturb the sleeping child in his arms.

Jessi rose. ''I'll take him up.''

''That's all right,'' Wes said. ''I can handle it.'' He looked up from the baby, noticed the surprised gazes of his siblings and shrugged. ''Passing him around would wake him up, is all.''

Jessi and Elliot smirked, but Wes ignored them, tiptoeing up the stairs with the infant. Jessi turned to Elliot. ''Guess I'll turn in, too. It's getting late.''

''Late?'' Elliot replied. ''It's only—''

Jessi kicked his shin and scowled at him.

''Oh. Hey, it's later than I realized,'' he amended without a single glance at his watch. ''Well, guess I'll hit the hay, as well. Goodnight, Chelsea. Garrett.''

''Night,'' Chelsea replied.

Garrett only frowned. Those two rarely took to their

beds before the late news, unless they were angry with him for something or other. Or up to no good. They hadn't been pouting, so he suspected the latter. The question was, what plot were those two villains hatching?

"I hope they understand," Chelsea said softly.

Garrett turned to her, stared into her forest green eyes and got lost for just a second. "Don't worry. They do."

"I should probably call that place tomorrow. Make arrangements to have Michele sent home."

"I could do that for you, if you—"

"No. No, Michele is my sister. The only family I have…had…except for Ethan. I'll take care of her."

He nodded, wishing this feeling of foreboding would leave the pit of his stomach. He really didn't have any legal grounds to keep Chelsea here. None at all. So he supposed he'd have to let her go.

The shrill of the telephone cut into his thoughts, and he got slowly to his feet to walk to the kitchen and pick it up. His greeting was cut off, as well, by a deep voice. A level voice. One he didn't recognize.

"The child's father is Vincent de Lorean. And he knows his son is with you."

"Who is this?" Garrett demanded, his grip tightening on the receiver.

"De Lorean wants Chelsea Brennan dead, Brand. She isn't safe. Not there and not in New York. She is the only person alive who could fight de Lorean for custody of that baby and stand a chance of winning. He wants to eliminate that possibility. He has men watching her apartment. They'll grab her the second she sets foot there. Do you understand?"

"How could he…"

"He's a powerful man, Brand. A dangerous man. Don't let the woman or the child out of your sight. Not for a second. If you do, he'll have them both."

"But—"

There was a click, then silence. Garrett jiggled the cutoff but to no avail. Finally, he hung up the phone, shaking his head, wondering what the hell he was supposed to do now.

"Garrett?"

Chelsea came to stand beside him, and she had to know damned well something was wrong. Garrett never had been any good at hiding his feelings.

"What is it?"

He shook his head. Not for all the world would he tell her anything that would put the ice-cold fear back into those pretty green eyes. He forced a smile. "Nothing, Chelsea. Nothing that can't wait until morning."

She relaxed a little. Still nervous. But calmer. It hit him that maybe she trusted him just a little bit. He vowed then and there he wouldn't let her down.

She yawned, and his smile became a genuine one. "You're sleepy. Go on up to bed, Chelsea. I'm gonna do the same myself soon as I lock up for the night."

She nodded, turned to go up the stairs, then stopped and faced him again. "You've been good to me and to Ethan," she said softly. "I owe you for that."

"You don't owe us a thing, Chelsea."

"I do. I'll repay you someday."

And she headed up the stairs without another word.

"Vincent de Lorean?" Wes shook his head, pacing the kitchen with a cup of coffee in his hand. The sun was barely peeking over the horizon, painting the ranch house's front windows a pale orange, like candle glow.

"None other. Biggest organized-crime figure in the state of Texas. Has ties to the Molinaire syndicate in New York."

"Well, hell, Garrett, we can't just let her go back there. She'd be walking right into their hands."

"Exactly. The question is, how do I convince her to stay?"

"You tell her the truth." Wes set his half-filled mug on the table and leaned over it, searching his brother's face.

"And see her go back to being terrified again?"

"What choice do you have? She's bound and determined to hop a jet for New York City at the first opportunity. Hell, Garrett, what else can you do?"

Garrett frowned. The same question had been nagging at him all night, and he thought he'd come up with some kind of solution. Not an easy one. But maybe the only one. "If I can do some digging, find evidence to tie de Lorean to Michele's murder, I can put him away, Wes."

"And since when are you some kind of supercop, big brother? You really think you can do what every cop in the state of Texas, not to mention the FBI, has been trying to do for five years or more? If it was that easy to get the dirt on de Lorean, he'd have been in prison years ago."

"So what would you suggest? Let her go to New York and read about her body being found the next day? Or maybe I tell her all this, and she takes off like a scared rabbit, goes into hiding somewhere with Ethan. How far did that kind of plan get her sister?"

Wes lowered his head and sighed. "Okay. Okay. When you're right, you're right. But while you dig up dirt on de Lorean, you have to find a way to keep

Chelsea Brennan right here, where we can protect her from that bastard. What brilliant plan have you come up with to accomplish that?''

''Nothing.'' Garrett shook his head, feeling panic well up in his gut...again.

''It's simple.'' Jessi stepped in from the dining room, and Garrett started in surprise.

''Dammit, Jes, did you ever hear of a private conversation?''

''No such thing as privacy in this family.'' She walked to the coffeepot, took a mug from the tree and filled it.

When Elliot came in after her, Garrett stifled a groan. ''Great. This is just great.''

''You oughtta be glad we overheard you, brother,'' Elliot quipped, pulling out a chair and lowering his lanky body into it. ''Sounded like you were fresh out of ideas.''

''Oh, and I suppose you two have the perfect solution?''

''Sure we do.'' Jessi added sugar to her coffee and stirred slowly, her eyes twinkling. ''If you want Chelsea to stay with us, Garret, all you have to do is give her a reason.''

Garrett rolled his eyes. ''Now why didn't I think of that?''

''Don't be sarcastic,'' Jessi said. ''Garrett, maybe you haven't noticed, but Chelsea Brennan...*likes* you.''

''She likes all of us, Jes—''

''No. I mean...she *really likes* you.''

Garrett went as still as stone as his little sister's meaning sank in. Then he battled an urge to strangle her. ''Don't be stupid.''

Jessi pouted. Elliot stretched his legs, leaned back in his chair and folded his hands behind his head. "Garrett Brand, you are one dense cowboy if you think Jessi's wrong about this. Hell, I didn't see Chelsea wrapped up in *Wes's* arms last night. Nor mine, either, for that matter. It was you she was clinging to while she cried."

Garrett felt his jaw drop and his eyes widen. "You—"

"Now, Garrett, we weren't snooping. Just coming in from the barn, and there you were, big as life, hugging the stuffin' outta that little lady."

"You got it all wrong!" Garrett walked away from them, pushing his hands through his hair. "Dammit, she was upset, is all—"

"It was more than that, Garrett." Jessi came up behind him, put her hands on his shoulders. "Women know about these things. She's soft on you, I can tell."

"That's gotta be the most ridiculous... Why would she...? I don't..." He gave up trying to speak, because words just plain deserted him. Confusion took over instead, and he turned a questioning gaze on Wes.

Wes shrugged. "They have a point. Look, Garrett, nobody's saying you gotta go cow-eyed over the woman. But maybe if you just sweet-talked her a little—"

"I can't believe you guys!" Garrett spun around, ready to tell them all how ridiculous the very notion was—and saw Chelsea just coming into the kitchen. Her hair was all tousled and her big green eyes were sleepy. When she looked at him, she smiled softly, and Garrett's big heart flipped upside down and began to fill with a kind of panic he'd never felt in his whole damned life.

"Good morning," she said, her voice deep and rusty.

Garrett mouthed "mornin'" but no sound came out. He cleared his throat and tried again.

"You're just in time," Jessi said, grinning from ear to ear. "We were just saying how rude we've been. Why, we haven't even shown you around the ranch yet. And it's really something to see."

Chelsea's auburn brows rose.

"Do you ride?" Elliot asked her.

Garrett held his breath.

"No," she replied, and Garrett sighed in relief. "But I've always wanted to try."

His heart performed some more acrobatics he hadn't realized it was capable of.

"Good for you," Elliot all but shouted. "Garrett rides the fence lines every morning to check things out. Perfect chance for you to try your seat. Isn't it, Garrett?"

"She can take Sugar. Oh, Chelsea, you'll love her. She's the most gentle mare on the place." Jessi's excitement was bubbling from her pores. "Wes, why don't you go saddle Sugar for Chelsea?"

Chelsea, too, seemed a bit caught up in their enthusiasm. But when she looked at Garrett, the smile left her face. "I really ought to stay here with Ethan," she said.

"Nah. Jessi can take charge of that little pistol for a while. I'll handle her chores for her," Elliot offered.

Garrett nearly choked. Elliot, offering to do extra chores?

Chelsea's eyes were still on him, and he squirmed. "It's okay. Really. I don't want to impose on your morning ride."

He lowered his head, feeling like a real snake. "No," he finally managed. "No, Chelsea, I'd really like you to come along."

"Really?"

When he looked into her eyes, he realized, a little slowly perhaps, that it was true. He would enjoy her company. "Yeah, really."

She smiled fully, almost blinding him.

"Come on upstairs, Chelsea," Jessi said, gripping Chelsea's arm and turning her around. "You need some jeans, and I have some that ought to fit you just fine. Might have to roll up the legs a little, but…oh, and some boots, too." Looking back over her shoulder, she sent Garrett a broad wink. "We'll be ready in ten minutes. Promise!"

When they disappeared up the stairs, Garrett pressed his fingertips to his forehead and groaned.

"Oh, come on, Garrett," Wes urged. "it isn't the end of the world."

"You can do this, big brother," Elliot added, a smug grin tugging at his lips, one he didn't try very hard to suppress. "And if you need any pointers on romancing a woman, you just come to me, okay?"

Garrett scowled at him, but Elliot and Wes just shared a laugh and headed out the door.

Chapter 8

The jeans were a bit long, but rolled up they were a fair fit. The boots were perfect. She and Jessi were both size seven, so their fit was comfy. Jessi had tossed in a rather tight-fitting tank top and a flannel shirt, insisting it would be hot by the time Chelsea returned, and she'd be glad to have the thin top underneath.

When Chelsea stepped out onto the front porch, two horses stood saddled and waiting. The gigantic dappled gray one she'd heard Garrett call Duke, and a smaller white mare with a handful of black spots on her rump, who had to be Sugar.

Garrett stood beside the horses, his big hand stroking Sugar's neck. He looked up at Chelsea, smiled a welcome, but she still had the niggling suspicion this little outing hadn't been his idea. And that he was less than happy about it.

She eyed the white horse, and her nerves jangled to life.

"Don't be scared, Chelsea. She's as gentle as a kitten. Come here." He held out a hand.

Chelsea went down the front steps and took it. When Garrett closed his fingers around her hand, he stilled for a second, staring down at their clasped hands as if in surprise. He drew her closer to the animal, laid her hand gently on the mare's neck, where his had been only seconds ago.

Chelsea stroked the animals' sleek neck and smiled. "She's beautiful."

"So are you."

She looked up quickly, only to see Garrett avert his face and pretend to tighten the girth straps.

"Now," he said, turning to face her again, "take hold of the pommel."

Licking her lips, she did.

"Put your foot in the stirrup."

She drew a breath and followed his instructions.

"Now swing your other leg over."

She nodded and pulled herself up. But the horse was tall, and she lost her momentum before she got her leg all the way over. Garrett's hands closed on her bottom, pushing her up, giving her enough of a lift to boost her into the saddle.

She felt her cheeks burn and couldn't look at him.

"Sorry," he muttered, handing her the reins. He walked around the mare, checking to be sure Chelsea had her foot firmly in the stirrup on the other side, then mounted his own horse in a move so smooth and effortless that watching him made her feel like a klutz. He held the reins loosely in one hand, and she imitated him. "Ready?"

She nodded once, then Garrett turned his horse and started across the lawn. Sugar didn't need Chelsea to tell her what to do. She turned, as well, and walked slow and easy beside Duke. They approached an open gate, and Wes, who was standing nearby, closed it behind them after they moved through.

"Squeeze your thighs around her, Chelsea," Garrett instructed, looking at her dangling legs.

She squeezed, and Sugar shot forward into a trot, causing Chelsea to bounce up and down until her teeth rattled. Garrett caught up to her within a few seconds, grabbed the reins and tugged gently. Sugar came to a halt.

"What did I do?" Chelsea asked, breathless.

"Dug your heels into her side. Just squeeze gently with your knees. You dig those heels in, she thinks you want to run."

Chelsea tried again, and this time the horse didn't take off. Garrett handed the reins back to her, his hand brushing hers as she took them. They started off again, side by side, and she knew he was going much more slowly than he probably would if he were alone. They rode into rolling green meadows, and soon she saw the curly coats of the white-faced Herefords dotting the grass in the distance. As they drew nearer, she saw calves running and jumping like children, and docile cows chewing lazily as if they hadn't a care in the world.

"They're something, aren't they?" Garrett remarked, drawing to a halt at a spot where they could look out over part of the herd.

Imitating Garrett again, Chelsea reined in her mount and followed his gaze. "I don't think I've ever seen anything that...peaceful."

It was true. Sitting here astride this gentle mare, beside this gentle man, with this gentle scene out before her, she felt that peace begin to fill her. This was a good place, this Texas Brand. A magical place. The vivid blue sky stretched wider than she'd ever seen it. And the sun beat down just as Jessi had predicted it would. Heat poured through her flannel shirt, and her skin dampened and prickled. Very carefully, she shrugged the shirt off one arm, but only got it partway down her shoulder before the horse danced a little, and she had to make a grab for the pommel.

"I...uh..." Garrett's horse sidled closer to hers. "I can get that." He reached out with one hand and pushed the shirt down her arm. She let go so he could tug it off, then held on with her other hand as Garrett's big, callused one pushed the shirt down from her opposite shoulder. His palm skimmed her arm all the way down, and she shivered. She closed her eyes without quite realizing she was doing so. She sensed him taking the shirt, and when she opened her eyes, she saw him staring at her. There was something in his gaze. Something new...and a little scary.

He blinked it away, tucking the shirt in front of him on the saddle, then nudged his horse into motion once more.

For an hour, they rode in silence, and Chelsea took in the beauty and tranquillity of the surroundings. The only sounds were the steady tromping of the horses' hooves, the creak of saddle leather, and once in a while, the gentle blowing sound made by the horses.

Garrett tugged Duke to a stop when they came to a small stream with a couple of trees on the far bank. He dismounted in one smooth motion and came to her side. "Better take a break," he said.

"Oh, but I'm fine."

He smiled, a big lopsided smile that made her stomach clench tight. "You think you're fine. But believe me, you're working muscles you didn't know you had. Come on, get down for a few minutes."

She nodded. "Okay, you're the expert." She braced one foot in the stirrup and tried to swing off the way he'd done. But Sugar sidestepped and she felt herself falling. Then two big hands curled around her waist from behind, lifting her gently, easily down. Her backside brushed over the front of him as he lowered her, and a shiver worked right up her spine. When her feet touched down, he didn't let go. Instead, his hands remained at her waist, holding her back against his body for a long moment.

"Damn," he whispered, and finally his hands fell away.

She turned around and stared up into his eyes. Dark brown, gentle eyes that held hers captive.

"Damn," he said again.

"Why do you keep saying that?"

He closed his eyes, breaking that tenuous hold, but only briefly. "Because I know you don't like being touched…and right now…" He shook his head in self-disgust. "I'm not good at this kind of thing, Chelsea. I don't know the kinds of pretty words that make women go soft inside. I'm a simple man, and I'm accustomed to just saying what's on my mind, straight out."

"So say it," she whispered, and her voice trembled, and fear danced in her veins. She felt more alive than she ever had.

"I want to kiss you."

She looked into his eyes, then at the expanse of green around them. They were alone here. But for some reason, she wasn't afraid. She'd never known a man as gentle as Garrett Brand. Not ever.

She tipped up her head and moved closer. "Then...go ahead and kiss me," she said, her words full of false bravado, but wavering all the same.

Garrett bent his head and touched his lips to hers. He didn't put his hands on her. He just kissed her slowly and gently, then lifted his head and searched her face.

"Again?" he murmured.

"Yes. Again."

This time his arms came up around her waist, his hands spanning the small of her back and easing her close to him. He kissed her again, nuzzling her lips until she parted them, then tracing their shape with his tongue.

Chelsea's pulse raced and nameless feelings swamped her mind. She put her hands on Garrett's broad shoulders and slipped them around him until her fingers tangled in his hair. She opened her mouth wider, ready now to experience more of this heady thing between them. Her heart pounded in her ears. Louder and louder, and when his tongue slowly slipped inside, it seemed the very ground under her feet trembled with—

He jerked away from her, eyes wide with alarm. And he swore.

"Garrett? Did I—"

"Stampede!"

His cry shocked her...then terrified her when its meaning became clear. She looked, and saw masses of frightened beasts churning the dust toward them. And even as Garrett reached for the horses, they bolted, wild-eyed, feet flying. Garrett's arm snagged her around the waist, propelling her forward. He shouted something at her, but the thundering hoofbeats of the cattle drowned out even his booming voice. As they splashed across the icy stream, she could smell the terrified cattle. Then her body was thrust against the trunk of a tree, and Garrett's ground tightly to her from behind, pinning her there. The animals were upon them, knocking into them on both sides, brushing, pushing. She felt Garrett's body being torn away from her and she turned to see, but couldn't.

Then she heard a shout and saw a horse at full gallop, pressing through the rampaging cows. A man she'd never seen before sat tall on a sable-colored, wide-eyed stallion. She watched as he bent low, reached down and pulled Garrett up. Garrett seemed to spring up from the ground and onto the back of that horse. His gaze was glued to the tree as the cattle flew past, and Chelsea clung to it with all her might as their bodies jostled hers. But one hit her too hard, and her palms scraped painfully over the rough bark as she fought to hold on. Her back hit the ground hard, and she automatically curled into a ball, covering her face with her arms as her body was pummeled again and again. It felt as if several strong men were surrounding her, hitting her with hammers.

The blows stopped at last. Then the thunder slowly died away. And all that remained was the blackened earth and torn grass and the sound of her own heart beating more loudly than those hooves had done. She uncurled cautiously, every movement hurting.

The rider came forward. Garrett leaped from the horse and ran to her, dropping to his knees beside her. His hands gripped her shoulders, pulled her close to his big chest. She could feel the pounding of his heart there, hear the raspy rush of his quickened breaths.

"Chelsea, dammit, are you all right?" He held her so hard, so tight, she could barely breathe.

He eased back a little when she didn't answer. Brown eyes flooded with worry scanned her body. His shirt was torn, one arm dripping blood, and there was another ugly cut high on his cheekbone. She lifted a hand toward him. "You're hurt."

She heard galloping and jerked her head around, only to see Elliot and Wes approaching at top speed.

"The hell with me! What about you? Damn, Chelsea, when I saw you fall—"

"I'm all right." She put her hands on his shoulders and pushed herself to her feet. She hurt. She hurt everywhere, but she didn't think anything was broken. At least her arms and hands and legs and feet seemed to be in working order.

Elliot and Wes had jumped from their horses and were running toward them now. There was real fear in their eyes, when they reached their brother.

"Garrett, are you okay?"

"What the hell happened?"

Garrett shook his head slowly, but his brown eyes narrowed dangerously as they found those of the stranger. "Something…or *someone*…spooked the cattle. Chelsea could have been killed."

The stranger said nothing. Just sat on that horse, holding Garrett's accusing stare. He was dark and whipcord lean, his face narrow and hard, with piercing pale blue eyes that even now seemed deathly calm. As Chelsea stared at him, something fluttered to the ground from his shirt pocket. A small slip of paper.

She pointed at it and started to tell him, but Garrett's angry voice made her go utterly still.

"Who the hell are you, mister?"

"Name's Lash," he replied, his face every bit as grim as Garrett's.

"It wasn't him, Garrett," Elliot said quickly. "He was with us."

Garrett gave Elliot a brief glance, then turned a questioning one on Wes.

"Elliot's right. Lash drove in right after you two left. Said he was looking for work. Since we're short-handed, I thought it wouldn't be a bad idea, and he was in a hurry to see you, so we saddled up and rode out here to run it by you."

"And it's a darned good thing we did, Garrett," Elliot added. "If Lash hadn't cut through that mess of frantic beefers to pull you up, you'd be hamburger."

"He saw you go down," Wes added. "We didn't."

Garrett heaved a thoughtful sigh, but his eyes remained wary. He walked over to the stranger, who'd dismounted by this time, and offered his hand. "Seems I'm indebted to you."

The man shook Garrett's hand. "You can repay me by hiring me on."

Garrett scowled. "Wish I could, friend, but this is a bad time—"

"Garrett, we could use the help."

Garrett turned to Elliot with a look that clearly told him to shut up. Elliot pursed his lips. "Hell, I'll go see if I can round up the horses." He headed for his own horse, jumped back into the saddle, wheeled around and rode off, leaving no one in any doubt as to his opinion of Garrett's decision.

Chelsea wondered why Garrett would be so distrustful of the man who'd probably saved his life. She knew Elliot was right. How many times had she heard them talking about how shorthanded they were right now?

"Like I said, it's a bad time," Garrett repeated, turning back to the stranger.

"I'm a good hand," Lash returned easily. "But if it's a bad time, it's a bad time." He shrugged as if he could care less. "You want some help herding those cattle back where they belong?"

"We can handle it."

"I got nowhere to go."

Garrett frowned. It wasn't like him to be rude, though Chelsea assumed that nearly being trampled to death would make even a saint grouchy.

"Fine. Ride along if you want." Elliot was riding toward them now, flanked by Duke and Sugar. Garrett returned to Chelsea and lifted a tender hand to push her hair away from her face. "You sure you're okay?"

"A few bruises, I think. Nothing serious."

"You up to the ride back to the house?"

She swallowed hard, but nodded. How else was she going to get back?

"The hell you are," he muttered.

Elliot jumped off his horse and led the other two mounts over to Garrett and Chelsea. "Garrett, why don't you take her back? The three of us can handle the cows. They've stopped running already. Tore through the north fence line, though. We'll drive 'em back in, repair the fence and meet you later at the house in time for lunch. All right?"

Garrett looked torn. For some reason, he didn't want to leave his brothers out here alone. Was he worried about the jumpy cows? From the wary look in his eyes,

Chelsea thought his concern lay elsewhere. With the stranger. Why?

He glanced at Chelsea again.

"I can make it back on my own, Garrett. You don't have to—"

"No. Not alone." His forefinger lazily brushed her cheek, and she wondered if there was a bruise forming there already. It felt as if there was. "I'll take you back."

He went over to Wes, who stood a bit away from the rest of them, just watching them all with those sharp, probing black eyes of his. Wes inclined his head as Garrett spoke softly. Then nodded. Lash, meanwhile, had ridden over to Elliot and was conversing with him. The slip of paper blew closer to Chelsea's feet, and she bent to pick it up, turning toward the stranger.

But Garrett came back to her at that moment, and without warning, he put his arms around her and scooped her right off her feet. He settled her in Duke's saddle, then swung up behind her. One arm came snugly around her waist. He touched the stallion's sides, and the horse took off at a brisk walk, back the way they'd come. Chelsea sighed in resignation and glanced at the name and address on the scrap of paper before stuffing it into her jeans pocket and vowing to return it to its owner later on.

Cattle did not stand around chewing peacefully one minute, then stampede the next. Garrett knew that. He'd only witnessed one stampede in his life and he'd been in the ranching business forever. It was rare. It didn't just happen.

Something had spooked those cattle. And spooked

them in the direction he and Chelsea had taken. Garrett couldn't convince himself it was a coincidence. Especially after that odd phone call last night. And that the appearance of this stranger—this *Lash*—could just be happenstance was a bit much to swallow.

Somebody wanted Chelsea Brennan dead. The voice on the phone had identified that somebody as Vincent de Lorean, a man as evil as Satan himself. And then she'd nearly been trampled to death. All within twenty-four hours.

No way could he have let her return to the house alone. And he couldn't trust her safety to his brothers. He had to see to it himself. Much as he disliked leaving Elliot and Wes out there with a stranger who might or might not be involved in all this, he'd had little choice. So he'd warned Wes about his suspicions. Wes could handle himself. Hell, Wes could handle himself and any six fighting men. He'd be all right.

Duke gave a little leap when he came out of the stream and started up the slight incline of the bank. Chelsea's bottom bounced down on the saddle, and she gave a little squeak of pain. Dammit, she was hurt, much as she might deny it.

"Don't sit so stiff," he instructed. "Just relax against me, and it won't hurt so much." He punctuated his advice by pulling her back closer to his chest. Her buttocks rocked between his legs, rubbing him in all the right places. Dammit, he should have left well enough alone.

No, he shouldn't. She leaned her head back against him. Oh, did he like that. He opened his palm on her flat belly. His hand itched to creep up higher. To cup her soft breasts, and squeeze them. His lips itched to kiss her. Her smooth-skinned neck was looking more tempting with every step Duke took.

"Why were you so suspicious of that man?" she asked softly.

Garrett clenched his jaw. He hadn't meant to be so obvious. The last thing he wanted was for her to think that the stampede had been an attempt on her life. He was afraid that knowledge would send her running scared. And if she ran, how the hell could he protect her?

"I don't like strangers nosing around," he tried.

"You took me in. Let me stay. *I'm* a stranger."

Garrett never had been any good at subterfuge. "You're a sight prettier than Lash is."

"Be honest with me, Garrett." As she said it, she turned her head so she could look up into his eyes. Her green ones searched and dug into his. Into his heart, too.

"I am being honest. You really *are* prettier."

She frowned at him.

"Okay," he said slowly, wondering how little he could get away with revealing. "We want it kept quiet that you're here, right? Why broadcast it to some drifter?"

She nodded, licked her lips. He ached to do the same. "So you really think Ethan's father will come after him if he finds out where we are?"

"He might. But—" Garrett cut himself off in mid-sentence as he was sharply, painfully reminded of Vincent de Lorean's other objective. His son. And Bubba was currently alone in the house with Jessi.

He tightened his grip on Chelsea. "Sorry about this, darlin'. Hold on." He kicked Duke's sides, and the horse obeyed instantly, beginning to gallop at a speed

Garrett hoped wouldn't send more spasms of pain through Chelsea's slender, bruised body.

When he jumped off Duke's back and ran up the front steps, leaving Chelsea sitting alone on a horse the size of a small elephant, she mentally cussed him.

But he only made it as far as the screen door. One look inside and his frown lines eased into a smile. "Everything okay here, Jessi?"

"Sure. Fine. Why wouldn't it be?"

"No reason." Garrett turned around, smiling. But his smile died when he saw Chelsea glaring at him from the saddle. "Sorry," he muttered, and came back to her, put his hands on her waist and lifted her down.

She shook her head. "You're crazy, Garrett Brand. What were you trying to do, making that mastodon run with me on his back? Kill me?"

"Course not! Hey, I just got worried about Jess and Bubba, is all."

"His *name* is Ethan, you big lug."

He opened his mouth.

"And why would you suddenly get so worried that you had to race all the way back here and scramble my insides in the process?" She poked him with a forefinger. "You are keeping something from me. Something about that stampede, and that stranger, and—"

"Stampede?" The screen door squeaked and Jessi stepped outside, Ethan anchored on her hip. "What stampede?"

"The one that almost killed us," Chelsea replied, still glaring at Garrett.

"Now, it wasn't that bad. Don't look like that, Jessi. Everything's fine. No one was hurt."

Jessi's gaze dipped to Garrett's torn and bloodied shirtsleeve. "Liar. Look at you! And you, too, Chelsea! What in all hell happened out there?"

"Watch your mouth," Garrett told her.

"I will not watch my mouth." She pouted, then shook her head. "Ah, get in here, both of you, and let me have a look. And while I'm looking, Garrett Ethan Brand, you better tell me what this is all about!" She spun around and slammed back into the house.

Chelsea took the first step, but Garrett gripped her shoulder gently, stopping her. "Wait."

She sighed, but turned to face him.

"Before all the craziness out there, Chelsea… something was…happening…between you and me."

She lowered her head. Something *had* been happening. Something that had been dizzying and wonderful at the time. But in hindsight, it scared the hell out of her.

"It's just as well we were interrupted," she whispered, but the words were coming hard.

"I have to disagree with you there."

She forced her head up and tried to hold on to his gaze, but couldn't. She had to look away again. "I'm not ready for anything like this. I don't *want* anything like this."

"Like what? Hell, Chelsea, I'm still trying to figure out what *this* is."

"It doesn't matter. It shouldn't have happened, and it's over. Let's just forget about it."

"I'm not real sure I can do that. Forget it, I mean." He searched her face, trying to smile, but it was bitter, and she thought maybe she'd hurt this big, gentle man.

But she barely knew him, after all. His gentleness

could fade as fast as the sun when a storm cloud rolls in. He could turn out to be as dangerous as her father had been. And she'd decided a long time ago that she would never trust any man long enough to find out. She would never fall in love. Besides, just because this man was physically attracted to her didn't mean he *felt* anything for her, so she was way ahead of herself anyway.

"It will be easier once Ethan and I are gone," she said.

His lips thinned. He seemed a little desperate and maybe at a loss for words. "I don't..."

"What?"

He lowered his head. "I don't want you to go, Chelsea."

She stared at him in surprise and more than a little confusion. What was he saying? He barely knew her, had only kissed her once, for God's sake. Well, okay, twice. How could he stand there and say—

"Will you two get in here already?" Jessi called.

"What do you mean, you don't want me to go? What do you want me to do, quit my job, give up my apartment and stay here? For a fling, Garrett? Well, I'm sorry to disappoint you. I don't do flings."

She turned away and marched up the steps and across the porch. But as she went, she heard his voice following her.

"Neither do I, Chelsea Brennan."

Chapter 9

Maybe one of those stupid cows had stomped on her head. That must be it. Maybe she had a concussion or brain damage or something. Or maybe Garrett did. Because she could have sworn the man she'd actually begun to see as some kind of big, honorable, gentle-as-a-teddy bear kind of guy had just propositioned her. Suggested she hang out at the ranch for a while, his meaning glimmering clearly in those formerly harmless brown eyes. He wanted her, the jerk. And he thought she was willing to put out. All on the basis of a couple of innocent kisses!

Man, his ego must be as big as he was!

She tried to hurry through the kitchen and dining room, straight on into the living room and up the stairway, but winced with every single step. It hurt, dammit. Him and his hormones! She should have known all along he only had one thing on his mind. Why hadn't she seen it coming? He'd probably only stopped the stupid horses so he could paw her, not so she could rest. And it was only just now occurring to her how utterly stupid she'd been to go along on that ride in the first place. Putting herself out of sight and shouting distance of anyone. Putting herself alone within reach of a man. Even this man. Because they were all the same underneath. Hadn't she learned anything?

A hot bath, she thought as she started up the stairs. It hurt to flex her thighs, and she grimaced. A long, hot bath. She tried envisioning it to get her up the next step. Her back screamed in protest. Steam, rolling off the water, she thought determinedly. Scented water. Hot, steamy, scented water and— She sucked air through her teeth at a new jab in her side. "Dammit!"

Big, strong arms swept under her, lifting her like a knight lifting a damsel in a fairy tale. Well, she was no damsel, and this horny lug was no knight. There were no such things as knights. Not even in Texas.

"Put me down."

"Not on your life, lady. Don't worry. I won't trouble you with my presence any longer than it takes to drop you on your bed."

"Drop me at my door, Hulk. I don't trust you anywhere near my bed."

Garrett took the stairs at a brisk pace. "I didn't say I wanted to sleep with you, woman."

"You want me to stay for what, then? My sparkling wit? My charm and sweetness?"

"What sweetness? You're as sour as a barrel of pickles." He set her on her feet, opened the bedroom door and waved a hand. "We'll talk about this later."

"I won't be here later."

"Fine."

"Fine." She slammed the door. Leaning shakily

against it, she closed her eyes hard in an effort to fight the fragile whisper of doubt that flitted through her mind, trying to make her wonder if maybe she'd jumped to the wrong conclusions about Garrett. But, hell, he'd been so uncharacteristically sweet—for a male—to her ever since she'd arrived. And now that she thought she knew the reason—that he was hoping for some easy sex—it made perfect sense.

Didn't it?

She groaned softly and hoped to God she was right. If she wasn't, she'd just made a total fool out of herself. She walked into the little bathroom, depressed the plunger and turned on the hot water. They'd moved her into the guest room where the baby had taken up residence, apparently having decided she could be trusted around her own flesh and blood.

As the water flowed into the bath, Chelsea remembered the way Garrett had looked in here yesterday, shirtless, soaking wet and grinning like a fool as he bathed little Ethan. And she tried to think of why he'd been so nice to the baby. What could he be hoping to get out of him?

Nothing, of course. And it couldn't have been to impress Chelsea because he hadn't known she'd be watching. How could he have known?

God, could it be the man was genuinely nice?

Nah.

Chelsea stripped off her clothes and sank into the bathtub, resting against the cool porcelain as the hot water slowly rose around her.

"Well, Jessi, so much for that stupid scheme you and Elliot came up with!"

Garrett slapped his dusty hat onto the back of a

chair. His little sister set Bubba down and promptly knocked Garrett into the same chair.

"Sit still so I can look at this." She promptly tore his shirtsleeve off, grimacing. "This is nasty, Garrett."

"It's nasty all right. I told her I wanted her to stay. Now she thinks I'm some kind of sex maniac."

Jessi pressed her lips tight, but a gurgle of laughter managed to escape anyway. She turned quickly to the sink, taking a clean cloth from a nearby drawer and wetting it down.

"Oh, yeah, you think you're so smart."

"Well jeez-louise, Garrett, you can't just blurt it out like that. You gotta build up to it. Give her some time."

"I don't have any damned time. She wants to leave today, for crying out loud!"

Jessi came over and pressed the damp cloth to the cut on his shoulder. "Sounds like that would really bother you."

"Only because it might get her killed."

Jessi's hands stilled on his shoulder. "Killed?"

"Vincent de Lorean would do anything to get his child back," he said grimly, "including murder."

Jessi's eyes opened wider. "God Almighty, Garrett, we can't let him!"

"No, we sure as hell can't. And we won't. We just have to convince Chelsea to stay put until I can figure out how."

"Guess you'll just have to sweep her off her feet."

He grunted. Then he stilled, searching her face. His little sister was dead serious here.

"Tell her she can't leave until tomorrow, Garrett. Make something up. Tell her the flights out today are all booked. Anything. Then, tonight—"

"Tonight she isn't speaking to me."

"Tonight you'll give her an evenin' she'll never forget."

Garrett shook his head. But his sister's eyes were sparkling, and he had a feeling he wasn't going to have much say in the matter.

"Now, about this stampede..." she began as if it were all settled. Sure. Just leave it to Jessi. She'd take care of everything. Oh, God help him now.

Dinner was a strained affair. Garrett was damned near squirming in his chair when he thought about what he had to do tonight. He wasn't eating with the others. Just sitting here for the company and the conversation, really. He'd eat later.

Jessi had worked it all out.

And there was this whole other matter to contend with. Lash. Elliot had been raving about how terrific the man had been with the spooked cattle. Even Wes had grudgingly admitted the guy knew his stuff. The damage to the fences had been worse than Elliot had realized, so the three had only come in briefly for a quick sandwich and then headed right out again. Elliot couldn't stop talking about Lash and his way with the cattle.

Even Jessi seemed impressed. She'd gone oddly quiet and suddenly learned some table manners. She was smiling more than usual, too.

Lash looked at her as if he were looking at a little kid, which was yet another mark in his favor.

Hell, Garrett would have hired the stranger in a minute under any circumstances. But with the threat of danger hanging over all their heads, he didn't think he could afford to trust a stranger.

Even one who'd saved his life.

Maybe later, after all this was worked out and Chelsea was safe.

Chelsea.

She hadn't come down for dinner. She'd said she'd rather skip the meal and go to bed early. He hoped that was because she was mad at him and not that she actually wanted to go to bed early. Because that was certainly not what she was going to do.

Chelsea wore an oversize T-shirt she'd snatched from the clothesline out back in response to the sweltering heat outside. She'd have preferred to remain wet and wear nothing at all, but there were simply too many males in this house. So she closed the bedroom door firmly and lay in the bed in the T-shirt, with the window wide open. She tried to rest, but she couldn't get comfortable no matter which way she turned. Everything hurt. She couldn't relax, either, because she kept expecting someone to come through the door to put little Ethan to bed.

It was late before she heard the hum of vehicles rumbling away. A few minutes later came footfalls on the stairs, then the knob turned and the door opened.

Garrett Brand stood in the doorway with his hat in his hands. "You awake?"

"Yeah."

He came the rest of the way inside, flicking on the light as he did. "We need to talk."

"You think so?"

"Yup." He nodded to a chair near the dressing table. "Mind if I sit?"

"It's your house."

He pulled the chair close to the bedside, sat down

slowly, then frowned, his gaze fixed on her bare thigh. She felt her blood rush a little more loudly in her ears. Then she followed his gaze and saw the vivid purple bruise and realized his look wasn't lecherous.

"I thought you said you didn't get hurt."

"It looks worse than it feels."

He got to his feet, headed out of the bedroom and returned within five seconds carrying a white plastic jar with a black lid. He didn't settle back in his chair again. Instead, he lowered his bulk to the edge of the bed, and Chelsea battled the urge to brace her feet against him and give a good shove.

He twisted the cap off the jar and scooped out a gob of ugly brown stuff with his fingers. She caught a whiff of it then and wrinkled her nose.

"What is that? It stinks."

"Liniment. Jessi made it up for the horses."

"The horses?"

"Yeah. They get stiff sometimes, go lame. It's good stuff. Trust me. Jessi's studying veterinary medicine, you know."

"I trust you about as far as I can throw you," she said.

And when he set the jar aside and moved his handful of goo toward her thigh, she pulled her leg away. "Wait a minute! You're not putting any horse liniment on me."

He met her eyes, and his held a definite twinkle. "Just lie still. It'll make you feel better."

She had a feeling this was a form of petty revenge for her determined low opinion of him. But she decided it might not be, and that maybe it was worth the risk. Anything was better than the way she ached right now.

He put his fingers on her thigh and gently rubbed some of the stuff onto the purple bruise. And though it should have hurt just to be touched there, it didn't. The ointment—or was it his fingers?—spread warmth over her flesh. Warmth that seemed to penetrate and slowly sink into her.

"Better already, isn't it?"

She released the breath she hadn't been aware she was holding and relaxed back on the pillows. "Yeah. It is."

"I told you." He scooped out more gunk and leaned over to her other leg, this time massaging the stuff onto the sore spot on her shin. Chelsea closed her eyes. Then his other hand slid behind her knee, lifting it until it bent upward. He started to rub some more of the liniment into the back of her calf, where some nasty cow had pinned it between a hard hoof and the ground.

An involuntary sigh escaped her. She bit her lip when she heard it, but it was too late.

"Where else?" he asked.

Her eyes flew open.

"Lift up the T-shirt, Chelsea."

His lips thinned. "You really think I'm gonna try something, don't you?"

She didn't answer, just looked into his eyes. But she saw nothing there to frighten her, or give her cause to mistrust him.

"I'm only trying to help you. You're hurting and I want to make it better." He shook his head, studying the brown gob on his fingertips. "Hell, maybe I am out of line. Taking care of people just...well, it's sort of ingrained in my bones, you know? Got so used to doin' it for the kids—"

"The kids?"

"Wes, Adam, Ben, Elliot...and Jessi. Especially Jessi."

She swallowed hard; he'd reminded her of who he was. The man who'd raised five children and kept a ranch going single-handedly after his parents had been killed. The man who treated a little old lady in town like the queen of Spain and even worried about her cat. The man who'd taken little Ethan in when it would have been just as easy to turn him over to the local social services. And who had sheltered her from the battering heads and hooves of a horde of crazed animals—sheltered her with his own body.

Did she *really* believe he was anything like her father?

"You were holding your back before. I just thought..." His words trailed into silence as Chelsea stared at him, probing his eyes for answers, finding only more questions. She chewed on her lower lip for a moment, then nodded once. She rolled onto her stomach and lifted the T-shirt above her waist.

"Damn, Chelsea, you look like you've been beat with a club."

"I feel like it, too."

His fingers touched her then. Warm. Soothing. He rubbed the stuff into her lower back, and it felt good. Maybe a little bit too good. When he stopped, she started to lower the shirt, but he covered her hand with his.

"Shhh. Just be still."

He began touching her once more, sliding one hand higher as he lifted her T-shirt with the other. He rubbed the ointment over both her shoulder blades and then the spot between them. She closed her eyes again, wondering if anything in her life had ever felt this soothing.

She'd never been touched this way before. She'd never expected a man's touch could be anything but hurtful and cruel. But Garrett's was gentle and healing and good.

He lowered the shirt down her back again. Chelsea rolled over, wincing as the gooey ointment stuck to the material.

"I'm ruining someone's T-shirt with this stuff," she said. She felt she had to say something, and that seemed like something safe.

"That's okay. I have others."

She blinked. "It's yours?"

His eyebrows rose. "Who else around here would need an extra-extra large?"

Her throat went dry. Why? What was so intimate about wearing Garrett's T-shirt? Why did she suddenly feel as if it were him wrapped around her, instead of just a piece of white cotton?

"What about your front?"

"I—"

But he was pushing the shirt up carefully and slowly. She didn't grab it and yank it back down. She waited, almost unable to breathe, telling herself this would be the proof she needed of what kind of man he truly was. When he yanked it up to her neck and tried to grope her breasts, she'd have no more room for doubt. And then…

He stopped, letting the shirt rest below her breasts. And though there was a definite yearning in his eyes as he gazed down at her bared waist, he didn't grope. He didn't make any lewd remarks. He didn't smirk.

"Your ribs are bruised to hell and gone. Damn,

Chelsea, maybe we oughtta drive into El Paso and get you some X rays.''

She shook her head. ''Nothing's broken.''

''You sure? Would you even know what a broken bone felt like? I mean, if you've never—''

''I've had plenty of broken bones, Garrett. I know what they feel like.''

''You...?'' He stopped without finishing the question, but it was in his eyes as they met hers, searching.

''Yeah. A wrist once. A couple of ribs another time. And then there was the collarbone.''

He swallowed so hard she saw the way his Adam's apple swelled and receded like a wave moving under his skin. ''Your father?'' The words were like a croak.

She only nodded.

Garrett closed his deep brown eyes very tight.

''It's okay,'' she said. ''I survived it in one piece.''

He opened his eyes, facing her, shaking his head. ''But you didn't, Chelsea. You think every man who cares for you is gonna hurt you somehow, and that just isn't true.''

''Isn't it? I don't know, Garrett. I think believing that is what got my sister killed.''

He sighed long and deep, but said nothing more. Instead, he looked again at her exposed skin and resumed the process of smoothing ointment over her bruises. His fingers trembled a little. But he finished, wiped his fingers on a rag and recapped the jar.

''I have something that needs saying,'' he told her. ''And I want you to listen and not think about your father or about your sister, if you can manage it. Just think about me and about you, okay?''

She nodded, but felt suspicion welling up in her heart.

Garrett cleared his throat. "When I said I wanted you to stay...it wasn't because I thought I could get you into bed. It was because...because I care about you. And I—"

"You can't care about me. You barely know me."

"Now, I thought you were gonna let me finish."

She clamped her lips together, crossed her arms over her chest and waited.

"I don't know you very well, that's true enough. The point is, I *want* to know you. I like being with you, Chelsea. I like spending time with you and I like the way I feel when I'm near you."

She stared at him, sure there was a punch line coming. But there didn't seem to be one imminent. His eyes were intense and so damned sincere that he almost had her believing this bull.

"How...how do you feel when you're near me?" she asked, surprised to find her voice had gone whispery soft.

He shook his head, his gaze turning inward. "I don't know...like...like maybe I'm more than just a stand-in parent to the kids. Like maybe I'm more than just the guy everybody brings their troubles to. More than just a small-town sheriff. I feel...I feel like a man. A flesh-and-blood man. I feel...alive."

She drew a deep breath and told herself his sweet talk wasn't working on her. Then she denied that her stomach had gone queasy at his words, or that her pulse was pounding in her temples. And that little shiver up her spine had certainly never happened.

"That's lust," she told him. "That's all it is."

"I know lust, Chelsea Brennan. I haven't lived like a monk, you know." He let his gaze roam down her body, but quickly jerked it back up to her eyes. "All right. It's lust. I won't deny that I want you. But it's more than that, too. There's something happening here, and I want to find out what it is, because it's something I've never felt before.''

She closed her eyes. ''Look, I don't think I want to hear any more of this right now.''

''Will you at least think about it?''

She nodded, because she knew there was nothing she could do to keep herself from thinking about it. Hadn't he told her he didn't know the kinds of pretty words that could make a woman go soft inside? Well, for someone who didn't know them, he was doing a pretty good job of reciting them all.

''Good. Now that that's settled, will you join me for dinner?''

Another surprise. The guy was full of them. ''The ointment helped, Garrett, but I'm still too sore to go out.''

''I know. That's why we're having dinner here.''

''I thought everyone had already eaten.'' She scowled at him, growing suspicious all over again.

''They did. And now they're gone. There's a big shebang in town tonight. Memorial Day lasts all week around here. Dancing and fireworks. Jessi took Ethan along.''

Chelsea felt her eyes widen.

''Don't worry. She's telling people he's our cousin. So what do you say, Chelsea? I want to be with you tonight. Just the two of us.''

Panic made her throat go dry.

''And just so you know, under no circumstances am I going to lay a hand on you tonight. I just want to spend some time. Get to know you. I promise, that's all.''

She was alone in this house with him. She ought to be bounding out of this bed right now and running away from him. But she wasn't. Instead, she was lying here, thinking about how much she could enjoy an evening in his company.

She must be losing her mind.

"All right," she heard herself say. "B-but I still have to leave tomorrow."

"You can make that decision tomorrow," he told her. Then he rose slowly from the edge of the bed without touching her. "I'll leave you to get dressed. Just come downstairs whenever you're ready."

She nodded and watched him as he left the room, closing the door gently behind him.

Oh, God, this was not what she'd expected. Never in her life had she thought any man would care enough to try so hard to work his way past her defenses. She didn't know how to deal with this. She didn't *want* a man in her life. Not ever!

All right, so she'd just explain that to him. He could be Prince Charming, she'd tell him, but it still wouldn't matter. She'd made a decision never to fall in love with a man, and it was a decision she was going to stick to. And if it hurt Garrett's feelings, then that wasn't her fault. He'd get over it.

Garrett closed the bedroom door, leaned back against it and wiped the beads of sweat from his forehead. Dammit, but he'd never felt more like a schoolboy than he did right now. And the scariest part of the entire experiment was that it had worked! He pulled the index cards from his pocket, scanning the lines quickly to be sure he'd covered everything.

Never felt like this before…like the way I feel when

I'm with you...more than just a small-town sheriff. Yup, he'd covered everything Jessi had written down. And tossed in some of his own lines to boot. He'd thought Jessi had gone plum out of her mind when she'd set him down to coach him on what to say. But maybe she knew a little something about what made women tick after all. Hell, she was one.

Imagine that. Little Jessi, a woman. He'd never thought of her that way before. But she obviously understood this stuff. She'd told him these kinds of words from a man would make her melt inside, then assured him they'd work just as well on Chelsea. And by heaven, she'd been right.

Garrett flipped through the cards to the ones yet to come.

Let's see. Music. Candles. Wine. And the compliments. Dammit, if they weren't the most flowery things he'd ever heard, he didn't know what were. But the other stuff seemed to have been effective.

Besides, he'd taken his own precautions as backup. He'd reserved every single seat on the two flights to New York tomorrow. Just in case.

Chelsea came down the stairs, and Garrett turned when he heard her steps. He was ready to tell her she was "a vision too beautiful to be real." But when he saw her, he forgot his lines. Everything rushed right out of his head because the sight of her hit him right between the eyes.

She wore a silk sundress that was the same deep green as her eyes. Thin straps held it up, and it fell over her slender curves like a caress. Her vivid red hair was caught up in the back, leaving delicate curls springing free around her face. The high heels made her legs seem like weapons, deadly weapons that could bring even a man his size right to his knees. For just a second, he felt they were aimed at him.

"Damn, you look good." Garrett bit his lip after the words escaped and tried to recall his lines. "I mean—"

"Thank you." Her face flushed with pleasure, and she smiled. Well, hell, he hadn't blown it with that slipup after all. She reached the bottom of the steps and gazed past him. "This is nice. You did all this for me?"

He turned to survey the transformed living room. There was a small fire snapping in the grate and a little round table set up by the picture window. Two tall candles glimmered on the table, their light sparkling off the bottle of chilled wine and the dishes set there.

Garrett would have preferred a cold beer, but hell, if it kept the lady alive…

"The music is nice, too. Did you pick that out?"

He listened to the crooning of some fella named Bryan—with a *Y* of all things—Adams, and thought he'd greatly prefer Hank, Jr. "Yeah. You like it?"

She nodded, then came forward.

Garrett racked his brain to figure out what came next. The wine, that was it! Oh, wait, she was heading for the table. He hurried after her to pull out her chair. Then he got lost looking down the front of her dress because the gentle swell of her bosom had captured his eyes and wouldn't let go.

Damn.

He shook himself, dragged his gaze away and reached for the wine, filling her glass first.

"Thank you."

Thank God Jessi hadn't suggested he drink some from her shoe. The things had open toes anyway.

She sipped, licked her lips. Garrett's mouth went dry. He picked up his glass and drained it, then poured more and finally sat himself down. He didn't think he'd be able to sit still for very long, though. He was damned nervous.

"So," he said.

"So?"

"So tell me about yourself, Chelsea." He belatedly remembered his lines. "I want to know everything there is to know about you."

She ducked her head quickly. "You already know all my secrets."

"I don't even know what you do back in New York."

"Oh. No, I guess you don't, do you? I work for an ad agency."

"Doing what?" He tried to inject sincere interest into his tone, tried to maintain eye contact, which was, Jessi had insisted, vital.

"I do the artwork for print ads."

His brows rose in surprise. "You're an artist?"

"Some would call me one. Others might argue." She shrugged. "I love to paint, though. But it's best when I'm at home and I can paint what I want instead of what's been assigned to me. My apartment gets great morning light to work by."

"I wish I could see your paintings," he said, forgetting about the lines he'd rehearsed. "What are they like?"

"They're children mostly. I like painting children. Happy children. Loved children."

He swallowed hard. "Because you never were. Happy. Loved."

"Maybe." She averted her eyes. "You did a wonderful thing for your family, Garrett. I don't know if you realize just how much they needed you after your parents died.''

"I needed them just as much,'' he said. Then he tilted his head. "What happened to you and Michele after your mamma went home?''

"Went home. That's a sweet way to put it, isn't it?''

He shrugged, unable to take his eyes off her. The candlelight made her green eyes shine, and he thought he might lose the entire thread of the conversation if he looked into them much longer.

"We went into the system. Foster care. Got shuffled around a lot until we were old enough to be on our own.'' She shook her head. "I wish we'd had a brother like you to watch out for us.''

"I don't want to be your brother, Chelsea.''

She bit her bottom lip, maybe a little frightened.

"But I'd like to watch out for you. You and Ethan. Even if you do go back to New York. You remember that, okay? If you ever need me, I'll be there in a heartbeat.''

Her green eyes widened a little. Then she shook her head. "You really are something, Garrett Brand.''

He wondered if she meant something good, or something bad. He was straying too far from Jessi's script here. Time to get back on track.

"Will you dance with me, Chelsea?''

She smiled a wavery little smile, took a sip of wine and slowly, gracefully, got to her feet.

Oh, God, that must mean yes. Garrett got up, too, and stepped close to her. He slipped his arms around her waist, but loosely, just anchoring his hands atop her hips. She clasped hers at the base of his neck, and he began to move with her in time to Bryan-with-a-*Y*

Adams as he crooned a heart-wrenching love song. Didn't the guy know anything else?

Chelsea sighed, and her breath fanned his throat. His stomach clenched into a hard knot, and he told himself it was just because he hadn't eaten. It was hard to keep that in mind, though, what with Chelsea so close and Bryan-with-a-*Y* singing about how to *really* love a woman. Come to think of it, the song was downright erotic if you listened to the words. And Garrett was listening. Mental pictures were forming in his mind. Pictures that distracted him from the lines he'd rehearsed and his step-by-step plan of how this evening was supposed to go.

"I have to tell you something, Garrett," Chelsea said, and her voice was as soft as goose down.

"What's that?"

She drew a breath, sighed again. Those damned sighs of hers were tickling his skin, and he battled the urge to pull her closer. So he could really *feel* her, as the singer kept suggesting.

"I'm scared."

She said it in a sudden gust as if forcing the words out. Garrett's feet stopped moving, and he looked down into her face. Her beautiful face. He was beginning to feel like a real jerk for leading her on like this. If it wasn't for the fact that she'd end up dead if she ran off, he'd cut the act here and now. It wasn't exactly the most chivalrous thing he'd ever done.

"Of me?"

"No. I tried to be, but...you're just not a very scary kind of man."

He lifted his brows. "Is that a compliment or a slam, lady?"

"Compliment. I've never met a man I wasn't afraid of, deservedly or not. But you...you're different."

"Different how?"

She shrugged and moved closer, laying her head on his shoulder, nudging him into motion again. He tightened his arms around her waist and held her close, then began dancing again.

But now the singer was advising him to really taste her, and it was beginning to get on his nerves.

She'd probably taste just like sugar.

"I'm not sure," she said, and he had to think a minute to remember the question. "You're gentle, for one thing. Everything you do, you do...gently."

"And you like that?"

"Mmm."

"Glad to hear it. I'm doing one thing right, then."

"More than one thing," she said, and her voice was beginning to take on a lazy quality that made him nervous. "You're also honest. You don't play games, just say what you mean straight out. I like that, too."

Garrett closed his eyes as a shaft of guilt the size of a Mack truck drove right through him.

"So the least I can do is be honest with you in return."

Taken aback, he stopped dancing again. Hell, she had been. Hadn't she? "About what?" he asked. He looked into her eyes again, saw them staring up at him, trusting him. He was scum.

"About...us. This...thing between us."

Wait a minute. There was *nothing* between them. He'd made that up. No, Jessi had.

"I feel it, too," Chelsea went on.

"You do?"

She nodded. "I..." She licked her lips, lowered her head. "I want you just as much as you want me."

"You do?" It was all Garrett could do not to stagger backward.

She looked up again, smiled just a little. "Yeah, I do. So you have to believe me when I tell you that if I were going to get involved with any man, it would be you."

"It would?" Dammit, couldn't he do more than repeat her every word?

"But I'm not. I made that decision a long time ago, Garrett. There will never be a man in my life. And I will never, ever, fall in love."

He sighed in abject relief. Thank God. At least this way, she wouldn't be hurt when she found out this had all been an act to get her to stay here.

"I just thought you should know that. So you won't be...you know...hurt. When I leave."

"Leave?"

Was there an echo in here?

"I'm glad you told me how you feel about me, Garrett. It's just one more reason for me to go. It will be easier on you when I'm back in New York."

"But Chelsea—"

"I can't stay, Garrett. Especially now." She lifted a hand to the side of his face. "You're a special man. You deserve so much more than I can ever give."

"I didn't ask you to give me anything," he said, which was, he figured, better than parroting her words and adding a question mark, but not by much.

"That's good, because I don't *have* anything."

He felt like swearing. Like stomping or hitting something. Jessi and her dumb ideas. All he'd done was give Chelsea another excuse to run off. Now what the hell was he supposed to do?

He gave himself a mental kick. "I moved in too fast, scared you, didn't I?" She shook her head in denial, but he caught her chin and stared down into her eyes. "Chelsea, I want you to stay. I want you to stay because I like you and because I'm nuts about Ethan. Because I'm scared to death of what will happen if you run off to New York alone. This maniac is still out there somewhere."

"I can take care of myself."

"I know you can. Hell, that's what you've been doing your whole life, isn't it? But this is different, Chelsea. You have to think about little Bubba now."

"I am thinking of him. And I owe it to him to see that his mother gets a proper burial—at home, where she belongs."

"Dammit, Chelsea, you can do it from right here. Ship the body. Make the arrangements over the phone."

"And miss my own sister's funeral?"

Garrett closed his eyes, trying hard to rein in his temper. She was frustrating!

"We can have a memorial service in Quinn. We can send a bushel of flowers. Hell, Chelsea, what do you think Michele would have wanted more? You and her son safe here with us, or standing beside a hole in the ground in New York waiting for that bastard to..." He bit his lip. Too late, though.

"What bastard?"

He shook his head.

"Garrett, you know something about Ethan's father, don't you? Something you're not telling me. What is it?"

The timer bell pinged from the kitchen.

"That's dinner." He said it with all the relief of a boxer teetering on the edge of consciousness and saved by the bell.

"I don't give a damn about dinner. What do you know?"

He sighed long and hard, seeing defeat in those sparking green eyes. "All right. I didn't want to tell you this because I knew it would scare you. But...I found out who Ethan's father is."

She stood away from him, braced and waiting.

He lifted his hands to her shoulders, but she pulled free. He cleared his throat. "Did you ever hear of Vincent De Lorean?"

"Maybe. The name is familiar, but... Should I?"

He drew another long breath. "He's one of the most wanted criminals in Texas, Chelsea."

She jerked back as the shock hit her. But she recovered fast, and he saw something else forming in her eyes. "Wanted...for what?"

"You name it. He's head of the biggest organized-crime syndicate in the state. A real mover and shaker in the drug trade. Suspected of tax evasion, conspiracy, fraud, extortion...and murder. But so far no one's ever been able to get enough evidence to put him away. He's a powerful man, with powerful connections."

She closed her eyes slowly, backing up until her legs hit the rocking chair and then sinking into it.

"He has people watching your place in N.Y., waiting for you to show up there with Bubba."

She swore, using words he never would have imagined were in her vocabulary.

"You can't go back there, Chelsea. Don't you see that by now?"

She swallowed hard and nodded.

"You're scared. God, I knew this would shake you. That's why I..."

Her head came up slowly. "That's why you what?" Then she swung her gaze around to the table, the candles, the wine. And he saw knowledge there he'd much rather not have seen. "That's what all this was about, then? You were trying to seduce me into staying here? You thought you could make me fall head over heels in love with you and never want to leave? Damn, Garrett, what the hell were you planning to do with me once the crisis was over?"

"Chelsea, it's not like that."

"Don't make it worse by lying even more. You arrogant son of a... God, you must really be vain to think a little attention from you would be enough to..." She shook her head hard, closed her eyes. "And I fell right into it, didn't I? Sinking into your arms and telling you..." She got to her feet, but not too steadily. "You and your brothers will have one hell of a belly laugh when you tell them what a sap I was, won't you, Garrett?"

"No! Dammit, Chelsea, shut up and listen for a minute."

"No, you listen. I'm leaving here. I'm taking Ethan and I'm leaving. But before I go, I need to know one thing."

He shook his head. She was not leaving. He wouldn't let her leave. Dammit, not when he knew she'd end up...

"Where does this bastard live?"

His thoughts came to a grinding halt at the pure venom he heard in Chelsea's voice.

"You can't—"

"I damn well can! And I damn well will, and if you won't tell me where to find this animal, I'll find someone else who can. I've waited almost twenty years to..." She stopped, breathing rapidly.

He shook his head and went to her, and he did touch her this time. He took her shoulders in her hands and stared hard at her. "Listen to yourself. Dammit, Chelsea, you're transferring all the rage you feel toward your father—rage you've been hanging on to way too long—onto a man you don't even know. What do you think you're gonna do? Hunt the man down and kill him?"

"Yes! Yes, dammit!"

"No. Chelsea, you gotta let go of this. It's eating you alive."

"I can't let go. They have to pay. Both of them. All of them. Every man who's ever lifted a hand to a woman...or a child.... God, Garrett, when is it going to end? Somebody has to stop them. Somebody has to say it's enough. It's over. No more. No more!"

She was shaking all over and was as white as a sheet. He pulled her tight against him, stroked her hair. "Chelsea, you're right, so right. Somebody has to stop them. But you can't do it alone. I know you want to, but you can't. No one can. And you can't do it by hunting every one of them down like the vermin they are. You might take out a few, but then you'd end up in prison and all the passion you feel for ending this nightmare would be wasted."

The first sob ripped through her, followed closely by another. It tore at his guts to feel the power of her pain wrenching through her small body. He ached, dammit. He bled inside.

"I...c-can get my father...and Vincent. And after th-th-that...it's all frosting...."

"No, baby, no. Not that way. Not that way."

"Then h-how?"

He hooked a finger under her chin, tipped her head up and saw the tears flooding her face. He meant to look into her eyes, try to see if he could make her see sense. But instead, he lowered his mouth to her trembling lips and kissed her. He tasted the salty tears. He tasted *her.* She shuddered with her inner anguish, but she held on to him. And she opened to him. He pushed his tongue between her moist lips and met hers. He licked the roof of her mouth and then drew her tongue into his, held it there, sucked at it. Wanted more.

Then she pushed him away, and he went. He released his grip on her at the first sign she'd had enough and stood there panting as she glared up at him.

"You don't have to pretend anymore, Garrett. It's not going to change my mind."

She turned and fled up the stairs.

Garrett sank into a chair, whispering the words that had leaped to his lips without rehearsal. Without one of Jessi's little cards. Without a well-laid plan.

"I wasn't pretending." He blinked, feeling as dazed as a shell-shocked warrior. "Hell and damnation, I wasn't pretending at all."

Chapter 10

Despite the liniment, Chelsea ached more in the morning than she had the night before. She rolled carefully out of bed, sending a jealous glance toward Ethan. He'd slept the night through in the hand-tooled hardwood cradle and still lay there, peaceful. Content. His legs drawn up underneath him made his little butt poke upward. Chelsea smiled, wondering how anyone could sleep in that position. He seemed comfortable, though.

She pulled on a bathrobe and slipped quietly out of the bedroom. Another steamy bath would have been nice, but the running water might disturb the baby. She'd just wait until later to soak her aching muscles again. Right now, she'd settle for a cup of coffee and the soothing feel of early morning.

The kitchen was deserted. Chelsea glanced at the little clock. Only 5:13. No wonder. The others wouldn't wake for a little while yet. She put on a fresh pot, located a cup and waited for the coffee to brew. When it was done, she took her steaming mug out onto the front porch. She sat down on the swing, leaned back and let the morning work its wonders on her. The new day crept in with its fresh, dewy air and its bird songs. The horizon glowed with brush strokes of fire and gold.

She sipped the coffee. It was beautiful here. Tranquil. But she couldn't stay. Not now.

Her serenity slipped a notch as she recalled what a fool she'd made of herself with Garrett last night. Telling him she wanted him. Confessing she had feelings for him. For God's sake, the man must be sadistic to let her go on like that when his side of the exchange had been no more than an act to keep her at the ranch. And that would have been reason enough to run. But what clinched it was the *reason* he wanted to keep her here. To protect her from an abuser and a killer. Just the way her mother used to step in and try to protect her.

And look where it had gotten Mom.

No, Chelsea didn't have it in her to watch anyone else, even someone as misguided as Garrett Brand, step in to take on a fight that belonged to her. She couldn't see another person hurt in her stead. And she most certainly couldn't stay here now.

Problem was, she couldn't go home, either.

She stared out at the horizon. There must be somewhere in the world that would be safe for her and Ethan. Somewhere, there must be a haven.

Then again, Michele had thought the same thing. She'd been running, searching for a safe haven, too. But this Vincent what's-his-name had found her anyway. And killed her.

A nicker came from the stable, just beyond the bigger barn. Then another.

Chelsea looked in that direction, frowning. A whinny followed, and she found herself getting to her feet, tilting her head, squinting. She knew next to nothing about horses. But what she'd heard struck her as odd. Not the normal, soft sounds animals made, but more a cry of alarm. Or something.

She took another sip from the mug and lowered it to the railing. Then she started down the front steps, pausing before she stepped into the still-moist grass to remove her slippers. No sense soaking them. She tossed them behind her onto the porch and hurried barefoot across the front lawn. The dew chilled her feet and sent a little shiver dancing up her spine. It felt good.

She reached the big front doors and lifted the crosspiece that held them closed, as she'd seen Garrett do. She tugged one of the huge doors open and stepped inside.

Dimmer in here. Cooler. The sweet smell of what must be grain, but smelled faintly of molasses, and the sharp odor of the animals themselves filled the place. Chelsea walked down the center between the stalls that lined either side of the stable. Huge brown eyes followed her progress as she moved slowly along. She spotted Sugar when she was almost all the way to the other end of the long, narrow building. She went over to her, stroked her white muzzle. But the horse seemed nervous and jumpy for some reason, dancing away, eyes too round.

Chelsea wrinkled her nose as she caught a faint whiff of something else. Something that shouldn't be here. But her attention was distracted from the task of putting a name to the scent when she heard a gentle creaking. She turned to see the big door she'd left open slowly swinging shut.

She blinked and her throat went dry.

"The wind," she whispered, sending the mare a nervous smile. "Just the wind." Wind or not, she'd had enough of this place. There was a door at the far end, exactly like the one she'd come through. It was closer than the other, so she headed toward it. Now that she'd checked and seen that the horses were fine, she could leave with a clear conscience.

The spotless concrete floor was cold on her damp feet anyway. She should have worn shoes. She walked quickly to the door, but it took only a single try to tell her that it was not going to budge. Probably a crosspiece, same as on the front door, holding it closed from the outside. Chelsea licked her lips. There was a smaller door on her left. Not an exit by the looks of it. Probably a tack room or something. Though... oddly, she didn't smell leather. More like...

She opened the door. Saw nothing out of the ordinary. But that smell. And...hey, that window was broken. What the...? She was only vaguely aware of a sudden movement outside the broken window. A pinprick of light, flicking from the window to the floor. Lightning bug. Only when the match landed in the puddle at her feet did she realize...

The gasoline on the floor made a *woof* sound and sent her sailing backward. She landed on the concrete floor, hitting it so hard she lost her breath. The fire followed her.

The baby was crying. And strangely enough, Chelsea hadn't done anything to stop him. Garrett grumbled under his breath, but dragged himself out of bed anyway. Even if Chelsea were mad enough to shoot him, she shouldn't take it out on little Bubba.

Nah. She *wouldn't* take it out on little Bubba. So what was up?

He pulled on his jeans. Ethan kept on yelling. He tugged on socks and stomped into his boots, waiting. Chelsea still hadn't picked the kid up. He gave her every opportunity, even shrugging on a shirt to put off the moment when he'd have to go into that bedroom and maybe see her lying there all sleepy and sexy. He didn't want to see her. Not after what she'd confessed last night.

That she wanted him.

Damn, but the look in her eyes when she'd said it had kept him awake all night. Haunting him like a ghost. Didn't matter if his eyes were open or closed, he could still see her there.

And he'd blown it. Sure as all hell, he'd blown it. He supposed he was a little bit slow. He must be, not to have realized it sooner that his part in this little play was more than just an act. The little hellcat meant something to him. Though he doubted he'd ever be able to convince her of it now.

Ethan howled, and Garrett sighed in defeat and stepped into the hall. Tapping once for politeness, he opened the guest-room door. Ethan sat up in the bed, playing with his toes and hollering largely for the pleasure of hearing his own voice, Garrett thought. He looked up when Garrett stepped inside and grinned his fool head off.

Garrett gathered him up and scanned the room, the unmade bed, the empty bathroom. Chelsea wasn't here. Frowning, Garrett looked around for the diaper bag.

"I'll get that, big brother." He spun to see Jessi, sleepy-eyed and ruffly-haired, smiling at him from the doorway. "Here, hand over the little pudge. I'll give him his morning bath. Meanwhile, you can tell me how last night went. You were already in bed by the time we came home."

Garrett frowned as a high-pitched whinny, which sounded an awful lot like Duke, drifted from the stable through the open bedroom window. "Later, Jes."

He handed her the baby on the way past, took the stairs at a trot and headed into the kitchen. Fresh coffee. Sugar out on the counter. A spoon.

"Chelsea?"

No answer. He frowned, studying the room, the beginnings of worry gnawing at his stomach. She shouldn't be out alone. Not with Vincent de Lorean after her. But as he glanced at the front door, he saw that it was unlocked. Somebody had gone out this morning. He crossed the kitchen quickly, opened the door and looked over at the porch swing, half-expecting to see her scowling at him.

She wasn't there. But a half-filled coffee mug sat on the railing. And her slippers lay on the steps.

Duke squealed again, drawing Garrett's gaze toward the stable. That's when he saw the smoke.

He turned just long enough to bellow, thankful for once for his booming voice. "Fire in the stable!" And then he was racing across the lawn, his heart in his throat. He told himself there was no reason in the world to think Chelsea was in that stable. But he believed it anyway. His heart damn near pounded a hole through his chest.

No. She couldn't be inside. The crosspiece still held the front doors closed. Garrett lifted it, tugged the doors open. Flames roared in front of him, a solid wall of fire blocking the entrance. Garrett turned away and raced around the side of the building, up the ladder to the second story where the grain was stored, and climbed inside. The place was sweltering and beginning to fill with smoke. But no flames licked at the granary. He got down on all fours, felt the searing heat scalding his palms as he searched for the trapdoor. He coughed, swiped sweat from his brow, found it and jerked it open.

Light, heat and smoke poured through. No flames, though. He couldn't see any directly below, so he swung his legs down through, and let himself drop.

The floor met him halfway, it seemed. Knocked the wind out of him. Damn. He coughed, wheezed, knuckled his stinging eyes and tried to see. He shouted Chelsea's name, but it was useless. The horses had taken to shrieking in terror. Walls of fire rose at both ends of the stable, blocking the exits, and the flames had spread, licking at the rafters and the stalls at either end.

Sugar reared and kicked the wall behind her again and again. Her stall was on fire, and she was crazed. Garrett staggered to his feet and started toward the frightened animal. Only then did he stumble on Chelsea. She lay on the floor, barely visible in the smoke haze that filled the place. If he hadn't tripped over her, he might never have found her.

Garrett bent down and scooped her up. She hung limply in his arms, head hanging backward. Her robe was smoldering, he realized with a start, and he quickly stripped if off her. Then he moved back to the trapdoor. He slung Chelsea over his shoulder, gripped the ladder and started up. Flames roaring in his ears now. Searing his flesh. Smoke choking him. He was weakening, dammit. Wheezing, gasping like an old man.

He emerged into the loft, but it was no longer any better here. Worse, if anything. Hotter. Smokier. Flames were now licking up through the floorboards here and there, and the roar was deafening. Horses screamed in an agony of panic.

He took a step toward the opening he'd come through. Then another. And then the floor beneath him just dissolved, and he and Chelsea crashed down into the hubs of hell.

"Garrett!" Jessi screamed. "Garrett!"

She stood as close as she could to the blazing stables, which wasn't close enough. But she had little Ethan on her hip and didn't dare go any closer. The place looked like a giant torch, and her beloved brother was inside. It was a nightmare. Elliot manned a hose, trying to soak down the blaze in the doorway enough to get inside. Wes had raced back to the house for a chain saw and now he was revving it and running, which was none too smart, but he did it anyway.

He headed around the side of the stable, and Jessi raced after him. Wes lifted the saw and sank its ripping teeth into the side of the building. The machine whined and growled. The horses shrieked and the fire roared. Ethan took to crying, too, and soon the noises all blended together.

Jessi dropped to her knees right there in the dirt, hugging the sobbing infant to her breast and praying out loud for the volunteer firemen to show up fast. She watched as her brother wielded the saw, and as soon as a jagged, gaping hole was made, Wes tossed the chain saw to the ground, lifted his arms over his face and charged right on inside.

"Wes, no!" Jessi shouted, but she knew it was useless before the words were out. Then Elliot came charging around the side of the burning building, as well, and dived inside after Wes. Blue stood beside Jessi, all four legs braced as he leaned forward, barking at the fire, the hair on his haunches bristling. The dog ran a few steps forward, then backed away, whimpering over and over again, torn between the age-old instinct of self-preservation and the love of his masters.

The fourth time he lunged forward, ol' Blue didn't come back. He leaped through the opening and vanished into the billowing gray smoke.

"Oh, Lord," Jessi cried, kneeling and rocking as unchecked tears flowed down her face. "Lord, don't take my brothers. Don't do that to me...please...."

She heard sirens. Time ticked by. Endless moments passed like hours, though it could only have been seconds between the time she heard the sirens and the time the trucks came barreling into the drive, bounding over the grass. Then men were running this way and that, voices yelling orders.

"Jessica?"

A warm, big hand closed on her shoulder, and she dragged her gaze from the fiery maw that had swallowed almost all of her family except Ben and Adam. She saw the worried face of the stranger who'd come to dinner last night.

"Lash...God, Lash, my brothers..."

His dark brows rose over those pale blue eyes. "In there?"

She nodded, returning her gaze to the hole, praying, hoping.

"There are people inside!" Lash yelled at the men who were even now manning fire hoses. He touched Jessi again. Both hands this time. "Come on. Get away from here before you and the baby end up hurt." He pulled her to her feet. But she tugged her arm free as soon as she was upright. "Jessi, there's nothing you can do here. Come on."

Fresh tears spilled over as he guided her away from the building at a run. He pointed her toward the house, then left her, heading back to join the fire fighters. Jessi didn't go far, only halfway, and she never took her eyes off the inferno. The room was ablaze now, as well. But the flames in the doorway had subsided. She caught her breath when she saw Lash don one of the heavy yellow coats and a helmet, then head inside with the others.

Only seconds later, big old Duke was led through that doorway with a neckerchief over his eyes. Behind him were Sugar, whose rump bore charred spots, and Paint dancing and kicking wildly. The man who led them out was Jason Pratt, a local merchant she'd known since kindergarten. He ran across the lawn, releasing the animals into the corral and closing the gate before hurrying back to the blazing stable.

Marisella's battered pickup bounced into the driveway, and the elderly woman jumped out with the agility of a sixteen-year-old. She ran up to Jessi. "Give the child to me before you drop him, *chica.* Here." She pried Ethan from Jessi's arms, and the baby stopped crying.

Then Lash came through the front door, half-dragging Elliot. Elliot's arm was wrapped around Lash's broad shoulders. They ran several yards from the stable, then Lash eased Elliot to the ground, whirled and raced back inside. One of the volunteers who hadn't gone in rushed over to Elliot with an oxygen tank and a mask. Jessi took a step forward, but Marisella's firm hand on her arm kept her from running to him, as well.

Two more men came out, Wes suspended between them, his face blackened with soot. He was coughing uncontrollably, and it looked as if he were fighting his rescuers. They dumped him on the ground and one of them stayed with him, trying to hold him there by all appearances, while the other rushed back inside. On his way in, this fire fighter passed another, coming out carrying Chelsea in his arms. He laid her beside Wes and Elliot.

Jessi did rush forward now, ignoring Marisella's warnings. She fell on the ground beside her brothers, not caring that she was in the way of the paramedics who tried to tend them.

"Elliot! Wes! God, I thought... Are you all right?"

Wes coughed some more, but tore the oxygen mask away from his face and struggled to his feet. Elliot lay on his back, blinking slowly and breathing deeply from the mask over his face.

"Garrett's still in there," Wes growled at the fire fighter holding his shoulders. "And you damned well can't stop me from going in after my brother."

Elliot muttered something that sounded like "Garrett" from beneath the mask. Jessi smoothed his sooty hair away from his black-streaked face. But her eyes were on the door. More horses emerged, then none. She counted them and knew they were all safe. But no sign of Garrett. She glanced Chelsea's way, but so many people were bending over her it was impossible to see. Fear gripped Jessi's heart.

Part of the roof fell in with a deafening roar and an explosion of sparks and cinders. The flames shot skyward, and Jessi screamed Garrett's name. Wes shoved the fire fighter so hard the man went flying and hit the ground, then Wes surged forward, running flat out toward the stable.

But he stopped short at the doorway. Garrett and Lash came stumbling out, and it was unclear who was helping whom. Blue lumbered along beside them. They staggered forward, and Jessi ran to meet them. Wes already had his arms around Garrett, so Jessi took hold of Lash and helped him back toward the others.

The remaining part of the roof and one whole side of the stable fell inward with a thunderous crash. But Jessi was too busy thanking God to notice it much.

''Chelsea...'' Garrett coughed and pushed the oxygen mask away from his face. He glanced once toward the burning building. Not much was left but a blazing framework. And then that even collapsed in on itself, leaving only charred ruins.

Jessi knelt beside him, crying, holding his hands. ''They got her, Garrett.'' She nodded to his left, and Garrett saw Chelsea lying there, surrounded by men who worked on her. But her eyes were closed and his heart turned over.

He drew a raspy breath, swallowed, but his throat felt raw. ''Wes and Elliot?''

''They're okay, Garrett.'' This from his left, and he turned to see Lash sitting upright, back bowed forward slightly, holding a mask to his face, breathing several times before moving it aside to speak again. ''They took in some smoke, but they're okay. We got all the horses out, too, I think.''

Garrett took only a second to look for his brothers. Elliot seemed shaken, dazed, but all right. Wes had wandered over to the corral and was trying to soothe the horses there. Garrett brought his gaze back to Lash and narrowed his stinging eyes. "What the hell are you doing here?"

"Garrett, he saved your life. Elliot's, too," Jessi said. "Thank God he was here."

Lash held Garrett's gaze. "I saw the fire trucks heading this way, and I followed."

"Why?"

Lash shrugged. "Thought I might be able to help. I used to do this crap for a living."

Garrett frowned. "You're a fire fighter?"

"Used to be. In Chicago."

Garrett nodded, digesting the information and still wondering what this stranger was really doing here. Why did he leave Chicago and show up in a speck on the map like Quinn? Why did he just happen to be around every time disaster struck?

Chelsea groaned, a hoarse, guttural sound, and putting his questions aside, he got to his feet and went to her. He knelt beside her, brushing her hair away from her face.

"She took in quite a bit of smoke, Garrett. Has a few burns, but nothing life threatening. We need to get her to the hospital."

He nodded to the anonymous voice of a paramedic, not bothering to link a name to it or to check the face of what was, in all likelihood, one of his neighbors.

"You could use some treatment yourself," the voice said.

"I'm fine. See to Chelsea." The man didn't argue. Garrett watched helplessly as Chelsea was bundled onto a gurney and rolled to a waiting ambulance. He turned once, found Wes and Jessi standing nearby. "You all right, Wes?"

Wes nodded, grim-faced. "Some of the horses have burns. They'll need tending."

"Can you and Jessi handle it?"

"Sure," Jessi said quickly. "I'll ask Marisella to stay and take care of Ethan for us."

"I want Elliot at the hospital. He doesn't look good."

"Neither do you," Wes replied. "I'll see he gets there."

"Send him along by ambulance. I want you to stay here, Wes. I'm thinking this fire was no accident."

Wes's black eyes narrowed, again reminding Garrett how appropriately his Comanche mother had named him. Raven Eyes. "Vincent de Lorean?"

"Probably."

"You think he'll try again?"

"He might."

"I'll watch things. He tries anything today, he's gonna be one hurting son of a—"

"You watch things. Don't let little Bubba out of your sight. Not for a second. I'm going with Chelsea."

Wes nodded, for once not making smart remarks about his love life. Garrett climbed into the back of the ambulance and found a seat. He clutched Chelsea's dirty hands in his and closed his eyes as the doors slammed shut. Then the vehicle bounded away, its sirens wailing.

She stirred awake. Pain seared her right arm and both feet. Her lungs burned. Her eyes stung, and it hurt to breathe. But all of that faded when she brought her vision into focus and saw Garrett sitting in a hard little chair beside her bed, staring down at her. Black soot coated his face and neck and arms. His dark hair curled unnaturally at the ends, singed, and she realized what had happened. She'd been trapped in the burning stable, and he had come in after her.

His brown eyes widened when they met hers. "Thank God Almighty, Chelsea. I was beginnin' to think you'd never come around."

She opened her mouth to speak, but only a hoarse croak emerged. She glanced down at herself. She lay in a white bed, wearing a pale blue hospital gown, and her right arm was bandaged and both her feet were wrapped in gauze. No soot coated her skin, and she realized someone had cleaned her up. No one tended to Garrett, though.

She cleared her throat. It hurt. "You're a mess," she whispered.

"You should have seen yourself."

She mustered a smile.

"Are you hurting, Chelsea?"

"A little." She closed her eyes, licked her parched lips. "A lot."

"I'll call a nurse, make them give you something for—"

"In a minute." She covered his hand as he reached for the call button clipped to the edge of her pillow. "Garrett, there was someone outside the barn."

"You saw someone?"

"I saw…a shape. Movement. I smelled gasoline, and…" She closed her eyes, shivering at the memory of the instant when she'd realized what was happening.

He left the chair, bending over the bed and enfolding her in his arms before the chill even left her spine. His big, solid chest was under her hands, and his strong arms held her gently. She thought she felt him tremble. And when he spoke, his voice was rough from more than just smoke he'd inhaled. "Dammit, Chelsea, you could have been killed. I could've...*we*...could've lost you."

She didn't fight her instinctive response to him. She let her arms slide around his waist and hugged him back, resting her head on his shoulder. He smelled smoky. But even that didn't make his embrace less soothing.

"I was scared, Garrett. I haven't been that scared since those nights when I'd sit in my bedroom and listen to my father's slaps and my mother's tears."

His sigh warmed her neck. Then he loosened his grip and moved back a little. He looked down at her and smiled softly. "I smudged your face." He took a tissue from the box on the bedside stand and wiped at a spot on her cheek.

She drew a calming breath, wishing she could steady her pattering heart, but finding it difficult.

Garrett dropped the tissue into the wastebasket and sat in his chair again. "So what were you doing in the stable, Chelsea?"

She shrugged. "The horses sounded jumpy. I thought I'd check on them." She studied his face as he listened carefully to her answer. "How did you know I was out there?"

"Saw the coffee on the porch, your slippers. Then the smoke." He shook his head and swore. "You'll never know how I felt when I yanked those doors open and saw that wall of fire."

"But you came inside anyway."

He held her gaze a long moment, his brown one

darkening. "Because I had this gut-deep feeling you were in there."

"You could have gotten yourself killed trying to get me out."

"What was the alternative, Chelsea? Just leave you there to burn to death?"

She shrugged. "I'm beginning to think my nephew would fare just as well being raised by you as by me. Maybe better."

"And you think your nephew is the only reason I risked my neck to get to you?"

She lifted her chin. "What else would I think?"

He hooked a finger beneath her chin to raise it, then settled his mouth over hers. His kiss was gentle. Healing, almost. Warmth and life seemed to flow through him into her. He lifted his head.

"Think that," he said softly.

She blinked up at him, confusion swirling like a tempest in her mind. "I don't..."

"Doesn't matter, Chelsea. We have time. Right now, all that matters is that you're okay and you're coming home with me."

She drew a slow breath as Garrett settled back in the chair. "I'm not sure that's such a great idea."

He frowned, didn't speak, just frowned and nodded at her to continue.

"Garrett, if that fire was deliberately set, then this Vincent character knows where I'm staying. He knows where Ethan is. And he'll keep trying until he gets to us."

"He can keep trying until hell freezes over, Chelsea. It won't do him any good. He's got a truckload of Brands to go through before he can get to you or Bubba, and he's gonna find that isn't exactly easy."

Chelsea closed her eyes. "That's exactly what I'm afraid of."

Garrett shook his head slowly, a puzzled look creasing his brow.

"You could have been killed in that fire, Garrett. Elliot or Wes—God, even Jessi—might have died today. I don't *want* all of you standing between this gangster and me. I don't want anyone else suffering because I showed up in your lives."

"No one's going to suffer—"

"No? Tell my mother that, Garrett. She died because she tried to protect my sister and me. I can't live with that happening to anyone else."

He stared down at her in silence as if he didn't know what to say. Finally, he just sighed hard. "We'll take precautions. I'll contact Ben and Adam, get them back here to help out. Everything will be just—"

"No."

He frowned at her, seeming unable to understand what she was getting at.

"He murdered my sister, Garrett. Not yours. This is between Vincent de Lorean and me, and nobody else."

"And Ethan," Garrett whispered. "Don't you forget about Ethan."

Licking her lips, swallowing hard on a decision that went down like a brick, she nodded. "I'm not forgetting him."

"Chelsea..." He shook his head, leaned over and took her hand in his. "All that crap before, the wine and the music, that wasn't me. It was bull. But I realized that night that—"

"I don't want to hear this. Not now, Garrett. Please."

He stared down at her, and she knew she'd hurt him.

God, could the big lug actually have developed a soft spot for her after all?

"You aren't alone anymore, Chelsea. Dammit straight to hell, I know you've had to be your whole life. I know every battle you fought, you fought by yourself. But you don't have to do that this time. Damn, woman, why won't you let me help you?"

Because I love you.

The words whispered through her mind like a sudden breeze, startling her enough to make her eyes widen. She loved him the way she'd loved her mother and her sister. She loved him in spite of the fact that he was a man and that she'd vowed never to love one of that gender. And she trusted him. There wasn't a single doubt in Chelsea's mind that he'd never harm a hair on her head. No doubt in her mind that he'd do everything in his power to protect her.

Her mother had tried to protect her, too. From a man a lot like Vincent. Her own father. Oh, Chelsea and Michele had taken beatings. Lots of them. But whenever she could, Mom had stepped in, diverted the bastard's rage away from her daughters, deliberately directing it at herself instead. And she'd died because of it.

And Michele. Michele had found a safe haven for her baby son and then run off in another direction. She'd become a moving target for Vincent's rage in order to save her son from the monster. And *she'd* died because of it.

Chelsea couldn't let someone—especially Garrett—try to take her place as the target of Vincent's vengeance. And she wouldn't run. Running didn't do any good. No place was safe as long as that man remained on this planet.

"Come here with me, Chelsea. The doc said you could leave whenever you felt up to it."

She nodded slowly. "Okay. I'll come." But she knew in her heart she was lying.

Chapter 11

Something was on her mind. Garrett knew it as well as he knew his own name, but she wouldn't open up. Wouldn't tell him about it. Wouldn't let him in.

And he wanted to get in more than a hairless pup in a blizzard. The more she withdrew, the more edgy he became. Until it seemed to Garrett that nothing in his life had ever been as important to him as his new mission. Getting to Chelsea Brennan. Making her let him help her. Let him see what she was thinking, what she was feeling. Let him…

Ah, hell, he didn't know what.

The stable was nothing more than soaking wet ashes and a few chunks of charred beams here and there. The horses were stuck in the corral for the night. Elliot was still complaining about his lungs hurting. Wes, Garrett suspected, was hurting a lot more than Elliot, but typically, he hadn't said a damned word to indicate it. Jessi was still shaky, jumping at shadows. He'd heard from Elliot that she'd been target shooting while he and Chelsea had been at the hospital. Target shooting, when they all knew damned well and good that Jessi could outshoot any of them. She didn't need to practice. He hated to see his tomboy sister all nerved up.

He'd been nerved up, too. So much so that he had a call in to the Texas Rangers asking for background information, an address and anything else they had on Vincent de Lorean. They hadn't got back to him yet, but Garrett thought it wouldn't be much longer. The second he knew where he could find the bastard, he planned to pay him a visit. And not a pleasant one.

Only Ethan seemed unaffected by it all. He played with the new set of soft-sided, brightly colored building blocks Wes had brought home from one of his trips into town. Kid loved the things. Especially seemed to like bopping ol' Blue on the head with them, not that Blue minded any. In fact, the old mutt had actually batted one across the floor a second ago the way a playful puppy might do.

Little Bubba had a way of making everyone feel younger, Garrett supposed. He glanced into the kitchen at Chelsea and swallowed hard. Yup. He knew he for one felt like an awkward twelve-year-old eyeing potential dance partners at his first boy-girl party.

He girded his loins and stomped into the kitchen. He'd taken a lot of pains today while Chelsea had been lying upstairs in bed recuperating. Now, dammit, he was going to give this thing one last, all-out shot.

"Chelsea?"

She turned toward him with a head of lettuce in her hand, auburn brows lifted. She'd trimmed off the edges of her hair where it had burned a bit, so now it framed her face in a way it hadn't before. He liked it. She seemed softer, and maybe a little more approachable. Her eyes were not hostile when they met his, and he thought they might've come to some kind of a truce back there at the hospital.

God, when he'd realized she might be trapped in that fire…when he'd seen her lying so still on the ground while those men worked on her…

His world had tilted. Looking into those deep green eyes, he felt that way again right now. Like looking way down into a pine-bordered lake. He could see himself in their reflection. He could see…

Good grief. He guessed he'd better get her alone before he made a damn fool of himself in front of everyone. They'd never let him hear the end of that. He took the lettuce from Chelsea and set it aside. Then he reached for her good hand, closed his around it and gave a gentle tug as he turned toward the door. "Come on. You and I are going out for dinner."

"We are?"

"Yup." He pulled her a few steps closer to the door.

"Don't you think you might have asked me first?"

"Nope."

"Shouldn't I at least change my clothes?"

He glanced down at the snug jeans and T-shirt she wore, smiled, then checked it so she wouldn't see what was in his eyes. Truth to tell, she looked a little bit too damned good. The jeans hugged and the T-shirt revealed and he wanted to touch her all over. But not if she was going to be cringing and getting all skittish with him. He wanted her to want his touch. He wanted her to…

He closed his eyes, drew a breath. "You're perfect, Chelsea. We're not going anywhere fancy."

She shrugged. "If I said no?"

"I'd stand outside your window and do my lonesome coyote impression until dawn."

Her lips curved into the delicate smile he'd been getting all too used to seeing. And even though he was getting used to it, that slow, slight curve of her lips made his stomach turn cartwheels and his heart break into a gallop.

"Then I guess we're going out," she said softly. "Though I might want to hear that lonesome coyote impression some other time."

He grinned at her and pulled her to the door. Duke and Paint stood saddled and waiting.

Chelsea frowned. "Where's Sugar?"

"Burned her rump a little bit this morning. Nothing too serious. Jessi tended her and she'll be fine. But a saddle would chafe."

Chelsea stroked Paint's neck and moved around to the left side. Garrett helped her into the saddle.

"Isn't this Wes's horse?"

"Yup."

"Won't he mind?"

"He insisted. Said Paint was the most well-trained, intelligent animal on the place, and if you were riding at all, you ought to be riding him."

"He said that?"

Garrett nodded. "My brother pretends to be made of stone, Chelsea, but he isn't really. It's just tough to crack through that granite shell sometimes."

"Wasn't very tough for Ethan, though."

"No, Ethan got to him right off. We could all see it." Garrett checked the bulging saddlebags and then swung into the saddle.

"What makes him like that? So…hot tempered and hard?"

Garrett glanced sideways at her as the horses turned side by side and started across the lawn, not toward what used to be the stable this time, but around the house, behind it and across the back lawn, as well, toward the sparse clusters of little trees scattered here and there.

"My brother spent two years in prison, Chelsea. That's enough to harden a man."

She opened her mouth, closed it again and stared at him. "Wes?"

"Yup. Some guys he was hanging with robbed a bar. Beat the hell out of the owner. Wes had left them before it happened, but he got blamed all the same."

"You mean he was innocent?"

"I'd stake my life on it."

"But..."

"I wasn't a sheriff then. The circumstantial evidence was stacked against him so high, I'm not sure I could've done anything even if I had been. Bought him the best lawyer in the state, for what it was worth. But he ended up being sentenced to five years hard time. We got him paroled after two, though. I'm not sure that would have happened, either, except one of the men on the parole board was a friend of my daddy's a hundred years ago."

"That's awful." She turned in the saddle, looking back toward the house and shaking her head. There was real regret in her eyes. "Two years for nothing."

"After Wes went up, I ran for sheriff. Figured if I couldn't beat the damn system, I might as well join it and try to change things from the inside. My brother...well, it's taken him a while to understand that. He was none too happy to come home and see me wearing a badge."

"I can imagine. He must have thought you'd joined the enemy."

Garrett nodded, studying her face. "You have a way of nailing things right down, Chelsea. That's exactly how he felt."

She stared into his eyes, and he could see her feeling for him, as well as for his brother. She had a heart as big as all outdoors. Though she didn't even realize that. Odd the way she could feel for the pain of others, but couldn't let anyone else—couldn't let *him*—feel for her. Share her hurts.

She did once, though. She did when she told him about the night her mamma died.

"What about now?" she asked. "Does he understand now?"

Garrett had to blink and focus hard before he came back to the subject at hand. "I think so. There's something…something lacking in Wes's soul." Garrett walked Duke up to a little tree and drew him to a halt. "I've raised him just like the others, but it wasn't enough somehow."

He slid from the saddle, pulled off the bridle and didn't bother picketing Duke. He wouldn't wander far. He removed the saddlebags and slung them over his shoulder.

"But, Garrett, Wes isn't just like the others."

"No?"

She shook her head. "Elliot told me he's half Comanche."

Garrett nodded, not minding at all that Elliot had told Chelsea about it. "My father left us for a time. It was before Elliot and Jessi were born, and I was just a kid. Never did know the whole story until a good deal later."

He slipped his free arm around Chelsea's shoulders, moving a little bit away from the horses and into a shady spot as he spoke. Compelled for some reason to tell her everything about himself, about his family.

"What was the whole story?' she asked in that deep, soft voice that sent chills up his nape.

Garrett cleared his throat. "Her name was Stands Alone," he said, "and I wish to God I'd known her. She was one hell of a woman, Wes's mother."

She frowned at him. "I'm surprised you'd feel that way about the woman your father had an affair with."

Garrett shrugged. "She was orphaned as a child, married young and widowed a short time later. Hence the name. But she never knew my father was married. They had a brief affair, and she fell deeply in love with him. But she was a wise woman and she knew, somehow, that his heart belonged to someone else. When she called him on it, he told her the truth. Then she sat that man down and gave him hell. Told him she wanted nothing to do with a man who would betray a good woman who bore him sons. Lectured him on the value of a good man. On how honor and trust and fidelity were more precious than riches, and how a man's children should mean more to him than his own life. She made him feel about two inches tall and sent him home to us, telling him not to ever try to see her again. What she didn't tell him was that she was pregnant with his son."

He looked into Chelsea's eyes, saw them wide and interested.

"How did your father ever find out about Wes?"

"He didn't," Garrett told her. "My mother did. Stands Alone changed my father. When he came back to us, he was the most devoted husband and father anyone could ask for. He felt bad for hurting our mother and did his damnedest to make up for it. Some years later, my mother heard talk of a young Comanche woman who'd died and left her son, Raven Eyes, alone."

"Raven Eyes?" Chelsea said it softly, then nodded. "That fits him."

"Mamma claimed she had a feeling, and to her dying day she swore that feeling was the spirit of Stands Alone, whispering to her. Whatever it was, she went to the Comanche village and asked around. Before long, she learned the truth—that Raven Eyes was my father's illegitimate son. She brought him home and treated him like one of her own, right from day one."

"How old was he then?" Chelsea asked.

"Seven."

She nodded.

"He seemed happy enough. But there's always been that shadow in his eyes. I just wish I knew what it was." He looked down at her, saw her gnawing her lower lip. "What? You're thinking something. I can see it. Go ahead. Tell me."

Chelsea nodded. "He spent the first seven years of his life in an entirely different culture. Then, just like that, he's removed from it. If it were me, I'd feel as if I were missing half my identity. He doesn't even seem to acknowledge the Native American blood running in his veins, but he must know it's there. He must remember his life before, but he acts as if it never happened."

Garrett moved closer to her, taking her waist in his hands, so she faced him. "You think that's what it is?"

"A tree can't grow without roots, Garrett. Your brother only has half of them and a whole pile of anger to boot. I'd say that's it. He probably doesn't even know that's what's bothering him, but I'll bet if he were to spend some time getting in touch with his heritage, he'd realize what he's been lacking in a heartbeat.''

Garrett nodded, studying her pretty face and wise eyes. Pained still, but wise. ''How can anyone be so smart about other people's demons, Chelsea, and so blind to their own?''

Her smile died slowly, and she averted her face. ''I'm not blind to them. I just...'' She shook her head.

''Just don't like looking at them.''

She nodded.

''I want to make this better for you, Chelsea. I want to make it all go away so you can heal.''

''Why?''

He lowered his forehead until it rested lightly against hers. ''A broken heart can't be filled. It just keeps leaking. I want those cracks all patched up, Chelsea.''

She looked down. But he kissed her anyway. He nudged her lips into parting, he tasted her mouth, he slipped his arms around her and held her tight. The way he'd wanted to all day.

''I think I might be—''

''Don't.'' She pulled free of him and turned back to her patient mount, pulling the bridle off the way Garrett had done with Duke. ''Not yet, Garrett. I'm not ready.''

''Okay.''

She faced him, bridle dangling from one hand. ''Okay? That's it?''

''Yup.''

Her eyes were wary, then relaxed and maybe even just a little bit grateful.

He slung an arm around her shoulders and walked her along a trail, leaving the horses to graze. ''Come here. I want to show you something.''

Chelsea walked along beside him, and he thought she seemed a little better since coming out here. Maybe this would help. ''What are you going to show me?''

''This.'' He led her around the last tree and waved an arm toward the huge pond that filled what was once just a small valley before Garrett and his brothers had diverted a tiny stream to fill it. The shore was grassy and level, and she took a deep breath, eyes glittering, lips curving.

''It's beautiful.''

''Yeah, I thought so, too. Until I saw you.''

She blushed a pretty shade of pink, and Garrett felt his chest swell a little. Maybe he didn't need Jessi and her silly cards after all.

''You know the other night, all that candlelight and wine and crystal and china?''

She lifted her brows, nodded.

Garrett cleared his throat. ''Well, uh, none of that was me. I mean, it wasn't...genuine. You know?''

''I think so.''

He nodded toward the pond again. ''This is me.''

Her eyes narrowed a little, but she nodded.

Garrett let the saddlebags slide from his shoulder to the ground. He hunkered down, unfastened the straps and opened them up. Then he pulled out a folded gray-and-white checkered tablecloth, took it by the edges and gave it a shake.

Smiling, Chelsea grabbed the opposite edges and helped him settle the cloth smoothly over the grass. Then she sat on it, curling her legs underneath her.

Garrett allowed himself the pleasure of watching her

sit, then dived back into the bags for the paper plates and plastic utensils. Then a big Tupperware bowl full of cold fried chicken and another one with leftover chili. And one with fresh tossed salad. And a pitcher of iced tea that was all dewy on the outside. And two plastic tumblers. Some pita bread. Some cheese. And a saltshaker.

By the time he finished, Chelsea was laughing very softly, and he slanted her a sideways glance. "What?"

She shook her head. "Just wondered if you left anything at all in the fridge for the others."

He grinned at her. "I only took as much as I could carry." He continued arranging the food on the blanket. Then sat back, surveyed it and nodded once. "See this spread?" he asked.

"Yeah."

"*This* is me. I'd a hundred times rather have a picnic under the sky than a fancy-schmancy candlelight dinner indoors."

"Oh."

Holding his plastic cup in one hand, he poured it full of iced tea with the other. Then he held the cup up. "See this?"

She nodded. "Is that you, too?"

"Uh-huh. Nothing comes close when the sun's been beating down for days on end. I don't even like wine. I wouldn't know a blush from a rosé, nor would I care to. Don't know which kind you'd have with chicken. Don't rightly give a damn, either. Give me a tall glass of good, sweet water, or some iced tea, or an ice-cold beer on occasion, and I'm a happy man."

"I see."

Garrett handed her the glass of tea and filled another for himself. He swallowed it in one gulp. Then he reached into one of the bags and pulled out a little portable radio. He flicked it on. Mellow country music came from the tiny speaker. Whining steel guitar, then some fiddle, and a plaintive voice that could break a heart.

"Hear that?"

She smiled. "Not really a Bryan Adams fan, are you?"

Shaking his head, he frowned and said, "Well, actually, that song we were dancing to the other night began to grow on me. But this is what I'd have picked." He reached down and snapped the radio off. "Or maybe not. 'Cause this is the real music." She frowned. He held up a hand. "Shhh. Just listen."

He knew she was doing what he told her. And he was glad. He watched her pick out the sounds one by one. The gentle grinding sound the horses made as they chewed grass. The lapping of the pond when the breeze pushed at it. The occasional banjo strum of a bullfrog. The birds. The rustling leaves. The horses, moving their hoofs against the grass. The whirring wings of a dragonfly. All of it.

"You're right," she whispered. "This is the real music."

He sat there, stared at her and was plunged into a depth of longing he'd never experienced in his life. Her eyes closed. Her head tilted as she listened, and the slight breeze wafted through her hair, like invisible fingers threading through it to feel its silkiness.

It occurred to Garrett that she belonged here. Right here, right in this very spot. It was as if it had been created just for her. And she belonged in this family. She was good for them. She saw things he couldn't see, hadn't seen. And something else occurred to him, too. Something that made him feel like he was coming down with a bad stomach virus.

Chelsea opened her eyes only to see Garrett looking a bit sickly. His face had gone unusually pale, and his eyes looked unfocused and distant, maybe a little shellshocked.

"Anything wrong?"

"What? Uh, no, nothing's...I'm fine. Here, have some chicken before it gets cold." He pushed the bowl toward her.

Chelsea grinned. "Garrett, it already *is* cold."

"Oh. Yeah, right." He yanked out a drumstick, looked at it and grimaced.

"Are you sick or something?" She felt a new worry creeping up on her. He really didn't look well, and she thought of all the smoke he'd inhaled and wondered if he might be having some delayed reaction to it.

"Probably just a stomach bug," he said, and set the chicken down on his plate. He refilled his glass and took another swig of iced tea. "You go ahead. Don't want all this food to go to waste."

Chelsea frowned at him, but helped herself to a bit of everything and ate. Garrett mostly shoved food around on his paper plate and watched her. He took a bite or two, but looked as if he were eating cardboard sandwiches filled with sand. Chelsea had witnessed this man's appetite firsthand. He did not pick at food. He inhaled it.

She finished eating and started cleaning up. Garrett's hand covered hers, stopping her. "Let me get that."

"No, it's okay. I don't mind." She went on with what she'd been doing. Garrett finally shrugged and joined in. When everything was packed away, she stood and stretched, gazing out at the pond again.

She'd like to take a closer look, but if Garrett didn't feel well…

"Pull off your shoes, Chelsea. Put your feet in."

"But you're sick."

He waved a dismissive hand. "Go on. Coming out here and being with you is the best medicine for what ails me."

She met his eyes, but he blinked and looked away. Chelsea shrugged and sat down, pulled off her shoes and socks and rolled up the legs of her jeans. Then she walked slowly toward the water's edge.

She stuck one foot—the one that was no longer bandaged and sore—in the cool water, down onto the smooth pebbles at the bottom. Something slippery brushed her ankle and she jumped backward with a gasp.

Garret's booming laugh reached her just before he did. "Just a little fish, Chelsea. Don't tell me you're scared of a little fish. Didn't you ever swim in a pond before?"

She slanted him a narrow-eyed glare. "No. Only pools where you can see all the way to the bottom." She glanced warily at the water again. "What else is in here?"

He shrugged. "A few frogs. Maybe a mud turtle or two."

"Turtles?" She took another step backward.

"Nothing that will hurt you, Chelsea."

She turned slowly, tilting her head. "You sure?"

"Nothing's ever gonna hurt you. Not when you're with me."

Only, she wasn't going to be with him much longer, was she? She bit her lower lip, let her chin drop down. He came closer, caught it and lifted it again. His brown eyes scanned her face. Chelsea stared up into them. Then at his lips. She wanted to kiss him more than she'd ever wanted anything. The knowledge surprised her. He'd kissed her, yes. He'd even asked permission to kiss her, and she'd given it. But for her to want to touch his mouth with hers badly enough to take the initiative was something entirely foreign to her. Hadn't she decided the touch of a man was something she could live without? Something she didn't need? She needed it now.

And he knew. She could tell he knew. Because his eyes darkened as they plumbed the depths of hers. But he didn't move. Just stood there, waiting, the picture of patience and kindness and understanding. But with his eyes, he spoke to her, encouraged, invited, even dared. And without a word, he drew her closer. A force beyond understanding pulled at her, until she stood on tiptoe and lifted her face to his, then fitted her mouth to his and tasted his lips.

They trembled so slightly she barely felt it. A faint ripple seemed to emanate from somewhere deep inside his big body and from his lips to hers, and then it echoed right to her soul. Her hands slid up his chest to curl around his neck, and Garrett bowed over her, gathered her close and moaned deeply and softly as he kissed her. She parted her lips to him, and he touched her with his tongue, tentatively at first, then boldly, probing her mouth in tender strokes that sent fire searing down into her spine and weakened her knees.

His lips slid over her mouth, skimming her cheek and jawline, then the hollows underneath. She shivered, letting her head fall backward to ease the way for his explorations. He kissed a path down the column of her throat, nuzzled the collar of her blouse out of the way, then tasted the skin over her collarbone and along the top of her shoulder. His hands pressed flat to her back, and he kissed the uppermost curve of her breasts and the spot in between them. Then he trailed hot, wet kisses back up the front of her, not missing an inch of skin on the trip to her mouth. His hands slid upward, tangling in her hair. Chelsea ached with a burning need she'd never felt for any man. A need she'd vowed she never would feel.

She kissed him back, not wanting this forbidden feeling to end. Not ever. When his mouth left hers again, she moved over his throat the way he had moved over hers. She felt every corded muscle under her lips. She tasted the salt of his skin. His pulse thudded wildly against her mouth, filling her and melding with her own rapid heartbeat until she couldn't distinguish one from the other. And she wasn't sure she wanted to.

His hands rose to cup her head, and gently he pulled her away. He was breathing rapidly now, and all of his color had come back and then some.

''Chelsea, if we don't stop—''

''I don't want to stop,'' she blurted, surprised she'd said it so fast. But it was like that with Garrett. She could say anything to him and know he wouldn't laugh at her or use the knowledge against her. He wasn't that kind of man.

''What *do* you want?''

Her answer was to crush herself against his chest and lift her head in search of his lips once more. He didn't hesitate to answer her quest. As he kissed her, he slipped his arms underneath her and lifted her up. Still kissing her, holding her, cradling her in his strength, he took long strides, bending once to snatch up the checkered tablecloth, then continuing along the shore. When she felt the sun's absence from her heated flesh, she opened her eyes to see a small cluster of scraggly trees surrounding a blanket of grass. He let the tablecloth fall and lowered her on top of it. He knelt beside her, bent over her and kissed her mouth some more. As if feeding on it, he drew on her tongue and lips as if they tasted sweeter than honey. A sweetness he craved. Hurriedly, he smoothed out the cloth before he lay down beside her, wrapped her in his arms and gently eased her off the hard ground until she lay only on his body.

The sensation was intense. The rugged length of him beneath her. Her breasts crushed to his chest. His hands slipped up underneath her shirt, roughened palms sliding over the skin of her back, up to her shoulders to pull her closer. Hold her tighter. Lick more deeply into her mouth. Let her more deeply into his. Still, it wasn't enough. She wanted to feel his flesh. She wanted to be naked with him. She wanted him inside her.

She braced herself up with one hand, tugged at the buttons of his shirt with the other. Her hurried movements made her clumsy. His big hand covered hers.

"Easy. It's all right, beautiful Chelsea. We have all night."

She met his blazing hot gaze, nodded once and tried again to free a button. His hand remained on top of hers, eyes locked with hers, as she released it and moved lower to the next and then the next. When the last button was freed, she pushed his shirt open, ran her hand over his muscled chest and felt the fine hairs there tickling her palm. She ran her fingertips over his nipple, and he clenched his jaw, grating his teeth. A rush of desire surged through her at the way his face changed just by her touch. She wanted more of that, so she scratched gently at his nipple with her nails, and he closed his eyes, drew three quick, openmouthed breaths.

It was good to do this to him. To make him gasp with pleasure. It was something she'd never dreamed of doing to a man. The thrill of it coursed through her like a drug, adding to her own arousal until she felt herself quivering like the reed of an instrument when its player's lips are over it. She moved her hand aside, lowered her head and kissed his chest. She flicked her tongue over his hard little nipple and scraped her teeth over it, too, while she used her hand to torture its mate.

His chin pointed skyward, and he panted, his chest rising and falling under her. His arms stretched out to either side, and she knew he was letting her lead the way in this. Letting her do what she wanted. Letting her call the shots. Because he didn't want to push her or scare her or…

"Chelsea…*dammit,* Chelsea, you're killing me…." But his words were only hoarse whispers.

She sat up, staring down at him, feeling a power filling her. Feeling more alive, more utterly female than she ever had.

He lifted his hands to her blouse, took hold of the top button, searched her eyes. "Can I?"

Nodding, she sat still as he released every button. He put his hands on her shoulders and pushed the blouse open then down her arms. Lowering his eyes to look at her, he stared at her unbound breasts with something like reverence in his eyes. She didn't tell him to stop. The heels of his hands and then his palms slipped downward over her breasts, and her nipples stiffened and pressed against his hands. She understood then the cause of his rapid breathing because she could barely control her own. Closing her eyes, she fought to regain it. Warmth and a tingling sensation rose up from the core of her and seemed to pool where he touched her. He drew his fingers downward, closed them on her nipples, the slight pressure and movement causing her to gasp.

He slid his hands around to her back and pulled her gently lower, and lower still, so that she was over him where he lay on the ground. She didn't resist. She could do this. She could let him guide her, let him have some of her, because she trusted him as she'd never trusted another man.

When she'd bent so low his warm breath caressed her breasts, he lifted his head to kiss the very tips. One and then the other. The contact too brief and too light. But his head remained there, close to her, and he parted his lips and ran his tongue over one yearning nipple, pushing it this way and that for a moment, only to leave it wet and aching for more as he moved to the other. Only when she felt ready to cry in sweet anguish, did he finally capture one of those throbbing nubs in his mouth. He suckled her, very gently at first. Then with more pressure and still more. It felt good. It felt so, so good. Her hands caught his head to hold him there, and she fed him her breasts for a long time. When he lay back, they were wet from his mouth, and the soft breeze wafted over their sensitized peaks and he watched them lengthen as if reaching for him.

Her mind began spinning because the longing wasn't just where he'd fed on her. It was everywhere. It was all through her body. And the epicenter was between her legs, where she felt hot and wet and empty. Straddling his body, she rubbed herself against him and felt his answering hardness bulging and pushing at her there.

She slid down a little to look at him, swelling behind the jeans he wore. With hands that trembled and a heart that did likewise, she touched the shape of him. As he'd done before, he lay still, arms returning to that nonthreatening position, stretched out at his sides. He let her touch him. Let her run her fingers along the swollen length of him and finally stop at the button of his jeans. Licking her lips, Chelsea freed it. And carefully she lowered the zipper. Parted the fly. Saw his shape and size and hardness even more clearly, outlined in white briefs.

She took hold of the jeans at the waist and pushed downward. Garrett obligingly lifted his hips, but when he arched up that way she almost forgot what she'd been doing. She pushed the jeans down to his knees, then pulled away the white fabric and pushed that down, as well. She sat there, astride his magnificent thighs and looked at him. Smooth and dark and so aroused. She moved her fingers closer, touched, traced his length right to the tip, then over it and down the other side. He groaned, and she looked up at his face to see undisguised agony twisting his features. She used her nails, very lightly, on the tip of him, and he lifted his hips off the ground in supplication. She bent her head and kissed him there. That skin tasted different somehow. Musky and male. Erotic. She followed the path her fingers had taken, with her tongue this time, and he moved and twisted and clenched his hands into trembling fists at his sides. If it killed him, she knew he'd let her explore him and learn him until she was ready to take the next step. Whatever she asked of him, he'd do. Whatever she needed, he'd give to her. It was just the way he was.

She cupped him underneath, massaging gently as she closed her lips around him in the most intimate kiss imaginable. And only then did he pull away from her lips, shaking his head when she looked up in question.

"Give...me...a minute," he gasped. She nodded, amazed she could reduce this giant of a man to this. She sat still, waiting for him to compose himself. He opened his eyes, met hers, smiled at her. "Okay. All right. Is it my turn now?"

A tiny ripple of nerves danced along her spine, but she nodded. She could give as well as take.

He caught her waist in his hands and lifted her up onto her knees. Then he undid her jeans and pushed them down. Chelsea twisted her body to the side and took the jeans off for him. He kicked his off, too, his eyes never leaving hers. When she began to move toward him once more, he whispered, "Wait. The panties, too. I want to see you, Chelsea."

Her throat had gone as dry as sandpaper. Not from fear—from sheer, gut-wrenching desire. She stood while he lay there watching, and she pushed her panties down and stepped out of them. Garrett blinked as if a sudden bright light had flashed in his eyes as he took in all of her from head to toe, utterly naked.

"You're...you're...you're perfect, Chelsea."

"I'm not—"

"Shh. Don't argue, baby. I know perfect when I see it and you're it."

She sat down, feeling too exposed standing while he burned her with his gaze.

"Lie down on your back for me, Chelsea. Will you do that for me? The way I did for you?"

She faced him, eyes widening.

"Do you trust me, Chelsea?"

She nodded. Slowly, she lay back on the ground with her thighs pressed tightly together.

Garrett rose up on his knees, near her feet. "Let me look at you. Let me kiss you, Chelsea. I want you to feel the way I was feeling a second ago. Let me give you that." His hands touched her inner thighs. "Open for me, sweet Chelsea."

Shivering with passion and nerves and who knew what else, she spread her legs for him. Garrett's eyes focused on the center of her. Then he lowered his head and kissed her there. His hands moved to open her wide, making her feel utterly vulnerable. Part of her wanted to push him away and cover herself as he looked at her. But he'd remained still for her and she would do the same for him. She kept her hands to the ground on either side of her. And he kissed her again, this time touching places that made her shake and burn and cry. Again and again he pressed his mouth to her. Then his tongue stroked over her in a hot path of fire. He drank from the very depths of her like a man possessed. Craving more. Until she cried out for him to stop because she felt herself losing all control.

So he stopped and he lifted his head. Her body ached for something she couldn't understand. It yearned and pleaded for fulfillment.

He met her eyes. "I want to be inside you, Chelsea. I want it now. But only if you—"

"Yes!"

She reached for him, and he lowered himself onto her, nudging the tip of his arousal into her wet opening.

She planted her feet and arched to receive him further. Garrett slid his hands under her buttocks, held her tight and tipped her up. Smoothly, gently, he sheathed himself completely inside her.

She felt a momentary flare of pain. But Garrett moved slowly, pulling back until she quivered with need, only to plunge himself to the very hilt again. And then again. She found herself moving with him, arching to meet his every thrust, her hands clawing at his backside, clenching and kneading. He claimed her mouth. Took it, this time. She knew now he was beyond thinking about asking permission. His tongue filled her mouth as he drove her to some point beyond rational thought, her insides twisting tightly as he moved within her. And then she exploded around him, crying his name aloud without a thought to whoever might hear. He drove into her again and again until he went stiff all over, shuddering violently.

Then his muscles uncoiled, and he lowered himself down, not on top of her, but beside her. He pulled her head down to his chest, and whispered something she didn't want to hear. So she pretended she'd imagined it, then climbed on top of him and started kissing him again.

Chapter 12

Mercy.

Chelsea curled in the crook of his arm, naked as the day she was born except for his denim work shirt, which he'd used to cover her a short while ago. Her head rested on his chest, and her fiery hair tickled his skin. Her breaths were slow and rhythmic. Waves of air rushing into her, rolling down to the furthest reaches of her lungs, pausing, and then slowly receding back out to sea as she exhaled.

He hadn't seen her this relaxed since he'd met her. Which hadn't been all that long ago. A fact that made him wince. This kind of thing wasn't like him. Outside, in front of God and everybody, and he'd done things with her he'd never done with any woman.

Outside, for heaven's sake! And though she was covered—from her shoulders to her thighs at least—*he* was still lying under the stars fully exposed.

He reached for his Stetson and settled it over his

most vulnerable area before laying his head back down on the ground.

She sure had been something.

One of his hands came up to stroke that reddish gold hair of hers, and Garrett closed his eyes, sighing inwardly. Hell, he hadn't thought it would ever happen. Not to him. Not like this.

She stirred in his arms, and he could tell by the change in her breathing that she was awake. He kept stroking, liking the feel of the silky strands under his palm. And he rather thought she was liking it, too.

"What time is it?" she asked, her voice husky.

Garrett peered up at the stars for a second. "Almost midnight."

She sat up, his big shirt slid down her back to the ground. Her breasts moved freely and he found himself wanting her again.

Again?

Yup.

"Garrett, what are the others going to think?"

He smiled at her. "They'll probably think exactly...this."

She groaned and pulled the shirt over her again. "We'd better get back."

He frowned as she got to her feet and started pawing the ground in search of her clothes. "I kind of thought we ought to...maybe...talk first."

She located her blouse, and it seemed to him that she was real careful to keep her face averted. "About what, Garrett?"

"Well...about this. About...you know...*this.*"

She found her jeans next and stepped into them. "This? You mean the sex?"

The way she said the word made it sound like something simple. Like eating or breathing or something. It wasn't, though. Hell, Garrett's entire world had been altered here tonight. "Yeah," he said. "About the sex."

She pulled on her blouse and tossed his shirt to him. "There's nothing to talk about," she told him. "It was just sex. Gee, Garrett, you didn't think it was anything more than that, did you? I mean, I already explained it to you. I'm not going to get involved with a man. Not any man. Not ever. And just because we had a little fun tonight doesn't mean I've changed my mind about that."

He took the blow admirably, he thought. Felt an awful lot like it had landed hard, right in the solar plexus, and he did lose his breath and feel like throwing up. But he managed not to double over or gasp aloud like a fish out of water. He figured those were major coups by themselves. This was all wrong. He knew it was all wrong on the practical plane of his mind, but the problem was, on the emotional plane of his heart, he was too busy bleeding to notice what the practical side was saying.

She'd hurt him. Taken a blade and driven it in right to the hilt, then given a little twist for good measure. She gathered up the tablecloth they'd been lying on, wadded it into a little ball and carried it back to the spot where they'd had their picnic a lifetime ago. She stuffed it into his saddlebag without pause. Garrett would have folded it with exquisite care, stroking the fabric where her body had touched it. Wondering if the material could retain some of the magic that had happened between them tonight.

But it was pretty obvious the magic was all in his

head. She thought they'd had a little fun. Nothing more. And damned if he hadn't thought she was anything *but* that kind of woman. He'd believed her to be a lady. A wounded, frightened innocent. An injured doe he could nurture and care for and maybe, if he were lucky, make his own.

Well, he'd been a fool, hadn't he?

He dressed quickly, yanking his clothes on, taking his anger out on them. Then he went for the horses. They'd wandered off, but not too far. Hell, in the heights of ecstasy, he'd forgotten all about them. He doubted Chelsea had been anywhere near as moved.

He walked the horses back to the pond, saddled Paint up for Chelsea and quickly did the same with Duke. When he went to help her climb on, it was to see her swing herself into that saddle all on her own. Quick learner, he thought. Damn her. She hadn't learned half-enough. Garrett swung onto his own horse and dug his heels in. It was only as Duke leaped into a gallop that Garrett caught hold of his temper and throttled it until it cooled. He couldn't run ahead and leave Chelsea to play catch-up. Cold as she might be, Vincent de Lorean was still after her. He reined Duke to a halt and waited. When Chelsea rode up beside him, he started off again, at a walk this time.

But nothing could make him look at her. Or talk to her. Not now. If he so much as opened his mouth, he was going to make a blubbering fool out of himself by telling her what had happened to him tonight. And she'd probably laugh at him. Hell, the way she acted, it was easy to imagine she'd had plenty of sex, with plenty of men. Men she hadn't cared for any more than she cared for Garrett. She probably thought he was just a big, dumb cowboy. *He* probably thought she was right. He *must* be pretty dumb to let himself fall so hard.

If Garrett so much as looked at her, she'd lose it. She knew she would. If he said a word, those gut-wrenching sobs she was battling would break loose and tear her apart.

She'd never dreamed she could trust any man enough to do…what they'd done. She'd never believed herself capable of letting herself be utterly free and unreserved in a man's arms. But she had been just that with Garrett. And it was only possible because of his exquisite tenderness, the caring in his eyes when he looked at her, the gentleness of his every touch.

There would never be another man like him.

She hoped to God little Ethan would try to emulate the big, gentle man who was going to raise him. It was the right decision. It was what Michele had wanted, what she'd known all along. Her sister must have sensed how perfect Garrett would be for Ethan. Somehow, she'd known.

Chelsea was no good for him, because she was too filled with anger. Only the anger had changed now. It had eased and softened. It was no longer the futile raging of an abused child against an omnipotent parent.

This was different. Not wild and undirected anymore. She knew Vincent de Lorean had murdered her sister. But that wasn't why she had to kill him. The need for revenge had somehow lost its force. Or maybe she'd just lost her taste for it.

No. Her reasons now were utterly different. Ethan. Little Ethan would never be safe until Vincent de Lorean was out of the picture. Utterly eliminated from the baby's life. It had to happen. If it didn't, Ethan might grow up the way Michele and Chelsea had. Oh, not the poverty. De Lorean was a wealthy man, Chelsea knew that. But the abuse. The lack of love. The broken heart. She couldn't let that happen.

And as long as de Lorean lived, no one who cared for Ethan would be safe from his wrath. Not Chelsea, even if she took the baby and ran away and hid. Not Garrett. Not any of the Brands. De Lorean would extract his own kind of vengeance on every one of them. And that would destroy them. All of them.

It was up to Chelsea. This was her ball game, and she was calling the shots. By herself. Just the way it had always been.

The horses stopped in front of the house, and she slipped down. Garrett took the reins from her without a single word and headed out toward the pasture where the other horses grazed. Chelsea watched him go, blinking back tears. Then she went inside and directly up to Garrett's room.

The house had a still, eerie feeling that told her everyone inside was asleep. Garrett would be a while coming back inside. He'd rub those horses down and hang the saddles and bridles along the split-rail fence, where the few others that had survived the fire were already hanging. He'd go out to that big barrel Wes had filled with grain from the feed store, and he'd scoop some out and feed the horses. Then he'd check their watering trough to be sure it was filled.

He'd take care of everything, Garrett would. He'd take care of her, too, if she'd let him. Just the way Mom always had. And he'd probably get himself killed the way she had, too.

Chelsea opened Garrett's nightstand drawer and took out his revolver. As an afterthought, she grabbed a box of bullets. Then she slipped out of the room and across the hall, ducking into the guest room she'd begun to think of as her own. Well, hers and Ethan's. She tucked the gun and bullets into her purse before turning to the cradle. She stood staring down at the sleeping angel inside. Her fingers stroked his satiny dark hair, and a single tear dropped from her cheek to dampen Ethan's. "I love you, baby," she whispered. "And I'm gonna make this world safe for you. I promise. You're never gonna go through what your mamma and I did. You'll be raised with love. You'll have a real family just like I promised you, Ethan. Right here."

She bent low and gently kissed his pudgy cheek. Then she turned back to the bed and sat down, pulled out a notepad and pencil from the stand beside it and began her note to Garrett.

"I have to leave," she wrote, struggling because her hands were shaking and because she couldn't say the things she was longing to tell him. If she did, he'd come after her. He'd never stop until he found her.

"I have a life to get back to. And I know Ethan will be better off here with you than he could ever be with me. Don't try to find me. I'm going to change my name and start over somewhere fresh, where de Lorean can never find me. Thanks for the laughs. Chelsea."

She'd like to add a warning about Lash because she'd finally remembered why the name de Lorean had sounded familiar to her when Garrett had first mentioned it. But that might give too much away. She'd just handle Lash the way she did everything else. Alone.

She dug out the slip of paper he'd dropped, unfolded it again, staring at the name and address, memorizing it. Vincent de Lorean. 705 Fairview, Ellis, Texas. She hadn't known this name when she'd found the note. And then she'd tucked it away and forgotten about it. But now…

She sat very still and quiet, waiting for the sound of Garrett's tired footfalls on the stairs. His steps paused outside her door…briefly. And then moved on, over to his own room. Hinges creaked. The door closed. Bedsprings squeaked. Two boots thudded to the hardwood floor. She waited longer. And still longer. And then, carrying her shoes and her bag, she slipped down the stairs.

Lash answered the door wearing a pair of white boxers and a frown. Bleary, pale blue eyes and tousled brown hair completed the look, and he stared at her, shaking his head. "What do you want?"

"I want you to get out of town," Chelsea said, thinking that she sounded like an old spaghetti Western.

"Huh?"

"I know about your connection to de Lorean," she went on. For emphasis she handed him the slip of paper. "You dropped this the other day."

He took it from her, blinked down at it and came more fully awake. His eyes sharpened as they scanned her face. "Why didn't you just hand it over to the Brand brothers?"

"Because they'd have probably killed you. They'd probably assume…as I do…that you were behind that stampede. And the fire in the stable. My guess is that you're just hanging around, doing de Lorean's bidding and waiting for the chance to kidnap a helpless baby. Hell, I oughtta kill you myself."

"Now wait a minute. You don't know—"

"I know plenty. I know if I tell Garrett about you, your hide will end up nailed to the barn wall. Or at least sitting in the town jail. So you get out of town. Tonight. If I see you again, I'll tell him everything."

His blue eyes narrowed, and he glanced past her at the car that sat alongside the curb. "How come you're out at this time of night alone?"

"None of your business."

"Where are you going, Chelsea?"

"I told you—"

His hand shot up fast, gripping her arm as if to haul her inside. Panic gripped her, especially since she knew this creep worked for a killer. She brought her knee up hard and fast into his groin, and he grunted at the impact, stumbled away from her and doubled over. His face turned six shades of purple as he gasped and swore. But still he forced himself to straighten up and take an unsteady step toward her.

Until he saw the gun in her wavering hand, pointing dead center at his leanly muscled chest.

"Damn it straight to hell, what are you—"

"Shut up!"

He shut up.

"Now just step back in there and stay there. I mean it. If you so much as poke your head out the door, I'll—"

"I get the idea."

"And you be gone from Quinn by morning, Lash. You be gone or I'll be back."

"How am I s'posed to leave town if I can't poke my head out the—"

"Shut up!"

He lifted his hands and shoulders in compliance and

stepped away from the door. Chelsea backed all the way to the car, got inside and shot away into the night.

There. Safe. She'd done it. She didn't think Lash whatever-his-name-was would dare show his pretty face on the Texas Brand again. Once she accomplished her mission, Chelsea would call or send a note telling Garrett of Lash's duplicity, just in case. But if she'd told Garrett now, he'd have known she was leaving and tried to stop her.

Garrett lay on his bed feeling sorry for himself for a very short time. Then he gave himself a mental kick in the seat of the pants. Because the whole time he'd been lying there, he'd been remembering every single second of his time with Chelsea tonight, and one instant kept coming back to him. That second he'd held her to him and pushed himself inside her. That incredible feeling of completion, of union, of rightness.

But gradually, he realized those feelings were only his own—she'd reacted a little differently. She'd been real enthusiastic before he entered her. And seconds afterward, she'd been as into it as he had. But at that moment in between, there'd been the slightest hint of resistance. She'd stiffened a little. Her fingernails had dug into his skin, and she'd bit her lip. And he'd felt something.

Something…

Garrett sat up in bed, blinking. Couldn't have been that, though. Couldn't have been…

Frowning, he got up and trotted down the stairs again. He'd tossed the saddlebags into the corner after unpacking them earlier and dumping the leftover food into ol' Blue's dish. The tablecloth lay atop the garbage pail, where Garrett had thrown it in an act of sheer, foolish pride. He reached for it now, held it up by two corners and let it fall open.

He saw the small red stain that told him all he needed to know. He'd been Chelsea Brennan's first lover. She'd trusted him that much. And there was no way in hell she felt as casual about what had happened tonight as she was pretending to feel.

Garrett dropped the tablecloth again and started up the stairs. But when he got to Chelsea's room, she wasn't there. His heart slowly broke, and the only thing that kept it from shattering completely was the happy gurgle coming from the cradle beside her bed.

"Bubba?"

"Dadadadadadadada," the little squirt sang, and his arms began to flail in time with his music.

The relief that surged through Garrett was tinged with bitter sadness. Thank the good Lord Chelsea hadn't taken this child away from him. But God, what it must have done to her to leave him behind.

Garrett went to the cradle and bent over it, reaching down to check the diaper and stroke the silky fuzz that passed for Bubba's hair. Ethan blinked slowly, his eyes still sleepy, but he smiled a little bit all the same. Gently, Garrett turned him over so he lay on his tummy, and then he ran his hand in the slow, clockwise circles that he knew the boy loved. His palm skimmed the baby's small back over and over, and those heavy eyes fell closed more often between peeks at Garrett.

Without stopping, Garrett reached for the sheet of paper Chelsea had left on her pillow. Then he sank onto the edge of the bed, still rubbing that little back and wondering now why the action was as soothing to him as it seemed to be for Bubba. He leaned back against the headboard, reading her callous goodbye. A note that said nothing. Not one damn thing he needed to hear. Like how she felt about what had happened between them. Like why she'd so willingly given him something as precious as her virginity, and why she hadn't told him, and whether she had ever really felt a damned thing for him at all.

A soft sight from Bubba, and Garrett looked at the sleeping child.

Must have felt something *for you, Garrett. She left Bubba with you. That's two priceless gifts in under a day.* He scowled, swinging his head back to the note. He was indulging in wishful thinking. She didn't feel a thing for him. Or for Bubba. If she had, she'd have stuck around and fought for them.

That's right, she would. Chelsea Brennan isn't the kind of woman to give anything up without a fight.

Which kind of added to the theory that she didn't give a rat's—

His head snapped around when he heard tires rolling over the well-worn driveway. Headlights moved across the window, and Garrett was halfway down the stairs before he gave himself a chance to wonder if it were really her. Dammit, he hadn't ought to be sitting around feeling sorry for himself. He ought to be worried. He'd let her out of his sight. Out there alone, she'd be a walking target for Vincent de Lorean and his squadron of goons. Thank God she'd changed her mind and come back. Thank—

Garrett skidded to a stop in the kitchen. The face peering through the window at him was not Chelsea's. Lash. And damned if his normally full load of calm didn't look a brick or two shy.

Fighting to keep the utter disappointment from

showing on his face, Garrett opened the door. "What the hell brings you clear out here this time of night?"

Lash licked his lips. "Trouble, Garrett. And I'm sore afraid it's trouble with a capital *C.*"

"A capital..." Garrett's brows came down fast. "Chelsea?"

Lash nodded slowly. "Do me a favor and listen to the whole thing before you break my face, okay, big fella?"

Light footsteps on the stairs. A soft voice. "Garrett, you down here? I thought I heard—"

"What whole thing?" Garrett asked, ignoring Jessi.

"That for the past few months, I've been—technically speaking, at least—employed by Vincent de Lorean. But it isn't what it—"

Garrett's big fist connected soundly with most of the front portion of Lash's face. Bone crunched. Blood spurted. Jessi screamed. Lash sort of bounced off the door behind him into Garrett's chest, then slumped to the floor.

Stampeding feet crashed down the stairs at Jessi's scream. Wes bounded to her side, his bowie in his hand and fire in his onyx eyes, while Elliot stood at the bottom of the stairs looking around and blinking in confusion.

Jessi lunged into the kitchen and fell to her knees beside the incapacitated Lash, though with all that blood, Garrett wondered if she even knew who he was. She was crying and swearing, using words Garrett didn't know she even knew. And most of them were aimed at him. She stomped away, but he knew she'd be back.

Lash didn't so much as wiggle.

"You kill him?" Wes asked, looking down at the

mess at Garrett's feet as he slid the bowie back into his boot.

"Nah."

Wes frowned hard and poked Lash in the ribs with the toe of his boot. No response. He looked up at Garrett again. "You sure?"

"I'm sure. Look, he's breathin'."

Wes stared for a minute. "How can you tell with all that blood?"

"I can tell."

"Get the hell away from him, the both of you!" Jessi shouted, shoving through them and dropping down beside Lash again. You'd have thought he was one of her brothers the way she was acting. She started dabbing the blood away from his nose and lips with a wet cloth. She'd brought bandages and various ointments back with her, too. Looked like she intended to doctor him up thoroughly.

Garrett glanced at the inert man once more, shook his head and stepped toward the table and out of Jessi's way.

Wes joined him, fixing a pot of coffee to brew as Garrett sat down. "So what happened to your infamous, endless, unshakable temper, big brother?"

"I lost it."

Wes set the carafe under the basket and flipped the On button. "Why?"

"He said he'd been working for de Lorean."

Wes nodded, sending a glance toward the stranger when he moaned softly. "You suspected that all along, though. Shouldn't have come as such a surprise."

"Chelsea's missing, Wes. She just took off tonight. Left a note. I got no idea where the hell she is—"

"So you took it out on Lash, hmm?"

Garrett watched as Jessi cleaned the blood away, revealing a split lip and a nose that was probably broken, judging from the odd angle of it.

"I shouldn't have hit him that hard."

"'Cause he didn't deserve it?"

"Hell, no. 'Cause I have a feeling he might know where Chelsea is. Now I can't even ask him until he comes around."

"Oh." Wes pulled the half-filled pot out from under the drip and shoved a cup under there to catch the still-brewing coffee while he filled two others. Then he yanked the third cup away and shoved the pot back underneath, all without spilling a drop. "We gotta get one of those new ones that stops dripping when you move the pot," he muttered, handing Garrett a cup. He took a seat and joined Garrett in watching their little sister work her veterinary wonders on a horse's backside.

"You think she's sweet on him, Wes?" Garrett asked.

"Who, Jessi? Nah. No way in hell." Wes watched her hand stroke Lash's hair away from his forehead. "Besides, if he ever laid a finger on her..."

"Yeah," Garrett agreed, rubbing his slightly sore knuckles absently. "Me, too."

Elliot stood in the doorway, looking from Jessi and Lash to Garrett and Wes, and shaking his head.

"You mind going back up and guarding little Bubba?" Garrett asked him. "I don't like him being alone, under the circumstances."

Elliot swallowed audibly and nodded toward the man on the floor. "What about him?"

"I want to talk to him. Soon as he comes around."

"You...uh..." Elliot shifted his feet. "You aren't gonna hit him again, are you?"

"I'll make sure he doesn't hit him again, Elliot," Wes assured his younger brother.

"Hell, Wes, your temper is ten times worse than Garrett's!"

"Yeah, but it isn't my ladylove who's run off. So I'm not as likely to lose it with Lash."

Elliot looked around slowly, taking it all in. Finally, he nodded and turned to head upstairs to the baby's room.

Chapter 13

Chelsea drove out of town, pulled the car off the road and opened the map that was still in her glove compartment—the one she'd bought at that convenience store before she'd come to this dusty little Tex-Mex town. It seemed like a lifetime ago now.

Still, with a little help from the overhead light, she was able to make out the town called Ellis—which looked like a crossroad right on the border. Less than twenty miles away, using her fingers to measure by. She took a moment to check out her rental car, making sure there was still plenty of gas and double-checking the water level in the radiator. Everything was fine, just as she'd left it the night she'd arrived on the Texas Brand. No one had touched the car except to move it out of the middle of the driveway.

She started the car again, heading directly along the route she'd already plotted out in her mind. She was going to find this Vincent de Lorean. And she was going to kill him.

Lash was lying on the couch, Jessi hovering over him like Florence Nightingale or something, when he opened his eyes. He met Garrett's, and they narrowed dangerously.

"I'll get you back for that, Brand. You gorilla."

Garrett only shrugged. "Tell me something, Lash. You the one who spooked those cattle after all? Hmm? Was it de Lorean who gave the order to burn down the stable or was that on your own initiative?"

"You're dumber than you look if you think I came all the way out here to tell a damned giant that I burned down his stable."

"I told you so, Garrett," Jessi snapped, closing her hands around one of Lash's. Lash looked at her and frowned as if he was seeing in her eyes something he hadn't noticed before. The look of discovery and surprise on his face made Garrett even more uneasy than he already was.

Wes reached over and gently tugged Jessi's hands away. "Go on upstairs and check on Elliot and Bubba, hon."

"But I—"

"Go."

Jessi stood reluctantly and eyed her two brothers. "If you hurt him—"

"We won't lay a finger on him. Promise," Wes said.

She glared at Garrett until he nodded agreement. Then she sent a tender gaze down at Lash. "If you need me, just call."

"I...er..." He sent wary glances at the two other men and squirmed a little. "Thanks."

As soon as she was gone, Wes knelt beside the couch. "Just for the record, Lash, regardless of the outcome of this conversation, I don't ever wanna see any part of your person make contact with any part of my little sister ever again. If I do, the part in question is gonna get cut off. Got it?"

Lash swallowed hard, but nodded. "She's a kid. I got no interest in kids."

"Exceptin' for Bubba, right?"

Lash shot a defiant glare at Garrett. "If you'd let me finish what I started to say before, you'd have your answers by now. I was working for de Lorean so I could gather enough evidence against him to bring him down."

Garrett's mouth suddenly went dry. "You're a cop?"

"No. I'm an ex-fire fighter from Chicago, just like I told you."

"Then why—"

"Why doesn't matter. It's my private business and I have no intention of discussing it with the likes of you. Now do you want to hear what I have to tell you or not?"

Garrett's knees bent, and he fell into a chair. Wes stood to one side, shaking his head slowly.

"De Lorean was getting suspicious of me. I still didn't have enough on him. But I knew he was after Chelsea and the baby, so I stuck around. Kept trying to feed him false leads and throw him off track. I knew from the beginning where she was. I was the one assigned to tail her from the morgue. But I told de Lorean I'd lost her."

"You..." Garrett whispered. "It was you who called me that night."

Lash nodded. ''De Lorean found out where she was just as I'd figured he would, with or without my help. Chelsea called her apartment manager and left an address where she could have her mail forwarded. That was one of the bases de Lorean had covered. He had the address within a few hours after Chelsea hung up. I called to warn you as soon as I realized it. Well, since the jerk was already suspicious of me, it seemed there was no more I could do on that end, short of maybe getting myself shot once between the eyes. So I headed out here. Thought I could help protect her and the kid from that bastard.''

''The stampede?''

Lash shook his head. ''When I arrived in town, I spotted a vehicle belonging to one of de Lorean's goons heading from this direction. So I made a beeline out here and came up with the first excuse I could think of to ride out and catch up to you and Chelsea.''

''And you saved our butts.''

''I'm *sure* you'd have done the same for me,'' Lash said, lightly touching his broken nose.

''And the fire?''

''When I saw the trucks heading out here, I knew damn well...'' He shrugged. ''I followed to try and help. Hell, it was half-instinctive. It's what I did for a good portion of my life.''

Garrett shook his head in disbelief.

''No need to thank me,'' Lash quipped.

Garrett looked him square in the eye. ''What do you know about Chelsea?''

''She came to see me tonight. Seems I got careless that day in the stampede. I dropped...'' He lifted himself into a sitting position with a grunt and shoved a hand into his blood-smattered T-shirt's pocket. Pulling out a slip of paper, he handed it to Garrett. "This. She found it and must've thought I was really one of the bad guys. What I can't figure is why she didn't tell you in the beginning."

"She didn't even know de Lorean's name until yesterday," Garrett muttered, cussing himself for keeping it from her.

Lash nodded. "Anyway, she told me to get out of town tonight. Told me if I set foot near you or the baby again, she'd tell you I was working for de Lorean and let you toss me in jail...or worse." He pressed a finger to his split lip, drew it away and checked it for fresh blood.

Garrett nodded. "Before she left us, she wanted to be sure you didn't pose a threat."

"She *is* gone, then?" Lash asked.

"Yeah. Said she wanted to start over someplace fresh. Said she thought little Bubba would be better off here with us."

"She lied through her teeth, Brand. She's gone after de Lorean."

Garrett's head snapped up. "What the hell makes you think she'd do that?"

Lash rolled his eyes. "Wake up, big fella. One, she knows where he lives." He ticked the points off on his fingers as he went on. "Two, she threatened me to be sure you and the baby would be safe, so it stands to reason she'd want to protect you all from him, as well. Three, she was heading that way when she left. And four, she was brandishing a handgun the size of a damn cannon. I seriously doubt she brought it along because it went so nicely with her shoes."

Wes swore, slamming a fist against the wall.

Garrett felt the bottom fall out of his stomach. He

glanced at the slip of paper again. "Ellis. Lord, she could be there already."

"We have to go after her, Garrett," Lash said. "De Lorean is a snake. He'll hurt her, dammit. He wants her out of the way so there'll never be a challenge to his keeping custody of the kid."

Garrett swore. But ran upstairs to grab a shirt and fill Elliot and Jessi in on what was going on.

The place was like something straight out of "Lifestyles of the Rich and Famous," Chelsea thought. Chelsea parked the car, lifted the gun and headed up the brick path to the front door of de Lorean's home—a Spanish-style mansion, with adobe-brick arches and stucco everywhere. A tall wrought-iron fence surrounded the place, but the gate between the towering center columns stood open. Almost as if de Lorean was expecting someone.

Chelsea walked softly, eyes wide and alert. Around her, night birds chattered and chirped. Other than that, though, there wasn't a sound. No movement. Not even a breeze. She tiptoed up the front steps and peered at the stained-glass panels in the door, but couldn't see through them. Her hand was slick with sweat when she closed it on the ornate door handle. She started in surprise when she turned the thing and found no resistance.

Pushing the door slightly, she peered inside. The entry hall towered and glittered. Her glance took in chandeliers and arched ceilings and marble tiles on the floor. On the far side of the room, she saw a silvery-haired man, reclining in a chaise, his back to her as he lifted a crystal glass to his lips.

She glanced to either side but saw no one else. She

listened and heard only the soft strains of a Spanish guitar floating from a hidden speaker.

Swallowing hard, Chelsea stepped inside. She lifted the gun, leveled its barrel at the back of the man's head and moved closer. He still showed no sign he was aware of her presence. She curled her forefinger around the trigger, drew a deep breath.

"Vincent de Lorean?" she asked to be sure.

"That's correct." His voice was deep and smooth. He didn't seem surprised or even unnerved. "Come in, Chelsea. The least you can do is look me in the eye when you kill me." He rose in one smooth movement and turned to flash a brilliant white smile from beneath a thin, salt-and-pepper mustache. His deeply tanned skin didn't sport a single wrinkle or flaw. "May I offer you a drink first? From the way that gun barrel is wavering, I think you could use one."

She glanced down at her shaking hands, fought to steady them. "How do you know who I am?"

"I know," he said softly. "I have ways of knowing everything." And without batting an eye, he sipped his drink again. One hand remained casually in the pocket of his satin robe. He didn't seem the least bit nervous.

"You killed my sister." Her voice was trembling now.

He only shrugged. "A drink would really bolster you, Chelsea. They don't call it liquid courage for nothing, you know."

"I don't want any damned drink."

Again, the careless shrug, accompanied by a tilt of his head. "I suppose you should get on with it, then. You came here to kill me, I assume?"

She blinked the moisture from her eyes. She hadn't

expected it to be this hard. Again, she steadied the gun, sighting the barrel at the center of his chest.

"It's going to make a terrible mess, you know. That's a rather large caliber weapon you're holding. A forty-four, I believe. You shouldn't have to fire it more than once." He took a step closer, downed the last of his drink and set the glass on a marble table. Then, with one hand, he pulled the robe open, exposing his bare chest to her. "Go ahead. Pull the hammer back. And lift the barrel just a little. Your aim seems a bit low. I'd really prefer to die right away rather than lie around with a bullet in me and suffer untold agony...wouldn't you?"

Chelsea stared at his exposed skin and imagined the bloody hole she was about to put in it. The bullet would rip right through the man's body. There would be blood. There would be a lot of blood.

She lifted the barrel.

Her hands shook even harder. Why was this so difficult? Why couldn't she just pull the trigger and end this? It was for Ethan, for Garrett and his family. She had to kill this man. She'd be doing the world a favor.

"Some would say, Chelsea, that you have a lot of your father in you. It surprises me, really. I didn't expect it. But here you are, ready to kill like a vengeful god. You've decided I'm not worthy of living, so—"

"Shut up!" She gave her head a shake, blinked again. The damned tears were blurring her vision.

"You have a killer's genes in you, Chelsea. We're a lot alike, you and I. We do what needs doing, with no—"

"I said shut up!"

She lifted the gun higher, and her finger tightened a

little on the trigger. Kill him, she screamed at herself. Just do it!

"Don't act so surprised, Chelsea. You've always known there was a lot of your father in you, haven't you? Isn't that the fear that's been haunting you all your life, the fear that deep inside, you might be just like him? Isn't that what made you believe you could come here tonight and execute me for my sins?"

She bit her lip, refusing to listen to his words, refusing to consider them. She steadied the gun, put a little more pressure on the trigger…

She couldn't do it. There was *nothing* of her father in her, and Chelsea knew that now. She'd been afraid of the anger inside her, of the rage. She'd always had this horrible feeling she could be just as cruel, just as violent.

But she simply wasn't. And taking a life, any life, was beyond her. Even now, with so much at stake. There had to be another way. There had to. She'd seen too much violence, too much death. She couldn't bear to be the instrument of still more.

Slowly, she lowered the gun. De Lorean's smile grew wider. "A wise decision, Chelsea," he purred. And before she'd even seen him move, he'd pulled his own gun from the deep pocket of his robe. She realized it had been aimed at her the whole time. No wonder he hadn't been afraid. "Don't lift that Magnum again, *chica.* If you do anything other than drop it on the floor, you'll find yourself in excruciating pain. I know how to inflict it. Believe me."

She swallowed hard, closed her eyes, and let the heavy weapon fall from her hands to the floor. It didn't matter now. He'd kill her anyway.

"Very good. I believe I have finally figured out how

to get my son back, Chelsea. And you've helped me. I thank you for that.'' He grabbed her arm, bruising it with the force of his grip. He pulled her forward and shoved her down into the chaise where he'd been sitting before. ''Now, if you'll just be still for a moment, I have an important call to make.''

Garrett's earlier ascent upstairs had been stopped cold by the ringing of the phone. Now, he stood at the foot of the stairs, feeling sick to his stomach just from the look in Wes's eyes as his brother swore into the receiver and finally slammed it down. ''What is it, Wes? Who was on the phone?''

''De Lorean.''

Garrett closed his eyes.

''He has Chelsea, Garrett,'' Wes went on. ''Says he's gonna kill her unless we hand little Ethan over to him.''

Garrett's legs wouldn't hold him. He sank down onto the bottom step feeling as if all the bones in his body had just dissolved. The air rushed from his lungs.

''What else?''

''We're supposed to keep quiet. No police. No Feds, or he'll kill her anyway.''

''And he'll know about it if you do report this, Garrett,'' Lash added. ''He has enough turncoats on his payroll that he'll know. We have to handle this ourselves.''

A sob from the top of the stairs drew Garrett's gaze upward. Jessi was standing there, her face colorless and damp. ''Dammit, Garrett, what are we gonna do?''

''I don't know.'' Garrett turned back to Wes. ''When is this supposed to happen?''

"He said he'd contact us in twenty-four hours to tell us where to meet him for the exchange."

That brought Garrett to his feet. "He expects me to wait that long? To leave Chelsea alone with that bastard for—"

"You'll have to, Garrett. You try to go after him now, you'll be signing Chelsea's death warrant." Lash paced the living room, shaking his head. "He won't kill her. Not yet, when he sees her as the key to getting his son back."

"You sure about that?" Wes asked.

"As sure as I can be."

"I can't just wait," Garrett said tightly. "I can't just sit here and wait."

"Don't wait, Garrett." Jessi came down the stairs and slid her arms around her brother's waist from behind, hugging him hard. "Use the time to plan. We have to be ready. We have to get Chelsea out of this alive, and we all know we can't hand our sweet little Ethan over to that animal." She released him and he turned to face her. "We need help, Garrett."

"No." He answered her before she said what he knew she was going to say. "Jessi, I don't want any more people I love risking their lives over this."

"Adam and Ben will never forgive you if you don't let them help. And you'll never forgive yourself if something goes wrong. They'd be here in a heartbeat if they knew what was going on. We have to tell them, Garrett."

He shook his head.

"She's right," Wes said. "This involves all of us now, Garrett. Not just you and Chelsea. We're family. We stick together."

Garrett met Wes's eyes, and again his heart damn

near burst with pride at the way his brothers and his baby sister had turned out.

"That's true," Lash said. "Even if de Lorean gets what he wants, he's going to have to get rid of everyone who knows what went down. And I'm afraid that includes all of you."

"Which is why I'm going to send them all away."

Jessi gasped. Elliot had joined them in the middle of the conversation, and as Jessi quickly brought him up to date, he stared at Garrett with accusing eyes.

"Don't argue, Elliot. You have to go. You, Wes, Jessi and little Bubba, as well. I want you all to get as far away from Texas as you can until this is over one way or another. Lash, if you had half a brain, you'd take off, as well. This is my fight. I don't want anyone else getting caught in the crossfire."

"Garrett—" Jessi began to protest.

Elliot silenced her with one hand on her arm. "Come on, sis. There's no sense talking to him when he gets like this. Let's go check on the little one."

Garrett watched them go, his heart twisting. Then he turned to Wes. "I'll book a flight for you in the morning. You can all go visit Adam in New York for a few days."

"They can go, you mean," Wes said, his voice level and deadly. "If you think you can bully me the way you can the kids, you'd better think again, brother. I'm staying. You want me on some flight out, you're gonna have to knock me out cold to get me on the plane. And we both know that won't be easy."

Lash's eyes widened a little at that.

Garrett saw it and shook his head. "What I have in size, Wes has twice in speed and pure meanness," he explained. "I'd hate like hell to have to find out who'd still be standing if we ever went at it."

"So don't force me to show you," Wes said. "I'm staying."

Garrett nodded once. He'd known Wes would argue, just hadn't been sure how hard. "It might get ugly."

"You're my brother, Garrett."

And with those four words, Garrett knew the tension between him and Wes was over. Buried. A thing of the past. One of the burdens weighing on his shoulders floated away. Too bad the remaining ones were threatening to break his back.

It was the longest night of Chelsea's life. She spent it in a locked room with no windows and nothing on the walls but a yellowish brown paint. The only piece of furniture was a small, twin-size bed with a bare, striped mattress and no pillows or blankets. An ugly room, out of place in an opulent mansion. She guessed de Lorean used the room especially for guests like her. Prisoners. She knew instinctively she wasn't the first to be held here. She cringed at the thought that Michele might have spent endless hours in this cell-like room.

She'd heard other voices shortly after de Lorean had dumped her here, so she knew he had brought in reinforcements. She'd been present when he'd placed his threatening phone call and realized that Garrett now knew what a fool she'd been. He knew—and he'd try to rescue her. He would never turn Ethan over; Garrett loved that child as if it were his own. But, God, he wouldn't stand by and let de Lorean murder her, either. Maybe he'd call the police. Maybe they'd bring in a SWAT team or something and storm this place. Maybe…

Chelsea closed her eyes and sank onto the bed. She couldn't just sit here. She had to do something. She'd put Garrett right in the middle of this, when all she'd wanted to do was protect him. She couldn't just wait around for him to get himself killed trying to save her.

She couldn't live through that again.

Because she loved him.

At dawn, as planned, Marisella's battered old pickup truck pulled in close to the front porch. Garrett paced nervously, hoping this damned plan of Lash's wouldn't backfire. Still, he couldn't have come up with a better one. Lash figured de Lorean probably had some men watching the place. They'd have to be doing so from a distance or they'd be obvious. So in order to send Jessi, Elliot and little Ethan to safety, they'd have to be sneaky about it. If de Lorean knew they'd moved the baby, he'd also know they were up to something. And that would put Chelsea in even greater danger.

Blue whined at the door but stayed put at Garrett's sharp command. Wes led two horses up just behind the pickup and made a big show of rubbing them down. Their true purpose was to block anyone's view. Elliot carried two suitcases and slung them into the back of the pickup before climbing in himself. He was none too happy about his forced vacation and he let Garrett know it every time he glanced his way. Jessi came out next, carrying the baby. She handed Ethan over to Elliot, then climbed in herself. They lay down in the pickup bed. Garrett spread the tarp over them. Then, as planned, Wes led the horses back to the corral and turned them loose. Garrett stood on the porch, talking to Marisella as if he'd been right there all along, doing just that. In a few minutes, Marisella climbed back into her truck and left. She would drive carefully home, pull the truck into her garage, close the door and get the kids out. They'd wait an hour, then drive to the airport and take a flight to New York. It was all arranged.

As the pickup rolled out of sight, Garrett breathed a sigh of relief. At least three of his charges were safe. Thank God. Now all he had to do was come up with a way he could single-handedly confront Vincent de Lorean and a horde of his thugs and still manage to get Chelsea out alive.

He shook his head at the enormity of the task.

Chapter 14

Garrett had never been so torn in his life. He'd always been the responsible one. The one who looked out for his family. Made sure they were all right. To let Wes come along when he pitted himself against Vincent de Lorean was going against everything he'd been practicing his whole life. To drag a stranger like Lash in on it and maybe risk his life, as well, was not something he would have considered.

But Chelsea was at risk. Dammit, if he took them along, he risked their lives, and if he didn't…if he didn't he might just be risking Chelsea's.

The choice had been taken firmly from his hands when Wes and Lash had steadfastly insisted they were coming with him, no matter what he said or did. But he still worried.

And then, unexpectedly, the choice was dropped right back into his lap again. Wes and Lash had gone into Quinn—Wes to call Adam in New York just to be sure the kids arrived there safely. They didn't dare use the phone at the ranch because Lash had suggested it might be tapped. Lash wanted to pick up a few things from his place. Weapons, Garrett figured. Most men were more comfortable using their own guns when push came to shove. Lash was probably no different.

So Garrett was left alone in the house. He had the niggling suspicion it was fate that had arranged things this way. Garrett never had been one to argue with fate.

He sat in the rocker in the living room, holding his big denim shirt. It was the one he'd used to cover Chelsea's body with last night when they'd fallen asleep under the stars. Her scent remained on the shirt, its very softness making him think of her. He sat there, running it through his hands, pressing it to his face to inhale her fragrance.

Chelsea. She'd been hurt and he'd made a vow to himself that he'd never let that woman be hurt again. But maybe she was being hurt right now. Maybe de Lorean…

He'd kill the bastard.

Images of her frightened eyes haunted Garrett. He hoped to God this episode didn't scar her injured heart still further. Damn, it wasn't fair for one woman to have to go through so much! The crap she'd been fed all her life had left her incapable of trusting him, of loving him. Men like her father and de Lorean had robbed her, and in doing so, they'd robbed Garrett, as well. He'd been denied something more precious than life—Chelsea Brennan's heart. Garrett realized then that it wasn't her fault she couldn't feel anything for him. It was selfish of him to have let himself get so angry over it.

Didn't matter that she was incapable of loving him.

Didn't matter at all. All that mattered was getting her out of this mess alive and unharmed. If de Lorean hurt her, he'd—

The telephone snapped Garrett out of the chair like a shot. He snatched up the receiver before it even finished ringing.

"Garrett Brand?"

"De Lorean," Garrett growled. "Where is Chelsea? I want to speak to her."

"Do you have my son?" de Lorean asked, that calm, smooth voice flowing through the phone lines like honey. "Are you ready to return him to me?"

"Whatever it takes." A bald-faced lie, yes. Garrett had no compunction about lying to a killer.

"Good. Now, I want you to meet me—"

"No way, de Lorean. Not until I talk to her."

There was a long pause. A ripple in the bastard's unshakable calm? "All right."

Another pause, this one brief. "Garrett?"

Every cell in his body came to life at the sound of her voice. "Chelsea, are you all right? Has he—"

"I'm sorry, Garrett. This is all my fault. I was so—"

"It's not your fault," he told her quickly. "I'm coming for you, Chelsea. It's gonna be—"

"No! Don't do this, Garrett. Don't risk your life for me. I'm not worth—"

Her words were suddenly cut off. De Lorean's voice came back on the line. "I wouldn't advise you to take the lady's advice, Brand. It could prove very unhealthy for her."

"If you hurt her, de Lorean, I swear to God—"

"You'll come alone," the man continued as if Garrett hadn't spoken. "If I get even an inkling you haven't followed my instructions to the letter, I'll put a bullet in Miss Brennan's pretty face. The only person with you will be my son. Is that understood?''

''Perfectly.''

''Good. You'll meet me in one hour at Thompson Gorge. Alone. When I have my son in my arms, I'll release Miss Brennan. Then we can all go our separate ways. Agreed?''

The creep was lying through his teeth. There was no way in hell he intended to let Garrett leave Thompson Gorge alive. The very fact he'd chosen a box canyon with only one way in and out, a place only accessible on horseback, was proof enough of that. Garrett swallowed his rage. ''Agreed.''

There was a click, and then the silence of a dead phone line. Garrett held the receiver in his hand for a long time. He had one chance, and one chance only. He had to get there first, find himself some cover and hope to God he could get Chelsea behind a rock before the shooting started. And he was going in alone. Leaving before Wes and Lash returned. They'd have no way of knowing where he'd headed. By the time they figured out where he'd gone, if they ever did, it would be over.

Garrett put the phone down and crossed the room to unlock the gun cabinet.

Lash knew something was up the second he and Wes walked into the empty house. Garrett had refused to leave the house with them in case Chelsea or de Lorean called. He wouldn't have left now. Not unless...

Wes cussed, and Lash turned to see his black eyes narrow as he scanned the gun cabinet in the corner.

''What is it?''

Wes took off his Stetson and slammed it onto the

back of the couch. ''Some of the guns are missing. Two forty-fives and the Winchester. Dammit, de Lorean must have called early.''

''But Garrett's pickup is still out front.'' Lash parted the curtains to look again, just to verify he'd seen the big truck the first time.

''Come on.'' Wes snatched his hat and strode out of the room. Lash followed. He had an inkling, but it was confirmed when Wes stomped out the door, crossed the front lawn and stopped at the corral where the horses grazed. The scowl on Wes's face was all the confirmation Lash needed. ''Garrett's horse and saddle are gone. Damn him, he's taken off on his own. I should have known better than to leave him for a second. The oversize, overprotective, damned—''

''Who the hell…?'' Lash interrupted Wes's tirade when he saw the old pickup bounding into the driveway, passengers in both the front and back.

Wes followed Lash's gaze and started swearing all over again as the pickup came to a halt and people started piling out. Two men Lash didn't recognize—one so big and blond that Lash thought he must be some out-of-time Viking, and the other smaller, but powerfully built and dark like Garrett. Then came Elliot. And Jessi.

Pretty, stubborn, long-legged Jessi, with her jaw set and her chin up high. Looked like she was ready for a fight and more than willing.

Wes continued swearing, but shut up when the two men approached, grim-faced.

Jessi made a beeline for Lash. Her hand closed on his forearm and she stood too damned close for comfort. The last thing he needed was hot-tempered Wes thinking Lash had eyes for his little sister.

''Lash, these are my brothers, Adam and Ben,'' Jessi said. ''Guys, this is Lash. The one I told you about.''

Oh, great, Lash thought. *More* Brand brothers. Just what he needed.

''Where's Garrett?'' She turned her big brown eyes on Lash, and he thought he'd rather take on all her brothers than tell her.

''Took off on his own,'' Wes said, not too tactfully elbowing his way between them and taking Jessi's arm. ''I'm afraid he's gone to meet de Lorean.''

Her eyes widened, and the others muttered. ''He'll get himself killed, Wes! Why did you let him—''

''I didn't *let* him, Jessi. He gave us the slip the second we turned our backs. You know how he is.''

''What the hell are we gonna do?''

''Watch your mouth, Jessi,'' the Viking told her. Ben, Lash reminded himself.

''Look, we only know he didn't go too far away. He took Duke,'' Wes explained.

''Duke can cover a lot of ground.'' Jessi gnawed her lower lip…her very full and rather sensual-looking lower lip, Lash noticed, then kicked himself for noticing. She nodded twice, firmly. ''Okay, we'll have to track him. Wes, you and Ben go inside and grab some weapons. Adam and Elliot, saddle up six horses. Lash and I will take a look and see if we can spot Duke's tracks.''

Adam and Ben exchanged surprised glances, maybe because of their baby sister's take-charge attitude and no-nonsense tone.

''Five horses,'' Wes said, not moving a muscle. ''Jessi, you're staying here.''

''The hell I am.''

''The hell you aren't.''

The two faced each other, almost nose-to-nose. "Dammit, Wes, there's not one of you who's a better shot than I am and you all know it. Not to mention that I'm the best tracker. You gonna risk Garrett's life just so you can keep your image of your innocent, helpless baby sister intact?"

"Damn straight I am."

"Fine." She crossed her arms over her chest and stared at him. "You all just saddle up and go on without me. Two minutes after you leave, I'll be heading out on my own. And the way you guys read signs, I'll probably find Garrett and this de Lorean jerk before you do. But I'm sure my big brother and I can handle it on our own. Don't you worry about us."

Damn, but she was something else, this girl. Er, woman, Lash reminded himself. But she couldn't be very old. What, twenty-two or twenty-three at the most? Really just a kid.

She sure as hell wasn't acting like a kid, though.

Wes was looking scared he might just lose this battle. "What about little Ethan?" he asked, and Lash recognized it as a last-ditch effort.

"Safe and sound with Marisella. Now are you gonna stand here arguing while Garrett gets himself killed, or are we going after him?"

"We're going after him." It wasn't Wes who spoke, but Ben—the blond one. He came forward and put an arm around Jessi's shoulders. "You've grown up, little sister."

"I'm glad *somebody* noticed," she snapped. "Now let's move. Come on, Lash. Let's go look for those tracks."

"Help the boys saddle those horses, Lash," Wes ordered. "I'll help Jes look for the trail." At his sister's killing glance, he added, "It's in my blood, sis. Don't forget I'm half-Comanche."

He sent a sideways glance at Lash that said plainly he would also be willing to scalp his enemies should the need arise. Lash swallowed hard, walked to the corral and grabbed a saddle.

Garrett crouched behind a boulder about five yards in from the canyon's entrance. A steep, rocky wall rose at his back. There was another one just like it fifty yards to his right and another one across from him. On his left was the opening—the only way in. And the only way out. That was the direction he watched. De Lorean would have to enter from there.

A couple of times, as he crouched there, Garrett heard the telltale clatter of pebbles and dirt tumbling down the canyon walls. Someone was on the ledge above, no doubt about that. Probably several someones. De Lorean's men. The back of Garrett's neck prickled, and his back felt sorely exposed. He didn't think they'd seen him yet. But if they did, he would be an easy shot. And once they saw he didn't have the baby, they wouldn't hesitate.

No breeze stirred in the canyon. It was darker here, Garrett thought, than any place on earth. No moon tonight. And though he could see a rectangle of star-dotted sky above him, its light didn't make the place any brighter. Every sound echoed endlessly. The Comanche believed the place to be bad medicine. And no wonder. Many an ambush had occurred within these towering stone walls. A lot of blood had soaked the ground here.

He looked up again, eyes scanning the rim. But it was too dark. Even if they were up there, he wouldn't be able to see them. He crouched until his thigh muscles screamed, checked his watch time and again.

Finally, ten minutes early, the headlights of a Jeep bounced into view. Garrett grimaced in surprise. De Lorean must have had the thing customized for rough terrain. No normal vehicle, even a four-wheel-drive one, could handle the trek out here. The vehicle came to a stop at the canyon's entrance. The lights remained on, effectively blinding Garrett to the people beyond them. He only knew they got out when he heard the doors slam. And then he heard de Lorean's voice.

"Brand. Are you here?"

"Turn off the lights," Garrett replied. "Or you'll never see your son."

De Lorean's laugh was low and ominous, and it bounced from the stone and rolled through the canyon. "You're in no position to be giving orders. Step out where I can see you."

Garrett drew a breath. "We can argue about it all night. I don't move until the lights go out."

"I don't think we'll argue about it at all, Brand. You see, I have Miss Brennan, and I have a very short temper. Oh, but you can't see me, can you? Well, then, listen."

Chelsea cried out. Not loudly. It was obvious she was struggling not to make a sound. But the bastard hurt her enough so the cry was torn from her throat, and Garrett's stomach clenched so hard and fast he thought he'd vomit.

If he stepped out from behind this rock, he was a dead man. The men on the rim above would pick him off so quick he'd never know what hit him. But if he remained hidden and safe, the bastard would torture Chelsea. Damn, if only he'd shut those headlights off.

Garrett eyed a group of boulders closer to the canyon's entrance and the wide stretch of coverless ground in between. If he could make it there, the lights wouldn't be in his eyes. He might be able to get a shot. But he might not be fast enough. And for the first few yards, those headlights would make him a sitting duck. Still, he had to try.

Grating his teeth, he pushed off and ran.

True to her claim, Jessi Brand turned out to be one hell of a tracker. They picked up the trail right away and rode for all they were worth, only stopping when Wes held up a hand.

The horses stopped in a cloud of dust as Wes tilted his head in a listening posture.

"What is it?" Lash whispered.

"I heard a vehicle."

"Thompson Gorge is up ahead," Jessi said softly. "God, Wes, Garrett wouldn't have gone there, would he? He'd have to know it was a trap."

"He'd go," Wes replied, his tone grim. "If it was for Chelsea, he'd go. Dammit, de Lorean will have snipers lining the rim of that godforsaken canyon."

"Not for long, he won't," Adam said. His eyes met each of his brothers in turn, making his meaning clear.

Ben nodded his blond head in agreement. "We take them out. At least give Garrett a fighting chance."

"Leave the horses here," Wes said. "We'll go in on foot."

Elliot lifted the neatly looped rope from his saddle and ran his hands over it. He dismounted and the others followed suit.

Lash got down, too, but his throat was suddenly very

dry. ‘‘You…uh…we aren’t going to just kill them, are we?’’

Wes grinned at him. ‘‘Only if we have to. What’s a matter, Lash, you got a weak stomach?’’

‘‘Shut up, Wes,’’ Jessi snapped. ‘‘Lash, we aren’t going to kill anyone. Contrary to first impressions, the Brands are not barbarians.’’

‘‘Speak for yourself, Jes,’’ Wes returned sharply. But then his voice softened. ‘‘I don’t suppose I could convince you to stay here with the horses, could I?’’

Jessi shook her head firmly and poked a bullet into the chamber of her rifle to emphasize the point.

Wes sighed hard, but started off at a quick, silent pace. When they could make out the shapes of horses in the darkness ahead, Wes whispered, ‘‘Fan out. Adam and Ben, work around to the far side of the canyon. Elliot and Lash, you take the end. Jes, you and I will work in from this side. Move in and take them out fast and quiet, then move on to see if you’re needed elsewhere.’’

‘‘Seven horses,’’ Jessi whispered from her crouching position on the ground. ‘‘One of us will have to handle two men. Be ready for that.’’

They broke up and slowly worked their way around the canyon. Lash kept one eye on young Jessi. He was worried about her, and if he’d been her brother, he thought he’d have argued harder against her coming along. Not that it would have done much good. He could still make out her form in the darkness as she crept from boulder to bush, working her way closer and closer to the canyon’s edge. And when he looked off in the direction she moved, he saw a man standing there, his back to her, a rifle cradled in his arms. He shivered.

Elliot's elbow dug into Lash's rib cage, "Pay attention to your own problems, Lash. Jessi can handle herself."

Lash followed Elliot's pointed gaze and spotted two more armed men standing at the lip, about ten yards apart.

Lash swallowed hard and started off after the closest man. He only turned once when he heard a soft, whirring sound. Then he saw Elliot's rope sail through the night, settle around the second man, and jerk sharply backward. The man was yanked off his feet, landing hard on his back with a low grunt. Before he could utter a cry, Elliot had pounced on him. Lash heard the thud of knuckles connecting with flesh just once. The guy didn't move again.

Lash wanted to check on Jessi, but there was no time. He moved forward rapidly, and grabbed the man hard, one hand covering his mouth, the other pressing the gun barrel into his spine. "Not a sound, pal, or you'll be singing with the angels."

The man nodded. Lash liberated the man from his weapon, then snatched the duct tape from his belt and managed to tear a strip off with his teeth. He sealed the man's lips, then bound him hand and foot and left him on the ground. He quickly made his way back to where Jessi was just moving up on her target. He wasn't close enough to intervene, though he tried to hurry.

She moved like a panther, he thought as he watched her in awe. Those long limbs stretched out to bring her closer and closer to her prey, soundless and deadly. Not a hint of hesitation or fear. But damn, he couldn't stand to see it and not try to help. He moved still faster and stepped on a twig. The snap seemed as loud as cannon fire. The man whirled on Lash, gun raised. Jessi launched herself at him. She landed on his back, knocking him facedown in the dirt, and his gun skidded away from him. She gave him one sharp crack on the head with the butt end of her rifle.

Voices floated up from below. De Lorean's. Garrett's. Then Chelsea cried out in pain.

Jessi ran to the edge and Lash followed just in time to see Garrett's fully illuminated form rush out from behind some rocks right into the open. From the corner of his eye, Lash spotted movement and turned to see another sniper raising his rifle, sighting it on Garrett. Lash took a single step, but it was unnecessary. A huge knife sailed out of nowhere, flying end over end and sinking deep between the sniper's shoulder blades. The man groaned and sank to his knees. The rifle fell at his feet. Wes stepped out from behind some brush, came forward, bent down and yanked the bowie knife from the dead man's back. Then he calmly wiped the bloody blade clean on a patch of crabgrass before replacing it in his boot.

Below, in the canyon, Garrett dived behind another group of boulders.

"You're trying my patience, Brand!" De Lorean's voice rang clearly from below, and then Chelsea screamed again.

"Come on," Wes whispered. "Let's get over to the other side. That bastard keeps hurting her, Garrett's gonna lose it and probably get himself killed."

The four of them ran around the back of the canyon, then crept up the other side. They only halted when they spotted Adam and Ben surrounded by four, not three, of de Lorean's goons.

"Damn, I must have missed a horse! I only counted

seven sets of tracks!'' Jessi shouldered her rifle. Lash saw her. Everyone else was too busy watching the fight. Seemed he was the only one whose eyes were constantly on Jessi. He covered her hands with his and pushed the gun down. ''If de Lorean hears a shot, he might kill Chelsea then and there, Jes.''

Wes's head snapped around. ''He's right. The only way we can help Adam and Ben is if we can get close enough to jump the bastards.''

''Help Ben, you mean,'' Elliot whispered as they all moved closer. ''Look.''

A meaty fist had connected with Adam's jaw, and he'd fallen backward, his head hitting a boulder. He didn't move again.

''I'll kill that oversize son of a—''

Jessi's threat was cut off then, because Ben seemed to launch himself into the air, kicking high with one leg, snapping one man's head back so hard Lash thought he'd broken the guy's neck. When he landed, Ben ducked another blow, rolled, sprang to his feet and grabbed another man. The man flew through the air and landed with a heavy thud. Ben never stopped moving. He whirled like a maddened dervish, and with his foot, *his foot,* he delivered so many rapid-fire, hard blows to the face that his lumberjack-size opponents were left teetering and blinking and dazed. And then, one by one they collapsed.

Ben lowered his hands to his sides, turned and bent over his brother. The others joined him there.

''Just what in the Sam Hill was *that?*'' Wes demanded. But he, too, bent over the unconscious Adam, examining the cut on his head. ''I've never seen a guy as big as you move like that!''

"Just something I picked up," Ben said. "Never thought I'd have to use it in a fight, though."

"What the hell else would you use it for?"

Ben lifted his pain-filled eyes to meet Wes's. "Peace," he said softly.

Lash knew, because Jessi had told him, about Ben's short marriage to the woman he'd known was dying from the day he'd met her. And he knew Ben had taken off right after he'd buried his young wife. Gone into seclusion in the wilds of Tennessee.

"Did it work?" Wes asked, his voice soft, husky.

Ben lowered his eyes. "Not yet."

Adam groaned a little, and his eyes fluttered open.

"You'd best not spend too much more time in New York City," Wes said, gripping his hand and pulling him to his feet. "It's making you soft."

"He caught me by surprise," Adam argued, but he looked rather sheepish as he dusted himself off.

From below in the canyon, Chelsea cried out again, and every eye turned in that direction.

"We'd better get down there," Jessi said. "And we'd better make it fast."

Chapter 15

De Lorean held Chelsea to his chest in a crushing grip, his head bent close to her ear. ''He's surrounded, you know. But you'd already guessed that, hadn't you? That's why you're trying so hard to keep quiet. Isn't it, Chelsea Brennan? That's why you've bitten your lip until it bleeds, because you know the second he steps into the open he's a dead man. He's going to join all the others who've died here in this canyon down through the ages. The Comanches say it's haunted, you know. They say the spirits of the murdered still linger here.''

He'd twisted her arm behind her back, trying to make her cry out. Trying to make her scream, so Garrett would step out of the sheltering rocks. And she'd grated her teeth, refusing to make a sound. Until she'd felt the popping of her shoulder, and her cry had been wrenched from her unwilling lips.

Garrett lunged from the cover of the boulders and

dashed across an open expanse, and she would have shouted a warning if de Lorean's hand hadn't been clamped firmly over her mouth. His paw covered her nose, as well, and she couldn't draw a breath. But the panic of not being able to breathe paled beside her fear for Garrett. She kept her gaze on him as he ran, fully expecting to see him cut down at any second. But somehow...somehow he made it. He dived behind another cluster of boulders, this one not bathed in white light as the other had been.

De Lorean's hand on her mouth eased its pressure, and she dragged a gulp of air into her lungs, then released it slowly in relief. She felt de Lorean's head moving as he scanned the ledge above, and he cursed in hot whispers that made her skin crawl. Why hadn't his men fired at Garrett? It was obvious he'd expect them to.

Her shoulder screamed, though the pressure on it had eased. Her eyes watered, making it even harder to see through the inky darkness to where Garrett now crouched.

De Lorean seemed to compose himself. He straightened a little, turning slightly so her body still remained directly behind him and the boulders sheltering Garrett. A human shield, she thought, and hoped that wouldn't stop Garrett from shooting. He ought to shoot right through her to get this bastard.

But Garrett wouldn't. He was no more like her father than she saw. She accepted that knowledge slowly, with dawning wonder, though she guessed she'd known it all along. Garrett was nothing like her father. Nothing like de Lorean. Nothing like any other man she'd ever known. She'd thought she could never love a man because of all she'd witnessed of that gender. But she'd been wrong.

''Very impressive, Brand,'' De Lorean called, not so loudly as before since Garrett was closer. ''But I didn't see my son cradled in your arms as you sprinted past. And unless I see him soon, Miss Brennan is going to join her sister in heaven.''

Garrett said nothing, didn't make a sound. Chelsea was glad. No use in his giving those killers above anything to shoot at—not even the sound of his voice.

Then de Lorean wrenched her already-throbbing arm still higher behind her back. She hadn't been expecting that, and she cried out again, but quickly bit down on the scream. Damn! The fingers of her right hand were within reach of her left ear, and they were tingling and slowly going numb. Sweat popped out on her face, trickling into her eyes, and pain made her breathing quick and shallow. It hurt! The entire right-half of her torso was on fire. Even drawing too deep a breath brought more intense pain.

De Lorean gave one more tug, and dizziness swamped her. Her stomach convulsed, and her inability to move with the spasm only resulted in more agony. She thought she was going to vomit soon.

''You'll never see your son unless you let her go. Now, de Lorean! Let her go!''

So he could see her now. She realized that, and as she did, she lifted her head and straightened up as much as her captor would allow and tried to force her facial muscles to relax. She didn't want to do anything to help the lowlife who held her.

''You didn't bring him, did you, Brand?'' de Lorean observed flatly. ''I should have known better than to trust you.''

"De Lorean—"

"Pity. Now I'll have to kill you both. I, you see, *am* a man of my word." He lifted his gun to the side of Chelsea's head. She felt the cold steel, the circular shape of the barrel pressed tight to her scalp.

"No!" Garrett leaped out of his hiding place and ran forward.

In slow motion, it seemed, de Lorean's gun swung toward him, away from Chelsea, and his other arm fell away from her, as well. Leaving her free to sink to her knees in agony, or to run for her life. And in the split second she had to decide which to do, she knew that had been Garrett's intention all along. To distract de Lorean and give her the chance to escape. To take the violence that was directed at her, to take it himself in her place.

Just the way her mother had done.

Rage filled her and escaped in the form of a tortured cry that sounded only half-human as it split the night and echoed from the canyon walls.

Chelsea hurled herself at de Lorean while her battle cry still floated skyward, and at the instant she hit him, the gun he held spit fire and death. An earsplitting explosion was followed by the acrid scent of sulphur. Garrett jerked backward, his eyes wide, then closing as he staggered, teetered and fell like a giant redwood. Chelsea screamed, clinging to de Lorean's back, kicking and clawing him with renewed vigor. De Lorean wrenched her free and slammed her to the ground. She landed on her wounded shoulder, the wind knocked out of her, and fought for breath even as she scrambled to her feet again. De Lorean walked forward slowly until he stood right over Garrett's big, prostrate form.

"Where is my son, you bastard!"

But Garrett didn't answer.

"Die, then," the monster said, and he pointed the barrel downward.

She couldn't get there in time. She couldn't...

Two things happened at once. A knife came flipping through the dark, and a lasso sailed into view. The blade embedded itself in de Lorean's right arm, and he screamed aloud even as the lasso settled around him and was pulled tight. His gun fell and landed on Garrett's chest, and Chelsea wondered for a moment if the spirits said to haunt this place had come to Garrett's aid.

Then with a jerk of that spectral rope, the criminal was yanked right off his feet. He landed with a thud and a grunt. And as Chelsea looked on, shocked, forms took shape in the darkness. She only realized they were actual human beings when she heard a voice she recognized.

And then it didn't matter. She ran forward to where Garrett had fallen, and flung herself on him, heedless of the raw pain slicing her shoulder to ribbons. The tears she cried dampened his face. But there was more on his face than just her tears. Blood. Lots of blood. So much she couldn't even see his features. God, he'd been shot in the head. Chelsea went cold all over as nightmarish memories swamped her. For an instant she was a frightened little girl again, clinging to the lifeless body of her mother. That same sickening horror engulfed her now as she realized that her worst fears had come true. Garrett had stepped in to protect her, just as her mother had. And just as her mother had, he'd...

"No," she whispered. She gripped his shoulders, shaking him. "No, Garrett. Not this time. Not you, too!"

A warm hand closed on her shoulder. "Easy, Chelsea," Wes said softly, bending over her, touching his brother with his other hand. "He's still alive."

Chelsea collapsed on Garrett's chest, sliding her arms beneath him and holding him to her as she sobbed in a terrifying mixture of relief and fear. "Please, Garrett. Please be all right. Just open your eyes and tell me you're all right."

But he didn't. And it took several pairs of hands to pull her away from his still body so his brothers could get close enough to inspect the damage, stanch the blood flow, then lift him into de Lorean's Jeep.

Jessi was there, climbing into the back with Garrett. And Lash, who told her he could help. Wes firmly guided Chelsea to the passenger seat, though she'd wanted to climb into the back with Garrett. Then Wes went to the driver's side and started the vehicle.

He shouted at his brothers through the open window. "Hog-tie that bastard and get him into town. Lock him up and notify the Rangers. If I stick around here, I'm liable to kill him. Leave the others. One's dead, and the rest will keep. They aren't going anywhere."

"Don't worry, Wes, we can handle them. Take care of Garrett," Elliot replied, sounding older than he ever had.

And then the Jeep was bounding over the trackless ground.

"...hospital," Jessi was whispering in the back.

"Moving him any more than we have to is liable to kill him, Jes," Lash argued gently. "We can't even see how bad the damage is! Let's get him to the house and call for help."

Chelsea turned in her seat, reaching over it to lay a hand on Garrett's face. She had to touch him, to cling to him, as if doing so could somehow keep him from leaving her. She closed her eyes, a feeling of dread such as she'd never known settling in the pit of her stomach. She couldn't live with another death on her conscience. She simply couldn't. And she found she didn't really want to. Not without Garrett.

Something was pressed into her free hand, and she glanced down to see a cellular phone. De Lorean's.

"Call for help, Chelsea," Wes instructed. "Tell them to meet us at the ranch."

She blinked up at the hoarse tone of Wes's voice and saw unashamed tears glistening on his dark lashes.

"I'm sorry," she whispered.

"Sorry?" He shook his head and reached for her, stroking the hair away from her face with a gentleness that surprised her. "Hell, Chelsea, he'd have been dead for sure if it hadn't been for you. De Lorean had him point-blank when you jumped on him. You saved my brother's life. I'm not gonna forget that any time soon. None of us are."

"B-but...if it wasn't for me, he wouldn't be...he *shouldn't.* Why didn't he just..." Her throat closed then, making it impossible to speak.

"Because it isn't in him, that's why."

Wes's hand touched her good shoulder, squeezed a little. It reminded her of the way she might have touched her own sister once upon a time. A reassuring shoulder squeeze—sometimes it worked wonders.

"Now stop your blubbering and make the call, okay?" He sniffed and took his hand away to knuckle his own eyes dry.

Garrett's head seemed to be engulfed in a cloud of pain. The waves of throbbing encompassed his skull and even reached down into the base of his neck. He couldn't pinpoint the epicenter from which the waves emanated. It hurt *everywhere.* And his brain didn't seem to be functioning on all eight cylinders. Because it was a full minute before he heard the soft crying, and he still wasn't sure where it was coming from. And it was still longer before he smelled the combination antiseptic-and-mothball aroma that seemed to cling to Doc wherever he went, or felt a pair of old, leathery hands pressing against his head and causing even more pain.

It took even longer for him to think to open his eyes, and when he did, it took a while for his eyes to get the message.

''He was lucky,'' Doc was saying in his thick Spanish accent. ''The bullet, it only grazed him. Lots of blood, but little damage.''

''Guess we can call off the medevac chopper,'' said a voice that sounded an awful lot like his brother Ben.

''Hell, I can still use it. I think that jerk broke my jaw,'' said another, that sounded an awful lot like his brother Adam.

''So maybe you'll learn to duck when some Neanderthal takes a swing at you.'' Ah, now that voice made more sense. Wes.

''Now, Señorita Brennan,'' Doc said, ''you will let me take a look at that shoulder of yours. And I will not take no for an answer this time.''

''But, Doctor, he's still unconscious.'' Ah, that was Chelsea's voice. The one he'd been waiting to hear. He sighed inwardly in relief. ''Surely if it's only a graze and not serious, he should be awake by now.''

Gee, she sounded awfully worried about him. He

tried to smile at the thought, but wasn't sure if his facial muscles responded or not.

"That bullet hit him like a hammer, Chelsea," Jessi said softly. "He probably has a concussion, but—"

"But nothing. I want him in a hospital! I want him x-rayed and CAT scanned and—"

"Garrett, he will be fine," Doc said. "His head is harder than the brick."

"You're hurt, Chelsea," Jessi coaxed. "Let Doc have a look at you."

That was Jessi, all right. Always... Wait a minute. Hurt? Chelsea was hurt?

Garrett's eyes opened wide, and he found it wasn't quite the struggle it had been before. He fought to bring the room into focus. Not his room. The living room. He was at home at the ranch, sprawled on the couch like a sack of feed.

Wetness coated his palm and he shifted his focus to see ol' Blue licking his hand. The dog looked back at him and whined.

"Garrett?" Chelsea dropped to her knees right in front of him. He was relieved. Shifting his eyes around looking for her was making him dizzy. "Garrett, you're awake."

Tear tracks marred her beautiful face, and her hair was even wilder than usual. Her swollen, puffy eyes searched his face, and she lifted one hand to his cheek. Her other arm hung oddly. She sort of clutched it against her side. And her shoulder looked funny.

"You..." He licked his lips, swallowed hard and tried again. "You hurt?"

"No. I wrenched my arm a little, but it's fine. No big deal."

He didn't think he believed her. But he had to know

everything. ‘‘Bubba?’’ he asked when his painful scan of the room didn’t produce any signs of the child.

‘‘Marisella just arrived with him, Garrett. He’s upstairs napping. She’s watching over him. He’s fine. Just fine.’’

‘‘De Lorean?’’ Garrett asked, angry that it took so much work to make his lips move.

‘‘In jail where she belongs,’’ Wes said. ‘‘And you can have all the time you want with your girlfriend here, big brother, but not until Doc takes a look at that shoulder of hers. And that’s an order!’’

Garrett frowned at her, gave her a nod, or tried to. ‘‘Go.’’ Reluctantly, Chelsea took her hand away from Garrett’s face and rose. Doc led her away, and Garrett tried to focus on Wes again, but found it difficult. Things were blurry and tough to look at for long. ‘‘Thought I heard the boys. Adam and Ben…’’

‘‘That’s because we’re here,’’ Adam said, and took Chelsea’s former position beside the couch. ‘‘You didn’t really think Jessi and Elliot would follow orders, did you?’’

‘‘And lucky for you they didn’t, you big lug,’’ Ben added, leaning over the couch from behind so that his shaggy blond hair hung forward. ‘‘Don’t tell me you didn’t know there were snipers lining that ridge.’’

Garrett smiled, but it felt as if only one side of his mouth was working. ‘‘Wondered…why they didn’t…pick me off.’’

‘‘’Cause we picked them off first,’’ Ben told him. ‘‘And don’t think baby sis didn’t get in on the act. She made at least one guy sorry he messed with this family.’’

‘‘Yeah,’’ Jessi said from somewhere beyond Garrett’s range of vision. ‘‘Might say I Branded him.’’

Laughter surrounded him. Garrett relaxed a little because that sound—his sister and his brothers laughing in this living room—told him more than anything else ever could that everything was really all right. Finally all right.

"That's it, Garrett," Ben said, his voice softening. "You go on back to sleep. Just don't expect me to carry you up to your room. A hernia, I don't need."

Another round of laughter. This punctuated by a happy whine from Blue and the sound of Ethan's gurgles as Marisella brought him down the stairs. He heard Chelsea speaking softly with Doc in the background. The kitchen, maybe. She sounded just fine.

And he fell into a contented sleep.

"Good," she said. "You're awake."

He blinked, noting first that Chelsea wore a sling on her arm, and then that she was freshly showered and dressed, and that her hair was tamed down a bit. He slanted his gaze toward the window. Late morning at the earliest. Gosh, how long had he slept?

"Chelsea…" He stopped himself, noticing as he sat up that there was a suitcase on the floor beside her chair. His heart hurt worse than his head. And *that* was saying something.

"I wanted to talk to you before I left. I've been waiting for hours."

She'd been crying. Not violently or hysterically like yesterday. But the signs were there. Her eyes started swimming again, even as he watched her.

"That's good, because I want to talk to you, too. I want to tell you—"

"Wait." She held up her good hand, and he fell

silent. She bit her lip, looked ceilingward, took a deep breath. "Just let me get this out, okay?"

"Okay." He leaned back on his pillows.

"I need..." She cleared her throat and met his eyes again. "I need to thank you, Garrett."

"I'm the sheriff, Chelsea. It's my job to rescue—"

"No, not for that."

He frowned, but waited.

"Garrett, before I met you I thought...I thought every man I ever met would turn out to be just like my father. You showed me...how wrong I was about that."

"That's good to know."

"I was angry at first that all that...that courting you did was only an act. Just a ploy to keep me and Ethan here where we were safe. But even so—"

"Now hold on a minute! I—"

"Please, will you just let me finish?"

He stared at her, jaw gaping, and decided it could wait. Maybe. At least until she'd let him get a word in edgewise. He lifted his hand, palm up, to tell her to go on.

She sighed, pushing her good hand through her hair. She rose from her chair and paced the room. "There's more. I also never thought I could trust a man enough to...enough to be with him...the way we were the other night. But you showed me that I could."

Silence wouldn't cut it anymore. "Chelsea, you tried to make me believe it didn't mean anything. But I was your first, wasn't I?"

She nodded. "I lied. It meant something. But you really have to be quiet, Garrett, or I'm never going to get to the point here."

"I'm trying." He smiled at her, and she closed her

eyes as if in pain. "Is it your arm?" he asked, suddenly concerned.

"No. The arm is fine, just a dislocated shoulder. Doc gave me something for the pain."

"Then why do you look like you're still hurting?"

She opened her eyes, licked her lips. "Quiet."

"I'm quiet. Go on."

She cleared her throat, then turned her back to him, pretending to look out the window. "I didn't think I could ever love a man," she said softly.

"Dammit, Chelsea, it doesn't matter." He flung back the covers and swung his feet to the floor and, gripping the arm of the couch, stood up. "It's selfish of me to ask you to. I don't care, Chelsea Brennan." He went up behind her, gripped her good shoulder and bent his head low, speaking soft and close to her ear. "I don't care if you can't love me the way I love you. I'll take whatever you can give and count myself lucky to have it, honey. If only you'll stay."

Chelsea went utterly still. It was as if she'd frozen in place. "I thought," she whispered, still not turning to face him, "that I asked you to keep quiet and let me finish." Her voice wavered, and Garrett figured it was damned near time to give up hope. She was gonna shoot him down here and now.

"Sorry," he told her, giving her shoulder one last squeeze. "I had to get it said."

"I was trying to tell you, Garrett, that I never thought I could love a man." She turned very slowly, and when she looked up into his eyes, hers were brimming with tears. A shaky smile toyed with her lips. "But you proved me wrong once again. Because I do. I love you, Garrett Ethan Brand."

The grin that split his face must have been a mile wide. Sure as hell felt like it was.

"Hot damn! You do?"

She nodded.

And Garrett kissed her like he'd never stop. But he did stop. Because he wasn't finished talking yet. There was one more thing that needed to be said.

He lifted his head, clasped her hand in his and lowered himself down on one knee. "You belong here, Chelsea. Do you know that yet? You're good for this family, and I think the Brands are good for you, too. I want…I want you to marry me, Chelsea. I want you to stay right here on the Texas Brand as my wife, and I want Bubba to be my boy. I'll love the two of you like nobody else ever could. I'll make you happy. I promise you that."

She smiled down at him as her tears spilled over. "I'm gonna hold you to that promise, Garrett. Forever."

"Forever," he echoed, and then he pulled her into his arms.

* * * * *

THE BADDEST VIRGIN IN TEXAS

Prologue

Little Lash Monroe sat in the hard wooden pew in the front row and listened to his foster father, the Reverend Ezekiel Stanton, pontificate in a loud, booming voice about the wages of sin and the wrath of the Almighty. Hellfire and damnation tended to be at the heart of most of the preacher's sermons. And Lash, being only nine, supposed one day he'd understand why the bumper sticker on the back of the Reverend Mr. Stanton's battered pickup truck read God Is Love when he talked about God as if He were a fire-breathing dragon from a horrific fairy tale. His words sent chills down Lash's spine.

And the light in the preacher's eyes gleamed like…like that new gray-blue cat's-eye marble Lash had won this morning from Gulliver Scuttle. Lash smiled and tucked his hand into his pocket to feel the cool, smooth marble he'd been gunning for all these weeks. His at last. Then the smile leaped from his face when the preacher struck his fist hard on the podium in front of him to punctuate the word *Vengeance* in the quote Lash figured must be his favorite, "Vengeance is mine, sayeth the Lord."

Lash met the preacher's piercing gaze, and forced himself to stop thinking about the marble, and the shooting match this morning, and to pay attention. After all, the preacher wasn't so bad. Strict, yes, but not mean. It wasn't his fault Lash was miserable living with him and Missus Olive, who would have blown away in a strong wind or fainted at the sound of a cuss word. Yeah, they were wearing on him some. Especially her, being so helpless and delicate and requiring a houseful of men and boys just to take care of her every little need. Lash had never known a whinier, more dependent woman in his life. But still and all, she was better than his own mom, who'd been drunk most of the time, and even more helpless. So helpless she'd said she couldn't take care of two boys all alone, and dumped Lash and Jimmy off at a shelter one night.

Jimmy had been sent to live with a family in Texas. And Lash had been brought here, to the preacher, who wanted plenty of sons, and his wife, who was unable to give him any. And really, despite their shortcomings, they'd treated him just swell.

It was the boys he couldn't stand. They were the ones who made his life pure misery in every way they could think of. All older than him, all bigger, and every one of them way meaner. Especially Zane, the oldest, biggest, meanest, of them all. Zane was twelve, Jack eleven, and Peter—who claimed his name was really Pedro and that he had a rich uncle in Mexico who would come for him one day—was ten. Peter made them all call him Pedro when the Stantons weren't within earshot. And if they forgot, they were liable to get clubbed for it. Lash tended to call him Petey, despite the repercussions, just because it bugged the other boy so much. Rich relatives, indeed. The king of beef, Peter said they called his uncle. Sure. The kid was full of blue mud.

In comparison to Lash's measly nine years of age, they were practically grown-ups. They didn't act that way, though. Lash still had sore ribs from the minor beating they'd given him last week, when Zane ordered Lash to do his share of the chores, and Lash was foolish enough to refuse. He'd ended up doing Zane's chores anyway, only doing them while hurting like crazy. Next time he'd just agree right off the bat.

But he had a feeling that wouldn't be enough to satisfy Zane. He thought Zane *liked* tormenting him.

It was as this thought entered Lash's mind that he first felt the itching, creeping sensation around his ankles and calves...and then higher. He dropped one hand to scratch his leg, all the while keeping his eyes respectfully focused on the preacher. But the itch didn't go away. In fact, it spread higher. And then, all of a sudden, it became a pinching feeling. Lash slapped hard at his legs, jerking his gaze floorward at the same moment. Oddly, he noticed several other members of the congregation itching and slapping themselves, too.

And then he saw them. Ants. There must have been a million of 'em. It looked as if someone had scattered handfuls of them across the floor near the front pew. A hundred of the shiny black buggers—some the size of guinea pigs, Lash noted with alarm—were swarming over his shoes and disappearing beneath the hem of his pant legs. He jumped to his feet, howling out loud and hopping up and down like a Mexican jumping bean, slapping his legs as if they were on fire. And he barely noticed at least six other people doing a similar jig. They looked like Indians from a John Wayne movie doing a war dance before the big shoot-'em-up scene. Mrs. Potter threw her walker so high and so hard that it formed a perfect arch in the air before coming down hard on the three people in the pew behind her. Sally Kenyon was standing in her seat, screaming at the top of her lungs and tugging on her blond ringlets. Girls. Sheesh, did she really think all that fussin' was going to help anything? Old Leroy LaRue just stood there, stooped as always, nailing ants one by one with his walking stick, just lifting it up and jamming it down, again and again. With his snow-white hair sticking up and his beak of a nose crinkling, he grinned toothlessly. "Gotcha, ya sneaky little buggers!" *Bam, bam, bam.* "There! Ha! Gotcha!" *Bam-bam!* "An' you, too! I see ya sneaking away!" *Bam-bam-bam-bam.*

Lash would've laughed at Leroy's counterattack if he hadn't been so busy trying to shake the entire ant army out of his pant legs. He managed to kick off his shoes in a frenzied effort to rid himself of the biting little demons. The shoes flew forward, and one hit the Reverend Mr. Stanton square dead center of his forehead. The second one landed on the podium, no doubt leaving a dirty mark all over the fire-and-brimstone sermon the preacher had spent all week composing. Lash barely noticed that the fire and brimstone from the sermon was becoming apparent in the Reverend Stanton's face. He was too busy hopping on one foot to peel off the other sock and then reversing the procedure.

It was only as Lash accomplished this and danced his bare feet away from the platoon of ants trooping over the church floor, that he noticed Zane, sitting safely two rows back. He was doubled over, clutching his spare-tire belly and laughing so hard his face was beet red and tears squeezed from the corners of his eyes.

And then Lash's view was blocked by the members of the congregation, all rising and making their way toward the exits, to avoid being attacked by Zane's killer ants.

Safe for the moment, Lash stood there shaking his head. And then a heavy hand clapped down on his shoulder from behind, and he knew full well whose hand it was. And he also knew he was in major trouble. Because of all the boys in the preacher's household, Lash was the only one with an ant farm. And even if he denied responsibility for this, it wouldn't hold water when Zane and Jack and Peter gave their version of things. They'd make sure their stories matched, and they'd make sure Lash was implicated. They always did.

"I think," said the Reverend Mr. Stanton, "that you are going to have some new Bible verses to memorize."

Lash glanced up at the preacher, and he could have sworn that behind that weathered, stern face, the preacher was battling against the urge to grin. But he couldn't be, Lash reasoned. The preacher was too upstanding to find any of this funny. Still, Lash found himself awfully glad that memorizing Bible verses was the most severe punishment in the man's collection. It wouldn't be so bad.

"How many this time, sir?" Lash asked.

The preacher's bushy brows rose. "For this? Oh, I'd say...a hundred might be sufficient."

"A hundred!"

The preacher nodded. "You may recite them before the entire congregation next Sunday—after you've delivered your apology to them, of course."

With a heavy sigh, Lash nodded. "Yes, sir."

"I swear, Lash, I've never come upon a boy with such a love of mischief-making as you. But I'm bound to reform you, son. Or die trying." His hand, leathery and firm, gave Lash's shoulder a squeeze.

He'd die trying, Lash thought. Lord, but *he* wasn't the one who was supposed to learn a hundred Bible verses in one week's time. *He* wasn't the one who'd be embarrassed right to the roots of his teeth getting up in front of all these people, who'd probably still be itching from their ant bites, to apologize and recite all those verses. Lash was. But Lash *wasn't* the one who'd orchestrated this whole fiasco in the first place.

He met Zane's triumphant beady little eyes across the room. An ant bit hard, and Lash jumped and slapped at his leg, and when he did, that pretty gray-blue cat's eye marble he'd been trying to win for a month popped right out of his pocket, rolled under the pew behind him and kept on rolling. And before he could get hold of it again, pudgy Zane with his ugly mug was knocking people out of the way to wedge himself under a pew two rows back. When he got up again, he held that marble between his thumb and forefinger and admired it, just to be sure Lash would see. Then he dropped it into his own pocket, and turned to saunter out of the church, acting like he wasn't even aware of all the hopping and slapping and shouting going on around him.

Silently Lash vowed that he would never, never for the rest of his life, want to be plunked down into the middle of a huge family. Especially one with so many older, bigger, meaner brothers! Never!

He made his way out of the church, and on the way, he caught the pale gaze of Olive Stanton, his foster mom, and he knew just by looking at her that she'd seen what Zane had just done. She knew that Lash wasn't the one responsible for all of this. Heck, as far as brains went, she had twice as many as her husband, even if he *was* a preacher and all.

But all Missus Stanton did was shake her head sadly and send a reproachful look toward Zane's retreating back. She wouldn't say anything. The woman didn't have any backbone at all when it came to telling her husband—or anyone else, for that matter—that they were wrong. She'd sooner be hung by her toes than disagree with anyone, and she never raised her voice above a whisper. Lash wasn't sure if that was because she appreciated all their coddling so much she didn't want to seem ungrateful, or if she just didn't have a lick of courage. But he did know he didn't want to be around females who got themselves used to being waited on. It made them soft and yellow, as far as he was concerned. Nope. Once Lash grew up and moved away from the Stantons of Maplewood, Illinois, he was going to keep himself clear of coddled girls, big families and older brothers for the rest of his life...and maybe even longer than that!

He didn't like having chores to do, Bible verses to memorize. He didn't like having to answer to the Reverend Mr. Stanton. He detested having to wait on Missus Olive. He just plain hated having to watch his every step in case he crossed those bullies he was forced to live with.

When he grew up, Lash was never going to have to

answer to anybody. He'd be free as a bird. Why, when he got tired of living in one place, he'd just throw his stuff in a bag and head off to someplace new and different. Every trip would be a brand-new adventure. Life was going to be fun and carefree, not an endless cycle of rules to be followed and orders to be obeyed. Not for Lash.

He was kinda hoping he could look up his real brother, Jimmy, who was in Texas now, and talk him into going along with this plan. They'd be drifters. Free and happy. No women or families allowed.

Meanwhile...Lash picked up his Bible, riffled the pages to be sure no ants were waiting in ambush inside, and then opened it to see if he could find a hundred verses the preacher hadn't already made him memorize. As often as he got himself into trouble—with plenty of help from Zane and Petey the beef prince—he kinda doubted he'd find that many.

Chapter 1

Jessica Brand caught hold of the calf's slippery, translucent front hooves and pulled as the cow strained. The animal was a first-calf heifer. She'd never been through this ordeal before, and she might not make it through this time. The cow was small, dammit. Jessi's brothers never should have kept her as breeding stock.

Jessi tightened her grip on the calf's tiny forefeet and tugged, but her hands slipped. She flew backward, landing butt first on the barn's concrete floor and cussing as those tiny feet vanished back into the haven of its mother. The cow bellowed loud enough to wake the dead.

"Hush, cow! The last thing I need is my brothers out here worrying I might break a nail. I'm a veterinarian now. And I could've handled this even without my brand-new license. Now be quiet and *push.*"

She shoved herself to her feet, using her elbows instead of her hands. She didn't want germs all over the latex gloves. Bracing one forearm across the cow's rump, she delved into the birth canal with her free hand, found those tiny cloven hooves and began pulling again.

"That's the most disgusting thing I've ever seen in my life." The deep voice came from the open front doors, and Jessi turned quickly, sighing in relief when she saw Lash lounging there grimacing at her. Better him than one of her oversize, overprotective brothers.

Of course, it couldn't have been one of her brothers. Any of *them* would have rushed her by now, shouting at her for standing close enough to be kicked, scolding that she wasn't strong enough to pull a stubborn calf into the world, yelling at her for even being out in the barn all alone in the middle of the night. She rolled her eyes at the thought of it. Thank God it wasn't them.

It was almost irritating, though, that Lash did none of those things. He just stood there, not so much as offering to lift a finger.

"Get in here and close the door," she told him. "If my brothers see the barn lights on, they'll be swarming all over this place."

"So what? If they swarm, then you get to hand this mess over to them. Seems like an appealing prospect, from where I'm standing."

"If I wanted to hand it all over to them, Lash, I would have just yelled for 'em in the first place. Now close the door."

With a slight frown and a glance over his shoulder, toward the house, Lash complied. Then he moved closer, but the look of distaste on his face only grew more and more pronounced.

"You're just a big fraud, aren't you, Lash?" Jessi said as she pulled, tugged and turned the calf slightly, trying to work him free before he suffocated. "You're no ranch hand."

"Never claimed to be," he said. "I told you before, I'm a firefighter. Or I was, till I came down here." He pursed his lips and narrowed his eyes. "I hate like hell to ask, but is there...something I can do to help?"

"Yeah," she said, glancing sideways at him, seeing the alarm flash in his pale blue eyes. Those eyes of his reminded her of an arctic wolf's. Alarmingly at odds with his silky sable hair. Hair she'd fantasized about running her fingers through...

"Jessi?"

She dragged her gaze from his hair and blinked. "Hmm?"

"You were gonna tell me how I could help?" he said, then glanced at where her hands were and made a face.

She laughed at him. "Don't worry. I want you on the other end. Stroke this big girl's head, or talk to her, or something. Scratch her ears. She's so damn tensed up she's gonna crush the calf instead of birthing him."

Nodding hard, Lash hurried around to the front of the cow and proceeded to stroke her head and whisper sweet nothings in her ear. The cow relaxed slightly. Jessi didn't blame her. That man could melt butter. Well, he could melt *her,* anyway. Jessi smiled when the cow relaxed still more. She could see the calf's wet pink nose now. "You're good at that," she said.

"I'm fair with animals. That's why I offered to stay on and help out while Garrett and Chelsea took their honeymoon." He glanced over the top of the cow to meet her gaze. "Never volunteered for that end of things, though."

Jessi smiled at him. "Well, now that I'm a full-fledged vet, I suppose I'll have to get used to this end of things.''

He shook his head. ''Makes me feel ancient. A kid like you is barely old enough to know what that end of things is for,'' he quipped, and went back to stroking the cow's face, calming her. Too bad he had the opposite effect on Jessi. She felt her face heating, and battled the urge to peel off her latex gloves and slap his face with them. Kid, indeed.

Then she was distracted by the animal actually pushing for once. The calf's head cleared so far she could see the closed eyes and pale lashes. ''That's good,'' she called. ''Whatever you're doing, keep doing it.''

She got a better grip on the newborn's forelegs, and waited. This time, when the cow pushed, Jessi was ready, and she pulled in sync. The calf's entire head emerged, and Jessi immediately cleared its airways, relieved when the tiny animal made wheezing sounds. But the calf was now hung up at the shoulders. This was the toughest part for the mother, she knew, and she used her hands again, wincing at the viselike pressure on her fingers as she probed. But she had to be sure the calf could emerge.

''So tell me,'' she said as she explored the poor, long-suffering animal, ''Why did you really come here in the first place? I know, you said you had an old score to settle with that maniac who almost killed *my* brother. But you never said what.''

Speaking softly, as if still soothing the pain-racked cow, Lash said, ''That maniac...killed *my* brother.''

Jessi was so startled that she paused in her examination of the animal and looked at him. He only nodded, his hand scratching the cow behind the ear. ''Jimmy was with the DEA, investigating Vincent de

Lorean's drug trade. De Lorean found out and had him killed.''

''And you quit your job at the Chicago Fire Department to come to Texas and make him pay?'' She shook her head. ''And my brothers call me impulsive and reckless!''

''It wasn't reckless. Hell, it worked. We got him, didn't we?''

Jessi nodded and resumed probing, not wanting to dwell on recent events that had nearly cost her oldest brother his life. ''So what now?'' she asked, trying not to sound overly interested in his answer, although she was.

He only frowned at her.

''You got de Lorean,'' she clarified. ''You stayed on here to help out while Garrett took his honeymoon. But he and Chelsea will be back tomorrow. So what are you going to do next?''

He shrugged. ''No idea.''

Jessi dipped her head quickly to hide her sudden smile from him. The birth canal was clear, so she gripped the calf's legs again, preparing to pull when the cow pushed. Soft baby-brown eyes blinked open and stared at her, unfocused and shining.

''You could stay here,'' she said. Then she peered around the cow to see his reaction. ''We were short-handed even before Garrett left.''

''Your brother Ben is home now,'' Lash said. ''You have plenty of hands.''

''Adam isn't. He insisted he had to get back to that city-slickin' job of his in New York. Though we all know it's really just that he's scared to death of running into Kirstin Armstrong and finally having to ask her why she left him at the altar and married old...''

The cow pushed, and Jessi pulled. The calf's shoulders passed through. "That's it, girl. Once more. Just once more."

"Come on, girl," Lash said to the cow. "You're doing great."

"Anyway," Jessi continued, as she awaited what would, she hoped, be the final push. "We could use you here. I know *I* could." He glanced at her sharply, eyes narrowed. "You're a natural with the animals," she said quickly. "Why, we could even put you in the extra bedroom up at—"

"Not on your life," Lash said. And again, Jessi popped up to meet his eyes.

"You think there's something *wrong* with my house, Lash Monroe?"

"Just a bit crowded, is all," he told her. "Been there. Done that. Didn't like it."

She scowled at him, but he went on.

"No, ma'am, Lash Monroe doesn't like crowds. And he doesn't like ties, either. Family or otherwise. I may stick around for a while, but then again, I might just pull up stakes and flit off as soon as your brother comes back. I pride myself, you see, on being just as free as a bird. That's all I want out of life, and so far, it's exactly what I got. I aim to keep it that way."

The cow pushed. Jessi pulled. The calf slid into the world with a *whoosh,* and Jessi hefted the hundred-pound baby bull in her arms, not letting him hit the floor. She eased him gently into the fresh hay she had waiting. "Untie her, Lash, so she can meet her newborn."

Lash loosened the halter ropes, and the cow turned around fast, bending her long neck and licking at her infant calf with so much vigor the newborn was knocked over sideways with every swipe of his mother's tongue.

Jessi turned and peeled off the gloves, then headed into the room at the far end of the barn to deposit them in the wastebasket, and scrub her hands thoroughly at the sink there. She hadn't liked Lash's response to her question. Then again, there wasn't much he said or did that she did like. He insisted on seeing her as a kid, just the way her brothers did. It was damned infuriating. Especially when it was coming from him—the one man she'd ever met who made her want to come across as one hundred percent pure Texas woman. Not that she'd shown it. Not yet, anyway. She had to figure out how to proceed first.

"So you're ready to move on, eh?" she asked, pretending it was only small talk. "Well, I can't say as I blame you. The work here is tough."

"I didn't say I minded hard work."

"Right," she said as she cranked off the faucets and reached for a paper towel. "Must be the dirt. You're from the city, after all. Can't blame you for going wishy-washy when it comes to the good fresh smell of cattle, can we?"

"Dirt doesn't bother me in the least," he said. "I was a firefighter, for crying—"

"Yes, but how long ago was that? I mean, you couldn't go back to it now, could you? Feeling as *ancient* as you do, and all."

"Now hold on a—"

"And it stands to reason that if you're getting too old and decrepit to fight fires, then ranching can't be much more to your liking." She sighed as he narrowed his eyes on her. "Probably you'll look for a nice easy job you can do from behind a desk, your butt cushioned by a soft chair as it slowly turns to flab.'' She deliberately craned her neck and focused on the part of his anatomy in question, shaking her head and clicking her tongue. ''Cryin' shame, too.'' She tossed her head and moved past him into the barn. The cow had licked the calf until his curly red-and-white coat stuck up in all directions. The little one had even managed to get to his feet.

''Did I do something to make you mad, Jessi?'' Lash asked, coming up behind her.

She glanced over her shoulder. '''Course not.'' Then she lifted the calf in her arms and carried it around its mother. ''Talk to her again, Lash. Let's see if this little fella is hungry.'' It was always a trial showing a newborn calf where to find nourishment for the first time, but even more of a trial getting a first-calf heifer to let her newborn suck.

Of course, Jessi suspected Lash had no clue about any of that. She listened to him crooning at the cow as she guided the little one's head to its mother's udder.

At the first taste, the calf began sucking madly, then suddenly jammed his head upward, in an action known as ''bunting'' that seemed to be an instinctive one among calves. Unfortunately, his mother did not appreciate her swollen, sore udder being so rudely treated. The cow jumped and kicked. Her hoof caught Jessi along her right temple and felt something like a sledgehammer. Jessi sailed backward from the force of the blow, and hit the floor with an impact that knocked the wind out of her, but good.

''Jessi!'' Lash lunged forward, falling on his knees beside her, and though his face swam before her eyes, she could see the alarm in his expression. She supposed it was directly related to the warm trickle she felt on the side of her head.

He tugged the bandanna from around his Stetson and pressed it to the wound, sliding his other arm beneath her shoulders and lifting her from the floor, searching her face. "Damn, you split your head. Are you okay? Can you see me? How many fingers am I holding up?"

She blinked her vision clear, and stared up into his eyes. Oh, man, she did like this. It was almost worth getting kicked. Lash holding her this way, bending over her—she could easily imagine that he was about to kiss her senseless, instead of just looking after a nasty wound. And she liked the fantasy so much that she moistened her lips, and lifted one hand to fan her fingers into the hair just above his nape. It felt every bit as good as she'd imagined it would. She liked the feel of it on her fingers.

"Jessi?" he asked, and he blinked in confusion. She smiled very slightly, and his eyes showed utter shock. They widened, then narrowed again. His brows drew together, and his gaze shifted downward to her lips. And then he couldn't seem to look anywhere else.

"Just what in the *hell* is all this?"

Lash dropped her so suddenly she nearly cracked her head again. Jessi suppressed a growl of utter frustration, and glanced over to see the calf now feeding happily on his own, the cow twitching and dancing a bit, but no longer fighting so hard. And beyond that, in the once again open doorway of the barn, she saw three big shapes silhouetted by moonlight and angry as all get-out.

"Just what in the *hell* does it look like?" she snapped. "I got kicked. But I'm fine." She got to her feet, ignoring the throbbing pain and the still slightly floaty sensation buzzing around in her head. She didn't forget to send a disgusted glare at Lash as she brushed the hay from her jeans, and then from her hair.

Wes didn't look as if he believed her. His dark Comanche eyes narrowed on her, then on Lash. Elliot just leaned against the barn door, grinning. Ben stood there without a hint of how he felt showing in his blue eyes. His shaggy blond mane moved with the breeze. Gosh, he was so quiet these days. She never knew what he was thinking.

To ease their minds, she lifted Lash's neckerchief away from her head, felt the bleeding start up again, saw her three brothers instantly pale and surge forward. They were so predictable, and all shouting at once.

"Jeez, Lash, how could you let this happen?"

"Damn cow is headed for auction first chance I have!"

"What the hell you doin' under a damned first-calf heifer anyway, Jess? You should have asked one of us for help."

Ben scooped her off her feet and started toward the house. Elliot rushed on ahead to call Doc. Wes headed into the barn to install the mother and newborn in the holding pen in the back for the night.

"Put me down," Jessi ordered. "Dammit, Benjamin, I mean it!" But Ben just shook his head and smiled gently at her, carrying her the rest of the way inside.

"Relax and enjoy it, honey. You're bleeding, and that's no little cut. So tell me, what was our hired hand doing out there, just now?"

Jessi rolled her eyes. "Trying to stop the blood from oozing outta my skull, you big nosy lug. What did it look like?"

Ben shrugged. "Looked like he was fixin' to kiss you, baby sister. And I can tell you, the day he does will be the day he's hitting the road. *Comprende?*"

"Don't sweat it, Ben. He's already planning to hit the road. Any day now, as a matter of fact. You got nothing to worry about." She stared into his blue eyes—dark blue, like the Gulf at midnight, instead of pale silvery blue like Lash's—then she poked him in the chest. "But I'll tell you one thing, big guy. I'm gonna kiss who I want, when I want, and how I want, and if you try to butt in, it's gonna be your rear end hitting the road. And I'll be behind you, kicking it from here to El Paso."

He smiled at her, or came as close to smiling as he ever did since his wife died, then reached down to ruffle her hair.

Jessi let her head fall backward and rolled her eyes. She was going to go stark raving *mad* if she didn't find a way to change the attitudes of the males on the Texas Brand. One male in particular.

She glanced back toward the barn, saw Lash standing in the doorway, staring after her and looking a little confused. Damn. What would it take to make him—to make all of them—see her as a grown woman with a mind of her own?

What?

Chapter 2

Lash stood there watching Ben carry his kid sister into the house, and he wondered what the hell had come over him just now. For a second there, when he was leaning over Jessi, with her head cradled in the crook of his arm, he'd felt something...something really unexpected. Her shining brown eyes—as big and innocent as the newborn calf's—had met his and held them. Her tongue had darted out to moisten those full lips of hers. And...if he wasn't mistaken...her fingers had threaded into his hair in a purely sensual way. For the barest instant, the thought of pressing his mouth to hers had crept into his mind with an undeniable insistence.

He swept his hat from his head with one hand and pushed the other one through his hair. She was trouble, that Jessi Brand. Trouble with a capital *T*. Good thing her oldest brother would be back tomorrow and Lash's services here would no longer be needed. The sooner he got away from her...and her brothers...the better.

They were bad news. Arrogant and macho, every last one of them, and they tended to remind him of the boys he'd been raised with a bit more than was comfortable.

Well, all except for Garrett, of course. Lash and that big lug had sort of become friends. And friends didn't go around having impure thoughts about a friend's baby sister, now did they?

"Hey, Lash, you wanna give me a hand in here?"

Lash turned, sighing. Wes had installed the cow and calf in the pen. Now he was carrying a pail of warm water toward the pen, the hay having already been there waiting.

Wes didn't need any help. So he must want to talk, and that was the last thing Lash felt like doing just now. Hell, Wes was the hottest-tempered of them all. They all joked it was the Comanche blood in him that made him so, but Lash suspected it was nothing more than pure meanness. And while he was only Jessi's half brother, he took the role as seriously as any of her full brothers did.

Lash replaced the Stetson he'd taken to wearing since coming to Texas, sauntered into the barn and scooped molasses-scented grain from a bin to take back to the cow, since it seemed the only chore left to be done. As Lash lowered the grain into the pen, Wes said, "How old are you, Lash?"

He felt the hairs on his nape prickle. Mean or not, he'd like to grab hold of Wes Brand and shake him, and he didn't give a damn about the bowie knife the guy carried in his boot, or his skill at throwing it, either. This really wasn't any of Wes's business, though he supposed the bastard would disagree.

"Thirty-four," he said, and he faced his accuser

squarely, leaning against the pen as if he hadn't a care in the world.

"Thirty-four," Wes repeated, black eyes piercing. "Jessi's twenty-three. You know that, right?"

"I know it."

Wes nodded. "Just checking. Wouldn't want you to forget it."

"I'm not likely to forget it," Lash replied. And he was telling the truth. He wasn't going to forget it. Jessi was far too young for him. And besides all that, she was exactly the kind of woman he *didn't* want. She was so used to being treated like a fragile princess, to being coddled and spoiled and protected by her big brothers, that she probably couldn't live without it. Why would he be attracted to her, even for that brief, insane instant? It was nuts!

"Garrett will be back tomorrow," Wes went on. He checked the gate on the pen to be sure it was fastened and started across the barn toward the door.

"I didn't forget that, either," Lash said. So Wes intended to give Lash his walking papers, did he?

"You planning to move on once he's back here?"

Lash nodded, heading for the door, as well. "That's the plan." And it was looking like a better plan with every second that ticked by. He was getting tired of the smell of cattle and fresh hay and horseflesh.

And that fresh sunshine-and-green-grass scent Jessi always seemed to exude. He was tired of that, as well.

Wes glanced over his shoulder. "Good," he said. "That's real good, Lash. For the best, I figure." He flicked off the barn lights and stepped outside.

Jessi had three stitches in her temple, a pounding headache and a bad attitude. The stitches hadn't been necessary. She could've slapped a handful of gummy pine tar on the cut and covered it with a bandage and been just fine. But no, her bossy brothers had insisted. And then they'd hustled her up to her bedroom and into her bed as if she were a six-year-old with the sniffles. They'd fussed over her until Doc arrived to throw them all out. And while Doc disappeared into her bathroom to scrub his hands, she'd slipped out of bed, tossing the ruffly pink comforter aside with a grimace and made her way to the window, with its matching ruffly pink curtains, to peer below.

Lash's decrepit-looking black car—the convertible from hell, she liked to call it—had still been parked outside. So he'd stayed. To make sure she was all right?

She scanned the darkness, and then she spotted him. He was perched on a bale of hay near the pasture gate, and every few minutes he glanced up toward her bedroom window.

She smiled broadly. He cared a little bit, then. Maybe. Or maybe he was thinking about that almost-kiss back in the barn. It had been an almost-kiss. She was sure of it.

Then Doc had returned and ordered her back to bed, and she'd suffered through a long night of being fussed over in the room her big brothers had decorated for her. If it wouldn't break their big, dumb hearts, she'd probably burn the furniture and paint the walls olive drab, just for a break from all the frills. But that would hurt them, and she wouldn't do that for the world.

It had been a long night.

This morning had been worse yet. They'd brought her breakfast in bed and informed her she'd be confined to her room. Doc, the old pain in the backside, had said she might have a mild concussion and advised twenty-four hours of bed rest. So Ben had gone off to the airport to pick up Chelsea and Garrett without her. And, dammit, she'd wanted to go along!

Despite Doc's silly orders, she wasn't in bed. She'd risen, showered and dressed and was now sitting in front of the prissy vanity her brothers had bought her, brushing her short rust-colored hair so that it covered the ugly white patch on the side of her head. Barely. With a sigh of disgust, she put the brush down and got up, went to the window and parted the stupid lacy curtains to look outside. She wondered what Lash was doing right now. Had he arrived yet this morning, or was he still at that apartment he insisted on keeping in town? And then she wondered what would have happened if her brothers hadn't burst into the barn when they did.

She'd seen something change in Lash's eyes as he stared down into hers. Something subtle, but real, she was sure of that. And she thought maybe he *had* been thinking about kissing her.

She wanted that man, dammit. Had wanted him since the first day he'd shown up on their doorstep. And what Jessi Brand wanted, Jessi Brand got.

Most of the time.

She wasn't going to give up on Lash. Of course, if he packed up and left town today, she would be doomed to failure.

She was just letting the curtains fall back into place when she saw the dust rising in the distance. Her heartbeat quickened, and she squinted at the road that stretched out beyond the arch over the driveway. And sure enough, Garrett's big old pickup truck bounced into view. Hot damn, Garrett was back!

She whirled around and raced into the hall and down the stairs. Elliot rose from his chair at her arrival. Little Ethan looked up from where he sat on the floor in his diaper and drool-spotted T-shirt and smiled at her, showing off his first two baby teeth. Ol' Blue lifted his head tiredly, but didn't leave his station, right beside the baby, as always. The hound dog acted as if he were Ethan's parent.

"They're back," Jessi said, pausing only long enough to scoop the baby up as she passed. She was on the front porch, baby on her hip, before the pickup came to a dusty stop out front. Then Ben emerged, followed by Chelsea and Garrett.

God, but those two looked happy. That woman was surely the best thing that had ever happened to her big brother. "Look, honey," she cooed to little Ethan. "Your aunt Chelsea and uncle Garrett are back!"

Garrett headed up the porch steps and wrapped Jessi in a bear hug that included the baby. Then he swept the little one from her arms. "Hey, Bubba! You've grown like a weed, haven't you?"

"Bubububububu!"

Chelsea came right on his heels, and she hugged Jessi, as well. "How is everything?" she asked. "Did he give you any trouble?"

"Depends on which *he* you're referring to, hon. The baby was a perfect angel. Can't say the same for the rest of these lugheads."

Wes was heading across the driveway from the nearby barn, Lash at his side. They looked up, spotted Garrett and Chelsea and both smiled. Wes's white grin was bright from within his tanned face, and Jessi wished he'd get over his hotheaded attitude and smile more often. Sure he'd done time for a crime he didn't commit, but it was over and it was time he let it go.

Then she met Lash's gaze. His smile faltered a little, but his gaze held hers tight. There was a little hint of alarm that drifted in and out of his eyes, and then he looked away.

There was noise and laughter and plenty of hugging as everyone talked at once. They wound up in the living room, drinking iced tea and hearing the full report on the honeymoon cruise to the Bahamas while Chelsea doled out the gifts she'd brought back for everyone. And that was when the subject finally turned to the big white bandage on the side of Jessi's head, and the entire incident in the barn last night, with Wes making it sound as if she'd taken her life in her hands just by birthing a calf. Lash didn't say much. Just sat in the far corner of the room. But his gaze strayed to Jessi's more than once, though he looked away quickly each time she met it.

Jessi sat quietly, pursed her lips and refused to scream at her brother. Not for the world would she have spoiled this homecoming by starting a brawl. Every time the urge to club Wes upside the head hit her, she took a big gulp of icy-cold tea to distract herself. She'd gone through half the glass already.

"It was pure foolishness," Wes was saying. "Besides risking herself, it was risky for the animals. Jess should've called a vet—"

"Wes," Chelsea said, frowning, "your sister *is* a vet."

"Come on, Chelsea, I meant a *real*..." Wes had the good sense not to finish the sentence. He met Jessi's gaze. "I mean—"

"I know what you mean," she said. She got to her

feet, her hand closing around her glass, crossed the room and poured the tea, ice cubes and all, into Wes's lap. She slammed the empty glass down on the table beside him, turned and left the room to go back upstairs to her own. Her head hurt, and she just wasn't up to dealing with her brothers right now.

Chelsea's voice followed her up the stairs. "Weston Brand, that had to be the most insensitive hogwash I've ever—" And then she heard the tap of Chelsea's feet crossing the floor and heading upstairs after her.

She barely had time to brush the hurt, angry tears away before she heard the gentle tap on her bedroom door. "Who is it?" she asked, just in case she was wrong and it was one of her brothers. If it was, she had every intention of telling them to go to hell.

"It's Chelsea."

Jessi opened the door, and met her sister-in-law's eyes.

"You wanna talk about it?" Chelsea asked.

The tears came fresh and fast, and the next thing Jessi knew she was wrapped up tight in the smaller woman's arms. "I hate this," she said, straightening away and swiping angrily at her eyes. "I never cry."

"I know you don't," Chelsea said. "But those brothers of yours bring it out in the best of us."

"You got that right."

"At least Lash set them straight," Chelsea said.

Jessi blinked and stared at her. "He did?"

Chelsea nodded. "Told them you pulled that calf like a pro. Said he knew he couldn't have done it, and doubted any other vet could've done better."

Jessi averted her eyes, hoping Chelsea wouldn't see how much pleasure that gave her. "Doubt it made any difference to them," she said.

''Probably not. In fact, Wes was sort of glaring at him when I left the room.'' She paced farther into the bedroom and sat down on the edge of the bed. ''It's just because they love you, you know. You'll always be their baby sister.''

''But, Chelsea, I'm an adult. When are they going to see that?''

Chelsea shrugged. ''They aren't...unless you force them to.''

''Yeah, that's pretty much the way I figure it, too.'' She sighed and went to the vanity, pulled open its drawer and extracted a letter. ''Something happened while you were gone,'' she said, and she turned to face Chelsea again. ''Marisella Cordoba...she passed away.''

''Oh, no.'' Chelsea looked stricken. ''That sweet lady? Oh, Jessi, I'm sorry. I know how close she was to you.''

''Closer than I realized, I guess.'' She handed Chelsea the letter, and Chelsea, frowning, pulled it from its envelope and unfolded it.

Her eyes scanned the page, then met Jessi's again. ''She named you as her sole heiress?''

Jessi nodded. ''Her lawyer said she had no family. And I guess she was grateful to me for always taking care of that old cat of hers. She wanted me to turn the house into a veterinary clinic, Chelsea. And the money she had in the bank will be enough to do it, too.'' Jessi shook her head slowly. ''She believed in me that much.''

''Of course she did. Anyone with half a brain would.''

Jessi smiled. ''She left me the cat, too.''

''There's always a catch, isn't there?'' Chelsea

grinned and Jessi smiled, feeling a bit better. "So where's that old beast now?"

"At the lawyer's house, in town. I'm supposed to pick him up today, when I go in to sign some papers making all this official." She lowered her head and sighed. "Chels, I haven't told anyone about this yet."

Chelsea nodded. "Because you think they'll try to talk you out of it?"

"Yeah. They'll say I'm too young, too inexperienced, too...too everything. But I'm going to do it. And if they give me too much grief...then..." She bit her lip, lowered her head. "Then I'm going to leave. The house Marisella left me is big enough for me to live in, as well as run a clinic from. And I will, Chelsea, if they force me."

"But if you do, you won't be running into Lash Monroe around the ranch every day, will you Jess?"

Jessi's head came up fast. "How did you—?"

"Oh, come on, sweetie. It's written all over your face every time you're in the same room with him."

Jessi felt her face heat. But in a moment she was shaking her head. "Doesn't matter," she said. "Lash is probably going to be leaving, anyway, now that Garrett's home."

"Don't be too sure of that. Garrett's planning to ask Lash to stay on."

Jessi felt her brows arch. "He is?"

"We had a message while we were away. There's been some rustling going on in the area, and Garrett's duties as sheriff are going to keep him busy until he puts a stop to it. He isn't going to have as much time as he'd hoped to help out here on the ranch. And besides all that, he wants Lash to help him with the investigation. I guess he was pretty impressed with

Lash's performance in tracking down Vincent de Lorean.''

Jessi licked her lips. ''You think Lash will agree?''

Chelsea shrugged. ''You know him better than I do. What do you think?''

Jessi smiled slowly. ''He'll agree. If I have anything to say about it...and believe me, I will.''

''That's more like the Jessi I know and love.''

''It's the Brand in me coming out,'' she said. ''Now, if I could just get my brothers to see it.''

Chelsea looked Jessi over, head to toe. ''Well, we can start right now. You say you're going into town today, to see that lawyer? Well, this is a business trip. You can't go in jeans.''

''Gee, Chelsea, I don't own much else.''

''I do. You need a power suit today, Jessica. And you might as well be wearing it when you face those bundles of testosterone downstairs to tell them about all this. You're a career woman now. So dress the part.'' She pursed her lips. ''I think my skirts will be quite a bit shorter on you than me.'' Then she smiled. ''All the better.'' And with a wink, she took Jessi's hand in hers and pulled her down the hall and into the master bedroom, which had once belonged to Jessi's parents, but now had been passed on to Chelsea and Garrett. Several new drawings and paintings hung on the walls. Chelsea's handiwork. She'd made a living as an artist before she came here. Now she divided her time between the ranch and volunteering over at the Women's Crisis Center in El Paso. Fighting domestic violence was one of Chelsea's passions.

Jessi surrendered herself to her sister-in-law's ministrations. A short time later, Jessi looked at herself in the full-length mirror and shook her head. She wore a pencil-slim emerald-green silk skirt that made her legs look endlessly long and slender. The matching jacket was cropped short, showing off her narrow waist. The cream-colored blouse underneath was nothing less than classy. Sheer nylons covered her legs, and she wore a pair of shiny black pumps on her feet. Chelsea had helped her with a light coat of makeup, barely visible, but somehow enhancing her cheekbones and wide-set eyes.

"What about my hair?" she said, giving her head a shake. "It's so tomboyish."

"You've gotta be kidding. Most women would kill for that shade of auburn, Jess. And the cut is what's known as 'short and sassy.' Very chic." She picked up a pair of earrings with green stones set in an intricate gold design and handed them to her. "You look fabulous. All you need is a briefcase."

"A veterinary bag," Jessi corrected. "And I already have one."

"Good. Now for the grand entrance."

"Yeah," Jessi said. "The one where I have to ask my brother for permission to use his pickup."

"Hey, I married him. It's my pickup too." Chelsea fished in her purse for the keys.

Jessi took the keys from her hand, bit her lip and blinked her eyes dry. "You don't know how much..."

"Sure I do."

"I was so young when our parents were killed. I can't even remember having another woman around to...to talk to, you know?"

"I know. Don't forget, I lost my mom, too. And then my sister."

Jessi nodded. "But you have another sister now."

Chelsea met her eyes, and Jessi saw them moistening. ''That means a lot to me, Jess.''

''Hey, don't get too happy. Remember, you got a houseful of brothers as part of the deal.''

''Five brothers and little Ethan. So the Brand women are outnumbered by the men, six to two.'' Chelsea smiled and gave Jessi a wink. ''They don't stand a chance.''

Lash had battled the urge to grab Wes Brand by the front of his shirt and shake him after seeing the tears spring to Jessi's eyes—tears caused by her brother's thoughtless remark. Heck, the kid didn't deserve that. And she had done a hell of a job with that calf last night. She might be young, but there was no question she was very good at what she did. Lash had seen her in action too often this past month to doubt that. What he couldn't figure out was why her brothers did. They'd been around her a heck of a lot longer than Lash had.

But he satisfied himself with a few words in her defense, and managed to keep his temper in check. Odd, the way the sight of her tears had roused it to such an unusual level. He was normally slow to anger. He shook his head, and thought it was a damned good thing he'd decided to move on.

The brothers had adjourned to the kitchen and now sat around the table with filled coffee mugs and a heap of doughnuts that seemed to be shrinking at an alarming rate. Lash didn't sit. Instead, he cleared his throat and, when Garrett looked at him, spoke. ''Now that you're back, Garrett, I'm thinking it's time for me to be heading out.''

It was Wes who replied. "Been nice havin' you here, Lash. You have a nice trip, now."

Elliot shook his head and took a quick sip of his coffee. Looked to Lash as if he did so to hide the grin he was battling. Ben said nothing. The guy never did say much. Seemed locked in a perpetual state of mourning over the death of his young wife, Penny. Jessi had filled Lash in on that sad event, but she'd also told him it had happened over a year ago, and that she was pretty worried about Ben's seeming inability to get past it. Or even to crack an occasional smile.

Garrett sat thoughtfully for a moment. Then he drew a breath. "Lash, is there something pressing you need to see to? Someplace you have to be?"

The question took Lash by surprise. "Well, no, not really. I just thought it was time."

"And you thought right," Wes said.

Garrett shot his brother a quelling glance before returning his attention to Lash. "Then I have a proposition for you." Garrett got to his feet, yanked another mug from the tree and filled it, then set it in front of an empty chair.

Taking his cue, Lash took the seat, and the mug.

"Lash, I could still use you here," Garrett began. Wes rolled his eyes and heaved a sigh, but as a deterrent it was ineffective. "There's been some rustling going on, and it's going to take more than one small-town sheriff to get to the bottom of it."

Lash choked on his coffee, lowered the mug with a bang and swiped at his mouth with his shirtsleeve. "You gotta be kidding me."

Garrett smiled at him. "You did a hell of a job with the whole de Lorean thing. No fed could've done better."

"I'm no lawman, Garrett."

"Neither was I, till they pinned this badge on me. I need a deputy, Lash. Not only that, but I'm still gonna need your help here on the ranch. Especially with rustlers prowling the pastures."

"Damnation," Wes muttered. Garrett glanced toward him, and Wes shook his head. "I don't suppose it ever occurred to you to ask one of us," he snapped.

"It occurred to me. Wes, you have a record, justified or not. You've also got a temper hot enough to melt glaciers, and the whole town knows it. Sorry, but with your reputation, they'd never sit still for me pinning a badge on your chest and handing you a loaded gun." Wes's face reddened a little, but he couldn't very well argue his brother's points. "Elliot's young yet. Maybe not too young, but we all know he can't hit the broad side of a barn with a pistol. 'Course, if he could rope the bad guys, we'd be in good shape, but it's safe to figure they'll be carrying weapons more lethal than lassos. And Ben..." Garrett glanced at the blond man sitting quietly with his head slightly lowered. "Ben's mind wouldn't be on the job. Lash has proven he's damn good at this kind of work, and I want him with me in this."

Finally he met Lash's eyes again. "So what do you say?"

Lash drew a breath and sighed hard. What could he say? Garrett had treated him like family...well, except for that one misunderstanding when he'd damn near broken Lash's nose and Jessi had just about screamed the house down over it.

Jessi. She was his reason for leaving. He wanted to get away from her, because he was sorely afraid she might be developing some silly crush on him. And she was too pretty, too able to make him feel a twinge of temptation every now and then, though he hadn't fully realized the danger she posed until last night.

On the other hand, he owed Garrett Brand. Owed him big. If not for the big guy, Jimmy's murderer might still be walking around a free man.

So which was more important? Risking a little temptation or doing right by a friend?

And, as it often did, the voice of the Reverend Stanton rang through Lash's mind like some kind of born-again Jiminy Cricket, acting as his conscience. "'*...Is this thy kindness to thy friend? Why wentest thou not with thy friend?' Second Samuel sixteen–seventeen, Lash, my boy. Memorize it.*"

Lash sighed and wondered if he'd ever find an occasion in life that didn't call some applicable verse to mind. Heck, probably not. He'd memorized most of the good book before he grew old enough to move out of the Stanton house. It came in handy at times. At others, it just gave him twinges of guilt.

Like now. A twinge just big enough to make him do the right thing.

He sighed once more, and finally nodded. "All right, Garrett. I'll stick around. But understand that this is temporary, okay? Once this rustling thing is over, I'll be leaving."

Garrett's face split in a broad smile. "Understood."

Lash reached his hand across the table to shake Garrett's. Then he caught Wes's eye and knew the man still didn't approve.

"Well, Lash, since you're staying on," Wes said, "maybe you can take the pickup into town for that load of feed that's waiting to be collected. It'll give me a chance to have a talk with my brothers."

"Be glad to," Lash said, but he knew his smile didn't reach his eyes. He and Wes were going to have to come to an understanding, and Lash suspected it wasn't going to be pretty. Fact was, he was eager to get out of here and think about what he'd just agreed to, and how the hell he was going to deal with it. By staying away from Jessi Brand, that was how. Damn, he'd been sure he would have shaken the Texas dirt off his boots by sundown.

"Sorry, boys, but the pickup is already spoken for." The voice was Chelsea's, and it came from the doorway.

All heads turned in her direction, but it wasn't Chelsea who caused their jaws to drop, one by one. It was Jessi. Chelsea stepped aside to let her walk by into the kitchen, and Lash felt his throat go dry. She looked... Dang...she looked gorgeous. Luscious. Sexy. And *very* grown-up.

Lash's eyes roamed from the low-slung collar of the creamy blouse to the swells of her breasts beneath it. His gaze lowered, following the sleek curves down to legs that would bring a man crashing right down to his trembling knees. Good Lord, he'd had no idea what she was hiding under those jeans and flannel shirts she usually wore.

"Where the hell do you think you're going all gussied up like that, Jessi?" Wes blurted, but even his voice sounded a bit hoarse.

"I have an appointment in town," she said, and her voice drew Lash's gaze back up to her face. Funny how he'd never noticed that her eyes were hypnotic, that her lips were as full and sensual as any Hollywood starlet's. Beyond all that, he noticed that she was nervous. Her eyes were not just incredible and deeper than the velvety brown of a doe's eyes, but wide and darting and glittering. She moistened her lips and went on. "But before I go, I have a little announcement to make."

Lash couldn't take his eyes off her. He lost track of her brothers' reactions, because he couldn't focus on anything but the world-class beauty standing at center stage.

"Go ahead, Jess," Garrett said softly.

Jessi nodded at him, smiling shakily. "Marisella left me everything she had," she said. "Including the house in town, and a sizable chunk of money."

She gave it a second to sink in. Lash saw the brothers focusing on her sharply, lifting their chins, interest lighting their eyes.

"And she left it for a reason," Jessi went on. "She wanted me to set up my veterinary clinic there, and I've decided to do it. I'm going into Quinn today to meet with her attorney and sign the necessary papers."

Wes got out of his chair fast. "Oh, for crying out loud, Jessi, you don't know the first thing about—"

"Weston Brand, you sit down and shut up, because I'm not finished yet."

Lash did manage to look away from her, briefly. Just long enough to see Wes's eyes widen, and his face pale just a bit. He didn't speak.

"I'm a grown woman, with a degree in veterinary medicine. I own my own house and have my own money, soon to be supplemented by the income from my clinic. Now I'm going to say this once, and once only. That house is plenty big enough to support a clinic *and* a home."

This time Garrett was the one who rose, shaking his

head slowly. "Honey...you aren't saying you're... you're moving out?"

"Not yet," she said. Lash noticed that she bit her lower lip, and he suspected that leaving this houseful of Brands would be as traumatic for her as for the rest of them. "But I will if any of you start riding me about this. Marisella believed in me. And so does Chelsea. And I'm not ashamed to tell you that it hurts like hell to know that my own brothers don't. But I'm not going to let it hold me back. Not anymore."

And as the Brand men all started blurting denials at once, Jessi sauntered past them, heels clicking across the floor tiles, and headed right out the front door.

Garrett and Wes both lunged, as if to go after her.

"Don't you even think about it," Chelsea said, and her voice was so loud and so firm that both of them stopped in their tracks. "Just you sit right back down. Jessi might be finished with you, but I haven't even started." Then she came forward and tapped Lash's shoulder. He'd been fixated on watching that little hell-cat climb into the pickup, her long legs revealed in their full glory.

"Lash, get your rear end out there. I believe the foreman here gave you a job to do."

"I didn't mean—" Wes began, but a glare from Chelsea stopped him.

"The grain, Lash. Wes told you to take the pickup into town and collect that load of grain."

"My car—" he blurted.

"Isn't big enough, and you know it. Ride with Jess. Go on. Move."

"Then Jess can take my car," Lash said, rushing on.

"Waste of gas." Chelsea put her hands on her hips and nodded her head toward the door. "Git."

She didn't leave much room for argument, and Lash suspected he was being sent away for far different reasons. Chelsea was good and riled about the state these fellows had put their sister in, and she was going to let them have it with both barrels. He ought to be glad to be out of the line of fire. But instead he was sweating bullets.

He nodded once to Chelsea, saw a smile hiding in her eyes, and then headed out the door to jump into the passenger side of the pickup truck before it could get away without him. And as he did he vowed to himself that he wouldn't even *look* at those long legs of Jessi Brand's.

Chapter 3

"What are you doing in here?" Jessi asked him.

Lash told himself not to look at her. He looked at her anyway. Ah, damn, there were tears brimming in her eyes again. He hated seeing tears in those pretty eyes.

"I...uh... Chelsea... I mean, Wes wants me to pick up a load of feed."

"Oh." She slid the shift easily into gear and eased up on the clutch. Lash's gaze fixed itself on her legs, which were parted slightly, of necessity, to reach both the accelerator and the clutch. Her skirt was riding high, showing to fullest advantage a pair of thighs so creamy and smooth he wanted to taste them.

No, he didn't. Damn, if the preacher could see him now, he'd tell him to memorize ten thousand Bible verses. At *least!* Old Ezekiel Stanton had always promised Lash they'd come in handy someday.

Exodus 20:17, Lash thought desperately. *Thou shalt*

not covet thy neighbor's wife, nor his manservant, nor his maidservant, nor his ox, nor his ass, nor any thing that is thy neighbor's. Including his sister. Lash recited the verse in his mind, closing his eyes and adding the final sentence, since he was sure it must have been included on the original stone tablet. God wouldn't skip over something this important.

"Lash?"

Swallowing hard, he opened his eyes and faced her. And, dammit, he still coveted.

"Did Garrett ask you to stay on?" she asked, her eyes on the road, instead of on him. Her hands on the wheel, instead of on him.

"Yeah," he croaked. "How did you know?"

"Chelsea filled me in…on the rustling and all." He nodded and said nothing. She glanced his way, and he noticed a tiny smudge of makeup under her eye, right in a spot he bet would be very sensitive, should he press his lips to it. "So? Are you going to?"

"Going to what?"

"Stay on," she said.

"Oh. Yeah, I told him I would."

Her eyes on the road again, she smiled. "I'm glad."

Wonderful. He didn't want her to be glad.

"So what do you think?"

What did he think? He thought he'd better get out of this pickup soon, because she was lifting her beautiful thigh, and then extending it to depress the clutch again, and he was getting turned on.

"About what?"

"My announcement back there," she said. "My clinic."

He smiled at the memory, frankly glad to have something to distract him from thinking about the way she looked. Must be the dress. The stockings. The makeup. He'd only seen her in jeans and work clothes before, and usually with dirt streaked across her face. He'd never looked at her as...well, as a woman. And it was hitting him hard and fast and all at once. It was downright flabbergasting.

"To tell the truth," he said slowly, "I didn't know you had it in you."

"To start a clinic?"

"To stand up to your brothers." Lord knew she'd put Olive Stanton right to shame with that little speech she'd just made. "I was beginning to think you enjoyed having them at your beck and call. Little princess, with her own army of knights protecting her from every threat."

She swung her head around, brown eyes flashing. "That's what you think of me?" Her face flushed with angry color.

"Well...see, I knew a woman like that once, and you were showing all the signs, so I—"

"I oughtta stop this truck and make you walk into town and carry the damned feed home on your back, Lash Monroe!"

She did have a temper. Made her cheeks hot and pink, and her eyes gleam. Made her look like pure fire.

"I didn't say I was right, okay?"

"You didn't say you were wrong, either."

He shrugged. "Maybe I'm reserving judgment."

She glared at him. "So you think you *were* right. You think I'm just some spoiled kid who likes having her brothers treating her like a fragile china doll."

He tilted his head. "Well, you put up with it for this long. Who knows, you go getting all independent now and you might just find you miss having all those men catering to your every need.''

''You got a lot to learn about me, Lash. A lot to learn.'' She shook her head slowly as she said it, and focused on her driving again.

He felt mean. Truth to tell, he was beginning to think he'd been way off base about Jessi Brand. She wasn't turning out to be as much like his foster mother, the helpless and dependent Olive Stanton, as he'd thought she was. But hell, he couldn't very well tell her so, could he? He didn't want her reading anything into it.

''For what it's worth, Jessi, I think you're one hell of a vet.''

''For a kid, you mean?''

He didn't answer that loaded question. She turned the truck expertly into the parking lot of the small clapboard law office and killed the motor.

''Look at me, Lash.''

Hell, was she nuts? He'd been doing nothing *but* look at her for the whole damned trip. Still, he complied, largely because he couldn't do otherwise.

''My mama was married, with two babies, by the time she was my age. Did you know that?''

He shook his head mutely.

''Do I look like a kid to you?'' she asked him point-blank. Right between the eyes. She'd been right awhile back when she'd claimed to be the best shot in the family.

''No, you don't.''

Her eyes dipped to focus very briefly on his mouth, and he felt that gaze like a red-hot branding iron. ''Well,'' she said softly. ''That's a start.''

A start? A start to what?

She opened her door, leaving the keys dangling from the switch as she climbed out. "You can go ahead and take the pickup to collect that feed, Lash. By the time you get back here, I should be ready to go."

Lash nodded, sliding across the seat to the driver's side. But he didn't leave right away. Instead, he sat there and watched as she walked away from the truck. Watched her hips moving back and forth, those long legs eating up the distance. Lord, but she was something. And he knew that he was in trouble.

But I say unto you that whosoever looketh on a woman to lust after her hath committed adultery with her already in his heart. The preacher's voice echoed in his mind. He could even hear the sound of that fist pounding down on the Bible.

Stop thinking about her, that was the key. Just put Jessi Brand right out of his mind. He could do that, couldn't he?

When she disappeared inside the lawyer's office, Lash started the truck and backed out of the lot. He headed toward the feed store two blocks away, but he was still thinking about Jessi when he got there. He backed up to the loading dock and went inside long enough to request the feed and ask that it be charged to the Texas Brand account. Then he went out back to help with the loading. Maybe a little physical labor would distract his wayward thoughts.

The feed was stacked in hundred-pound burlap bags. Lash slung one over his shoulder, and it emitted a puff of fragrant dust he knew would remain on his shirt all day. He tossed it into the pickup bed and went back for another. Already the sun was sending heat waves down to toast his flesh, and after the third trip he was coated in sweat, as well as feed dust. Fifteen bags later, his back was starting to protest. His heart was thudding in his chest, and he was out of breath. And he was still thinking about Jessi Brand. He dreaded the ride back to the ranch, and hoped it would go quickly. Hoped he could keep his thoughts to himself until they got back. Hoped he could keep his *hands* to himself, as well.

Ah, hell.

He drove back to the law office. And there she was, standing outside, in the sunshine that made her hair gleam like copper. She had a manila envelope in one hand, and a black-and-white cat cradled against her chest. She kept bending to stroke her cheek over the cat's head, and there was something so damned sexy about the act that he almost stalled the truck.

She sauntered over to the passenger side, and Lash leaned across to open the door for her. The cat came first, settling itself down on the seat beside Lash. Jessi climbed in beside the animal and slammed the door. "This is Pedro," she said.

"I knew a Pedro once. Didn't much like him, though. He come with the house?"

Jessi nodded and smiled, but it was a nervous smile. "Yeah. And so did Marisella's old truck." She turned toward him, grimaced, then slowly reached out a hand and brushed the dust from his hair.

Lash didn't know whether to duck away from her touch, or close his eyes and lean into it. Damn, he liked the way her hands felt in his hair.

"You're a mess," she said.

"You got that right." She frowned at him, but he didn't explain his meaning. "So, back to the ranch?"

She chewed her lower lip, then shook her head. "If you're not in a big hurry to get back, Lash, I'd like to stop by Marisella's place. Take a look around."

"Oh." More time alone with her. Great.

"That way I can drive her...my new pickup truck home."

"Or I can tow it home. As I recall, that thing's at least as old as this cat appears to be."

"Older," she said. "But it runs." She turned her attention back to the cat, stroking his head, and Lash felt a twinge of envy.

He ignored it and steered the truck toward the edge of town, and the house Jessi had just inherited.

Lash had never been inside Marisella's house. It was a red adobe cottage, with a matching garage beside it that was nearly as big as the house itself. A front lawn rolled gently between the two buildings and the road, and an even bigger one unfolded in the back.

Jessi took the keys and went to the door, setting the cat gently on the ground as she unlocked it. Lash sat right where he was until she glanced over her shoulder at him, smiled that killer smile of hers, and waved a hand at him to come on. Okay. Everything was okay. He could handle this.

Lash got out of the truck and followed her inside.

The place looked as if Marisella had just left for the day. Pedro followed them through the front door and meowed plaintively for his owner. "Poor thing," Jessi said, speaking in hushed tones. "He doesn't understand where she's gone."

Lash nodded and reached down to pet the cat, but Pedro shot away from him, running through the house, probably in search of Marisella. Jessi looked around the small kitchen area, with its white cupboards and spotless countertop, its small round oak table and matching chairs, its ancient-looking refrigerator.

"I'd have to tear it apart to turn it into a clinic,"

she said, still speaking very softly. "I'm not sure I can bring myself to do it." She ran a hand over the countertop. "There's so much of Marisella still here. And she was one hell of a lady. I don't want to lose that sense of her."

"Then don't," Lash said. Jessi turned to face him, brows lifted. He shrugged. "I mean...well, the garage is plenty big enough for a clinic," he went on. "Put in a few partitions, do a little wiring in there. It wouldn't be all that difficult."

Her eyes narrowed as she watched him. Then she nodded slowly. "It's a good idea." She turned away then, walking through the kitchen and into the small living room, with its cozy furniture and its countless embroidered samplers decorating the walls. She looked around and nodded. "It really is a good idea. This place should be someone's home, not a sterile clinic, you know? There should be a family here. God, Marisella would love the idea of kids running around her house, getting into mischief, making noise." Her smile was whimsical, as if she were envisioning it all in her mind.

"Thinking of renting it out to some family like that?"

She shook her head. "Thinking of the future, Lash. My own family. My own kids."

Lash felt his brows lift in surprise. "Getting a little ahead of yourself, aren't you?"

She only shrugged. "I don't believe in waiting for what I want," she said. "Maybe it's because my parents died so young and so suddenly, or maybe it's just me. But I've always figured you ought to go after your dreams just as hard and as fast as you possibly can. You never know when fate might step in and take away your chance.'' She stepped to the window and looked out over a wide, overgrown expanse of grass. ''Besides, this backyard was made for children.''

Lash almost asked her if she had a husband in mind, but decided against it. He didn't want to know if she was already planning her marriage to some local good ol' boy. He did take a moment to pity the poor fool, whoever he was. Imagine having those overprotective brothers of hers to contend with. Hell, he wouldn't be in that slob's shoes for all the tea in China.

She turned her back to the window, leaning against the sill, and looked at him with a gleam in her eyes that made him squirm clear to his boots.

Lash cleared his throat. ''I...er...thought you wanted to keep living out at the ranch.''

''For now,'' she said. ''But I know better than to think of staying there forever. Especially if I ever—I mean, *when* I get married. Lord, Lash, can you imagine the way my brothers would feel about the poor guy? They'd probably be as hostile as...as they were with you at first.''

He shifted uncomfortably. ''Yeah. That's pretty easy to imagine.''

''C'mon,'' she said. ''I'll show you the rest. There are two bedrooms, and—''

''I think we oughtta take a look at that garage.''

If he'd blurted it too fast, it couldn't be helped. No way was he going anywhere *near* a bedroom with Jessi Brand. Uh-uh. What did she think he was, totally stupid?

She sent him a sidelong glance that said she knew every thought that went through his mind, which was impossible, of course. ''Okay,'' she said.

She scooped up the cat and led the way outside,

locking the door behind her. Pedro yowled enough to break a heart, and it looked as if it was breaking Jessi's. She rubbed his head, kissed his face. "It's gonna be all right, kitty. I promise."

The cat settled down some after that. And Lash figured if she'd rubbed *his* head and kissed *his* face like that, he'd probably be lying on his back and purring, as well, by now.

She deposited the animal in the pickup on the way to the garage, then headed there to unlock the overhead door. She tugged on it, too, bending over right in front of Lash and making his pulse rate skyrocket with the thoughts that action invoked. He tapped her shoulder so she'd straighten up and quit torturing him. Then he reached past her to yank the sticky door upward.

And then she groaned audibly.

Marisella's old pickup sat in the only place it possibly could. Around it, the garage was packed full. Piles of boxes and bags loomed higher than Lash's head. There were stacks and stacks of cases and trunks and containers of every shape imaginable.

"Looks like Marisella was a closet pack rat," he observed.

Jessi shook her head slowly and picked her way inside, seeking out a path between the piles. She pulled the flap of one box aside to peer at its contents. "Magazines," she said, turning to face him. "Old ones. I can't imagine why she kept..."

He didn't hear the rest. The box she'd tugged on was in the middle of a ten-foot stack, and that stack was teetering now, tipping, right above her pretty head.

Lash lunged forward as the stack fell. His body hit Jessi's, and they both sailed out of harm's way as the pile of boxes came crashing down right in the spot where she'd been standing.

Only the danger hadn't passed. Not by a long shot. Because Lash was lying facedown on top of Jessi, where she'd landed, atop a heap of plastic bags. Every inch of his body was pressed intimately to every inch of hers. And his hand had come to rest, for some damned inexplicable reason, against her firm, nylon-encased thigh.

He didn't move. Couldn't move, even when he tried to tell himself he should. He lifted his head and looked into her eyes, and the heat he saw in those big pools of melted chocolate seared him right to his toes. "You...uh...okay?"

"Fine," she said in a deep, sultry whisper. "Maybe even better than fine. How about you?"

"Um...yeah, I'm okay, too."

She shifted her hips a little, then blinked up at him. "So, are you carrying a pistol, Lash, or are you just glad to see me?"

He closed his eyes and grimaced, embarrassed to the roots of his hair. "You're a mouthy little thing, you know that?"

She only smiled—a slow, sexy smile that made him want to groan aloud. "Yeah, I've been told that before." She held his gaze. He couldn't look away. "So, Lash, what's it gonna be? You gonna get off me, or kiss me?"

He looked down into her eyes, and it hit him that she *wanted* him to kiss her. Dammit, wasn't it bad enough that he was having these bouts of lust for her? Did she have to go and start having them for him, as well?

He pushed himself up with his hands.

''Chicken,'' she said.

''Cut it out, Jessi.'' He got to his feet, with some effort, and reached a hand down to help her up, as well. She took it and got up, but he thought she looked a little hurt, or disappointed, or something. He shook his head and heaved a sigh. ''Look, just so you know, you don't have to go trying to convince me you're all grown up, okay? I got the message.''

''You think that's what I was doing?''

He turned away and began moving boxes aside to clear a path out of the garage. ''I know damned well that's what you were doing. And you can save it. I'm convinced already. So you can quit with the nonsense.''

He moved one last box and stepped out into the sunlight again.

She stayed where she was. ''And what if it wasn't nonsense?''

He went still, feeling a shiver race right up his spine. ''That's all it can be, Jessi. I'm leaving here as soon as Garrett and I put a stop to this rustling. Besides that, I'm old enough to be your—''

''My lover?''

He spun around. She shrugged innocently. ''Well, you couldn't say 'father,' 'cause it would be bull. And I already have plenty of brothers. Sure don't need another one of those. So what's left?''

''Friend,'' he said.

''Oh.''

He didn't like the look in her eyes, so he averted his own, glancing at the battered old pickup instead of at her face. ''How about if I drive this clunker back to the ranch, and you take Garrett's truck?''

''Why?''

She still hadn't moved, and she was still looking at him like a panther looks at an unsuspecting rabbit.

"Well, because I can tell by driving it what kind of work it might need."

"And what makes you think I can't?" she asked him.

He bit his lip. Damn. He supposed he'd underestimated her...again. "Fine, you drive it. I'll follow, in case it breaks down."

"Well, now, isn't that just *friendly* of you." She finally clambered out from between the piles of junk and made her way to the old red pickup truck. She opened the door and climbed behind the wheel. "It's going to run just fine," she told him, inserting the key.

"How can you be so sure?"

She smiled at him. "I want it to. And you know me, right, friend? I'm that spoiled little princess, the darling baby sister of the Brand brothers. I *always* get what I want."

As Lash stood there with his throat going just as dry as the desert sand, Jessi turned the key, and the pickup roared to life like an angry bull. She slipped it into gear and drove it slowly out of the garage, then past him, onto the road heading back toward the ranch.

Lash closed and locked the garage, then returned to Garrett's pickup to follow her. He felt a little sick to his stomach. But he wasn't sure why.

He wants me!

Jessi couldn't stop smiling as she ground the ancient pickup truck into a higher gear and bounced down the road. The thing steered like a tank, and she was leaving a smoke trail behind her that would have choked a horse. But none of that dampened her mood. Lash

Monroe had given himself away today. He could deny it till hell froze over, but he couldn't convince her that she'd imagined what had happened between them back there. No way. He'd been turned on. Aroused. Attracted.

She smiled even more. *Hard.*

Yup, he wanted her, all right. But him wanting her was only half the battle. He was going to have to *love* her. And soon, before he and Garrett solved this rustling thing and he got it into his head to go running away from her again. It had to be before that happened.

She settled deeper in her seat and glanced at her own determined eyes in the rearview mirror. "I'm gonna make that man my very own, if it's the last thing I do."

The voice sounded certain, but a hint of doubt crept into her reflection's gaze. Jessi bit her lip as a slight bout of worry assailed her. What if she couldn't do it? What if all Lash felt for her was a physical longing, and nothing more? What if he was too hell-bent on retaining his precious freedom to let himself feel anything else?

Just how in hell did a woman go about making a man fall in love with her? How did she make a confirmed bachelor change his ways? How did she make a drifter decide to settle down?

Lord, she needed a plan. And she needed it quick. Before those damned rustlers were caught and tossed behind bars and Lash flitted off like a goose in winter.

The truck bounded into the driveway and under the arches of the Texas Brand, and Jessi brought it to a whining stop and killed the engine. It died slow, as if it didn't quite want to let go just yet. It coughed, gasped, backfired once, and then finally gave up the ghost. She glanced up to see Garrett on the front porch, shaking his head and waving one hand as if to clear the smoke away, though it was nowhere near him. Chelsea sat on the porch swing beside him, and she gave him a nudge in the ribs with her elbow.

As Jessi got out of the pickup, Garrett rose and came to meet her. ''How'd it go?''

''Went fine,'' she said. ''It's gonna be a lot of work, Garrett, but I can do it.'' She lifted her chin a little as she said it, certain he was going to disagree.

''I know you can.''

Jessi blinked. ''You do?''

''Hell, you're a Brand, aren't you?''

For now, she thought, and she glanced over her shoulder in time to see Lash behind the wheel of Garrett's pickup, backing the load of grain up to the barn door. Above him, the sky was darkening with ominous-looking clouds. It had been hot and dry for a while now, and she knew too well how dangerous a sudden cloudburst could be. What they needed was a slow, steady rain. The ground-soaking kind. Not a downpour.

''Look, Jess,'' Garrett said, interrupting her inspection of the horizon, and of the man out near the barn. ''I'm sorry if we've given you the feeling that we're not behind you. It's just that...well, you're our baby sister, you know?''

She dragged her attention from the dark clouds and battled the worry skittering up her spine. ''How could I not know?''

Garrett smiled a bit sheepishly. ''If you're determined to do this, let us help you.''

She faced him again, squaring her shoulders. ''I don't think so. Look, don't get all offended, big brother, but I want to do this on my own. I don't want anyone thinking I couldn't have made it work without my brothers' help. And besides, you guys have your hands full as it is."

"But, Jessi—"

Chelsea cleared her throat from the porch, and Garrett cut off his protest.

"Okay, Jess. If that's the way you want it. Just know we're here for you, okay? And don't think that asking for advice is a sign of weakness. That's what family's for, you know."

"I know," she told him. Then he hugged her hard, and she hugged him back.

When he released her, he stared down at her, searching her face. "Now, about Lash…"

Jessi frowned. "What about Lash?"

Garrett shifted his stance a bit. "I, uh…that is, Wes seems to think there might be…er…"

"Might be…what?"

"Look, Jess, he's a drifter. He's told us all flat out that he's leaving here soon. And besides all that, he's ten years older than you, and—"

"Eleven, Garrett. He's eleven years older than me."

Garrett just bunched up his eyebrows and tilted his head.

"So, Jessi," Chelsea said loudly, shouldering her way between brother and sister to drape an arm around Jessi's shoulders and begin leading her into the house. "Tell me all about your plans for the clinic. And don't leave anything out."

Jessi let Chelsea draw her away, but she glanced back over her shoulder at Garrett. "I'm a grown woman now," she said. "I can take care of myself."

"I just don't want to see you get hurt," he said.

She sighed hard and shook her head. Damn. Things around here would never change.

Upstairs in her room, Jessi spent some time at her computer, making detailed plans for her clinic. She kept the radio playing, hoping for a weather report, but only half listening. And pretty soon it didn't matter, because she heard the thunder in the distance and saw those clouds rolling in thicker all the time. They were in for a whopper of a storm, and damned if the ground wasn't too parched to absorb it. Could be a mess.

But if there was, they'd deal with it. They always had.

She put the possible repercussions of a storm out of her mind and worked on her plans. She'd added up all the cash she'd inherited and started formulating a budget. She knew more about the costs of equipment for the clinic than she did about the price of construction for the garage, so that was where she began, thumbing through her countless veterinary-supply catalogs and making lists of what she'd need, then subtracting the cost from the available funds. She'd have to earmark most of the rest for the remodeling, she had little doubt of that. There would be none left over for a better vehicle, and she'd need a good pickup truck for this venture.

Well, she'd have to make do. Maybe she could get some work done on the truck she had. It sounded to her as if it could use a new muffler, and probably plugs and points. A little tune-up, an oil change, new filters and belts—heck, she could probably make it run like new again.

Right.

Sighing, she got to her feet and wandered to the window to part the curtains and look outside.

Then she caught her breath and gnawed her lower lip.

Lash was out there by the barn now. He'd stripped off his shirt in deference to the moisture-laden heat, and he was unloading the heavy bags of grain and handing them off to Wes. Wes then carried them a few yards and handed them off to someone else, inside the barn. Elliot or Ben or Garrett. Didn't matter. And it didn't matter that Wes was shirtless as well, or that his rugged Comanche build usually made other men pale in comparison. It was Lash who'd captured her attention. God, but he was a beautiful man. Lean and firm and strong. Not bulging with muscle, but rippling instead. Subtle power slid under his skin, and she sucked a breath through her teeth when she saw the thin sheen of sweat coating his chest. It was dark outside, and the air was heavy and sizzling hot, the approaching storm acting like a woolen blanket, holding the heat beneath it.

"Damn," she muttered.

"Damn, what?" Chelsea asked, popping into the room and coming up to the window beside her. She followed Jessi's gaze and said, "Oh."

"So, what do you think?" Jessi asked.

Chelsea shrugged and leaned against the window. "Not bad. Not bad at all." She looked at Jessi and winked. "So how did the trip into town go?"

"You mean with the lawyer?" Jessi asked innocently.

"You know perfectly well what I mean. Tell me everything."

Jessi grinned. "I thought you'd never ask," she said.

"But I'm gonna have to save it for later. I mean, I really oughtta go out there and help my poor brothers unload that heavy grain, don't you think?"

"Not in that outfit, you're not. Talk fast, while you change. Then you can take those poor, hot, sweaty-looking fellas out something cold to drink."

Lash glanced up to see Jessi, back in her usual jeans and a ribbed tank top, making her way across the yard toward the barns with a six-pack of dewy bottles in one hand. He licked his lips, unsure if it was the thought of that icy-cold soda that made him do it, or the way she looked. Lean and curvy and fresh. She didn't look the same way she'd looked before, but suddenly he was seeing her so differently.

She came right up to him, leaned one hip on the pickup's lowered tailgate and freed one of the bottles of soda from the pack. "You're looking..." Her mischievous brown eyes slid all the way down his sweaty chest, pausing on the snap of his jeans and moving slowly back up again. "Hot," she finished.

His throat went three times drier than it had been. "Yeah, it's a scorcher today. Muggy."

"Mmm... I think we're in for a storm." She twisted the cap off the bottle. "You want a drink?"

"Sure, if it's good an' cold." A slow rumble of thunder rolled over them and then faded.

She smiled and held the bottle out. He reached for it, and she moved it quickly past his hand, pressing its chilly glass against his belly. He yelped and jumped back.

"Cold enough?" Damn, she was sparkling like a gemstone today.

"Plenty," he told her, and he couldn't help smiling

at her. She wanted to play. He could see that. If her brothers wouldn't take offense, he might just oblige her. Sling her right over his shoulder and haul her butt to the pond to toss her in. Oh, yeah, he could play.

But then she'd stand up, and that little tank shirt she wore would be transparent, it would be so wet. And that cold water would do things to her body. Make him notice it even more than he was already noticing it, and dammit, he was already noticing it way more than he should. And…ah, hell, maybe the pond wasn't such a good idea.

"What's the matter, Lash?"

"Huh?" He met her eyes.

"You were staring at my chest. Just wondering if I had something on me, or—"

He shook his head and averted his eyes, searching for a change of subject and latching on to the first one that came to him. "Garrett's worried about flash flooding. Said it's been known to happen when a big storm rolls in after such a long dry spell."

"Yeah, it has been. But Garrett tends to worry too much." She glanced inside the dim, fragrant barn. "Where is he, anyway?"

Lash sighed. Stupid way to change the subject. Now he had to inform her that they were alone in this big old barn together. Maybe he should just lie.

She held his gaze and drew the truth out of him like mud will draw the stinger out of a bee sting. "He had to go inside to take a phone call. Didn't you hear Chelsea holler for him?"

She shook her head. "No. I was distracted. So, what about the others?"

He licked his lips. "They headed down to that lower pasture that runs alongside the creek. Garrett said he wanted them to move the heifers to higher ground, just in case.''

''Like I said, he worries too much.'' Her eyes scanned the barn's dark interior, as if to confirm that her brothers were gone.

Lash tried distracting her with a new subject again. ''That cat...Pedro...he's in the truck. Best get him out, before he gets too warm in there.''

''Okay.'' She turned and walked away from him. He reached into the truck to haul out the last bag of grain. He hoped Garrett's phone call was a brief one. He was alone out here with Jessi, and he didn't like it.

Or maybe he did. And maybe he shouldn't.

She opened the pickup door, and Pedro shot out so fast he appeared no more than a black-and-white streak. He ran between Lash's feet, shot into the barn and scrambled up through the opening, into the hayloft.

''Damn,'' Jessi said, slamming the truck's door. She started right through that barn, and stopped at the ladder. ''Well, c'mon, Lash,'' she called. ''I'll never catch him by myself. Give me a hand, will you?''

Lash looked at her. Then he looked at the darkness above her, beyond the opening in the ceiling. Darkness and soft, fragrant hay. Silence and solitude. Hot, sultry, sticky air, smelling of fresh hay and Jessi Brand. Oh, man.

She put her foot on the lowest rung of the ladder. Lash set the bag of feed down, and moved as if he had no control over his body. As if he were operating on autopilot or something. His brain was telling him to stay where he was, but his brain was no longer running this show. His libido was, and that part of him wanted nothing more than to follow Jessi Brand up into that hayloft. Hell, that part of him wanted to follow her to the ends of the earth, and all she'd have to do would be to crook her little finger.

Lord, but he was in over his head here. And he was beginning to wonder if there was one damn thing he could do about it.

Chapter 4

Lash got to the ladder just as Jessi started climbing. Her shapely, denim-encased backside moved higher, right past his face, and then disappeared into the darkness above. And he heard her feet moving in the hay, and he heard her calling, "Here, kitty-kitty. Come on, Pedro."

He sighed softly, gripped the ladder and clambered up it after her.

It was dim, but not pitch-dark. The place smelled so strongly of hay that the air felt thick with it. In fact, it probably was slightly thick with it, judging by the dust floating into his lungs. And it was hotter up here than it was below. Hotter than the hellfire he was gonna burn in if he didn't watch himself. Hotter than the combined tempers of the Brand brothers. And dark. Damn, but it was dark. Like dusk, instead of a summer afternoon.

"There he is," Jessi said, and he squinted until he

could see where she was pointing, then followed her finger. The cat was perched on the top of a stack of hay. He couldn't have seen the beast well at all, if not for the white spots. And Jessi headed over to climb up after him.

Lash was right behind her. "Hold on, now, you'll pull that whole stack down on top of you."

"Not if I go up on this side. It's solid here."

He examined the stack of bales she proposed to climb, then gave a tug on them to assure himself of their stability. "It's also straight up and down, Jess. There's nothing to climb on here."

"Sure there is." To prove her point, she gripped high above her, fingers sinking into the hay, and then she picked up one foot and jammed her toe into the bale, creating her own toehold. She repeated the process with the other foot, then began moving, hands and feet alternately higher, like a rock climber, only slower.

"You're gonna break your neck," he warned.

"You're right."

"Huh?"

"I'm gonna fall!" she yelled suddenly.

Lash reached up and pressed his hands to her to keep her from falling. Only the result was that he ended up with her firm little backside in the palms of his hands.

Oh, damn. She felt good.

"I've got the cat," she called. "Can you sort of...lower me down?"

"I don't think so," he said, and the words were breathless and choked.

"Well, Lash, I can't climb back down. My hands are full."

"So are mine," he said.

She laughed softly. "That best not have been an insult, pal."

"I'd sooner insult the *Mona Lisa,*" he muttered, and he managed to lower her some. Then he moved his hands, one at a time, up to her waist, and brought her down some more. But he hadn't figured on those tight buns of hers sliding so intimately down the front of him.

Lord, he'd never smell hay again and not remember this. The girl was killing him. Slowly. Deliciously. She stood still for a moment, there in front of him. And, holding the cat in her arms, she leaned just slightly back against him.

And Lash bent his head, just a bit. So that his nose hovered really close to her hair, and he could inhale the scent of it. And then he battled the urge to bend even lower and maybe trace his lips over her neck, or taste her tender earlobe. It was bad enough his arms had decided to snug themselves around her waist. As if he were hugging her. Very intimate.

She tipped her head back, so that it rested on his shoulder, and he could see that her eyes were closed. "Damn, Lash, this feels *so* nice," she said softly.

He blinked and gave himself a mental shake. Then he took his arms from around her, though it was hell to let her go. He could have bent over her just now and kissed her. It would have been so easy. So...so good.

She sighed, as if in disappointment. "You really are stubborn," she said.

He didn't reply. Best to let her think he didn't have a clue what she was talking about.

She shook her head hard. "C'mon, then, let's get Pedro in the house before this storm cuts loose," she said in an exasperated tone. "My brothers catch you up here with me, Lash, and they'll think we were—"

"I can imagine what they would think," he said, not wanting to hear whatever colorful euphemism she'd come up with. Fearing that if he heard her say it, he'd see it even more clearly in his mind. As things turned out, he ended up seeing it in his mind anyway, so it was a wasted effort.

The cat stood at one end of the living room, eyeing Blue, who lay at the other end, eyeing the cat. Jessi glanced from one animal to the other, and hoped the two would learn to be friends eventually. So far, they just stared. At least they weren't fighting. They didn't move, and she gave up on them, turning instead to the window to gaze outside.

And she paused there, because she saw Ben. He stood alone, facing the approaching storm, moving in slow, graceful patterns that almost seemed like some ancient dance. She'd had no idea her big lug of a brother could move like that.

"T'ai chi," Elliot whispered in her ear. "When he was off playing hermit in the hills of Tennessee, he studied it. Said it helped, a little. Gave him peace or something."

"Poor Ben," Jessi whispered. "I wish he could get over his grief and move on." She swallowed hard, and reached up to close the curtains. Let Ben have his privacy. Let him mourn in his own way.

Lash was washing up in the kitchen, and Garrett was out there, too, having just finished with a phone call. Apparently it had been business, bad business. Garrett was saying something about another rustling incident at a neighboring ranch. It sounded to Jessi as if he and

Lash would be heading over to investigate shortly. Damn. There went any excuse she might have had to spend time with Lash tonight.

Then Garrett popped his head through the arched doorway into the living room. "You busy, Jess?"

She perked up instantly. "No. Why, you need me for something?"

"Bar-L had some stock stolen tonight. The boys rode up on the rustlers and the bastards took a few shots at them. Hit one of their horses."

"My God, Garrett! The rustlers *shot* at the Loomis boys? But one of 'em is just a kid!"

Garrett nodded, his face grim. "Yeah. These guys are dangerous. Luckily, they only hit a horse, but it's one of their best mounts. Paul Loomis just called, and I'm headed over there. Can you come?"

"Of course I'm coming. Let me grab some supplies. You know how bad the animal's hurt?"

Garrett shook his head. "Hurry, okay? It's gonna storm like crazy tonight, and I'd just as soon you be safe back home before it hits."

Jessi rolled her eyes at him, but refrained from arguing. Instead, she nodded and raced up the stairs to haul her bag out of her closet. She rummaged through the box of supplies she had on hand, and tossed in anything she thought she might need, including a case of sterile surgical instruments, a vial of tranquilizer and a selection of antibiotics. She was very glad to have already changed back into her jeans. Chelsea's nice clothes might look great on her, but they were just not suitable for work. She snapped the bag shut and headed downstairs again, muttering under her breath about the heartless bastards who'd shoot a horse, much less try to harm a teenage boy and his brothers, who were both around her age, more or less, just to steal a few head of cattle. The jerks would be sorry when Garrett and Lash caught up with them.

She slung her bag into the pickup's bed, then jumped into the front seat beside her brother. Lash got in next to her, and she realized that in her anger and worry over the poor, suffering animal, she'd forgotten all about her plan to seduce him. Didn't matter. Not tonight. This was business. This was what she lived for. She'd worry about roping and branding her man later.

They were barely under way when Garrett hit a bump in the road, and Jessi was jostled tight to Lash's side. She felt a hard bulge beneath his clothes, and bit her lip. Shoot, this time he *was* carrying a gun.

Thunder cracked like a rifle shot, and lightning split the night. In an instant the sky broke loose in a deluge that seemed to Jessi to be of biblical proportions.

Lash handed the heavy bag to Jess and watched as she raced through the pounding rain toward the spot Paul Loomis pointed out. Paul had climbed into the back of Garrett's pickup as soon as it rolled to a stop in his driveway. He'd shouted directions above the noise of the storm as Garrett drove over the rain-wet paths to the distant field. They'd stopped three times to let Paul climb down and open a gate, then close it behind them when they splashed through.

Garrett had been right about the storm. It was a big one, and the ground wasn't absorbing the water. Instead, the rain seemed to be bouncing off the earth, then gathering into miniature streams and running off in a hundred directions.

They'd driven far from the ranch house and the

barns. A handful of cattle stood alert and restless, dripping-wet, watching the proceedings, as three young men knelt around the fallen horse. The mare was a shadowy shape rising from the dark, rainy field, her sides rising and falling rapidly with her labored breathing, steam rising from her wet coat, as well as her flared nostrils.

Two other horses waited, dancing and pawing occasionally, no more at ease than anyone else. Animals could sense trouble, and these were no exception.

Garrett and Lash moved forward at a slower pace as Paul, the father of the three boys, a big man with square shoulders, a thick mustache and a face that could have been carved from granite, filled them in on what had happened.

''The dogs were taking on,'' he was saying. ''The boys decided to ride out to check on things. I should have gone with them.'' He shook his head. ''Damn, Garrett, that could be one of my *sons* lying there with a bullet in him.''

Garrett slapped a hand down on Paul Loomis's shoulder, splashing rain from the back of his yellow slicker. ''You had no way of knowing what they were riding into,'' he said. ''Hell, Paul, they've been riding your place all their lives without you hovering over them. This isn't your fault.''

Paul nodded, as if he knew it, but still felt guilty. Lightning flashed, illuminating his face, and Lash could see the horrible ''What if?'' expression that haunted his eyes. ''They say they came up over this 'ere rise,'' Paul went on, ''and saw a half-dozen men or more, mounted and herding our cattle north.''

Lash looked off in the direction Paul indicated,

squinting through the pouring rain, and frowning at what he saw there. "What, off into that scrub lot?"

"Yep," Paul said. "My guess is, they were heading them through that brush as a shortcut outta here. Only way to move cattle off the place without marching 'em right on past the house. There's an old road out there…been closed for years. But it's the nearest place I can figure where a man could load that many head."

"How many, Paul?" Garrett asked.

The older man shook his head, water beading and rolling from the brim of his hat. "I had a hundred head in this pasture. You can see what's left." He nodded toward the small group of cows in the distance. No more than twenty white-faced cattle remained. "'Course, a few probably scattered when the shootin' started."

Garrett nodded and pulled out a flashlight, snapping it on and shining it on the ground. The beam illuminated the muddy tracks of horses and cows, all mingled together. Garrett lifted the light and moved forward, well past the spot where Jessi was working on the horse. Lash pulled out his own light and followed. Near the scrub lot, he stopped. "Garrett, here's where they went through. The fence has been cut."

Garrett nodded. "I'm gonna follow, see if I can see anything."

"Not alone, you're not," Lash said.

Garrett glanced back at Jessi, then shot a serious look at Lash. "Lash, I don't want her here alone. These bastards haven't been gone all that long, and for all we know, they might not have gone far. Stay with her."

Lash saw the point and nodded. He wasn't about to leave Jessi vulnerable to the type of men they were dealing with. And while there were four Loomis men surrounding her, Lash knew they probably weren't armed. He was. "All right, Garrett. But be careful. You see anything, come back for me."

"Gee, Lash, I'm touched," Garrett quipped.

"Hell, I just don't want to be the one to have to tell that houseful of Brands that I let their brother get hurt."

Garrett smiled, then ducked into the dripping brush and scraggly trees, and soon disappeared from sight.

Lash went back to see if there was anything he could do to help Jessi.

She looked up before he got near, almost as if she could sense him coming toward her. Rain glistened on her cheeks and glimmered like diamonds on her eyelashes. Her hair was plastered to her face, dripping wet. She wore a yellow raincoat, like the rest of them, but she'd let the hood fall back, apparently not even aware of its absence.

"I need you, Lash," she said. Only the words came out chopped and forceful, not slow and sexy, the way he'd like to hear her say them.

Hell, what was he thinking along those lines for?

He hurried close and knelt beside her in the mud. Without a word, he plucked the Stetson from his own head and plopped it down on hers.

She sent him a quick look, the slightest smile acknowledging the hat, then turned her full attention back to the wet, pain-racked horse.

The animal's labored breathing and wide, wild eyes told Lash all he needed to know of its pain and fear. Instinctively, he stroked the smooth, wet neck, and leaned closer to speak soothingly to the horse.

He felt the animal's tense muscles relax a bit under his hand.

Then he felt Jessi's wide eyes on him. He slanted a glance her way as she shook her head. "I still can't get over it," she muttered.

"What?"

"Just keep doin' what you're doin'." Then she turned to the eldest Loomis brother. "Alan, you hold the light. Keith, Richard, you two stand back. She's liable to kick like a mule."

Lash didn't like the sounds of that. If Jessi went and got herself kicked again, he'd find himself in the uncomfortable position of having to explain to her overprotective brothers just how he'd managed to let her get hurt. It'd be especially uncomfortable since Garrett had left him behind to make sure she didn't.

"Be careful, Jessi," he told her, blinking rainwater from his eyes and pushing his now wet hair off his face.

She grunted, and he was sure she barely heard. Even more sure she would pay no attention to him, whether she'd heard him or not.

"Small-caliber gun, by the size of this hole in her shoulder. Twenty-two, probably. That's good." She fiddled around, and it was tough for Lash to see what she was doing. But he knew a second later, when the mare went rigid and released a choked, surprised sound of protest. Her hind leg jerked forward in a reflex action, and Lash left his post to lean sideways, thrusting his arm between the hoof and the small of Jessi's back.

His reward was a blow to the forearm that would no doubt leave a hoof-shaped bruise.

Jessi withdrew the hypodermic and turned around to frown at him. His arm remained wrapped tight around her, and he realized that it looked as if he were putting the moves on her. Sliding his arm around her waist for a quick cuddle in the midst of chaos. And he didn't want her thinking that. No way did he want her thinking that.

He moved his arm away. "She almost kicked you," he said, by way of explanation.

She offered him a slight smile. "No need to make up excuses, darlin'." Then she winked.

"I— Jess, I wasn't—"

She gave her head a quick shake and returned her attention to her patient. The mirth quickly faded from her eyes. They seemed troubled now, instead of mischievous. "If I can't stop the bleeding, we'll lose her." She nodded toward the mare's head. "How's she doing?"

Lash dragged his eyes away from Jessi, and returned to his position beside the horse's head just as the animal let it fall gently to the short, scraggly bed of wet grass. Her eyes closed, opened slowly, then closed again.

"Oh, Lord, is she dying?" the youngest Loomis cried. Lash thought his name was Keith, and he appeared to be around sixteen.

"It's just a tranquilizer," Jessi soothed.

"It's working, Jess," Lash told her. "She's relaxed now."

"Good. Lift that light higher, Alan. No, to the right. Yes, right there." She dug in her bag again, and raindrops glistened from the black leather as Alan shone the light down on it for her. "Lash, keep her calm. The tranquilizer will help some, but I don't dare give her too much just now. I have to get this bleeding stopped, and it's gonna hurt."

"Damn," Lash said, but he stroked and soothed and made soft sounds that the animal seemed to respond to. Jessi probed with some instrument, and the horse occasionally stiffened or jerked, but for the most part she remained still.

"How's he do that?" Alan Loomis asked.

"Has a way with women," Jessi replied, and Lash heard the two younger boys chuckle nervously. Good for Jessi, relieving their stress a little, even if it was at his expense. Then, Jessi said, "Okay, I've got it. The bullet's right here, wedged against bone. If I can get it out..." Surgical steel clanged as she changed tools, and then the horse went rigid again, its eyes flying open.

"Easy, girl, hold on now. It's gonna be just fine. Yeah. That's it." Lash stroked and spoke softly.

"I've got it!"

There was more clattering as she dropped the bullet into a waiting receptacle. By the time Garrett came back toward them, boots slapping the rain-wet ground to announce his presence, Jessi had already stitched up the wound and was applying thick layers of bandages to the mare's front shoulder. She finished and got to her feet, holding her bloodied gloves up in front of her.

"There's a stream where you can clean up a little," Alan Loomis offered. He took Jessi's arm and led her away into the darkness.

"You be careful near that stream," Garrett called after them. "This rain keeps up like this, and we're gonna be seeing trouble."

"Don't you worry, Garrett," Alan called. "I ain't gonna let nothing happen to this one."

Lash didn't like the friendly hand the man placed at the small of Jessi's back, or the way he could hear Alan's gushing compliments on her talents...then her beauty...as they walked away in the downpour.

"The mare?" Garrett asked, drawing Lash back to attention.

"Er...yeah. Right. Jess got the bullet out and stopped the bleeding. I think she'll be okay." He heard a soft laugh, and glanced off into the rainy darkness where Jessi had gone with that cow-eyed cowboy.

"Paul's theory was right," Garrett said. "Looks like they herded the cattle through that scrub lot to the old dirt road on the far side. There are tire tracks in the mud out there. Dualies."

"Dualies?" Lash echoed.

"Dual tires," Garrett clarified. "Had a semi out there. Maybe two."

"Damn. This is no small-time operation then."

"Nope. These boys are serious."

Voices carried on a stray wet breeze, and Lash heard Alan Loomis clearly. "The boys and I would be thrilled to come help you clean out that garage of Marisella's, sugar. We owe you for this."

Sugar?

"Thanks, Alan. And I won't be taking any pay for tending to the mare. You guys help me clean out that garage, and we'll call it even."

"You bet," he said. And this time, as they strolled into view, the jerk's arm was around her middle, and he turned to give her a big manly cowboy sort of hug. With them both wearing raincoats, it shouldn't have seemed as intimate as it did, but it still made Lash grate his teeth. "That mare's my pride and joy, hon. And I'd have lost her if it hadn't been for you."

Hon?

"That's my job, Alan."

Lash cleared his throat, and then wished he hadn't.

It not only got Jessi's attention, it got her big brother's, as well. Garrett was looking at him a little strangely.

"Isn't it time we get going?" Lash asked.

Jessi frowned at him. Garrett saved him, though. "Lash is right. I gotta get into town and alert the Rangers to be on the lookout for a couple of tractor-trailers full of prime beefers. Sooner the better."

Jessi nodded. "She shouldn't be walking on that leg at all," she told Paul. "And you have to get her in out of this rain. She needs to be warm and dry. I have a sling at home for lifting downed animals, if you—"

"We got one, too, Jessi. This ain't the first mishap we've had with a critter too big to toss over your shoulder. We'll bring out a wagon, and get her back to the stables nice and gentle. Don't you worry."

"I'll come by tomorrow to check on her," she said. "She'll need another shot of antibiotics, and clean bandages."

Alan grinned…in anticipation, Lash thought. "I'll be here, Jessi. You can show me how to take proper care of that wound until it heals."

Jessi nodded.

"Yeah," Lash said, without even realizing his mouth was running without brakes. "And I'll come along, too, in case you need any more help." Everyone looked at him. He cleared his throat. "I'd…er…like to get a look at this crime scene in daylight."

Garrett who'd rejoined the group shook his head, sent Lash a worried glance and then climbed into the pickup, which he'd left running. "I'll do everything I can to get those cows back to you, Paul."

"I know you will, Garrett. If there's anything I can do to help, you know where to find me."

Garrett touched the brim of his hat and turned the

wipers up a notch as Jessi and Lash climbed in the passenger side. Garrett didn't head back toward the ranch, but into the town of Quinn, and his office, instead. The rain just kept coming, and the creek was already running alarmingly high when they crossed the bridge just outside town. As they drove, Lash heard thunder rolling constantly, like the thundering hooves of a thousand stampeding cattle. The wind was picking up now, as well, adding to the chaos outside. It whipped tree limbs and weeds viciously, and sent the raindrops into a horizontal, slashing pattern. Those slate-dark clouds had thickened over the face of the moon until they obliterated it.

"Hell of a storm," Garrett observed. "I don't like it."

"I hope they get the mare inside fast." Jessi looked over her shoulder, as if she could still see the Loomis ranch, which of course she couldn't. "And they'd better remember to rub her down till she's completely dry," she went on. "Damn, I should have stayed."

"You couldn't do anything more, Jess," Lash said, hating the worry he heard in her tone. "They'll do right by the horse. Hell, Alan seemed as smitten with that animal as he is with you."

Jessi blinked twice and turned wide eyes on him. "What kind of an asinine remark is that?"

Lash shrugged. "Just an observation."

Garrett made a sound that was half grunt, half growl. "Jessi ain't interested in Alan Loomis."

Now Jessi glared at her brother instead of Lash. "Who says I'm not?"

"Hell, Jess, he drinks. Everybody knows that. And when he drinks he gets ornery." Garrett steered around a deep-looking puddle. The wipers slapped in time with the conversation.

"Well, maybe I like 'em ornery."

Garrett's jaw twitched, and Lash thought he was grating his teeth behind his thin lips. "He's trouble. Understand, Jessi? Trouble. You stay away from him."

"Or what?" she snapped, eyes flashing fire.

"Or I'll break his arm off at the shoulder and beat him over the head with it, hon." For some reason, Garrett's words made Lash grimace. Too damned visual. "The guy's got a mean streak, and I don't aim to see it turned loose on you."

"Garrett Brand, I'm a grown woman, and it's high time you stop treating me like a little girl. I'll see any man I want, you understand? Sooner or later I'm gonna marry someone, and I hate to be the one to tell you this, honey, but you and the boys *don't* get the privilege of picking him out for me. You aren't going to have any say at all, matter of fact."

Garrett grimaced and pulled into the small space in front of the sheriff's office. Rain was streaming from the eaves like rivers. "I know you're a grown woman, and I know you're gonna see men. Hell, Jess, it's tough for me to see fellas looking at you...the way they been lately. But I'll get used to it, I suppose. Still and all, that doesn't mean I can stand by and watch you make a mistake that could get you hurt. Please, hon. Tell me you ain't carrying a torch for that Loomis fella. He ain't good enough for you."

"Then who is?" She crossed her arms over her chest, leaned back in the seat and stared straight through the window. "Let's see, what about his brothers? Richard or Keith?"

"Richard's lazy. He'll never amount to anything. And Keith's too young for you, Jessi. You know that."

She shook her head. "So what about Freddy Ortega?"

"Freddy? The *bartender?* C'mon, Jess, you can do better than—"

"Bobby Joe Hawthorne?" she asked, interrupting him.

"That fool? Gambles away every nickel he earns, and—"

"Sam Bonander?"

"Sam's a womanizer. You watch out for that—"

"Lash Monroe?" she shouted.

Garrett stopped talking and just gaped at her. Lash's throat went so dry he couldn't have swallowed if he tried. Then Garrett looked at him, almost accusingly, and then he looked back at his sister in disbelief.

"Lash is too old for you," Garrett said, very softly. "And besides that, he's a drifter. He's gonna be leaving here soon." He looked past her again, at Lash. "Right, Lash?"

"Right. Absolutely. I always hated being in one place for too long, and—"

"So basically, big brother, you've eliminated just about every single Quinn male between the ages of eighteen and eighty. What you're saying is that no man in this town is good enough for me, right? So maybe I should join a convent, or turn gay, or something."

"Jess!"

She turned her back to Lash to poke her brother in the chest with her forefinger. "Let me tell you something, Garrett Brand. No one is going to pick my man for me, because I've already picked one out all by myself. You aren't going to have anything to say about it.''

''What man?'' Garrett asked. ''Who?''

She tossed her head, turned the other way, and poked Lash's chest, as well. ''And neither are you!''

''Hey, I'm just along for the ride, Jessi! This isn't my fight.''

''The hell it isn't,'' she muttered. Then she leaned across him, and she was warm and close and soft. Damn. But all she was doing was shoving his door open and glaring at him as she waited to be let out. He stared at her face in the glow of the dash lights, eyes flashing, cheeks red, lips parted. She was looking at him from underneath his too-big hat, her skin still rain-water fresh, and he thought he'd never known a woman who could compare. Not ever.

He got out, and held the door for her while the rain pummeled him. He couldn't take his eyes off her as she dashed to the front steps. He just stood there like an idiot, getting soaked to the skin.

Garrett tapped him on the shoulder, snapping him out of his little trance, and searched his face with a curious expression. Curious, and maybe a little bit worried.

Lash felt his face heat under Garrett's probing stare. ''Stop looking at me like that, Garrett. I don't have any more clue what she's talking about than you do.''

''Yeah, well, let's hope it stays that way. Otherwise...you and I are gonna have some serious talkin' to do.''

''Talking, huh?'' Lash refrained from rubbing his nose as he recalled the last time Garrett Brand had felt ''serious talkin''' was called for.

Garrett frowned at him one last time, and then gave

his head a shake and lit out, racing through the deluge to the office door, where his sister stood waiting, sheltered by the eaves. Lash followed, and only got himself more thoroughly soaked for his trouble by the time he ducked inside behind the other two. He could hear the rain drumming against the roof and slashing over the windows. The wind had taken to howling like a banshee.

Garrett reached for the thermostat on one wall and cranked it up. The tiny furnace hidden away in the small office-slash-jailhouse rattled and clanked to life, and in a few seconds Lash dared to peel off his yellow raincoat, shake some of the water off it and hang it on a hook near the door. Jessi and Garrett did likewise. Lash took the chance to venture up beside Jessi where she stood warming herself over the baseboard register.

Garrett had plopped down behind the desk and put in a call to the nearest Ranger station, asking them to set up roadblocks and keep an eye out for cattle trucks with questionable manifests. He reached out to turn on his computer.

Jessi marched across the room, letting Lash have the heat all to himself while she reached out to turn the computer off.

''What the—''

''You big lug, you can't go using a PC during a thunderstorm,'' she told her brother.

''I have a surge protector,'' he countered, turning it on again.

''Which is useless against lightning,'' she said. ''You get zapped and you'll be spending precious time shipping this thing off to be repaired.''

Sighing heavily, Garrett switched the monitor off once more. ''For a little chicken, you sure do a good job of playing the mother hen. Fine, you win. I'll do this the old-fashioned way.'' He reached for the file drawer, removed several folders, then armed himself with a pen.

''So what can I do to help?'' Lash offered, stepping closer to the desk to see that the files were those on each rustling incident in the area over the past six months. Garrett was apparently going to review them.

Garrett divided the stack in half and handed one pile to Lash. ''Gotta go over these cases until we know 'em by heart, Lash. There has to be something connecting them, some clue or *something* we're missing.''

Lash nodded, pulled up a wooden chair and bent over the files. He sat on the opposite side of the desk from Garrett, and he read until his eyes burned.

Sometime later, the aroma of fresh coffee tickled his nostrils and made his mouth water. Jessi leaned over him to set a steaming mug down on the desk. She handed a second mug to her brother. Lash looked up at her, noting the damp spots on her shirt and the darker color of her jeans below the knees. Her hair had dried a little, but damn, she had to be freezing. He was chilled himself.

''Anything else I can do to help here?'' she asked.

Before Garrett could answer, Jessi went on. '''Cause if there isn't, and it's all the same to you two, I'm thinkin' I'd just as soon head home.''

''I don't think so, Jess.'' Garrett's tone was gentle, but his words didn't sit any better with his sister for that.

''Why not?'' she asked. ''I can send one of the boys back with your pickup, so it isn't like I'd be leaving you stranded. Elliot's been dying to get involved in this case, anyway. He'd be glad to come—''

"You won't be leaving me stranded, kiddo, 'cause you won't be leaving me at all. Not in this." Garrett nodded toward the nearest window. As if to punctuate his warning, the lightning chose that moment to flash again, and the thunderclap that followed shook the entire building.

"It's just a thunderstorm. Jeez, Garrett, I've driven in worse."

"If you have, this is the first I've heard of it."

"Surprise, big brother—I don't tell you everything."

He glared. She glared right back.

"Garrett, I have so much to do. Lists to make, supplies to order—"

Sighing hard, Garrett shook his head. Then he looked at Lash, who felt like a spectator at a close boxing match. "You mind running her home for me, Lash?"

Jessi sputtered, as if to argue, then bit her lower lip as if to halt the words from coming forth. And Lash knew damn well she was furious at her brother for thinking she needed a chaperon to get home safely. Which made him wonder why she'd bitten back her fury.

She slid a sideways glance at Lash, and he could see the wheels turning behind those cunning, sexy-as-hell eyes. What was she up to?

"Oh, all right," she finally said. "If you insist, Garrett, I'll let Lash drive me home."

Garrett had noticed the change in her attitude, as well, it seemed, because he narrowed his eyes on her, then shifted his meaningful gaze to Lash. "Take my truck, see she gets safely inside, and then meet me back here. Shouldn't take you more than—'' he glanced at his watch ''—an hour. *At the most.*''

Lash nodded, getting the full gist of the man's message. No pulling off the road into some secluded, rain-veiled glen for a little one-on-one with Garrett's baby sister. Right. As if he needed that warning.

''Forty-five minutes, tops,'' Lash said, taking the keys from Garrett's outstretched hand.

Jessi stood looking from one to the other, and if Lash wasn't mistaken, the best word for the look she sent them was *glower.*

Lash went to the hook near the door and retrieved their yellow vinyl slickers. He handed one to Jessi and pulled the other over his head, poncho-style. It was still damp, and he winced at the chill.

With a final nod to Garrett, Lash dropped his hat on his head, reached out to yank Jessi's hood up so that it covered hers, opened the door and made a dash for the pickup. When he jumped in behind the wheel and slammed his door, Jessi was already clambering in the other side and slamming hers. Quick as a fox and twice as clever, he thought, turning the key, switching on the headlights and wipers. Then he watched her push her yellow hood down and swipe the droplets from her face with a delicate brush of her hand. She missed some. Her lashes still glistened with a diamond or two. The dash lights made them glow magically, made him want to kiss them away…

''Lash, you gonna sit there looking at me all night, or drive? I'm sure Garrett's set some kind of timer by now.''

Lash blinked, cleared his throat, then tore his gaze away from her. He shifted the truck into reverse and backed carefully out of the parking space. There was no traffic in town tonight. The weather had worsened dramatically while they'd been inside going over files. Even though a while ago, Lash wouldn't have thought it could get much worse. Only a lunatic would be out in this nasty weather. He had to drive slowly, and even then he could barely see. God, he hadn't realized it from inside Garrett's safe, dry office, but the storm was probably the most severe he'd ever seen. The rain came down in sheets over the windshield. The wipers, slapping at their highest speed, were barely effective at all.

"This is ridiculous," he muttered.

"Oh, I don't know. I think it's kinda nice," she said. She reached out a hand and flicked the radio on, fiddling with the buttons until a slow country song came wafting in to fill the space between them. Didn't seem to bother her in the least that the song was interrupted by crackling static with every flash of lightning. He could feel her eyes on him. But he didn't dare look at her. And it wasn't just because he was afraid to take his eyes off the road.

"It's getting worse," he announced, though he was sure she could see that perfectly well without being told. Lightning split the sky, and the radio crackled again before returning to its crooning melody.

"You can always pull off and wait for it to let up a little," she suggested.

Yeah, right. That would be brilliant. Take little Jessi Brand out parking in a thunderstorm. He kept driving. It took fifteen minutes to leave the town behind them, and the weather only worsened. He realized a short while later that he'd have been better off listening to her, because at least then they'd have been in town, with houses nearby, and maybe a phone to call Garrett from. Now they were on the long, deserted, muddy stretch of road that led back to the ranch, creeping along at a snail's pace. He glanced at his watch's luminous dial and groaned inwardly. Thirty minutes had passed. He wasn't going to make Garrett's deadline. Lord knew what the big cowboy would be thinking.

They approached the tiny bridge that spanned the usually small and slow-running creek. Lash noted with alarm that the water was high, way higher than normal, and way higher than it had been a couple of hours ago, when they drove in. He slowed the truck even further.

"It'll be fine," she said. "That bridge has held up during flooding before."

"You sure?" he asked.

"Sure I'm sure. Just go over it quickly. Gun it, Lash."

He stepped down on the accelerator, and the pickup lurched forward onto the surface of the bridge. Then Jessi screamed, "Stop!"

He jammed the brakes in a knee-jerk reaction to her shout, and looked at her to ask what the hell she was shouting about. But Jessi was already jumping out of the truck. Lash was baffled until he looked through the windshield again. There, huddled right in the center of the bridge, was a shivering, dripping-wet animal that appeared to be mostly made of rainwater and brown legs. Rolling his eyes and cussing, Lash got out of the truck, as well. Rain pounded him, and rivers of it ran down the sides of the poncho he wore, soaking his jeans and his boots in a matter of seconds. When he reached Jess, she was slowly creeping closer to the trembling fawn. She reached out for it, but it sprang to its spindly legs and stumbled backward, eyes wide, rainwater rolling from its sides. Jessi held out her hands. ‘‘Easy, now. Are you hurt, little one? Or just cold and afraid? There now. I’m not gonna hurt you.’’

Lash came up slowly beside her, and wanted to scold her for jumping out in the rain like that, but he couldn’t. She was too beautiful, even dripping-wet. The fawn had stopped retreating now. Its white-spotted coat twitched as it shivered, though, and the animal stared with eyes huge and afraid.

Those big brown eyes were heartbreaking.

‘‘She’s beautiful,’’ Jess was saying. ‘‘Oh, yes, you are. You’re beautiful.’’

‘‘Prettiest drowned rat I’ve ever seen,’’ Lash said. He had to speak loudly to be heard over the rain, and the animal flinched in response to his voice. ‘‘Let’s just grab her and put her in the truck, Jess, and get out of here.’’

She nodded, but just as she stepped close enough to make a grab at the fawn, the animal’s head came up and turned to the right. Its delicate ears perked forward, and its baby-size tail flashed up straight. It whirled and ran gracefully off the bridge, disappearing into the rain-drenched woods on the far side. Jessi squinted off in the direction it had gone, then pointed, smiling. Lash saw the flash of a larger tail running along beside the little one. Nodding, he met Jessi’s eyes. ‘‘Looks like she found her mama,’’ he said. He took her arm, turning her toward the pickup. Then he paused, because there was a roar in his ears. Different from the howl of the wind, and definitely not thunder. ‘‘What the—’’

He turned his head in the direction the sound seemed to be coming from, and then frowned, because he wasn’t sure what he was seeing. It looked like…

‘‘Flash flood!’’ Jessi shouted.

Lash reached out for her just as the wall of water

unleashed its fury on the tiny bridge. His hand caught hers. A torrent flooded over them, slamming into his side and washing up around his waist, the current fierce and pulling at him, pulling at her, as if determined to snatch her away from his grip. Lash held tight to her hand, yelling at her to hold on. He tried to hold his footing, tried to back off the damned bridge and onto solid ground before it was too late, but the force of the water just kept shoving at him, trying to knock him off balance.

He sought for something to hold on to, something to grab to pull them both to safety, but there was only Jessi's cold, wet hand in his, and the roar of the water, and the pressure of it. And her eyes meeting his, filled with a terror that made his stomach clench.

There was a cracking sound as the bridge gave way, and the wood under his feet dissolved beneath the onslaught. He and Jessi were hurled forward, pitched into the frigid turmoil of the flood, tossed up and sucked back under the waves again and again as they were dragged downstream. He managed to get an arm around Jessi, then another, and he held tight to her as he struggled to get their heads above water. But it was no use. He was at the mercy of the flood. He only hoped they'd both survive.

Chapter 5

Garrett looked at his watch for the tenth time in as many minutes. The hour he'd given Lash to get back to the office was up, and then some. Of course, the rain had gotten worse. Weather might be holding them up. But he just couldn't shake the nagging feeling that something was up. And though he'd told Wes he didn't believe his suspicion about Jessí having a crush on Lash, he couldn't get the thought out of his mind now.

If Lash so much as—

The telephone on his desk interrupted his thoughts with a soft bleat, and Garrett snatched it up.

"Oh, good, you're still there."

It was Chelsea's voice and, as always, it put a dreamy smile on his face. He settled back in his chair, the worry fading. "That's not good at all," he told her. "I'd rather be home with you."

"Yes, but I'm glad I caught you all the same. We just got a bulletin over the radio. There are flash flood warnings posted for Sycamore creek. So you'd best take the long way home.''

His smile died a sudden death. ''Honey, did Jessi and Lash make it back there yet?''

Silence.

''Honey?''

''No. Garrett, were they taking—''

''They're fine,'' he said, hearing the panic in her voice. ''I'm sure they're fine. Look, just to be safe, why don't you send the boys out? I'll meet them at the bridge. All right?''

''Garrett, you don't think—''

''Don't worry, darlin'.'' But she was worried. He knew her too well to think otherwise. And he was worried, too. ''Send the boys. I'll call you as soon as we find them.''

''Be careful, Garrett.''

''Always,'' he told her. ''I love you, Chelsea.''

''Me too.''

Garrett put the phone down, and looked again at the rain slashing against the windows. ''Damn.'' He grabbed a raincoat and a flashlight, then headed out to borrow a car from the first person he could rouse.

Jessi clung to Lash with everything in her, stark terror giving her additional strength. The cold water filled her nose and mouth and blinded her eyes, dragging her into its tumultuous depths again and again, despite her struggles. The two of them pitched and rolled at the whim of the waves, and there was nothing she could do but hold on and wait it out. Each time the current forced her to the surface, she dragged in desperate gulps of precious air, only to be sucked beneath the frigid, filthy waters once more. More than once she was slammed against debris, and she never knew for sure just what had hit her—logs or limbs or what. And each time her body was yanked forcefully, Lash would only tighten his grip on her. He refused to let go. No matter what hit them, he refused to let her go.

The weight of the raincoat was tugging her down, and it seemed Lash knew. Somehow he wrested it away from her and let the current carry it off. He'd lost his, as well, she realized, or maybe he'd shed it deliberately.

They were battered and dragged and pounded in the water's fury for what seemed like hours, though it could have only been minutes. And then, suddenly, the force eased, and it was Lash who was pulling her, tugging her through the still-rushing water. She was barely aware of the shallows, the stony bottom dragging beneath her legs, the lack of water over her head, the rain pounding down on her. Still drenched by the floodwaters, it took a full minute for her to realize that she was no longer immersed in them. Instead, she was stretched out on the muddy bank, Lash lying beside her, raised up on one elbow to bend over her, his face inches from her own. Water dripped from his chin into the hollow of her neck as she blinked her eyes open and met his. She shivered. God, she'd never been so cold.

"Jessi? God, Jessi, are you all right? Come on, darlin', talk to me. Tell me you're okay."

She closed her eyes, coughed, and nodded slowly.

Lash sighed loudly, and it was as if his body melted, in relief or in exhaustion. She wasn't sure which. Maybe a combination of the two. But the result was the same. His upper body lowered to rest atop hers, his arms anchored around her as if they were still clinging to one another for dear life. She slipped her arms around his waist, feeling the water squeeze from his shirt in response to the pressure of her embrace. "I thought we… God, Lash, I've never been so frightened in my life."

"I know," he whispered, his fingers threading through her wet hair. She could feel his warmth seeping through their wet clothing, infusing her chilled flesh, and she clung tighter when he moved as if to get up.

"Don't," she told him. "Please, Lash, don't go running away from me this time. Just hold me…just for a minute."

Head lifted, he stared down into her eyes. He didn't want to get up. She could see that very clearly.

"I'm cold, Lash. I'm freezing."

"Me too."

"You didn't let me go," she whispered, blinking up into his eyes. "I can't believe you didn't let me go."

"I'd have to be nuts to let you go," he replied, and seemed as surprised to be blurting out those words as she was to be hearing them.

He touched her face, just a slight caress of his chilled fingertips across her cheek. And it was so intimate, so honest, that touch. It was her undoing.

"Will you kiss me this time, Lash?"

Very slowly, he lowered his mouth to hers. Gently, he kissed her, and she could taste the cold water on his lips. She parted her own, and felt him tremble. She wondered if it was from the cold, or something else. Something like the finger of heat that was sending tremors of longing through her.

When he would have lifted his head away, she slipped her hands up over his wet shoulders, higher, into his hair, and pressed her mouth tighter to his. With her tongue, she touched his lips, and when they parted she slipped inside the inviting warmth of his mouth.

He groaned softly, deeply, and his weight shifted, his body moving to cover hers completely. Instinctively, she moved her hips against his, and felt the answering motion of his, arching against her. His hands slid under her, then down to cup her buttocks, and he squeezed and pressed her tight to him, moving intimately. She parted her thighs to bring him to the place where she longed for him to be. She shuddered, clinging, kissing, moaning softly as her hips moved with his in the age-old rhythm of woman and man. The rain pounded down on their heated bodies as they mimicked the act of lovemaking, fully clothed, pressing urgently against one another without consummating their desire.

But she knew it was going to happen. And she wanted it to happen. And she knew he wanted it, too. The hardness pressing insistently between her legs was more than he could deny this time. And she didn't think he'd even try.

He ground against her, his mouth devouring hers as if he were starving for the taste of her. Jessi pulled her hands from around him, and slipped them between their bodies, pulling the snap and zipper of her jeans until they came open, tugging at the buttons of her shirt until they tore free.

Lash stiffened, and slowly lifted his head. And then his body, up and away from hers, leaving her cold and alone. He stared down at her—blouse gaping, breasts naked and tingling beneath his heated gaze, jeans parted as if in invitation. He stared down at her, and with one trembling hand, he reached out, touched her breast, his thumb running slowly over the aching peak. Jessi closed her eyes and arched her back.

The hand moved away.

"I can't do this, Jessi."

It was like a slap in the face.

Her eyes flashed open, and she felt her cheeks warm. He was still kneeling beside her, staring down at her, and she felt vulnerable and exposed to those eyes, instead of aroused and caressed by them, as before. "I d-don't understand." It was difficult to speak. She was breathless, her heart hammering against her ribs so loudly he had to hear it. She'd never been this aroused. Never.

"Jessi..." He shook his head, then averted his eyes. "I can't. Look, this is just stress. The aftermath of damned near drowning together. Understand? This isn't—"

"Liar!"

He shook his head, keeping his eyes averted.

"Look at me, dammit."

He did. He turned his head, slowly, and looked at her, and his gaze dropped from her eyes to her lips, to her still-uncovered breasts. She shivered at the chill touch of the wind on her nipples. "Jesus, Jessi, fix your shirt." But his gaze didn't change its focus.

She sat up, leaning back on her hands, leaving her blouse just the way it was. "You want me just as much as I want you, Lash Monroe. Admit it."

Lash licked his lips. He shook his head in denial, but continued staring. "It isn't right, Jessi."

"Feels right to me." She got up onto her knees, bringing her exposed chest up to eye level for him. Let him deny it now, she thought. "You're gonna say it's wrong because you're older, aren't you?"

Eyes transfixed, he nodded.

"But ten years isn't all that much older. And you know that as well as I do."

"It's not just that."

"No?"

His tongue darted out to moisten his lips again. "I'm a drifter, Jessi. You know that. I can't stay—"

"I didn't ask you to stay," she whispered, and she reached down to slip her fingers into his hair. He moved his head a little closer, closed his eyes, bit his lip.

"Please fix your shirt, Jessi. I'm begging—"

"Tell me you want me," she told him.

"You're killing me."

She leaned in, just enough. Her taut nipple brushed his lips, and then she backed away again.

Lash's eyes flew open, and they blazed. His hands clasped her waist, hard and without warning, and he jerked her close, capturing her breast in his mouth as he trembled from head to toe. Jessi clutched handfuls of his hair as his tongue flayed her nipple, his lips capturing it, suckling it. His teeth catching it and pinching with delicious pressure. She closed her eyes and let her head fall backward, pulling him closer, holding him to her breast and craving things she'd never even thought about before.

"Jessi! Lash!"

At the sounds of male voices shouting their names, Jessi's eyes flew open, and Lash jerked away from her as if he'd been electrocuted.

His eyes met hers, unspoken need flashing from their pale, silver-blue depths. She released a shuddering sigh, got to her feet, and righted her clothes as best she could. She could easily have screamed in frustration, but she resisted the impulse. Barely.

She heard a low barking, and turned to see Ol' Blue's tall, sagging shape loping toward them from farther up the slope. Behind it, bobbing beams of light showed the location of her brothers. She waved half-heartedly, knowing they'd be worried, and knowing she had to reassure them. And yet wishing she could take Lash by the hand and run off into the night where no one could find them. No one could stop them. Damn, she'd been so close!

"Here," she called. "We're here. We're all right."

"Jessi!"

The beams of light bobbed faster, and then her brothers ran into view. Wes reached her first, sweeping her into his arms and hugging the breath out of her. He kissed her wet hair and held her tight, while Ol' Blue barked at her and raced around her legs, moving more enthusiastically than she'd ever seen him move. He'd be exhausted when he got home. And chilled through, as well. She stroked his wet fur. "You're too old to be playing hero, Blue."

"You okay?" Wes asked.

"Yeah," she breathed. "Lash pulled me out. If he hadn't..." She lowered her eyes, shaking her head.

Elliot slammed Lash's shoulder. "Good man," he announced. Jessi looked at Lash and saw the horrible guilt on his face. It was eating him alive. "Hell," Elliot went on, "Garrett will probably even forgive you for the pickup."

Lash looked at Elliot, brows lifted in an unspoken question, and Jessi, too, frowned at her brother. "I kind of lost track of the truck," Lash said. "Is it—?"

"Nose down in the creek, a mile upstream," Ben

said softly. "When we spotted it, we thought..." He didn't finish. Instead, he pried Jessi from Wes's arms and hugged her himself.

"There's Garrett," Wes said, pointing to another flashlight beam on the opposite bank. Cupping his hands around his mouth, he shouted, "Garrett! We found them! They're okay!"

The beam of light on the other side stopped moving, then lifted in an effort to reach them. Wes shone his light on Jessi so that Garrett could see for himself that she was in one piece. Then Garrett's voice drifted across the rapid water. "Take them home. I'll meet you there."

Jessi bit her lip, and hoped no one would notice the missing buttons on her blouse. The old hound dog barked once more, and she looked down to see Blue sitting at her feet, looking up at her with a question in his big brown eyes. "Yes," she said. "You done good, old boy." And she stroked his ears and whispered, "But your timing could have been better."

Lash's head came around, and his eyes met hers, letting her know he'd heard that remark. She held his gaze, and wished to God she could tell what he was thinking. But she couldn't read the man. He was better at hiding his feelings than anyone she'd ever known.

Damn. Was he regretting the untimely interruption? Or maybe regretting that he'd lost his stoic resistance to her for just a moment?

Jessi was soaking in a hot bath, and Lash knew she'd be all right. Chelsea was dancing attendance on her, as if she were a fragile little china doll in danger of shattering in a strong wind. Ol' Blue had taken up residence in Jessi's room, and he was convinced the hound had decided to watch over her until *he* assured himself she was okay. Damn dog was close to human. And as protective of Jess as if he were one of her brothers.

She didn't need their help, though. Lash was only just beginning to get a feel for the real Jessi Brand. And she was tougher than he'd given her credit for.

Smarter, too. There was no longer any doubt in Lash's mind about what Jessi had meant when she told her brother that she had chosen her own man. She'd meant *him.* It scared the hell out of him. Especially when he thought about certain other remarks she'd dropped his way lately. Like that one about her always getting what she wanted.

Damn. If the boys hadn't come along when they had, he'd have…he'd have…

Damn.

Walk in the Spirit, and ye shall not fulfil the lust of the flesh, he thought to himself. It didn't help. He still lusted. And Jessi was right, ten years or so wasn't all that big an age difference. But for crying out loud, Lash Monroe had known what he wanted all his life. Freedom. Solitude. He wanted to be untethered, able to roam where the wind took him, whenever he pleased. He didn't want a relationship, and he knew better than to think Jessi had a casual fling on her mind. No, she'd want more. She'd want commitment. Imagine, Lash thought, just imagine being crazy enough to plunk himself down in the midst of another big family. A family chock-full of older brothers, all of whom would hate his guts for soiling their baby sister with his unworthy touch. Imagine the tension, the arguments. Damn, this thing with Jessi would end up making *all* of them miserable, himself included.

Besides, it wasn't as if he loved her. Any red-blooded male would respond to her. She was gorgeous, and sexy as hell, and clearly attracted to him. And damned if he could figure where she'd managed to learn it, with her brothers as guard dogs, but she sure as hell knew what she was doing.

So, he wasn't acting illogically to want her. He was only human. Hell, Saint Francis of Assisi would want her! But that was as far as it went. And Lash needed to keep that in mind. Maybe find himself a casual fling in town to relieve the pressure. And keep his distance from Jessi Brand at all costs.

He thought then about the women he'd met while he'd been here in Quinn. Beautiful sloe-eyed Mexican women who could keep a man awake nights. Blue-eyed Texas girls with big hair and bright smiles and bodies to die for. He thought hard about those girls. And he felt cold inside. Couldn't even work up enough interest to dwell on any one of them for more than a second.

Who the hell was he kidding? He didn't want any other woman. He wanted this one. He'd never been hit as forcefully with desire's hammer until right now. He felt as if he were under some sort of spell, one that wouldn't let go.

But he owed Garrett. Owed him a lot. And Lash wasn't the kind of man who could pay back his debt by committing what would be seen as the ultimate betrayal.

And that was final. Even if it killed him.

He resolved not to think any more about what it might be like to make love to Jessi Brand, to hold her hot, naked body close to his own. To run his hands along those firm thighs, and taste, just once more, those round, luscious breasts, and kiss those plump lips.

He shifted in his seat, and tried real hard to bring his attention back to the conversation taking place around him.

"Might as well spend the night here, Lash," Garrett was saying. "No sense trying to drive back to town now."

Lash swallowed hard. Maybe he ought to *walk* back into town. "I'm real sorry about your pickup. I never would have stopped on that bridge, Garrett, but there was this baby deer lying there, and—"

"I know. You've already explained all that." Garrett smiled crookedly and dropped a big hand onto Lash's shoulder. "The pickup's insured, Lash. I don't give a damn about that. Jessi said you could have probably dragged yourself out of the current a hell of a lot sooner, just by letting go of her. But you didn't, Lash." The hand on Lash's shoulder squeezed. "You saved my sister's life. And I think you know that there's not much on this planet I hold closer to my heart than that hellcat baby sister of mine. You're one hell of a good friend. Feel free to drown my pickup any old time."

Lash couldn't look Garrett in the eye. His stomach twisted up in knots, and guilt washed over him just as forcefully as that flash flood had done. Damn.

"Consider yourself part of the family from here on in," Elliot said.

"Anything you need, Lash," Ben added. "Anytime, anywhere, you call on us. You hear?"

Lash forced himself to meet their gazes, one by one, and he nodded. Last, he faced Wes. His dark onyx eyes were glinting.

Wes took a step forward, drew a thoughtful breath, and finally extended a hand. Lash blinked in surprise, but took it, and returned Wes's firm shake. Wes never said a word. But he didn't have to.

Lash felt ill. These men were not the bullies of his childhood, out to cause him trouble and make him miserable. These were good, honest men who thought of him as a friend, welcomed him into their midst, treated him like a brother, for God's sake. They *trusted* him.

The telephone rang. Garrett picked it up and spoke softly, then glanced toward Lash and held it out. "You have an aunt Kate?"

"My foster mother's sister," Lash muttered, and took the phone, feeling his self-appointed aunt couldn't have picked a worse time to call.

He covered the receiver with one hand and glanced at the brothers. "Sorry for the interruption. This might be a while. She feels it's her civic duty to check on every one of us periodically and grill us about every aspect of our lives. No matter where I go, she manages to track me down."

"I'm heading up to bed anyway," Garrett said. "Why don't you take Adam's old bedroom, Lash? There are some of his clothes in the closet, so you can get dry. They oughtta fit."

"Thanks," Lash said, eager to get out from under their grateful eyes. Adam was the one missing brother, the one still living in New York and working for an international bank. But with Lash's luck, he'd show up in time for the lynching. He watched the brothers head toward the stairs, then covered the phone again, briefly. "Which room would that be?"

"Second to the last one on the right," Elliot said. "Right between mine and Jessi's."

Lash's heart tripped over itself, and he felt heat creep up his neck and into his ears. "Oh."

He dragged his gaze from theirs, though he could still feel their eyes on him as they marched up the stairs. Then he drew the phone to his ear. ''Hello, Aunt Kate,'' he said.

He could still hear the Brand brothers talking upstairs. Extolling his virtues and his heroism, he imagined, groaning. Damn, if they knew the truth…

He answered Kate's questions without thinking. Told her he really wasn't interested in hearing what his so-called ''brothers'' were up to, and finally put the phone down.

It didn't matter that the Brands didn't know the truth, he thought, because he wasn't going to so much as *think* about touching Jessi again. It was simple. Mind over matter. Willpower. He could do this.

He sat there a long time, telling himself just how easy it would be. Then he headed up to his assigned bedroom, took a long, hot shower, changed into some dry duds and crawled into the welcome warmth of the bed. And thought about Jessi lying in her own bed, naked, maybe, thinking of him, maybe. Touching herself gently and closing her eyes and whispering his name. Just a wall away from him.

Lord!

When he finally fell asleep, his willpower dissolved along with his consciousness.

The dream spun its seductive web around him. He was on that same bank with Jessi, only this time it was grassy and lush instead of mud-slick and cold. The creek ran calm, and glittered beneath a blazing white sun. But the storm raging inside him was a fierce one. They were naked, the two of them, arms and legs twined as they undulated in a chaos of passion. He could feel her body tight around the length of him, and he was so close...so close...

And then a lasso settled around his neck from some unseen place, and yanked him away from her. He heard Jessi cry out...and he stared back at her...but she faded, slowly, like a damp mist evaporating in the sun. And then he saw himself, sitting atop a great black horse. And he was dressed oddly...like some saddle tramp from an old western flick. The horse stood still beneath a giant oak tree, and Lash forced himself to look up at the sturdy branch that stretched above his head. A noose dangled from it, swaying softly in the breeze.

It lowered to eye level. He wanted to bat it away, but his hands were bound behind his back. The ghostly noose settled itself around his neck, pulled itself tight with a sudden jerk that left him gasping.

He lowered his gaze, tried to swallow and couldn't.

Around him, the Brand brothers—all five of them, even the missing Adam—sat their mounts. They wore long, time-yellowed dusters and had six-shooters strapped to their hips. None of them had taken the time to shave this morning, by the looks of them.

Garrett puffed on a hand-rolled smoke, then flicked it to the ground. "Any last words, Monroe?"

Lash tried to speak, but couldn't. The damned noose was too tight.

"Didn't think so," Garrett said. Then he nudged his horse up beside Lash's, leaned over and raised up a hand. He slapped the rump of Lash's mount hard, and the horse reared beneath him, and then bolted right out from under him.

Lash felt himself falling and he closed his eyes, waiting for the snap of his neck that would come when he reached the end of this rope. Falling, falling, falling...

He jerked upright in the bed, gasping for air and clawing at his neck. But there was no rope there, and no lynching tree in sight.

There was only Jessi Brand, smiling sweetly behind her seductress's eyes. He blinked to clear the dream away, but she remained. He was awake. And she was here, in his bedroom.

"It just occurred to me," she said, very softly. "I never thanked you properly...for saving my life."

Chapter 6

"You shouldn't be in here," he said. His voice was hoarse, but he attributed that to last night's cold water, and the fact that he'd just dreamed of slow strangulation. "Your brothers—"

"It's morning, Lash. Garrett and Wes have gone to see about the pickup and to help the crew repairing the bridge. Garrett had to return the car he borrowed in town to come home last night, too. Elliot and Ben are out checking the stock, and Chelsea took the baby into town for his checkup." She moved closer and sat on the edge of the bed. "She had to take the long way around."

Lash swallowed hard and slid toward the other side.

"When you didn't get up in time for breakfast, I was afraid something might be wrong," she whispered. She reached up, as if to untie the sash of the satiny pink robe she wore. But instead, she just toyed with the dangling ends of it, arousing him more than if she'd yanked it off and sat there naked.

"Guess I was tired," Lash stammered. Dammit, he couldn't stand much more of this. He could see she wasn't wearing a thing beneath that robe. Her breasts were perfect, and he could taste them again just by looking at their shape, so clearly outlined in the thin fabric. If she crawled into this bed…if she touched him…

"Yeah, me too," she said with a careless shrug. "I don't know, though, it seems I haven't been sleeping much at all lately."

Damn. He hadn't been sleeping well, either, and he knew she was well aware of that fact. She had to be. She was the cause of it. And he'd pretty much revealed the direction of his thoughts last night.

He cleared his throat. "So, uh, how are you?"

"Bruised in all the places I can see, and it feels even worse in the places I can't." She smiled at him, a devilish look in her eyes. "But I'd have been a heck of a lot worse off if it hadn't been for you."

"I didn't do anything any other man wouldn't have done."

"Only if the other man were one of my brothers." She turned around and leaned her back against his headboard, drawing her knees up so that she could wrap her arms around them. "I think that's why I'm so drawn to you, Lash. 'Cause I never expected to find any man who could measure up to those brothers of mine. But then I met you, and you do it in spades."

He sensed she was being sincere with him. Not laying it on to soften him up. And it touched him, in spite of himself. "That's probably the nicest compliment anyone's ever given me,'' he told her. ''Especially since I think so highly of your brothers, Jessi.''

She nodded. ''I know you do. That makes all this kinda hard on you, doesn't it?''

Damn. Straight to the point, again. She sure didn't pull punches or play games. ''Yeah, it does. Friendship is something sacred, Jessi. A person would be foolish to let something as fleeting as…as lust get in the way of it.''

''So you're pretty sure that's all there is between us? Just…lust? Just two people who can't stop thinking about tearing each other's clothes off and—''

''Don't.'' He met her big brown eyes and felt it again. Desire, rushing through him like some internal brand of hellfire. Searing-hot.

''I love my brothers, too, you know,'' she told him, holding his gaze trapped in her own. ''But not enough to let them run my life, Lash. And I can't quite swallow that you care more for my brothers than even I do. So I'm thinking there's something else bothering you.''

He drew a breath, then looked away.

''You wanna tell me about it?''

He shook his head, but heard himself talking to her all the same. ''I was raised by a foster family, Jessi. A great big oversize family, just like this one.''

''And it was terrible?''

''No, it wasn't terrible,'' he said quickly, but he lowered his head when he said it.

She dipped her head, searching his face.

''Okay, parts of it were pretty awful, but parts were okay. It's just that it was enough to convince me that a settled-down life with a dependent little wife and a bunch of relatives tripping over each other wasn't what I wanted. I want freedom, Jess. I want to be able to sling my stuff in a bag and take off whenever the urge hits me. Go wherever my feet feel like taking me. No guilt trips or balls and chains dragging me down. No anchors holding me still."

"That all sounds real nice."

He nodded. "It has been."

"So you think I'm looking to hook myself around your throat like an anchor, Lash? You think I'm gonna cry to my brothers if you and I do what we both want to do, and then you up and walk away?" She pierced him with her eyes. "C'mon, do you really think I'd do that to you?"

He spoke, but his voice was so hoarse his words came out unintelligible. He cleared his throat and tried again. "I don't know. I guess…I guess I don't think you'd do that. But—"

"And you want me, right?"

He closed his eyes. "One of the good things about being raised by the Reverend Mr. Stanton, Jess, was that he taught me right from wrong."

"And you think making love to me would be wrong?"

"I know it would."

She drew a breath, then let it out all at once. "You know something, Lash, I don't think I believe you. I think you're afraid of me. Afraid that once wouldn't be enough, and that being with me might just smash that drifter's way of life right to smithereens."

His eyes widened, and he felt as if she'd hit him between the eyes with a mallet. Could she be—? No. No way in hell. She wasn't even close to the truth.

She got slowly to her feet, straightened her robe, and started back to the door, but paused there, facing him again. "But I'll tell you this much. I know it's real, because I feel it in my gut. It's going to happen, Lash. If not now, then later. You know it as well as I do. I want you, and I'm not ashamed to admit it. You want me, too, though you're having a little more trouble accepting it. We're both adults, and you don't have one thing to be afraid of. Not me, and not my brothers. I think what you're really scared of is yourself. But this thing between us isn't gonna go away, you know, no matter how much you try to ignore it." Her hand touched the knob, like a caress. He couldn't breathe. "When you're ready for me, Lash, you just let me know. But don't wait too long, 'cause I'm not going to."

Then she slipped away and he managed to breathe again. Damn, he was in trouble here. Deep trouble. It would take a saint to resist that woman.

And Lash Monroe was no saint.

She was wearing him down. She sensed it.

The morning sun had burned off the dark clouds of the night before, and dried the rain-ravaged ground. Jessi was grateful to be alone in the house as she washed up the breakfast dishes and did a load of laundry. The boys had refused to let her work in the barns today, insisting she sleep late and take it easy after her episode last night. So she'd just make up for it by doing some of the indoor chores. It was hot already. The coming day was going to be the scorcher after the storm, she predicted, and she dressed accordingly: cut-off shorts and a sleeveless tank that hugged her curves. Funny, she'd never noticed whether her clothes hugged her curves before. It was Lash, she decided. He made her feel like…like a woman. A sexy, desirable woman. And the reason he made her feel that way was that he wanted her. He wanted her so much it scared him witless. Wanted her even though he was determined not to. Wanted her so much he wasn't sleeping nights thinking about it.

Oh, yeah, she knew. She couldn't help but know. It was in his eyes every time he looked at her, and getting more and more evident all the time. Hell, it was going to be obvious to everyone in the house pretty soon.

She was at the sink, drying coffee mugs with a dish towel, when she sensed him behind her. She took her time about turning to acknowledge his presence. Let him look his fill, she thought, feeling a little trill of excitement sing through her veins. She *liked* this feeling. It was so new, so thrilling.

He cleared his throat, so she finally glanced over her shoulder at him. "Oh. You're up."

"Your brothers will skin you for dressing like that," he observed.

Jessi frowned at him. "It's how I always dress when it's hot outside. Gee, Lash, you've seen me in shorts before."

His gaze slid down her legs, slowly, and came back up again. "Maybe I have," he muttered.

"Maybe it's different now that you know you want me, though."

"Jessi, don't—"

The screen door banged and Elliot traipsed in, followed closely by Ben. They looked at Jessi, then at Lash, then at each other. Ben shrugged. Elliot grinned, and came forward to take the dish towel away from her.

"Thought we told you to take it easy today, sis. You never could follow an order."

"And probably never will," she said, but she filled

a cup with the fresh coffee she'd made and sauntered to the table, electing to sit before one of them told her to, in which case she'd be forced to remain standing, just on principle. "Have you heard from Garrett?"

"Yeah, he called from the office. Damage to the bridge wasn't as bad as they thought, and the repairs ought to be finished by tomorrow. Meanwhile, he got a loaner from the dealer, so he has wheels again while he waits for the insurance company to settle up on his pickup." Elliot's grin was infectious.

"What's so funny about that?" Jessi asked.

Elliot shook his head. It was Ben who said, "The loaner is a little bit of a car that looks, according to Garrett, like a toaster on wheels. He can barely sit upright in it."

Jessi laughed out loud at the image, and Elliot did, as well. A low hissing sound came from the living room, and Jessi frowned and went to check it out. "Uh-oh. Look at this, you guys."

Her brothers and Lash followed her, and paused at the sight of the scene being played out on the floor. The old cat, Pedro, was poised, rear end in the air, chest to the floor, hissing and batting a paw at Ol' Blue. The big hound lifted one eyebrow, then closed his eyes again with a tired sigh.

"Blue, you lazy dog, he wants to play," Jessi said.

Blue made a groaning sound and didn't stir.

"Either that or he wants to fight," Elliot said. "You sure that old cat isn't gonna claw Blue's eyes out?"

"He's just feeling him out, seeing how much he'll put up with," Jessi told him. She walked into the living room, coffee mug in hand, to bend down and stroke the hound dog's head. "Blue, how come you're ignoring Pedro?"

Blue lifted his head high enough to reach up and lick her face.

''Hell, Jessi, I think Blue's just jealous. He never showed you so much affection until you came lugging that cat home,'' Elliot said.

''Could be that he knows how close he came to losing you in that flood last night,'' Ben put in, speaking low and soft. She knew he was thinking about his wife, and how much it hurt to lose someone you loved. But her brain quickly jumped back to what Elliot had said. About Blue loving her more now because of the competition. Maybe that thought merited some more study.

''Well, guys, I have to leave you now. Keep an eye on these two for me, will you?''

The three of them frowned. It was Lash who spoke. ''Where to?''

''Marisella's house...my house, I mean. The Loomis boys are supposed to help me hoe out that garage today to pay me back for taking care of that mare. And I have a contractor coming at noon to check the place out and give me an estimate on the remodeling. I'll be out most of the day. I want to check on the Loomises' mare while I'm at it. And if it gets too late, I'll probably just spend the night at my soon-to-be new clinic. So if I don't come home, don't go calling out the National Guard, okay?'' She paused near the door, where her overnight bag was packed and waiting.

Ben shook his head. ''You had a rough night, Jess. Maybe you ought—''

''I had a wonderful night,'' she said. ''Damn near a perfect one.'' Her gaze slanted deliberately toward Lash, but he quickly looked away.

''Nearly drowning agrees with you, huh, sis?'' Elliot asked.

"*Not* drowning is what agrees with me. I could have died last night, but I didn't. And today I feel like a new woman."

"And I suppose you're taking that old clunker of a truck," Ben asked.

"That's what it's for, brother dear."

"You...um...oughtta change first."

She paused on her way to the door to stare at Lash, who seemed to be rather surprised that he'd just blurted what he had. As if he had any right to express an opinion about what she wore. "Why would I want to change? It'll be ninety-five by noon."

Lash shrugged. "You want those Loomis boys concentrating on what they're doing, don't you?"

She smiled. Maybe Elliot had been right. "I think I'll take that as a compliment. See you guys later." And she would. She'd see Lash later, at least. Because she had let him know she'd be there, alone, all night, in Marisella's house. Or at least she knew she'd be there alone. He might wonder. Maybe enough to stop by later, just to check in and reassure himself. Lord, she could only hope.

Lash fixed fence, counted cattle and repaired a loose shingle on the barn roof. Then he took his own car into town—the long way around, since the bridge wasn't fixed yet—and spent the afternoon going over the rustling incidents with Garrett in his office. They pieced together the bits of information until they had a pretty good picture of the men responsible. It was a big-time operation, judging by the hundreds of head that had been stolen over the past weeks. And in order to make such an operation profitable, there had to be a steady market for the stolen cattle. One not so far away as to make transporting them too costly. All signs pointed south. Garrett suspected the cows were being smuggled across the border and marketed in Mexico. But where, and by whom?

Though Lash fought hard to keep his mind on the case, he couldn't stop thinking about Jessi, and the way she'd looked when she left the ranch this morning. She'd changed in the past few days. It was as if all of a sudden she knew just how attractive she was, and it seemed to make her giddy with the power of it. She used to look innocent and cute in cutoff shorts and tank tops. Now she looked like some man's secret fantasy. Beguiling. Seductive. A siren. A fox.

Or…maybe she only looked that way to him. Maybe he was the one who'd changed. He'd certainly become aware of her as more than his boss's baby sister.

Thing was, he had a feeling those Loomis boys had noticed that about her a long time ago. And he didn't like the notion of their eyes feasting on those long, gorgeous legs of hers, or of the thoughts that might be racing through their minds. Suppose one of them put his hands on her? Suppose she didn't object? Hell, she was going to be in that damned empty house all alone tonight.

Waiting for him. He'd received her message this morning loud and clear. Kept seeing it flashing in her big, sultry eyes, over and over again. Hearing it in her voice. Damn.

"You with me, Lash?" Garrett asked, breaking into his thoughts. Lash looked up fast. "You seem… distracted."

"Sorry." Lash jerked himself away from the window he'd been staring absently through, and turned to cross the office. There was another desk now. An old, dark wooden one that looked as if it belonged in a one-room schoolhouse from days gone by. He ran one hand over the gleaming, freshly polished wood, feeling guilty as hell. ''It was nice of you, dragging this desk in here for me, the way you did,'' he said.

''Hell, it was sitting home in the attic collecting dust. I figured it might as well get some use. No big deal.''

But it was a big deal. The desk had belonged to Maria Brand, Garrett's mother, and it was most certainly a big deal. Lash didn't imagine the Brand brothers would consent to letting just anyone use it. And someone had taken pains to restore the gleam to that wood.

They treated him like family. Especially Garrett.

''You okay, Lash?''

Lash gave his head a shake. ''Just wondering how you managed to haul this thing over here without your truck.''

When Garrett didn't answer, Lash looked up to see him grinning and shaking his head. ''That damn toaster-car is a hatchback. I drove over here with the desk half in, half out, and the rear end squatting so low I think we were throwing sparks from the back bumper.'' Garrett closed the file folder he had been perusing and slipped it into its spot in the drawer. ''What say we call it a night? It's getting late, anyway. The boys probably have chores finished by now.''

Lash glanced at his watch, noting the late hour with surprise. Time flies when you're obsessing, he thought.

''Okay. Guess I'll head home, then.'' Sure you will, he thought miserably.

''You can come to supper if you want. Chelsea's making her fried chicken tonight.''

He thought of the last time he'd joined the Brands for fried chicken. Sitting across the table from Jessi, watching her lick her fingers. Lash compressed his lips into a hard line. ''No, thanks. I'm beat. Think I'll turn in early.''

''Okay. See you in the morning, then?''

''Sure.'' Lash snatched his hat from the back of his chair and headed out. He drove his noisy black convertible back to his lonely apartment in town. His haven of solitude.

It was waiting there for him, empty and dark. He shoved his door open, stepped inside, and the thought flitted through his mind that the place was as quiet as a graveyard. And then he frowned. ''Since when did quiet bother me? Hell, I *like* quiet.''

He went inside and tried to enjoy the quiet. One of the best parts of his freedom, he reminded himself over a solitary dinner consisting of a cold meat sandwich and a beer. But the quiet got on his nerves tonight. He found himself flicking on the little portable TV set he barely ever watched, turning the volume up loud. But the tinny voices and canned laughter didn't do the trick. Damn those Brands. He must be getting so used to being around them, being immersed in that big familial den of chaos, that he actually missed it when he wasn't. Imagine that.

Maybe he oughtta get a dog.

He tossed his paper plate into the trash, drained his beer and opened a second. He carried the can with him into the living room to sink onto the little easy chair and stare sightlessly at the television.

Was this what he truly wanted out of life? Endless nights like this one? Alone, bored.

"But free," he muttered, and lifted his can in a mocking toast to freedom.

It was that damned Jessi, making him feel restless and frustrated and itchy. Her and all her suggestive glances.

Her and her hot kisses. Her and her talk about the clinic and the house and the family she'd have there one day.

He didn't want that, dammit.

But he did want her.

His shower that night was a cool one. He dived into bed still wet, hoping the dampness would keep the oppressive heat from smothering him. And after a third beer, he fell into a jerky, restless sleep.

But she didn't leave him alone then, either. She was there, haunting his dreams, touching him, kissing him, teasing him, as he lay there paralyzed and unable to reciprocate. He thrashed in agony, his head whipping back and forth, his body coated in sweat. Invisible chains held him immobile as Jessi leaned over him, trailing her fingers slowly up and down his body, touching lightly, and moving away. Repeating the torture with her lips. Laughing at him for his helplessness.

He woke shouting her name. And then he blinked the dream away and sat in his bed, shuddering with need, coated in a cold sweat. The phone was ringing. And he knew better than to pick it up. But he picked it up anyway.

"Are you ready yet, Lash?"

"Jessi?" He frowned into the receiver, and then her words registered, and he started sweating all over again.

"You sound sleepy. Were you sleeping? I haven't been able to."

"No?" he asked, telling himself to put the phone down now.

"No," she breathed. "It's so hot, and I'm just...I don't know, jittery, I guess."

"Jittery," he repeated. "And hot."

"Mmmm... Every time I slide between the cool sheets and close my eyes, all I can see is...you. The way we were on the bank of Sycamore Creek. The way your mouth felt when you—"

"Why won't you leave me alone, Jess?" He asked it softly, feeling desperation clog his throat.

"I thought you'd stop by tonight. I'm here, you know. I'm alone. And I've been waiting. Damn, Lash, when are you going to quit disappointing me?"

"I'm hanging up the phone now," he told her. But he didn't do it.

"I'm sorry if I'm making this hard on you," she whispered. "Maybe I ought to be ashamed of myself, but I'm not, you know. I want you so much I can't—"

"I'm human," he muttered. "Dammit to hell, I'm only human." He slammed the phone down, flung back the covers and reached for his jeans.

Jessi had replaced the receiver, and sighed. He wasn't coming. Okay. She could live with that...for now. But she sure as hell couldn't sleep.

So now she was balanced precariously on a rickety step ladder, screwing a new light bulb into an old socket in the now empty garage. The Loomis boys had worked like wild men for her today, and between the three of them, they'd had the entire contents of the garage sorted, packed and hauled away to a storage shed on their ranch—which they'd insisted she use for as long as she needed—in a matter of a few hours.

They were grateful to her, and they showed it. The mare was on her feet today, and doing well. Jessi had gone out to their spread at lunchtime to check on her. She'd be all right. Jessi felt good about that.

She also felt perfectly all right about the little stop she'd made on her way back here. At Mr. Henry's Drug Store. She'd gathered up her courage, and for the first time in her life, she'd purchased condoms. No easy task, what with a mischievous-looking nine-year-old boy peering at her and giggling every few seconds, with his carrot-colored curls and his faceful of freckles. But he was too young to know what the little foil packets were. She hoped. She had bought three, individually wrapped, and had silently hoped Lash would come to her...tonight. Well, he hadn't, but he would. Soon. And when he did, she'd be prepared.

She'd fully expected him to come to her tonight, and her disappointment burned. She wouldn't sleep before dawn, she was sure of it. It was still early. But if he hadn't shown by now, he wasn't going to.

She'd been so ready for tonight. She'd thought of everything. The peach-colored silk teddy still hugged her secretly beneath the robe she'd pulled over it when it became obvious Lash wasn't going to come over. The condoms were still in the robe's pocket. She'd soaked in a scented bath that left her skin silky-soft and smelling faintly of honeysuckle. In the bedroom, she'd had soft music playing, and candles glowing. But he hadn't come to her. Even her little wake-up call hadn't convinced him. And dammit, she'd been too wound up to sleep. So she'd come out here to get some work done.

Beginning with new light bulbs.

The garage was pretty much empty now. Aside from

the ladder on which she stood, there were only a few items scattered around—things she'd decided to keep for her own use. The rusty toolbox in the corner containing a valuable selection of tools that were in surprisingly good condition. A brass magazine rack she planned to use in the clinic's waiting room. A box full of antique books.

She reached overhead to twist the new bulb in tighter. The ladder wobbled. Her balance faltered. And two strong hands clasped around her waist to steady her.

She knew those hands. Knew the familiar warm pressure of each callused fingertip. "Lash," she breathed.

He didn't say anything. Just lifted her gently, and lowered her to the floor. Her body brushed his on the way down. Her knees felt weak, and when she was standing, she leaned back against him, feeling the heat of him, relaxing against him. His arms hesitated, then slowly slid around her waist. His head bowed, and he spoke softly, very close to her ear. "What the hell am I ever going to do with you, Jess?"

She turned in his arms, tipped her head back, stared up into his eyes. "You know the answer to that just as well as I do."

"You're driving me crazy," he whispered, his eyes roaming over her face. "I can't sleep nights anymore. You're like a siren, Jessi, and I think you know it. I think you're actually *trying* to drive me right out of my mind."

"No, Lash. I only want to drive you into my arms."

He threaded his fingers in her hair, touching it, rubbing locks of it, bringing it to his face to inhale its scent. "Dammit, Jess, I don't want—"

"Yeah, you do," she said. "You know perfectly well you do, Lash. Just as much as I do. So why don't you just shut up and kiss me?"

Chapter 7

He shook his head slowly, slightly, and he searched her eyes. Then he kissed her. And she knew that her plan was going to work. He was going to make love to her. He was going to see how perfect they were together. He wouldn't be able to stay away from her after this. And when his job with Garrett was finished, and it came time for him to leave, he'd realize that he had fallen in love with her. He'd decide he had to stay. He was going to love her. It was going to work.

"I can't stay," he muttered between kisses. "You have to know that up front, Jessi. I'm not a settling-down kind of guy."

"I didn't ask you to stay," she told him. "Just this. Just tonight. This is all I want," she lied.

He lifted his head, probing her eyes, and she knew that he knew she was lying. For just an instant, she saw the hesitation—the second thoughts clouding his eyes. So she took a single step backward, pulling out of his arms, and she parted the robe she wore, letting it slide from her shoulders, down her arms, to pool around her feet.

And Lash's lips parted and his eyes widened and his Adam's apple swelled and receded again as he swallowed hard. His gaze moved slowly down the silky teddy, back up again. He drew a shallow breath. "Mercy," he muttered, and she thought maybe he meant it.

Too bad if he did. She wasn't going to show him *any* mercy tonight.

She moved close to him again, pressed her body to his, caught both of his hands in hers, and kissed him. And when she finished, he was shuddering and shivering and sweating. Best of all, he was kissing her back. He trailed his lips over her chin, down to her throat, and then her shoulder, pushing the teddy's silken strap aside with his mouth as he did. His hands kneaded her buttocks, pulling her tight to him as he arched against her. Her fingers sifted his hair, urging his head lower, until he worked her breast free of its confines to suckle it thoroughly.

He was hers. All hers now. She knew it a second later, when he let go of her, eyes blazing, and tore his shirt open, struggling out of it hurriedly. She smiled softly when he reached for the button fly of his jeans, as well.

But her smile died when he paused. "Dammit, what the hell am I thinking?"

"Don't think," she whispered. "You think way too much as it is, Lash. This isn't about thinking. It's about *feeling,* Lash."

He gave his head a shake. "We can't do this," he muttered, turning slowly away from her, pushing one hand through his hair and messing it up endearingly. ''I didn't bring... I don't have...''

''Oh,'' she said. ''You don't have...protection? Is that what you mean?'' Jessi crouched and slipped her hand into the pocket of her robe, emerging with one of the small foil packets and holding it up. ''But I do.''

He blinked, eyes narrowing. ''You were that sure of yourself, were you?''

She shrugged and tossed him the packet. He caught it, still staring at her. Still having second thoughts, she was afraid. So she pushed the straps of the teddy the rest of the way down, and let it fall to her feet. She stepped out of it, catching the peach silk on the end of one toe and flinging that at him, too.

He didn't catch it, though. The teddy hit him in the center of his glorious chest, and fell to the garage floor, forgotten. Lash didn't seem to notice it. His gaze slid, very slowly, all the way down her naked body, and then up again. And then he whispered, ''I'm gonna burn in hell, Jessi Brand, but not until I've loved every inch of you.''

He pulled her against him, kissing her deeply, hungrily, and lowering her to the floor atop her soft robe. He pushed her down on her back, and held her arms at her sides, and kissed her all over. It was incredible, the way he made her feel. And all Jessi wanted was more of this magic. She didn't let herself tremble, even when a tiny whisper of fear—fear of the unknown—tiptoed through her mind. Instead she played the role of seductress, the one she'd written and then cast herself in, to the hilt. She kissed him and trailed her hands down his hard back. She touched him everywhere, and when he sucked air through his teeth, she knew she was doing it right.

His fingers dipped and probed and parted her, and Jessi shivered with a forbidden pleasure as she parted her thighs for him. ''Now, Lash,'' she whispered. ''We've waited long enough. Do it now.''

She wrapped her legs around him, moved her hips against him, and he did what she asked. She felt him nudging his way inside her, bit by bit. And then she felt filled and stretched, and there was a brief stab of pain that made her go stiff all over and had her eyes flying wide open.

He stilled. ''Jessi?''

No, he wasn't going to stop. Not now. She closed her hands on his firm buttocks and pulled him to her, and into her, and she moved against him, and in a few seconds he was hers again. All hers. No second thoughts about repercussions could hold him the way she could. He was hers, dammit. And he might as well get used to the idea, because he was going to stay hers.

It wouldn't be long. *Couldn't* be. Not if he was feeling a tenth of what she was right now. It was as if...as if they'd become one.

When he moved inside her, she arched to receive him. When he turned his head in search of her mouth, he found it there, waiting for his kiss. No words, no signals—nothing was needed, because the connection between them was so strong. He held her hard and tight, as if he'd never let her go, and she wished it could go on forever.

And then her mind whirled out of the realm of cognizance, as the feelings he was stirring took over. Sensation enveloped her. There was nothing else, only pleasure, mounting pleasure, pleasure so intense she wanted to scream with it.

And then she did scream with it, words tumbling

from her lips in a rush, driven by a passion so intense she wasn't even sure what she was saying.

He bucked harder and then drove into her, holding her tight to take him. He shuddered, and she did, as well. And it was a long time before he relaxed enough to move again. A long time before she came back to earth and realized what she'd shouted when the climax swept her away.

She closed her eyes and prayed she hadn't ruined everything. Maybe…maybe he'd been too carried away to notice the words she said.

Or…maybe not.

Jessi had curled into his arms, pulling his discarded flannel shirt over her. She lay relaxed and warm and sated against him. Flesh to flesh. Body to body. And he couldn't deny that it had been incredible. The best sex he'd ever had in his life.

And it had also been, he realized, the biggest mistake.

Lash relived the experience, knowing the precise moment when he should have stopped. He should be horsewhipped. He wouldn't blame her brothers for lynching him now. He wouldn't blame them a bit.

He stared down at the scarlet proof of what he should have known all along, staining the pale pink satin of Jessi's crumpled robe. The pink of a tea rose. The pink of innocence.

"You should have told me," he said, and his voice was strained.

She snuggled closer to his side, tugging at him as if she wanted him to lie down again. "Told you what?"

"Dammit, Jessi, you were… I was…"

"You were my first," she said, and she smiled up

at him. It was a sleepy, sexy smile in the too-bright light of the single bare bulb. "And if you'd get back down here with me, you could be my second...and my third and m—"

"Dammit," he muttered again, and this time he eased himself out of her embrace and got to his feet. He pulled his jeans on hurriedly, while she looked on, her doe eyes round and hurting. Of course she was hurting. He was a bastard.

He averted his eyes and paced the barren garage in broad strides, sweeping his hand through his hair. "I never would have...if I'd known...we shouldn't..."

She sat up, tilting her head to one side. "Don't tell me you thought I was in the habit of—" she glanced down at the robe, the dirty floor, her fallen teddy "—of this."

"Well, hell, Jess, you were too good at it to be an amateur. I didn't stand a chance, once you set your mind to—" He bit off the rest when he met her gaze by accident and saw fresh pain flash in her eyes. But it vanished fast.

Chased away by anger.

"Forgive me," she said. "I kinda got the idea that you were willing."

"You know damn well what I meant. I didn't want this... I mean, I *did,* but I wouldn't have...not if you'd left me the hell alone when I told you to. Damn, Jessi, what the hell am I supposed to do now?"

She got slowly to her feet, pulling his shirtsleeves over her arms, jerking it closed in the front. "You can always have me arrested," she snapped. "Charge me with rape, seeing as how I gave you no choice and ignored you a while ago when you were screaming no. Hell, you probably have a good case, right? So you decide, Lash. Meanwhile, why don't you get the hell out of my garage, off my property and out of my life."

"Gladly." He snatched up his boots, put them on haphazardly and fled. As if the devil himself were on his heels, Lash stomped to his car, slammed the door and spit gravel in his wake when he headed home. But he couldn't run fast enough or far enough. He'd been raised better than this. The Reverend Mr. Stanton had taught him far, far better than this. But even so, he'd given in to his baser urges. He'd told himself they were two consenting adults and that so long as she understood up front that this meant nothing, it would be all right. Hell, she'd even had condoms on hand.

But he'd been wrong. She was an innocent, no matter how effective her seduction. *An innocent.* She didn't know anything about sex or men or...

What should he do? What the hell should he do? He pulled the car into the spot in front of his apartment, killed the engine and sat there cursing himself. He closed his eyes and saw Reverend Stanton at the pulpit, fist slamming down on the open Bible, fire and brimstone in his eyes. "You have to marry her, boy! It's the only honorable thing you *can* do. You sullied an innocent, defiled her, deflowered her. And, boy, the blame for that is only half hers, and you know it."

"You're right," Lash muttered. And he knew it was true. Sure, she'd acted as if she knew what was what. But if he'd searched his soul, he'd have known it was all bluster. All an act.

She'd told him she loved him. She was an innocent young girl who thought she was in love with him. And if he hadn't been so busy lusting after her, he'd have seen love shining from those big brown eyes. He'd have seen it and he'd have run like hell. She thought she loved him. And because of that, she'd given him something more precious than gold, and she'd sure as hell regret it some day.

He owed her. He owed her brothers. He had to do what was right.

Jessi was stunned.

After what they'd shared, she'd thought he'd have to know they were meant for each other. How could he not know it, after that? How?

She closed her eyes. God, it had been…it had been like nothing she'd ever dreamed of. The way they fit together. They'd been so close, so insane with wanting and giving and feeling. How could he still not know?

Jessi sighed and pulled his shirt tighter around her, hugging her waist. She'd thought he would understand that they were meant to be together once they made love. But she'd been wrong. He hadn't understood anything. He'd acted angry, instead of moved. Instead of in love, he'd been in what looked and felt like mortal fear of her.

Were all men this dense, or only Lash?

Or maybe…maybe she was the one who wasn't getting it. Lash had been with other women. Maybe being with her hadn't been anything so special for him. Maybe it had been just like the rest, and not the earth-shattering experience it had been for her.

That thought made more sense than any other. Maybe she was the one who'd been a total fool. She picked up her bathrobe, balled it up and carried it under her arm. Her chin lowered to her chest, she walked through the darkness back into the house and stuffed it into her overnight bag. Then she showered, letting steaming-hot water pound her sore body, telling herself to let it rinse away this heartache that had settled over her like a heavy shroud.

It didn't. And the quiet of the empty house only made it worse. She didn't want to be alone tonight. If she were, she'd just spend the night bawling like some weak-kneed female, and she *hated* women like that. No, better to find some distraction. Something else to think about.

She threw on some fresh jeans, snatched up her bag and headed to the one place where she knew she could always find comfort. And love. And chaos. Home. The Texas Brand. Even if she slipped up to her room without seeing anyone, just being there would be enough. Just hearing all that noise, feeling the warmth that big house was always filled with, would be enough. It would be better to lick her wounds there than here, alone. And maybe then she could make some sense out of all of these strange feelings swirling around in her heart, and decide what she was supposed to do next.

There was an unfamiliar car in the driveway when she arrived, and she figured someone had company. Part of her wanted to creep into the house through the back door and sneak unseen up to her room. Most of her, though, wanted to shake this dark cloud from over her head and march in with her head held high. She had nothing to be ashamed of. Lash should have been happy to learn he was her first. He should have been thrilled. And if he had half a brain, he'd have understood what an honor it was that she'd bestowed on him. She'd wanted him to be her first. She'd waited all her life for him.

And he'd been furious about it.

"Well, to hell with him."

She was hurt, but there was a lot more to it than

that. She was mad as hell. And sniveling her way through the house as if she had something to be ashamed of was not her way of dealing with it. Because she wasn't ashamed. She'd done nothing wrong.

Besides, her brothers would sense something was up if she didn't act like her usual self. So she did.

She burst through the front door, small bag in her hand, plastering a smile on her face and acting as if she were on top of the world. But she paused when she saw a harried-looking woman who seemed to be on her way out. The woman had a boy in tow. A carrot-topped, freckle-faced little boy. Jessi recognized him at once and frowned, wondering what on earth was going on. Her first thought was that the kid *had* known what those foil packets were, and that he'd ratted her out to her older brothers. And the bottom fell out of her stomach as she looked up at Garrett.

But Garrett was smiling as he and Chelsea saw the woman and the boy off. "Don't let it happen again, you hear? And Mrs. Peterson, don't you worry about the late hour. I'm glad you came to me, and you did the right thing by letting Mr. Henry know right away. I'm sure no harm's been done."

The woman nodded, red-faced, never quite meeting Garrett's eyes. "I just can't imagine what came over him, Sheriff Brand. But I was always taught confession is good for the soul. Now that he's owned up to it and you had that little talk with him, I'm sure he'll mend his ways."

"Don't be too hard on him, ma'am. Boys tend toward mischief, you know. They can't help it much."

The woman scowled at her son and hustled him out of the house to their waiting car.

Jessi stood just inside the screen door, watching as

the two left. When they were gone, she looked at her brother, frowning. "What was all that about?"

"Hardened criminal," Garrett said. "His mom caught him in the act and made him confess to the sheriff." He shook his head, grinning. "I gave him a talkin'-to. I don't think he's gonna mess up again."

"Oh." Jessi nodded. "I heard you mention Mr. Henry. What did the kid do, shoplift something from the drugstore?"

Garrett shook his head, and she could see that he was battling a gut-deep chuckle. Chelsea elbowed him in the ribs. "It's not one bit funny, you big lug."

He sobered. "You're right, of course. I was just wondering if little Bubba's gonna be as much of a heller as that one is. Thank goodness his mama caught him and let ol' Mr. Henry know what he'd done."

"That bad, huh?" Jessi asked.

"You bet," Garrett said. "His mama caught him in the prophylactic aisle with a sewing needle in his hand. Seems his friends dared him to poke holes in the condoms."

Jessi's blood rushed to her feet so fast she felt dizzy. "P-poke…*holes?*" Her hand clenched tighter around the handle of her small bag.

"Little feller annihilated a dozen or more before she caught him. Seems he was at it all afternoon."

Jessi put one hand on her belly to calm it. This was just silly. She was just being silly. What were the odds that the ones she'd bought had been—?

"Well, I hope he's learned his lesson," she said, but her voice lacked conviction, and it cracked a little. She wanted to chase the woman down and wring her child's freckled neck. "I'm heading upstairs. I'm tired out."

"But, Jess, you didn't tell us about the garage. How'd it go today? You get much done?"

She kept walking, speaking softly as she went, not turning around. She was operating on autopilot right now, while her brain reeled from the shock. The very thought... "Fine. It's coming along fine."

"Now what the heck do you suppose is ailing her?" she heard her brother mutter.

She hurried to her room, closed the door, turned the lock and raced to her bed, shaking the contents of her overnight bag onto the comforter. She grasped her robe when it rolled onto the bed, and shook it.

The two remaining foil packets spilled out in front of her, and her hands were trembling when she picked one of them up. She scanned the little sucker, front and back, straining her eyes. But there were no punctures. The packet was fine.

She dropped it, sighing in relief and grabbing up the second one. She'd been afraid for nothing. There'd been no reason to think that...

"Oh, my God."

She swallowed hard and stared at the series of tiny holes in the second packet, willing them to disappear. But they remained.

"Oh, my God, this is like Russian roulette. What about the third one? The one we...used?"

No way to tell. Lash had disposed of it, wrapper and all, though she had no idea what he'd done with it. She only knew she'd looked around the floor after he left, wanting to leave no telltale signs for her snoopy brothers to stumble upon. And she'd found nothing there. She'd be damned before she asked Lash what he'd done with it. She'd be damned before she even mentioned any of this to him.

She closed her eyes and pressed her palm to her forehead. Oh, God, what if…what if…?

No. It couldn't happen. It couldn't.

But there was no way she was going to stop worrying about it until she knew. And she couldn't know. Not yet. All she could do was wait…and try not to let her panic show in her eyes in the meantime.

Because if the worst *had* happened tonight… She closed her eyes, chewed her lower lip… Damn. Her brothers were going to skin Lash alive.

He knew what he *ought* to do, he just wasn't quite sure he could bring himself to go through with it. He hadn't heard a word from Jessi in three days, and he'd managed to avoid her so far. It might do to give her some time to get over him, he thought. After all, she might decide she wasn't in love with him, after all, and maybe she'd be okay, and he wouldn't have to sacrifice his freedom on the altar of her lost innocence.

He ought to be ashamed of himself. He really should. Hell, he *was*. He told himself, though, that it was better for Jessi not to rush into anything. To cool down and think it through first. And he figured he'd get a pretty good handle on how she was dealing with all of this any minute now. This morning Garrett had called to ask Lash to be at the ranch for breakfast. Said he wanted to get an early start as they headed out to a ranch forty miles east where another rustling incident had taken place recently. It would be easier if they left from the ranch in one vehicle.

And if every excuse Lash could think of hadn't sounded so lame in his mind, he might have tried using one or two of them.

He sat at the table in the Brand's kitchen, feeling

like Judas at the Last Supper. And maybe it was just him, but there seemed to be a pall hanging over all of them. Lash was used to Ben's solemn face and sad eyes. But it wasn't just Ben. Wes sat across from him, looking preoccupied. Elliot wasn't cracking jokes or grinning. Garrett rarely stopped frowning. Even Chelsea was unusually quiet.

He didn't think they knew. Hell, if they knew, he wouldn't be sitting here and they wouldn't be moping. He'd be running for his life and they'd be chasing him with blood in their eyes, more than likely. He cleared his throat and decided to face it head-on. "Why's everybody so glum?"

Garrett shook himself. "Hell, Lash, I forgot you haven't been out here for a few days."

"Nope," Wes said, and then his black eyes narrowed. "In fact, he hasn't been around since Jessi first started acting so strangely."

Chelsea's head came up, her eyes widening. "Wes, she told you, it's just a stomach bug. Flu, probably. It'll pass. She'll be fine."

Wes grunted, and Lash swallowed hard. "So something's wrong with Jessi?" he asked.

"Don't worry about it," Chelsea replied. And her eyes pierced his. "She's too tough to let any insignificant little *bug* keep her down."

Lash flinched. Damn, if no one else knew, it was obvious Chelsea at least had a pretty good idea of what was bothering Jess. He felt about two inches high. But he was worried. "Is she—"

"Here she comes," Elliot said. "See for yourself."

No sooner had he said it than Jessi sailed into the kitchen, chin high, overly bright smile on her face.

"Overslept again," she sang. "You guys should have woke me."

"Heard you up pacing till after midnight," Ben said softly. "Thought if you were finally sleeping, we oughtta let you have at it."

She smiled even harder, then caught sight of Lash, and her face froze, the smile dying slowly.

"Morning, Jessi," he managed.

She blinked the emotions from her eyes and turned her back to pour herself a cup of coffee. "Morning," she muttered.

When she faced them again, her smile was back in place, and every bit as phony as before. Maybe even a little bit more so now.

Something was sure as hell bothering her. She wouldn't look him in the eye, barely spoke more than a syllable in his direction at a time. She looked pale, and there were dark rings surrounding her eyes. From lack of sleep, no doubt. Up pacing till after midnight, indeed.

She picked at her food. Normally, that bundle of energy had an appetite like a horse, but this morning—and maybe for the past several mornings, judging by her family's worry—she pushed the food around on her plate, looking at it as if it held no appeal whatsoever. And Lash knew he wasn't imagining the haunted look in her eyes.

Looking at her, Lash lost his appetite, as well. She was a mess. Trying hard to hide it, but a mess all the same. Lash couldn't avoid the consequences of his actions. Not anymore. It was clear he'd hurt her. Hurt her bad. If he'd known she was a virgin, he'd never have assumed she could deal with a casual one-night stand. And he should have known. Thing was, he thought, he just plain hadn't wanted to know. He'd wanted her, and he'd had her, and now the poor little thing was devastated.

Probably she'd been harboring some fantasy about how it would all play out. Probably she'd thought he'd fall madly in love with her after having her once, and that he'd be hers forever. She was still in love with him, and he'd broken her innocent heart all to hell. Poor thing, falling apart over him.

Lord, but he'd messed up good this time.

She sipped her coffee, leaned back in her chair. "So you two are heading out to the Bar Z today?" She addressed her question to Garrett, acting as if Lash weren't even in the room.

"Yeah," Garrett said. "The rustling spree out their way last year bears some similarities to ours."

"That's great," she said. "Maybe you'll break this case wide open."

"That would be nice," Garrett said. "I'm sick of working on this thing into the wee hours night after night."

"You aren't the only one," Lash said.

Jessi looked right at him, those brown eyes locking on to his like laser beams. "That's right," she said. "Once this thing is over, you can be on your way. I know you can't wait."

Lash took the blow she dealt and didn't even rock backward under the impact, which he thought was admirable. "Actually," he said slowly, forcing the words out, "I was thinking about staying on."

There was, in that instant, a flicker in her eyes. Lash thought it might have been hope, or joy, or something. He thought maybe he'd caused it.

But it died quickly, and the sadness was back in her

eyes, or worry, or stress, or whatever it was. Darkness. That was what he saw. And she said, "Sure you are. And I'm thinking of running for mayor."

Lash gave his head a shake. "You don't believe me," he stated flatly.

"You shouldn't say things you don't mean, Lash."

"I meant it."

She held his gaze for a long moment, and Lash couldn't look away, even when he felt curious gazes on him. Speculative eyes. Hostile ones.

Finally, Jessi broke eye contact with a shrug. "Hell, it doesn't matter to me one way or another."

But it did. And he knew, dammit, he knew what he had to do.

"We'd best get a move on, Lash," Garrett said, pushing away from the table and snatching up his hat.

Lash nodded, his eyes on his boss's baby sister. "I'll see you later, Jessi," he said. Hoping she'd get the message. They had to talk. He had to do right by her.

But Jessi refused to so much as look at him as he stood near the door with his hat in his hand. And he had to give up, because he didn't want to have to deal with her brothers until after he'd fixed that pretty little heart he'd stupidly managed to break. And he was being pretty obvious here.

He plunked the hat on his head, nodded to the others and headed out the door.

Chapter 8

He tried to put the pain he'd seen in her eyes out of his mind by throwing himself into the rustling investigation up to his eyeballs. He and Garrett interviewed ranchers from one end of the county to the other. They examined tire tracks and hoof tracks, and Lash had an impromptu lesson from Garrett in making plaster molds of them for future reference. Almost as if Garrett might be taking seriously Lash's words about sticking around.

Hell.

He knew Jessi was doing the same, throwing herself into her work. By the time Lash and Garrett got back that night, the contractor she'd hired was out at her place in town. The guy was already raising hell with that garage. When Lash drove by on his way home, he saw crews of men. Muscular types, working shirtless. All of them tanned and rippling, the bastards. Jessi stood nearby, overseeing their progress, and never hesitated to correct them or boss them around. The lawn was a mess of lumber and sawhorses and pickup trucks and power tools and extension cords. These guys were pros, and they were going to town on the clinic. All of which made Lash suspect Jessi was deliberately hurrying the process along, just to divert her mind from the way he'd broken her poor, innocent heart.

He was truly a slug.

He pulled over, not really thinking about what he was doing or why. He sat in his car for a very long time, parked right across the street from her new place, and stared at the activity as the sun went down—like a kid hoping for a glimpse of a sweet at a candy store, but without the wherewithal to go inside. And all the while, the preacher's voice rang in his mind with Bible verses telling him the right thing to do.

No matter how tempting Jessi's advances had been, this was his own fault. He wasn't an animal. He could have said no, done the honorable thing and walked away from her. He'd wanted her as badly as she wanted him. Thing was, he was experienced, and she was innocent. He was older, and supposedly wiser. He was the man, she the woman. His role should have been to protect her, watch out for her, not to take advantage of her innocent feelings for him.

He'd crushed her. And no matter how he looked at it, there was only one way to fix this mess. Hell, marrying and settling down wasn't the way he'd planned to live his life, but it wouldn't be so bad. He liked Jessi. She was attractive—no, she was gorgeous—and smart. Fabulous in bed. God, more than fabulous. For a while there, she'd robbed him of his will to live without her body wrapped around his. And Quinn, Texas, wasn't such a terrible place to settle down, if a man was forced to settle down somewhere. And her brothers—hell, they'd come around. It wouldn't be so bad.

He sat there. She'd seen him, he knew that, but she pointedly ignored his presence. After a while, the contractors packed up their equipment, leaving the bigger items in the garage, then cleared out.

Jessi glanced across the way at him, shook her head, almost as if she were exasperated, and turned to walk into her house. It was time. Taking a deep breath and stiffening his spine, Lash wrenched open the door of his car and strode purposefully across the street and up the walk to the little house, eyeing it the way a newly condemned man eyes his prison cell. Silently he said goodbye to his dreams of roaming free and unfettered, wherever the wind would take him, and resigned himself to the mundane life of a married man. He felt pretty damned proud of himself for making this supreme sacrifice.

He knocked on the little door, knowing in his heart that the joy in Jessi's pretty eyes when he told her what he'd decided to do was going to be all the reward he needed.

Jessi opened the door and saw Lash standing there, looking at her as if she were a kid with a boo-boo and he had the only Band-Aid in town. She frowned, tilting her head to one side.

"Look, Lash, you said it was a one-night stand, and I agreed, okay? I don't remember offering seconds."

He lowered his eyes. "I just want to talk."

Her eyes narrowed suspiciously. "Talk, then."

"Can I come in?"

She heaved a sigh, shrugged and stepped back, away from the door, so that he could come inside. He did, looking around the place and nodding in approval. "Wow. You've been busy."

And she had. She'd scrubbed the place spotless, hung new curtains, had the furniture professionally cleaned, stored most of Marisella's personal things and moved in a whole lot of her own. She'd decided not to rent the house to strangers after all. She'd use it herself when she felt like it. And she'd stay at the ranch when she didn't. So there. In fact, she was going to do exactly what she wanted, when she wanted, where she wanted, from now until she died a spinster at eighty-something.

Mostly, though, all the work had been to pass the time until she could get rid of this gnawing worry over the possibly faulty condom. It would be two weeks before a pregnancy test could give any sort of accurate results. Once she got past that, and the stupid thing read negative—as it most certainly would—she'd be rid of this nervous energy. Until then, all she could do was direct it into something constructive, just to burn it off. It was the only way she could sleep at night. And even then, she tossed and turned, and slept in fits and starts.

The cottage was hers now. She'd made it hers. Forest-green curtains matched the new slipcovers on the sofa and chair. White throw pillows with green ruffles littered the sofa, and there were matching throw rugs on the hardwood floors, for accents. She'd placed a few of her treasures around the room. Knickknacks she'd collected over the years. Bowls full of flowers here and there. The shelves on the wall where Marisella used to pile her collection of trinkets were now Jessi's bookshelves, lined with most of her veterinary books. She'd even brought her PC over and installed it on its own desk, in the corner near the window that overlooked the front yard. That way she could work on her plans and budgeting and still be close enough to keep track of the workers outside.

She watched Lash look around the place, saw the approval in his eyes, and thought he'd better blurt the apology he'd been practicing, beg her forgiveness on bended knee and ask for the chance to start over with her pretty darned fast, or he'd find himself out on his ear.

"I've been worried about you," he said.

"No need for that. I'm just fine." She paced to the small sofa and sat down. Might as well resign herself to the fact that he would only get to his apology in his own good time.

"You don't look fine," he told her, and he stood in front of where she sat, looking down at her almost worriedly. But it was a paternal, or big-brotherly, sort of worry. "You've lost weight, haven't you?"

She shrugged and averted her eyes. Worry would do that. It was only three or four pounds. Nothing to get excited about. In fact, it was rather reassuring. Pregnant women *gained* weight, right? That she'd lost weight only added credence to her firm belief that she couldn't possibly be carrying Lash Monroe's baby.

Lash cleared his throat, drawing her gaze back to his again. He was holding his hat in his hand, now. Worrying the brim with kneading fingers. Ah, the apology must be forthcoming, she thought. Maybe she ought to make him kneel.

"I wasn't fair to you before, Jess. I mean, it would have been different if you were...you know, experienced, but you weren't, and I should have known that."

She shrugged and wondered when he'd get around to apologizing and asking for a second chance.

He turned slowly, taking a deep breath and paced to a nearby chair, one right across from her. Finally, he sat down and met her gaze again. "I take full responsibility for what happened between us, and I've decided to do the honorable thing and face up to the consequences."

She drew a swift gulp of air and lifted her brows. He couldn't possibly know about the condoms, could he? "Consequences?"

"Yes," he said, nodding firmly. "Look, just because I never intended to settle down, doesn't mean I can shirk my responsibilities. I screwed up, and I have no one to blame for that but myself."

Jessi frowned at him. "You act like you robbed a bank. We had sex, Lash. Pretty incredible sex, actually. Last I knew, incredible sex wasn't a capital crime."

He lowered his chin and his eyes simultaneously.

"Did you come here thinking you had to do some sort of penance?"

He nodded. "Something like that."

Jessi sighed hard and shook her head. "You're confusing the hell out of me. Just say what you came here to say, all right?"

"All right. I will." He stood up, took her hands in his and drew her to her feet. "Jessi, I'm going to marry you. It's really the only thing I can do to make this right, and I'm willing to do it."

She blinked in shock, feeling as if he'd slapped her. Her jaw dropped. She snapped it closed, drew a breath, resisted the urge to slam him upside the head and gave her own head a shake to clear out the confusion. "Let me get this straight," she managed. "You made a mistake by sleeping with a virgin. You feel guilty about it, and figure you have to pay for your crime. And marrying me is your sentence?''

''W-well, I don't know if I'd put it like that—''

''But that's the way you did put it, Lash. That is *exactly* the way you put it.''

''No, I didn't. What I meant was—''

''What about your precious freedom? What about you not being a 'settling-down kind of guy'?''

He shook his head, looking confused. ''I'll give all of that up, Jess. Look, I know I broke your heart, and I'm just trying to make it right.''

''*You* broke *my* heart?'' She blinked up at him, then shook her head and turned to pace away. ''Gee, it's the first I've heard of it. But thanks for being willing to sacrifice your life out of guilt, and thanks all to hell for being so very generous in offering to do hard time as my husband to make up for it.'' She whirled on him, hands clenched into trembling fists at her sides. ''I oughtta knock your teeth out, you arrogant, pious, self-righteous snake in the grass!''

''I— I—''

''What makes you think for one minute that Jessi Brand would even *consider* marrying a man who sees her as some kind of punishment? Hmm? What makes you think I'd settle for a man who doesn't love me?''

''But, Jessi, I thought—''

''Well, here's your answer, Lash. I wouldn't marry you if you were the last mammal on the planet. I wouldn't marry you if I were ninety years old and still single. I wouldn't marry you if you got down on your damned knees and begged! Now get the hell out of here before I throw you out.''

He took a step toward her. "Jessi, you don't understand what I—"

"Get out!" Her hand closed around the nearest item handy, which turned out to be a fake Aztec vase, and she hurled it at his head. He ducked, and the vase smashed against the wall beyond him. Jessi spun around in search of more ammunition.

"Just think about it, okay?" he said, heading for the door. "Just give yourself some time to calm down and think—"

A second item sailed over his head, a porcelain figurine of some sort. It sailed by him and smashed into the door. He yanked the door open before all the pieces hit the floor, ducked outside and closed it fast behind him.

"Damn you, Lash," she muttered. Then she sank onto the sofa, and lowered her head into her hands. To think she'd believed such an insensitive, dense S.O.B. could actually fall in love with her. God, she'd been an idiot!

She shook her head and refused to allow the tears burning in her eyes to spill over. "You're the one who's the fool, Lash," she whispered. "You could have had the best damned woman north of the Rio Grande, and you blew it, you jerk. You blew it all to hell."

Lash sat in his rather battered convertible, feeling as if he'd just been through a war, but with no idea what the fight was about, or on which side he was supposed to be fighting.

What the hell was wrong with Jessi? Why wasn't she glad he wanted to do the right thing by her?

Hell. Nothing was going the way he'd expected.

Even his own feelings were out of whack. He ought to be relieved that she'd let him off the hook. Relieved that he wouldn't have to make the supreme sacrifice after all, that he could continue with the freewheeling life-style he held so dear. That she wouldn't marry him if he was the last mammal on the planet.

So why was he feeling such an acute sense of disappointment? And why was he getting this urge to go back there and try everything he could think of to make her change her mind?

This was insane. Made no sense whatsoever. None. She was supposed to melt into his arms, maybe cry a little bit with joy. She was supposed to kiss him and tell him how happy he'd made her, and how miserable she'd been these past few days.

And she *had* been miserable. The rings around her eyes, the weight loss that made her cheeks slightly hollow, the sleepless nights and lack of appetite and fake smile, all pointed to that. But maybe she had some other reason to be upset besides him. Maybe he hadn't broken her little heart after all.

So if he hadn't, then what was wrong?

Jessi went back to the ranch that night. The next day was Sunday, so she didn't expect her construction crew to come around. And it was good to spend the day at home with her family. She felt a little battle-scarred, but maybe wiser than before. And she knew that the way she was feeling was partly her own fault. She'd seduced a man, thinking she could change him.

And that was always a mistake. Hadn't she seen enough talk shows to know that by now? She guessed a woman had to live it to really understand. You can't make someone love you. You can't change a drifter into a devoted husband just by luring him into your bed. It can't happen. Men don't change.

Breakfast was the usual boisterous occasion, with Ethan making a mess of his food, dropping lots of scraps to the floor, where Ol' Blue waited, frowning when the quick cat got to the bits of food before him. He was going to have to mend his lazy ways if he hoped to compete for table scraps with Pedro around.

"Goggy!" Ethan chirped, flailing his hands excitedly and aiming his crumbs at Blue, or so it seemed.

Blue shifted his position so that he was lying under the table beneath Ethan's feet, big brown eyes pleading for sustenance. When Ethan only stared back, the irritated old dog actually barked. Ethan laughed out loud. "Goggy eeet!" He tossed more scraps. Blue caught them as they came down, and it was the cat's turn to look irritated.

"There's more color in your cheeks this morning, Jess," Wes observed. "You feeling better?"

"Sure. It was just a bug. It's practically gone."

He nodded. "Glad to hear it. I was getting worried."

"You guys always worry about me. It's wasted energy. I'm tougher than any of you."

"Hell, Jess," Elliot said, "I'm beginning to believe it. Have you guys seen what she's done to that place of Marisella's?"

"I stopped by there yesterday," Garrett said. "It's looking great."

"I knew you could do it," Chelsea said.

Ben, quiet as always, got up from the table to go into the living room. When he returned, he carried a very large, flat cardboard box with a huge bow on top. He set it in front of Jessi.

"What's this?"

He shrugged. "I got to thinking, if Penny were here, this is exactly what she'd have done. So I did it for her."

Jessi blinked fast, so she wouldn't cry. Poor Ben was still hurting so much. And there didn't seem to be any way she could help him get over the pain of losing his young wife. It was always in his eyes, even on those rare occasions when he smiled.

She took the cover from the box and set in on the floor beside her chair. Then she pawed aside the tissue paper. Inside was a hand-tooled hardwood sign, gleaming with layers of painstakingly applied shellac. It was arched in exactly the shape of the big wooden arch over the ranch's driveway, and the lettering was the same, as well. The words Texas Brand curved across the arched top, and in the area beneath it read Veterinary Clinic. Another line below the first two read, "Jessica Lynn Brand, D.V.M."

Jessi's eyes brimmed and the tears she'd been battling spilled over. "Oh, Ben…"

"I figured if you couldn't have the clinic here on the ranch, you could take a little bit of the Texas Brand to the clinic."

She set the precious gift aside, pushed her chair away from the table and slung her arms around her big blond brother, hugging him hard. "You're the sweetest man alive, Ben."

"Just love my kid sister, is all," he said.

She stepped away from him, searching his sad eyes, and wishing with everything in her that he could find the happiness he so richly deserved. Someday, maybe… "I love you, too," she told him. "Thanks, Ben."

He nodded, and reached for his hat. "Gotta go," he

said, and headed out the door. Same as he'd done every Sunday since he came back from his year of solitude in the hills of Tennessee. He spent Sunday mornings at the cemetery where his young wife was buried. It was enough to make a grown woman bawl like a newborn calf.

Wes rose, breaking into her thoughts. "I'm headed out, too. Be back in time for chores tonight." He didn't offer any explanations, just left.

"Now what is he up to?" Garrett asked.

Chelsea tilted her head. "I know, but if you tell him I found out, I'll wring your neck." She sat back and sipped her coffee. "He's been spending time out near the Comanche reservation where he was born."

"Really?" Jessi was surprised. She'd never known Wes to show any inkling at all toward getting in touch with his roots on his mother's side. Hell, he'd lived here on the ranch since he was seven. Maria Brand had treated him as if he were her own child, and never once let him feel an outcast just because he was the product of her husband's infidelity.

Chelsea nodded and slipped a hand over Garrett's. "Don't be upset by this. I've said all along that Wes has something missing inside him, and you know as well as I do he needs to do this."

Garrett nodded. "I'm not upset, darlin'. Just amazed at how right you always manage to be." He leaned over and kissed her. "C'mon, Elliot. Looks like it's you and me riding the fencelines this morning."

Elliot wolfed down another sausage patty on his way out the door, slamming his hat on with his free hand. "Fine by me," he said around the food. "I can practice roping a few head."

Garrett shook his head in mock exasperation, with

just a hint of indulgence, and the two left. Minutes later, Jessi heard the gentle slapping of hooves as they rode away. She started clearing the table, with Pedro rubbing around her calves in a shameless effort to extract more scraps.

"So what's really been wrong with you these past few days?" Chelsea asked.

Jessi drew a breath. She'd known this was coming. But she wasn't going to tell Chelsea about the very slim chance she might be pregnant, because it was so very unlikely that there was no sense in worrying her. "I don't know," she said, instead. "I guess Lash just isn't the man I thought he was."

"Disappointed you, did he?"

Jess nodded.

"I know how that goes. Hell, I'll never forget your big lug of a brother trying to romance me just to keep me from leaving here and putting myself in danger. When I found out, I was sure that everything he was pretending to feel for me was only a part of his act. Of course, at the time, he thought so, too."

Jessi tilted her head. "Is there supposed to be some lesson in this tale for me?"

"Yeah," Chelsea said. "Men can be pretty stupid when it comes to matters of the heart, Jess. They can tell themselves all sorts of things, make up all kinds of excuses for the feelings they just don't understand. But in the end, they figure it out." She frowned. "Sometimes it takes clubbing them over the head, though."

Jessi laughed out loud for the first time in days. Clubbing Lash over the head held a wonderful appeal to her right now.

Their laughter was interrupted by a knock at the

screen door, and to Jessi's surprise, Ol' Blue got up from his nap under the kitchen table, faced the door and growled.

On the other side of the door, a bulky man with beady little black button eyes and a bit of a paunch around his middle peered at them. "This the Brand ranch?"

"Sure is," Jessi replied, moving to the door, but not opening it. She didn't want Blue to up and bite the stranger. "Can I help you with something?"

"I sure hope so." He smiled broadly. "Name's Zane, ma'am. I'm Lash Monroe's brother...well, foster brother, anyway."

Lash's foster brother? Jessi returned the smile and stepped out onto the porch, closing the door on the still-snarling hound dog and taking the beefy hand the man offered. "Well, I'll be. Lash never mentioned you. I'm Jessi Brand, Lash's...friend." She stumbled a little over the last word, then gave her head a shake and motioned the man to take a seat on the porch swing. "Can I get you a drink? Coffee, iced tea?"

"No, no, I'm fine, but thank you kindly. I was hoping to find Lash. Been a long time, you know."

No, she didn't know. "Sorry, but he's not here today. He's in town, probably at the sheriff's office. You can check there. Or...I could call him and tell him you're here."

"Naw, no need to bother him if he's busy. You say he's with the sheriff? That Lash. He always was one to get himself in trouble. I should have known he'd be in hot water."

Jessi blinked and, despite her anger at Lash, felt her hackles rise just a little. "Lash isn't in any trouble, Mr....uh...Zane. He's working as a deputy." Had her chin lifted just a little as she said that? "He's helping my brother Garrett—Garrett's the sheriff here—to solve a rash of cattle rustling in the area."

"Well, I'll be! Lash is a lawman? Imagine that."

"Doesn't seem so hard to imagine to me," she muttered.

The man chuckled. "Well, you didn't know him when I did. Close as two peas in a pod, we were. I adored the little runt. Damn, I'm sorry I missed him, but I just found out he was in town, and I couldn't resist the urge to stop by and find out what he's been doin' with himself. Heard he was working here on the ranch."

"Well, yes, he does that, too."

"Busy fella," Zane said. He stretched his arms along the back of the porch swing while gazing out at the horizon. "This looks like a mighty big spread. You run many cattle?"

"A thousand head," she said proudly.

"Well, now, I musta missed all those cattle driving in. I seen only a dozen or so heifers out in the pasture." He pointed. "Sure is a beautiful ranch, though."

He was a friendly, talkative sort, Jessi decided. And hell, so long as he was Lash's brother, she figured she ought to be friendly.

"A thousand head," he said, sighing and shaking his head in wonder. "Now that is one sight I'd give just about anything to see. Always wanted a ranch, myself. Maybe someday..."

"Do you ride, Zane?" she asked impulsively.

He smiled brightly, and gave her a nod.

It was a nice long chat they had as they rode side by side at a comfortable walk, and Jessi showed Zane around the ranch. He was so very polite, and genuinely interested in everything about the ranch, and her brothers, and her clinic. He seemed to hang on her every word, asking lots of questions, wanting to know everything about his brother's life of late. Jessi wondered why Lash had never mentioned him before.

When they finally said goodbye at the front porch, Jessi found herself inviting Zane back to visit anytime. She wished later that he'd talked more about himself and his childhood with Lash. Maybe she could have learned more about Zane's pigheaded foster brother that way. Ah, well, she thought, waving to the stranger as he drove away, maybe next time he visited he'd volunteer more.

He'd asked her to dinner. Flattering, but not a very attractive offer. She'd eased out of it with a noncommittal reply. But maybe if she accepted, she could get him to talk about Lash. Maybe she could figure out just why it was he was so damned hung up on freedom, and roaming, and so deathly against being tied down by anything or anyone.

Maybe she ought to go ahead and have that dinner with Zane. She'd think on it. It irked her to realize, that despite her claims to the contrary, she still hadn't given up on her hopelessly thickheaded drifter.

Not by a long shot.

Chapter 9

Lash leaned over the polished hardwood bar, nursing a beer and a headache brought on by thinking too much. He couldn't figure Jessi out, and he'd decided it was high time he quit trying. She didn't want him. Fine. He'd just consider it a narrow escape and get on with his life. The best thing to do, the way he figured it, was to avoid her as best he could until he and Garrett wrapped up this investigation, and then get the hell outta Dodge.

Unfortunately, all of those things were easier to decide, than to actually do. He still wanted her. Every time he saw that girl, he ached with wanting her. The memory of that one time he'd been with her haunted him. Bits of it, feelings, sensations, hearing her heartfelt declaration of love, in a voice rough and loud with passion, the way she'd touched him, the way it had *felt* to be inside her—all of it—drifted through his dreams at night, and kept his mind so stirred up by day that he couldn't think about anything else.

The longer he stayed away from her, the more he missed her. And yet, he avoided her. Because he didn't understand any of this. And to tell the truth, it scared him.

Garrett had told him Jessi was spending Sunday at the ranch when Lash stopped in that morning. He'd run into Garrett out near the pasture, saddling up to ride the fencelines, so he'd decided to avoid the house. He'd helped with the various tasks that needed doing around the place, and then he'd headed back into town, never once venturing near the house, where he might run into her. He didn't want a repeat of the other night being played out in front of her family. Vases sailing at his head might make them start asking questions.

Jessi had spent today at the clinic. Yeah, okay, he'd been keeping track of her. Avoiding her like the plague but for some reason unable to stop watching her without her knowing it. He was behaving like some crazed stalker, and he couldn't for the life of him figure out why he had this morbid need to look at her all the time. It only made him crave her touch all the more.

God, he couldn't believe how very badly he wanted to kiss her again!

Lash had seen the contractors packing up their gear, and most of them had left by noon today, with one or two men remaining to finish up with details. And then, early tonight, there had been a van backed up to the door with the name of a veterinary supply company painted on the side.

The garage no longer resembled a garage. The overhead door was gone, replaced by a wide front window. The smaller door served as the main entrance. Lash was dying to see the inside of the place, but didn't figure that would be a very good idea. But he had managed to come up with excuses to drive by often enough to keep tabs on its progress. And on Jessi.

He couldn't help but be worried about her. In fact, his concern for her was on his mind almost as much as his desire for her. He knew something was bothering her, something besides the fact that she'd decided he was the scum of the earth, that is. He'd thought it was a broken heart, but if it wasn't that, then it must be something else. And he was still—vainly, perhaps—convinced that whatever it was, it was his fault. The idea that he might have nothing to do with her odd mood bothered him too much even to consider.

He took another sip from the foamy mug, and nearly choked on the brew when a voice from the past drifted over the jukebox's country twang and the clink of glasses. "Well, well, if it isn't my kid brother."

Very carefully, Lash set the beer down, centering it in the damp ring it had left on the hardwood. He turned, telling himself that his worst nightmare from childhood hadn't just caught up with him. But it had. Zane smiled at him, but the grin didn't meet his piggish eyes as he sauntered forward to take a stool beside him.

"Been a long time, Lash."

"Not long enough," Lash said, and there was a prickling sensation dancing along his nape.

"Oh, hell, can't we let bygones be bygones, brother?"

"You're no brother of mine."

Zane shook his head slowly, clicking his tongue. "Crying shame, that. 'Cause let me tell you, Lash, that little kitten over at the Texas Brand would make one fantasy of a sister-in-law."

Lash's fists clenched, where they rested on the bar. "Maybe you'd like to tell me what the hell you're talking about?"

"Why, Miss Jessi Brand, of course. She gets that look in her eyes when your name comes up. Then again, you always did have a way with the females."

Teeth grated, Lash willed himself calm. "So, you've met Jessi."

"Ah, well, yeah, I suppose you would be curious about that, now wouldn't you? Smart fella. I spent several hours with her Sunday morning, just sitting in that porch swing beside her and chatting like old pals. And then that sweet little thing invited me to go ridin' with her, and of course, being a red-blooded male, I took her up on it."

Lash swallowed the sand in his throat.

"I always did have a knack for taking things that were yours, little brother."

"What the hell are you doing here, Zane?"

Zane just shrugged. "Missed you. Wanted to catch up. But you don't need to say much, because that pretty little thing filled me in nice and thorough. We rode all over that sprawling ranch of hers…all alone. Just the two of us. 'Course, she did most of the talking. I was mostly enjoying the view."

Lash stood up fast.

Zane held up his hands. "Now, Lash, no need getting all excited. I didn't lay a finger on that pretty little thing." He tilted his head. "Not yet, anyway. Have you?"

"You're slime, Zane, and I'm going to have to kick your ass for that. But before I do, maybe you'd like to tell me just what the hell you're really doing here. More importantly, are you gonna get out of town under your own steam, or am I gonna have to see to it that you leave in a pine box?''

Zane smiled, got to his feet, and swallowed the shot he'd ordered in one quick gulp. ''I'm here on business. Won't be for long. A few more days at most. So do you have any claims on the woman or not, Lash? I really need to know, 'cause you know, I think she kinda likes me. I asked her out—dinner's how I put it, but we both know it isn't food I'm gonna be devouring. Man, I can't remember when I've seen such a sweet, tight little—''

Lash's fist flashed out, connected with Zane's face, and the larger man rocked backward, falling over his stool to the floor. He gave his head a shake, rubbed his nose, then looked up at Lash and smiled. ''Then you do return the lady's feelings. Hell, all the more reason for me to show her how a real man would feel when he—''

Lash gripped the bastard's shirt and hauled him to his feet. ''Don't let me catch you anywhere near her, you son of a bitch!''

Grinning, Zane shook his head. Then he sucker-punched Lash in the belly. Lash released him and doubled over, but came up swinging.

''Sheriff Brand! Hurry up! There's trouble at La Cucaracha!''

Garrett shot up from behind the desk, grabbed his hat and headed out. He'd been working late in the office, again. This damned case was baffling him. He'd sent Lash home early, mostly because it was fairly obvious his mind wasn't on his work, anyway. Something was bothering his deputy. Lash wasn't himself at all.

Seemed distracted and brooding all the time. But Garrett supposed it was none of his business.

Well, maybe there was a silver lining in his being stuck here at the office late, yet again. He'd been close by to see to whatever little crisis had cropped up at the local bar.

He strode down the cracked sidewalk, ignoring the shiny new pickup, nearly identical to his old one, that sat outside his office. The insurance company had finally come through. And Garrett didn't miss the little toaster-car one bit. His long strides ate up the distance between his office and the bar. Then he walked inside the smoky room, heard glass smashing, and looked up to see his deputy holding his own in a brawling match with a man twice his size. Both men looked pretty bad, though, and Garrett shook his head slowly, battling a smile of admiration for Lash's spunk. He headed over to break it up.

He damn near took a fist to the head for his trouble. Ducking fast, Garrett spun around and caught the stranger's fist in his hand. "Care to explain what you're doing using my deputy for a punching bag, stranger?"

The big guy stopped, glanced down at the badge pinned to Garrett's chest and lowered his hand, panting, sweaty and bleeding from several locations on his face. Behind him, Lash stood in much the same condition. "He started it," the big guy said. "You ask anybody in here, Sheriff. Lash here hit me first."

Brows lifted, Garrett glanced at Freddy Ortega for confirmation.

The bartender piped up. "Yup, Garrett. I seen it all. Lash started the whole fight." He stood behind mahogany ridge, wiping glasses with a towel and acting utterly unruffled. ''Right after this 'ere stranger insulted your baby sister, wasn't it?'' he asked the beefy man.

Garrett's brows lifted. ''My sister, huh? Well, hell, didn't you know that's illegal here in Quinn?''

''Wha—''

''Hey, everybody, tell this fella about that law. How's it go again? Article four, section two. Hell, I oughtta have it memorized, seeing as how I just wrote it myself, right this minute.'' He spun the man around, twisting one arm behind his back, then pulled the other one to join it and snapped on a pair of handcuffs. Paul Loomis was sitting at a corner table, fighting a smile, and Garrett motioned to him. ''Paul, you mind taking this pile of garbage on over to the jail and shoving him in a cell for me? I need to talk with my deputy.''

Paul touched the brim of his hat, and got to his feet, gripping the guy's elbow and leading him out of the bar. The big guy didn't resist, just sent a menacing glance over his shoulder at Lash. Then he glanced at Garrett. ''You can't hold me for anything more serious than disorderly conduct,'' he called.

''Try assaulting an officer,'' Garrett told him as he was marched out the door.

As if on cue, the murmur of conversation and the clinking of ice in glasses resumed. Garrett turned to Lash. ''That forehead of yours will need stitching. You can tell me about this little incident on the way to Doc's office.''

''Doc's out of town tonight,'' the bartender called. ''Best take him on over to the clinic. Jessi's stitched up her brothers often enough to take care of that little cut.''

A chuckle went up from the patrons close enough

to hear. "Been hanging around them Brands so long, he's getting to be just like 'em," one said.

"Yep. Durn fool stranger ought to know better than to mess with that bunch." More hearty laughter followed as Garrett led Lash outside and along the sidewalk to the new pickup in front of the office.

Lash argued, but it did little good. He could feel the blood trickling down the side of his face from the deep cut just above his eyebrow, and he knew it needed stitching, but damn, he didn't want to see Jessi. Not like this.

Garrett took him inside the little house, since the clinic was still a jumble of unpacked boxes and equipment. He hollered for Jess, and she came out of the living room, took one look at Lash and scowled.

"Garrett, how could you!" she cried.

Garrett frowned, and Lash caught Jessi's eyes and shook his head slightly.

"How could I what?" Garrett asked.

Jessi's eyes narrowed. "You didn't do that to him?" she asked her brother.

Garrett blinked. "'Course not. Why would I—"

"What happened?"

"Some stranger insulted you, little sister. And since there were no Brand brothers at the bar to defend your honor, Lash stood in for us."

Jessi's eyes widened, and her hard expression softened as she searched Lash's face. He felt the touch of those big brown eyes on him. "You did that?" And she smiled just a little, and reached out to brush the hair away from the cut on his forehead. "You got this defending me?"

Lash nodded, then winced as Garrett slapped a hand

on his shoulder. "I gotta go see to my prisoner. You take care of that gash for him, okay, Jess?"

"Yeah," she muttered, and damned if she didn't look a little worried as she took Lash by the arm and led him to a kitchen chair.

Garrett hurried out. Lash had told him who Zane was on the way over. Now, he supposed, he'd have to repeat the whole damned story to Jessi.

She leaned over him, pushing the hair away from his forehead and examining the cut. She was touching him. Damn, but he liked her touching him. "Are you all right?" she asked him.

"Fine."

"You sure? No, just stay there. Sit. I'll get my bag. You look awful."

"Zane looks a lot worse than I do." It was male pride that made him say it, but he didn't take it back.

She had turned to retrieve her bag, but she paused with her back to him. While he could no longer see her face, he *felt* the warmth drain out of her. She wasn't soft toward him now. That straight spine spoke volumes. "You were duking it out with your *brother?*"

"Make no mistake, Jessi, that slimebag is no brother of mine."

"I can't believe you would beat up your own brother!" She fetched the bag and returned, tearing open alcohol wipes with her teeth. Then she began cleaning the cut, and it stung like crazy. Which was good, because it kept him from enjoying having her hands on him so much. Lash sucked in a breath and pulled his head away, but she caught it in one hand and held him still. "Why did you do it?" she asked. "Just because he asked me out to dinner?"

"He really did that?"

"Sure he did. And what's it to you, anyway?"

Lash shook his head, catching her arm in one hand and stilling her. "You stay away from him, Jessi." He stared up into her eyes, making his own hard and his voice firm. "He's trouble, you understand? Don't you go anywhere near him."

"I'll go near him if I want to, Lash Monroe. Since when did you decide you were one of my brothers? Don't I have enough men trying to run my life without you joining the ranks?"

"But, Jessi—"

"No buts. You don't want me for yourself, but you don't want any other man anywhere near me, either, is that it?"

"What the hell do you mean, I don't want you for myself? I offered to marry you, didn't I?"

"Lucky me," she snapped.

"Jessi, Zane's a bastard. He only wants you because of me," he stated.

Jessi stepped away, blinking down at him as if she'd never seen him before, and Lash knew he'd said the wrong thing, yet again.

"Gee, thanks for the compliment. I don't suppose it's even in the realm of reason that he might want me because of me, is it? No, of course not. So tell me, Lash, what is it about you that makes your brother—I'm sorry, *foster* brother—want me?"

"Because making me miserable is his reason for living," he said, shaking his head slowly. "Always has been. He thinks you mean something to me, so—"

"Oh. Well, then, there's no problem, is there? Because I *don't* mean anything to you. He's dead wrong about that. No harm, no foul, Lash. You beat him up for nothing. All you had to do was tell him that I was no more to you than a roll around the garage floor, and he'd have left me alone.''

''Dammit, Jessi, you know that isn't the way it is!''

She tilted her head, staring down at him. ''No? Suppose you tell me just what way it is, then, 'cause I sure as hell don't know.''

''I...I don't know. I don't know, Jessi. If I did...I'd tell you. But...hell, if nothing else, we're friends, aren't we? Or, hell, I thought we were.''

Her eyes fell closed, but not before he saw the little flash of pain that came into them. Hell, he'd gone and hurt her again.

''I got plenty of friends, Lash. I don't need another one.''

''Jess—''

''Just sit still. This is gonna hurt.''

He had no doubt she intended to make sure it hurt as much as possible. He grated his teeth while she readied some needles and silk thread.

''He came to the ranch, didn't he?'' he asked, to distract himself from the inevitable. Not the pain of the stitches she administered, but the pain of wanting nothing more than to pull her into his arms and kiss her senseless. Of wanting to scoop her up into his arms and carry her into that bedroom and love her...

Love her?

''Sure he did,'' she was saying as he blinked in shock and tried real hard to figure out why such a turn of phrase would pop into his mind. ''Sunday. We had a nice talk.''

''About what?''

She shrugged. ''Nothing in particular. Ranching, cattle. He didn't tell me any of your secrets, Lash.

Maybe he'll get to that when I have dinner with him, though.''

''Dammit, Jessi, I told you—''

She pinched the edges of the cut together and jabbed the needle through his flesh. He winced. ''I don't give a damn what you told me,'' she said. She tied off the stitch, snipped the thread with a tiny pair of scissors, then prepared to install another.

He looked up and met her eyes. ''Don't do this,'' he whispered.

''Give me one good reason why I shouldn't.'' And there was something in her eyes, something that should have told him what he was supposed to say, but he couldn't read it quite clearly.

He searched his mind, sought for the right words to convince her. ''He'll hurt you,'' he said. ''I don't want to see you get hurt, Jess.''

Her chin lowered, and her eyes fell away from his. ''Wrong reason,'' she told him, and then she put in another stitch.

A week later, she was still every bit as miserable as she'd been the night she stitched up Lash. He had avoided her as if she carried some deadly plague, and she told herself she didn't really care. She did, though. She must be a hundred kinds of fool, but she did. She hadn't had dinner with Zane, who'd spent one long night in Garrett's jail before her big brother turned him loose and told him he had one week to get out of town. She might have gone, if she'd had the time, just to see if it would make Lash realize that he belonged with her. But with the clinic coming together so fast, there hadn't been a free night yet. And today was her grand opening.

Chelsea had been helping her plan for this all week long. Lord knew she had plenty of time on her hands, what with Garrett so busy trying to track down the rustlers. There hadn't been another incident all week, and Jessi was of the opinion that the creeps had left to go prey on some other cow town, but her stubborn brother refused to let it go.

Monday morning came far too early. But Jessi couldn't have slept anyway, it being the biggest day of her life and all. She dressed quickly, and drove her smoke-belching pickup over to the clinic. The decorations were already in place. She and Chelsea had done all of that last night. Balloons and streamers danced in the early-morning breeze. Picnic tables lined the lawn out front, and that beautiful sign Ben had given her hung proudly over the clinic's front door. Jessi parked in the driveway, and walked slowly past the house, unlocked her clinic and stepped inside to take it in. Her dream come true.

The reception area was lined with chairs and a potted plant Elliot had brought over. A wide counter sectioned off the area where the receptionist would work, once she hired one. Meanwhile, she'd handle that job on her own. The phones were hooked up, lights had been installed, everything was done.

She had two treatment rooms, their cabinets stocked with supplies. She had a surgery room, with sterile instruments at the ready. She had a kennel area with pens of various sizes for overnight guests. And she had an office of her very own. Situated right on the spot where she and Lash had made love. Some demon had compelled her to put her own private space there, not wanting to share it with anyone else. It was her own precious memory, and she'd keep it here, safe.

Damn the man.

Jessi had also had a big metal box installed in the old pickup truck's bed, its dozens of drawers and compartments filled with still more tools of her trade. Most of her work would be with large animals, and it would be done from that truck, at the homes of her neighbors. But there would be plenty of business here, as well. Cats and dogs, mostly, she figured. And it would all begin today. In a couple of hours, half the town would start showing up with food for the celebration picnic. Freddy from La Cucaracha had promised to bring a keg of beer over. Chelsea would be hauling in the salads and casseroles she'd made. People would come to admire the clinic while eating, drinking and making merry.

She really ought to be happy. She really, really ought to be.

But there were a couple of things still undermining her happiness. One was Lash's indifference, of course. That was the main one. The second was the home pregnancy test she had tucked away in the bottom of her purse. She hadn't bought it at the local drugstore. She'd gone out of town for it yesterday, because Lord knew how tongues would have wagged around here if she was seen making such a purchase. Garrett would have known about it within the hour, she'd bet.

She hadn't used the thing yet. Hadn't been able to work up the nerve last night, and she'd told herself that she'd just go ahead and enjoy today's festivities first. That she'd rather not know the results until later. She'd been wrong, of course. She was only going to worry until she had the answer. It was cowardice that was keeping her from doing it right now and having it over with.

"The place looks great."

She sucked in a breath and turned fast. Lash leaned in the doorway, studying her. She felt the same old rush she always felt when he looked at her that way. Scanning her, head to toe, and maybe liking what he saw. At least he hadn't gone back to looking at her as a kid. Maybe he was even remembering…how it had been. She hoped he was. She hoped he wanted her so badly his teeth ached with it.

"And so do you," he said, finally. "Look great, that is."

She didn't. She knew damn well she didn't. She was pale and tired-looking, and she couldn't seem to keep those dark circles under her eyes from growing on a daily basis. But all that would change once she used the stupid kit in her purse and got the negative result she knew was inevitable. It was the not knowing that was getting to her. That kernel of doubt.

"So you showed up after all," she said.

"What, you didn't think I would?"

"The way you've been avoiding me, Lash, I figured you'd hole up in that stupid apartment of yours and stay there until the festivities were over and done."

He shrugged, his gaze falling away from her accusing one. "I thought it was for the best."

"Sure you did."

"Every time I see you, it seems like I say something that hurts you. I don't like hurting you, Jess."

"You don't care one way or the other, and we both know it."

"You're dead wrong on that score. Hell, I proposed to you, didn't I?"

"Yeah. As penance. It's real flattering to be considered the wages of sin, you know that? All that ol' Pharaoh got for his crimes against Israel were plagues and locusts. But you—you must be a far worse sinner than he was to think God would sentence you to something as horrible as marriage.'' She turned away from him as she spoke, but felt his hand on her shoulder a second later, pulling her around to face him again.

''If it sounded that way to you, Jess, then I'm sorry. It's not how I meant it.''

''No? Suppose you tell me just how you did mean it, then?''

He stared down into her eyes, and she could see the confusion in his. His hand eased on her arm, his palm rubbing the spot he'd been gripping before. ''You're like that apple must have been to Adam, you know that?''

''Lord, but we're full of biblical references today, aren't we?'' Her words lacked the acid she'd intended them to carry. It was the look in his eyes that was making them come out soft and whispery, instead of harsh and condemning.

''I still want you, Jess. Dammit, I know it's wrong. Your brothers have treated me like family. They trust me, and I'm surely gonna burn in hell for it, but I can't stop thinking about you…the way it was with us that night…''

His eyes closed. She saw the battle he was waging, saw the guilt in the little lines between his brows and at the corners of his mouth. And, like an idiot, she leaned up, and pressed her lips to his. Lash shuddered, and his arms slipped around her waist. He pulled her close, tight to his body, and he kissed her, long and slow. And Jessi thought there might still be a chance for them. The damn fool had to care a little. He must. He couldn't kiss her like this, hold her like this, if he didn't. He was just too dense to realize it, was all. And right now she didn't know whether to start tearing off his clothes, or smack him upside the head.

His hips arched against hers, and she leaned toward him. She could smack him later.

God, he tasted good. And his arms around her felt right. Strong and sure, as if they belonged there. Always. He tasted her with his tongue, threaded his fingers in her hair to tip her head to just the right angle as he fed from her mouth.

And then a horn sounded, followed shortly by the slamming of a car door. Lash straightened and moved away from her, albeit reluctantly. And as he did, he looked at her, confusion clouding his eyes. She just barely resisted the urge to say, "You're falling in love with me, you big dope. Don't worry, it's not fatal." But she said nothing. Because she wasn't at all sure that was the case, and besides, even if it was, he was going to have to realize it on his own.

The door opened and Garrett stepped inside. He stared from one to the other, and frowned.

"You're early," Jessi said, because it was the only thing that popped into her head to say.

"I'm right on time," he replied. "Apparently Lash is the one who's early."

"He just got here." She dragged her gaze from Lash's, and battled the insane surge of hope she felt trying to wash her sense of reality down the drain.

"Well, people are startin' to arrive, Jess. You ought to be outside to greet 'em."

She plastered a smile on her face and nodded at her brother. Then she went outside to join the festivities. As soon as she exited the clinic, she was hit full in the face with the cheerful noise of a mariachi band. They struck up the second they saw her. She smiled. A person couldn't help but smile when a mariachi band was playing in her face. And she turned to Garrett, blinking in surprise. "Where'd they come from?"

Garrett shrugged. So she glanced to her right, where Lash stood, looking slightly sheepish. "Surprise," he muttered.

Her heart felt as if some big hand were squeezing it. "I didn't know you had it in you to be so sweet," she said. "I can't believe you did this."

"Neither can I," Garrett put in, but the suspicion in his tone didn't break the hold Jessi's gaze had on Lash's, and if he saw the tiny tear that came to her eye, well, she couldn't help it, could she? It was a sweet gesture that touched her—probably a little more than it should.

And maybe she was reading more into his actions today than she should, but it seemed that maybe his heart was finally giving his brain a wake-up call.

Lash reached out to take her hand in his, and as soon as he did, the mariachis changed to a slower tune. And then he actually pulled her into his arms, and danced with her. Right there on the lawn in front of her clinic, with the entire town, and all her brothers, watching. He danced with her, and he leaned close and whispered in her ear, "Don't give up on me just yet, okay, Jessi?"

She tried to swallow and couldn't. "If you think I'm planning to give up, you don't know me very well."

He spun her around the grass until Freddy Ortega cut in. After that she danced with each of the Loomis boys, and then her brothers, except for Elliot, because Elliot hated to dance. And then she danced with Lash again.

The food was put out on the tables, and the music ended as everyone headed that way to eat. And Lash sat beside her during that picnic lunch. As if he belonged there. As if they were a couple or something.

Lord, if he was getting her hopes up like this only to let her down again, she'd never forgive him. Or herself. She had to be realistic here. She had to remember that he felt strongly about marrying her because he'd taken her virginity. And she'd turned him down, so maybe all of this was just his attempt at getting her to change her mind. So he could do the right thing and clear his conscience.

Or maybe…just maybe…he was falling in love with her after all.

It might not mean anything at all, this attention he was suddenly paying her. She told herself that over and over. But for some reason, she just couldn't quite make herself believe it.

At any rate, the party itself was a huge success. The entire town turned out. But Jessi noted one absence that disappointed her right to the toes of her boots. She'd made a point of inviting Zane to this event, having made up her mind that even a foster brother was a brother of sorts. He was the only family Lash had, so far as she knew. And Jessi felt strongly that no family should remain estranged when there was a Brand around to help fix things. She'd run into Zane in town one day, and she'd told him all about the party, talked it up as big as she could, hoping to entice him to attend so that she could try to help him and Lash patch things up at long last. They'd obviously been estranged for quite a while now. Too long, in Jessi's opinion.

She could just picture it all so clearly in her mind.

The joyful reunion. The manly hug. Lash's undying gratitude to her for intervening and saving his relationship with Zane after all these years.

She sighed, and kept watching each new group of people that arrived, looking for Lash's foster brother. But Zane never showed. And it wasn't until they all returned to the ranch much later that night that she finally understood exactly why.

The worst part was, she had no one to blame but herself.

Chapter 10

Lash knew something was wrong before he even hopped out of his car. It was obvious. Garrett's pickup had pulled in ahead of him, and Jessi's rolled in behind. And one by one they piled out of the vehicles and stood there, shaking their heads, brows furrowed in blatant confusion and dawning understanding. The barn doors were wide open, the gate to the south pasture was gaping, and the ground was scarred by tire tracks. Lash just stood there for a moment, gaping in disbelief as his eyes picked out the trail of flattened grass that led as far as the eye could see, without veering once, all the way to the pasture where the young stock grazed. Only he had a feeling they weren't grazing there now.

Jessi raced past him as her brothers swore in turns. It seemed to take the rest of them a second longer to convince their bodies to move. Chelsea—with little Ethan anchored on her hip—and the boys followed where Jessi led, and stood around the spot where she crouched.

"Dual tires," Jessi muttered. "Semis, and more than one. Been gone for at least a couple of hours by now. Maybe longer."

Wes swiped his black Stetson from his head and slammed it against his thigh. "Damn it straight to hell! Look at those tracks! It's like they knew exactly where they were going."

"More than that," Garrett said. "They knew exactly when we'd all be away from the ranch at the same time. I mean, come on. They drove right past the house, bold as brass. They wouldn't have done that if they'd thought anyone was home."

"But everyone in town was at the party," Elliot said. "Who could—"

"Not everyone," Jessi put in. And she turned remorseful eyes on Lash, and he knew right then what she was going to say. "I'm really sorry if I'm wrong about this, Lash, but...I think it was your brother."

"Foster brother, and it wouldn't surprise me. I told you he was trouble."

"But what makes you so suspicious of him, Jessi?" Garrett asked.

She closed her pretty eyes and sighed as if her heart was going to break. "God, Garrett, this is all my fault. He came over here last Sunday, all full of questions about the ranch and the cattle—how many head we ran and how the pastures were growing and how big our spread was. I thought he was just curious about us because Lash worked here, but I should have known. Jeez, I was stupid. I told him everything, even took him on a tour of the ranch and showed him the pastures where the beefers graze. Pointed out the young stock, showed off the prize bull…''

''And you told him about the party?'' Chelsea asked.

Jessi nodded, then slowly lowered her head. ''I thought if I could get him to come to the grand opening, he and Lash might be able to patch things up.'' She lifted her gaze, meeting his eyes. ''I didn't know how bad it was, Lash. I really didn't. I should've kept my nose out of your business. I'm so sorry.''

''You were only trying to help,'' he said. ''I should have figured you'd try something like that. Jessi, this isn't your fault. I should have been more clear about Zane when I tried to warn you about him, but I was just too damned jea—'' He broke off. Holy cow, he'd nearly said he was jealous. What was wrong with him?

Oh, Lord, it was worse than he'd thought. Now that he considered it, it was true. He actually *had* been jealous.

Jessi pressed her palms to her cheeks and stared out toward the pasture. ''Lord, this could ruin us.''

Wes put a hand on her shoulder. ''Hey, come on, kiddo, we can always mortgage your clinic to recoup the losses.'' She looked up at him, and he winked. ''C'mon, Ben,'' he said to the big, quiet Brand who just stood musing. ''Let's saddle up and see what the damage is.''

Ben nodded. ''Let's hope those trucks spooked the cattle so that at least a few of them ran off before they could herd them into the trailers.''

''Yeah.'' Wes headed for the house instead of the barns, and when Ben asked why, he said, ''Figure we'd better take a couple of shotguns, just in case.''

''Make it one,'' Ben said. ''I don't plan to kill a

man unless I have no choice, and if that's the case, my hands are all I need."

Everyone just stared at Ben for a moment, but the shocked reaction passed and was swallowed by the buzz of activity. Lash could hear the phone jangling insistently from inside the house. Chelsea went running off to answer it, the baby bouncing on her hip. Elliot joined Ben and Wes in checking on what cattle remained. And Jessi just stood there, her gorgeous face twisted into a mask of regret. Lash took a step toward her, with every intention of pulling her close to him and holding her and making her feel better any way he could—only to feel Garrett's heavy hand fall on his shoulder.

"She's gonna be just fine, Lash. We need to talk, you and I."

Lash swallowed hard. It almost sounded as if Garrett knew. "I never meant to hurt her," he managed.

Garrett frowned. "It's not your fault this Zane character robbed us blind. He's the one who hurt her—hurt all of us. Hell, Lash, you can't think we'd blame you for this."

A three-hundred-watt bulb flashed on above Lash's head then, and he realized it wasn't Jessi Garrett he wanted to have a talk with him about. It was Zane. He did his best to recover his fumble, and followed Garrett into the house.

Before they got through the door, Chelsea was holding the phone out toward Garrett. "It's Jimmy Rodriguez from the Circle-Bar-T. They got hit, too. Before he called, I heard from the Double Horseshoe. And, Garrett, the machine is blinking like crazy. I'll check the tape, but it looks to me like the bastards wiped out half the county."

Garrett closed his eyes. "Take down the details, darlin', and tell Jimmy I'm doing all I can."

Lash grated his teeth. "I might be able to find out something, Garrett, if I can make a few phone calls."

He nodded. "Looks like our line's gonna be tied up all night. And I'm afraid the phones in the office will be just as bad. Let's head over to your place and see what we can turn up."

Lash nodded and turned to Jessi as Garrett headed for his pickup truck. "Jess, honey, you gonna be okay?"

She met his eyes and blinked—maybe at what he'd just called her, because it had surprised him, too, to hear the endearment roll naturally off his tongue. "I'm fine. You go on."

He reached out to enfold her hand in his, squeezed it gently, and turned to join Garrett.

But what they turned up about Zane through the long hours of the night was definitely not good news. Turned out the bully had been a busy boy for the past twenty-odd years. No small-time larceny, either. He'd turned cattle rustling into big business, and he was wanted in five states. Garrett had the FBI fax him the information they had, and the theory the Feds developed was that he was smuggling the stolen cattle by the truckload over the border into Mexico. There the trail ended. No one knew who his Mexican buyer was or where he might be located. The Texas Rangers had an APB out on the big rigs, but if Jessi's tracking skills were as good as she claimed, those trucks were long since over the border.

But Lash had an idea.

"You know, Garrett," he said later as they sat over hot coffee in his apartment, wondering what the hell to do next. "I learned a little bit about this slob, being raised in the same house with him."

"You have my sympathies," Garrett muttered.

"He's a coward," Lash said. "Always loved trouble, but never had the balls to stir it up all by himself. He needed egging on. Needed a few other lowlifes around to show off for, or it wasn't worth the effort. Plus, when it was time to pay the piper, he could always be sure to have a scapegoat."

Garrett was sitting up a little straighter now. "So, you think you know who else might be involved?"

"This might be a long shot, but in those days it was always Jack and Peter who helped him pull his nonsense. Now, Peter's given name was Pedro Gonzales. The preacher—"

"The *preacher?*"

"Our foster father," Lash clarified. "He saw fit to give Pedro a more 'American'-sounding name. But as I recall, Pedro used to like to brag about his relatives in Mexico."

"So it's safe to assume he might have connections there," Garrett said.

"I can make a couple of phone calls."

"To your preacher?"

"No, he's gone now. No doubt thumping Bibles in that big pulpit in the sky, and probably ordering little angels to memorize verses when their wings are wrinkled. But his wife's sister is still living in Illinois, and she always did have a knack for keeping up on the family business."

"Don't tell me," Garrett said, "aunt Kate."

"You got it." Lash picked up the phone and dialed the string of numbers he knew by heart.

* * *

An hour later, Lash was packing his belongings. Then he slung his bag in the back of his beat-up convertible, thinking that it was almost as if he were drifting on to the next great adventure. Only this time, the idea didn't appeal to him in the least.

Garrett leaned on the driver's-side door, shaking his head. "I don't like this, Lash."

"Look, I'm not going to do anything. I'll just check it out. If Petey inherited his rich uncle's meat-packing business like aunt Kate says, then chances are that's where all the cattle are ending up. I'll call you as soon as I see for myself what's going on."

"You could get in over your head, Lash."

"But you understand it, don't you, Garrett? This is a family thing. An old grudge between Zane and me that goes back as far as I can remember. It's my fight, and I have to settle it on my own."

Garrett scowled, but nodded. "Yeah, I understand."

"I need to ask you a favor, Garrett. And it's a big one."

Garrett lifted his brows and waited.

"Don't tell Jessi I've left town, and even if she somehow finds out I'm gone, don't tell her where I went or why."

Garrett tilted his head. "You're gonna have to explain that one to me, Lash. Now, I been letting a lot of stuff between you and my sister slide lately, but this—"

"You know her," Lash said. "You know how she dives into trouble headfirst, without a thought about her own safety. Rushes in where angels fear to tread, right? If she finds out, Garrett, she's liable to decide I need help and come charging down there after me. And

I don't want her anywhere near my slimebag foster brother. More than that, I just don't want her getting hurt."

Garrett nodded. "All right, you make a good point. I won't tell her. But, Lash, we're going to have to talk about this...this whatever-it-is with you and Jessi—"

"When I get back," he said. "Promise."

Garrett scanned Lash's face, eyes narrowed, but eventually he nodded, and clasped Lash's hand. "Okay. You just be sure you come back in one piece so you can keep that promise."

"I will. And, Garrett, don't tell your brothers about this, either, okay? I don't want one of them doing something foolish, or slipping up and telling Jessi. This is just between you and me."

"You have my word on it. Call me when you get down there. And I mean the minute you get down there, Lash, so you can tell me where you're staying and how I can reach you."

Lash nodded. "Best set a time, so I can be sure you're the one who answers the phone." The thought of having to explain himself to Jessi didn't appeal to him. He wouldn't be any damned good at lying to her. He'd be seeing those big brown eyes in his mind, all hurt and damp and loving.

"Midnight tomorrow?" Garrett asked. "That give you enough time to get down there and find a phone?"

"Midnight tomorrow," Lash repeated. "Thanks, Garrett. For everything."

Garrett stood in the darkness, staring after him, as Lash pulled away.

Jessi couldn't stop pacing back and forth, endlessly, across the front porch. The telephone kept ringing inside, but Chelsea was covering the calls like a pro. Little Ethan was having a much-needed nap. Wes, Elliot and Ben were out checking on the cattle. And Lash was at his place with Garrett, chasing down leads. But they'd been gone quite a while now, and though she squinted into the distance, willing them to show up, there was no sign of them yet.

Lash had squeezed her hand before he left. He'd called her honey.

She gnawed her lower lip and wondered what she was supposed to make of that.

"You okay?" Chelsea asked softly from beyond the screen door. The phone had finally decided to give its ringer a break.

"Restless," Jessi replied. "I think I'm gonna take a drive. Look around."

"Heading south, by any chance?" Chelsea had crossed her arms over her chest and was looking her over thoroughly.

"Just driving. Not tracking rustlers. Hell, Chels, I wouldn't know where to begin."

"If you're not back in an hour, I'll send your brothers looking."

Jessi rolled her eyes. "You're ruthless, you know that?"

Chelsea only smiled and waved Jessi on her way. Jessi jumped into her pickup, then took a shortcut to reach Route 10. Her plan was to head south from there, until she found the most likely bridge for a half-dozen semis to use to cross the Rio Grande. The idea was stupid. There wasn't going to be any sign of the cattle trucks by now. But then again, she wasn't doing any good sitting at home, either. So she bounced and rattled over the dirt-road shortcut, turned onto the paved stretch that would get her to Route 10, then frowned into her rearview mirror.

The car coming up fast behind her looked like— Hell, it didn't just look like it, it was— Lash's old black convertible.

But he was supposed to be back in Quinn with Garrett and— She slammed the door on the thoughts that tried to come to her then. She wouldn't jump to conclusions. It was a bad habit she'd been meaning to break for quite a while, and now seemed like a good time to start. She blew her horn, and watched him in her rearview mirror. He flashed his headlights to let her know he'd recognized her. Okay, time to figure things out. Jessi put on her right turn signal and pulled off onto the shoulder. She watched as Lash did the same.

Then she got out of her truck. They were close to the highway. She could hear the traffic, even see the glow of headlights moving in the distance. But this side road was all but deserted. If a car passed once every half hour, it would be a busy night.

Thrusting her hands into her jeans pockets, she walked back toward Lash's car as he got out. The convertible's top was down. It was a beautiful night for a drive with the wind in your hair, she thought, and wished she'd been riding in there with him.

Lash shut his door and took a step toward her. Then, as if he'd just thought of something, turned to reach into the back seat. Frowning, Jessi saw him quickly toss a jacket over the suitcase that rested there. And her eager footsteps came to a halt.

So this was it. They knew who was behind the rustling, and he and Garrett had probably turned the whole case over to some higher authority. The Texas Rangers or the FBI or someone like that. And now that his job with Garrett was done, Lash was keeping his promise. He was leaving town, just like the drifter he'd claimed to be. He was moving on, just the way he'd warned her he would.

And he hadn't even said goodbye. Probably figured it would be easier on her this way. Hell, he knew she loved him. It wasn't his fault he didn't feel the same.

She was glad she hadn't told him about the damaged condoms, or the home pregnancy test she'd bought. At least he was doing what he wanted to do. At least this was honest. Real. Not that obligatory thing he was trying to foist on her before. Not his stupid, overdeveloped sense of duty.

She sighed as he turned to face her again. Hell, if this was the way he wanted to do it, fine. Let him go on thinking she hadn't seen that suitcase in the back. Let him slip away without having to face her and tell her he was leaving. What did she care?

She plastered a smile on her face and started walking toward him again, stopping when they stood toe-to-toe.

"What're you doing out here, Jessi?" he asked her, his voice low and soft. And his eyes were probing hers, seeing way more than she wanted them to.

"Just felt like a drive," she said. "You?"

"Following up on a lead. It shouldn't take long."

She closed her eyes, because his white lie hurt so much he'd have to see it reflected there. "Sure," she said. "A lead."

"I'm glad I ran into you, though," he told her. "We have to talk, Jess."

To say goodbye? she wondered. Was he going to tell her how he was leaving tonight, and how he'd probably never see her again?

Lash took her hand in his, and pulled her with him as he walked back to his car. He opened the passenger door for her, and she got in, steadfastly refusing to glance into the back seat. Then he got in the driver's side and closed the door. The top was still down, so the night air surrounded them. She could hear crickets starting up their nightly thrum, and gradually competing with the sounds of the highway not far away. Lash turned toward her, took off his hat and tossed it in the back before pushing one hand through his hair.

"I think you misunderstood me before," he began.

"I understood you just fine, Lash. You told me the truth, right from the start. I'm a big girl. I can handle it."

"That's not what I meant, Jessi."

She blinked when her eyes tried to fill, then lifted one hand to touch his face. "I don't want to do this," she whispered. "I don't want to talk." Not if talking meant telling him goodbye. She was strong, but she didn't think she was strong enough to do that.

"But, Jess, I—"

She leaned forward, and pressed her lips to his. And it was only an instant before she felt him beginning to respond. His mouth softened, his hands slipped around her neck, his fingers cradling her head so gently it made her want to cry. Those same fingers threaded upward, into her hair.

He lifted his mouth from hers. His eyes had turned to molten silver. "You're just about the sweetest thing I ever tasted," he murmured.

"Then taste me again, Lash."

He closed his eyes. "Damn, woman. I must've been out of my mind to think…"

"Shh…" she whispered. "No talking, Lash. Not tonight. Not when…" She stopped herself from saying, "not when it's the last night we'll have." She didn't want to ruin this with a confrontation. "Not when I want you so badly."

She watched his eyes open, saw his imminent surrender in those pale blue depths. He wasn't even going to try to deny her this time. He reached out to touch her, trailing his fingertips from her cheek, all the way down her neck and over her breast to her belly. She closed her eyes and sighed in longing.

And then he pulled her close and kissed her again, and it was so bittersweet that she had to battle tears. To love him this much, to know he was leaving her…she wanted to hate him, but she couldn't find it in her. He'd told her this was how it would be, after all. He'd warned her again and again, but she hadn't listened. She had no one to blame for her heartbreak but herself.

But she'd have this. One last night to cling to, to remember him by. She lowered her hands between them, and one by one opened the buttons of his shirt. Then she pushed the material away and pressed her palms to his chest. Warmth and firmness under her hands. His heart pounding, his breathing ragged.

His hands were at the hem of her shirt, and he pulled it off over her head. And then he pushed her back against the seat, and trailed his lips over her breasts, capturing one peak and suckling it as if he were feeding there. As if he needed this sustenance to survive.

Then he sat up slowly, eyes blazing. "I should put the top up," he whispered.

"I like it down."

"Someone could come along."

"I really don't care." She reached out and tugged

the button of his jeans loose, then carefully lowered the zipper.

"This time," he told her, "I brought protection."

"Hope you didn't buy them at Mr. Henry's."

"Why—"

"Shh..." she said, and she pushed his jeans down, skimming her hands over his hips. "It might not matter now, anyway," she whispered. "Make love to me, Lash." She pushed him down until he was sitting on the seat of the car. Then she knelt up and managed to kick free of her own jeans. She looked at him sitting there, aroused and waiting for her. And she slowly lowered her head into his lap, taking him into her mouth, working him with her lips until he was trembling and tangling his hands in her hair and making desperate, pleading noises deep in his throat.

She sat up again, and slowly, she straddled him, lowering herself over him, down into his lap, while she held his gaze with her own.

He closed his eyes and released a slow, long, shuddery sigh.

Her hands clasped his shoulders, nails digging slightly into his flesh, and she lifted herself up, lowered again, drew away, came back. Over and over she moved, her pace so slow it was agonizing. He clamped her waist, urging her faster. His head fell backward, and he grated his teeth, his lips parting in delicious anguish as she made him insane. She could see the cords in his neck standing out. She could feel his pulse skyrocketing.

His hands slid lower, cupping her buttocks and squeezing her. And then he brought his head up, caught her nipple in his teeth and suckled it as if trying to extract its nectar. She moved her hands to the back of his head to pull him closer, hold him to her breast, and she quickened her pace. He was moving, now, too. Arching himself up and into her, clinging to her, moaning her name. And then she didn't hear anything as the climax broke over her in waves, each one more powerful than the one preceding it. She whispered that this night would last her forever, and then she relaxed against him, sliding her arms around him and lowering her head onto his shoulder.

And he held her, just that way, stroking her hair, for a very long time. But she knew it couldn't last. And finally he said, "Jessi, I don't want to, honey, but I have to go."

"I know," she said. "I know." He'd told her all along, hadn't he? How could she not know?

She slowly got off him, reaching for her clothes.

"We're going to have that talk," he said. "But it's gonna have to wait, for now. If I wait too long—"

"It's all right, Lash. There's nothing you need to explain to me. I understand." She pulled her shirt on, climbed out of the car, where it was easier to stand, and yanked her jeans on. Lash was struggling into his inside the car. She smiled gently as she watched him. "Goodbye, Lash." She turned to start walking toward her pickup.

"Jessi?" He looked up as she left, still trying hard to right his clothes in the confines of the vehicle. His shirt hung open, his hat was on crooked, and his jeans were still undone when he jumped out to stand on the roadside.

A car buzzed by, and its occupants blew their horn at him and hollered something obscene out the window.

"Dammit, Jessi, wait. At least you have to know that when I said I wanted to marry you before, I—"

"I know," she whispered. "I already know." She blew him a kiss, climbed into her pickup, started the engine and drove away fast, heading for home instead of the highway. She had to get out of there before the tears started flowing. If he saw them, he'd go back to believing she was some innocent, naive little girl who couldn't handle reality.

Problem was, she was wishing she could be the naive girl he thought she was. But she couldn't. Not when reality was staring her squarely in the face. She loved him, and he was leaving. And there was still a slim chance she might be carrying his child.

Hell, reality was just no fun at all.

Jessi tried really hard to act perfectly normal at home, but she suspected her family saw right through her. And whenever anyone mentioned Lash's name, she had to avert her eyes so that she could have a minute to blink them dry.

"Speaking of Lash..." Wes said, after someone mentioned his name yet again, this time as they gathered for leftovers in the kitchen. No one could sleep, after the rustling, and now, at midnight, everyone was hungry. "Where the hell is he? I thought he'd be out here with you, Garrett, seeing as how we were the latest victims of the rustlers."

"No need of that," Garrett said. "We've pretty much figured it was that lowlife Zane who did it. Now all we have to do is track him down."

"Oh." Wes frowned and reached for another piece of fried chicken. "So why aren't we doing it?"

"I'm just waiting for some information to come in," Garrett said. "Don't worry, we'll get him."

Elliot tilted his head, observing and listening. "Not like you to be so vague, Garrett," he said.

"Not like you to be so curious," Garrett said quickly. "I'm goin' up to bed. Can't do any good to sit up all night."

"Me too," Jessi said softly, drawing all her brothers' eyes to her face, every set of them studying her worriedly.

"You getting sick again, Jessi?" Wes asked.

"You're so quiet," Ben added.

"You should talk, Ben," she replied, injecting a lightness she didn't feel into her tone. "My brother, the epitome of the 'strong, silent type.'" Ben smiled at her, and she smiled back, but it felt strained. Then she said good-night and headed up to her room, but she was far from ready to go to sleep.

She put on her nightgown, and actually crawled into bed. She lay there, wide awake and staring at the ceiling, for over an hour before she gave up the notion of getting any rest tonight. She couldn't even close her eyes.

Garrett must already know that Lash had moved on. After all, they'd solved the rustling. They knew now that Zane was the mastermind behind the whole thing, and since he'd no doubt left the state and maybe even the country, it was up to the FBI to bring him in. Lash's job was done. He'd only promised Garrett he'd stay until it was, and he'd probably turned in his badge tonight, when they went to his place in town.

But Garrett had his suspicions about Jessi and Lash, and he didn't have the heart to tell her the truth.

Poor Garrett. It would be easier on him if she told

him she knew, and that she was all right with it. But she wasn't quite sure she *was* all right with it yet. So she paced, and worried, and she figured she might as well just buck up and get used to the fact that she'd never see Lash Monroe again. It wasn't the end of the world...as much as it felt like it was.

Wes said over a hundred head of cattle had been taken. It was a terrible loss, but the ranch would probably survive. Still, she felt personally responsible for the loss. So as long as she was pacing anyway, she went ahead and worried about that, as well.

The pregnancy test was still in its wrapper in the bottom of her purse. So she paced still more, and she worried about that, above and beyond all else. She gnawed her lip and told herself she couldn't use it tonight. She stopped pacing, stared at her purse, took a step toward it, then shook her head hard and resumed moving along the path she was trying to wear in her carpet. She had enough on her mind tonight without knowing the results of that stupid pink pregnancy test kit. And what idiot decided to wrap them up in pink cellophane, anyway?

Ah, but if she knew the results were negative, it would be one *less* thing to worry about, right? And she had to do something. Anything productive.

"All right," she said, and nodded firmly. "What am I, a woman or a wimp?" She lifted her chin. "Woman. Pure Texas woman, toughest breed on the planet. Too tough to be so scared of a five-dollar package from the drugstore." She nodded hard. "So, let's do it."

She locked her bedroom door, took the kit from her purse, unwrapped it and read the instructions twice.

Then she went into the adjoining bathroom.

She came out a few minutes later and scuffed aimlessly until she found herself sinking onto the stool in front of her vanity. She focused her blurred vision and saw that her face was very pale and her eyes were huge as they stared back at her from the vanity mirror. In something like awe, she laid her palms very gently against her abdomen. "I can't believe it," she whispered, and a tear made of sheer emotion spilled from her eye and rolled silently down her cheek.

She'd expected to feel panic-stricken, devastated, frightened, when she looked down and saw the positive results so clearly showing in the test kit. But instead, she'd felt something entirely different. A wave of warm, soothing, overwhelming joy. A glowing feeling that seemed to fill her up from her head to her toes. She could almost believe it was shining from her eyes like the pale amber glow of light from an oil lamp on a stormy night.

She was going to have Lash Monroe's baby. She was carrying the child of the man she loved. And there was nothing frightening or devastating about it.

She looked into the mirror again, and this time she smiled.

Chapter 11

"So," Garrett said to Chelsea as they lay in bed, her snuggled so close to him that he could feel her heart beating. "This aunt Kate person told Lash that his other foster brother, Peter, had gone back to Mexico when his uncle died, leaving him—get this—lock-stock-and-barrel ownership of his meat-packing business."

"You're kidding me," she said. "Gosh, how many rotten bad-news foster brothers did that poor guy have to put up with, anyway?"

"Three," Garrett said. "He doesn't think the other one is involved, though. But it seems Zane and this Peter were always stirring up trouble together. So Lash figures Peter has to be Zane's connection. He got an address for the company, and he's going down there to check it out."

"All by himself?" Chelsea sat up a little, staring down at Garrett with a bit of censure in her eyes.

"Yeah, I didn't like that part of it, either. But Lash says he and Zane have a score to settle that goes back a long ways, and that it's their own private war, and he has to take care of this himself. I did make him promise to check in, though, and to let us know if he gets himself into trouble."

Chelsea nodded. "You know how many men Zane must have had working with him to pull off as many rustlings as he did yesterday?" she asked him.

Garrett grimaced, and closed his eyes. "I promised Lash I'd give him a chance to handle this on his own."

"He's going to get himself killed, going down there alone. He's walking into a snake pit."

"Sweetheart, he's not gonna try to take them down or anything. He's just gonna check the place out, see if any cattle are walking into the slaughterhouse with our brand on their hides, see if Zane is down there. Then he'll call in the cavalry."

"The cavalry being...?"

Garrett shook his head. "Wes, Elliot, Ben and me, of course."

"No Feds?"

Garrett shrugged. "Depends on Lash. If he wants me to bring them in, I will. But, hon, if he'd rather not, we'll handle it ourselves. Hell, Lash is like family."

"Maybe more like family than you think," she muttered.

He bunched up his brows and stared hard at her. "Now that sounds like maybe you know something I don't know. Chelsea...is there something going on between Lash and Jessi?"

She shrugged. "Wish I knew. It would be nice, though, wouldn't it?"

"Nice, hell!" He sat up in the bed. "He's too old, and he's a drifter, and—"

"And he's a hell of a good man, and you love him like a brother already. Calm down, you big lug. I swear, I never saw any man as resistant to Cupid's arrow as you! I had to damn near get myself killed before you figured out we belonged together, and now you're pretending to know what's best for your sister. You've got to learn to let love take its own course, honey. And even if you don't, it won't matter, because it's going to anyway."

He didn't like the sounds of this. Not one little bit.

"Chels, there's one more thing. Lash made me promise I wouldn't say a word to Jessi—or to the boys, either, for that matter—about where he went or why. He says he's seen the way she dives headfirst into trouble, and he's right. Remember when I was facing an ambush in that canyon and she insisted on coming along to help get me out of it? She could have been killed then—"

"I remember. I was there, too, you know. And the way I recall it, Jessi held her own and made a few of those criminals sorry she'd come along at all."

"She's just a kid, Chelsea."

"She's a grown woman with a career and a business of her own. You've got to get that through your head."

"Lash thought it best she not know what he was up to until it's over with. He doesn't want her rushing off half-cocked and getting hurt, and I agree with him."

"She'd realize how stupid and risky what he's doing is, same as I do," Chelsea said.

"She'd get herself hurt trying to go after him, especially if she's got some hare-brained notion that she's in love with him."

"Yeah. Hell of a hare-brained notion that would be."

"Don't tell her, Chelsea. Promise me?"

"What could I tell her? Mexico's a big country. And for that matter, how are you going to know where to go when Lash needs your help?"

"He's going to call tomorrow night at midnight. Sooner, if he gets into trouble. He'll tell me where he's at then. So do you promise to keep this from Jessi?"

"I promise," she said. "I won't tell her unless it becomes absolutely necessary."

Garrett frowned at her and tried to see just what mischief was working behind her eyes. But, as always, his Chelsea only revealed what she chose to reveal. Which most of the time was everything, at least to him. But once in a while it was not quite everything. He had a feeling this was one of those times.

Six times Lash caught himself driving way over the speed limit. He was in one hell of a hurry, and he told himself it was because he wanted to catch Zane red-handed with those cattle. But it was a lengthy drive, over deserted stretches of dark nighttime highway, and it gave a man time to think. Maybe a little too much time to think.

So he got to thinking, and he didn't like what it was he was thinking about. He blamed it on the heat, then the darkness and the lack of streetlights, and finally on the heartbreaking crooning of country music, which was all his radio could pick up for a while. Songs belted out by men who were hurting so bad their voices cracked, just as their hearts apparently had. Crying over that perfect woman they hadn't realized they loved until it was too late. Moaning about wishing for a second chance as they watched her walk down the aisle with somebody else. Sheesh, it was enough to drive a man nuts.

Of course, he didn't quite have enough willpower to lift his hand and turn that knob in search of a different station, though he couldn't figure out why. So he listened until he lost the signal a little while later. After that, all he got were Spanish-speaking stations, and the music they played ranged from sexy Tejano to hot Latin beats that only served to remind him of the look in Jessi's eyes just a little while ago, when she'd driven him out of his mind with sensations in the front seat of his car. And then there were the heartfelt, emotional ballads with Spanish guitar accompanying them, which reminded him of her eyes when she'd realized he was responsible for that mariachi band at her grand opening. And he remembered dancing with her later.

Hell, everything reminded him of Jessi Brand. And he was more convinced than ever that he had to do the right thing by her. He'd taken advantage of her, and he really ought to make up for that. And if she thought marrying her was some kind of punishment in his eyes, she was wrong. It wasn't punishment at all. It was compensation. And hell, it wouldn't be so bad to be Jessi Brand's husband.

Just who did he think he was kidding, anyway? It would be the closest thing to heaven.

"Jessica Lynn Brand Monroe," he muttered, and then he grinned. "Jessi Monroe." It had a nice ring to it. "Dr. Jessica Monroe, D.V.M."

Well, hell, there was no question about it. He had to at least try to convince her that this was the right thing to do. And what her brothers, with their old-fashioned sense of values, would expect them to do.

What the Reverend Mr. Stanton would have flat-out ordered him to do. Hell, it was what he expected himself to do. He'd been raised to do the right thing. And the good book said it was better for a man to marry than to be burning up with lust. And he certainly was that.

A little voice in his head whispered that it was more than any of those things he'd just listed in his mind. Marrying Jessi wasn't just what he *should* do. It was what he *wanted* to do. And maybe that was what she'd been needing to hear. Maybe if he told her that, she'd change her mind.

Maybe he should just tell her. He nodded his head. Yeah. He'd just tell her.

That decided, he started humming along to the tune of the music, and then he frowned. Considering what he was facing a few more miles to the south, he had to wonder just what in the hell he was feeling so good about.

"You have to tell me where he went," Jessi went on. "Chelsea, I wouldn't ask if it wasn't important."

"I promised Garrett I wouldn't say anything." Chelsea had every intention of saying something—Jessi could see it in her eyes.

"Look, this is silly. I know he left. I'm okay with that, but there's a reason I need to know where he is. I'm going to have to get in touch with him...when the time is right...and..." Jessi frowned then, and tilted her head. "Chelsea, why in the world wouldn't Garrett want me to know where Lash has gone?"

"Because they both think you'll go running after him."

Jessi's eyes widened. "Like I'm so desperate I need

to chase a man down and throw myself at him? God, Chelsea, you don't really believe that, do you?''

''No one believes that,'' she said. ''No one thinks you'd go after him to throw yourself at him. It's...'' She let her voice trail off.

Jessi frowned. She knew something more was going on than what she already knew. And if she couldn't find out what it was, her name wasn't Jessica Brand.

''If I wasn't chasing him to rope and brand him, Chelsea, why would I be going after him?''

Chelsea lowered her eyes.

''He's in trouble, isn't he?'' Jessi whispered, and she searched her sister-in-law's face.

''No. Not yet,'' Chelsea said.

She wanted to say more, Jessi could see it plainly, but she also knew that it was up to her to ask the right questions. Chelsea couldn't just break her promise to Garrett. It was one of the things Jessi respected most about her. That deep-running sense of loyalty.

''But he's in danger, isn't he, Chelsea?'' Chelsea didn't nod, but her eyes affirmed Jessi's guess. And then Jessi caught her breath. ''He went after that sleazy Zane, didn't he? I'm right, aren't I?''

Chelsea met her eyes and said nothing.

''Where?'' Jessi pressed.

''I can't tell you that, Jessi. I promised Garrett...''

''But...?''

''But if the phone should ring around midnight, and if you were to pick it up and be very quiet, you might find out exactly what's going on with Lash. I'm only saying so because I think you deserve to know and because...of this...''

She dipped a hand into her pocket, and Jessi heard the crinkle of cellophane. Then Chelsea pulled out the pink bit of wrapper and opened her palm to reveal the home pregnancy test's brand name across the front.

Jessi snatched it out of Chelsea's hand and jammed it into her jeans pocket, looking around them to be sure no one else had seen. "Where did you get that?"

"It was my turn for housework," Chelsea said. "I was taking out the trash, and it sort of fluttered out of a bag. Darn lucky it was me and not one of your brothers who picked it up."

Jessi closed her eyes and tried to slow her escalating heartbeat as she realized just how easily that might have happened. "It was those damned condoms that little freckle-faced monster poked full of holes," she confessed, her words emerging in a fast, harsh whisper. She rushed to get them out before she could change her mind.

"Oh, Jess," Chelsea muttered. She was watching Jessi's face, waiting, all but holding her breath. "Are you going to tell me?"

"Tell you…?"

"Jeez, Jessi, tell me the results! I'm dying here."

Jessi closed her eyes and lowered her chin to her chest.

"Positive," she whispered. "I'm pregnant, Chelsea."

Chelsea's arms came around her, pulled her close and held her hard. "Oh, baby, it's gonna be okay. I promise you that. This is between you and me for now, okay? No one's going to know until you're ready. And, honey, you know I'm gonna be here for you, no matter what you decide to do."

"Thanks," Jessi said, and then she let herself hug Chelsea back, and a few tears burned her eyes.

"Thanks. God, it's good to hear that. But I think I've already decided…I want to keep it, Chelsea."

Chelsea stroked her hair. "Then I'll help you. You're going to be all right." She stepped back just a little and looked down at Jessi's face, smiling. "Are you going to tell him?"

"No," she said. "No, I can't. Not yet. I want him to fall in love with me, Chels. If I tell him this, then he's going to say and do anything he thinks necessary to get me to marry him, and I want to know it's real. I won't marry a man who doesn't love me."

"But, honey, what about the baby?"

"What baby?" Garrett said from the doorway. Jessi stiffened and saw the look of shock in Chelsea's eyes. Then Chelsea painted her face with a great big smile and kept on talking as if she hadn't seen or heard her husband. "You going to watch that baby for me next weekend or not, Jessi? 'Cause if you can't, I need time to find someone else. I promised to fill in at the Women's Center."

"What? Oh…um, sure. I'd love to watch little Ethan for you. Anytime." Without turning around or even glancing her brother's way, Jessi hurried out of the house.

She closed her eyes in relief when she heard Lash's voice on the other end of the phone line at midnight that night. Her bag was already packed and waiting in the truck outside. She had a map. She'd filled the gas tank and checked the oil. She was ready.

She covered the mouthpiece with her hand so that neither Lash nor Garrett would hear her relieved sigh when Lash's voice—sounding perfectly normal—

reached her ears. She hadn't even realized she was holding her breath.

"It was Zane, all right," Lash told Garrett. "He's here, with about a dozen others I suspect are part of his rustling operation. Then there's Petey and his crew of cutthroats. All told, I'd say this is going to be a tough nut to crack."

"You'd better sit tight, then," Garrett said. "You got a room somewhere?"

"Yeah, fleabag hotel called Casa del Coronado. But I can't just sit here, Garrett. I have a feeling Zane and the boys are just gonna take the money and run. And we might never track them down if that happens."

"You stay where you are," Garrett said. "I'll call the Federales and get them started, and then the boys and I will be—"

"No, you guys stay out of this. I don't want to be responsible for Jessi losing one of her brothers. This is my fight."

"Hey, pal, those are my cattle about to become fajita filler, so how do you figure it's your fight?"

"It's a family thing, like I told you. I want you to stay out of it, Garrett."

Garrett muttered, but agreed. Jessi stood there gaping, not believing her brother would be such an idiot. Lash was going to end up dead!

"All right, pal, but wait for the Federales, okay?"

"Unless he makes like he's leaving town, I'll lay low."

"Good. Now give me the pertinent details, so I can get some help on the way."

Lash recited the address of the hotel where he was staying, and gave a phone number. Jessi grabbed for a pen and copied both down rapidly, then tore off the sheet of notepaper and jammed it into her pocket, where her pickup keys were digging into her thigh.

"Be careful," Garrett said.

"How's Jessi?" Lash asked. She was halfway to hanging up when she heard that, but she snapped the phone back to her ear.

"Still acting pretty darned strangely, Lash. And I can't figure her out. First she was depressed again, and then tonight, she seemed kind of…I dunno, wound up and tense or something. I was hoping she'd have snapped out of it by now, but—"

"You haven't told her where I am, have you, Garrett? You promised you—"

"Hell, no, I haven't told her."

"Oh." His voice sounded vaguely disappointed. "Then, she hasn't asked?"

"Asked? Hell, Lash, she demanded. You know Jessi. But I kept my word. I guess she figures you decided it was time to move on."

Lash was quiet for a long time.

"Lash? Did you hear me? I said, she figures—"

"I heard you. I didn't want her to go thinking that, either."

"Well, you know how she is. Jumps to conclusions quicker than a prairie dog diving for his hole."

"Do me a favor, Garrett?"

Jessi gripped the receiver a little tighter as she listened.

"You tell her I'm coming back. Just so she knows I didn't pull up and move on without even saying so long. Okay?"

"You know, Lash, I've been trying to wait on this, because you asked me to, and because I agreed in good faith, but I think it's about time you tell me about it."

"About what?"

"About Jessi. And you. I mean, it seems to me that you and she have—"

"Sorry, Garrett, you're gonna have to be patient just a little bit longer on that one. I told you we'd talk it out, and we will. But I think it's only fair I talk this through with Jessi first." There was some noise in the background, and then Lash came back on the line. "Just know I don't want to see Jessi hurt any more than you do, okay? Now I gotta go. There's a big Mexican here shaking his fist at me and shouting about *el teléfono,*" Lash said. "Goodbye, Garrett." And then the line went dead.

Jessi restrained herself from slamming the living-room extension down and hurrying on her way. Instead, she waited for Garrett to hang up first. Then she put the phone down quietly and walked to the pickup truck parked out front. She got inside, and pulled the door closed quietly.

She was not chasing after Lash Monroe. Her pride wouldn't allow it. And she wouldn't agree to marry him until she was sure he loved her, respected her and truly wanted her to be his wife. Not even if he got down on his knees and begged until his ears bled. No way. But maybe…maybe he was getting a little closer to loving her for real. Maybe he even did already, and just hadn't realized it yet. Maybe there was still a chance.

She bit her lip and told herself not to get her hopes up. She didn't need him. She wasn't worthy of the Brand name if she couldn't have her baby and raise it perfectly well on her own without any help from any man.

But, God, she wanted him. She wanted him so much

it hurt all the time, like a toothache that wouldn't go away. She even ached for him in her sleep.

But there was a whole other issue here. He was the father of the child she was carrying. And there was no way in hell she could sit safe and sound at home while her baby's father was out there getting himself killed. She had to do something. Lash wasn't going to rob her child of the chance to know its father.

Besides, she loved the damned fool.

Jessi coasted the pickup truck as far as it would go, and then she turned the key.

Garrett sat up in bed at the loud protests coming from the holes in Jessi's muffler. "Where the hell do you suppose she's off to at this time of the night?"

"Veterinary emergency?" Chelsea suggested.

"The phone didn't ring."

Chelsea was quiet for a very long moment, and Garrett reached out to flick on the lamp so that he could study her face. Damn. She had something to say. Something she was dying to get out. "Chelsea, hon?"

"The phone *did* ring, Garrett. And when the phone rings in the middle of the night, and you're a veterinarian, you probably tend to dive for it in case it's a veterinary emergency, wouldn't you think?"

Garrett just looked at her. Just sat in the bed and stared at her. She was telling him something. "If Jessi did pick up the phone, she would have said something."

"I don't know," Chelsea said. "I mean, if she picks it up and starts hearing the answers to questions she's been wondering about for a day or two, she might not say a word."

"She went down there after Lash, didn't she?"

"My goodness, I hope not!" Chelsea sat up in the bed. "I mean, it sounded to me like Lash was in trouble right up to his neck down there." Then she frowned. "Oh, but that can't be right. You didn't think it was necessary for you and your brothers to go help him out, so it must be perfectly safe for your baby sister, as well, right?"

Garrett closed his eyes, feeling the barb of guilt his wife had no doubt inflicted on purpose. He flung back the covers and pulled on his jeans, opened the bedroom door and hollered. "Ben, Elliot, Wes! Get up, and get dressed. Time for a road trip."

Jessi's old pickup truck wouldn't go above forty-five unless it was out of gear and going down a steep hill. Going uphill, she didn't think it would hit fifteen, but, thankfully, these roads were pretty much flat. There was another route that would have been a bit shorter, but there were one or two inclines on it that would have been too much for the old engine, so she chose the flat way, knowing it would be faster in the long run.

She'd breezed through customs without incident, though one young officer had advised her not to drive too far from home in *that truck.* Hell, the truck ran fine, just a little slowly, was all. Once she got past the border, she pulled off the road, turned on her dome light and consulted the map she'd purchased earlier. She was nothing if not prepared. She found the little town of Pueblo Bonito and mentally plotted out her route.

But then a pair of bounding high beams cut through the windshield, glaring into her eyes, and she couldn't see a thing. Panic seeped into her brain when the lights stopped, facing her, the vehicle having pulled off onto the shoulder, right in front of hers. Instinctively she reached out to lock both doors, and then she turned her key to crank the motor. She'd just back up, fast. All the way back to the border guys, if necessary. These lowlifes were going to be sorely disappointed if they thought they'd found some lost American female who'd make easy prey for their night's amusement. The dirty—

The headlights went out, and Jessi blinked in the sudden darkness. Was that—?

Four tall shapes emerged from the shiny new oversize pickup truck and sauntered toward her. Shapes she wished she didn't recognize. She thought about shifting into reverse and making a run for it anyway, but she knew she didn't stand a chance of outrunning Garrett in his brand-new umpteen-horsepower machine. Maybe they'd believe she was just out for a little evenin' drive.

She unlocked her door and rolled down her window. Garrett leaned his crossed forearms on the door, then smiled at her. "Honey, you gotta come home now."

"The hell I do," she said, instantly on the defensive, no matter how sweet his smile.

His smile turned to a frown. "What good do you think you can do down here? Hmm? You'd just get yourself hurt, and then Lash would have more to worry about than he already does."

Jessi wrenched on her door handle, shoved it open, pushing her oversize brother out of the way as she got out, and then slammed it again, standing toe-to-toe and nose-to-chest with him. "Seems to me I did *you* quite a bit of good when *you* were in trouble, Garrett Brand. Seems to me when one member of this family needs help, there are usually Brands coming out of the woodwork to see he gets it. And you and I both know that Lash is in trouble down here.''

Wes, standing off to one side, tilted his head and eyed Garrett. ''That true, brother?''

''He'll be fine so long as he keeps his head down.''

Elliot piped up. ''Well, sure, Garrett. But supposing he *don't* keep his head down?''

''You know, Garrett, he did get his face all busted up defending our sister's honor. Don't we kind of owe him one?'' Ben asked.

Garrett sighed heavily and turned to face them all. ''Look, guys, this isn't my decision. Lash made me promise to stay out of this. It's a family thing. A long-overdue showdown between him and his foster brother, and he wants to handle it alone. I gave him my word.''

''Yup,'' Wes said, voice deep and slow. ''Just like you made all of us give you our word not to get involved when you were walking into an ambush in that box canyon. But remember, Garrett, if we'd kept our word back then, you'd be dead right now. Maybe Chelsea would, too.''

''Exactly,'' Jessi said. ''Lash needs our help, and I'm going to give it to him. Whether he wants it or not is completely beside the point.''

Garrett shook his head. ''Look, I get the feeling this thing with him and Zane is private. It would be different if Lash were family, but he's not, and—''

''You're wrong about that,'' Jessi said, and then she bit her lip, because her brothers were all staring at her, waiting for—and probably fully expecting—her to have the last word. Only…they were gonna flip when they heard what that last word was. She closed her eyes and drew a breath. ''Technically, Lash *is* family.''

''How's that?'' Elliot asked innocently. She opened her eyes just to slits, and saw Wes and Garrett's tempers sizzling to life. Ben stood calmly, no emotion showing on his face.

She scrunched her face up tight, clenched her hands into trembling fists at her sides and blurted out, ''I'm carrying his baby.''

Silence. Dead, stony silence. She opened her eyes just enough to peek out at them. Their faces were shocked, but turning mean. Reddening. Jaws tight. Teeth grinding. And yet they didn't speak. It was so quiet she could hear the ghostly moan of a distant wind in the desert, and the crunching, skittering sound of a tumbleweed rolling around somewhere out there. It all felt like a scene in an old western film—the one just before the big showdown. That moment when all the townsfolk hustle their women and children off the streets, and the black-clothed gunslingers step out on opposite ends to face each other. Death seemed to hang on the air. It might be after midnight, but there was a definite ''high noon'' feeling to all of this.

Then, finally, someone spoke. It was Wes. He said, ''I'll *kill* him! I'll kill that double-dealing snake in the grass. I'll—''

''Can't kill him,'' Garrett said, and it tore at Jessi that his voice was a little choked with emotion. ''We can make him wish to God we'd kill him, but we can't kill him. 'Cause there has to be enough of him left to marry her.''

''Oh, no—''

''Man,'' Elliot said, ''I sure hope Zane has Lash in a coma or something before we get there. He'd be better off.''

Ben touched her shoulders. ''Are you okay, Jessi?''

"I'm gonna take my bullwhip to that yellow-bellied liar and strip every inch of hide off his sidewindin' body!" Wes threw his precious Stetson on the dusty road and stomped on it. "I'm gonna pull my bowie outta my boot and—"

Jessi put her fingers to her lips and cut loose with a piercing whistle that should have broken their eardrums—probably would have, too, if they hadn't all been so thickheaded.

"No! You boys are gonna listen to what I have to say if I have to hold you at gunpoint to make you do it! Now get this straight. I am in love with Lash Monroe. Have been ever since the day he first set foot on the Texas Brand. I wanted him, and I set about the business of getting him. If you doubt that, boys, just think about it for a minute. I always get what I want, don't I?" She glared at each of them in turn, but only paused a second, because if they started in again she'd never shut them up. "I seduced Lash, not the other way around. And I'm not one bit ashamed of it, either. He told me right from the start not to fall for him, but I did it anyway. He doesn't know about this baby, and I don't want him to know until I'm damned good and ready to tell him. You understand me? You keep your big fat mouths *shut!*"

Then she turned to Ben. "And yes, I'm okay. I'm just fine."

Ben nodded, big and gentle and accepting. "I'm glad, honey. But I'm gonna have to kick your boyfriend's ass for this."

Jessi rolled her eyes as her brothers all started talking at once, voices raised as they described what they were going to do to Lash in the most colorful terms possible. They swore and ranted and hollered. She sidled away from them, all the way up to that pretty new shiny red pickup truck, and peeked in to see the keys dangling from the switch. Glancing over her shoulder, she saw her brothers standing in a huddle the Dallas Cowboys would have been proud of, each one trying to top the other's threats. She opened the door and climbed behind the wheel. She closed the windows, secured the locks, released the emergency brake, slipped the shift into first, then depressed the clutch. All systems go.

She twisted the key. As soon as the motor came to life, her brothers turned like one collective testosterone-enhanced male entity. She waved and popped the clutch as they all surged forward. But it was too late. She pulled it into second gear, then glanced in the rear-view mirror and smiled at the distance the big lugs chased her before giving up. She faced front again, flicking on the headlights and shifting up another gear.

She could have taken the keys to her old pickup, leaving them stranded. It would have been intensely satisfying to think of them having to hoof it back to the border and use a phone to call Chelsea. Imagine them trying to explain that their little sister had stolen their big manly truck and left them high and dry. Ah, it was almost too good. But she'd denied herself the pleasure of that. She'd left them the keys. Because she had a feeling Lash was going to need a little bit more help than she could give him. So it was necessary for the boys to follow her on her journey south.

She turned on the radio and hoped this little town was far enough away to give her brothers plenty of time to cool down. One thing was for sure, she was going to have plenty of time to kill, waiting for them to catch up to her in that slowpoke of a truck. Which was good, in a way, because she was starved. Nice that she finally had her appetite back. Must be all this excitement.

Chapter 12

Lash had been holed up in the sleazy hotel for just about as long as he could stand, and no Federales had shown up yet. Zane was in a little cantina a few yards down the dirt track that passed for a road in this hole-in-the-wall town. Pueblo Bonito, indeed. If ever there had been a misnomer…

A good portion of Garrett's herd of prime beef stock—and those of many of his neighbors—were a bit farther down, penned up in open-air corrals and waiting for the morning shift to show up to slaughter them. Seven a.m. was when the workers would arrive to begin their gruesome task, or so Lash had been told when he asked around in stammering, very bad Spanish. That gave him barely four hours, and it wasn't going to be enough time.

He had to do something. He couldn't just keep on waiting for help to arrive. He'd scoped out the slaughterhouse yard, and seen men sorely in need of bathtubs and razor blades standing around the cattle pens holding rifles. He figured if he even got close, they'd use them.

The town was obviously poverty-stricken. Buildings were in tumbledown condition; brown water flowed from the faucets, when they chose to spew any at all. More interesting was the rat poison strategically placed underneath the sink. The few vehicles in town looked as if they were held together with coat hangers and baling twine. Broken windows were patched with large pieces of cardboard. The place reeked of despair.

But, hell, he couldn't sit around here much longer. He couldn't stand to. All he could think about was getting back to Texas. To the ranch. To Jessi.

And it had just started to occur to him that maybe he'd been wrong when he told her he wasn't a settling-down kind of guy. At first, he'd only thought he should marry her because it was the right thing to do, but then she'd gone and turned him down, and it had made him think. Long and hard. Hell, he'd been *disappointed* when she refused him. And when he pondered that feeling, he'd realized that if he'd only been proposing out of guilt or a sense of duty, then he'd have been relieved. But he hadn't been relieved at all. In fact, he'd been pretty crushed. He'd told himself he wasn't, but that had been bull. All he'd been doing since then was trying to think of how to talk her into changing her mind. Into saying yes. Into being his wife.

Being his wife. God, the phrase whispering through his brain made him feel warm and soft inside.

So the question remained—why? If it wasn't guilt or remorse—if suddenly the idea of jumping into his old car and heading for a new town and a new adventure seemed like a nightmare instead of a thrill—then why?

Damn. Could he actually be...*in love?*

Seemed beyond his wildest imaginings.

He settled down in a rickety chair behind the filthy window in his hotel room, watching the cantina's entrance through the hole where the glass was broken, because it was the only part he could see through. There was little activity in the streets, but the cantina was busy. Men staggered in and out. Rough-sounding Spanish and deep laughter spilled into the street. He watched it all, and pondered his feelings about Jessi Brand for a long while.

And then he leaped out of the chair so fast that it clattered to the floor behind him. He stared, aghast, out the window, rubbed his eyes and stared again. Because the girl he'd been thinking about had materialized right before his eyes. She was sauntering down that dusty road in a pair of straight-legged jeans that hugged her where they shouldn't, and tall slender boots that reached almost to her knees. She wore one of those sexy ribbed tank tops, glaring white, the ones that were made for a man, but did incredible things on a woman. Over it was a plaid flannel shirt, lightweight, unbuttoned and gaping, sleeves rolled to the elbows. She wore a hat, a Stetson like his, only hers was a soft brown felt that made the red in her hair look even prettier.

She was eating a fajita about a foot long as she walked, and she was looking around—probably for him, he figured.

He heard the wolf whistle, saw her stop and turn her head toward the cantina's swinging doors. She turned so fast that her short auburn hair kept swinging even after her head had come to a stop. He could see it brushing her shoulders in the shadow of her hat.

Lash pulled his handgun and, without taking his eyes off the street below, checked to see that it was fully loaded.

The swinging doors of the cantina flung outward and his nemesis, Zane, staggered out, said something obnoxious to Jessi and gripped her forearm. Jessi smashed what was left of her fajita into his leering face, and he laughed as he swiped it off.

The bastard. He pulled her inside. Lash whirled and ran, as fast as he could out of his room and down the hall. His booted feet landed so hard that chunks of plaster jarred loose from the walls as he passed. He slammed down the stairs, skipping the lowest one—the one with the missing board—so as not to break a leg, and headed out of the hotel. He could hear the cantina's radio blasting from here. A cloud of dust followed him across the road, and he burst into the noisy Mexican bar, pistol drawn and ready, to see Zane on a stool, with Jessi on his lap. She had a big, heavy beer glass in her hand, and Zane was telling her to be sociable and drink with him.

"Get your filthy hands off her, Zane."

Someone stopped the music. The laughter and talk in the place died a beat later.

Zane blinked a little drunkenly, finally located Lash's eyes, squinted at the gun and laughed. He waved a hand around the bar to the patrons there. *"Mi hermano,"* he sang out. Then to Lash he said, "Little brother, these are my friends. They love me, because I bring jobs to their impoverished little town. I could run for mayor here and win. So I suggest you put that gun down before you upset them."

Lash glanced around at the men. They were all wearing ponchos and beards. The stench of body odor and stale beer and cigarette smoke surrounded him. And the glare of hatred flashed from their eyes. Then he looked at Jessi, and her eyes were so beautiful and big and sparkling. And not scared. Not at all scared. She looked…excited. There was a twinkle in those brown eyes of hers. Mischief. Devilment. The hellion was planning something.

He sent her a message with his eyes, silently telling her to stay still, and not draw any undue attention to herself. He didn't want her getting hurt. She smiled very slightly at him, as if to say, "Yeah, right."

Swallowing hard, Lash faced his worst enemy again. "If they like you so much, Zane," he said, "they'll sit still and keep out of this. Otherwise, they'll see you with a big hole in your head."

"I don't think so, *amigo.*"

Jessi yelled, "Behind you, Lash!"

It was too late, though. The blow to the head took him by surprise, and as he staggered sideways, the gun was yanked out of his hand and tossed out into the street. The man who'd hit him loomed over him, and Lash pretended to cower, then hooked one leg behind the guy's feet and swept them right out from under him. Someone else jumped in front of him even as he got to his feet, but Lash came up swinging.

From the corner of his eye, he saw Jessi bring her giant beer mug down on top of Zane's head. Glass shattered, beer splashed and spilled, and Zane was bleeding. Zane gaped at her in disbelief, but only until she jabbed her elbow into his belly, hopped out of his lap, picked up a bar stool and swung it at him like a baseball bat.

The bartender ducked as a chair sailed over his head to smash the mirror that hung on the wall behind him. Then about eight guys jumped on Lash at once. But for some reason, they didn't stay long. He'd been holding his own, but, if truth be told, he had been getting pretty winded, ducking all those blows and taking a punch or two every now and then. He closed his hand around the neck of a bottle and broke it over one head. While that attacker sank to the floor, he turned with the broken bottle to face another. But before he could blink, a big hand closed on the guy's shoulder, spun him around and plowed a fist into his face with a teeth-shattering crunch.

Lash frowned and looked up at the owner of that beefy fist. Garrett looked back at him. Only he wasn't smiling. In fact, he looked as if he were planning to knock Lash's teeth out next.

What the hell—?

Another guy leaped on Lash from behind then, so he had to turn around and tend to business. But damn, Garrett had looked meaner than a bear with a toothache just now. What the hell was wrong with him?

Lash ducked as a small round table sailed past. It hit the guy he was fighting right in the chin. He crouched low and made his way back toward the bar, where he'd last seen Jessi, worrying about her being in the middle of the riot that had broken out. He had to stay low to avoid flying bottles, glasses, furniture and the occasional body sailing past. One guy got hurled right through the front window, landing on his back in the street. Damn fool got up and dived right back in again, swearing a blue streak in his native tongue and uttering some kind of battle cry.

He stepped on something soft that grunted in response. "Excuse me, pal," he muttered, and stepped over the body on the floor. Someone blocked his path, and a fist came toward his face. Lash grabbed the first thing he could close his hand on, and brought it up like a shield. Turned out to be somebody's dinner plate, and it smashed to bits. The owner of the fist howled and clutched his bleeding knuckles. Lash punched him in the nose and kept on going.

And then he saw her.

Jessi Brand was using an upturned table for cover, ducking behind it. Every time one of Zane's guys walked close enough to her, she popped up like some demonic jack-in-the-box and rapped him over the head with a full bottle of liquor. Seemed she had a cache of them back there. Lash made his way toward her, and when he got within reach she popped up again, bottle in hand, ready to add him to that pile of bodies lying in an unconscious, liquor-soaked heap all around her little battle station. Fortunately, he'd expected it, and he caught her wrist before the bottle could connect with his skull. "It's me, Jess."

"You big jerk, I oughtta clobber you anyway!"

He frowned, confused, but she twisted her hand around to grip his arm and yanked him behind the table with her, pulling him down low, so that they were both kneeling in the dubious safety provided by the toppled table.

She glared at him for a full minute, and then her face softened. "Damn, I'm glad to see you," she muttered, and she snapped her arms around his neck and kissed him full on the mouth.

Lash's arms slipped right around her waist, and he held her close, tasted those lips, and loved every second of it. The noise of the brawl faded, and a buzz of longing filled his head instead. He didn't want to stop kissing her. Not ever.

But he did, after a long moment. And he lifted his head in time to see a glass pitcher flying toward her. He pulled her out of its path and watched it crash to the floor. Then he shook his head. "Jessi, what the hell are you doing here?"

"What the hell am *I* doing here? Hell, Lash, you care to tell me how you were planning to get out of this mess on your own?"

"I wasn't planning to get *into* this mess on my own, you little hellion! You really think I'd have walked into a bar full of drunken men who see Zane as their hero if I hadn't seen the bastard yank you in here first?"

She blinked. "You saw that?"

"Sure I saw that."

"And you only came charging in here because of that?"

"Well, hell, Jessi, I couldn't just leave you here."

"And you knew all hell was going to break loose and that you'd be facing twenty-to-one odds?"

"I kinda figured."

She smiled. Then she slid her arms around his neck and she pressed her lips to his all over again. Man, she was going to kill him with kisses if she kept it up. She kissed him thoroughly, so thoroughly that it made his head swim and his gut clench and a sheen of sweat broke out on his forehead. And he thought he must have been a damn fool not to have been working his tail off to sweep this lady off her feet from day one.

A body sailed over the table and hit him on the way to the floor, jarring him away from Jessi's lips. And he looked into her eyes, and opened his mouth to say the words he'd been afraid to utter to any woman, ever. "Jessi, I—"

A whistle pierced the noise of the battle, and a pair of gunshots caused the combatants to cease and desist. Lash looked up to see what looked like a small army of Mexican police, shouting in Spanish and heavily accented English and hauling men to their feet and out the door.

Damn. They were arresting Jessi's brothers right along with everyone else. He had to do something.

But as he got up, one of the officers gripped his shoulder, and slapped a pair of handcuffs around his wrists.

Jessi couldn't believe her eyes. One by one, her brothers were hauled out the door by Mexican police, and so was Lash. While she was totally ignored.

She stepped outside, walked right up to the nearest uniformed man, a handsome, olive-skinned Don Juan with a cute mustache. She tapped his shoulder. "Hey. Why aren't you arresting me?"

He smiled charmingly down at her. "You are too pretty to be in jail, *chica.* Go home now."

"Now wait just a corn-shuckin' minute, here. I was fighting just the same as they were! Hell, *I'm* the one who started it. You have to arrest me! You can't *not* arrest me just because I'm a woman."

He shook his head, grinning indulgently. "You Americans! You make me to laugh." And he did laugh, and she thought that in about a minute he was going to ruffle her hair.

Then she peeked through the windows of the van where the guys had been installed and saw her brothers, all of them, looking at Lash as if he were a steak and they were a pack of hungry pit bulls. She tapped Don Juan again. ''You can't put them all in the same cell, okay? See that one, the one they're all glaring at? He ought to be in a cell by himself.''

''Why, pretty one? Is he a prince? A king?''

''No, but if they're alone with him, he's gonna be a dead man.''

The officer frowned, then shrugged. ''Women worry too much. Our space, it is small. You stop worrying now, and go home.'' And he turned and climbed behind the wheel. Then he blew her a kiss, sent her a wink and drove away.

Jessi stomped her foot and shouted after him. ''Chauvinist pig!''

Lash didn't claim his handgun when the officer showed it to him and asked if it was his. He figured he'd get in less trouble that way. Then he allowed himself to be led to a cell in the back of the crumbling structure that passed for a jail in this town. He was shoved inside an adobe room with a barred door, where Garrett, Ben, Wes and Elliot Brand all sat on benches. None of them said a word. None of them grinned. All of them looked suddenly meaner than a pack of junkyard dogs on the hottest day in July, and for one brief moment, he thought longingly of his childhood with the preacher and his houseful of bullies.

''Hey, guys,'' he said.

They said nothing.

''I really owe you for coming down here like this. I'd have been dog meat in that cantina if you hadn't showed up when you did.''

Garrett got up, nice and slow. Elliot reached up to

grab his arm, but Garrett shook him off and stepped forward.

"So I guess we got Zane by the short hairs, huh?" Lash said, and he took a step backward, only to meet up with the cold steel bars behind him. "I explained everything to that officer out there," he said, speaking quickly. "Just as soon as they confirm it all—and he's not gonna let 'em slaughter any cattle until they do—we can just send some rigs down here to fetch 'em back home and..."

Garrett gripped the front of Lash's shirt in both hands and picked him up off the floor, backing him against the bars.

"Gee, Garrett, is it just me, or have I done something to tick you off?"

Garrett said nothing. It was Wes who spoke up. "Jessi's pregnant, Lash. She says you got her that way."

"Jessi?" Lash blinked, his gaze swinging to Wes's, then back to Garrett. "Pregnant? She's pregnant?" He blinked slowly, some kind of warm yellow light filling him up inside from his head to his toes. "My God, she's carrying...my...my baby?"

"What the hell are you grinning about?" Garrett demanded. "Don't you feel the cold breath of the reaper on the back of your neck, son?"

"Jessi's gonna have my baby," he repeated. And he smiled even more. He couldn't seem to help himself. It was like a miracle. It *was* a miracle. And he loved her. *He loved her,* and had for quite a while now. It was going to be okay. Everything was going to be... just fabulous!

He dragged his gaze back to Garrett again. Well, it

was going to be fabulous, assuming he lived long enough to marry her.

"You're gonna do right by my sister, Lash Monroe. Make no mistake about this. You're gonna marry her, and not just because she's pregnant. You're gonna treat her like she's made of twenty-four-karat gold, pal."

"You're damn right I am," he said.

Garrett's eyes narrowed.

"I love her, Garrett," Lash said. "I love her so much I'd take on every one of you, if that's what it took to be with her. And maybe you'd break me up into little pieces before we were finished, or maybe you wouldn't. I've had some experience with bullies on the rampage, you know. But it wouldn't matter. I'm so high right now that I probably wouldn't feel it if you broke every bone in my body. So you gonna put me down, or you wanna take me on, here and now?"

Garrett's eyes widened. Then widened still further when his little sister's voice came to them, loud and low and mean as she shouted, "Open that cell door right now, mister, or prepare to meet your maker!"

He dropped Lash, and they all turned to stare through the bars at a guard with shaking hands held high above his head, and a pretty desperado with a neckerchief tied around her face, pointing his own gun at him. She backed the guard all the way to the cell and waggled the gun barrel at him. The guard put the key into the cell door, turned it and opened it.

"Good," she said. "Now, just so we're clear on this, those guys in that other cell are the criminals. These guys aren't guilty of anything. And I'd wait for you to figure that out for yourself, but I have pressing business to tend to, and it can't wait. You got it?"

The guard just nodded as the Brands and Lash

crowded out of the cell. "Truck's waiting out back. You boys pile in. In the back, dammit, or I'll leave you sitting here. Lash, you wait right here. You, *amigo—*" she dipped the gun toward the guard "—into the cell."

He moved into the cell and she locked it, then tossed the keys back down the hall. Then she popped the cylinder of the guard's gun open, and gave it a spin. "Just so you know, pal, it wasn't loaded. I'd never point a loaded gun at a peace officer. Even a chauvinist one." She dropped the gun on the floor. The boys were already piling into Garrett's pickup. She told Lash to get in the front, and then she got behind the wheel, yanked the neckerchief down to let it hang around her neck and pointed the vehicle toward the border. "I only hope we get past the checkpoint before they report us missing," she said. As she drove, she dug Lash's wallet out of her pocket and tossed it onto the seat. "Found this on that officer's desk. Didn't look like he'd been through it yet."

Lash couldn't take his eyes off her. Her cheeks were flushed with color, and her eyes just sparkled. And his gaze dipped down to her flat tummy and he thought about the tiny bit of life she was cradling inside her. And then he thought he was gonna just about burst with the love he felt for her. It was unbelievable to him that he hadn't ever recognized this feeling for what it was.

He *adored* this woman.

"Jessi," he said, and he slid closer, reached out and touched her hair.

She smiled at him. "We could get in big trouble for this," she said. "Garrett's a sheriff. I hope he had the good sense to give a false name. But I figure we can gift the town with some cattle. Breeding stock or something, to make up for their loss. Maybe with a show of goodwill like that, they'll let this little incident slide."

"Jessi," he said again, and he knew he was smiling stupidly.

"I found a prostitute outside the bar and gave her twenty bucks to drive my truck back to our side of the border. We can pick it up there tomorrow."

"I love you," he said.

She blinked, turned her head fast, and stared up at him.

"I want to marry you. Not as penance or out of guilt or anything else. I just want to marry you."

She smiled, and tears sprang to the surface of her brown eyes. "Lash…" But her voice trailed off, and that bright smile faded very quickly. The moisture in her eyes, though, remained. She looked away. "So my bigmouth brothers told you, did they?"

He didn't know what to say. So he decided to tell the truth. "Yes. I know about the baby."

He should have lied. He could see the tears that glittered in the glow of the dashboard lights. "That was so good, Lash, you know? For a minute there, I almost believed you."

"You have to believe me, Jessi. It's the truth."

"Hell, Lash, you were willing to marry me to pay for my virginity. Naturally you see it as even more necessary now. Your preacher sure as hell raised you right, I'll give you that much. But I'm sorry. It's not gonna work."

"You're wrong. Whatever you're thinking, you're dead wrong."

She braked so hard and fast that the Brands in the

back were jostled against the cab. Lash could hear the tears in her voice, see her distress. "Promise me…not one more word about this. We'll talk later, okay? I can't…discuss this right now. It's making me physically ill, to tell you the truth. I could just about…" She put a hand to her stomach and shook her head. "Just…just sit there and shut up, or I'll make you ride in the back with those idiots."

"Don't be mad at them, Jess. This isn't their—"

"The hell it isn't! Dammit, Lash, I was just beginning to think there might be some chance for us. And they ruined it! You'd say anything to get me to marry you now, and how the hell could I ever know if it was true?"

"Jessi, I—"

"No. No more. The last time we talked, you told me you didn't want to marry, to settle down, to have a family. You said you just weren't that kind, Lash. Now you say you've changed your mind. I'd be a fool to believe you. It's because of the baby. That's the only thing that's changed, the only thing you know now that you didn't know before. No. That's the end of it. Don't say any more."

He closed his eyes, and he knew that from where she was sitting, what she'd just said made perfect sense. And how the hell was he ever going to convince her now?

"Jessi, the thing I know now that I didn't know before is that I love you. I have all along. I've done nothing but think about you since I left, and it hit me like a—"

She clamped a hand over his mouth, reached past him and opened the door. "Get out."

Lash got out. Jessi did, too. She stepped up to the

pickup's bed and said, "Garrett, drive. Wes, you come up front with me. Lash, climb in with Ben and Elliot. Ben, if you lay a finger on him, I swear to God I'll leave you stranded in the desert. I've never asked you for a damn thing, but I'm asking now, and if you can't do this for me, then—"

"All right, all right. I got the message. I'll behave."

"Elliot, if he does anything, toss his oversize bulk right over the side."

Elliot gave her a two-fingered salute. "On your side, sis. Just like I always am."

She got back in the truck, Garrett and Wes doing just exactly what she'd asked them to.

Lash felt defeated. He'd hurt her, all over again. And maybe caused her to lose any trust she ever could have had in him. How in the world was he ever going to convince her that he really did love her? How?

He racked his brain all the way back to Texas, but didn't have any flashes of inspiration. He stared miserably at the back of Jessi's head through the glass that separated them. When she leaned tiredly back against it, he pressed his fingers to the glass, as if he could touch her hair.

"You said you loved her," Ben said softly. "Did you mean it?"

Lash lifted his head and met those perpetually sad blue eyes. "I meant it."

"Then don't give up," Ben said. "Life's too short, Lash."

Lash held his head in his hands, and wished to God he could win. But it looked to him as if the game were over, and he'd lost. He felt just like one of those damned country songs.

Chapter 13

Jessi had a pounding headache, and her stomach was churning. Maybe because she'd pretty much figured out how she was going to handle all of this. She needed to tell Lash exactly how it was going to be, and then she'd tell her brothers. But Lash first. It was only fair.

When Garrett pulled into the familiar driveway of the ranch, she started to cry. She just couldn't keep it in any longer. Wes looked as guilty as Garrett did, and he slid an arm around her shoulders and hugged her. "Aw, honey, it's gonna be all right."

"I wish my mother were here," she sobbed, and she lowered her head, dropping her face into the haven of her warm palms.

"I know you do, Jessi," Wes went on. "Look, we were hotheads down there. You know we're gonna stand by you. You know we'll treat Lash like family once he marries you."

"Ah, hell, Wes, you just don't understand anything,

do you?'' She lifted her face to stare at him, and saw his wide-eyed confusion. ''I can't marry him now. Don't you see that?''

Wes frowned at her. ''Damn straight I don't see it. Hell, Jessi, you have to marry him now more than ever. You're carrying—''

''Lord, Jessi,'' Garrett said, touching her shoulder. ''Honey, tell me you haven't decided to... I mean, I know, it's your decision. I know that. It's the nineties. But...honey...''

His stricken expression touched her, and she lowered her palms to her belly—damn, but it hurt. ''I'm keeping my baby, Garrett. I love that idiot. How could I not want his baby?''

Garrett sighed in relief. Wes, on the other side of her, swore softly. ''Dammit, Jessi, you aren't making any sense. If you love him, then why the hell can't you marry him?''

She met his eyes, wondering how he could be so dense. Then she just shook her head and got out. The guys piled out of the truck, and Chelsea stepped out of the house, onto the front porch, to greet them. Jessi was exhausted. Handling all these men was just too much. All she wanted to do was tell Lash her decision and collapse into her bed.

Chelsea met her eyes, and read them with that uncanny intuition of hers that sometimes gave Jessi the shivers. Chelsea nodded once and said, ''Okay, boys, it's nearing dawn and you all have a big day coming up. Get your butts in here and get some rest. Give your kid sister a break for once, okay?''

Garrett walked up onto the steps and met his wife's eyes. ''You knew about this, didn't you?'' he said.

She drew a breath and nodded. ''I gave your sister

my word I'd let her tell you when she was ready. And I love you too much—love *her* too much—to break a promise like that."

He closed his eyes slowly, nodding in understanding.

"It's gonna be okay, honey," Chelsea told him. "I promise you, it will." She hugged Garrett hard.

The others muttered in protest, but they went inside, and Chelsea kept one arm around Garrett, leading him in last of all.

Lash stayed outside with Jessi. She sat down on the topmost step of the porch, and he came over to sit beside her. "We really have to talk about this," he said.

"Yes, I guess we do, Lash. Because I've come to some important decisions, and you have a right to know what they are."

"But not to have any say in them?"

She met his eyes. He went silent. "Here's what I've decided," she said. "I've decided to keep the baby. I've got my own home, my own business, and I can support a child just fine all by myself. But if you want to chip in, I won't refuse you. And I'll give you all the visitation rights you could possibly want."

"Aw, honey, I don't want any damn visitation. I want us to be a family. Dammit, Jessi, you have to believe me."

She lifted her chin and looked him right in the eye. "I'm one hell of a woman, Lash Monroe. And there is no way in hell I'm gonna settle for a man who doesn't love me with every bone in his body. I shouldn't have to. You shouldn't ask me to."

"I'm not."

"Guess I'll never know for sure, will I?"

He let his chin fall to his chest. "I had my chance and I let you get away," he said. "I suppose I deserve this."

She shrugged.

"Jessi, I'm not giving up. My drifting days are over, and I'm gonna convince you that I meant what I said. I'll follow you around like a lonely pup. I'll camp out on your front porch. I'll serenade you in the moonlight, and buy you flowers and write you poetry. All the things I should've been doing in the first place. Damn, I never thought I was a fool, but it's pretty obvious now. I love you, Jessi. Sooner or later, I'm gonna convince you."

She smiled very slightly, feeling a little dizzy on top of everything else. "I hope so," she said. "But I don't see how you can." She got to her feet, staggered a bit, and gripped the railing for support.

"Jessi?"

"I'm going to bed. I just can't take any more tonight." She turned and went up the steps, but had to pause in the doorway to catch her breath and battle the dizziness. The sudden, violent urge to get into her own warm bed overcame her, and she managed to propel herself through the doorway, stumbled through the house to the stairway, and gripped the bannister.

Lash was right behind her, his hands coming to rest on her shoulders as she trembled. "Jessi, what's wrong?"

"I don't know... I feel—"

"Garrett," Lash called. "Chelsea! Get down here! Something's—"

The first cramp hit her, and she felt as if she'd been kicked in the belly by a mule. She doubled over, clutching her middle, and she cried out in pain.

That cry more than Lash's, she knew, brought her brothers and Chelsea running.

"God in heaven, don't let her lose the baby," Lash muttered. He bent over her, and scooped her up into his arms. "I'm taking her to the hospital," he told the others. "Hold on, Jessi. Hold on."

Lash carried her gently through the automatic double doors of the emergency room, whispering to her that it was going to be all right. That he loved her. That he wouldn't let anything happen to her. Once inside, he shouted, "Get me a doctor. She's pregnant, and—"

Jessi cried out again, clutching her middle, tears pouring down her cheeks. And Lash felt a warm wetness on his own face. Several nurses rushed forward, one dragging a gurney with her and instructing him to lower her down onto it. Then these strangers wheeled her away from him.

He lunged forward, but one of the nurses caught his arm and shook her head. "Please, sir. We can take better care of her if you wait out here. I know it's hard, but it's best for her, really."

Lash stood there staring until they'd wheeled her out of sight, through another set of doors. Then he pressed both hands to his head and turned in a circle. Damn! If he lost her now… God, this was probably his fault. If he hadn't gone to Mexico…if she hadn't come after him… Maybe she'd been hurt in that damned brawl in the cantina. Maybe the drive over those rutted roads had instigated this. Maybe it was the stress, or the hurt brought on by not being sure of his feelings.

The doors swung open again, and Lash looked up to see the entire Brand family surging through. The boys stopped where they were, staring him down.

Chelsea handed a sleepy-looking Ethan to Garrett and hurried forward, wrapping Lash in a warm hug. ''She's gonna be all right, Lash. You'll see. She's tough.''

''Toughest woman I've ever met,'' he said. ''Stubbornest, too. Damn, Chelsea, I can't lose her.''

''You won't.'' Chelsea stood back a bit. ''You look like hell, Lash.''

He closed his eyes and let her guide him to a chair. He took the coffee she brought him moments later.

He drank it, and watched those doors. Time ticked by, every second dragging out into a hundred of them. He got up and paced, stared at those doors some more, sat for a while, questioned a couple of nurses who knew nothing at all. And all the while, he felt the hostile eyes of Jessi's brothers on him. They blamed him for this. Hell, they ought to. He blamed himself.

Two hours later, he was on his third cup of stale, machine-generated coffee, and getting more nervous by the minute, when Garrett finally got around to saying what was on his mind. ''So you guys talked, before she got sick?''

''Yeah,'' Lash told him.

''And you convinced her to marry you?''

''Nope.'' Lash crumpled his paper cup in his fist and tossed it.

''Well, then, we will,'' Garrett said. ''She's gonna marry you, and that's final. We can't have her trying to raise a kid on her own.''

Lash got to his feet, very slowly. ''No,'' he said. He stared at each of the brothers, one by one. ''No, it's time you guys figured something out. Your sister is tough, smart, beautiful, and perfectly capable of taking care of herself. She doesn't think I love her. And she isn't going to marry a man unless she knows beyond any doubt that he loves her the way she deserves to be loved. So no, I'm not going to marry her. I'm not going to let you pressure her into accepting me. The only way I'm going to marry Jessi Brand is by working my tail off to convince her that I really do love her. And it might take a while, but I'm gonna do it. I'm gonna do it whether she..." He closed his eyes, swallowing hard. "Whether she loses this baby or not. I adore that woman, and she doesn't deserve not to be sure."

He glanced back toward the doors, blinked his eyes dry, and faced the boys again, nodding firmly. "That's the way it's gonna be. So if you don't like it, we all might as well step out into the parking lot right now, because I love her too much to let her marry me before she understands just how I feel. I want her to be sure. I want her to know that I'd walk barefoot over hot coals for her, baby or no baby. I want her to know that."

The angry frown vanished from Garrett's face, and even Wes had the good sense to stop glaring. In fact, their expressions turned, one by one, into looks of grudging admiration.

Chelsea smiled outright. "You'll convince her, Lash. Damn, I'm so glad she's got herself a man who loves her the way you do."

Then the boys all shifted their gazes to look past Lash, and Lash turned to see what they were focused on, and spotted a nurse who seemed to be very upset as she spoke to a doctor, who looked puzzled. The woman raised her voice a notch then, and they could all hear her.

"I don't know how, Doctor! We only left her alone for a second, and....well, we just lost her!"

Lash's heart froze in that moment. The rest of his

body dissolved and he sank to his knees. "No," he whispered. "God, no, not Jessi…"

Elliot, Garrett and Wes stampeded past him, crowding the startled pair in white and demanding answers. Behind him, he could hear Chelsea crying.

And then Ben, that big, quiet, saddest of all Brands, was kneeling beside him, and dropping a big hand on his shoulder, squeezing gently. And when Lash looked up, he saw Ben's face, wet with tears. And he knew Ben had lost his own young wife, and the pain he was feeling was reflected in this man's eyes.

"Not again," Ben said softly. "God, not again."

"This can't be happening," Lash whispered.

Ben's arms enfolded him, and the two knelt there together, sobbing like a couple of kids. Lash didn't think he'd ever be able to stand on his feet again.

A shrill, piercing whistle cut through the grief in that waiting room like a fire alarm, and Lash managed to look up, toward the sound.

Jessi stood at the far end of the waiting room, clad in a hospital gown, hands on her hips. "What in the Sam Hill is everybody bawling about?" she demanded.

Lash's strength surged back into his body. He sprang to his feet and ran the length of the room, scooping her into his arms and hugging her hard, clinging to her as if he'd never let go.

He vaguely heard the nurse apologizing for her poor choice of words, and explaining that her patient was missing, not dead. By then, though, no one was really listening. Jessi's brothers were crowding around her, hugging her and Lash all at once, and Lash kind of figured they'd pretty much gotten over the idea of beating him senseless in the parking lot. For tonight, at least.

Lash set her on her feet, anxiously searching her face to be sure she was really all right.

"You really need to spend the night, Miss Brand," the doctor was saying. "You shouldn't even be on your feet right now."

And some of that joyous relief faded from Lash's heart when he heard the concern in the doc's voice. "Jessi?" Lash scooped her up again. If the doc said she shouldn't be on her feet, she damned well wasn't going to be. He held her gently. "Sweetheart, what's wrong? Is it the baby? Is there—"

"The baby's fine," she told him, and he almost sank to his knees all over again in relief. Then she nodded to the doctor. "Tell him, Doc."

The man smiled. "Food poisoning. A mild case, fortunately, though I'm sure it didn't feel that way."

"It was that damned fajita," she muttered, and she let her head rest on Lash's shoulder. "But I'm glad it happened."

Garrett shook his head. "How can you be glad? Do you know what you just did to us?"

"You scared the hell out of us," Wes said.

"When that nurse said she'd lost you..." Garrett began.

"I died inside, Jessi," Lash finished. "I swear to God, I felt myself die inside."

She met his gaze, held it, and he saw new moisture in her eyes. Chelsea cleared her throat, and Jessi pulled her gaze away from Lash's. "They wanted to keep me overnight. I wanted out of here, so as soon as they weren't looking, I sneaked out to see if I could convince my big brothers to spring me." Her gaze came back to Lash's, something like wonder in her brown eyes as she reached up and ran one hand through his hair. "And I'm glad I did, because I got a front-row seat for that little speech of yours."

Lash blinked. "You did?"

She sniffed, and nodded. "Yeah, I did. You convinced me, Lash. It's really not just the baby, is it?"

"No, Jessi. It's got nothing to do with the baby. I love you, and I'd figured that out before your brothers ever told me about the baby. I was down there in Mexico, missing you with everything in me and trying to figure out how the hell to convince you to marry me. God, Jessi, I never knew I could feel this way. But I do. I swear to God, I do love you."

"Then I guess I'm gonna hafta marry myself a drifter," she said. "Because I've loved you all along. You know that, don't you, Lash?"

He shook his head in wonder. "I know it. I can't quite understand why, but I know it." Then his face split in a grin. "You're gonna marry me?"

She nodded.

He leaned forward and kissed her, gently but thoroughly.

Garrett nudged Wes with his elbow. "Looks like we just got ourselves another brother."

"Well, hell," Wes said. "I've been saying all along that he was the only man around good enough for our baby sister, haven't I?"

"No, actually, you haven't."

The two grinned foolishly. "Somebody better call Adam in New York," Elliot chirped. "He's gotta be here for this wedding."

In the corner, Ben remained silent, and reached up to wipe a single tear from his eye.

Epilogue

Jessi gripped the doctor by the front of his shirt and growled deep in her throat. "I told you, I don't like pain. Now give me something or die!"

Lash pried her hands away from the poor guy's white coat, brought them to his lips and kissed them. "Sweetheart, the doc says it's better for you to do this without drugs if you can. You can do it, can't you? Come on, now—"

"Where's my gun?"

"Oh, boy."

The doc patted him on the back. "Jessi Lynn Brand Monroe, you settle down. Drugs are no good for the baby, and I know perfectly well you don't want to hurt the baby, do you?"

She glared at him. Lash figured she probably thought the doc was lying, just to keep the drugs from her and make her suffer. Since she'd been in the third stage of labor, she seemed to have formed the opinion that every male in the place was getting some perverse pleasure from her pain.

Ben and Garrett and Elliot were all smiling at her and speaking soft, comforting words. Adam, who'd come in from New York on the first flight out when they called to tell him she was in labor, was pacing like a caged lion. In fact, there were so many Brands surrounding the bed that the doctor said they were in the way. None of them wanted to leave though, and they wouldn't, Lash thought, unless they were bodily removed.

Except Wes. He was toughing it out largely to save face, Lash thought. But he was looking decidedly queasy.

Chelsea was on her way. She'd had to drop Ethan off with a sitter before she could get here.

The pain seemed to ease, and Jessi's face relaxed. She clutched her husband's hand in hers. "We should have sold tickets to this event," she said, panting to catch her breath. "Coulda paid for college."

"It's sure standing room only."

She nodded. "Good thing you don't have lots of family here, too, isn't it?"

"My so-called family? Heck, they wouldn't let Petey and Zane out of prison just to attend a birthing, would they? Besides, they'd contaminate the place. I don't want them anywhere near you…or our baby."

"Doesn't matter," she said. "You've got all kinds of family now. In fact, you have that big crowd of relatives you never wanted."

"And I love every last one of 'em," he told her, and he leaned over and kissed her mouth. Felt it go tight against his, felt her breaths coming faster on his lips.

"I...I can feel it... I have to push!"

"Go ahead and push, then," the doctor said. Lash straightened, and felt his heart flip-flop. This was it. He turned to smile crookedly at Garrett, and then Elliot, and Ben, and... Hey, where was Wes?

Oh, there he was, out in the hall, back to the wall, shoulders slumped, Adam seemingly holding him up. He was white as a sheet. What was that nurse waving under his nose?

Jessi clutched Lash's hand hard enough to break the bones and grated her teeth, and Lash felt helpless and scared as he watched her battle the pain, drawing on that endless reserve of strength deep inside her to push their child into the world.

"Damn, sweetheart, I'd do it for you if I could," he told her, bathing her face with a cool cloth.

"No man could go through this and live," she said through gritted teeth.

It seemed forever...and then it seemed it had been no time at all, because the doc was lowering a pink, squirming, tiny human being into Lash's waiting arms. And Lash was looking down into the face of an angel. "A girl," he whispered, and he bent close to Jessi. "Our little girl."

Garrett, Elliot and Ben crowded close, cooing and making the most ridiculous faces and basically sounding like a bunch of lunatics.

Then the door opened, Adam coming in first, to join them at the bedside, looking alien in his suit and tie. And then Wes came in, real slow, his black eyes wide and wet. The others parted to give him a chance to meet his new niece. And he knelt beside the bed, reaching out, letting the little one grasp his forefinger.

He reached into a pocket with his free hand, and pulled out a tiny suede pouch fastened to a thong.

"What's this?" Lash asked.

"A gift from Turtle, the shaman over at the reservation," he said. He'd been learning a whole lot about his heritage, and he seemed to be gaining a peace he hadn't had before. "It's a medicine bag. Hang it in her room until she's old enough to wear it. It'll keep her safe, and happy and strong."

"That's so sweet, Wes."

He shrugged as if it were no big deal, then ran one hand down Jessi's cheek. "You did good, little sister."

"I did, didn't I?"

He nodded, then straightened, averting his face to swipe at his eyes. "Maybe we should clear out now, leave you two and your little girl alone to get acquainted."

"Thanks, Wes."

The boys each leaned down to kiss their sister, and then they left the room. Lash lowered the baby into Jessi's arms, and bent to kiss them both.

"What will we name her?" he whispered softly, stroking the soft, downy head of reddish hair.

"Maria," Jessi whispered. "After my mother."

"Maria," he said. "That's nice. And what about a middle name?"

Jessi shrugged, her big brown eyes just drinking in the sight of the baby in her arms. "You pick one."

"All right. Michele. After Chelsea's sister."

"Chelsea will like that."

Lash touched Jessi's chin, tipping her face up so that he could stare into those eyes. "I never thought I could be this happy," he told her. "But I am. Don't you ever doubt it, Jessi. I adore you."

She smiled, real slow, eyes sparkling. ''Hell, drifter, I knew it before you did.'' And she leaned up and kissed him.

* * * * *

BADLANDS BAD BOY

Chapter 1

Not so long ago Emerald Flat, this very spot, had been littered with painted tepees. On a clear, hot night like tonight, there probably would have been a huge fire in the center of the village. And men and women…even children, decked out in beaded ceremonial garb, would have been dancing in time with the steady throb of deep-voiced drums.

The vision was so vivid that for a second Taylor thought she could hear them. A drumbeat so faint it might have been imaginary. Or perhaps not. A flash of color in the distance, where the edges of this haven reached their green fingers out into the desert. And then another flicker, barely visible in the night. Animals? Birds?

Dancers?

Taylor McCoy rubbed her eyes, admitting it was probably nothing more than too many sleepless nights and a vivid imagination. Those things, and a little help from that old man who kept showing up. Turtle, he called himself. Said he was a Comanche shaman, and that it was his duty to observe her progress on the dig.

Funny that none of the tribal elders she'd spoken to had mentioned him. And neither had Dennis Hawthorne, the money behind the project. And the old fellow seemed more interested in telling stories late at night than in the progress—or lack of it—on the dig. Stories she'd rather not hear, and avoided listening to whenever possible.

No, none of her ancestors' ghosts were dancing in the desert tonight. And there were no beaded loincloths or painted tepees on the site. Tonight, and for the past two weeks, the oblong piece of Texas wildland that seemed to sit as a divider between the desert and the rest of the world was littered not with tepees, but with three modern dome tents. Instead of a central fire, there were a handful of portable cookstoves and Coleman lanterns. Sleeping bags instead of tanned hides. Boilable bags of dehydrated food instead of freshly killed game. ATVs instead of painted ponies.

Still it didn't seem to Taylor as if it had really been all that long.

Taylor sat down in the scraggly grass in front of her tent. A gas lantern hanging from a nearby tree bathed the area in white light nearly as bright as that back in her apartment in Dallas. Her temporary apartment. All her homes were temporary ones.

She picked a triangular piece of pottery from the boxful of bits the team had recovered today, and reached for the soft-bristled brush. Team. She grimaced at the word. Some team. Two grad students and one out-of-work archaeologist. The local big shot funding this dig wasn't exactly generous with his money.

Or with time. But since she'd been between jobs when the offer came in, she'd had little practical choice but to accept.

As she gently, reverently whisked the dirt away from the clay, she wondered about the hands that had formed it. She wondered about the person attached to those hands. A woman, more than likely. Had she been old, or young? A mother? A grandmother? A young girl in love?

Taylor drew the piece closer to examine the design, absently humming, and then singing very softly. Barely aware of the words she was using. Comanche words, from an age-old Comanche love song. Kelly and Scourge had retired into the haven of their dome tents, zipper doors sealed up for the night. She sat all alone as she studied the bits of the past dug up today. It was her favorite time here. The silence, broken only by the occasional hum or chirp of an insect or the sudden flutter of a night bird's wings. There had never been enough time for silence in her life. And sitting here surrounded by it, she thought this was exactly how it must have been in this spot centuries ago.

She hadn't wanted to come here. In her career she'd excavated countless Native American sites, but never one belonging to the Comanches. And she wasn't even fully certain why. Fear, maybe. Fear of discovering a people and a past she'd been isolated from for all her life. Of connecting to it...of connecting to anything, really.

During her last dig she'd been working for a university—last semester in Dallas, that had been. No tenure. Temporary position—her students had referred to her as Solitary McCoy. Behind her back, of course. She supposed she'd earned the nickname. It had made her wonder why she'd become as isolated—as lonely—as she had.

The nicker of a horse brought Taylor back to herself with a jolt. Her head shot up, her eyes narrowing as she tried to make out the form in the distance, there on the barren ground just beyond the place where the grass gradually ended.

Her fingers went stiff, and the pottery piece fell into the brittle grass as Taylor slowly rose to her feet. A magnificent horse danced and pawed where the desert began. A dark horse, with a dark rider.

The unnaturally bright light of the gas lantern hanging beside her made it impossible to see details of the man and his horse in the darkness. She could only see that the rider was bare chested, and that long tendrils of dark hair snapped like flags when the wind lifted them. The horse reared on its hind legs, and she realized the man was bare legged, as well. And wore… perhaps…a loincloth and little else.

A chill crept up her nape, and a whisper of the ghosts she'd been thinking about—and the one she'd thought she'd seen just before making the decision to come here—danced through her mind. She stood a little straighter, fought her own silly imagination. This was no ghost.

"Who is that?" she called, nervously brushing the loose grass and twigs from the seat of her pants. "What do you want?"

He sat exactly as he'd been, his hair dancing in the breeze. And she realized with a small shiver that there had been no breeze a moment ago. None that she could feel, anyway. She reached for the lamp to turn it off.

And then he spoke, and her hand froze in midair.

The depth and power of his voice made her shiver. "You desecrate sacred ground, Taylor McCoy."

She was trembling now, for no good reason. Who in the name of God was the man? "You're mistaken," she shouted. She forced herself to move, reached for the lamp, but instead of shutting it off she lifted it, held it high and out in front of her as if she could see his face by doing so. Naturally she couldn't. "I don't work that way. Look, I was hired to determine whether there is a sacred site here—at the request of the Comanches who own this land."

"Do you not hear them?" he said very softly, so softly she was surprised his words reached her ears from where he was.

"Hear...who?"

"The great shamans of the past! They scream in outrage."

"But—"

"There *is* sacred ground here, woman, but not for your prying eyes to find." Again the horse reared up.

She shivered, fought it. Heard the rustling coming from the other two tents, knew she wasn't alone. No reason to be afraid. Besides, she didn't believe in ghosts.

Then why have I seen two in one week?

"Why don't you stop behaving like a lunatic and talk to me about your concerns? You can start by telling me who you—"

"Wolf Shadow explains himself to no one!"

"But—"

"Aiieeeeeeee!" His war cry split the night, and as he uttered it, he lifted a war lance high above his head, holding it tight in his clenched fist, the feathers dancing in that breeze she couldn't feel. "Leave here, woman, while you can!"

The rustling sounds from the other tents changed to more-urgent noises as her assistants jolted to life. But by the time Scourge and Kelly came shooting out of their tents, he was gone. The horse had galloped off at the speed of light, and she belatedly realized she couldn't even hear the hoofbeats.

Taylor blinked and shook her head slowly. "What the hell was that?"

Scourge shook his head, scanning the horizon while Kelly rubbed an apparent chill away from her arms and came closer.

A gnarled hand fell on Taylor's shoulder, and she nearly jumped out of her skin as she whirled. Turtle. She hadn't even known he was still here. "God, you scared me half to death!"

He only smiled. "Your young helpers want to hear the tales of your people, Sky Dancer. Even if you do not."

Sky Dancer. He'd been calling her that since the first day he showed up here, uninvited. Said a Comanche woman needed a Comanche name, even if she did deny her heritage.

She bristled at his insistence on addressing her that way, but there were more-important things to do here than argue with an old man.

"What happened, Ms. McCoy?" Kelly asked. "We heard—"

"Are you all right?" Scourge came closer, twelve years her junior and nursing a bad crush, she suspected. She shook herself and tried not to look quite so terrified. Even if he cut that neon yellow dust mop and dumped the nose ring, she wouldn't want him playing hero to her damsel in distress. She was quite capable of being her own savior, thanks.

More calmly she asked, ''Did you see him?'' And she couldn't help looking toward where the horse and rider had been.

All three of her companions turned to follow her gaze.

''No,'' Turtle said softly.

''Did anyone else see him?'' She faced Kelly, then Scourge, hoping against hope. But it was silly to doubt herself like this, silly to need confirmation of what she'd seen with her two perfectly good eyes. Just because she'd awakened to soft sobbing one morning, opened hazy eyes to see a beautiful young Comanche woman silhouetted in morning sunlight near her bedroom window—a woman who'd faded as soon as Taylor rubbed her eyes—that was no reason to think she was suddenly prone to hallucinations.

And just because the phone had rung seconds later with this particular job offer didn't mean one event had a thing to do with the other.

Or with this latest…apparition.

Turtle's gnarled hand returned gently to Taylor's shoulder. ''You did not imagine him, Sky Dancer. We all heard his cry.'' It was as if he could read her thoughts.

''You heard him?'' she asked, searching Turtle's crinkled face, probing the faded eyes that resembled worn black denim.

He nodded hard, so hard his steel gray hair fell forward, so he had to push it away from his face. ''Wolf Shadow. Legend says he appears still, to keep the sacred grounds of The People from desecration. To keep the place where his lover lies beneath the earth from the touch of any outsider."

Taylor grabbed his arm, remembered his age and gentled her grip. "Turtle, your tribal elders assured me they believe this site was an ordinary Comanche village. Even if it is older than anything excavated to date, it shouldn't be considered sacred ground."

"The legend tells you otherwise," Turtle said slowly.

Taylor sighed hard. "But that's why they brought me here. To find out which is true."

And again he nodded. His movements were always slow, so deliberate they were almost graceful, so that when he nodded, his head bobbed like a rubber ball floating in gentle waves.

"If you find no evidence that the legend is true, they will sell this land to Hawthorne."

"Because they desperately need the money that sale will bring," she said quickly, and then wondered why she sounded defensive. Why should she? It wasn't her decision. She had nothing to do with it.

"But if you find the evidence, if you dig the past from the earth, it will no longer *be* sacred ground."

She shook her head, exasperated. "You're making this thing sound like some kind of Zen riddle."

He shrugged and got that look on his face. The thoughtful one he got sometimes just before blurting something deep. "The legend says that if this place is preserved, treated with honor, its magic will ensure the prosperity of The People."

"Yeah, well it hasn't done that so far, has it? I saw the community where your people—"

"Correction, Sky Dancer," he interrupted. "*Our* people."

"Fine. Whatever. I've seen where they're living. The school isn't even safe, let alone conducive to learning. The houses are in disrepair. I don't blame the elders a bit for wanting to take Hawthorne's offer on this land. And if I don't find anything to indicate it's some kind of sacred place to them, they'll be free to do it."

"And if you do, Sky Dancer? You have your clearance from the state. You are within your rights under the law to be here. You have the permission of the tribe. Hawthorne is paying you to dig up this ground. He hopes you'll find nothing here, because he wishes to own it. And the elders hope you'll find nothing here, because they wish to sell it. These motives are selfish. But what if it *is* sacred ground? Would it even matter to you, a woman who has turned her back on her—?"

"Don't you dare say that to me." She faced him suddenly, ignoring the two young people who stared as if transfixed by this exchange. But Turtle's solemn eyes held no malice. And they practically dared her to deny what he'd said. And of course, she couldn't. But she hadn't turned her back on anyone or anything. She'd simply been raised white, by loving parents who'd lied to her with nearly every breath. She'd had no connection to her heritage, and now that she was grown she didn't want or need one.

"Would it matter?" he asked her again.

"Of course it would matter," she snapped. And then he smiled serenely at her, closed his eyes, gave a single, slow nod that made her think he looked remarkably like his namesake.

"It would matter, Turtle, but only *if* I found legitimate evidence of it. I'm *not* going to be scared off by some jerk in full costume trying to make me believe he's a ghost."

Turtle's eyes opened again, looking worried. "Then...you don't believe in Wolf Shadow?"

She blinked, and tried to soften her expression. She'd been filled in about this local legend, even before Turtle had told it to her. Wolf Shadow was a Comanche shaman of incredible power. He'd fallen in love with Little Sparrow, daughter of a chief, and—in Turtle's version at least—a woman of such beauty it weakened a man's heart to look upon her. But before the two became one according to tribal custom, there was a raid on the village. Horse soldiers attacked in retaliation for some wrong they blamed on whatever Indian village was handy and nearby. And Little Sparrow was killed in that raid.

The legend went that Wolf Shadow carried her body to the spot where he had first kissed her. Where he'd given her a pendant he'd made with his own hands, and where he'd asked her to be his woman. He'd buried her there. It was said Wolf Shadow blessed the earth in which she rested, and called on the shamans of his village to protect that spot. He promised that if they did this, prosperity would rain down on their descendants. And then he shed his ceremonial garb and put on the clothes of a warrior. He left the village to avenge Little Sparrow's death, and spent the rest of his days seeking out the soldiers who had raided the village that day, and killing them, one by one. The whites put a price on Wolf Shadow's head, and he was killed a few years later, though no one knew what had been done with his remains.

Turtle claimed the spirits of Little Sparrow and Wolf Shadow were still not at peace. That because she was taken before the two became one, their spirits wandered endlessly, each searching for the other. And that only when one of Wolf Shadow's descendants found true love with one of Little Sparrow's would the two ancient lovers be reunited and know peace.

Taylor had heard the tale from the elders, as well as from Turtle—him giving the more romantically embellished version. Believing it, of course, was another matter. But Turtle was asking her again.

"Do you, Sky Dancer? Do you believe in Wolf Shadow? In the legend?"

She drew a breath. Looked sideways at Kelly, who seemed to have set Taylor up as some kind of role model, a position Taylor didn't ask for or feel comfortable in. And at Scourge, ready to jump should she crook a finger. It wouldn't do either of them any good to hear her put some silly legend ahead of the important work she was doing. Nor would it help them much to hear her, a scientist, admit she believed in ghosts.

She didn't.

"I didn't say that I *don't* believe in the legend, Turtle. I said I don't believe *that* was Wolf Shadow." She narrowed her eyes, searched Turtle's face. "Have you ever seen this ghostly rider, Turtle? Would you know what he looks like?"

Turtle shook his head slowly, then tilted it and studied her face as he spoke. Watching her a little too intently. "I am told he is a man so beautiful that the mere sight of him has weakened the hearts of many a woman. That his eyes are piercing and sharp, and his body as strong as that of his spirit brother, the wolf." He slanted her a sideways glance. "Was that how he looked to you?"

Kelly's soft sigh drew Taylor's gaze. The young woman lifted her brows and breathed, "Was it?"

Taylor thought of the powerful form she'd glimpsed, the black hair waving in the breeze. She licked her lips. "It seems a bit of an exaggerated description to me."

"He *wasn't* attractive to you, then?" Turtle asked.

"Well, I wouldn't say he was *un*attractive."

"Hmm." Turtle rubbed his chin. "It is said that Wolf Shadow appears only to the person in need of his warnings, Sky Dancer. He appeared tonight, only to you."

"Yeah, well, he'll think twice about pulling any more of this nonsense when I talk to the sheriff tomorrow."

"Good idea," Scourge said a little too quickly. "And I'll start keeping watch at night, outside your tent, if you—"

Kelly's elbow jabbed him in the rib cage. Scourge grunted, then shot her a confused glance. "What?"

"Subtle, Scourge," she said. "Real subtle."

His face reddened, and he averted his gaze.

Turtle smiled very slowly. "Talking to the sheriff is a good idea," he said. "Garrett Brand is a good man. He will help you if he can."

Taylor frowned. "If he can? What's that supposed to mean?"

"I must go, Sky Dancer. Sleep now. Perhaps your dreams know the answers."

Turtle turned and loped off into the darkness, in the opposite direction from the one the alleged Wolf Shadow had taken. And not for the first time, Taylor marveled at his agility and grace.

Then she brought her attention back to the matter at hand. Someone didn't want her completing this dig.

Someone with an incredible chest and a pair of muscled thighs that looked pretty good clenched tight around a horse. At least...as far as she could tell, it being so dark and all.

The question was, why?

"Never again," Wes growled as he kicked the horse into a gentle lope. "Never, *ever* again!" He rode away from that little camp out into the desert, then slowed the horse to a walk and turned to head back—the long way around. He skirted the site unseen, and reentered it on the lower side where he was shielded from sight by a small copse of trees. Once he got to the water hole he dismounted, and let his horse—scratch that, his *brother's* horse—take his fill of water. Lord help him if Garrett ever found out he'd "borrowed" Duke, much less *why*.

Wes sighed hard, hunkered down and scooped handfuls of chilled water onto his face, rubbing hard to scrub the ridiculous makeup off. It took some doing, and every few minutes a bird would flit from a tree, making enough noise to jolt him right to his toes thinking someone was coming up on him, about to catch him red-handed.

Eventually his face felt clean, and Wes felt a little less like a kid on Halloween. He tied his hair back in its usual style, with a thong. He hadn't cut it since he'd got out of prison. Probably never would. One more way of thumbing his nose at the conventions of society, he figured.

He changed clothes next. And when he was finally rid of the entire getup, he rolled up the loincloth and stuffed it into the duffel bag he'd left hidden here.

Finished, he tucked the war lance and the duffel bag

full of makeup and his skimpy costume into their hiding place—the small cave near the east end of the pond. Then he mounted up and rode around the lower side of the dig area, giving it a wide berth, and heading down toward the dirt road below and his friend's place. He had every intention of strangling the old coot.

This was a bad idea. Worst idea he'd ever let himself get talked into. Worse even than going out drinking with that band of rowdies who'd pulled a holdup after he'd left them, and then let him take the rap along with them.

Well, he'd tried it. It hadn't worked. That Dr. McCoy woman hadn't seemed the least bit afraid of his Wolf Shadow routine. The dig was going to go on, and there wasn't a damned thing Wes could do to stop it. And just because over the past year he'd let himself get closer to that old man than he'd ever been to anyone, didn't mean he had to go painting himself up and parading around half-naked for him. It was damned humiliating.

He emerged onto the deserted dirt lane and rode along its edge, the horse's hooves kicking up a slight dust in his wake. And as they rode, he remembered the first time he'd met the old Indian who claimed to be a Comanche shaman. The fellow had been sitting along the roadside in a battered pickup that looked to be rustier and less dependable than Wes's baby sister's was. And that was saying something. Just sitting there. As Wes had driven past, he'd seen the flat tire, and glanced again at the leathery face of the man inside. A twinge of conscience, and he'd stopped to offer a hand changing the tire.

That had been the beginning. Just a coincidence, Wes had said. But the old nut—Turtle, he called himself—had said there was no such thing as coincidence. That he'd been waiting for Wes for quite some time. And since he seemed so in need of a friend, Wes had visited with him for a while. And then he'd gone back.

That was probably the mistake, right there. He never should have gone back.

The mobile home came into sight, looking old and shabby. Pickup truck drooping in the driveway as if it might shed a part or two if they got much heavier. The circular area in the middle of the lawn was blackened and littered with cinders and partially burned lumps of wood. Nearby, a metal barrel with the top cut out of it brimmed with beer cans, the cumulative results of all their nights together around a campfire, sipping a cold one while Turtle told those stories. All told, the beer cans were the only things in sight that weren't rusted.

Wes tied the horse up out back and walked inside without knocking.

But his anger faded when he caught sight of Turtle lying on the sagging couch, his face flushed and tiny beads of perspiration clinging to his brow. Wes frowned and leaned forward to press a hand to Turtle's face. He felt heat there.

"You're feverish, pal. What is it? Are you getting worse?"

Turtle closed his serene eyes, shook his head. "Tell me about your mission, Raven Eyes. Were you successful?"

Wes sighed, rolling his eyes heavenward. "Yeah, I was successful, all right. Successful in making a complete fool outta myself. Dammit, Turtle, I told you this would never work. I must've been nuts to let you talk me into prancing around half-naked and whooping it up like a goldern coyote! That professor woman wasn't any more scared of me than a grizzly bear would've been. And I can tell you right now, there is no way in hell I'm ever going to do anything so stupid again. No way in—''

''You saw her, then?''

Wes bit off his words, and recalled her sitting there on the ground in the lamplight. Jet hair pulled back in a tight little knot, except for the few strands that had escaped. Huge dark eyes glowing. He'd had a good look at her, there in that pool of white light. ''Yeah. I saw her.''

''And?''

''And what? I was surprised, I suppose. I didn't expect someone named McCoy to look...''

''Like us?'' Turtle asked.

Wes nodded and searched Turtle's face. ''How'd you know that?''

Turtle only shrugged. ''I'm a shaman. I know things. She is Comanche, though not raised as one. Is she beautiful?''

Wes thought about her eyes, flashing like onyx in the glow of the lamplight. Her stance straightening and her small chin lifting as she challenged him. ''Yeah, I suppose you could call her beautiful. Though what that has to do with any of this, I don't—''

Turtle groaned softly, and Wes's words came to a stop.

''This is crazy,'' he said, but his voice was softer now. ''Dammit, Turtle, you're not going to die just because somebody digs up some old dirt. It's ridiculous!''

But he was worried. The old man was obviously slipping. And maybe the fact that he *believed* this would kill him could make it actually happen. For crying out loud, he was as hot and sticky right now as if he'd just run a footrace.

"Look, there has to be another way."

Turtle shook his head. "I have told you, Raven Eyes, I am the last shaman of my clan. A small bit of that land was sacred to the shamans of my line. We were sworn to protect it. If it is violated, I will die."

Wes shook his head. "The McCoy woman doesn't seem to believe any of that. And the state of Texas must not, either, or they'd have at least objected. Hell, Turtle, even the Comanche people haven't raised a stink about this dig—"

"The sacred place is there," Turtle insisted. "She must believe it is there, and convince The People not to sell to this Hawthorne. But she must believe it without finding it, without violating it, or its magic will be lost."

"But why don't the tribal elders know more about it, if it's so damned important? Why don't they know—?"

"The secret of that place was handed down through the shamans of my clan. And of those, Raven Eyes, I am the only one left. I alone know where Little Sparrow lies. You must stop the woman from disturbing that ground, or..."

"Or?"

Turtle closed his eyes and shook his head slowly. "It is good that we found one another when we did," he said. "All the time we had, to sit beside the fire outside while I told you the stories of your people and your heritage. It was good. We had a good year together, didn't we, my friend?"

Wes closed his eyes and thought, Here we go again.

"When my time comes, I will gather all I need and go out into the desert. And there I'll wait for the Great Spirit to take me...."

"No. Dammit, Turtle, no, you're not gonna do that. You do, and I promise I'll ride out there and find you, and I'll haul your butt right back here. You understand?"

Turtle met Wes's eyes. "If the sacred ground of my people is violated, then—"

Wes yanked his hat off the rack and slammed it down on his head. "Your sacred ground isn't gonna be violated, all right? I'll see to it."

"But you said..."

"I said I'd see to it and I will. And while I'm at it, I'm gonna see about having you looked at by a doctor. And I don't want any damned arguments about that, either, you stubborn goat."

Turtle sighed in misery, but nodded. "You are a good friend to me, Wes Brand."

"Yeah, and you're a pain in the backside." He looked back and sighed. "Anything I can get for you before I go? Maybe you should eat something. Or..."

"Go. Your brothers need you at the ranch. Go on. I will sleep. I'm very tired, you know."

Grimacing, Wes reached for the blanket on the back of the couch, and tried to feign carelessness as he draped it over Turtle's old body and tucked it around him. He was worried. Damn, he'd never seen Turtle looking this fragile and weak. Was the old man really going to will himself to die just because of this dig?

Wes took a long look at the man who had become more than a friend to him. Then he shook his head and left for the night.

* * *

When Turtle heard the receding hoofbeats and knew Wes had gone, he flung the blanket back and pulled the remote control out from under the couch cushion. He could still catch the last quarter of the football game. As the screen lit up, he headed into the small kitchen, opened the fridge and pulled out a can of beer and a slice of cold pizza. Then he strode back to the couch, whistling the "Monday Night Football" theme song.

His plan was unorthodox, to say the least. But he had promises to keep. One promise in particular, made to a wonderful woman as she lay dying a very long time ago. Beyond that, he had an ancient mission to fulfill. Keep the sacred spot safe, and yet keep The People from selling it. And make sure the rest of Wolf Shadow's legend came full circle. As the last shaman of his clan, it was all up to him. He'd lived for 107 years. And he knew full well why he'd been allowed such a long life. For this. All for this.

He took a big bite of cold pizza, leaned back on the couch and watched the Dallas Cowboys begin one of their famous fourth-quarter comebacks.

Chapter 2

"Hey, Wes. You're up early."

Wes was halfway out the screen door onto the front porch of the Texas Brand when his baby sister's voice put an automatic smile on his face. She was sitting all alone on the porch swing, looking kinda somber, he thought as he looked her over. And he felt his smile die slowly as he moved toward her. She got up to greet him with a bear hug.

He squeezed her tight, then stood back a little so he could see her. "What're you doing here this early in the morning, Jessi?"

"Gee, I thought you'd be glad to see me." She thrust her lower lip out and gave him her best puppy-dog eyes.

"Well, I am. Hell, we miss you like crazy around here since you moved out. Only see you—what—two, three times a day?"

She punched him in the shoulder. "Just 'cause we

have our own place doesn't mean I gave this one up, you big lug.''

''It had better not,'' he told her. But he got serious again in a hurry. ''So, what's going on? You usually wait till we're at least awake and at the breakfast table to visit. Is little Maria okay?''

''The baby's fine, Wes. And—''

''So it's Lash, then. If he's giving you grief, little sister, just say the word and I'll—''

''Wes, for crying out loud, you won't do anything! Lash is fabulous, the best husband I could even imagine. Gosh, you've seen the way he spoils Maria-Michele, and he's almost as bad with me.''

Wes searched her eyes, decided she was telling the truth and shrugged. ''So, then what're you doing here so early?''

She turned toward the horizon and smiled very gently. ''I just had a hankerin' to see the sunrise from this porch swing like I used to, is all. It's silly, me being only a few miles away and still getting so darned homesick.''

''Yeah,'' he said, and he followed her gaze to where the red-orange sun painted the sky with fire so it looked like an abstract painting of yellows and golds and reds instead of the blue it would be later on. ''I guess I understand that. This place…it gets into your blood.'' And for just a moment he thought maybe he knew why Turtle might be reacting so badly to having the land of his forebears invaded by outsiders. ''I'm gonna miss it, too.''

She looked at him sharply. ''You goin' somewhere, Wes?''

He smiled at her. ''Not far, kiddo. Not far. I hadn't

mentioned this to anyone yet, but I'm thinking about buying the old Cumberland place."

"Over near where those scientists are digging up the Comanche village?" Her brows rose high, eyes wide but interested. "But, Wes, that place is falling down. It's not even livable."

"Not now. But it's smack in the middle of some of the finest grazing pastures north of the Rio Grande, kid. The land is perfect. The house and barn…well, they can be fixed up. And the price is gonna be low, I can almost guarantee it."

"You mean you don't know what they want for it?"

"State took possession for back taxes," he said. "The place was abandoned for years even before that. The suits just got around to making their minds up to auction it off and cut their losses. I already talked to the bank. I'm putting a bid in today."

"Oh." She tilted her head to one side. "You gonna run cattle?"

"Nope," he said, and he pushed his Stetson back a little. "Horses. Appaloosas. Gonna start out with a few head, and breed the best horses to be found."

She grinned up at him suddenly. "You'll do it, too."

"Damned straight I will," he said. And he didn't tell her that part of the reason he wanted this particular place was that he knew his ancestors had once lived on its lands. Hunted there. Fought and even died there. Funny how his Comanche blood had never mattered much to him before. Not until he'd met Turtle. The old man had a way of making the stories come alive, and of relating them to Wes personally.

"So, you gonna tell me why you're up so early?"

He shrugged, not telling her he was eager to check in on his aging friend this morning. He hadn't confided to his family about Turtle. Not yet. He didn't know why, except that it was a little too personal right now, the things he was learning, the things he was feeling. "Just wanted to get an early start on the chores, kid. You wanna give me a hand?"

"Just like old times?" she said with a grin. "Sure. That husband of mine can handle the baby just fine for a while."

Wes searched her eyes and gave a slow nod. His sister looked happy. Really happy.

She'd better be, or her husband would have him to answer to.

They headed out to the barns together, but stopped short when a khaki-colored Jeep bounced into sight, rolling under the arching Texas Brand over the driveway and raising a heck of a dust cloud.

He and Jessi turned as one when the Jeep came to a stop and its driver's door opened. And then *she* got out, and Wes almost choked on his next breath. Taylor McCoy. What the hell was she doing here? Had she somehow recognized him underneath all that paint and the protective cover of darkness last night? But how could she? She'd never even met him before.

She wore pleated khaki trousers and a matching short-sleeved shirt. But the loose-fitting clothes couldn't hide the long, slender lines of her. She was tall, willowy. And her ebony hair was twisted into a tight knot again, only this morning there were no loose tendrils framing her regal face. Instead a pair of black-rimmed glasses, round ones, tried to hide her almond eyes.

Wes swallowed hard, recalling the other reason he hadn't slept well last night. He'd kept picturing her the way he'd first seen her. Sitting outside the dome tent caressing a broken piece of pottery as if it were the Hope diamond. And when he'd seen her face, he'd wondered if she knew all the things he'd never known about his own people. But Turtle had answered that question for him. She knew as little as Wes had known a year ago. She'd been raised away from that world. And maybe this dig of hers was her way of searching for it. Just as Wes's nights around the fire with Turtle were his.

"Hello," she said. "Mr. Brand?"

He just kept staring. Wondering if she knew about his foolish attempt to frighten her last night. Wondering what she was going to say. Her black eyes met his, held them. And he felt something…something he couldn't define.

Jessi elbowed him in the rib cage. He started out of his stupor, blinked and managed to say, "Yeah. What can I do for you?"

"I'm Dr. Taylor McCoy," she said, extending a long and elegant hand. "I'm supervising the archaeological dig over at Emerald Flat."

"Yeah, I know." He took her hand in his. Warm, firm. There were a few calluses. A woman who knew about hard work and wasn't a bit afraid of it, he thought.

She glanced down at their clasped hands, and he realized he was still holding hers and abruptly let go. Damn. Since when did he get all flabbergasted around women? Usually they were the ones tripping over themselves at a glance from him. He *hated* that.

No danger of it with this one, though.

"I have to apologize for bothering you at home, Sheriff Brand, but I just couldn't wait for office hours. This is important and I—"

"Whoa, wait a minute, Doc," Jessi cut in. "This isn't—"

"That's okay, Jessi," Wes said quickly. "Let the lady talk. Meanwhile, didn't you say you had something to do in the house?"

Jessi's eyes bulged so widely Wes wondered if they wouldn't pop their sockets. When she finished gaping at him, she turned toward the woman, and her gaze got narrower as she gave her the once-over. "You sure you're up to this?" she asked the woman.

"Excuse me?" Taylor McCoy frowned in confusion.

Jessi shook her head. "Nothing. Never mind. I'll be inside, Wes." Then Jessi headed back to the house. Wes figured he had about five minutes to figure out what it was the good doc had to say to his brother the sheriff. By then Jessi would have blabbed and Garrett would be out here giving it all away.

"So," he began, and then he met her eyes and forgot what he was saying again. She stared into his eyes for a long moment. As if she couldn't look away. And then she blinked and shook herself a little.

"I...um...don't think your wife liked me bothering you at home."

"My wife?" He blinked. "Oh, you mean Jessi? That's my baby sister. I don't have a wife."

She frowned and took a step backward. "That's funny..."

"What is?"

"The guy at the gas station over in town told me I could find the sheriff out here, where he lived with his wife and little boy." She narrowed her eyes until she was almost squinting at him. "Have I met you before? You look—"

"Nope. No chance of that. Listen, I didn't mean to mislead you. Garrett is the lawman, not me. But he's probably not even up yet, and I...sometimes help him out with things."

"Oh. Then you're *not* the sheriff."

He shook his head. "I'm his brother. Wes Brand, ma'am."

She studied his face, tilted her head. "You're Native American, aren't you?"

"Half," he told her.

"Comanche?" she asked, and he nodded. "Maybe you *can* help me, then. Look, what do you know about the site of that village I'm excavating?"

He shook his head. "Next to nothing." He lowered his eyes, and felt a twinge of guilt that made little sense. "I'm not as knowledgeable about my heritage as I should be, I suppose. But I'm trying to change that."

When he looked up again, there was a solemn understanding in her dark eyes, and they held his in a grip that wouldn't let go. A warm breeze stirred the dust in little whorls around his feet, and her hair danced in slow motion. "I'm...not, either," she said, very softly. "Very knowledgeable about...them."

"But you're an archaeologist."

She nodded and looked away.

Wes frowned. "I kinda figured you'd be an expert on the subject."

She shrugged, still not meeting his eyes. "I'm an expert on Native American cultures," she said, picking her words carefully, he thought. "Every one *except* the Comanches." She looked a little guilty when she said it.

"Why is that, Taylor?"

She looked up, met his eyes squarely. And he felt something…some kind of connection to her, as if he knew her…or should know her…or something.

The screen door creaked, then banged, and heavy-booted feet tramped down the steps. She turned to look at Garrett loping across the lawn with a stride that ate up the distance. Wes glimpsed his brother once, but his gaze was drawn right back to Taylor again. The definition of her cheekbones. Her small, proud chin, and strong jawline. The way the sun painted her black hair with glimmering light as it climbed higher in the sky.

"Dr. McCoy," Garrett said when he reached her and clasped her hand in greeting.

"You must be Sheriff Brand," she said with an easy smile. Broad and white and stunning. Her eyes glowed when she smiled. If she'd felt anything just now, she was hiding it well. Either that or it had all been in Wes's mind. But he didn't think so.

Garrett sent a quick glance toward Wes, and Wes nodded. Garrett returned his attention to the doc. "Call me Garrett. I see you've already met Wes. Why don't you come on inside and join us for some breakfast, ma'am, and you can tell me what it is I can help you with."

She shook her head quickly. "Thanks, but I don't have time for all that. We had an incident out at the site on Emerald Flat last night, Sheriff, and I'm not sure what to do about it."

"An incident?" Garrett frowned worriedly.

Wes tried real hard to look innocent.

The doc opened her mouth, closed it again and shook her head. "It's going to sound a little crazy."

Garrett smiled at her, that big, gentle smile he used

when he was trying to make smaller creatures feel comfortable around him, and not intimidated by his size. "I've heard crazy before," he said.

"Okay." She took off her glasses and polished the lenses with a tissue she pulled from her pocket. A way, Wes thought, of avoiding their eyes while she told them her crazy story. "You ever hear the legend the local Comanches have about a man they call Wolf Shadow?"

Garrett nodded. "Sure. We've all heard that one. No one really believes it anymore, but—"

"Well, last night Wolf Shadow was at the site."

Garrett's brows went up. "Come again?"

"He—or someone trying to impersonate him—rode up to the edge of the site on a black horse the size of…of that one over there." She pointed and nodded toward the horse grazing now in the paddock. Wes's heart fell to his feet, and he choked noisily.

Garrett frowned at the horse, then at his brother. He slammed Wes on the back, and nodded at Taylor to go on.

"He said we were desecrating sacred ground and that we should leave while we still could," she said.

"And?" Garrett asked. Wes had stopped choking, but he really didn't want to be here for this. He should have skinned out the minute he'd seen her coming.

"And nothing," she said. "He rode off. I was hoping you could come out to the site with me, see if you can make any sense out of this."

Garrett nodded. "I have a ton on my schedule today, Taylor," he said, calling her by her first name as easily and naturally as if she were an old friend. "And with my deputy off caring for his new baby half the time…" Garrett grinned a little lopsidedly when he mentioned his brand-new niece, then seemed to shake himself. "I'll get out there later on today and have a look around."

Taylor lowered her head. "I don't want you to just take a look around." She raised her head, met Garrett's eyes and slipped her glasses into her shirt pocket with deliberate motions. "Look, this scared me. I want someone up there with me in case this lunatic comes back."

Garrett frowned, and Wes felt more guilty by the minute.

"Did this guy threaten you in any way?" Garrett asked.

She shifted her stance and looked irritated. "I sort of took that 'leave while you still can' part as a threat."

"I don't blame you," Garrett said. "I just don't know that I can pack up and move onto the site to watch out for you. I've got a wife and a boy and a ranch to run, and right now I'm the only law in this town." He shook his head. "I'm sure you're not in any danger. I'll investigate today and—"

"Look, this might not seem very important to you, Sheriff Brand, but this dig represents a lot of hard prep work and research for me, and I'm not going to let some lunatic in a loincloth screw it up." She turned fast to face Wes. "What about you?"

He blinked. "What *about* me?"

"You said you help your brother out from time to time."

"You did?" Garrett blurted, but Taylor rushed right on.

"So how about camping at the site for a few nights to check this out?"

"Well, I...I mean, what I meant was—it's just that—"

"I want someone out there. I want some kind of investigation started and I want some form of protection."

"Now, ma'am, I'm not sure you're in need of any *protection*," Garrett said.

"Insane people are dangerous, Sheriff. And sane people do not paint their faces and play ghostly avenger in the middle of the night. Now, you can help me out with this, or...or I'll just go back into town, buy myself a rifle and the next time someone rides up to my site in the dark—"

"Now, hold on a minute!" Garrett lifted both hands defensively.

Taylor stopped talking and nodded. "I thought that might get your attention," she said in a calmer voice. Then she sighed hard, shook her head. "Look, I'm not going to go shooting at shadows, gentlemen, but I really am concerned. This shook me. Sheriff Brand, what if it was your wife or your little sister up there in a tent with no protection, and some lunatic was showing up at midnight with war whoops and veiled threats? Would you take this more seriously then?"

Garrett nodded. "You're right, and I'm sorry."

"I have two students with me up there," she told him. "I can't risk anything happening to them. And frankly...I doubt they'd be much help to me if this guy decided to get violent."

"I'll take care of it," Garrett began.

"No." Wes cleared his throat as they both looked his way. "No, I'll take care of it. In fact, I think you had the best idea, Doc."

Wes looked from one to the other. Taylor seemed

relieved. Garrett…suspicious. But he couldn't risk Garrett going up there and uncovering his ploy. And besides, what better way to make sure Turtle's precious sacred ground didn't get violated than to be right there at the dig?

"I'll pack up some gear and head out to the site," Wes said, instantly wondering if he would live to regret it. "Hang out there for a few days. Garrett, with Elliot and Ben here, you can get by without me for a short while."

"I don't know," Garrett said. Then he frowned. "Chelsea *is* always saying how she thinks you oughtta get in touch with your Comanche heritage, though. This might be something you ought to do."

"Chelsea's taking her psychology classes way too serious," Wes muttered, not bothering to tell his brother he'd been doing just that for the past year.

Garrett glanced at Taylor. "You realize, my brother isn't a lawman. But I'd trust him with my life. Have, a time or two, in fact, and I'm still here to tell about it."

"That's good enough for me," Taylor said.

Garrett finally nodded. "Good, then. It's settled." He slapped Wes's shoulder. "Thanks for jumping in like this, Wes. Little Bubba's toddling around into everything, and Chelsea's busy with the women's crisis center and her psych classes. We got cows ready to freshen and fence to repair. Those damned rustlers we caught in Mexico last year are coming to trial, and I have to testify. Jessi's busy with the new baby, and Lash is up nights so much with her that he's not worth much in the daylight these days, even if I can convince him to come into the office." He nodded, as if reassuring himself. "Yup, this is the perfect solution."

Wes glanced once again at Taylor McCoy, who stood looking at him with her big dark eyes. ''All right, then,'' he said. ''But don't be thinking you're gonna pin any badge on me, big brother, 'cause it's not gonna happen.''

''Wouldn't dream of it,'' Garrett said. ''This will be unofficial. Okay?''

Wes nodded. Garrett tipped his hat to the lady, and then headed out to the barns, leaving Wes alone with the woman once more. He faced her, suddenly uncomfortable, not sure what to say.

''I...appreciate this,'' she said. ''I know it's a lot to ask, but—''

''It's the least I can do,'' Wes said. And it was. He was the one who'd scared the woman so badly, after all.

''I'll come on out to the site later on. I need time to pack up some gear and I got a...an errand to run in town.''

''All right,'' she said. But she didn't turn to go. He gave her a questioning glance, and she lowered her eyes. ''Will you...be there before dark?''

Hell, she really was scared. He hadn't thought Wolf Shadow's appearance had shaken her in the least, but he'd been wrong. ''Yeah,'' he said. ''Well before dark. Promise.''

She nodded. ''Good,'' she said. ''That's good.''

Wes Brand had eyes that could burn holes right through her, she thought as she bounded over the rutted roads in her Jeep. He'd seemed a little unnerved by her presence. Or maybe it was her story that bothered him.

So what was it about *him* that bothered *her?*

There was something about him. Something that made her feel warm and jittery. But he also wore this aura like a glowing sign that flashed Stay Away to anyone who got too close. She pegged him as a loner.

And then she realized that she had been pegged that way, too. Most of her life. All through college and graduate studies, she'd immersed herself in her work to the exclusion of a social life, much less any romantic attachments. She'd attributed that to the need for focusing on her career. But she knew there was more to it. She knew what lay beneath her detachment. She just hadn't taken the time to examine it closely, or to try to work through it. Old hurts didn't matter. They had nothing to do with the present.

What made Wes Brand a loner? she wondered idly.

He was one beautiful man. Strikingly so. Made her think twice about having him come up to the site instead of his big but safe-looking brother. He could very easily become a distraction, which was utterly hilarious when she thought about it, because she'd never once met a man who could compete with her work for her attention.

Well, there was a first time for everything. But she could handle it. She'd just put on her professor face, and keep a cool, clinical distance between the two of them.

If only she could do the same with the mysterious Wolf Shadow. But it was harder with him, because he was a phantom. A ghost. And last night after he'd gone, he'd returned to her in dreams no cool, clinical scientist ought to be having.

Pretty strange, she thought. Good ol' Solitary McCoy feeling…oddly drawn to two different men in the space of twenty-four hours, when she usually didn't even notice men.

Very strange. She felt a little worried about that as she headed back to the site.

''Well, well, well,'' Jessi chirped when Wes went back inside. She was sitting at the table, but he had no doubt she'd been watching him with Taylor McCoy the whole time.

''She's got to be the most stunningly beautiful woman I've ever seen,'' Chelsea said. Garrett's wife gave Wes a mischievous grin and a wink. ''Not that you probably noticed.''

''She looks like Pocahontas did in the Disney movie,'' Jessi said.

''Since when do you watch Disney movies?'' was the only safe comeback he could think of.

Little Bubba came running across the floor, arms flailing as if he were a little bird trying to fly, and when he reached Chelsea's legs, he hugged them hard, laughing out loud.

Chelsea scooped him up in her arms and kissed his face. ''You little speed demon,'' she said. ''You just learned to walk and now all you do is run!''

''Wun!'' Bubba said.

''So, Wes,'' Jessi said, ''you gonna tell me what's goin' on with you and the pretty professor?''

''Nothing,'' he told his little sister. ''And that's the last time I want to hear about it.'' He gave them a warning look, shook his head. ''I gotta pack.'' He tromped through the house, heading for the stairs. Jessi followed. So did Chelsea, with Bubba anchored on her hip.

''So where you going, then?'' Jessi asked.

"Garrett wants me to camp out at the site for a few days. They've had some trouble. He'll fill you in. God knows you won't leave him alone until he does."

Jessi laughed. "So you're going camping with a drop-dead gorgeous woman who looks at you like you're a rare steak and she's coming off a hunger strike—and nothing's going to happen between you two?"

He pointed his finger at her like a gun and cocked his thumb. "Bull's-eye," he told her. "And she didn't look at me like anything."

Jessi turned to Chelsea with a huge grin. "Isn't it great, Chelsea? He's in denial."

"Yeah, and he couldn't even *see* the way *he* was looking at *her*," Chelsea said. "Like a sailor lost at sea looks at a distant island."

"Ooh, that's a good one," Jessi said. "Or like a drowning man looks at a life preserver."

"Or like a brown bear looks at a honeycomb."

The two women laughed out loud. Wes just groaned and went into his room to pack.

Chapter 3

Taylor glanced up from the screen through which she'd been sifting dirt, her gaze drawn by something she couldn't have named. She half expected to see Wolf Shadow looming above her, closer and more real than before. But instead she saw Wes Brand with a duffel bag in his hand and a pack slung over one sturdy shoulder. In his tight jeans and Western shirt, that black Stetson shadowing his face, he looked more cowboy than Indian, and for some reason that thought made her hackles rise slightly in resentment.

She shook the feeling away with a puzzled frown, handed the screen to the nearest pair of hands and nearly dropped it when the student didn't react.

Swinging her head around sharply, Taylor saw the girl beside her staring at Wes Brand as if he were the second coming or something. Her brown eyes swam, and her lips curved in a dreamy smile.

"Kelly? Do you mind?"

Kelly snapped out of it long enough to focus briefly on Taylor, take the screen from her hands and go right back to staring at the man. Taylor shook her head in frustration, brushed the dirt from her hands and climbed out of the square, roped-off area where she'd been digging. "Thanks for coming," she told him, and she was extremely careful to keep her voice cool and her expression professional. She didn't want to look the way Kelly did. Not in this lifetime.

"No problem." He shifted the pack on his shoulder a little. It looked heavy. Her gaze lingered on his face—bronzed skin, hard features, that hands-off look he wore. His eyes gleamed. And they kept dipping to focus on her mouth, then jerking up again.

She cleared her throat. "This is Kelly, by the way."

"Kelly Mallone," her assistant said, dropping the screen too hard, and reaching a dirty hand out to shake Wes's.

"Wes Brand," he replied.

"Mr. Brand will be camping with us for a few days," Taylor explained. "In case our...visitor shows up again."

Kelly's lashes fluttered. "I'll feel so much safer now," she breathed.

Wes's jaw went a little tighter, and he averted his gaze from Kelly's blatantly interested one. So his way with the ladies bothered him, did it?

Then he looked at Taylor, and she schooled her features to cool professionalism again. "I'll...uh...show you where to put that stuff." He said nothing, so she set off up the slight incline to the flat area where three dome tents dotted the ground. The sticky heat seemed worse somehow than it had been only moments before, and she wiped the damp hairs from her cheeks, and shrugged. "Just pick a spot, I guess."

"Which tent is yours?"

She whirled to face him, eyes going wide.

He smiled slightly, almost as if he knew what sort of thoughts had jolted through her head just for an instant. "I want to pitch mine close to it, Doc."

"W-why?" Okay, so while she was at it, why didn't she ask herself why her stomach was clenching and relaxing like an overstimulated heart muscle?

"The kid I saw when I got here told me you were the only one who saw this...*ghost.* I want to be sure I'm within shoutin' distance if you see it again."

"Oh." She pushed another loose tendril of hair behind her ear. "What kid?" Did it matter? No, but she hated awkward silences.

"Didn't get his name," he said. "Scrawny. Hairball. Earring in his nose like some kinda damned fruitcake."

Her chin came up fast, and she gave him her best glare, while trying not to laugh at his description. "I'd never have guessed you were the judgmental type," she said. "Scourge happens to be one of the most gifted students I've ever worked with."

"Scourge?" He looked at her as if she were crazy.

Taylor almost smiled at his reaction. She bit her lip instead. "It's a nickname. His real name's Stanley, and he hates it."

Wes grinned at her, shook his head. "And *Scourge* is such an attractive alternative."

She did smile this time. She couldn't help it. She'd been razzing Scourge about his choice in nicknames since she'd met him.

After a moment of sharing that smile, Wes said, "So you're a teacher?"

His rapid change of subjects took her off guard. She didn't answer. Instead she turned to lead him to her tent. "This one's mine," she said.

He dropped his duffel, slung the pack from his shoulder to the ground, then hunkered down to pull the neatly rolled tent from inside it. And when he hunkered that way, his jeans got a whole lot tighter around his backside. He glanced up at her, over his shoulder, caught her looking before she managed to steer her gaze back where it belonged and pretended not to notice. "Then you're *not* a teacher," he said.

"I teach. But I'm not a teacher."

"Sounds deep," he said, and when she looked at him, he paused in unrolling the tent and stared at her. "I'll take a stab, though. You teach to pay the bills. But what you love is digging for bones and broken dishes."

She couldn't seem to take her eyes from his. "You're not even close."

"I didn't think so." And still he held her gaze.

To break the tension, she got up and went to the opposite end of the nylon circle, gripping the edges and pulling it out flat. Wes reached back into his pack for the flexible poles, and quickly inserted them through the fabric.

"A woman of mystery," he quipped as he worked.

She helped him raise the tent, a perfect black dome standing neatly beside her gray one. So close she imagined if she poked her hand into the side of her tent, and he did the same from within his own, they could touch through the fabric.

It was a silly thought. A silly thought that made her tingle somewhere deep. He was looking at her, waiting. "I wasn't trying to be mysterious," she said. "Truth is, I still don't know what I am.'' She lowered her head, knowing it probably sounded lame.

''And this digging up the past is your way of trying to find out.''

She brought her head up fast, because his words were so accurate. It startled her. ''It never was,'' she said softly. And silently she added, *Until now.* Then she scratched that idea. She wasn't here to learn about herself, her past, her so-called heritage. She was here to do a job. Period.

Besides, she didn't need to look very far to find herself. Her heart was being boarded on a beautiful ranch in Oklahoma. Someday she'd have a home—a real home, not one of these temporary apartments. And she'd bring Jasper there. Feed her carrots and ride her at sunrise, instead of spending the odd weekend with her, between jobs. That was what she wanted out of life. All she wanted, really. Enough money to have that place, for her and her horse. She didn't need anyone else.

''I study the past because I'm good at it,'' she said finally. ''And I learn enough along the way to make me qualified to teach it to others.''

''But not enough to let you stop looking.''

She blinked and looked away to avoid his eyes. ''I dig, I teach, I write now and then. Whatever pays the rent.'' She glanced past him to see Kelly and Scourge watching the two of them intently, although when she looked, they both got back to work.

Wes unzipped the arched doorway of his tent, slung his duffel bag inside. Then zipped it closed again. ''For what it's worth, Doc, I don't think you're gonna find yourself in that dirt you've been sifting.''

She met his black eyes, and they made her burn.

Because it was as if he knew. As if he knew exactly the lost kind of feeling she'd never really been without. The sense that he could see things she'd rather not share made her uncomfortable. She gave her head a shake. "I'm looking for artifacts, Mr. Brand, nothing more." She lowered her eyes. "And since we're swapping unasked-for advice, I don't think *you're* going to find this trespassing ghostly warrior by standing around talking to me."

"Good point," he said, and he touched the brim of his hat in a mock salute. "So why don't you show me where you saw him?"

She nodded, turned and walked. And Wes followed. She took him to the slight rise in the ground where the warrior had appeared. "He was right here."

"On a horse, right?" Wes asked.

"Yes. A big black. A stallion, I think. Probably four years old, or more."

The man frowned at her. "How can you possibly—?"

"Well, it was dark, but I could see some," she told him. "That horse was no colt. Didn't have that lean, sleek line to him. In fact, he looked a bit overweight."

"I'll be damned." He stared at her, shoved his hat back a bit, stared some more. "So you know horses as well as history?"

She smiled, thinking of Jasper. "Yeah, I know horses."

Shaking his head, Wes knelt, and she saw him examining the ground. Then he shrugged and got up. "No hoofprints."

She frowned. "Well, the ground is hard here. He might not have left any."

"Okay," he said. She got the feeling he was humoring her.

"You are aware that skilled warriors, when they wanted to employ the element of surprise, would wrap their horses' hooves in cloth to muffle the sound. When they did that, there were seldom any clear tracks."

Wes straightened up, searching her face. "You get that from a history book, Doc?"

"No," she said softly. "I got that from a Louis L'Amour book."

"I'll be damned."

"That's the second time you've said that," she told him, but he was looking at her in some kind of mingling of surprise and…she wasn't sure, but it looked like a hint of panic.

"Is something wrong, Mr.—?"

"Wes," he said. Then he shook himself. "Er, how well did you see him?"

"The horse?"

"The rider."

She tapped a forefinger against her chin and thought back, lowering her lashes to conceal her eyes. "Well enough." Well enough so that she'd seen him again, in her dreams.

"Can you describe him to me?" Wes asked.

He was going through the motions, she thought. He didn't believe she'd seen a thing, probably thought it was all in her imagination. And it made her angry, but she nodded anyway.

"He was wearing paint on his face. His hair was long and dark, and he wore it loose." She tipped her head sideways, examining the hair tied behind Wes's head. "As long as yours is, I think," she said. Then she frowned. "You know, with hair like that, I don't know how you could call Scourge a hairball."

"Scourge looks like he's wearing a lemon yellow dust mop on his head."

She almost choked on her laugh, because she'd thought the same thing about Scourge's hair so often.

"Go on," Wes said, while she swallowed her mirth. "What was this ghost wearing?"

"Not a hell of a lot." She smiled a little. "Then again, I figure any man who looked like he did would probably prefer going naked." He glanced at her sharply, and she lowered her head. "That was stupid. Sorry." She peered up at him again, but he seemed totally at a loss for words.

She cleared her throat and reminded herself this was serious. Good as the rider looked, the man could have been dangerous. And he might come back. "He was wearing some sort of loincloth, I think. His arms and chest were bare, and so were his legs, clear to the hip."

Wes licked his lips. "I thought you said it was dark."

"Well, there was moonlight. And once I put my back to my gas lamp, I could see a little better."

"Oh."

She tilted her head.

"So," Wes said, "you say he looked to be in...er... fairly good shape."

"He looked like he belonged on a calendar." She pursed her lips in thought. "Maybe he really was a ghost after all," she said. "I never saw a real man look that good." Then she walked a few steps to the east, her back to Wes. "He rode off in this direction, and that was...uh...Wes?"

He looked up, seemingly surprised to see that she'd

moved on and continued speaking. He was still standing in the same spot, blinking in what looked like shock and looking as if the heat was getting to him a bit, judging by the flush of color in his face.

"Yeah. I'm with you," he said. And he hurried up to join her.

The way she described Wolf Shadow had shaken Wes right to the core. And the way she looked when she described him was even worse.

For God's sake, she acted turned on by the guy.

But *the guy* was *him!*

Only, she didn't know that. And he didn't seem to know much of anything. And besides, she was scared, too. Scared enough so that she'd made him promise to arrive here before dark. Scared enough so that hint of fear in her eyes had been all it took to extract that promise, and maybe his liver, if she'd asked for it, as well.

He'd finished chores in record time after she'd gone. Then packed up his things and tossed them into the back of his Bronco. He'd gone back inside just long enough to write down his bid on the old Cumberland place, and then he'd sealed it in an envelope and dropped it off at the town clerk's office. After that he'd made a quick stop to check in on Turtle.

He'd arrived at Turtle's place shortly after noon, and the old goat was actually out of bed and dressed for a change. Seeing him looking more like his old self chased a good portion of the troubling thoughts from Wes's mind, and he even smiled. "You're looking better!"

"Because I know you intend to set up camp at the site, Raven Eyes," Turtle said. "And because I know you'll remain there until you've found a way to protect the sacred ground."

Wes shook his head slowly and took a seat at the small Formica-topped table in the trailer's kitchen. Turtle took a cold beer from the ancient fridge, handed it to Wes and sat opposite him. He sipped tea, and that alone let Wes know he wasn't completely recovered yet. "I'm going to try, Turtle, but I can't promise it's going to work. Taylor says—"

"Taylor?"

"Doc McCoy. She's the one in charge of the dig."

"Ah...Sky Dancer."

Wes searched Turtle's face, brows raised in question.

Turtle's only answer was, "It is a good name."

Blinking, Wes shook himself. "Okay, if you say so. Anyway, she didn't say a thing about finding evidence that Emerald Flat was ever anything other than a regular village."

"It was," Turtle said, interrupting him. "It was sacred to the shamans of my clan. It is sacred to me."

"But why are you so sure all this is true?"

Turtle closed his eyes slowly, then opened them again. "I believe it is true. The why does not matter."

Wes sipped his beer and counted to ten. Then, as calmly as he could, he said, "The Wolf Shadow thing isn't going to work, Turtle. She isn't all *that* afraid of him."

"Yes, she is," Turtle said as if he knew it beyond any doubt.

Wes took a breath, bit his tongue. "Okay, she's a little afraid, but there's more."

"She's attracted to him," Turtle said.

Wes gaped.

"This is good, my friend. If she fears him, his power over her is strong, but if she wants him, it is even stronger. You must appear to her again as Wolf Shadow. Soon."

Wes shook his head. "She wants me out there so she'll have protection from him…er…me," he said. "She even made me promise to be there before dark. If that ghost shows up and I'm not in my tent, she's going to want to know why."

"Then lure her away. Away from the camp. And while she's away, appear to her then. She can't blame you for not being close by if she's the one who leaves."

Wes grated his teeth, shook his head. "She'll never go for it. Look, my setting up housekeeping out there on the flat is supposed to end the need for this Wolf Shadow nonsense. If I'm right there to watch what—"

"It's not enough." Turtle smiled serenely, sipped his tea. Then he closed his eyes and pressed a hand to his forehead. "I'm feeling weak again, my friend. Perhaps I got up too soon."

Wes's frown vanished, swept away by concern for his friend. "We shouldn't even be talking about this," he said, getting to his feet, taking Turtle by the arm. "It gets you all stirred up. Come on, lie down. Take it easy. Don't worry about any of this, Turtle, I'm gonna take care of it."

He put an arm around Turtle's fragile shoulders and eased him into the living area, three steps from the kitchen area in this cubbyhole of a place. He helped the old man onto the green-tartan couch that sagged in the middle, and pulled a woven horse blanket off the back to cover him.

Turtle asked, "Tonight, Raven Eyes? You'll try again tonight?"

"Yeah, tonight, sure," Wes said. "If it's humanly possible. Now rest, okay? Just relax. It's gonna be okay."

After assuring himself Turtle was all right, for the time being at least, Wes had continued on his way here. To look into the huge ebony eyes of the woman he was supposed to be scaring off. And to learn that she liked horses and Western novels, and had a sense of humor, and was afraid of something. Something besides his ghostly visit. Herself, he thought. Her past. Her blood. She was afraid of it.

There was no way in hell he could lure the doc away from the camp that night. He watched and waited for an opportunity, stuck close to her side all evening, just in case she'd wander off, giving him an opening. He could get into costume in five minutes flat. There would be no time to "borrow" his brother's oversize horse this time, but if she knew horseflesh as well as she seemed to, that probably wouldn't be a good idea, anyway. Besides, he didn't need the horse. All he needed was an opportunity.

He watched her when the sun began its spectacular descent, sinking lower on the western horizon, painting the desert with a blaze orange brush. He saw the way she fidgeted and kept glancing off in the direction where his alter ego had made his first appearance. Getting nervous by the look of things. Pacing back and forth in front of her tent. Wes sat on the ground in front of his own tent, with an open notebook in one hand and a pencil in the other. He had planning to do, careful planning. The bank loan wasn't quite enough to cover the cost of all the renovations that old Cumberland place would need, if he were lucky enough to have put in the winning bid. He'd have to make the money stretch, cover the necessities first, and save the frills for later on.

Every once in a while he felt Taylor's eyes on him, glanced up fast to catch her looking at him. As if to assure herself he was still there. Close by. But when he met her gaze, she quickly covered whatever she was feeling with an "I couldn't care less" sort of expression.

Wes set his notebook aside and walked up to her anyway, nodded down at her small camp stove and the pan of water boiling on its single butane burner, and said, "It's gonna boil dry pretty soon."

She glanced down, frowned. "I forgot about it."

"Well, you have a lot on your mind."

She drummed up a scowl for him, and he wondered if he were right in assuming he'd been the thing distracting her.

Or maybe not. Maybe it was Wolf Shadow she'd been thinking of just now.

She ducked into her tent and emerged again with a sealed plastic bag full of dehydrated food, which she apparently intended to drop into the water for her dinner. He must have made a face, because she paused over the camp stove, and sent him a questioning glance. "What?"

Wes shrugged. "I just didn't expect you'd be so... citified."

"Citified?"

"Modern. Civilized. I mean, you're the one trying to find yourself in the past, aren't you?"

"You said that. I didn't." She glanced down at the

bag of food, then back at him, and she looked puzzled. She was cute when she was puzzled, he discovered. ‘‘And what does that have to do with this, anyway?’’ she asked, lifting the bag.

He shrugged. ‘‘Maybe nothing. Or maybe…’’ Giving his head a shake, he looked at the area around him, dimmer now, bathed in the last pale blush of the setting sun. Scruffy-looking trees, and a small patch of forest to the northwest, with that pond and the cave where he'd hidden his props nestled inside. To the east was civilization. Walking that way would bring you to the dirt road and Turtle's trailer, and beyond that actual towns began springing up. To the south was desert. Not the kind of place most people thought of when they thought of desert. No sand or dunes. Just hard-packed ground and rock formations rising up like living things. Nothing much grew out there. Arid, barren land. Folks around here called this patch of nowhere the Badlands. And whether it was technically accurate or not, Wes thought it fit.

This flat was like an oasis. A gentle haven set within the harsh country. Lush greenery and life, right in the middle of no-man's-land.

‘‘What is it, Wes?’’ she asked, coming to stand closer to him, searching his face, the plastic bag of food forgotten.

‘‘I was just wondering…what it was like here a hundred years ago. Or two hundred.’’

‘‘Or six,’’ she said in a voice softer than he'd ever heard her use. ‘‘I was wondering about it myself, just last night. Six centuries ago is when the first Comanche people set up camp here on this flat.’’

He shook his head. ‘‘Bet they didn't eat from any boilable bags, Doc.’’

She frowned at him. "Of course not. They cooked over a central fire, over there." And she pointed.

"So why don't we?"

She blinked, surprised maybe by his suggestion. "Wes, it's dry here. It would be dangerous to…" But her words trailed off as she gazed toward the spot she'd indicated, and he thought she was picturing it, maybe.

"We dig down a little," Wes said, "surround the fire with stones the way our ancestors did."

Her eyes glowed in the dying breath of sunlight, just before it slipped lower and vanished amid the barren hills to the west. "We could have a few pails of water standing by, just in case."

Wes smiled. He couldn't imagine why he was smiling, or why he was so enthused over something as simple as a campfire. He and Turtle sat beside a campfire more often than not. So what was the big deal here?

"I'll gather some deadfall," he told her. "There's plenty in that little stand of woods."

"I'll get Scourge to help dig a trench. Let's keep it small, Wes." She looked up at him just before he turned away, and when their eyes met, something moved between them. A childlike excitement, a sense of adventure, something new. She smiled gently at him, and Wes's throat went dry. Then he turned and headed out in search of firewood.

And as he gathered branches and twigs from beneath gnarled, mystical-looking trees, Wes asked himself what the hell he was doing. He wasn't supposed to be playing Cub Scout with Doc McCoy; he was supposed to be convincing her the legend was real and then scaring her the hell away from here. But damn, when she flashed those big onyx eyes his way, it was tough to remember that. Okay, so he'd do the campfire thing. At this point it would look pretty suspicious if he didn't. But after that, it was back to the matter at hand. His best friend's life might very well depend on it.

Chapter 4

Why she agreed to the idea of building a fire in the midst of the site, she couldn't have said. There was really no logical reason for it. Then again, there was no real reason not to do it. The location of the central fire had already been excavated, and with the pails of water Wes had hauled up from the pond, any risk of the fire spreading was eliminated.

Still she wasn't prone to mixing work with pleasure, and a campfire was that. Pleasure.

Such pleasure.

Wes took her by the hand, a casual gesture that really shouldn't have sent her pulse rate skittering. Then he knelt and patiently showed her just how to arrange the dried leaves and twigs he'd gathered up. He added large twigs in a tepee shape above the kindling. Then he took two stones from his pocket, pressing one of them into her hand.

"What is it?" she asked, mesmerized.

"Flint," he told her as she handed it back to him. "Watch." Bending low, he struck the stones together, holding them close to the edge of a dry leaf. They produced a spark with each strike, until finally the leaf began to smolder, and then to glow. Wes bent closer and blew gently on the newborn fire until tongues of flame came to life. Then he straightened, facing her. "That's the way our ancestors did it."

She averted her eyes, just a bit uncomfortable.

Then her hands were caught in his larger ones, and the stones gently enfolded in her palms. But his touch was lingering and warm. Like a lover's caress, and it made her shiver. "Keep them," he said. "You never know when you might need them."

He took his hands away slowly, as if he regretted doing so, looked up into her eyes with a slightly puzzled expression in his—as if his actions had surprised him as much as they had her. Then he gave himself a shake and sat down to enjoy the fire. And Taylor did, too.

How had she lived this long and never known how good it felt just to sit under the stars beside an open fire?

The firelight painted every face with dancing light and flickering shadow. Full darkness bathed the camp all around them, and Kelly seemed to be enjoying the fire as much as Taylor was. In fact, sitting crosslegged on the ground, the desert's chill rippling up and down her back, while the fire's warmth blanketed her front, she found it easy to imagine that the dark shapes of the dome tents around her were actually pointy-topped tepees. And that the people sitting around the fire wore animal hides instead of denim and flannel.

Scourge wasn't as enthusiastic. Not at first, anyway.

He sat there glumly, as if he were only doing so under protest. The looks he sent Wes's way when Wes wasn't looking were less than friendly, bordering on suspicious, in fact.

Wes sat beside Taylor. And she wondered if he had a clue what sorts of things were going through her mind right now. And whether he'd planned it this way. Maybe he was in cahoots with old Turtle. Subtly steering her toward things she'd avoided until now. Of course, knowledge about Comanche ways had been a necessity before even beginning this job. But the things she'd let herself study were words in books. Clinical accounts of the past. This…this was different.

If she closed her eyes, and just let herself float away in sensation—the pungency of the wood smoke, the snap and crackle and hiss of the fire, the heat of it on her face—she could almost feel them all around her. A village filled with people. Her ancestors. And instead of chilling her, the sensation warmed her.

But the warmth made her wary. She found herself mistrusting it.

"Our ancestors told stories on nights like this," Wes said, his voice deep and slow, making her think he was feeling the same things she did. But that was impossible, of course.

She nodded. "I don't know their stories nearly as well as you do, I'm sure," she said softly. Kelly was talking softly to Scourge, while he stared in silent contemplation of the flames. "I can recite facts and figures, tell you what they ate and how they cooked it. But the legends…" She sighed. "The People were later in developing a written form of their language than many other tribes. So much of what they believed in has been lost."

"Not as much as you think," Wes said, searching her face. "But what survived, survived because of nights like this one, and people gathered around a fire, sharing their tales, the old telling them to the young, generation after generation."

When he looked at her, the reflection of the flames danced in his black eyes. And she didn't say anything, so he went on. "Imagine what would have happened if the young refused to listen to those stories."

He was referring, of course, to her. She'd told him how she'd avoided studying the Comanche ways all her life. "Then the stories might have been lost."

"Not 'might have been.' Would have been," Wes said. "It's the oral tradition that's kept them alive. The stories, the history of a people."

She nodded, knew what he was getting at. She was doing a disservice to her ancestors and maybe to her descendants by refusing to listen, to know.

"For a long time I didn't think it made a difference. Maybe to *them,* you know. But not to me, personally." He paused there, waiting.

"And what changed your mind?" she asked. Kelly and Scourge had moved closer, abandoning their own conversation in favor of listening to hers and Wes's.

"I met an old man who liked to tell the stories. And I was either too polite or too dumb not to listen."

Taylor nodded slowly, watching his eyes. Seemed once a person looked into those dark eyes, it got unreasonably difficult to look away again. "And did it? Make a difference to you, personally?"

He dipped a hand into his jeans pocket, and pulled out a small woven pouch of black and bright red. The drawstring was knotted around one of his belt loops, she noticed. "Made a lot of difference," he said. "I know who I am now. Know where I come from."

She was mesmerized by the way his big hand cupped the small pouch. Long fingers stroking the weave. And maybe it was the firelight, or the night air...but it seemed sensual, somehow. And she forgot to breathe for a minute, staring at the way his fingers moved.

"Could you tell us some of those stories?" Kelly chirped, jarring Taylor right out of the spell the night—and Wes—had spun.

Wes didn't answer her. He was staring at Taylor. "They're nothing to be afraid of," he said, very softly, so softly she wasn't certain whether the other two could hear him, or if his words reached her ears alone.

"I'm not afraid of any tales of the past," she whispered, but as she said it, a shiver ran up her spine.

"Then ask, and I'll tell you. Say stop and I'll stop."

She bit her lip, glanced over the flames at Scourge, who seemed to be straining to hear the words they spoke softly to one another. At Kelly, practically bouncing on the ground in anticipation. At her tent, out of reach on the other side. But not really out of reach. She could get up, walk away, let him tell his stories to the kids and try hard not to hear, the way she did when Turtle came and insisted on talking of the past, and The People and the old ways.

She met Wes's eyes again, and there was warmth there, assurance. He wouldn't say anything that would hurt her, his eyes seemed to promise. She swallowed the lump in her throat.

"Tell me," she said softly.

And he smiled. Taylor felt as if she'd overcome some kind of obstacle. It was one of those moments when you sensed your life—your world—was about to change. And a warm hand crept over hers where it rested on the cool ground, closed around it and squeezed. And when she looked up at Wes, he was looking away, as if he was deep in thought and totally unaware of the intimate gesture.

His hand moved away a second later, and he spoke in a voice that carried around the fire. "My friend, an old shaman, tells this one over and over again," he said. "I think it's his favorite."

Without thinking about it first, Taylor moved closer to him. She couldn't take her eyes from his face as he spoke. And he reached up, without warning, to gently remove her glasses, fold the arms and drop them into her shirt pocket.

"There was a woman, long ago, who had a vision. An eagle landed on the limb of a tall tree and spoke to her. And the things the eagle said frightened the woman to the core of her, but they brought her hope, as well. 'Hard times lay ahead for The People,' the eagle told her. 'And before your generation leaves this world, you will see such hardship and strife that very few of you will survive. Many of the ways of The People will be lost, forever.'"

Taylor nodded. "Smart eagle," she said softly. "He was all too right."

Wes looked serious as he went on. "This troubled the woman. But she remained where she was and bade the eagle go on. 'You,' he told her, 'will bear a daughter, who will bear a daughter, who will bear a daughter. And this child, the great-granddaughter of your heart, is destined to restore the past to The People to whom it belongs. For no tree can exist without all of its roots. And no people can flourish without all of its past.'"

Taylor almost winced at the way those words cut to the quick. She'd been trying to flourish without her roots, but all she felt was lost and alone. But her isolation was self-imposed. She didn't trust because she chose not to trust. It was easier—safer—than believing and being betrayed again.

"The woman asked the eagle how her great-granddaughter would accomplish such a thing, but the eagle only uttered the name of the young warrior the girl was to take as husband one day, a warrior not even born yet, and then he said no more. He spread his mighty wings and took flight.

"Part of what the eagle told the woman did indeed come to pass. She had a daughter. And her daughter had a daughter. And finally her granddaughter had a daughter.

"But the granddaughter died while her child was still young, and her relatives had no wealth to give to the child. Times were dire for The People then. Thinking they were doing what was best, they sent the young one away from her tribe and her people, and she was raised in the white man's world, learning only white men's ways."

Taylor shifted uncomfortably. "You're making this up for my benefit, aren't you?"

Wes frowned at her. "This is exactly the way it was told to me, I swear." Then he tilted his head. "Why do you think—?"

"Because it could easily be my story."

He held up both hands. "Hold on. Wait. I know, you think I'm making up a story around your life to guilt you into something you don't want to do. I know. I accused my old friend of the same thing when he told it to me."

She tilted her head, eyed him suspiciously.

"It could be my story, too, Taylor, with some very minor changes. I used to think that's why the old crock was so fond of telling it to me. I've decided otherwise, though. It's just one of a hundred tales he's told me over the past year."

She lowered her head, a little embarrassed at having accused him. And then lifted it again, because what he said was sinking in. If it could be his story, as well, then…

"So…we have one thing in common, you and I," she said.

"More than one thing." His eyes gripped hers for a moment, but then he lowered them. "Should I stop?"

It was just a story, she told herself. It couldn't hurt her. "No. Go on. What happened?"

She thought he might have sighed in relief, but she wasn't sure. When he looked up again, his eyes were distant, in the past, maybe. "The great-grandmother knew of the death of her granddaughter, and that the child was given to whites, for she saw these things in her dreams as she lay on her deathbed. Yet she didn't know where the child was taken, or how to reach her. She called the village shaman to her bedside, and she told him of all the eagle had said. And with her dying breath, she whispered the name of the young warrior her great-granddaughter was to marry, according to the words of the eagle. She begged the shaman to see to it that all would happen as the eagle had said it should, and he gave his word, that she might cross to the summerland in peace.

"But the shaman was afraid of the enormous task set upon his shoulders. To find this girl, and somehow bring her back to her homelands. To teach her the ways of her people, and convince her to take upon herself the task the eagle had said would be hers…much less to convince her to marry a young man she didn't know, one he might never be able to find…all of this seemed impossible."

Kelly was smiling and wide-eyed and rapt. Even Scourge was leaning forward a bit, listening.

"The shaman went on a vision quest on the night of the old woman's death. And he saw the Great Spirit, in the form of an eagle, just as the old woman had. The eagle spoke to him and said these words, 'You will not see death until you have fulfilled your vow.' To this day that shaman still lives. And still he seeks to complete his mission."

Wes fell silent, and sat staring into the flames. Taylor stared at his face for a long time, the shadows the fire created making him seem harder and more mysterious than before. When she finally looked away from him, it was to see the others around the fire, both staring at him exactly the way she'd been doing. Kelly looked as if she wanted to wrap up in his arms. Scourge seemed mesmerized.

"It's a beautiful story," Taylor whispered.

"It's intense," Scourge said. "Mr. Brand, you said a shaman told you this tale."

Wes blinked and looked up, as if he'd been lost in thought. Then he nodded. "Yeah. There aren't that many Comanche shamans left now, but I believe this one's genuine."

Scourge bit his lip. Wes frowned across the flames at him. "I can see there's something on your mind, kid. Spit it out."

Nodding fast, Scourge said, "I've read accounts claiming that the…er…the magic practiced by Native

American shamans is...well, uh...beyond explanation.'' He shrugged. ''It makes a person wonder, is all. Have you seen anything that...would make you...you know, wonder?''

Wes glanced sideways at Taylor, and she realized she hadn't taken her eyes off him, and wondered if she looked as moonstruck as poor lovesick Kelly did. There was a question in his eyes.

''I'd like to know, too,'' she told him.

Wes drew a breath. ''You asked for it. But the first one of you who so much as chuckles, gets staked out in the desert for the night. Understood?''

Kelly shifted nervously. Scourge licked his lips and swallowed hard, but nodded.

Wes glanced at Taylor, as if he were speaking only to her, but his voice carried to everyone as it had before. ''I was a skeptic. Never believed in anything I couldn't see. So when this shaman friend of mine started talking about magic, I just smiled and nodded. Figured I'd humor him. Turtle is an old man after all, and I—''

''Turtle?'' Taylor blinked in surprise. ''Turtle is this shaman you're talking about?''

Wes frowned, tilting his head and searching her face. ''You know Turtle?''

''I've met him, yes. He just showed up here a few times for no apparent reason. I never did figure out what he wanted. He seemed harmless enough, and he was friendly, so I didn't mind.''

Wes seemed thoroughly surprised by her revelation.

''I'm sorry,'' she said, and she reached out, impulsively, touching his hand, covering it with her own. It was such a natural act, she did it without thinking, as if she'd been touching him this way for years. And when she did it, he looked down at her hand on his and blinked. Taylor felt her face heat, and drew her hand away.

Something was happening here. Something...potent. And totally unexpected. What *was* this?

"I didn't mean to distract you," she said, but her voice was coarse and unsteady. "Please, go on. You said you were skeptical when he talked about magic."

"Magic," he repeated, still staring at her hand. Then he blinked and seemed to shake himself. "Right, magic. When Turtle talked about magic, I didn't argue, but I didn't buy it, either. I hadn't figured out yet that he could see right through me. So, one night when I was visiting him, I noticed he'd let the campfire burn down to nothing but a heap of cherry red coals. I reached for a log to toss on, but he stopped me. And he told me to sit and be quiet."

Wes paused, looked around. When he did, Taylor did, too. Kelly and Scourge were rapt. Wes picked up a stray length of wood, stretched out his arm and poked at a nest of glowing coals beneath the fire. "They were like these, those embers," he said softly. "Red-hot." He stared at the coals for a moment, then shook his head. "So I sat and waited. And Turtle, he stood looking at that bed of heat for a minute or two. I thought he was meditating or something. Then he closed his eyes. And then he just...he just stepped forward...into the hot coals. And I realized then that he was barefoot."

Kelly squeaked in alarm. Even Scourge's jaw dropped.

"I thought my heart stopped when I saw that," Wes said. "It turned my stomach over, and I had to bite my lip to keep from yelling out loud and startling him into falling flat on his face or something. I jumped to my feet, reached for him, but he just held up a hand, and gave me this serene look. And for some reason I stood still. And old Turtle...he just walked across those coals like he was walking barefoot through the cool green grass.''

Scourge swore. Kelly elbowed him. Taylor had fallen into some kind of a trance. ''Go on,'' she whispered, and this time her hand closed tight around his, as if by holding on to him she could hold on to the magic he was casting around her. It was the third time their hands had joined almost of their own volition tonight, but this time he turned his, threaded his fingers with hers, held on gently, before she could pull her hand away.

When he met her eyes, she saw that whatever this thing was she felt, he was aware of it. Feeling it, too, and knowing she did. Her heart rate increased, and her stomach felt knotted with fear. She barely knew this man.

''Not much more to tell,'' he said, speaking low. Still holding on, his thumb now idly moving up and down on the back of her hand. ''As soon as Turtle stepped onto solid ground again, I made him sit and I got down on my knees to examine his feet and tried to remember the number for 911.''

Scourge chuckled at that remark. But Wes's eyes never left Taylor's. ''But there wasn't a mark on him. Not a burn, not a blister. Nothing.'' Wes drew a deep breath. ''Turtle pats me on the head like I'm a little kid or something and says, 'Raven Eyes, you have much to learn about shamanism.'''

''And that was it?'' Kelly asked.

''That was it,'' Wes said. ''He just sat down in his

usual spot, opened a fresh beer and acted like nothing had happened."

The fire popped loudly, and Kelly jumped a foot off the ground. Scourge leaned closer to her and said, "Boo," but she only scowled at him. Then Scourge shook his shaggy head and said, "That's intense."

"Yeah, it was intense, all right," Wes said. "Shook me up pretty thoroughly, I can tell you that much."

"It gave me chills just listening to you tell it," Taylor whispered, and when he looked at her, she knew exactly what he was thinking. That the chills running through her right now were not from his story, and that he was perfectly aware of it.

She gently took her hand from Wes's, and avoided his eyes. It was ridiculous, this sense that she knew him. That she…

Ridiculous.

The small group around the fire fell into a contemplative silence for a while, and first Kelly, and then Scourge withdrew into their tents, yawning and stretching as they went. The sounds of nylon zippers broke the incredible tone of the evening for Taylor, but she couldn't bring herself to call an end to it. Not yet. Not even when every alarm bell in her brain was ringing, and her practical mind was screaming at her to put some distance between herself and this mesmerizing man.

Instead she turned to him, studied his face, his black eyes. "Raven Eyes," she said softly. "Is that—?"

"It's the name I was born with," Wes said. "My mother gave it to me before she took ill and died."

"I'm sorry," she whispered. "But how did you end up with the Brands?"

He smiled. "I'm only half-Comanche, Doc. The

other half is pure Brand.'' She frowned and tilted her head. ''It's a long story.''

''It's early yet.''

His eyes danced over her face. ''It's midnight.'' And then he touched her cheek with a forefinger. ''And you don't like stories, remember?''

Taylor looked at her watch, and shook her head in disbelief. The time had flown past.

''But I'll save that one for another time,'' he said. ''And as much as I'm enjoying sitting out here with you...''

''I know. You must be half-asleep.''

''I've never been more awake in my life.''

She felt her eyes widen, her pulse skip. ''I...um...''

With one hand he touched her hair, very tentatively, just with his fingertips, catching a lock between them and rubbing it. He closed his eyes. ''Where the hell did this come from, Doc?''

Panic took hold. Taylor got to her feet, reached for a pail of water and poured it on the fire, symbolically dousing the flames licking to life in her belly. ''I'm not sure what you're talking about,'' she said, reaching for another.

''Yeah, you are.'' He heaved the third bucket onto the smoldering coals. The water smothered the fire, turning instantly into hissing steam. Wes stirred the remaining embers with the long stick he'd been poking the fire with all night. ''But it's okay. You know you can bank the fire, but the heat's gonna stay around for a long while.''

She didn't look at him. Couldn't. ''Tonight was... unexpected.''

''I know. For me, too,'' he said. Seemed as if he was going to let her off the hook then. Whatever this thing was between them, they didn't have to discuss it, analyze it, admit to it out loud. She didn't have to be vulnerable to him.

She *wouldn't let* herself be vulnerable to him. To anyone.

But even as she reminded herself of that, there was a part of her thinking how she'd never in her life enjoyed an evening the way she'd enjoyed this one.

"Our ancestors," she said softly, "really knew how to live."

Wes smiled at her, easing the tension with the warmth in his eyes. "That's arguable," he said. "Our ancestors would have followed this late night up with a freezing-cold bath in the water hole around dawn."

"Well, nobody's perfect." She examined the fire again, satisfied herself that it was safely extinguished and turned toward her tent. But she paused at the doorway. "You won't...leave or anything...during the night, will you, Wes?"

He turned from his tent flap to catch her gaze. "I'll be right here, Doc. I'll be right here."

She nodded once. "Thanks." Then she ducked through the opening of her dome tent, and pulled the zipper down to shut out the cold.

Chapter 5

Wes Brand was scared half to death. He'd known a hell of a lot of women. Hell, he'd *had* a lot of women. But he'd never once felt this kind of chill set into his bones, way down deep where a man couldn't do a thing to chase it away. He'd never once looked into a woman's eyes and seen…

What had he seen in those onyx eyes that had him so thoroughly shaken? He closed his eyes and brought those gemstones into focus in his mind. And it was just like looking into them again. And he was seeing—himself, only the missing part of himself, that empty place that even finding his heritage hadn't filled. And he was seeing—damn, he was seeing hearts and flowers. Wanting a woman was one thing, but this was damned *dangerous.*

In his mind he looked deep into her eyes again. And he was seeing…

Babies!

Wes jumped to his feet, forgetting he was in a dome tent too short to accommodate his height, and poked his head into the top. Holy mother of God, what was the matter with him?

Lord help him, he was losing his mind.

He took some deep breaths and tried to keep from hyperventilating as he very slowly lay back down and slid into his sleeping bag. He just wouldn't think about her. That was all. He'd just think about the ranch. The old…uh…Cumberland spread. He'd plan—that was what he'd do. He'd lie here and plan his future until he fell asleep.

He didn't fall asleep. He couldn't focus on the ranch when he kept seeing her eyes, and the firelight on her face. And lying there alone, in the dark, his thoughts turned from hearts and flowers and—God help him—babies, to things of a more earthy nature. His mind wandered where it damned well shouldn't, so that every time he came close to drifting off to sleep, he started to dream of what she'd look like with all that hair hanging loose over her shoulders instead of bundled up in back the way she wore it. He'd start to wonder what she'd feel like naked and twined around him, and what kinds of sounds she'd make, and what her mouth might taste like, and…

And then he'd be wide-awake again, and aching. And wondering just when any man had been hit as hard and as fast as she'd hit him, like a mallet between the eyes.

All right, so he wanted her. Bad. It wasn't the end of the world. And it was no reason to give up on the job he'd come here to do. Right? No. In fact it was just an added motive to get the job done. He had to scare her away from here in order to save Turtle's life and—if he were very lucky—preserve his own sanity. And while he was at it, he might as well attempt to keep his hands and his thoughts to himself. All of which might be too much for one ordinary man. It surely would be too much for any man he knew.

But, he reminded himself, he wasn't one ordinary man. He was two men. Hot-tempered Wes Brand, *and*—stepping into a nearby phone booth—the mystical, legendary Wolf Shadow!

Surely between the two of them, one could manage to get the woman the hell out of here before it was too late.

Too late for what? he wondered.

He pulled his sleeping bag up to his neck and tried to get some shut-eye. But as dawn crept over the encampment, he was still wide-awake.

She dreamed again that night. As she slept, Taylor felt the woman she'd always been slowly peeling away, layer by layer, until the woman who remained wasn't Taylor McCoy at all. She was Sky Dancer, a Comanche woman, sitting at the central fire of her village and listening to a brave named Raven Eyes tell stories that fascinated her. And she couldn't take her eyes from him, and she realized that he was looking at her just as often, just as intensely. He was the most intriguing man she'd ever known. And she wanted him.

This woman, this Sky Dancer, wasn't afraid of her feelings at all. So when the others retired to their beds for the night, and Raven Eyes rose to go to his own, she took his hand, and she told him with her eyes what she was feeling as she drew him slowly to her painted tepee.

He followed her, his dark eyes blazing, and inside, in the dimness, he swept her into his arms, and he kissed her hungrily, greedily, taking her mouth in a mimicry of lovemaking that made her insides melt and bubble. She threaded her hands through his hair, tugging loose the band that held it tied back. And when the satin masses spilled free, and he lifted his head slightly, she looked up at him…

And saw Wolf Shadow. His face frightening beneath its fearsome war paint. His eyes hard and distant. His touch cold, and his breath smelling of death.

She sat up in her tent, eyes flying wide, and she screamed in stark terror.

Almost before the sound died, her tent's zipper was yanked upward, and the flap shoved open. And then Wes Brand was inside with her, gripping her shoulders in the darkness, touching her face, asking her if she were all right. She didn't need the light to know who he was. The sound of his voice was burned into her mind, after hearing him tell those stories the night before. She knew him when he spoke. And she shamelessly clung to him, burying her face against his broad chest, holding him hard and trying not to cry.

She hated for *anyone* to see her cry.

He stiffened a little at first, but only briefly. In a moment his hands were stroking her hair, and her back and her shoulders, and he was speaking softly. "It's okay, Doc. Look, it was just a bad dream, all right? There's no one out there. And I'm right here. Okay? Hmm?"

Sniffling like a child, she nodded against his chest. Her nose and wet cheeks and lips brushing the bare skin as she did. Tasting the salt of it. Feeling its warmth. She went still, and so did he. Heat uncoiled in her middle and spread upward, downward, everywhere. She was sitting up, her legs folded to one side, her sleeping bag tangled beneath her. Apparently she'd fought free of it during the dream. He was kneeling, one hand at the small of her back, where only a tank top lay between her flesh and his. The other hand buried in her hair at the back. Her own arms had twined around his waist, and her face remained pressed to his hard, bare chest.

It was embarrassing to behave like this. She was a scientist. A professional.

She was burning up inside for a man she barely knew.

Her own breathing was getting soft and shallow. His heart pounded against her face.

"Are you okay?" he whispered.

"I...I think so."

"I'm glad one of us is."

He was waiting. Waiting for her. To move. To touch him, to kiss him or to pull away. Some signal. Some sign of what she wanted. And if she knew what she wanted, she might have given it to him.

Still he waited. And finally he said, "Doc, I'm clinging to my last shred of chivalry with my toenails. Another second and I'm gone."

Her fingers moved. Not away, though. Just splayed across his back. She moved her lips to speak, but only managed to caress his chest with them, emitting soft air and no words.

"There it goes," he whispered. He pulled back just slightly, looking down, catching her chin in one hand and tipping her head up. Parting his lips and moving nearer, and she thought that in an instant he'd be kissing her mouth, and then he'd push her back onto the sleeping bag, and he'd…

He stopped a hairbreadth from her lips. Clenched his jaw. Swore. "You're trembling. Your eyes are as wide as the Rio Grande. I'm scaring the hell outta you." And he backed away, took his hands away, his warmth, his touch. He sat there and pushed a hand through his hair, blowing air through his teeth.

Taylor was shaking even harder now. So she pulled the sleeping bag up over her shoulders. "I…I don't know what's happening to me."

"You're not the only one, Doc." He gave his head a shake, met her eyes. "You okay?"

She closed her eyes and nodded. "It was just a bad dream."

He looked around, fumbling until he found her lamp and some matches. He filled the tent with light, carefully set the lamp on a small stool and then turned to zip the flap closed. She sent him a startled look when he did that, and he said, "Bugs. Light draws them."

"Oh." She swiped at her cheeks, embarrassed by the tearstains he might see there. And she noticed he was wearing a pair of boxers, and not another stitch. He was incredible. Firm and lean and muscular. And she revised her earlier opinion that no man alive could look as good half-naked as Wolf Shadow did. Because the living proof was right in front of her.

Wow.

When she got around to focusing on his eyes again, she noticed they were glued to her chest. And she remembered she wasn't wearing much more than he was. A snug-fitting tank top and a pair of panties. No bra, and she figured he knew that by now. It was none too warm in here, and he'd been staring at her chest plenty long enough to see the obvious. Besides, a second ago he'd probably felt the obvious. She pulled the bag around her more thoroughly.

He met her eyes again. And his hair was loose. And she realized with a start just how much this little scene was starting to resemble her dream.

"I'm sorry I woke you," she said.

"I'm not." He looked her up and down. "I've been wondering what your hair looks like when it isn't bundled up in a knot."

Her hand closed reflexively around a tendril that hung down below her shoulder. "I—"

"Maybe I should stay," he said. "Maybe you'd sleep better. Hell, maybe we both would."

She felt her eyes widen and her heart trip over itself. "I...no. Look, I don't do this kind of thing, Wes."

She closed her eyes, shocked by her own blunt statement. But at least she'd made it plain. "I don't even know you."

He nodded. "That's not what it feels like."

"I know." She bit her lip, shook her head slowly. "I didn't come out here looking for...I don't even want..."

"And you're scared witless. What I can't quite figure out, Taylor, is what scares you most. Wolf Shadow? Me? Or yourself?"

"You don't need to figure that out, Wes. It doesn't matter. Because this kind of thing isn't going to happen again."

"Are you sure? 'Cause I'm sure as hell not."

She didn't answer. Instead she got up, too hot, needing air, leaving the sleeping bag to puddle on the floor. She pushed the tent flap open and gazed outside. "The sun's going to be up in a few minutes," she said softly.

A low groan brought her head around, and she saw Wes's eyes roaming up and down her body. She bit her lip, reached for an olive drab button-down shirt and pulled it on. "Sorry," she said. But the wanting was still in his eyes, and she was more shaken by it than by Wolf Shadow in all his glory. "I think I'll do what my ancestors did and take a dip in the pond this morning."

"It'll be freezing," he told her.

"The colder the better," she said.

"I heard that."

She swallowed hard. "I just need to be by myself for a while. You…um…you aren't what I expected to find out here. This is all coming out of left field for me."

"Me, too," he told her. "Just so you know. I'm as…I'm as blown away by whatever the hell this is as you are." He drew a deep breath, closed his eyes in resignation.

A deep fear gnawed at her stomach. Taylor met his eyes. "Don't be. This is nothing. Look, Wes, I don't want to mislead you. I don't…I don't *do* relationships."

A frown creased his brow, but he said nothing, just watched her, waiting.

"I came here to do a job. When it's over, I'm leaving."

"I see." But he didn't. He couldn't. She was confused as hell, because she was feeling something here, something she hadn't felt before. But it was physical; that was all. So her hormones were raging, raising hell after a lifetime of lying around all but dormant. This didn't mean anything. It couldn't. She wouldn't let it.

When you loved…when you trusted…when you believed in other people, you got hurt. It was the way it was. She'd spent years drumming that lesson into her heart, and she wasn't going to forget it now. Not now. Not ever.

Wes was still studying her face. But after a long moment he sighed heavily and turned toward the flap. "I'll get the hell out of here and leave you alone, Doc. I didn't mean to…shoot, maybe I'll take the next turn at that icy pond water."

"Just so long as you wait until I get back here first," she said. "And do me a favor, Wes? Keep the A-Team from wandering out there for a while?"

"They'll wander out there over my dead body, lady." He smiled at her, but it wasn't a real smile. All for show. He seemed as mixed up right now as she felt. But the sight of that fake smile made her stomach clench all the same. Then he ducked out into the graying dawn.

Do it. This is your chance.

Dammit, Wes thought. I can't. I *can't.* There's something about her…I want her. I want to…

No. I have to get her the hell out of here. Make her leave. I don't like the way I feel when I look at her. It's too intense, too…

But she was leaving anyway. She'd made that perfectly clear, and Wes was damned if he knew why the idea bothered him so much. It was what he wanted. And it would be better for him, far better for him, if she left here sooner rather than later. Because if she stuck around much longer…

He wasn't going to want to let her go.

It would be cruel of him to frighten her again. She was already so shaken up she was having nightmares.

He thought of Turtle lying on that cheap couch, wasting slowly away. Turtle, begging Wes to save his life. Surely if the choice were between frightening Taylor McCoy and losing Turtle to death, it was obvious what he had to do. The risk to Turtle was far greater. The consequences to Taylor, far less severe. What was a little fear when a man's life was at stake?

Besides, if he scared her, she'd leave. Soon. Before this horrible feeling writhing around in the pit of his stomach got any worse.

He waited until she was out of sight, and then he sneaked around the outer edge of the woods, reentering beyond her, and making his way to the cave where he'd hidden his supplies.

Taylor looked around carefully. A little niggle of fear rushed up her spine when she thought of bathing in the water hole, out in the open like this. But it was dawn. Wes would keep Kelly and Scourge from wandering down here. And that nut who wanted her to believe he was a ghost wasn't likely to show up in the daylight. He'd wait until dark to bother her.

She thought about her dream, about the way she'd felt in it. Wild and free, unfettered by shyness or fear. The way the Comanche women who'd lived their lives here had been.

Her ancestors. Surely some of their blood ran in her veins.

She blinked at that thought. It was the first time she'd consciously acknowledged that she was of the same blood. It must be this place. It was getting to her. And maybe that was part of the reason she'd reacted to Wes Brand the way she had. Just some of her long-nurtured inhibitions dissolving away.

She shouldn't be ashamed of wanting a man. It was natural. She was a healthy woman. Why shouldn't her body react to the touch of a handsome man? Why shouldn't it? It would be the same with any man she found attractive. There was nothing special with Wes. It was chemistry, pure and simple. No more than that.

She felt better having convinced herself of it. Relationships scared the hell out of her. Chemistry, she could handle. She was the one in control of her own body, after all. She could deal with it, keep it in check.

But a tiny voice in the back of her mind was telling her there was something more than the physical going on here. Something deeper. She didn't want to hear that voice, so she silenced it, refusing to even consider what it had to say. But the doubt remained. She just wished she knew for sure.

She stripped off her clothes, stepped up to the edge of the water and dipped one toe in. The chilly water embraced her skin, and she drew a harsh breath. Cold. Freezing. If she hesitated, she'd never get in, and suddenly she wanted to. She didn't know if she were trying to prove something to herself…to Wes and Turtle, who probably didn't think she was worthy of calling herself Comanche. It didn't matter. She wanted to do it.

Drawing a deep breath, backing up a few steps, Taylor ran forward and jumped into the water, sinking under the frigid surface as her warm skin screamed with shock. When she came up again, every nerve ending in her body was tingling and goose bumps crawled over her arms and legs. She felt alive. More alive than she ever had.

By the time he heard Taylor splashing in the water, Wes's face was hidden beneath layers of brilliant paint, an eagle feather was braided into his hair and he was wearing, once again, a loincloth and a string of bear claws around his neck.

He felt pretty much naked. And it wasn't as dark this time as it had been before. She'd see him a lot more clearly. Bared flanks and all. He could imagine how amused she'd be if she recognized him. His face heated, no doubt in reaction to the idea of her laughing at it. But for Turtle, he could do this. And for himself. She couldn't stay here. He could make her leave. It was just a matter of getting into character.

I *am* Wolf Shadow, he told himself. I'm a legendary warrior, noble, fearless, doing what's right.

Yeah, right.

Stiffening his spine and assuming a more noble, warriorlike posture, Wes stepped out of the sheltering trees and up to the water's edge. And then he realized what he should have realized sooner. She was naked, too. More naked than he was, as a matter of fact.

Why that didn't make him feel any more at ease, he could only guess. No, scratch that. It would be better not to speculate on the reasons for that clenching and tightening going on all over him.

He caught glimpses of her dark skin as she moved and played in the water and told himself to avert his eyes. But he couldn't look away. He could only stand there on the shore, in the mists of early morning, watching her as if mesmerized. She was a different woman out here. Almost childlike in her frolicking. Smiling. She was smiling. And he stood there in silence, wishing he knew everything about her, watching her and trying to figure out the change. Until finally she turned and saw him.

She went still, one hand flying to her mouth as if to catch the startled cry that squeaked out of her. Her smile died, and the fear that crept into her eyes was too much for him.

"I won't harm you," he told her, deliberately speaking in a lower than normal tone of voice. "I couldn't."

She blinked, and her brows drew together. "As if I'd believe that. Why should I trust a word you say?"

"Because I say you can."

Again her eyes narrowed. Then they traveled down his body, and lingered. She drew her gaze upward to meet his again, and now she seemed more confused or puzzled than angry. "Pretend to be a gentleman," she said. "Turn around, let me get out of here and..."

Wes turned his back to her before she could finish the sentence. And he heard the water rippling as she moved toward shore. But having his back toward her did little good. He could envision her body, gloriously naked, beaded with water and goose bumps, nipples erect and hard. He bit his lip, and turned around again. She'd wrapped a large towel around her, under her arms.

She scowled at him. "You could at least give me time to get dressed."

"What I have to say to you will not take long," he said softly. Too softly. That kind of catch in his voice wasn't going to scare her. He was supposed to be intimidating her. So he added, "Besides, I like the way you look. Dress after I'm gone."

"Bastard," she said. And she took a step toward him.

Startled, Wes took a step backward, and held up one hand like some extra in an old Western, about to say "How." Only his line was, "Stay where you are."

She frowned, tilting her head to one side. "Why?"

Uh-oh. She looked suspicious. Time to pull out the big guns. Or arrows, as the case may be. "I've warned you to stop this digging, to leave this place." He made his voice deep and scary. He hoped. "You have ignored my words. What happens to you should you ignore them again will be no one's fault but your own."

"So you came here to threaten me again?"

Wes grated his teeth. Why was it she seemed so afraid of Wolf Shadow when he *wasn't* around, but when he *was,* she stood up to him like a bulldog guarding a T-bone?

"It's no threat, Taylor McCoy. It is only the truth. A warning. I have told you the sacred place is here, on this site. That has to be enough for you. Tell the elders not to sell the land. And then leave here. Today."

There. Any minute now he ought to see the fear creeping back into those black eyes. And maybe it was mean, but it would get rid of her before his mental state deteriorated more than it already had. And it would save Turtle's life.

The fear didn't come. In fact her expression got about 360 degrees angrier. Not liking the way this was going, Wes turned to walk away. His intent was to vanish into the mists as any self-respecting noble warrior would do, and then hightail it back to his tent.

It took him completely by surprise when a small hand gripped his shoulder from behind and spun him around. Taylor stood toe-to-toe and nose-to-chest, glaring up at him. "Don't you *dare* walk away from me, dammit. I want to know who you are, and what the hell you really want, or I'll—"

He'd only meant to set her away from him. To get

some distance between them and protect his identity from that piercing ebony gaze. But his fingers somehow tangled in the towel, and it fell to the ground. Taylor stood in front of him naked, chest heaving, cheeks flaming. Her fists clenched at her sides as he stood there, paralyzed, unable to move or take his eyes off her incredible body. Every cell in his brain went to sleep, and every cell in the rest of his body came to screaming, aching life. Looking at her was like glimpsing heaven. And he couldn't think. He wanted....

"Damn you," she whispered, and she bent to retrieve the towel. Unfortunately, at the same moment, his knees gave out, and he dropped down onto them. She tugged at the towel, but since he was kneeling on it, it was useless. His eyes feasted on her breasts. And then she went still, and he saw the anger in her face easing, changing, and he saw something else replacing it.

He lifted his hands slowly, so slowly he was barely aware they were moving. As if they were floating upward on their own, until they closed around her small waist. She inhaled, a short, wavering gasp. But she didn't move away. Her wide eyes held his, no anger in them at all. Not anymore. There was something else. A curiosity. A question, though he wasn't sure *what* question.

"Never in my life," he whispered, his voice harsh, "have I seen anything I wanted to touch the way I want to touch you."

He slid his hands upward until his thumbs could run along the bottom curve of her breasts, and then higher, brushing over her nipples. A sound came from her. Not one of objection, but one of need. And when he met her eyes again, he saw the excitement burning in them, the ever so slight flare of her nostrils as the breaths rushed in and out of her.

He pulled her downward, and she dropped to her knees. And with one last look at the fire in her eyes, he lost himself. He wrapped his arms completely around her, pulling her tight to him, one hand closing on her buttocks, one threading through her hair. Her breasts touched his naked chest, and he pressed tight to her, bending her backward and lowering his mouth to hers.

Ah, God, she tasted good. Salty and sweet and warm. He ached for her. Ached in a way he never had. Her body, totally naked, utterly vulnerable to him in every way. Her mouth, parting to let him take what he wanted, her tongue responding to each caress of his. He pushed her down farther, until her nude body stretched on the ground, and he lowered his own atop it, still feeding from her succulent mouth. He wedged his knee between hers, parting her legs, and lowering himself between them. He was hard, throbbing, and he pressed himself into her and cursed the loincloth and thanked his stars it was the only thing between them. She arched her hips against him, and he thought he would die of wanting. He reached down with his hand, parting her folds and thrusting a possessive finger inside her. When she stiffened, he pushed deeper, and she was hot inside, hot and quivering and wet for him. He yanked the loincloth aside, lowered his hips to hers. The tip of him touched her and pushed the merest fraction of an inch into her hungry body.

And someone—Kelly, he thought—yelled, "Ms. McCoy! Ms. McCoy, are you there?"

She stiffened, palms flattening to his chest and shoving at him. And Wes jerked away from her, wondering just what sort of insanity had claimed him. But he shouldn't wonder. He knew. Who was it who'd said God gave man a penis and a brain, and only enough blood to flow to one of them at a time? Whoever it was had been right. He sure as hell hadn't been thinking with his brain just now.

Taylor looked bewildered. Like a sleepwalker just waking up and wondering how she'd got where she was.

Twigs snapped under approaching footfalls. Wes looked up fast to see Kelly making her way toward them at a steady pace. But she hadn't spotted them yet. Then he looked down at Taylor, lying there naked and hungry and confused, panting with reaction and wide-eyed with fear all at once. He knelt, snatched up her towel and draped it over her body. Then he turned and ran off into the mists, disappearing just the way he'd planned to do.

Chapter 6

She sat up, wrapping herself in the towel, scrambling backward over the prickly grass to snag her shirt and panties from where she'd left them. She tugged them on frantically and clumsily, because her hands were chilled numb and trembling.

What had she done? What had she *almost* done? What had come over her just now? For the past hour she'd been analyzing her attraction to Wes Brand, telling herself over and over it was only physical and meant nothing, and doubting the truth of that mantra. When Wolf Shadow touched her, when he looked at her, she'd felt the same sizzling desire she'd felt for Wes. And she'd thought…she could let him kiss her. Just once, to prove to herself that her reaction would be the same. Prove to herself it would feel no different. That any attractive man could probably elicit a response in her, now that her sleeping libido had finally decided to wake up. She was thirty-five. Didn't they say women reached their sexual peak around this age? Wasn't that the one and only reason she felt the least bit attracted to the two men who'd dropped into her life out of nowhere?

Well, she had her proof. She was right; it was physical. Because Wolf Shadow's kiss and the delicious press of his body against hers had aroused her as much as Wes's touch had done. But my God, she'd let herself get lost in it. She'd kissed him back. She'd lost her mind for a few brief seconds. If Kelly hadn't come along when she had...

"There you are!" Kelly said, hurrying forward. "I was worried about you. After that thing with that Wolf Shadow character and all, I thought you shouldn't be out here all al— Ms. McCoy? Gosh, are you all right?"

"What? Oh. Fine."

Taylor was kneeling, buttoning up her shirt, but she paused to look at the way her own hands trembled. And she wondered what her face must look like. Her eyes.

"You look scared to death," Kelly said, confirming Taylor's suspicions, as she knelt in front of her. "Did you see that ghost again? Oh, gosh, you did, didn't you?"

"I..." Taylor blinked, searched the girl's face and finally shook her head slowly. "No. Of course not. It's just the water, it's freezing. I dove in without realizing how cold it would be, and it jolted me." She hugged herself, rubbing her arms for effect. If she frightened the students with much more of this Wolf Shadow nonsense, they'd want to pull the plug and leave. Might even run out on her. And she couldn't risk that.

Kelly frowned, her big blue eyes probing, worried. She was a sweet girl, even if she was making eyes at the same guy Taylor was interested in. No. The guy she *wasn't* interested in. It was her body that wanted him. There was nothing else there.

And how could Taylor possibly feel even that one brief stab of jealousy, when she'd just been making out with another man?

She couldn't believe this. All through school she'd been a loner. An island. A solitary woman with more interest in dusty tomes and historical accounts than human beings. She'd avoided getting personally involved with anyone. Male or female. Sexually or otherwise. She didn't even care enough to have any real enemies.

Now she was turning into a grade-A slut. Burning up for two men, neither one of whom she knew well enough to call an acquaintance. What was the matter with her? Maybe she should see a doctor. Maybe raging hormones could be controlled with a little pill.

She gathered up her towel, and the T-shirt she hadn't put back on. Wearing her long button-down and her towel, she started back for camp. She hoped she wouldn't see Wes. Wouldn't have to explain her appearance to him. He was so sweet. And maybe interested in her. And patient when she'd explained that nothing could happen between them. What kind of woman must she be to behave this way? How would he feel about her if he knew?

Didn't make any difference, she told herself. It didn't matter how he felt about her, because she didn't have any feelings for him.

She couldn't face him. Not yet.

"Did you notice that hollow in the ground over there?" she asked, grasping at straws. Stalling for time. She had to pull herself together.

"Where?"

Pushing her hands through her wet hair, Taylor led the younger woman to a perfectly natural dip in the ground, and pretended to examine it, rattling on about possible reasons for it being there while her mind raced everywhere else.

Kelly fell for it for a while, but soon she was looking at Taylor a little oddly. ''Ms. McCoy, is there some reason you don't want to go back to camp?''

''What? No. What a silly thing to ask.'' Taylor avoided the girl's eyes.

''Oh. 'Cause I thought maybe…well, that Wes Brand…''

''What about him?'' She'd asked it too quickly, her tone too sharp. Stupid.

Kelly shrugged. ''I've seen the way he looks at you. That's all. But if it's him you're avoiding, you don't have to worry. He's not there.''

Taylor blinked and stared at the girl blankly. ''Not…''

''He left right after you wandered down here. At least, I think so. He seemed to be heading out when I glimpsed him, and I didn't see him again after that.''

But he'd promised to keep everyone away while she… Oh, hell, what difference did it make? It certainly wasn't the biggest promise made to her that had ever been broken.

Taylor gave her head a shake, turned away from the girl and started back toward camp. Kelly kept pace with her. As they emerged among the tents, she saw no sign of Wes. Maybe Kelly was right and he had taken off. Thank goodness. She turned to Kelly. ''Thanks for worrying about me,'' she said.

Kelly nodded. ''You'd better dry off, or you'll catch your death.'' Then she glanced at the sun, a fiery ball peering up over the horizon. "Then again, it'll be sweltering here in no time anyway. Maybe you should just stay wet." She smiled and headed back toward her own tent. Scourge was sitting near the fire with a cup of coffee in his hand, and he nodded hello as Taylor passed.

Closing her eyes in relief, Taylor headed for her tent, peeling back the flap, ducking inside and sinking to the floor to lower her head to her hands.

"Doc?"

Taylor jerked her head up fast to see Wes Brand sitting on the small stool in her tent, looking genuinely concerned. His face was red, as if he'd just scrubbed it. And his hair was pulled back into its customary queue, held in place with that thong of his. He wore a ribbed tank top, with a denim shirt tossed over it, hanging unbuttoned, sleeves clumsily rolled to just below his elbows. And black jeans that fit so snugly they ought to be illegal.

She felt so guilty she couldn't look him in the eye. And why, for God's sake? It wasn't as if there was anything between them. Not really.

Then why did it feel as if she'd betrayed him?

"Are you okay?" he asked, getting up, coming closer. "Did something happen?"

"No!" She bit her lip, realizing how defensive she sounded. "I'm just...jumpy. That's all. I shouldn't go walking off by myself when I'm so keyed up. I jump out of my skin every time a rabbit scampers by."

He frowned. "But you're okay," he asked. "You didn't see that Wolf Shadow character again, or anything."

"No, of course not." She averted her eyes as she said it.

"Okay," he said. And something in his tone made her head come up slowly.

He was quiet for a moment, searching her face. Then he averted his. "If you did see him, Taylor, and you're not telling me—for whatever reason—" He gave his head a shake.

Did he know? Had he...oh, God, had he wandered down to the water hole and seen...?

She turned her back to him abruptly, pressing her fingers to her lips.

"Look, I'm not prying," he said softly. "It's just that if I'm going to find out what's behind all this, Doc, you're going to have to be honest with me. If you don't trust me enough to tell me everything, then I might as well give up the investigation and—"

"I do trust you," she said, interrupting him, so guilt ridden she could barely stand it. And for no good reason. She schooled her features to what she hoped was a semblance of calm, and faced him again. "Really. It's myself I'm having trouble with." When he frowned and searched her face, she opened her mouth to speak, only to stop when movement outside caught her attention. She turned to see Scourge and Kelly outside, fixing their morning meals, pouring more coffee. "And you're right, something did happen this morning."

"But you don't want to tell me about it," he said slowly.

She lifted her chin, swallowed hard. "You came out here to look into this when you had plenty of better things to do. The least I can do is tell you what you need to know to do it right."

"So...?"

She closed her eyes. ‘‘If there’s one thing I can’t stand, it’s dishonesty.’’

‘‘Then you’re going to tell me.’’ He looked down, and something crossed his face. Looked as if he felt badly about something.

‘‘I don’t want to talk about this here,’’ she said. ‘‘Can we go somewhere...private?’’

‘‘Sure,’’ he said. ‘‘All right, Doc. Okay. C’mon, I know a place.’’

What devil was driving him to ask her about what happened this morning? He must be totally insane.

And why the hell was it he felt compelled to take her where he was taking her?

He didn’t know. He didn’t know much of anything anymore. She was driving him so crazy he wasn’t sure what he wanted from one minute to the next.

Wes drove the little khaki-colored Jeep because Taylor asked him to. He opened the door, got in and adjusted the seat. She sent him a frown. ‘‘What?’’ he asked.

She shook her head and faced front.

He started it up and pulled out, heading over the rough terrain that skirted the woods, and around them until he emerged onto the dirt trail that passed for a road. And when he pulled onto it, he reached up to adjust the mirror.

She swung her head toward him, making an irritated sound, but then bit her lip and looked away.

Wes tilted his head to one side, and his troubled mind eased just a bit. Or he was distracted from it at least. Because he’d made another discovery about Taylor McCoy.

"You don't usually let anyone drive this baby but you, do you, Doc?"

She shrugged, staring through the windshield, but not seeing anything, he thought. Not the Texas sage or the gradual leveling off of landscape, that buzzard circling some roadkill up ahead or the increasing greenery they were heading into.

"I think I'll change your radio station now."

She blinked and looked at him. Gave her head a shake. "Sorry. I was somewhere else."

"Where?"

She closed her eyes, lowered her chin an inch or two. Was that guilt she was feeling?

Wes squirmed inwardly. He was the one who ought to feel guilty, first for trying to scare her, then for losing his sanity out there in the woods with her. And then for asking her to tell him what had happened when he knew exactly what had happened. He supposed it was some sick, morbid curiosity on his part. He wanted to know how she felt about damned near making it with him.

No. Scratch that. With Wolf Shadow. Not him.

And he wasn't even sure what he was hoping to hear. Would he be gloating or green-eyed if she confessed to having relished every sizzling second in his arms? In *his* arms.

Sighing, he shifted down a gear and took a turn onto an even less traveled dirt road, heading up a slight incline. Taylor glanced up at him, her eyes exotic and wide and curious. The guilt or whatever she'd been feeling, momentarily gone. "Where are we going?"

Good. A change of subject. He was sick of thinking about his alter ego. "It's just ahead," he told her. And then he braced himself for her reaction when the Jeep bounded over the crest of the hill and the level ground rolled out like a lush green carpet for as far as the eye could see. When he'd brought his baby sister up here to see it, long before he'd ever decided to buy the place, she'd focused in on the dilapidated barn, listing slightly to one side, boards gray with age, roof flapping in the slightest breeze. And the house, with the shutters hanging crookedly like broken glasses on filmy, myopic eyes. The railing, clinging to the porch in places, sagging in others, sections missing. The peeling flecks of paint where there was any paint at all.

Jessi's reaction had been a grimace. As if she'd eaten some bad meat.

He pulled the Jeep to a stop in what had once been a driveway and now was bits of hard-pack in between patches of weeds. And then he turned to see what Taylor thought.

Her back was toward him, though. She was opening the door and getting out. And as bothered as she'd been before about their near copulation in the woods, she seemed to have forgotten all about it now. He got out, too, and walked around to join her, eagerly searching her face.

She wasn't looking at the barn or the house. She was looking beyond them, at the gently rolling fields, and beyond that to where the creek meandered lazily, a blue coil bisecting the green, glittering like diamonds in the Texas sunshine.

She opened her mouth, but all that came out was a whisper of breath. And then she blinked. "I don't think…I don't think I've ever seen anything this beautiful in my life, Wes."

He smiled so hard his face hurt. "You're kidding."

"No." She turned to face him. "How much land is attached to this place?"

"Five hundred acres." He waved an arm to encompass the area. "As far as you can see. It's nowhere near as big as the Texas Brand, but—"

She trotted forward without warning, heading up the rickety steps to the porch, and then pushed the door, testing it, pushing it some more. It squealed in protest, but she was stepping inside by the time Wes caught up with her. Rapping the walls with a fist. Running a hand along the time-worn, dirt-stained woodwork.

"Look at this workmanship," she said. "And it could be restored, I think. There's no sign of rot."

"I thought the same thing." He couldn't believe her face. It glowed. Her eyes lit and sparkled, and she couldn't seem to stop smiling.

"The foundation..." she began.

"Solid as a rock."

"And the roof?"

"Needs replacing. Wiring, too. Plumbing's in great shape, though, and the house is structurally sound. Most of the fixing up will be cosmetic."

She'd stepped into the large front room, and was staring up at cathedral ceilings with chipping plaster, the same awestruck look on her face he imagined most people got when looking at the ceiling in the Sistine Chapel. But she paused to bring her head level when he spoke. "Will be? Have you bought this place, then?" Her voice echoed in the emptiness.

"Not yet. But I've put in a bid on it."

"Well, if I had the money, Wes, I think I would, too."

"Like it that much?"

She moved her gaze from one end of the room to

the other, then walked slowly through to the wide bay window in the back, chipped casing and all, and stared through at the view. "If I found a place like this," she said softly, leaning forward, elbows on the sill, "I don't think I'd ever want to leave."

And he thought, *Maybe I should give it to her, then.* But wait a minute. He *wanted* her to leave.

Didn't he?

"I'd stay here always. Fix it up, a little at a time. Barn first, though. The house could wait." She pushed herself away from the windowsill and turned to head back outside. Wes trailed along like a lovesick pup as she stepped lightly down the porch steps and turned to inspect the barn. "Is it in pretty good shape, as well?"

"Water and power were never put in," Wes said. "We'd have to—" He stopped short, and his jaw dropped. He blinked. Lord have mercy, what had he just said? Had he just said *we?*

"What?" she asked, turning, looking as if she hadn't noticed.

He licked his lips. "I'll have to wire it from scratch and run a water line to it. You can see the roof is bad. But the framework is sound. Just needs work."

"That would be what I'd do first," she said. "Fix up the barn."

He moved up beside her. "That's exactly what I plan to do," he told her, a little amazed she'd agree. "My sister said I was nuts. That the house is more important." They walked side by side as they talked, slowly, arms swinging.

"Depends on who you ask. If it were me, the barn would be the first priority. Because I'd fill it just as soon as I could."

Wes stopped, crossed his arms on the top of a wobbly fence post. "And what would you fill it with, Doc?"

She smiled, and he thought she had the prettiest smile he'd ever seen in his life. "You'll bring in cattle, no doubt. Beefers like your family raises. But not me. I'd raise horses."

His arm slipped, and he almost fell forward. Caught himself just in time to keep from slamming his chin on that post. "H-horses?"

"Appaloosas," she told him.

And he just stood there gaping.

Taylor leaned back against another fence post, this one looking a little more solid. Her hair was loose today for some reason, and the breeze up here pushed it around a bit, so it seemed alive. "I have a mare, you know. Jasper. Oh, and she is the finest mare you've ever seen in your life."

She looked at him, but since he'd lost the ability to speak, he kept quiet. Just nodded at her to go on.

"I have to board her, of course. I don't even have a permanent home. I don't get to see her nearly as often as I'd like to. But someday…"

"S-someday?" he prompted, glad he'd regained the talent for uttering one-word sentences, at least.

"Ever since I was a little girl, I've wanted a big place. Like this one. Maybe not quite this big. Just big enough for Jasper and me." She looked around, shaking her head. "Now that I've seen this, though, I think I'd expand on that dream a little. Heck, with a spread this big, I could raise them."

He tried to speak, cleared his throat, tried again. "You'd want to raise Appaloosas?"

She smiled at him, nodding hard. "Silly, isn't it? I'm an archaeology teacher without tenure anywhere, and I'm still dreaming those little-girl dreams.'' She shrugged and sighed deeply, gazing off into the distance. And the dream in her eyes was so real he could see it there. What startled him most was that he was seeing his own dream there, as well. ''But you know, I've spent a lot of time waiting to find something better, and I haven't. Maybe I knew more about who I was as a little girl than I've managed to figure out since.''

''You ever have her bred?'' She brought her gaze back to him, and he added, ''The mare?''

''Oh. No, not yet. I will someday, when I have a place of my own and room for a colt. But you know, the stallion would have to be something special.''

''I...um...I have one.''

Her brows came together. ''A stallion?''

He only nodded.

''An Appaloosa?''

Another nod. My, but his conversational skills were honed to a razor edge today! ''Actually that's what I want this place for. That's why I bought him. He's going to be the beginning of my herd.''

Her lips parting slightly, she shook her head. ''I can't believe this.'' But the look of wonder died, and one of confusion replaced it. ''It's almost scary, isn't it?''

''What, how many things we have in common?'' He lowered his head. ''Freaking terrifying.''

She came closer, laying one hand on his chest, so lightly it felt like a nervous little bird, ready to take flight at the slightest hint of danger. Swallowing hard, Wes lifted his own hand to lay atop it. And then he met her eyes and thought she looked more scared now than she had when he'd been *trying* to frighten her.

"I...I don't think it means anything," she said, as if trying to convince herself. "It's just chemistry. And coincidence. It doesn't mean anything."

"What if it does?"

She drew a breath, lifted her chin higher. "I came out here to tell you about this morning."

Guilt hit him hard in the belly. He dropped his gaze, shook his head. "No, Taylor, look, you don't have to—"

"He kissed me." She blurted it. And then she pulled her hand away and turned her back to him. "He more than kissed me. And I kissed him back."

"Taylor, it doesn't—"

"Yeah, it does," she said. "Or...I thought it did at the time." Facing him again, looking like a criminal facing the jury, she lifted her chin. "I don't know what's come over me lately, Wes. I don't act that way. I've *never* acted that way. And the only time I've even come close to feeling that kind of...thing...has been with you. So I thought it was just my body telling me it had been too long and it was time and it didn't matter who..." She closed her eyes, gave her head a shake.

"And what do you think now?" he asked her.

"I don't know." She blinked up at him. "When I'm with you I think...maybe...it's something more. But it's something I don't want. Something I've never wanted."

"Like you thought you never wanted to know about your people, Taylor? Your past?"

She lowered her head quickly. "Maybe."

Her hair fell over her face like a curtain, and impulsively Wes brushed it away. "Would it help to know I never thought I wanted it, either?"

"I'm afraid of this," she said softly.

"I'm terrified of this," he told her, and it was the truth.

"I thought when I told you…about Wolf Shadow, about this morning, you'd…"

He felt like an assassin. Like a liar. Like a fool. "It's okay." He lifted his hand to touch her cheek. If he'd blown his chances with this woman because of all that Wolf Shadow nonsense, he would never forgive himself. Ever. "Let's forget it happened, Taylor. Let's start over, right here, today."

Her smile was tremulous when she faced him again. "At least it's out in the open. Whatever this might be…" She sighed, shrugged. "If it starts with honesty, maybe it will be all right."

Honesty.

How many times a day did she use that word in a sentence, anyway? It was important to her. Vital, he sensed that. Then he went warm inside, because she leaned up, and she kissed him softly on the mouth.

A kiss he deserved less than any man on the planet. Except maybe Wolf Shadow.

"Wes?"

He opened his eyes, met her wary, uncertain gaze.

"Will you take me to the Texas Brand? I'd like to meet your horse."

"You might have to put up with meeting the rest of my family while you're at it," he said.

"I think I can stand that."

He slipped his arm around her shoulders, and turning, walked with her back to the Jeep. It was an odd feeling, this thing. This new thing where he could put his arm around a woman's shoulders as casually as this. Or hold her hand. Or lean down and kiss her cheek. This…Lord, this was turning into a *relation-*

ship. And Taylor had told him, up front, that she didn't *do* relationships. And until now, he'd pretty much felt the same on that score.

But he was worried. Scared out of his mind, really. Because he liked this thing, and he wanted this thing. But if his secret identity came out…it would be over. He'd lose her before he'd ever really had her.

It was amazing how much the thought of that hurt.

Chapter 7

They had to head back to the site first. Taylor said she needed to put in several hours at work on the dig before she could leave. Her time was limited. That reminder jabbed at Wes's gut. Things were changing. Everything was changing for him.

By the time they headed to the Texas Brand, it was getting toward noon. Taylor was too conscientious to take a break before lunch hour, even though she wasn't punching a time clock and Wes was pretty sure the kids could have handled the morning on their own.

It would be just like that family of his to invite her to stay to lunch. And he was real nervous about that. He didn't want his siblings needling him about past mistakes or his infamous temper, or telling her stories that would curl her hair. His past was a sore subject, and he wasn't sure enough of Taylor yet. Hell, the whole town had pretty much turned against him after the robbery. Even when the conviction was overturned,

Wes suspected most folks hadn't changed their opinion of him. And he didn't want Taylor to judge him the way the others had. Couldn't bear the idea that she might change her mind about him, once she knew the truth.

They took his Bronco this time, and Wes climbed into the passenger side before she could beat him to it. She paused beside the door and looked down at him, her long straight hair hanging through the open window. He wanted to stroke it, but resisted. He didn't want to scare her by coming on too strong. She'd been hesitant when he'd nearly kissed her in the tent before.

But she hadn't been hesitant at all with Wolf Shadow. Damn, he was being stupid. But it was true. She was different with him.

"So what is this," she asked, "you tired of driving?"

"I drove yours, so you get to drive mine." He smiled up at her, hiding the doubts that kept creeping in. "Besides, I want to make sure you know the way… so you can come back."

She smiled back at him and headed around to the driver's side. When she got in, she adjusted his seat, fiddled with his mirrors and twisted the radio dial though it wasn't even turned on yet. He was, though. "There," she said. "Now we're even." And she cranked the engine to life.

Wes gave directions for the shortest route to the ranch, and she drove, smiling in pleasure when the Bronco bounced beneath the arch and into the driveway. She nodded in pleasure. "What a place," she said. "Just as impressive as the first time I saw it."

"You like it better than the other one?" Why was he suddenly so sensitive about everything she said?

"Not by a long shot, but this is nice, too."

He almost sighed in relief. She brought the car to a stop behind Garrett's gargantuan pickup truck, and looked at Wes a little nervously.

Wes jumped out and hurried around to her side, opening her door. "Come on," he said. "If you meet my horse before my family, they'll feel slighted."

"Wouldn't want that." She took the hand he offered and got to her feet, and then she paused, looking down at their joined hands, blinking as if she was seeing something she'd never seen before. Then she met his eyes and he knew. It wasn't something she'd never *seen,* but something she'd never *felt.* He was feeling it, too. He'd have laughed in the face of anyone who told him love at first sight could happen to him, but he was beginning to think this thing with Taylor was damned close to that.

The screen door creaked, then it banged. "Wes? Hey, I didn't know you were coming home for lunch. And you brought company!" Chelsea smiled and wiped her hands on the apron she was wearing. "You're in luck," she said, smiling her killer smile at Taylor. "It was my turn to cook."

"Is that a slam on the Brand men's culinary talents?" Wes asked. Then he glanced down at Taylor. "Don't let her fool you with that housemother getup she's wearing. Chelsea's a lot more than chief cook and bottle washer around here. Even if she *hasn't* acquired a respectable Texas drawl just yet." He sent Chelsea a wink.

She came down the steps and extended a hand. "I'm Chelsea Brand," she said. "You must be Taylor. I've heard a lot about you."

Taylor shook her hand. "I can't imagine how."

"Oh, I get around. Actually I'm studying for a psychology degree over at the university. The professors there have been bandying your name about campus since you started on the Emerald Flat dig. You have a terrific reputation."

"That's good to know," Taylor said, and Wes saw her chin lift just a little. She was proud of that reputation, and she should be.

The door banged again, and little Bubba toddled onto the steps, reached for his mother, teetered. Wes lunged quickly and scooped the pudge up before he could take a tumble. "Hey, Bubba! How's my best buddy doin?" He tickled Bubba's ribs, and got a squeal out of him.

"Eat," Bubba said.

"You *always* wanna eat," Wes returned.

Chelsea shook her head. "Taylor, meet my little boy, Ethan. Though the men in this house refuse to call him by his proper name."

"Hello, Ethan." Taylor came closer and stuck out her hand. Bubba shook it, apparently quite pleased at being treated like a grown-up.

"Who?" he said.

"Taylor," she told him. "Tay-lor. Can you say 'Taylor'?"

He grinned at her. "Tay-*lo!*" he said. Then he turned very seriously to his uncle, his little brows furrowed as he lowered his forehead to Wes's and stared him square in the eyes.

"He likes her," Chelsea said.

"Me, too," Wes replied. Then wished he hadn't, because Chelsea, when he glanced her way again, was grinning as if she'd just won the lottery. Lord help him now.

''Well, come on inside and let's feed this starving toddler before he wastes away,'' she sang, and she slipped an arm through Taylor's and walked her up the steps and into the house as if she were a long-lost sister.

By the time Wes carried Bubba inside, Taylor was being ushered into a chair at the kitchen table, and Chelsea was sending silent messages to Garrett with her eyes. Wes's brothers were already sitting, and it looked as if they were all picking up on Chelsea's unspoken announcement that Wes had finally found a woman he liked.

They rose as Taylor sat. Two giant maples and a whipcord sapling, all inspecting the poor woman as if she were a cow they were considering buying. All smiling and nodding at one another as if they'd decided she'd be good for the herd.

Wes tucked Bubba into his high chair and performed the introductions. ''You've already met Garrett,'' he said to Taylor, pointing.

''Chelsea's husband, right?'' Taylor smiled. ''Good to see you again.''

''Pleasure's all mine, Taylor,'' he said, and they all sat down.

''The big blonde in need of a good barber is my brother Ben,'' Wes said, ''and the puny one there is Elliot, runt of the litter.''

''Thanks a lot, big brother,'' Elliot said. But he sent Taylor a grin.

Wes took the only seat they'd left him, the one next to Taylor, and Garrett started passing dishes around. Taylor said, ''This isn't everyone, is it? I remember I met a sister...Jessi, wasn't it?''

''Yeah. Jessi lives in town with her husband, Lash,

and their new baby girl,'' Chelsea filled in. ''She's a veterinarian.''

''Right, I think I drove past her clinic one day. Her husband is your deputy, right, Garrett?''

''He is when I can get him to give up daddy duty long enough to be. Right now he's more into changing diapers than keeping the peace. Fortunately we don't have a lot of crime around here.''

Chelsea nodded hard. ''Quinn, Texas, is the best place in the world to raise a family.''

Wes sent her a scowl. Gee, next she'd be ordering invitations. ''I have another brother,'' he said. ''Adam works for a bank in New York City.''

''I'll never keep everyone straight.'' Taylor smiled and helped herself to a scoop of mashed-potato pie.

''Sure, you will,'' Chelsea said. ''But we're talking too much about us. We're all dying to hear more about you. Where are you from, Taylor?''

''I grew up in Indiana,'' she said. ''But now I don't really call any one place home. My work takes me all over.''

Chelsea frowned. ''As highly as they speak of you at the university, I figured you must have tenure somewhere.''

Taylor shook her head. ''I haven't wanted tenure. Been waiting to find the perfect place first.''

Chelsea smiled and glanced at Wes knowingly.

''And how is the dig going?'' Garrett asked. ''Any more trouble from your ghostly visitor?''

Taylor's eyes met Wes's. ''Not really,'' she said. And he knew she didn't want to talk about Wolf Shadow with his family right now. He couldn't say he blamed her.

''I'm watching things,'' Wes said, to save her from

having to say any more. ‘‘I don’t think he’s gonna bother Taylor again.’’ Truth was, he meant it. His Wolf Shadow days were over.

After lunch Wes managed to extract Taylor from the grip of his family—though they seemed reluctant to let her go. He walked with her out past the stable to where the horses grazed in the back pasture, and she leaned on the gate beside him when he whistled to Paint.

The stallion galloped toward them, slowing to a high-stepping trot as he approached, shaking his mane. The show-off.

Taylor reached up to stroke his neck. ‘‘Look at him,’’ she said. ‘‘Wes, he’s fabulous.’’

‘‘I know.’’ The horse blew and stomped when Taylor stopped petting him, fussing until she started up again. That made her laugh, a sound like ice and crystal. Wes swallowed hard. ‘‘I have an idea, if you want to hear it.’’

‘‘I think I know what it is already,’’ she said. ‘‘But tell me anyway.’’

Wes turned to lean his back against the gate, scuffing the dust with the heel of his boot. ‘‘Well, you said you were boarding your mare someplace. I was thinking, once I get that barn in shape, you might want to have her trucked out here. I’d keep her for you for nothing.’’

‘‘And breed her to Paint, here,’’ she said, nodding. ‘‘But not for nothing, Wes. I couldn’t do that.’’

‘‘Sure you could. I—’’

‘‘No.’’ She turned, too, leaning back against the gate just as he was. Paint leaned his head over and nuzzled her hair. Smart horse. ‘‘I’d have to pay you.’’ She laughed at the horse’s attention and reached up to rub his face. ‘‘I’d give you the foal.’’

Wes straightened and pushed his Stetson back farther on his head. "I couldn't take your colt, Doc."

"Sure, you could. Heck, Wes, I can't care for one horse, let alone two. What would I do with it?"

He drew a breath and sighed. Taylor straightened up and thrust her hand out. "So do we have a deal, or what?"

He looked down at the toes of his boots, looked up at her again. "Okay. Deal," he said. And he clasped her hand in his. But instead of shaking, he drew her slowly forward, and pressed his mouth to hers. Light and gentle. Long and lingering. But careful.

When she lifted her head, she looked as bewildered and enchanted as he felt. Lord, but he was sinking fast with this woman.

"You know what I like about you?" she asked softly.

Wes shook his head. "I can't even imagine."

She smiled a little. "You're gentle," she told him. "You kiss me like you're afraid I might break. And you're real."

"Real?"

"Straightforward," she said. "No games or acts. Just...honest. That means everything to me, you know. Honesty."

Wes swallowed hard and tried to still the panic in his belly. She was sincere, meant what she was saying. But in her eyes he thought he saw more. Anticipation. Eagerness. She wanted to explore the feelings flowing like a deep river between them as badly as he did. Wanted to know just how deep that water was, and what lay at the bottom...and where that river was going to take them.

Wes just hoped there wasn't white water waiting around the bend.

There wasn't, of course. It was more like Niagara Falls.

Wes was a special man. It didn't take much to see that. He was gentle. He was sweet and kind and so, so very gentle. She'd seen him with his little nephew. The careful, expert way he'd held the chubby toddler as if it were something he'd been doing for a long time. And when little Ethan looked up at his uncle, there was adoration in his eyes.

She liked everything about him. Everything. His family. Their teasing did nothing to conceal the love that lay underneath. It was something she'd never had, that closeness.

That afternoon she rejoined her group, and they wrapped up work on the quadrants where they'd been digging, and set up guidelines for the next. Small squares, roped off with light string. Wes had said he had to leave for a while. Didn't say where he'd gone. Didn't say what he was doing. It didn't matter.

Good God, was she saying that she *trusted* him? It was amazing to her that she could know a man for so short a time and trust him even slightly. She'd vowed *never* to put herself on the line like this for any man—or for anyone at all. Was she beginning to trust Wes? And was she putting herself at risk as she'd sworn she would never do by letting herself?

As the day wore on into late afternoon, with Taylor crouching in the square she'd assigned herself, sifting earth through a screened tray, breaking clumps of soil with her fingers and tossing pebbles aside, her fingers closed on something hard. Frowning, she grasped it carefully, setting the tray aside and reaching for her small brush, and methodically she began brushing the dirt away. Slowly a medallion emerged. An uneven oval of metal…gold, she thought, pounded flat. Symbols and designs had been carved into the gold all around. And in the center an almond-shaped, smooth piece of turquoise, with a perfect black circle painted in its center. Like an eye, set in gold. With a small black pupil. There were holes bored into either end of the oval, and she suspected a thong had been threaded through each end, to hold the eye around its owner's neck.

It was beautiful. And her first thought was that she couldn't wait to show it to Wes.

That made her pause and blink in surprise as her fingers caressed the smooth turquoise. Usually her first thought would be radiocarbon testing of the metal to determine its age, or perhaps what the stone had signi fied. Now it was of Wes. Lord, the way he'd crept into her thoughts was incredible. And frightening. And maybe…maybe right.

And at the same time, completely without her permission, an image flew into her mind. Of Wolf Shadow, sitting tall on his magnificent horse, this pendant gleaming on his naked, muscled chest. His eyes boring into hers and glazed with desire. His hands on her body. His mouth…

"Dammit, what's wrong with me?" She ordered the image away, but not before she'd felt the effects of it. Her body heated and her belly clenched. How could she be feeling so much—for the first time in her life—for one man, and still be so powerfully hungry for the touch of another? How could she care emotionally, as well as physically for Wes, and want to make wild love to someone else? It made no sense. Wes and that other man were total opposites. Wes was so tender, so sensitive. Wolf Shadow was wild and untamed, and dangerous.

"Where's Mr. Brand?" Scourge's voice interrupted her confusing, faithless thoughts. Guiltily she closed her hand around the pendant, dropping it into the deep pocket of her khaki trousers before turning to face him. Kelly stood by his side, shifting from one foot to the other a little nervously.

"He had some things to do," she said. "He'll be back later on. Why, is something wrong?" The two certainly looked as if there was. Kelly chewed her lower lip, and Scourge couldn't quite meet her eyes.

"Well, come on, speak up. What is it?"

Kelly drew a breath, looked at Scourge and sighed. "We went into town today, to pick up some bottled water. We were running low."

"And?"

"Well, we mentioned to the man in the store that Wes Brand was up here helping us out. And the guy just started talking."

Scourge cleared his throat. "It isn't like we were asking about him or anything, the guy just...he just talked. You know how older people like to talk."

Taylor frowned, waiting for them to go on.

"Ms. McCoy, you aren't like getting involved with this guy, are you?"

"Kelly, I really don't think that's an appropriate question." Taylor averted her eyes. "Just what did this fellow in town say to get you two so stirred up?"

Scourge lowered his head. "He said Wes was the black sheep of his family. That he'd done time in prison for robbing a bar and beating the owner half to death.''

Taylor sucked in a fast, loud breath. Closed her eyes. It wasn't true. Not Wes. Not the gentle man she'd been getting so close to. ''You shouldn't listen to gossip.'' But she turned away.

''He also said Wes killed a man a little over a year ago. With a knife.''

''It's ridiculous!'' She faced them again, getting angry now. ''Don't you think he'd be in jail if any of this were true?''

''Maybe not...his brother being the sheriff.''

''Oh, for the love of—''

''He does carry a knife. A big one, tucked in his boot. You must've noticed it,'' Scourge said slowly, not meeting her eyes.

She'd noticed it. But that didn't mean... ''I don't want to hear any more slander about Wes Brand. I can't believe you two listening to small-town gossip and swallowing it whole like this. You're old enough to know better.''

''But, Ms. McCoy, the man wasn't slandering Wes. He was...it was like he was praising him or something. Said if he ever had trouble he'd want Wes on his side and—''

''And that alone should tell you his story is nothing but garbage. Kelly, Wes Brand came here to protect us, for heaven's sake! He put his own responsibilities aside to spend time here, just to be sure we'd all be safe. He...'' She pushed one hand through her hair and shook her head. ''Look, that's enough. I'm not going to discuss this anymore. Gather up what you've got and get busy cataloging it. We'll stop in an hour for something to eat, okay?''

Scourge shook his head and made a disgusted sound in his throat as he turned and stomped away. Kelly started to go, too, then turned back. "It's just that we're concerned about you, Ms. McCoy. We didn't mean to upset you. I mean...we've never seen you look at a man the way you look at Wes. And if he's bad news...well, we just thought you ought to know."

Taylor looked at the innocence in Kelly's blue eyes, and her anger cooled to a simmer. "I'm glad you're looking out for me," she said. "But that's *my* job, remember? I'm a grown-up. I've been doing it for a while now."

"Okay. But...be careful."

She nodded. When Kelly left, Taylor brushed off her hands and headed for the solitude of her own tent. And then she sat down on her sleeping bag, grated her teeth and prayed that Wes didn't have some secret side he'd been hiding from her. She'd begun to let herself think that maybe he was the man she was meant to find. But what if she hadn't seen the man he really was?

And if she had to ask him directly, and it turned out to be true, how could she trust him to be honest with her about anything else? How would she know when he wasn't lying, but simply hiding the truth?

And if she asked him about this and it turned out to be a pile of lies...would he forgive her for being so suspicious?

She gnawed on her lower lip. How could she handle this? How?

"It's over, Turtle. She's not leaving the site, and this Wolf Shadow nonsense isn't going to convince her to. I can't do it to her. Not anymore."

Turtle sat outside tonight. Wes had encouraged him

to get up off the ratty plaid couch and come out under the stars to sit beside a fire as they'd made a habit of doing for the past year. The fire Wes built snapped and danced, and Turtle sat on his favorite lawn chair with a woven blanket wrapped around his shoulders. He sipped tea again tonight. And Wes was still very worried about him.

"Why, my friend?" he asked, then he closed his eyes, and the firelight painted his papery lids. "No, don't tell me. I'm still a shaman. I can see."

Wes frowned and sat still in the other seat, an old metal folding chair that had seen better days. He took another sip of his beer and waited.

"You care for her," Turtle said.

Wes choked on the beer.

Turtle's eyes came open, and he smiled slightly. "It is good," he said.

"Not if it means you're going to wander off into the desert and sit there until you die of dehydration and exposure, old friend. I'm here to tell you, I won't stand for that."

Turtle nodded slowly. "I've had a vision, Raven Eyes," he said. "It might be that my failure to protect the land will be forgiven…if you will remain there. Watch over it. See that the possessions of our ancestors are treated with respect, and honor."

Wes set his empty beer can aside and stared at Turtle. "Taylor wouldn't treat them any other way," he said. "You have my word on that."

"Not enough. You must be there. Remain until she is finished with her digging into the past."

The firelight danced on his face, making it appear red and orange rather than weathered bronze.

"And if I do, you're not going to go on this death march of yours? I have your word on it?"

Turtle blinked slowly. Very turtlelike. "If the time comes when I must go to await the spirits, my friend, I will come to you to say goodbye."

"Guess I can't ask for more than that," Wes said, but he was thinking that he'd hogtie the old shaman if that were what it would take to keep him safe.

"It's dark," Turtle told him. "You should go to her now."

Wes nodded and got to his feet, picked up his empty beer can and tossed it into the barrel that was overflowing with them. "Gotta empty that for you next time I come over," he said. "Remind me, will you?"

Turtle nodded again, and turned to stare solemnly into the flames.

When Wes had gone, Turtle slung his blanket off his shoulders. It was working. The long-ago words of the eagle to Sky Dancer's great-grandmother were being fulfilled. She would marry the man chosen for her. She would marry Raven Eyes. And then Turtle would teach them the old ways, together. He'd keep the promise he'd made to her grandmother as the woman lay dying.

There was still more to be done. So much more. He had to be sure Sky Dancer could be trusted not to violate the sacred ground, should she find it. He had to be sure the elders wouldn't sell the land to Hawthorne, in case she didn't find it. But he wouldn't take any action just yet. He had a feeling Raven Eyes and Sky Dancer must be the ones to work all of this out. To make the legend come full circle. Then prosperity would surely come to The People. And the spirits of

Wolf Shadow and Little Sparrow would find one another, and peace.

He took a hasty sip from his cup, grimaced and spit in the fire. Tea. Awful stuff! He reached for a beer from the six-pack on the ground, took a long swallow and set it aside. Then Turtle got to his feet and began to move. Slowly at first, in rhythmic steps danced for centuries. A dance of celebration. His voice rose to the skies in the tongue of his ancestors, and his pace increased as he danced in joy around the fire.

Chapter 8

It was dark and he hadn't returned. And part of her was afraid Wolf Shadow would show up before Wes did. And part of her hoped he would. The guilt that rinsed through her over that thought was sickening.

Then her tent flap opened and Wes stuck his head inside, and Taylor sighed in what she sincerely hoped was relief.

"You're back."

"Sorry it took so long. I had to check in on a sick friend." He came closer, sat beside her.

She smelled beer on his breath. Sick friend? Then she closed her eyes and told herself not to let Kelly and Scourge's gossip make her start doubting every word Wes said. So he'd had a beer while he'd been gone. So what?

"Is anything wrong, Doc?"

She looked up at him, faked a smile. "No," she lied. Then she sighed. "I don't know."

Looking worried, Wes searched her face. "Tell me."

Taylor drew a deep breath. "I guess...this thing is moving a little too fast for me, Wes. I have all these feelings and..."

"And?"

She closed her eyes. "And I barely know you." She opened her eyes and looked at him. "I really don't know anything about you. Your past, or..."

Wes sighed, lowering his head. "My past." He said it softly, and she knew then that there was something. A chill went up her spine. Wes licked his lips and met her eyes again. "It isn't pretty, Doc. Truth is...I didn't want to tell you."

"Why?" she whispered.

Wes reached out, stroked her hair. "Because I'm scared to death of losing you before we find out...just what we have here. I'm afraid you'll change your mind about me the way everyone else in this town did."

He was really afraid she would. His dark eyes were so vulnerable right now. She gave her head a shake. "Honesty is more important to me than any mistakes you might have made in your past, Wes." And right then, she meant it. "I'm not going to change my mind."

"Yeah, well, don't say that with so much conviction just yet."

"All right." She shifted a little closer to him. This need to be near him, to be touching him, was overwhelming, and new and frightening. "Then tell me. But...hold me while you do."

Wes slipped his arm around her, and she leaned back and sideways, her head cradled on his shoulder. It felt good to be held in his strong arms. So good.

"I've done time in prison, Taylor."

She closed her eyes. Damn. It was true. She should have known nothing this good came without a price.

"I've never been known as a reasonable man," he told her slowly. "And for a while, I ran with a pretty rough crowd. I must've been about seventeen when some of the boys and I were drinking and raising hell one night. We got tossed out of the bar by the owner, and he was none too gentle with us. Well, I spent that night trying to stay on my horse long enough to get home. See, the one thing I did have in my brain back then was enough sense to take the horse instead of the car when I knew I'd be drinking. But to tell the truth, it was probably less out of any sense of right and wrong than it was because I knew Garrett would kick my young butt black and blue if I did otherwise."

She thought she heard a smile in his voice. Maybe what he had to say wouldn't be so bad. "And what happened?"

He held her a little tighter. "The boys went back to that bar after closing. Beat the owner within an inch of his life and cleaned out the cash box. It was dark. The owner swore up and down all of us had come back that night, but I swear to you, Taylor, I wasn't with them. Course, I had no witnesses, no alibi. Got myself convicted and did two years' hard time before one of the boys finally admitted the truth. I got a new trial, and the conviction was overturned."

She sat up a little, turned and looked into his eyes. He was telling the truth. She could see it. "That's it?"

He nodded.

"And you thought…" She shook her head slowly.

"Most people around here don't believe me," he told her. "And they've known me all my life. You've only just started to get to know me. Why should you believe me when—?''

''I believe you,'' she said.

Wes stared so hard into her eyes she thought he was seeing into her soul. ''Why? Taylor, you said I was gentle, honest. But I'm not. I've got a terrible temper. The whole town knows it. And I doubt there's a gentle bone in my body.''

''You're gentle with me,'' she said.

He licked his lips, shook his head. ''I'm different when I'm with you. I've been different since I laid eyes on you, Doc.''

''I know. I've been changing, too. It's not like me to trust someone, Wes, but...I'm finding myself... trusting you.''

He averted his face when she said that, and a niggling doubt crept up her spine. There was more he was keeping from her. She knew it right then. And maybe it had to do with that other bit of gossip Scourge had so willingly passed along. That he'd killed a man. But it couldn't be true. He was opening up to her, being honest with her. She had to let herself trust him. And pray it wouldn't be a mistake. It was time, she told herself. It was time to believe in someone again.

''You keep saying that,'' he said after a moment. ''About trust...about honesty being so important to you.'' He met her eyes. ''You've been lied to in the past, haven't you, Taylor?''

''Hasn't everyone?'' She blinked and looked away. But then she bit her lip and faced him again. He'd shared some of his secrets with her. Maybe not all of them...yet...but some. If she were going to make this work, she was going to have to do the same.

She returned to her former position, settling back

into his arms. ‘‘My parents—the McCoys—they never told me I was adopted.’’ She drew a deep breath and let it out slowly. ‘‘I think I was around eight or nine when the questions started occurring to me. I was so different from them. My skin and my hair. But when I asked them about it, they just changed the subject, completely avoided the issue.’’

‘‘Aw, hell, Taylor. What were they thinking?’’ His big hand stroked slowly down her hair. And again.

‘‘But I could never get past the feeling that there was this big secret being kept from me. And it seemed like everyone was in on it but me. Kids in school, teachers, parents of my friends when I visited. I could sense it, you know?’’

She felt him nod, and snuggled closer. ‘‘In seventh-grade health class we were studying genetics. And according to what I was reading from the textbook and hearing from the teachers, there was no way in hell a copper-skinned, black-eyed, raven-haired baby could be produced by a blue-eyed blonde and a blue-eyed redhead.’’ She felt a tiny twisting in her stomach. It still hurt now and then, even after all this time. ‘‘I think I suspected it before then, but to have it confirmed like that…in school…all my friends looking at me like they'd known all along. The teacher suddenly backpedaling and trying to cover. But they knew. I could see it so clearly. I ran out of the classroom in tears. Mom had to come to school and take me home. And they still didn't want to tell me the truth. I had to practically force it out of them.’’

Wes shifted, pulling away from her for a moment and moving so that she reclined in the V of his legs, resting her back against his chest. His hands locked at her waist. He bent to kiss the top of her head. ‘‘It was because they loved you,'' he said. ''They were afraid of losing something by telling you.''

''I know that now. But then...well, I was pretty devastated.'' She laid her hands over his, squeezed them. ''I guess that's why honesty is so important to me. It has been ever since then. Maybe it gets too important sometimes. If someone lies to me...I just can't ever trust them again.''

He stiffened a little. She turned his hands over and threaded her fingers with his. ''It was about that time I started to withdraw. I don't need a psychologist to explain that to me. I just didn't like being close to people anymore. I think I was subconsciously wondering what they were hiding from me, what secrets they were keeping. After all, if the people I trusted most in the world had lied to me, how could I believe there was anyone who wouldn't?''

''So you were a loner. Just like me.''

''Yeah. But after a while I thought I could get past it, learn to trust again. I saw a therapist, for quite a long time, and eventually I opened myself up again. Let myself trust him. Told him everything I felt and thought and wanted and dreamed of.''

''And it helped?'' Wes asked.

Taylor drew a breath and sighed. ''I had an affair with him.'' She said it quickly, to get it over with. She'd never told a soul about this. ''I thought I was in love with him. And he encouraged it, talked to me about our future together, used all my dreams against me.'' She shook her head, closed her eyes. ''Then I found out he was married.''

Wes swore softly, held her a little tighter.

''I withdrew more than ever after that. Just sank inside myself, poured all the energy I used to spend on relationships into my studies, my degree and later my career. But it's never been enough. I thought it was. For so long I thought it was all I needed. Just me. No connections, not with people, not with my…my heritage. But now…'' She turned in his arms, looked into his eyes. ''Now I want more. And I think…I think I want it with you.''

He ran his hands up her back, under her hair, fingers sliding over her nape and sending chills down her spine. And then he kissed her. As tenderly as before.

Taylor put her hands on his head to cling closer, and the kiss deepened. He slipped his tongue between her lips and tasted her mouth. And Taylor thought finally…finally he was making her feel the way she'd felt with Wolf Shadow. Aroused, and liquid, and shivery. She kissed him back. She touched his tongue with her own, and twisted his hair around her fingers.

And then she lifted her head away, staring into his shining eyes.

''I don't deserve you,'' he told her. ''They say I have the worst temper in seven counties, Doc. You sure you want me?''

''Are you trying to scare me away, Wes?''

''No.'' His gaze roamed from her forehead to her chin and up to her eyes again. ''I won't hurt you, Taylor. I couldn't.''

And in that instant his voice sounded exactly the way Wolf Shadow's had. He'd said those same words to her, in almost exactly the same way. And he'd sounded…

''Are you ready to make love to me?'' he asked her, and now his voice was softer, raspier. A whisper.

She blinked, unsure, confused. ''I…I'm not sure.''

He closed his eyes, drew a breath, then opened them

again. Leaning forward, he kissed her forehead. "If you're not sure, then you're not ready." He smiled gently at her. "And that's okay by me. I'll wait forever if I have to. But I think it might be best if I headed out of this tent now."

"Oh."

He kissed her nose. Then her lips, lingering there, suckling upper, then lower in turn. Then he released her with a sigh, and got to his feet. "We have a lot more to talk about, Doc. There are still things about me..." He closed his eyes, shook his head. "But we have time."

And he left, calling good-night over his shoulder as the tent flap fell behind him.

She *did* want him. She *was* ready.

No. No, she wasn't. Wes was right; they had time. And there was still something he hadn't told her about. It was shadowing his eyes tonight. She'd spotted the secret first when she'd told him how important honesty was to her, and again when he'd said there was more they had to talk about. She knew that look. That look of a secret hiding in a person's eyes. She'd grown up with that shadow peering out at her from the eyes of her parents. She'd seen it, sensed it there.

"Right, and I've been suspicious of every person I've met since." She pounded her fist into the sleeping bag beneath her, turned over, closed her eyes. Told herself she was overreacting. Wes had no secrets. He wasn't hiding anything. It was her. And she was going to ruin what could be the best thing that had ever happened to her if she kept doubting him this way.

She knew she would. She'd ruined budding friendships, even a couple of relationships with men after only a couple of dates, by being so untrusting of everyone she knew.

She had to get past this. Maybe talk to someone. She'd always vowed never to try therapy again, after her devastating experience with it in the past. But maybe it was time she tried it again. Because she didn't want to take chances with this fragile, precious thing. She couldn't risk it.

Maybe…maybe she could talk to Chelsea.

Yes. That was it. She'd felt instinctively drawn to that small, auburn-haired woman. And Chelsea was studying for a degree in psychology. So maybe… maybe it would be worth trying. Before she screwed everything up with Wes.

Wes. The man she thought she might be falling in love with.

Chelsea refilled Taylor's cup with coffee, and returned to her seat in Jessi's kitchen. Taylor marveled again at the closeness of this Brand family. Chelsea had simply told Jessica that she needed a private place to talk, and Jessi hadn't batted an eye or asked a question. Just opened her door and let them both come in. Said Lash had taken the baby to the pediatrician for her immunizations, and that she would be out in the clinic if they needed her. And that was that.

It must be nice to be able to count on people the way this family could count on each other, Taylor thought, with a twinge of envy. She'd never been able to convince herself anyone would be that trustworthy, there for her, no questions asked, for any little thing that might come up. It was incredible. She'd lost the ability to trust fully in her parents. Oh, they'd mended things, saw each other often, got along well. And she loved them. But it just wasn't the same as it had been before.

And this closeness, this intimacy, was something she craved.

"This isn't really my area of expertise," Chelsea said, stirring her coffee and leaning back in her chair. "But I want to tell you how much it means to me that you could come to me with all this."

Taylor lifted her brows.

"I mean it, Taylor. No matter what happens, or doesn't happen with you and Wes, I want you to think of me as a friend. And anything you say to me isn't going any further. I promise."

Taylor nodded. "So what is your area?" she asked, sipping the coffee, enjoying her time away from the site and wondering how soon she'd screw up this new friendship Chelsea seemed to be offering her. "I don't think you said before."

"No, I didn't. I specialize in domestic violence. When I first came out here, I…well, I was a lot like you, actually. But it was only men I couldn't trust. Garrett included."

Taylor blinked in surprise, stopping with her cup halfway to her mouth. "You…you'd been…?"

"Battered?" She closed her eyes briefly. "I saw my mother die when my father took his rage too far. And then my sister was murdered by a man who'd claimed to love her. Little Ethan was her baby…his father was her killer."

"My God." Taylor's hand snaked across the table to close around Chelsea's before she'd even realized she was moving it.

"I'm okay now," she said. "Really. And so is Ethan. I like to think my mom and sister are, too, somewhere. Anyway, after I married Garrett, I saw a need in this area. So many small towns with so few resources. So I got involved with a domestic-violence hot line, and got some basic training in how to counsel the women who called. It wasn't long before I realized I didn't know as much about how to help them as I would have liked. Garrett encouraged me to go after this degree, if it was what I really wanted. And it was."

Taylor shook her head slowly. "You must be an incredible woman, Chelsea Brand."

Chelsea smiled. "I like to think so."

They both laughed, and Taylor thought she felt more relaxed than she had in ages.

"Actually, Taylor, I don't think your inability to trust is an unusual reaction to the kind of betrayal you felt your parents had dealt you. And that therapist should be in prison for what he did. It's amazing you don't have more problems than just this."

"So what should I do?"

Chelsea tilted her head. "Not to sound biased, but Wes is as honest as the day is long, Taylor. If there's something you want to know about him, just ask him."

"But he might think I don't trust him."

"Well, you don't. You can't just yet, because of what you've been through. Be honest with him about that. That kind of trust is something that has to be nurtured and it will grow over time. I guarantee it."

"I still think he's keeping something from me."

Chelsea frowned. "I can't imagine what. You said he told you about his prison time. That's been a thorn in his side for a long time, I can tell you that. But he's been different since you've been around. Calmer. More serene or something. Actually he's been steadily getting over his rotten temper for even longer. I think that old Indian who befriended him has a lot to do with that.'' She sipped her coffee. ''Of course, Wes thinks the rest of us don't know about that. But he'll tell us, when he's ready. Why don't you tell me what you think it is? I can see in your eyes there's something.''

Sighing, Taylor lowered her head. ''You'll think I'm horrible just for asking.''

Chelsea laughed, bringing Taylor's gaze sharply back to her. ''Honey, when I met Garrett, I punched him in the face and accused him of murdering my sister. You got nothing on me. Now spill.''

''You didn't.''

Chelsea nodded.

Taylor took a deep breath. ''Some of the students heard a rumor in town that Wes had killed a man a year ago, with a knife. And I've seen that bowie he carries in his boot.'' There. It was out. She studied Chelsea's face, but there was no shocked reaction. No outrage. No righteous indignation.

''Oh, hell, *that* can't be the big secret you think he's keeping. Listen, I was there.''

''So was I,'' a deep voice said. Taylor stiffened and turned to see a man she'd never met before, whipcord lean and handsome, carrying a pudgy baby girl with dark swirls of hair and huge blue eyes. He had to be Lash, Jessi's husband. He held up one hand. ''Didn't mean to barge in. Honest. And I just came in this minute, all I heard was what you two just said. Scout's honor.''

Chelsea smiled and shook her head. ''I gotta get an office or something. Lash, meet—''

''Taylor McCoy,'' Lash said. ''I'd know her anywhere. Jessi's done nothing but talk about the beautiful woman who's got her hotheaded brother acting like a pussycat.'' He smiled, his brown eyes warm. ''Now that I've seen her, I think I understand how such a miracle could come about.''

Taylor sat still, not sure what to say or how to act.

''I'm assuming this was a private conversation. Look, I won't repeat a word, but as long as I'm here, can I tell you about that day, Taylor?''

Taylor opened her mouth, closed it again, nodded once.

''Good.'' He came inside and settled the baby in her cradle and handed her a rattle. ''Maria-Michele, you be good while Dad gets Uncle Wes outta hot water, okay?''

The baby gurgled and cooed in response to her father's voice, and Lash ran a hand over her curls before turning to join them at the table.

''Lash can give you a better version of events than I can anyway,'' Chelsea said. ''See, I was busy being held at gunpoint by the man who killed my sister. And Garrett was trying to get to me in time to save my life.''

Before Taylor could choke out her surprise, Lash went on. ''Right. But the maniac had snipers lined up to take Garrett out. Wes and the rest of us were trying to remove them from the equation. Now, Jessi had just tackled one guy when—''

''Jessi?'' Taylor gaped, wide-eyed.

''Oh, yeah. She's a hellion when someone she loves is at stake. Hell, that's why I take little Maria in for her shots. I'm afraid Jessi would punch out the doc for pricking her.'' He grinned and winked. ''Anyway, she took one guy out, and I turned to see another one lifting his rifle and taking aim at Garrett. I couldn't get to the guy in time, and Garrett didn't even know he was there. Wes spotted him, though, pulled his knife and threw it just as the guy's gun went off.''

Taylor looked from Lash to Chelsea and back again.

Chelsea said, ''If Wes hadn't done what he did, my husband would be dead right now. Even the FBI agreed no charges should be filed against Wes. He just did what he had to do to save his brother's life.''

Taylor lowered her head and shook it slowly. ''I feel so horrible for thinking…even for a minute…''

''Hey, Wes is no angel,'' Lash said. ''But he's a decent guy.''

''But, Taylor, if you're sure he's keeping something from you, it's obvious this isn't it. He'd tell you all of this just as readily as we would. It's not a secret. The whole town knows about it.'' Chelsea shook her head. ''So if he *is* keeping something hidden, it must be something even *we* don't know about.''

The front door opened, and Jessi came in, made a straight line for her husband and ended up wrapped tight in his arms. They kissed like lovers. And when he released her he said, ''I was just telling Taylor that she ought to come by for dinner sometime.''

Jessi grinned. ''Oh, she will. I've got a feeling we're gonna be seeing a lot of her. *If* my brother has half a brain, anyway.''

Taylor lowered her chin to hide the way her cheeks heated. ''Thanks for that, Jessi.''

''Stick around for a while?'' Jessi asked. ''You can help me feed Maria her lunch. I might even make you a sandwich.'' She winked. ''I want to get to know you better, make sure you're up to the Brand-family standards and all that.''

''Watch it, Taylor,'' Chelsea said. ''Once she decided I passed muster, she wouldn't let me leave until I married into the family."

Taylor smiled. "I think I like you people," she said. "I'll stay if I get to hold the baby."

Taylor was thoroughly disgusted with herself for thinking there was even a slight chance the things Kelly and Scourge had told her about Wes were true. She must be sicker than she thought to mistrust a man like him. He was honest. And kind. And with a family like the one he had, how could he be anything else? No, the more she thought about it, the more certain she was that Wes wasn't keeping any secrets. And that meant the problem was all hers, and by God, she was going to deal with it this time. Get over this habit of being so suspicious.

Because he meant something to her. He meant…a whole lot to her.

And maybe, just maybe, this lingering attraction she still felt for Wolf Shadow was just one more way she was subconsciously trying to sabotage her own happiness. It was probably all some very deep psychological thing that she couldn't untangle alone. But she would. Chelsea would help her.

She came back to camp feeling guilty, but determined not to wrong Wes with her suspicious mind again. And then she remembered the medallion she'd uncovered yesterday. She hadn't cataloged it yet, because she'd wanted to show it to him. And now would be the perfect time. It was the least she could do to make up for the rotten things she'd been thinking.

She got the turquoise eye from her tent, emerged and scanned the area, but saw no sign of him. The kids were doing paperwork in the shade, and she knew they'd attack the actual digging again in a short while when the sun wasn't beating down quite so fiercely. But Wes wasn't with them. Shrugging, she headed to his tent. The flap was unzipped, so she pushed it aside and stepped in.

No Wes. She felt a rush of disappointment, but told herself she shouldn't expect the man to be here at her beck and call at any given moment of the day or night. She turned to leave, tripped on the tent flap and caught herself before she fell, but the medallion flew from her hands, landing in a muddy bit of dirt directly in front of Wes's tent.

"Damn!" Taylor knelt, snatching it up, checking it quickly for damage and scowling at the mud all over its surface. She ducked quickly back into Wes's tent, searching for something to wipe the pendant clean, and spotted a washbasin in the corner, with a cloth tossed inside it. Snatching the cloth up, she carefully wiped the bits of dirt and mud from the pendant, sighing in relief when it seemed to be unharmed by her clumsiness.

But then she frowned, because the cloth left a streak of yellow on the stone. What the hell…?

Taylor rubbed the stain off with her thumb, then shook the washcloth out and stared at the odd blotches of color smeared all over it. It looked like…

She blinked in shock. It looked like the paint Wolf Shadow wore on his face. It looked like…

"No." She slapped the cloth back into its basin and backed away from it as if it could infect her. "It's my cynical brain working overtime again. He couldn't be…"

But what else would explain this? It isn't like he's been painting in here. It isn't Halloween. He's not an actor. So why's he got bright-colored stains all over his washcloth?

But what sense did it make to think Wes had been the man behind the makeup? Why would he want to scare her away?

God, had it been Wes she'd very nearly made love to in that quiet glade? *Have I been feeling guilty for being attracted to two men, who are really one and the same?*

Taylor pressed a hand to her suddenly throbbing forehead. This was ridiculous! How was she supposed to know when she was using her common sense and seeing the obvious, and when she was letting past betrayals make her unduly suspicious? And how the hell was she going to find out for sure which was the case this time?

But how could she doubt it, when the proof was right before her eyes? She recalled Wes's words to her the night before, the way they'd sounded so much like Wolf Shadow's. And his kiss…and the way his touch fired her body to life just the way…

Was it true? Oh, God, he had lied to her. She'd let herself trust him, and he'd lied. The pain that twisted her insides was nearly unbearable, and tears burned hot paths down her face.

But what if…what if there was the slightest chance she might be wrong? How could she be sure?

It came to her slowly, but it came.

She had to see Wolf Shadow again.

And when she did, she'd look into his eyes and she would know. She couldn't look into Wes's eyes and not know him, not after all this.

God help him if he'd been deceiving her all this time.

And God help her.

Chapter 9

Wes had bundled up all his Wolf Shadow paraphernalia and got it the hell away from the site. It had been tucked in that cave near the pond, but that was far too close for comfort. Under his bed, back at the ranch was the best he could do for now. And there it would stay, until he could find time to toss it into a bonfire, at least. He didn't want to risk what he had going with Taylor. And he wasn't going to. She'd never find out the truth. And now there was nothing standing in the way. He was going to wine that woman and dine that woman until she melted in his arms; that was what he was going to do.

A finger of guilt tickled at the back of his neck. He knew he ought to just tell her. Just come clean and have it over with. Hell, she'd probably react to just about anything better than she'd react to being lied to.

But what if he told her, and lost her?

Maybe he should wait. Tell her later, after they were on more solid ground. Maybe if she…if she…

He was a rat. He never should have started all this. But he'd make it up to her. He'd sweep her off her feet. He'd make her see that it didn't matter, that what was growing between them was more important than any stupid mistake he'd made. And he'd start tonight.

He was practically rubbing his hands together in anticipation as he traipsed up over the slight incline and headed overland to Emerald Flat that evening wearing his newest pair of Wrangler jeans and his best boots.

She was sitting near a campfire. Seemed she'd taken a liking to campfires since he'd built one the other night. She—or somebody—had built another in the same spot, though it wasn't even dark yet. And Taylor sat on a seasoned log and stared unseeingly into the flames. She looked worried.

He aimed himself in her direction, only to be stopped by a scrawny hand on his shoulder, and turned to see the hairball looking at him with what he probably thought was a mean look on his face. From Wes's point of view, it looked more like indigestion, but he didn't think that was the kid's intent.

Wes stopped, glanced down at the hand on his shoulder and narrowed his eyes. The hand fell away. Wes turned his gaze on the kid. "You got something you need to say to me, son?"

"I'm not your son, mister."

"You got that right," Wes said. "No son of mine would be traipsing around with an earring in his nose, unless he wanted it replaced with a bull ring." Wes started to walk past him. The hand landed on his shoulder again.

"You know, Stanley, you keep sticking that hand where it don't belong, you're liable to lose it."

The kid flinched at Wes's use of his given name, rather than his nickname. "I want to talk to you," he blurted, but the hand fell to his side again.

Wes's temper bubbled up a little. But he managed to keep it to a simmer. The doc seemed to like Scourge, and Wes wasn't about to mess things up with her over the punk. "So what's on your mind?"

"Ms. McCoy."

Wes grinned a little. "Well, forget it. I got there first."

"I'm serious here, Brand. You better watch your step with her."

The simmer changed to a boil. "And just why is that?"

"'Cause I don't want to see her getting hurt, that's why. And I'm not gonna stand by and watch you keep jerking her around the way you've been doing."

Jerking her around? "Kid, I'm restraining the urge to kick your skinny ass for you here. But maybe it'd be nice if you'd tell me what the *hell* you're talking about now, while you're still able, just in case."

The kid swallowed hard, but lifted his chin. "She's been sitting there like that for over an hour. And I think she was crying earlier, in her tent. And she doesn't deserve..."

Wes swung his gaze to Taylor, shoved the kid aside and strode up to her, suddenly feeling the cold fingers of panic poking him in the gut. "Doc?"

She blinked and looked up at him. And damned if it didn't look as if maybe she *had* shed a tear or two today. She worked up a welcoming smile for him, but it was about as steady as a hummingbird in a hurricane.

He dropped down on one knee in front of her, searched her face. "Taylor, what's wrong?"

She sniffed, shook her head. But when she met his eyes, there was something there that scared the life out of him. "I hope you won't hate me for this," she said.

"Not a chance, lady." He clasped both her hands in his. They were cold, trembling. "Come on, tell me what's wrong. It's not going to be as bad as you think."

She closed her eyes. "You won't say that after you hear what it is."

Wes went stiff. God, was she going to tell him to take a walk? That she didn't want to see him anymore? That she'd changed her mind?

She lifted a hand, stroked his face. "I can't go on with this relationship," she said softly, tears brimming in her beautiful eyes. "Not until I…" Biting her lower lip, she shook her head.

"Not until you what, Taylor? Damn, don't leave me hanging this way." His heart had already dropped to the vicinity of his stomach. He was sorely afraid she was about to drop a boulder on top of it.

"Not until I see *him* again."

"Him?"

She took a deep breath, lifted her chin. "Wolf Shadow."

Wes blinked and managed not to let his jaw hit the ground when it fell.

"Wes, what I feel for you is…is so powerful, so intense. But…but you deserve more."

"I didn't ask for more," he said. "Taylor, you don't have to—"

"Yes, I do. Wes, I have to see him one more time. I have to prove to myself that whatever odd attraction he stirred in me is dead now that we're...together. For my own peace of mind, Wes. Can you understand that?''

He looked at the toes of his boots, shook his head. ''No,'' he said softly. ''No, ma'am, I sure don't understand.''

''I'm sorry, Wes. I think...I think this will be good for us. Once I put him behind me...I'll be free of him forever. And there won't be anything in the way of you and me.''

''It doesn't make any sense to me,'' he said, staring into her eyes, a plea in his own.

''Lord forgive me if I'm wrong,'' she muttered.

''Taylor?''

''Please, Wes. Just give me some time. I need time to think and to sort out my feelings. And seeing him will be all the verification I need. I can't commit to you the way I think I want to until I prove to myself that I can live up to that commitment. Be as faithful as you deserve me to be. I have to see him, calmly tell him that it's you I want. If I can do that, then I'll know I'm okay.''

He let his chin fall to his chest, sighing in resignation. ''If you have to, you have to.''

She nodded. ''Maybe...since there's no way of telling when I'll see him again...or even if I will—''

''Oh, you will.'' He clamped his mouth shut after he said it.

''But who knows when? I think it might be easier if you moved back to the ranch until—''

''Forget it. I'm not leaving so that bastard can waltz in here and—'' Wes stopped talking, replayed what he'd just said in his mind and frowned. Damn. ''I'm losing my freaking mind here.''

He turned and went into his tent, angry and hurt and jealous as all hell. Of himself.

Wes strode into the house that night without a word to anyone, heading straight up the stairs to his room. He felt the eyes on him. Garrett's curious gaze, and Chelsea's concerned one. But neither spoke, and maybe they sensed the turmoil going on inside him.

He couldn't believe it had come to this. That Taylor felt she had to see Wolf Shadow. It gnawed at him, and he couldn't shake the idea that maybe she preferred his alter ego to him. That maybe it was that legendary ghost she really wanted, and had been him all along. And it was stupid to feel that way; he knew that. But dammit, if she were so determined to see Wolf Shadow again, then he had no choice but to don the costume one last time.

He slung his bedroom door open and stalked inside, knelt beside the bed and groped underneath for the bundle that held his secrets safe from prying eyes.

And there was nothing there.

"You wouldn't be looking for this, now, would you, big brother?"

He came to his feet and whirled to see Jessi standing in the doorway with his satchel dangling from one hand. His temper heated up. "What are you doing with that?" He surged forward and snatched it from her hand. "Dammit, Jess, you know better than—"

"Than what? Huh? To worry about my brother and try to find out what's wrong?"

"To snoop." He tucked the bag under his arm, hoping to heaven she hadn't gone through it.

She stared at him hard, crossing her arms over her chest. "How could you do it to her, Wes?"

Hell, she had gone through the bag, then. "Look, you don't have a clue what's going on, so just—"

"The heck I don't! You're the one who scared that woman half out of her wits in that godawful getup. What I don't have a clue about is why. And I'm not leaving this room until you tell me."

"I'm not telling you anything. This isn't your business, Jessi." He tried to keep his temper in check. He adored his little sister, but her meddlesome ways could make a saint see red. "Leave it alone, Jess."

She thrust her chin out, and he knew damned well she wasn't going to oblige him. "You can talk to me, or you can talk to Garrett," she said. "But I can tell you now, he won't be too pleased to have to arrest his own brother for trespassing and whatever else you've been up to out there at Emerald Flat. So what's going on? Why are you trying so hard to ruin the best thing that's ever happened to you, Wes?"

Sighing hard, Wes sank onto the edge of his bed, closed his eyes. "I'm not tryin' to ruin it. I'm tryin' to save it." He peered up at Jessi, but she was still standing there with that stubborn look in her eye, so he told her. He told her everything, and it actually felt good to get it off his chest. When he finished, she came to sit down beside him, and she looked up at him, shaking her head.

"You're going at this all wrong," she told him. "What you gotta do is throw this dang costume away and tell Taylor the truth."

"Hell, I can't do that."

"She'd understand, Wes. Just tell her the way you told me. Tell her about old Turtle and his illness and all. Tell her—"

"You don't get it. She *likes* the guy."

Jessi cocked her head. "Turtle?"

"No. Wolf Shadow. She...she's attracted to him."

His sister made a fist and knocked lightly on the top of his head. "Hello? Anybody home in there? The guy is you, Wes."

"Yeah, but she doesn't know that."

Frowning hard, Jessi said, "I wouldn't be so sure about that theory. The woman isn't stupid."

"She doesn't know. I'm sure of it, and dammit, Jess, I have to keep it that way. She wants to see him one more time, and by God, I'm gonna see to it she does. Let her get the damned ghost out of her system so we can get on with things."

"And you think that's what's gonna happen?"

He lowered his head. "I hope that's what's gonna happen."

Jessi shook her head. "I never realized just how clueless the Brand men were. Lord, but you all need keepers."

"I have to go." He got to his feet, satchel still tucked under his arm.

"Don't do this, Wes. It's bound to blow up in your face, I'm telling you."

He shook his head. "I got no choice." And he headed out without waiting for her arguments, because they made too much sense and he was already scared witless about what he was going to do. She was wrong, no matter how logical she sounded. Dead wrong.

He hoped.

Taylor waited until Wes was out of sight, and then she followed him. On foot. She cut through the woods to watch as he walked down to his car and took the long way around, the only way on and off the flat by car. And then she stationed herself there, where she'd be sure to see him when he came back.

It was over an hour. But he did return. He pulled the truck off the trail into a copse of brush almost as if he wanted it hidden, and then he got out, slung a pack of some kind over his shoulder and began hiking toward the woods where she crouched.

Catching her breath, Taylor ducked behind some deadfall, and waited for him to pass. He hadn't seen her. Good. His steps never faltered. And he walked like a man who knew exactly where he was going. She gave him a few seconds, and then she crept out of her hiding place and followed.

Once she stepped on a twig, and it snapped. She lunged for a tree, flattening herself to its bark for cover, and when she peered out, she saw Wes standing in the distance, looking back, listening. She all but held her breath as she waited, and waited. But eventually he gave his head a shake and turned away again.

Relief made her almost too limp to move, but she was determined to know the truth. For sure. Tonight.

And in a few more minutes she did. Wes clambered up a shallow slope not far from the pond, and then disappeared. Taylor crept closer, pushing tangled undergrowth aside to find the entrance to a cave. And there was a light coming from within. Narrowing her eyes, she peered around the corner to see Wes sitting cross-legged on the stone floor, a kerosene lamp glowing in front of him, a mirror propped up against a rock. As she looked on, he pulled his hair free of its usual thong. Then he dipped his fingers into a jar of color, and smeared stripes of bright yellow over his face. Before her very eyes, Wes turned into Wolf Shadow. And it was good that she'd seen it because she never would have believed it otherwise.

She withdrew in silence, lowered her head, felt the burn of tears in her eyes, but only for a moment. Seconds later anger surged up to overwhelm the disappointment. Damn him. He obviously had some ulterior motive here, some hidden reason for wanting to sabotage the dig. And she couldn't help but wonder if his alleged feelings for her were as phony as the costume he was wearing tonight. Just another part of his scheme. A way of putting himself right in the middle of the dig, maybe getting in position to resort to some other means of stopping the project in case his scare tactics didn't work.

Why? She couldn't for the life of her imagine why.

But maybe the why of it didn't even matter. He'd lied to her. He'd betrayed her, when she'd trusted him in a way she hadn't trusted anyone in a very long time. And it hurt to feel this disillusioned yet again. But she'd deal with the hurt later. Right now the man needed to be taught a lesson he wouldn't soon forget. How could she ever have thought she could be falling in love with him?

She slipped down to the edge of the pond, brushed the tears from her eyes, and she waited. And within a short while, his footsteps came softly on the dried leaves and bristly grass behind her. Drawing a breath, telling herself she could play at this game of charades as well as he could—better than he could—she got to her feet and turned to face him.

She had never looked more beautiful, Wes thought, or more vulnerable, than she did right now. He felt like slime. Lower than that. But dammit, what choice had she given him? He was doing this for her…for them.

She looked at him as if she were seeing him for the first time, and he thought she set her jaw. "I was hoping you'd come tonight," she said, her voice barely more than a whisper.

"For the last time," he told her. "I can't come to you again after this." He didn't move closer. God forbid she should recognize him now, when he was about to put this stupid scam to rest forever.

"Why?" Taylor came closer, but stopped two feet from him, those piercing dark eyes of hers skimming his face.

"I am not real, Taylor. I'm a phantom. A myth. I don't even exist."

"We both know that's a lie." She came still closer, and this time she touched him, her palm skimming lightly up his outer arm. "You're as real as I am."

He drew slightly away, because her touch rekindled memories of the last time he'd been with her here. What had nearly happened between them. And he wanted her so much he ached with it. But not as some ghostly apparition. Not like that.

"You're wrong. I only came tonight to say goodbye," he said, and his voice had gone hoarse. "You deserve more. A real man, who can give you all that I can't. I'm going, Taylor, and you won't see me again."

She swallowed hard, met his eyes. "If that's the way it has to be."

He nodded. "It is."

"Will you do one thing for me before you go?"

So close. So close to ending this charade. Wes felt a shiver dance up his spine. "If I can."

"You can," she said, and she averted her eyes. "I

need to know that what I…feel for you…is as nonexistent as you claim to be."

"It is, Taylor. It's only a fantasy."

"Prove it to me, Wolf Shadow." She lifted her head, met his eyes and came closer, until her toes touched his. And he realized for the first time that she was barefoot, as he was, and damned near moaned at the erotic thrill that rushed through him at that simple contact. Skin to skin. Warmth and softness. "Kiss me," she said. "Just kiss me once more. A goodbye kiss."

He shook his head from side to side, told himself to move away from her, and remained standing right where he was. "It would prove nothing," he whispered, even as her hands crept up around his neck and her fingers threaded into his hair.

"Maybe not." She pressed her body to his. "Maybe I just want to make sure you know what you'll be missing." She fit her mouth to his, and she kissed him, gently, softly. Too softly. She drew away to stare into his eyes, and then she kissed him again. Drew away again. Kissed him again. Drew away. "C'mon," she whispered. "You know you want to."

When her lips danced over his yet again, Wes lost whatever willpower he'd had. And most of his sanity, as well. His arms locked around her waist, and he bowed over her, covering her mouth with his. Her taste drove him mad, and he pulled her tighter to him, his tongue diving inside her mouth, his hands anchoring her hips to his.

Her hands rose between them to push him away, but he ignored their gentle pressure, and kept kissing her. And finally she pulled her head to the side, muttered, "Stop. Enough, it's enough."

But Wes didn't think it would ever be enough. Still

he let his hands fall to his sides. She was breathless, wide-eyed, and if she wanted him as much as she seemed to, he'd probably just blown his plan all to hell.

She took a step away from him. "Goodbye, Wolf Shadow," she said.

And he was left to frown after her, puzzled, confused, disgusted with himself for ruining everything and with her for letting him. Didn't she have any sense of loyalty at all?

She turned once more to look back at him. "Maybe some night when you're so lonely you can hardly bear it, you'll realize what you gave up tonight."

"I already do," he muttered, but she was already hurrying back through the woods out of sight. Damn. He'd lost her. He'd…

No, wait a minute. Wolf Shadow had lost her. Maybe that meant there was still a chance…for Wes.

Taylor slammed into her dome tent, yanked the zipper closed and fumbled in the darkness for a gas lamp until she finally got the thing lit.

Damn him!

And damn *her*. How could she still feel so crazy in his arms when she knew full well how he'd tricked her and lied to her? How could she have lost herself in his kiss the way she had? God, she still wanted the bastard. Even knowing the truth.

She was sick. She was seriously sick to feel anything for him now.

But she did. Leaving him behind in the forest had been the hardest thing she'd ever done. She should have been repulsed and disgusted to have to carry out her act. Instead she was more turned on this time than she had been before. And maybe that was because she knew the man she was kissing was really Wes Brand. So that now all the things she'd felt for him, and all the things she'd felt for Wolf Shadow, had combined into a burning desire for them both—for one man who had for some reason tricked her into believing he was really two.

Dammit, she hated feeling this way.

But she could control it. She could get past it. She'd dealt with lies and betrayals before and survived it, hadn't she? She could do it again. But nothing, *nothing* infuriated her more than being made a fool of. And this time she was going to get a pound of flesh in return. Wes was going to live to regret the day he'd tried to pull one over on Taylor McCoy.

Damn. Why did it hurt so much?

She cried herself to sleep. And she dreamed a very strange dream. In which she saw a woman who looked like her, lying very still on the cold ground. Eyes open, but unseeing. And a man—a man who looked like Wolf Shadow—kneeling beside her, crying. The dream wrenched at her on a deep level she didn't understand, and she woke with a start, sitting up fast and wide-eyed.

"Just a dream," she muttered, pushing her hair out of her eyes. She sat still, consciously calming her breathing, waiting for her heart to slow down to a normal rate again. But there was a smell. Wood smoke, pungent and soothing somehow. A fire's glow painted the front of her tent from without. The yellow flicker managed to permeate the fabric, and she could feel the warmth making its way inside, as well. And the invitation was too much to resist. A glance at her watch told her there were only a couple of hours until morning. No one would be out there. Hard to believe the kids would have built up a campfire and left it burning, but apparently someone had.

She slid out of her sleeping bag, and slowly pushed the tent flap open to peer outside. No one was there, so she stepped out, drawn closer to the fire's warmth and the snapping and crackling that was like a night song. She stood close, her back chilled while the front of her soaked up the heat.

And then a woolen blanket was gently draped over her shoulders, and she caught her breath, looking up quickly. Wes smiled down at her, but the smile didn't reach his eyes. Her heart started to melt. She hardened it. He'd lied to her, deceived her, probably hadn't felt a thing for her at all. She couldn't forget that. No matter how the firelight painted the angles of his face or lit up his eyes.

He lifted a hand to her face, ran the pad of his thumb over her cheek. "You've been crying," he said.

She shrugged and averted her eyes. "The dig's been a big disappointment. I haven't found anything but what I'd expect to find in a normal Comanche village. It's...frustrating."

"But that's not what's bothering you."

Taylor stared into the flames, because it was easier than looking into his eyes and wishing he'd just tell her the truth. "No."

He pressed a palm to her cheek, turning her head toward him, probing her eyes with his. "Tell me."

Taylor drew a breath, fought to keep her chin high, to make her voice firm and emotionless. "I saw him tonight. Wolf Shadow. He said he wouldn't be coming back again, and I believe him." In spite of herself, her gaze lowered to the ground. "So there's no reason for you to stay on the site any longer."

He was quiet for a long moment. Not touching her. Just standing there, so close she wished he would. Then he said, "I would have said there was a damned good reason for me to stay." He bent a little, dipping his head so he could get a look at her lowered eyes. "But maybe I was wrong about that."

"Maybe you were." The breath rushed out of him. Taylor looked up to see him standing there, eyes closed tight as if he were in pain.

Without opening them, he whispered, "Is it because of him? Are you—?"

"Am I what? In love with him?"

Wes's eyes flashed open, and she saw the jealousy flash in their depths so plainly it was unmistakable. She frowned in confusion. How could he be jealous of her feelings for a man who was…who was him?

"Are you?" he asked, and he held her gaze, his own burning.

"How could I be? I've told you how important honesty is to me, Wes. How could I possibly fall in love with a man who won't tell me who he really is, or why he wants me to leave this place? A man who claims to be a ghost when I know perfectly well he's as real as…as real as you are."

It was Wes's turn to look away. Was he ashamed, then? She hoped so. He ought to be.

"If it isn't him," he said, his voice low and measured, "then what, Taylor? I thought…I thought we had something."

She shook her head slowly. "Maybe we did. Or maybe it was wishful thinking. I don't really know what I believe anymore. This whole thing with Wolf Shadow has me questioning everything I think is real."

"I don't—"

"I'm the only one who saw him, Wes. He says he isn't real, so what if it's true? What if he isn't real? What if nothing I think of as reality is real? How can I trust my own feelings? And if I don't trust mine, how can I trust yours?"

"You aren't making any sense."

"I'm making perfect sense and you know it."

He went still, silent, searching her face.

"I think you've been keeping as many secrets from me as Wolf Shadow has, Wes." She lowered her head. "So there it is. I won't be lied to. I won't. I can't."

Silence. Long, tense silence, and she waited. His hand came to her shoulder, but she shrugged it away, took a step to put distance between them, turned to look at him. "So are you ready to tell me the truth yet?"

And he was starting to get it. She could see it in his eyes, a slowly dawning horror. "What do you want to know?"

She shrugged. "Oh, I don't know. Maybe you can start by explaining why you felt it necessary to make a complete fool of me. To make me believe I was falling for two men, when they were actually one and the same."

It was as if all the life went out of him. His shoulders slumped, his head lowered. "You know." It was a flat, toneless statement.

"Yeah," she said. "I know." She turned toward her tent.

Wes caught her shoulders and turned her to face him again. "I don't know what you're thinking, Taylor, but it's wrong. I can explain all this. Once you understand, you—"

"It's too late for that."

"It's not."

She put her hands on his, removing them from her shoulders, and dropped them at his sides. "The time to explain all this, Wes, was the first time you kissed me and made me think it was real. Or when you took me up to that ranch and convinced me we shared the same dreams. Or when—"

"Dammit, Taylor, all of that *was* real."

"It was a fantasy," she said. "That's how our friend Wolf Shadow put it, wasn't it? I think I'd call it something else, though. A lie. It was all a lie."

Again she turned. And again his hand came to stop her, on her arm this time. Facing her back, he said, "I don't want to lose you, Doc."

"You never had me, Wes. So losing me isn't an option."

He ran his hand gently up and down her outer arm. Taylor shivered and drew away. "You still want me," he said.

"Go to hell."

"I will. If you walk away now, I will."

She didn't turn, because if she had, he'd have seen the rivers of tears gliding silently down her face. She just went forward, into her tent, zipped it tight and left him standing there.

Chapter 10

When she emerged from her tent again, Wes's tent and belongings were gone, along with his truck. Taylor stood by the blackened logs and snowy ash of the dead fire, and for just a moment let herself wallow in disappointment. He'd left. She'd told him to go, and he'd just packed up and gone. Somehow she hadn't pegged Wes as a man who would throw in the towel so easily. She'd expected him to stay. To try to explain himself. Maybe lose that hot temper she kept hearing everyone talk about, but had yet to see firsthand.

But he'd done none of those things. And she shouldn't care. She'd read Wes all wrong. Had never really known him after all. He was a quitter, readily accepting her statement that it was over, that it was too late.

Or maybe he'd never really cared enough to keep trying.

"Damn you, Wes," she whispered. "I thought you'd at least explain..."

Her head came up sharply at the odd little tremors she felt beneath her feet. A sound, like distant thunder rolling nearer, made her frown and squint into the rising sun in the distance. And then she paused, because the sunrise was so stunning. A giant red-orange ball rising slowly from the desert, painting everything from the sky to the trees to the parched ground with color. As she watched, something took shape near the very center of the spectacular fireball. A form, growing larger, right where the sun kissed the desert floor.

Taylor shielded her eyes with her hands. It was a man on a galloping horse. With the sun behind him like some artist's concept of the perfect backdrop, she could only see the man in silhouette. Like a shadow, black hair flying loose in the wind as he leaned over his horse, urging it faster, racing nearer. Man and animal moving as one magnificent shadow.

Shadow. Wolf Shadow?

Her eyes burned from staring into the sun that way, and she had to avert them. But when she did, it seemed those hoofbeats got suddenly louder and the ground vibrated with them. And when she looked up again, Wes was bearing down on her. His hair wild, his chest bare, his skin reddish gold in the blush of sunlight. But he wore faded blue jeans, and there was no paint on his face. She glimpsed something around his neck, a pouch of some sort, on a thong. And then she realized she should have been moving instead of staring at him this way. Because he suddenly let out a cry worthy of any legendary warrior, and leaned sideways as his horse thundered past. Taylor felt an iron grip around her waist and then she was hoisted right off her feet, and deposited again on the horse's back. She was awkwardly balanced between Wes's legs in a bad imitation of riding sidesaddle, and her hands gripped his shoulders in a knee-jerk reaction to keep from falling to the ground.

Not that there had been any danger of that. His hard forearm still pressed to the front of her waist, forcing her body tight to his unclothed chest. He whooped again, kicked the stallion's flanks, and they surged forward at dizzying speeds. She was vaguely aware of Kelly and Scourge lunging out of their tents and shouting after her. And then all that was behind them.

It was with a little shiver of apprehension…and something else…that she realized where they were heading. The animal's hooves were throwing parched dust up behind them now, as they galloped out into the desert, into the Badlands, toward the rising sun.

She lifted her head, fixed a glare on her face, though it was difficult with the wind whipping her hair into her eyes, and making it dance around Wes's face, as well. "What in hell do you think you're doing?"

"Did you think I was just going to walk away?"

She'd thought exactly that, but she refrained from saying so. "Wes, this isn't going to make any difference."

"No?" He slowed the horse a bit, drawing back on the reins, angling him in a new direction. Slowing some more until the Appaloosa stopped running, and was trotting instead. The running was easier. Now she was bounced up and down like a Mexican jumping bean.

"Dammit, I'm going to fall."

"Sit astride, then," he said, and without waiting for her answer, he closed his big hand on her inner thigh, and pulled her leg over the horse's back. Only she wound up sitting backward, facing Wes, one of her legs anchored over each of his. She might be sitting astride the horse now, but she was basically straddling Wes, as well. And he'd planned it that way.

Damn him.

"I brought you out here to show you something."

"I'll bet."

The horse stumbled, jarring her up and down again. Wes's hands closed on her hips, and she would have believed it was an instinctive reaction on his part, except that they tightened there, pulling her to the hardness of him. Pressing her close. And he closed his eyes, and swore softly. And then he kissed her.

One hand slid slowly up her back until his fingers spread through her hair to hold her head. The other remained on her backside, kneading gently, keeping her close. His lips nudged hers apart, and his tongue slid into her mouth. And while her mind was telling her that she hated him, her body was responding the way it had before. Her blood heated and her heart hammered in her chest. Her arms crept around him, hands pressing to warm skin and hard muscle. Her lips opened to let him inside. Her hips moved when his did. The horse had stopped moving, but she was barely aware of that. She only knew Wes was making her forget everything except the fire between them. Making her want him when she didn't want to let herself.

He pressed himself to her, and she let him, and it made her angry that she still wanted him this much. And then he drew his head away from hers, looking down at her, his eyes as glazed and passion filled as hers must have been. He closed them slowly, releasing his breath in a soul-deep sigh. "That wasn't part of my plan," he said.

She couldn't look at him. Wasn't even sure what she was feeling. "You have to tell me why."

But before he could answer, she heard a voice, very distant and faint. A chanting song, in perfect Comanche, sung by a voice hoarse with age.

"I'll show you why," Wes said, and gently he turned her around so that her back was toward him. Then he nudged the horse's sides, and they moved up into the rocky, barren hills, ever higher over twisting, barely discernible paths. Pebbles clattered behind them.

She saw a thin ribbon of gray smoke ahead, and then, as they drew nearer, the painted tepee that had been erected, and the form hunched before it. An old man, sitting on the ground near his small fire, chanting in his native tongue.

Wes drew the horse to a stop and got down. Then he closed his hands around Taylor's small waist and lifted her to the ground. Turtle didn't seem to notice them there. The minute he'd gone to the old man's trailer and found it empty and locked up tight, he'd known where he would find him. Damn.

"What's this all about?" Taylor asked, but Wes shook his head, took her arm and drew her forward.

Without looking up, Turtle said, "I knew you would find me, Raven Eyes. But why have you brought Sky Dancer with you?"

Wes sat down beside his friend, and Taylor followed suit, sitting, as well. "Turtle, I'm not going to let you do this."

But the old one only shook his head. "I am a shaman whose medicine has turned bad,'' he said. ''This is the only thing I can do. My time has come.''

''Look, we tried this your way. It didn't work. Now we're going to try it my way. Talk to her, Turtle. Tell her why she has to stop digging on the flat. It's what you should have done in the first place.''

For the first time Turtle lifted his head, his faded black eyes leveling on Taylor. Wes could see her scanning his face.

''If Turtle had something to tell me, he would have told me before now. Instead of just telling tales and giving out nicknames.''

''Sky Dancer is your name,'' Turtle said. ''Not a nickname. Your true name.''

Her brows came together. ''I don't understand.''

''You don't want to understand. You come here to do your white man's work, but all the time you fear your own soul. You fear the touch of your ancestors. You pray you'll never know them.''

Taylor blinked, got to her feet, turned toward the horse. ''I don't have a clue what new game this is you've cooked up, Wes, but I'm going back. On foot if necessary. I'm not falling for any more of your tricks.''

''Taylor—'' Wes began, but the old voice interrupted him.

''I was there when you were born, Sky Dancer. I knew your mother. And your grandmother before her.''

Taylor went utterly rigid. ''My *mother* was Leandra McCoy.''

''Loving the one does not mean you cannot come to know of the other.'' Turtle turned to Wes, while Taylor stood there, back to them, hair flying like a satin flag in the desert breeze. "I will take your advice, my friend. I will tell her the story. If she will listen."

Wes nodded, got to his feet and went to her. "Taylor, please. Hear what he has to say. Please."

She remained stiff, but slowly she turned. "All right. I'll listen. But don't think any yarns you cook up are going to make me stop this project. I've been made a fool of once. It isn't going to happen again."

Turtle nodded slowly, patting the ground beside him. Taylor sat down. Wes could see the wariness in her eyes, the suspicion. God. She didn't trust him now as far as she could throw him.

And Turtle began.

"Wolf Shadow was a shaman. Young, but taught at the feet of the old wise men of our clan for most of his life. His parents knew from the time he learned to speak, that this was the path he would walk, and so he learned. He knew the ways of good medicine and bad. He was a healer. And the spirits spoke to him in visions few other men had the power to see. But the spirit of the wolf called him brother, and he could see. He knew where our hunting parties would find success. He knew when disaster was about to befall them. And his prophecies always came true."

Taylor glanced at Wes, but he only shrugged. "This is new to me, as well." Then he turned his gaze back to Turtle. "Go on, old friend."

Turtle nodded. "Wolf Shadow fell in love with a young woman. And he set about to win her for his own. But the girl was an odd one. Determined to remain alone, to live her days without a man or children. And some said it was her very strangeness that made Wolf Shadow as devoted as he was. He brought gifts for her. Meat and ponies and blankets. Yet she denied him. He tried to impress her with his strength and skill in riding and fighting, but to no avail. It was only when Wolf Shadow took ill that her heart softened. She cared for him herself, refusing to allow any others into his tepee, and it's said that she fell in love with him then. When he was well again, the two were as one, never apart. And their happiness was said to fill the entire village with joy just at seeing it. Everyone became involved in the preparations for the ceremony that would join them."

Taylor had heard the story before. But Turtle was embellishing more this time, she thought. Turtle fell silent for a moment, staring into the dying flames of his small fire, breathing deeply. It was almost as if he could see the story he told, unfolding in the fire.

"But before they were joined, she was killed when the white man's horse soldiers raided the village. It was said they attacked to avenge some Indian raid on their towns, but our village was a peace-loving one. At least, it had been, until then. Wolf Shadow never smiled again, after that day. He became a warrior, raining vengeance upon the soldiers at every opportunity."

"You've told me this before, Turtle," Taylor said. "They were never married."

"Wolf Shadow spent days at her burial spot, hiding away many of the things sacred to the two of them. The heart he'd shaped of turquoise and given to her, the beaded moccasins she'd made for him. He declared that spot to be sacred, and vowed no one should set foot there or desecrate the ground. Before he set out on the raid that would be his last, Wolf Shadow told the villagers of a vision he'd seen while mourning over the body of his love. He said that because their love had never been consummated, neither of their spirits would find peace. He claimed he could only be freed when one of his descendants found true love with one of hers, completing the circle begun so long ago.''

''Descendants?'' Taylor glanced toward Wes, who'd gone still and silent.

''One of Wolf Shadow's nieces was given to Little Sparrow's nephew. But it was never true love. Only the village shamans knew, of course, but the spirits of the two lovers remained in turmoil. Ever seeking, but unable to find one another.''

He looked Taylor in the eye, his own eyes clouded and sad. ''Her resting place is in danger, Sky Dancer. You must stop this digging. Wolf Shadow has suffered enough. Moreover he charged the shamans of our line with the task of keeping that place safe, and I am the last of those. If I fail...''

Taylor got to her feet, paced toward the fire, stopped. ''Turtle, you could have told me all of this a long time ago. I asked you, and other Comanche elders, if there were objections to excavating Emerald Flat. You all said there was nothing. The elders *asked* me to come here.''

''Umm.'' Turtle nodded, lowering his gaze again. ''They were determined to go through with the sale to Hawthorne unless they found proof that Little Sparrow's resting place was here. Hawthorne wanted a team of his own choosing. I was able to convince the elders to agree to the dig only if they could choose the scientist themselves. Hawthorne has his own reasons for wanting this land, none of which are known to us. It was I who told the elders to contact you, Sky Dancer.''

''You...?''

''The legend of Wolf Shadow and Little Sparrow is

sacred, and told again only to Comanches descended from their village and clan. And again there was the chance that once you knew of the sacred articles to be found, you would seek all the harder for the place where they've lain since the time of my grandfathers' grandfathers."

She turned slowly to face Turtle, brows lifting. "It's been that long?"

"Three centuries, and more," Turtle told her.

And she slanted a suspicious gaze toward Wes. "But the artifacts we've been uncovering on the flat are less than half that old. My research says the village is far older, but so far I've found nothing to indicate—"

"The village remained," Turtle said, nodding slowly. "The People lived there, each generation after the one before. Until they were herded like cattle onto the reservation. But that spot where Wolf Shadow buried Little Sparrow went untouched from the time she was lain down. And eventually the whites saw fit to return this bit of land to The People, because they saw it as barren and of little use to them."

Taylor nodded slowly. "Then this sacred spot wasn't *in* the village, but somewhere outside it."

"Taylor?" Wes searched her face when she turned to look his way. "For God's sake, you aren't seriously considering looking for it, are you? Not after what Turtle just told you. You can't—"

"If I don't find the spot, the land will be sold anyway," Taylor said. "Besides, how can I believe all of this isn't another lie? I want to know the real reason you two want me out of here. Until I do, the dig goes on as planned."

Turtle lowered his head. "Then I've failed."

For just a minute Taylor looked alarmed. But then

she gave her head a shake. ''Everyone knows you two are best friends,'' she said to Wes, with a nod toward the old man on the ground. ''You cooked this up as another way of scaring me off. I'm not falling for it, okay? You think you can lie and trick me the way you have and then expect me to fall for the very next game you set up?'' She shook her head, her eyes flashing. ''No way. I'm the least gullible woman you're ever likely to meet, Wes.''

When she turned to begin trudging off toward the flat, Wes shot forward, gripped her shoulders, made her face him. ''This isn't a game, dammit. *Look* at him. He's waiting to die, Taylor. If you go on with this dig…'' He let his words trail off, because he saw no hint of surrender in her eyes. ''You really don't believe a word he said, do you?''

''Not a word.'' She looked away. ''And I can't believe you'd try to take the things I told you and twist them around to use against me this way. But I don't suppose I should be surprised.''

''Taylor, that's not what this is about.''

''The hell it isn't. It's one big guilt trip. Heap it on and you figure I'll buckle just to make up for neglecting my heritage all these years. Ignoring it. Well, I don't want it, Wes. For a while I thought I did, but…'' She shook her head. ''I'm damned well not going to give up on this dig out of guilt. So forget it.''

She meant it. He'd destroyed any hope she'd trust a word he said, and Turtle was apparently judged guilty by association. He glanced toward where his horse stood patiently. ''Take the horse,'' he said. ''Get back to camp where you belong. I'll take care of Turtle.''

''Fine. You two can sit here and start plotting your next scam.'' She walked away from him, mounted the horse with ease and whirled him around toward the site. With one last glance back at Turtle, she dug in her heels.

The dig continued at the village site through the day. Aside from a few bits of pottery, nothing major came of it. Taylor let Kelly and Scourge work, and closeted herself in her tent. Scourge had begun work on a map of the village based on what they'd found, and Taylor studied it, trying to decide where this so-called sacred spot might be located, if it even existed. Chances were it was as bogus as the rest of Turtle's tale.

But as determined as she was to ignore the old man's story, it kept coming back to her. So much so that she was compelled to go through every account she'd brought with her, concerning the history of the Comanches in this area. Nowhere did she find mention of the location of Little Sparrow's resting place. The question was, what was the real reason Wes and Turtle were conspiring against her? What hidden truths were their lies covering up?

And what if she was wrong?

She closed her eyes and thought of the dream she'd had, of Wolf Shadow crying beside Little Sparrow's grave.

God, what if she was wrong?

There was no convincing Turtle to leave his morbid vigil. Wes tried everything from pleading with him to screaming at him, but nothing helped. At least he'd convinced his friend to eat something. He'd bagged a rabbit and cooked it over the fire, and Turtle had eaten a healthy portion. He was drinking the water Wes had brought out here, as well. But the fire was pathetic, and there wasn't a hell of a lot of wood to be found in the area, so keeping it any warmer would be impossible. He draped blankets over Turtle's shoulders and walked off through the rocks in search of more fuel. He'd been talking until he was hoarse, all day, trying to get Turtle to give in, but to no avail. It would be dark soon. The old man would freeze without a decent fire to keep him warm. And Wes wasn't willing to let that happen.

He was furious with Taylor. Wanted to shake her until she understood that this was for real. But every time his anger reached the boiling point, he reminded himself that her skepticism was his own fault. He'd courted her trust, and then broken it. Even knowing how much it galled her to be lied to. And she was right. She had told him things in confidence. Only to find out he'd been lying through his teeth all along. Could he really blame her?

He spotted some rotting branches that had fallen from a scrawny, sickly tree that had somehow grown here among the rocks, and he bent to begin picking them up, one by one. One branch seemed anchored in the ground beneath a huge boulder, and Wes yanked hard on it to pull it free. When it came, a shower of pebbles and dirt tumbled free with it, and Wes saw the concave shape that had been painstakingly chiseled into the rock, then covered over with smaller stones.

He went still. There was something in there. Something… Wes reached his hand into the opening and touched it. And the shape was smooth and cool against his fingers. He drew the item out, and saw it. The turquoise heart Turtle had described. With the figure of a sparrow etched into its blue-green face.

His heart beat faster as the stone seemed to warm in his hand. Wes quickly replaced it where it had been before, and shoved the pebbles in around it to hide it again. My God, this was the place. This was where Little Sparrow had been buried, and where her lover had sat for days mourning her. This was the spot no white man was ever to defile.

And here he was, invading it.

A sound made him whirl almost guiltily, and Wes glimpsed a man standing in the distance. For a second he thought he was looking into a mirror. But that would only have been right if he'd braided an eagle's feather into his hair, and wore buckskins instead of blue jeans. Aside from that, though, the image was his own. Standing about a hundred yards away, just staring at him, with eyes that looked haunted and unspeakably sad.

Wes blinked, rubbed his eyes and looked again. But this time there was nothing there.

"It's the desert," he muttered. "Been hotter than hell all day, and I probably didn't drink enough. Mirage. That's all."

Again he checked to be sure he'd concealed the treasure he'd found. And then he gathered up the wood he'd dropped, and returned to Turtle.

He could wait this thing out, hope Taylor never found the pendant. She'd pack up and leave, and when she did, Turtle would quit with this death watch he was on. She'd leave. She'd walk away believing he'd lied to her again. Believing he'd used her deepest feelings against her.

Or he could show her what he'd found. It would prove he'd been on the level and maybe give him another chance with her, which was what he wanted more than anything in the world. And if she knew it were true, she'd do the right thing.

Wouldn't she?

Could he risk that she might not?

He thought about the look in the apparition's eyes. Thought about the heartbreaking story Turtle had told him. And wondered just what in hell was the right thing to do.

Taylor waited until everyone was asleep to pull on her parka and hoist the heavy pack onto her back. Wes's horse was grazing contentedly where she'd picketed him, near the pond, but she'd have to see to it he got back to the ranch tomorrow. She'd kind of figured Wes would come back for him today, but he hadn't. And more and more, doubts were creeping into her mind.

She couldn't rest. Not until she just checked in. Just in case she was wrong, she had to make sure that old man was still all right. No dig was worth him losing his life over, even if she did think his story was just another ploy to get rid of her.

When Wes kissed her...God, he kissed her as if he meant it. It had felt as if...as if it were right somehow, being with him, being cradled in his arms. How could he kiss her like that just as a prelude to setting her up for his best scam yet? How could it feel so genuine if it were nothing more than a small part of a very big lie?

As much as she wanted to forget that kiss, she couldn't stop replaying it in her mind. Living it again. Feeling his hands in her hair and his mouth on hers.

She walked into the desert, under the moon, leaving the horse behind because he might make some noise and give her away. And part of her insisted it was just to check on the old man. But she knew deep down that she was really looking for a way to believe. She wanted to believe. Wes had made her want that. And she was probably just setting herself up for one more disappointment. But if there was a chance…if there was a chance…

Sky Dancer is your true name.

She had to see Turtle again, find out what he'd meant by that. She'd said she didn't want to know… and maybe she didn't.

But want to or not, she had to know.

She had to know.

Chapter 11

"You found wood." Turtle spoke softly, stating the obvious while Wes added a couple of branches to the dwindling campfire.

"Yeah."

"And?"

Wes pulled his gaze from the fire long enough to send a startled look Turtle's way. "And nothing. I found wood. We'll need it before the night's out."

Turtle didn't answer, didn't nod in his usual slow-motion manner. He narrowed his eyes instead, probing until Wes had to look away.

"If you'd agree to come back to the trailer, pal, I wouldn't need to be hunting high and low for wood in the first place."

"You don't need to. I've told you to go."

Wes resumed pacing. "If I go, you'll sit here and freeze to death, you stubborn son of a—"

"You saw something. Besides wood," Turtle said.

Wes stopped in midstride, turning slowly to face the old man. Turtle met his gaze and smiled. "It's in your eyes. Don't worry. Wolf Shadow would not object to your being there."

Drawing a breath and letting it out slowly, Wes moved over to where Turtle sat and hunkered down beside him. "You know, sometimes you have me all but convinced you're pulling my leg, and then you turn around and haul some mystical rabbit out of your hat and make me crazy."

"I am Turtle, last shaman of the Emerald Flat Clan. I'm surprised you still doubt me at all."

Wes lowered his head and ran a hand across his face. "Yeah. Well. This latest thing...having me put on that getup and try to scare her off...it wasn't like you."

Turtle lowered his head quickly. "People say desperate times call for desperate measures."

"Still..."

"Would it ease your mind to know I am not certain I was brought here to die?"

Wes frowned. "I don't get it. I thought that was the whole idea...."

Turtle shook his head. "I saw him," he said very softly, watching Wes's face as he said it.

Wes drew a blank. "You saw who?"

"Wolf Shadow."

Tipping his head skyward, Wes rolled his eyes. But despite himself, a shiver ran up his spine. "Don't you think that horse is dead, Turtle?"

"I saw him. He told me to come here and to wait. I assumed it was death I was awaiting, but now I'm not so sure. Perhaps there was some other reason."

"What other reason?" Wes started to get to his feet to resume pacing. Pacing was good. Kept him from thinking about Taylor, and how damned much he wanted her. How much he missed her now that she'd decided to hate his guts. "To drive Wes Brand nuts, maybe? To give the both of us pneumonia?"

"To make Sky Dancer stay here."

He stopped short, his back to Turtle. "Make her stay? Hell, Turtle, this whole scheme of yours has only made her detest the sight of me."

"Not true." Turtle got to his feet and walked slowly toward Wes. "It was my scheme that brought her here."

"Yeah, so I gathered. Maybe it's time you told me why."

Turtle shrugged and turned away. "I promised her grandmother, as she lay dying, that I would see Sky Dancer returned here, and that she take as husband the man her family had chosen."

Wes turned. "You brought her here to marry her off to one of your relatives on the reservation?"

Turtle only looked at him with a slow, turtlelike blink.

Wes felt his jaw go stiff. "The hell you will."

"I must. I gave my word. She is the last descendant of Little Sparrow's family. She's the last chance there will ever be to bring peace to Wolf Shadow's spirit."

"Taylor?" Wes took a second to digest that. Taylor, the woman so afraid to embrace her heritage. Talk about irony. "So you've got some husband all picked out for her, have you?"

Turtle smiled while Wes reminded himself that beating the old coot senseless wouldn't do either of them any good.

"Yes. If I can bring the two together, then I haven't failed after all. It's as much a part of my destiny as protecting the sacred ground where Little Sparrow lies waiting for her spirit's release.''

Wes was simmering. He'd be boiling over soon. All this time, all this scheming, and Turtle had an ulterior motive all along. Damn him. He'd sat still and watched Wes fall head over heels for the woman, while plotting to fix her up with someone else. The rotten, scheming, conniving goat.

''Maybe you'd better tell me who this guy is,'' Wes said. ''So I can kick his ass up front and get it over with.''

Turtle returned to his place and sat down.

''He is pleasing to the eye. Young women seem drawn to him. Besides, it is her destiny. She will agree.'' From somewhere under the blankets around his shoulders, Turtle pulled out some herbs and tossed them into the flames. A soft plume of fragrant smoke puffed out as they ignited, and Turtle used his hand to cup the smoke and pull it toward him, smoothing it over his face and head.

Wes lowered his head. ''You're crazy, you know that? There's no way she'd…'' He brought his head up again, eyes narrowed. ''Has she met this guy yet?''

Turtle sat a bit straighter, eyeing the smoke as if he saw something there. Then he turned to Wes. ''She is out there. You should go to her.''

Wes tilted his head. ''Yeah, I'll just waltz right up to her tent and tell her she's gotta marry some—''

''No,'' Turtle said. And he waved an arm toward the desert. ''Out there.''

''Out there,'' Wes repeated, frowning. Then his heart tripped over itself, and his blood chilled. ''Out *there?*''

* * *

Stupid, stupid, stupid. Taylor thought it would be a simple matter to hike out through the Badlands and spot the cluster of boulders that grew into a rocky hill. Problem was, there was more than one rocky hill out here. She hadn't realized. So she'd walked straight to the first one she'd spotted, which, as it turned out, had been the wrong thing to do. Now it was getting dark, and the chill was seeping straight through her clothes. She couldn't see her footprints in the patches of barren ground that stretched between clumps of solid rock, and every cactus looked the same.

She figured she had two choices. Try heading back the way she'd come and hope she didn't veer off track in the darkness, or camp here for the night and make the best of it until dawn. She was truly torn over which choice to make. The confident professional in her thought she could probably find her way. The little girl she seldom acknowledged was afraid of getting lost in the wasteland. But there was another part of her, a new part, telling her that spending the night out here would be okay. Her ancestors had lived here. They'd survived. It might even be exciting.

Okay, then. She'd stay. Spend the night right here in the wilderness, under the stars, no one for company but herself. And maybe…her past.

She closed her eyes, battling a shiver of unease and shaking her thoughts away. If she were staying, she'd need to do some things. She remembered Wes building the fire at the campsite, showing her the old way of stacking the wood, and using two flint rocks to spark the kindling to life. Could she do it? She didn't have a match or a lighter on her, so she supposed she had no choice but to try.

Hoisting her pack higher on her shoulder, Taylor

walked higher up into the shelter of the rocks, looking around for a perfect spot. She found it in a half circle of boulders that stood like guardians, keeping out the wind. Good. She shrugged free of her backpack and dropped it to the ground. Something moved where it landed, and she shuddered as a snake uncoiled and slithered away, disappearing beneath a nearby boulder. Too nearby. She took her pack to the farthest point from where the slimy thing had vanished, scanned the ground warily and dropped the pack again. Now, for the fire.

She looked at the barren, rocky ground with a sinking sensation in her belly. Where was she going to find kindling or wood out here?

She supposed she could get by without a fire at all. She had a warm coat, and blankets in her pack. She'd intended them for the old man. As she thought of him a finger of guilt wriggled up the back of her neck. Damn. She hoped he was all right. But Wes was with him, right? Wes wouldn't go off and leave him alone if he really were waiting to die out there. Not that she believed any of that, but…

A coyote's heartbroken wail drifted from somewhere nearby, and she bit her lip. Maybe it wasn't a coyote. Maybe it was a wolf. Blankets or no blankets, she wanted a fire. To keep the critters at bay.

She started off, keeping careful track of where she was going and looking behind her often so she could find her way back. It wasn't pitch-dark. The moonlight made for great illumination, but it never hurt to be cautious. She wouldn't wander far. If she could find some wood nearby, great. If not…

Sky Dancer…

She came to a dead stop, bringing her head up

sharply. What the hell was that? Her eyes scanned the moonlit rock formations as her heart accelerated. It had sounded as if someone had whispered that name the old man had given her.

No. It had to be the wind. And her own suddenly active imagination. Nothing more.

Sky Dancer…here…

The coyote—or wolf—yipped brokenly and then settled into a warbling howl. His relatives decided to join in. Taylor was beginning to feel as if she were playing an extra in some old black-and-white werewolf flick. Or was this Wes, up to his old tricks again?

She caught a flicker of movement, higher on the hill. And for just a moment the moon seemed to illuminate a form. Delicate and feminine, wearing a doeskin dress, bleached nearly white, with fringe dancing in the breeze just as her long hair was doing.

Taylor's heart flipped over. She'd seen this woman before. But… She lunged closer. But the form was gone.

Wes. Now he'd employed some female assistance for his ridiculous mind games. She clenched her fists at her sides and stomped forward. "Damn you, Wes Brand, when I get my hands on you I'll—"

Soft laughter filled her ears…or maybe it was her mind. And she realized she'd never told Wes about having seen the woman. He didn't know. So how could it have been part of his plan? She stilled again, straining to hear, but the sound faded until it became part of the wind whispering through the branches of a gnarled and twisted tree.

A tree. And a couple of others just beyond it. That meant wood.

Taylor rubbed her arms and looked around her as

she walked on. And when she reached the small copse of stunted trees, she noticed an elongated rock formation that was nearly white. It stood upright and had a shape that from a distance, she supposed, might look like a person.

Yeah. A person with hair and a fringed dress. And a whispery soft voice. "You're losing it, Taylor."

She sighed. She really didn't want to believe Wes was still trying to frighten her with ghostly visitations, but she didn't want to think she was imagining things, either. The third possibility didn't even bear consideration.

It was Wes. It had to be. He was such a jerk.

She strode ahead and found a treasure trove of broken limbs and piles of tiny twigs and dried leaves for kindling. She carried these back to her spot, and made several more trips, until she had a nice-looking supply of firewood for the night.

The canine chorus was getting more raucous by the minute. Sounded as if they were working themselves up for a night of hell-raising, to her. She just hoped she wasn't on their list of things to do, under the appetizer category.

She bent over her pile of twigs and leaves, gathering bunches of them into her hands and piling them carefully in the center of the spot she'd chosen for her fire. Then she added larger twigs, leaning them against one another tepee style with the kindling beneath them. She left room enough for her hands on one side. Then, kneeling beside her creation, she took the flint from her pocket. And against her will, she remembered watching Wes as he used the stones with so much skill. Remembered his hands touching hers in a deliberate caress as he gave them to her. And the way the firelight had painted his face and danced in his eyes.

She closed her eyes and licked her lips. This was no way to get over the lying sneak. Just light the damned fire, she told herself. She struck the stones together once, twice, again. The third time produced a spark. Okay, good. She struck them again, and this time the spark caught one tiny edge of a dried leaf. A red glow ate into the leaf, and she bent closer, blowing gently, until a thread of smoke rose from the pile. Then a single tongue of flame licked to life, and it caught at the kindling. Taylor sat back on her heels, smiling as she watched the fire grow. It was slow, but steady, and soon the twigs were burning with loud snapping sounds and an aroma so sweet she could almost taste it.

She went to her woodpile for some large pieces, bending to grab what looked like the perfect limb—and then she froze in place, arm still extended, as the rattling sound pierced her nerves like a blade. Moving only her eyes, Taylor looked around her. The snake was coiled very close to where her hand still hovered, its tail vibrating. Her heart stilled, and she held her breath. It was within striking distance of her hand and maybe her forearm. She knew enough about rattlers to know that she would never make it back to camp if it bit her. But if she pulled her hand back quickly enough, it might miss. Might not even strike at all. If she could just jerk her arm out of reach, she might be okay. All right, then. On three. One…two…th—

"Don't move, Taylor."

Wes. Her breath rushed out of her, and her hands began to shake. "Jesus, what took you so long?"

"Stay still. Stay perfectly still."

She didn't look toward him, didn't answer him again. She heard a soft hiss, something against leather, she thought. Then before she could draw another breath, something flashed in her peripheral vision, and then thudded into the woodpile. The rattling stopped abruptly. Still frozen in place, she looked toward the snake again. It lay still, its head cleanly severed. A large silvery knife stood embedded in the branch she'd been reaching for, its handle still quivering from the impact.

"You can move now."

"Speak for yourself."

Wes's hands closed on her shoulders, and he turned her around, pulled her close as her body lost its fear-induced stiffness and went limp instead. He held her hard, and she let him, for the moment. It felt too damned good to object. "You okay?"

"Yeah." She hated to do it, but she pulled herself out of his incredible embrace and stood facing him.

"Nice fire," he said.

She glanced at the fire, then at the woodpile. Damned if she was going to stick her hands in that direction again. Wes seemed to read her thoughts, though, and he picked up a few larger branches to add to the flames. Then he settled himself down on the ground as if he planned to stay and visit awhile.

"So what are you doing out here," she asked him. "Shouldn't you be with your partner?"

Wes looked up, no doubt hearing the sarcasm in her tone. "What, you're not gonna thank me?" She glared. He shrugged. "Turtle said you were out here somewhere and sent me after you. Good thing, too." And he nodded toward the decapitated reptile.

Taylor shuddered. "Could you get rid of that thing?"

"Could," he said. "Depends on how hungry you are. Rattlesnake tastes—"

"Just like chicken?"

Wes grinned at her, and she caught herself smiling back for a second. She sighed heavily and looked away. Damn, why did he have to turn out to be a liar? It could have been something special with him.

Wes got up, pulled his blade from the log and used it to lift the snake's remains and toss them out into the darkness. "Waste of a perfect dinner if you ask me." He wiped the blade on some of her dry leaves and then replaced it in his boot.

"I'd rather go hungry," she said. "But since I have plenty of food with me, I won't have to."

"Oh, yeah?" Without asking permission, he bent to unzip her pack, and began pulling out the contents. "I guess you do have supplies here. Food. Water. Blankets." He glanced her way, waiting for an explanation, she guessed. She only shrugged and looked away.

"Looks like you were either planning a little camping trip…or bringing this stuff out to Turtle and me."

She rolled her eyes. "Turtle," she said. "You could sit there and starve for all I care."

"I knew you were just a softy under all that ice, Doc. You were worried about us. Admit it."

"I was worried about the old man," she said.

"So you thought you might have been wrong when you called him a liar?"

"I never called him—"

"Did so. Maybe not in so many words, but that's what it amounted to." Wes spread one of the blankets on the ground in front of the fire, sat down on it and patted the spot beside him. She hesitated. ''Hey, I'm not gonna bite you. Besides, I want you close by in case another snake comes along.''

Taylor betrayed herself by quickly scanning the ground around her feet.

''Or a scorpion. Nasty little buggers, you know.''

''You just never get tired of trying to scare me, do you?'' But she did sit down beside him. And then she wished she hadn't. Being close to him was no good for her. Made her want to be closer.

''Taylor.''

She turned to look up at him, and that damned firelight was making his eyes shine like before. He must know how good he looked in firelight, she figured.

''I'm sorry. No, don't look like that. I mean it.'' He pushed one hand through his hair, and she noticed that it was loose. He hadn't tied it back. ''I don't know how the hell I let Turtle talk me into going along with that damned plan, but I did. He's…he's important to me. When you care about somebody, well, it's awful easy to screw up.''

She sighed and looked away. Looking into his eyes was too much.

''Like I screwed up with you,'' he said softly. ''If I could take it back, Doc, I would.''

Without looking at him, she said, ''Then what was tonight all about?''

''Tonight?'' He shrugged. ''I guess I thought if you saw how serious Turtle was about all this, you'd understand why I—''

''No, not Turtle and his deathwatch and his stories. I'm talking about tonight, here. That little act out on the bluff.'' She turned to look at him and saw nothing but confusion in his eyes.

"I don't know what you're talking about," he said.

She sighed in disgust. "Sure, you don't."

"Taylor, I just got here. I left Turtle two hours ago, hiked back to the site and then followed what was left of your trail from there." He searched her face. "Did something happen, Doc?"

She closed her eyes, shook her head.

"Stupid question," he said. "If nothing happened, you wouldn't be asking me about it, would you?"

She shrugged. "I saw something. Or I thought I did. Hell, Wes, it was either you and your head games or my own imagination, and at this point I'm not even sure how I'd know."

His hand touched her hair, stroked it away from her face. "I did a number on you, didn't I? Doc, I swear, whatever you saw, I wasn't involved. You're getting nothing but the truth from me, from here on. I promise."

She lifted her head, his hand still lingering in her hair, and met his eyes. "I'd really like to believe that."

"What can I do to convince you?"

Her breath came out in a slow sigh. "Nothing, Wes. Not unless you can take away all the lies I've ever been told. All the times I trusted when I shouldn't have."

"No," he said. "There's a way. And I'm gonna find it, Doc. I messed this thing up and I'm damned well gonna fix it."

The coyotes wailed, sounding closer than before, and Taylor stiffened.

"You want to go back to camp?"

She shook her head. "I want to spend the night here, like my ancestors did." She saw his eyes widen in surprise. "I'm thinking...maybe...it's time."

He smiled slowly. ‘‘I’m staying with you, then.’’

‘‘I didn’t mean—’’

‘‘I know. I didn’t, either.’’ His thumb stroked a slow circle on her cheek, and then his hand fell away. ‘‘I’m just here for the snakes.’’

‘‘And the scorpions,’’ she said, and she felt lighter than she had before. The confusion, the emptiness she’d always felt inside her, seemed to melt away tonight, under the stars. And she had a feeling being with this man might have a lot to do with it.

‘‘Turtle...he told me some things after you left. Things you maybe ought to know.’’

He was asking permission, she realized. She reached for her pack and the food she’d brought along, dragging it closer, taking out the packets of dehydrated meals. ‘‘You can tell me over dinner. I brought enough for two.’’

‘‘Even though you were only worried about Turtle, and I could starve for all you cared?’’ There was a gleam of mischief in his eyes.

‘‘Hey, you can always go after that perfectly good rattlesnake you threw away.’’

He made a face. ‘‘I never was much for chicken.’’

They ate, and Wes told her everything Turtle had said to him. About her famous ancestor, Little Sparrow, and about her being the last blood relative of her line. And finally about Turtle’s belief that she should marry one of Wolf Shadow’s descendants to free the spirits of the star-crossed lovers.

She took it all pretty well, he thought. Though she seemed to lose her appetite about halfway through his account. When he finished, she was quiet for a long time. And then she said, ‘‘Turtle...said he made this promise to see that I came back here and fulfilled what he calls...my destiny?''

''Yeah, that's what he said. And for what it's worth, I believe him. I know him pretty well, Taylor. And I can't think of any reason for him to make all this up.''

''But you said he was the one who put you up to scaring me off. It doesn't make sense.''

Wes nodded, and hoped he hadn't just blown any chance he had of regaining her trust in him. ''I know. I asked him the same thing. Seems while he saw it as his mission in life to get you back here, he also made a vow to keep Little Sparrow's resting place undisturbed until her spirit is free again. I guess getting you here was fine, but having you digging on that particular spot wasn't. He was hoping to convince you the legend was real, and that the site was there, without you actually having to find it. He wants you to tell the elders the spot is here, so they won't sell.''

''I can't do that,'' she said. ''It would be dishonest, if I didn't know for sure. And, Wes, those people need the money they'll get from this sale.''

''I know,'' he said. And the guilt loomed up in him. Maybe he should just tell her where the site was. But what would that do to Turtle?

Staring into the flames, she nodded slowly. ''I suppose his thinking makes some kind of sense.''

''To Turtle, it does.''

She turned her face to his, and Wes found himself marveling again at the depth of her dark lashes, the intelligence in her black eyes. ''Who did he make this promise to? The one about me, I mean.''

Wes drew a breath. ''You sure you want to hear all this?''

She nodded.

"Okay. He said he promised your grandmother. Said he knew her, was with your mother when you were born."

She blinked several times, but that was her only reaction. "He knew my birth mother." Then she lowered her head. "The woman who gave me up."

"The woman who gave you life, Taylor. And she didn't give you up. She was sick, dying. And she knew it. She did everything she could to find a loving home for you. A good home. And hell, Taylor, back then times were pretty bleak for the Comanches on the reservation. So she sent you away from all that. She wanted you to have everything. But your grandmother made Turtle promise to see to it you came back someday. She wanted you to know where you came from, get in touch with your roots."

Taylor searched his eyes, and hers were narrow, and unless it was a trick of the firelight, slightly damp. "Turtle told you all that?"

"Yeah. He did." He wanted to pull her into his arms and kiss her pain away, because he could see how much she was hurting. He hated seeing her hurt. "But that's about all he told me. Doc, if you want to know about your family, I imagine Turtle could tell you just about everything there is to know."

She sniffed, averting her face. "All this time I thought she just didn't want me. I thought she just gave me away. And I blamed her...."

"For what, Taylor?"

She shook her head, bit her lip.

"Come on, talk to me. Don't you think all this baggage has been weighing you down long enough? Unload it, Doc. Dump it right here." He patted his shoulder. "Right here."

She looked at his shoulders, then looked away. ''It was tough, you know? I went to a small school. Not another Native American in the place. And the kids—hell, Wes, you know how kids can be—they started making remarks about my red-haired dad and my blond, blue-eyed mother. Saying I must've been left by Gypsies and garbage like that.''

He could feel her pain, hear it in her voice. It wasn't a grown-up kind of hurt; he knew that. It was the pain of a little girl, confused and lied to. She looked up at him, eyes huge and glittering. ''I loved my parents. Trusted them. So I believed them.'' She lowered her head and shook it slowly.

Wes sighed. Damn. It was still with her, the memory of that hurt. As fresh as if it were yesterday, he could tell. ''It must have torn you apart,'' he said, and he stroked her hair again. Seemed he couldn't get enough of its silky texture sliding across his palm, around his fingers.

''It wasn't the knowledge that I was adopted,'' she said. ''It was the betrayal. It was suddenly knowing the two people I'd trusted most in the world had lied to me, for all of my life. And I think I blamed my birth mother, in a way. I think that's when I decided I'd never want any part of my heritage.''

''That's not surprising.''

''It's screwed up a lot of friendships, this thing I have about trust. Every time I get close to anyone, it gets in the way. Either I think they're lying when they aren't, or I catch them in some harmless fib and over-react.'' She met his gaze head-on. ''Or I actually start to trust them, and they...''

''They let you down,'' he said. ''God, I'm sorry, Taylor. I'm so sorry.''

"You can stop apologizing," she said. "I believe you."

Wes's heart leapt. "You believe me?"

And her gaze went wary. "I believe you're sorry. I don't know what else might happen, Wes, but I don't want you to spend every minute apologizing to me."

"I'd apologize till hell froze over if it would help."

She drew a breath, licked her lips. "I want to get past this," she said. "I want to trust you again, Wes. I really do. I just…"

"Just…?"

She closed her eyes. "Just don't know if I can."

"Ah, Taylor…"

Her eyes opened and met his, and maybe she saw him thinking about kissing her. Maybe she noticed the way his gaze kept dipping down to her lips, caressing them, tasting them in his mind. Because she stiffened her shoulders and moved a bit farther away from him. She stretched out on the blanket he'd put on the ground, pulling her backpack under her head for a pillow. "I don't want to think about my problems or your shenanigans any more tonight, okay?"

"Okay. We'll talk about something else. Anything you want."

Her eyes were closed. Wes got up and grabbed the second blanket, still folded on the ground. He shook it out, and spread it over her, and when he did, she hunched up her shoulders like a cat when you pet it just right. She looked relaxed, more relaxed than he'd seen her. And beautiful. Her hair spread like a black pool around her, and all he could do was stand there and stare, and think if he couldn't get her back, he'd never get over it. He'd see her like this every night, in his dreams, for as long as he lived.

"Tell me about your ranch," she said.

"The Texas Brand?"

She shook her head slightly, not opening her eyes. "No. *Your* ranch. The one you're buying."

"Ah, that one. Well, fact is, I bought it."

Her eyes popped open. "You did?"

"Yeah. The bids were opened today, and I won. Not that I imagine there was much competition. The loan from the bank will be enough to get started on the renovations, too."

"Barn first," she reminded him.

"Barn first," he said with a nod. "I've already ordered the supplies. I'll be able to start work any day now."

She smiled. Lips curving seductively upward, laugh lines deepening at the corners of her eyes. "It's going to be something."

"Sure is."

"What are you going to call it? Texas Brand Two?"

Wes rubbed his chin with one hand. "No. Actually it deserves a name as beautiful as the land that it's a part of, don't you think?"

"You have something in mind?"

Her voice was getting sleepy. Slower and thicker. Sexy as hell. "Yeah. I think I'm gonna call it Sky Dancer Ranch."

Her eyes opened suddenly. They met his, held them, but she didn't speak.

"Turtle says it is your real name. The name your birth mother gave you."

"I didn't realize...."

"There's a lot you don't realize just yet, Sky Dancer. A whole lot." He reached out, closed his hand around hers and just sat beside her, feeling its smallness, its warmth. Then Taylor opened her hand to lace her fingers with his, and she squeezed.

She fell asleep that way, while Wes sat there, looking at her, aching clear to his bones and hoping to God there was still a chance for him.

Chapter 12

A snuffling sound woke her. She had no idea how long she'd been lying there, sound asleep. Wes lay beside her, very close beside her. And beneath her. She'd cuddled closer in her sleep, so her head rested on his shoulder and his arm curled around hers. He was warm, and he smelled good. Wood smoke clung to his skin, but there was something more. His shoulder was bare beneath her face. And if she moved slightly, she could taste his skin on her lips. For a long moment she lay there debating the wisdom of doing just that.

She still wanted him. Whatever else happened, she thought she probably always would.

Then that snuffling sound came again, and she went a little stiff, and turned her head slowly. The fire had died to mere embers. And an animal was pawing at her backpack, no more than a yard from where she lay. Sniffing and pawing. Its head halfway inside the thing. It looked like an underfed dog, but she knew better.

Wes's arm tightened around her. The moonlight had fled now. It must be nearly dawn.

Moving slowly, Wes turned until his lips brushed her ear, and whispered, "No sudden moves, okay?"

She nodded once. And Wes pulled his arm from beneath her and sat up slowly. The animal yanked its head from the backpack and looked at him. Wes sat perfectly still and looked back.

It seemed like a standoff.

Taylor lay still, shivering under the blanket, though not from the cold. "Coyote?" she whispered.

And Wes gave his head a nearly imperceptible shake, side to side. No. Not a coyote, then. So that left…

"Wolf?" Her voice was a squeak, and the animal's ears pricked forward.

Wes kept his gaze focused on the wolf's eyes. Held them hard, even when the animal bared its teeth in a snarl and the fur on its back seemed to bristle upward. It lowered its head and shoulders slightly, as if in preparation to spring on them, and emitted a low and endless growl.

Wes didn't move. He just sat there, staring. Taylor wanted to tell him to get that damned knife out of his boot and make use of it. But she didn't dare to speak, and doubted she'd manage more than a meaningless grunt if she tried. Her throat seemed to swell shut with fear. She could barely breathe, let alone speak.

Very slowly Wes got to his feet. How he managed it in such slow motion was beyond her, but he did. Inch by inch he straightened until it seemed he towered above her from her vantage point, flat on her back. Then he moved forward, stepping over her, first with one leg, and then the other. So that he stood between

Taylor and the wolf. And all the while he never broke eye contact.

The growling stopped. Peering around Wes's legs, she could still see the wolf. Its snarl died, and its head tipped upward as it stared into Wes's eyes. It spent a long moment like that. Neither moving, nor making a sound. And then suddenly the wolf simply spun around and ran away into the darkness. Taylor glimpsed its upturned tail as it bounded away, and then nothing more.

She lay still, shaking her head slowly. "What did you just do?"

When Wes sat down again, he did it suddenly. As if his muscles had just decided to go limp. Taylor pulled herself into a sitting position, getting in front of him so she could see his face. His eyes were closed, and he sighed heavily.

"Wes?"

He looked at her, shook his head. "I don't know, exactly. It's something Turtle taught me. Damn, I'm glad it worked."

"Glad…what worked?"

In something like wonder he was looking off in the direction the wolf had taken. "I'd tried it with horses. An eagle once. But hell, I didn't really think it…" Again he shook his head, pushing both hands backward through his hair. "A wolf. Never thought I'd have call to try it with a wolf. Damn."

He was talking more to himself than to her. She reached out, touched his face, just to remind him she was there. It worked. He looked into her eyes, and she could see he was shaken. Maybe more shaken than she was.

"Wes. Tell me what just happened here."

He closed his eyes, opened them again. "I talked to him."

"You talked to him." She frowned and looked at where the animal had been crouching. Then back at Wes. "To the wolf."

He nodded. And he looked dead serious. Taylor battled a shiver, and then forced a smile that had to be shaky at best. "What did you say? 'Please don't eat us'?"

Wes shook his head and looked at the ground. "I sound like a lunatic."

"Not unless the wolf talked back," she said, trying for a light tone, even though she still couldn't stop shaking.

Without looking up he said, "He did."

She threaded her fingers into his hair, tipping his head up again. "Okay. So you're a lunatic. A lunatic who saved my life twice in one night." A little of the tension faded from his face. "You stepped in front of me," she said. "That animal could have—"

He pressed his forefinger to her lips. "I'd step in front of a train for you, Doc. Haven't you figured that out yet?"

He took his finger away from her mouth, staring into her eyes. And then he lowered his head, and put his lips there instead.

It was so right. So perfect. And she didn't care that he'd lied to her, or that he talked to wolves. It didn't matter. All that mattered was this. Touching him. Kissing him. Wanting him with everything in her.

She slipped her arms around his shoulders. His crept tighter around her waist. When his lips nudged hers apart, she shivered, and when his tongue slid over hers, her heart seemed to melt. She was in his arms, and it was where she wanted to be. Where she'd wanted to be for some time now. And she held him close to her as she lay down, so that he came with her, his body covering hers. When he moved his hips, she felt his hardness pressing into her, and when he took his mouth away, he whispered, "Tell me to stop, Taylor."

He stared down into her eyes, and his were on fire. Black fire. Raven Eyes. It didn't have to mean forever. He knew she wasn't ready for that. He wouldn't expect anything. Just this…just tonight.

She ran her palms over his chest. And then she said, "Make love to me, Wes."

His jaw went tight. He closed his eyes. And then he kissed her again. Deeply, thoroughly, and the gentleness in his touch grew into something more as he tugged her T-shirt up and put his hands on her breasts. And then he was kissing them, too. Suckling her, groaning deep in his throat. She tipped her head back, closing her eyes and letting him feed at her nipples. Her breathing ragged, she ran her hands over his chest, and his back, and then lower, slipping a hand between his legs and caressing the hardness there. She freed him from his jeans, and touched him. Hot and ridged and hard. She closed her hand around the tip of him, and he shivered. And then he backed away, sitting up, and he reached slowly down to pull her shirt over her head.

She shivered in the cold. Wes took her hands and drew her to her feet. But he remained kneeling down. And then he reached for her pants, unfastening them, sliding them down over her hips, looking at her as he did. She shuddered, but without shyness, stepped out of them. And then he peeled her panties away in the same slow manner, his eyes devouring her. When she kicked the panties aside, he touched her there, and he whispered, "I want to taste you."

Her stomach clenched. He put his hands on her buttocks and drew her closer. And then he pressed his mouth to her, nuzzling her there, pushing her open with his mouth, and then tasting her with his tongue.

Fire shot through her body, and her knees trembled and then buckled. She fell to the ground, but he followed, parting her legs with his hands, and burying his face between them. Stroking deeper with his tongue until she clasped his head and moaned softly in the night.

He kissed a path up her body, putting his hand where his mouth had been seconds ago, stroking up inside her, making her shudder and cry. And then he pressed himself into her, and she felt filled, not just physically, but spiritually. When he sank himself all the way into her body, she arched her hips to take him. And he wrapped her up tight in his arms and kissed her again as he moved. She knew it had never been like this for her before, and never would be again. She moved with him, arching against him, holding him with every part of her. And when she climaxed, he did, too. And it felt as if their souls were fused together in this fire. As if they'd never be able to exist again on their own.

Wes lay beside her, holding her close, as the sun rose over the desert. A ball of fire. Every sunrise here was a spectacular light show. Wes wondered if the sunrises would be visible from his ranch. He thought so. What an incredible way to wake up each morning.

If she were there beside him.

Without Taylor's face, bathed in the fiery glow of dawn, the sunrises would lose their appeal.

He was in love with her.

The thought of losing her, of spending his life without her, became nightmarish to him then. And without warning, he thought of his brother Ben, and he nearly choked on the sudden tightness in his throat. Ben still mourned his wife, Penny. Every day he must think of her. Every morning he must wake up alone and remember waking with her in his arms. And the urge to hug his oversize brother hit Wes almost as powerfully as the urge to stay where he was, with Taylor snuggled close to him.

Then she sat up, and pulled the blanket over her, a little self-consciously. She looked nervous. Sated, but scared.

''It's okay,'' he told her, reaching up to stroke her hair. ''I know it didn't mean anything.''

And she lowered her head. ''It meant something, Wes. It just didn't mean…everything.''

He understood. He'd won her body, and even her affection. But not her trust, and not her heart. Not yet. ''There's one thing you might not know about me, lady,'' he said with a smile.

''You mean besides the fact that you double as Dr. Doolittle and talk to animals?'' She smiled back, seemingly relieved that he wasn't asking for promises, that he was taking last night for what it was and nothing more.

''That I thrive on challenges,'' he told her.

''But you're wrong,'' she said. ''I'd already figured that out. I knew it the second you showed me that ranch of yours.''

''You calling my new place a challenge?''

She shrugged. Wes sat up and sighed. ''Better than my kid sister. She called it a dump.''

The sun rose higher, and their smiles died as he got lost in her eyes. And before he slipped and said something stupid way too soon, scaring her off for good, Wes tore his gaze away. "We ought to get back. Your kids will be worried sick. Scourge might even decide to play hero and go wandering into the desert looking for you. I don't have time to hunt for hairballs."

"He wouldn't do that," she said. "He's too smart."

"He has a crush on you," Wes said. "Bad enough I have to compete with whatever Comanche stud Turtle has picked out for you. I have to contend with a Don Juan with peach fuzz to boot."

"Don't forget about my ghostly admirer," she said. "I really kind of like him." Her eyes were filled with mischief.

He chucked her under the chin. "He really kind of likes you, too," he said. "Damned if I ever thought I'd be jealous of myself."

She laughed softly. "Serves you right."

"You're right, it does."

He liked this. This easiness that had returned between them. And it was more than it had been before. Deeper. She seemed comfortable with him, relaxed. As for him, well, he was falling harder with every smart-ass quip she tossed his way. The guarded, solitary scientist had melted away. The woman underneath was so irresistible he could barely keep his hands off her.

"Better get dressed," he said. "Search party could show up any time." He got up, buck naked, and walked around picking up her clothes, which had somehow ended up scattered hither and yon. Then he brought them to her, and saw her eyes devouring him. He swallowed hard.

"Take away the clothes," she said, "And there's

really no difference between Wes Brand and Wolf Shadow.''

''Just a few hundred years is all. Or am I sagging more than I realized?'' He pulled on his jeans.

She didn't return his grin this time. Instead her eyes narrowed. ''Wes, will you tell me something?''

''Anything. I told you, nothing but honesty from now on.''

She nodded, and he thought maybe she was about to put his vow to the test. ''What did that wolf say to you last night?''

He blinked. Then drew a deep breath, lifting his head, and bringing his gaze level with hers again. ''He...uh...he called me 'brother.'''

Biting her lower lip, she nodded slowly.

''Am I going to regret being honest, Doc? You going to recommend I talk to a shrink now?''

''No, Wes. Not when I...''

''Not when you what?''

She shook her head. ''It'll sound foolish.''

''More foolish than talking to wolves? C'mon, Taylor, this honesty thing has to work both ways.''

She met his eyes, nodded hard. ''You're right. It does.'' She lifted her chin. ''I think I saw...Little Sparrow last night.'' She turned then, and pulled on her shirt, maybe to avoid his eyes.

''That's what you were talking about when I first got here.''

She nodded and picked up her khaki trousers.

''And you thought it was me? What, in drag?''

Pulling the pants up to her hips, she stood and tucked her shirt in, then fastened them up. ''No. I guess I thought you'd drafted another conspirator. But I shouldn't have, because...''

"Because?"

Dropping her hands to her sides, she faced him. "Because it wasn't the first time. I saw her once before, just prior to coming down here for this dig." She frowned hard. "Wes, it was like looking into a mirror. Only, translucent. And then she just faded like mist."

He thought then that he should tell her about his own encounter with someone he thought might have been Wolf Shadow. The real one, not his own little interpretation of the role. But then he thought better of it. Honesty was fine, but she didn't trust him yet. And if he blurted this out, she might chalk it up to yet another trick on his part. He'd tell her, yes. But not just yet.

It was like looking into a mirror.

Her words rang in his ears. He'd had the same eerie sensation at the single glimpse he'd had of…whatever he'd seen last night.

"I think," she said, "that you should talk to Turtle about this wolf thing."

"I was thinking the same thing." He finished dressing himself, and began shaking out and folding the blankets, stuffing them into her pack, slinging it over his own shoulder when it was filled. He took a long drink from the canteen and then handed it to her. "I'll take you back to camp, and then I'll head out to check on him. I don't like him out there alone, especially with a pack of wolves so nearby."

"It was only one wolf," she reminded him. "Besides, Wes, if you can talk a wolf out of attacking, old Turtle can probably make him roll over and play dead. He's a shaman after all. Shamans are known for their animal broth—" She bit her lip and met his eyes, her own widening.

"Animal brothers." Wes finished her sentence for

her. And he didn't blame her for the wide-eyed look. He was feeling pretty wide-eyed himself. He didn't know what all this meant, and frankly he wasn't sure he wanted to know. It was scaring the hell out of him. Almost as much as his feelings for Taylor were doing.

Chapter 13

Wes walked Taylor back to the camp, received a scathing glance from Scourge and grinned at the kid in return. He borrowed a few supplies from the site, stuffing them into Taylor's backpack. Then he turned to the woman he'd made up his mind was going to be his own. "I'll be back later on."

She nodded. "Go on, go see about Turtle. I'm as worried about him as you are."

Impulsively Wes swayed forward and brushed her lips with his. Then he turned toward where Taylor had his horse anchored for the night and climbed aboard. "I know you hate my guts for this, Paint. We'll head home for your morning oats soon, I promise."

Paint shook his mane and nickered as Wes untied him, slipped his bridle in place and then mounted. He glanced back at Taylor once as he headed back into the desert. She was speaking rapidly to the kids, gesturing, her face firm. Not defending that kiss, he hoped.

More likely telling them to mind their own business. And he smiled.

As if she felt his eyes on her, she turned, and met his gaze. And for a long moment they remained that way. Just looking at one another. Wes could feel something moving between them. From her eyes to his and then back again, like a current gaining amps with every circuit. He touched the brim of his hat, and rode away, though it was the last thing in the world he wanted to do.

But she needed time. And he needed Turtle. Because something very strange was happening, and he needed to talk it through.

He found his mentor still sitting in the same spot near the fire. He must have moved once or twice, because the fire hadn't dwindled. He'd tossed logs on, then. But to look at him, you wouldn't have thought so. He was like a wooden sculpture, sitting cross-legged on the ground with the woven blanket draped over his shoulders. If his voice—slightly hoarse now—hadn't been raised slightly in song, Wes might have been startled to see him sitting so still.

Wes drew Paint to a halt and slid from the smooth white back. And as he did, Turtle stopped chanting and looked up. "You found her," he said.

Wes nodded and turned to the pack he'd slung over the horse's rump, pulled it off, then unbuckled and opened the flap. He pulled out a battered old coffeepot, the canteen full of water and a can with some coffee inside. The items rattled and clanked as he found the two tin cups in the pack, and with his arms loaded, he strode over to the fire. "Taylor's fine. She took it into her head to bring some supplies out here last night, and took a wrong turn. Wound up camping out at No

Man's Bluff.'' Hunkering down, Wes dropped the items on the ground, opened the canteen and filled the coffeepot.

''You stayed with her?''

Wes heard the speculation in Turtle's voice and glanced up sharply. ''Yeah.''

The old man averted his eyes, but Wes thought he'd spotted a twinkle in them first. Couldn't be sure, though. He hadn't expected it. He'd figured Turtle would be angry, if anything, at the idea of Wes spending the night with her. Screwing things up for the prospective bridegroom Turtle had picked out for Taylor.

Odd. Wes poured coffee into the pot's basket, guessing at the amount since he hadn't brought a spoon to measure it. Then he slapped the lid on and settled the pot on a thick forked limb amid the flames.

''Something is on your mind,'' Turtle said. ''Sit down and tell me.''

Wes sat, eyeing Turtle and wondering yet again about the old man's instincts. He always knew what Wes was thinking, or it seemed that way to him. ''Yeah, there is something,'' he said. ''A wolf got into Taylor's camp last night.''

Turtle nodded slowly. ''Only one?''

''Only one.''

''You had a fire?''

''It was burning low, but still burning.'' Wes sighed. ''I tried that thing you taught me. Holding his eyes and speaking to him with my mind.''

''Ah,'' Turtle said.

''And I thought he answered me.''

Turtle's head came up, eyes narrowed on Wes's face. ''He called you brother?'' the old man asked.

Wes frowned hard. ''How could you know that?''

The old face split in a grin of long, straight teeth. "Because it is what the Tortoise called me when he came to me seventy years ago."

Wes grinned. "Sure, he did. We don't have any tortoises in these parts. You're playing with me again, aren't you, pal?"

Turtle shook his head. "It wasn't a tortoise. It was the spirit of the tortoise. I was napping in the sunlight when a shadow fell over my face, and I opened my eyes to see him standing beside me, blinking slowly. And I saw his powerful beak and thought he might snap my hand off if it pleased him."

Wes studied Turtle's face. "You aren't kidding, are you? So is that why they called you Turtle?"

"I was born early, and weak, and wasn't expected to survive. But I lived all the same. So my mother named me for the animal she knew as the survivor, for his hard shell of protection, and for the longevity of the creature."

"I see." But Wes wasn't really sure he did.

"Raven Eyes, do you know that every shaman has a spirit guide? Some have many. Some, only one. The animal spirit presents itself to the shaman in its own time, and often tests his courage. As the spirit tortoise tested mine. As the spirit wolf tested yours."

Wes looked at Turtle sharply. "Hold on a minute. That's all well and good for you, pal, but don't forget, I'm no shaman."

"Nor was I, until the shamanic spirit came to me in the form of the tortoise."

Wes shook his head slowly.

"It was not an ordinary wolf, my friend. He was alone, not in a pack. He didn't fear the fire of your camp. He spoke to you."

"That doesn't mean…"

"Let me tell you a story, Raven Eyes."

Wes opened his mouth to object, then bit his lip. Let Turtle talk. Maybe…maybe some of this would make sense if he listened.

"There was an old shaman living alone, with no descendants and no young man with the spirit shining in his eyes. He knew his time in this world would come to an end soon, but he'd vowed to pass his wisdom along to a young shaman before he died. To give the next generation the traditions to cling to, and keep alive."

Wes stared at the coffeepot as it started to bubble, at the condensation hissing on the outside of the tin.

"The old shaman made a fire, and danced around it, and he called on the old gods, and on the spirit of the tortoise, to bring a young man to him. The one they brought would become his student, and he would teach him the old ways, and make of him a fine and worthy shaman to take his place when this life ended."

"Turtle, listen—"

"The old shaman prayed for this all night, and made powerful medicine, and he knew his student would come to him the next day. But as that day burned low, no young man came. And growing restless, the old shaman drove in his truck for some distance along the road, to see if any stranger seemed to be heading his way. The truck's tire went flat. At first the old man thought he'd made a mistake. That now he would be away from home for too long, and might miss the young man's arrival there. But he soon knew it was the work of the gods. Because the young man came to him there on the road, and fixed his tire for him, and followed him back home."

Wes couldn't do much more than sit there shaking his head in disbelief.

"All I have taught you, Raven Eyes, all the stories I have told you and the ways you have learned, all have been to prepare you for this day. The day when your spirit guide came to you, tested you and accepted you by calling you brother."

Wes rubbed his temples with his forefingers. "I can't believe this."

Turtle shrugged. "It is not so different. But now you can ask the spirits for advice directly. And if you listen, they will guide your steps."

Wes nodded. "Good. First thing I'll ask them is the name of the guy you say is Wolf Shadow's descendant, so I can make sure he never gets within a hundred feet of Taylor."

Turtle smiled. "The spirits might tell you that. Or perhaps they, like me, will decide it is something you must learn for yourself."

Wes lowered his head, gnawed his lip, couldn't decide whether he felt foolish or skeptical or excited. But what if it were true? What if he could get some kind of direct line to…to some higher power? He could find out what he should do with the last secret he was keeping from Taylor. Whether he should tell her he'd found Little Sparrow's resting place.

He cleared his throat. "How…uh…does one go about…asking?"

A gnarled, warm hand fell on his shoulder. "Come to me tonight, my friend."

Wes sighed. "Good. It's just as well. I need some time to digest all this." Then he eyed the rising sun, burning down, scorching already. "But if you sit out here all day again, I doubt you'll be around when I come back tonight. Turtle, you have to—''

Turtle held up a hand, shook his head. ''It's time for me to return home,'' Turtle said. ''My stay here has served its purpose.''

Wes blew a sigh of pure relief. ''Thank God for that. If I had to make the trek out here one more time, I'd have hogtied you and hauled your butt back there.'' He softened his words with a smile. ''So you aren't about to die after all?'' he asked, and if his voice broke just a little with the words, then he supposed it was understandable. He hadn't realized just how afraid he was of losing the old goat, until now, when it seemed he wasn't going to lose him at all.

''Not just yet, at least,'' Turtle said, and he smiled broadly. ''The spirits wouldn't leave so clueless a shaman here to bungle things on his own.''

''So you get to stick around and help me bungle things?''

Turtle got to his feet and blinked a couple times, averting his face. ''I am as proud as if you were my own blood, Raven Eyes.'' He made a show of brushing the dirt from his pants legs, but Wes sensed he was just avoiding looking him in the face.

''Makes sense,'' Wes said. ''It's been a long time since I've been as close to a man as I am to you. Since before my father died.''

Turtle looked up at him, and their eyes met. Uncomfortable, they both looked away at the same time.

Wes shook his head and turned toward the fire. In another second they'd have been hugging or some ridiculous female thing like that. ''Let's have that coffee,'' he said in his most macho voice. ''Then we'll pack up and head back.''

* * *

A young stranger arrived at the camp around noon, handed a letter to Taylor and then left without a word.

Frowning and battling a creepy sense of foreboding, Taylor opened the envelope, extracted the sheet of expensive notepaper and looked it over. Dennis Hawthorne's name gleamed in gold script across the top. There was no greeting.

> I'd like a progress report soon. Don't forget, my funding for this project stops on Sunday. Unless you've found evidence of this alleged sacred site by then, I fully expect you to inform the tribal elders that it doesn't exist so that my purchase of the property can go ahead on schedule.

It was signed with a nearly illegible scribble she thought was supposed to resemble an *H.*

She crumpled the sheet in her hand. "Damn, why do I get the feeling that man is up to no good?"

Scourge approached then, and narrowed his eyes at her. "Ms. McCoy…I…that is, Kelly and I…were wondering…about you and Mr. Brand, that is, if—"

She lifted her head. "Stop wondering." And she turned to go into her tent. And then she sat slowly on the floor, because she was wondering, too. She'd made love to Wes last night, and it had been an experience like nothing she'd ever known. But a physical one. She still got the feeling he wasn't telling her everything. About himself. About this place. About so many things, including his true feelings for her.

How could she love a man she didn't trust? And how could she prevent herself from doing just that? Her heart ached for him every second they spent apart, but her mind constantly rebelled. He'd lied to her, deceived her, might very well still be doing so.

So why did she want to forget all of that and surrender to her heart? Why was it so hard to keep resisting him? And what the hell was she going to do when this dig was over, in a few short days?

Wes talked Taylor into joining him at the house for dinner that night. Of course, when he made the invitation, she'd thought he meant the Texas Brand, with the family. And he'd deliberately let her go on thinking it. But as he drove over the roads leading to the ranch he'd finally made his own, he could see the understanding dawning on her pretty face.

"You do like your practical jokes, don't you?" she asked him, and Wes bit his lip. Had he screwed up yet again?

"It's not a joke, Doc. It's a surprise." Then he lowered his head. "I thought..."

"No." She touched his hand. "I'm being oversensitive again. I'm sorry." She looked through the windshield as the tumbledown house came into view. "It's a nice surprise. I love this place—you know that."

"I'm learning, Taylor. I'll try to keep a handle on the urge to surprise you from now on, okay?"

She closed her eyes slowly and nodded. "Just so long as you know I'm the one with the problem, not you."

"You don't like being surprised. I'm filing it away. I won't forget again." He stopped the vehicle, then reached into the back to pull out a picnic basket before getting out.

Taylor got out on her side and stood for a moment, taking in the view. "My mare is going to love it here."

"My brothers and I have been stringing some fence," Wes told her, and he pointed out beyond the barn. "We've got a good hunk of grazing land secured and ready. Once the barn is done, I can start bringing horses in here."

Taylor squinted, shielding her eyes with one hand. "When have you had the time?"

Wes shrugged. "Four men can get a lot done with a couple of hours here and a couple of hours there."

She nodded. "The stream runs right through the section you fenced in. It's perfect, Wes."

"It's progress," he said. "The only perfect thing on this place right now is you."

She smiled and dipped her head.

"So where do you want to eat? Outside under the sky?"

She shook her head. "I've been eating outside every day," she said. "Why don't we dust off a place in the house? That spot with the bay windows in the back would be perfect."

"You don't mind the cobwebs?"

She rolled her eyes. "I live for cobwebs."

Wes grinned at her and took her hand, hefting the basket in the other and heading up the rickety front steps and across the porch. He set the basket down to unlock the door, and then waited for her to precede him inside.

She made a beeline for the big room with the fabulous view, and cautiously opened a couple of the windows there. Wes set the basket down and looked around. "There's an old table here. We could clean it off a bit and—"

"What would we clean it with?"

He reached into the cupboard beneath a very old

stainless-steel sink and pulled out a pail brimming with cleaning supplies. ‘‘My sister put these together for me and told me to be sure to use them. So far they’ve just been keeping the cupboard company.’’

Taylor smiled and drew closer, looking into the big plastic pail, pawing the contents. Sponges and cloths, window cleaner and oil soap and several other cleansers. Taylor nodded and met his eyes. ‘‘If she gave you a broom, too, then she thought of everything.’’

Wes nodded toward the brand-new broom, dustpan and mop leaning in one corner. ‘‘Jessi *always* thinks of everything. She’s bound and determined I’m going to clean the place up.’’

Taylor tilted her head. ‘‘She does have a point.’’ And she looked around her, and he could see her eyes sparkling. ‘‘You know we could really go to town on this mess tonight.’’

Shaking his head, Wes said, ‘‘I didn’t bring you here to put you to work, Doc.’’

‘‘But it would be fun!’’ She reached to the sink to crank one of the faucets there, but frowned when nothing happened.

‘‘Electricity isn’t turned on yet,’’ he explained. ‘‘I need to double-check the wiring first.’’

She shrugged. ‘‘There’s a hand pump out front, though.’’

He grimaced. Cleaning wasn’t what he’d wanted to spend the night doing with Taylor. But she seemed so animated about it. She snatched the pail right out of his hand and dumped its contents onto one side of the sink. Then she headed outside, leaving him no choice but to follow. ‘‘Okay, just the table, then,’’ he said. ‘‘We clean the old table and then we eat.’’

‘‘Whatever you say.’’ She trotted down the steps,

around the side of the house, set the pail down and began pumping on the handle. There was gurgling, spitting, and finally water rushing from the spout.

Five hours later Wes's hands were beginning to resemble prunes. The big room, which he was now sure would have to be the living room, was all but sparkling, and Taylor was standing in the middle of it looking around and beaming.

"It's even more wonderful than I realized," she said.

"Do you know it's ten o'clock?" he asked.

"You know this room really is in great shape."

Wes looked up at the place where the plaster had fallen from the ceiling, leaving ancient lath visible, and the spot where old cloth-coated wires stuck down with no light fixture attached.

"We could patch that hole in no time flat," Taylor said, and he realized she was looking at him, following his doubtful gaze. And then he realized she'd said *We*.

"And can you just see it when we replace the old wiring and put some fabulous chandelier up there? Nothing too fancy. Maybe one of those wagon-wheel types, you know?"

He frowned, picturing the fixture above his head, and then he nodded. "That would work."

"No carpeting, though. These hardwood floors are fabulous. Just need some sanding and a few coats of varnish. Some throw rugs maybe, here and there, but we wouldn't want to cover up these great floors."

He hadn't even known the place *had* hardwood floors until Taylor had shouted out the news as she mopped. But as she went on, talking about valances instead of curtains on those windows to preserve the view, and the banister on the staircase that curved up out of this room to the second floor, and what kind of furniture would look perfect here, he could see it all very clearly. And he liked what he saw. For the first time he was thinking of this place as a home, instead of just a great place to raise Appaloosas.

And then he realized that it was because she was here. When Taylor was here, with him, the house wasn't a ruin; it was a home. Warm and wonderful, comforting and so serene. Without her, though, it would just be a pile of boards and nails again. A shell. No matter what he did to it, if he rebuilt it to look like a castle, it would still be empty and lifeless.

He needed her.

She looked at him, and he opened his mouth to tell her just that. But before he got a single word out, the front door slammed, and Jessi called, "Wes? You here?"

Smiling, Taylor turned. "In here, Jessi," she called.

Wes sighed and lowered his head, and then Jessi and Ben came in, and Jessi looked around the room and grinned. "Hot damn, this place has some potential after all!"

"Your donation helped," Wes said. Then he nodded to Ben, who was looking around the place and nodding approval. Not smiling, though. Ben rarely smiled anymore. And Wes remembered that desolate feeling that had crept over him when he'd thought about losing Taylor forever, and impulsively hugged his brother.

Ben slapped him on the back, then stood back and blinked at him. "You okay, Wes?"

Feeling foolish, Wes just shook his head, then turned to Jessi. "So what brings you out here this time of night?"

"Lookin' for you, of course," she said. "You

weren't at home, so I checked over at the site, and when I didn't find you there, either, I figured you must be here.''

''Persistent, aren't you?''

Her brows rose at his tone. Then fell again. ''Oh, heck, Wes, we're not...interrupting...anything, are we?''

''Of course not,'' Taylor said. ''We've just been cleaning. It looks great, doesn't it?''

And Jessi tilted her head. ''Well...'great' might not be quite the right word...'' Then she gave her head a shake. ''But I brought you some news that is better than great.'' She looked at Wes a little doubtfully. ''I just hope I didn't...overstep.''

No one could overstep like Wes's baby sister, and he groaned inwardly. ''What did you do?''

She smiled at him. ''First I called the lumberyard to check on those supplies you ordered for the barn. They said they couldn't deliver for three days, but I... *discussed* it with them—''

''You bitched at them,'' Ben clarified. He glanced at Taylor. ''I could hear her yelling clear out in the stable.''

''You're exaggerating,'' Jessi said. ''But anyway, Wes, they'll be delivering the stuff tomorrow.''

Wes couldn't help himself. He chuckled aloud. ''Leave it to Jessi Brand to put the fear of God into a man.'' Then he frowned. ''Still there was no hurry. I won't have time to work on the barn much until...''

''Saturday,'' she said, and she said it firmly.

A little foreboding tiptoed up Wes's spine. ''Why Saturday?''

''Because on Saturday, big brother, we are having a good ol'-fashioned barn raising!'' She clapped her hands together, practically bouncing up and down in excitement.

Wes blinked, then glanced at Ben, who only nodded in agreement. ''A barn raising.'' Then he shook his head, and put one hand on his sister's shoulder. ''Look, Jess, it's a fabulous idea and all, but don't go getting your hopes up. I'm not exactly the most popular guy in town.''

''Don't be silly, Wes.''

''I'm not,'' he told her. ''Look, I may be a Brand, but that doesn't mean people like me. Hell, a lot of 'em still believe that time I did in prison was well deserved.''

''Oh, Wes, that's bull. Everyone knows you were set up. Besides, it's ancient history. And I'll tell you, they might not vote you Mr. Congeniality around here, but there's not one person in the county who wouldn't want you on their side if they were in trouble. And most of 'em know you'd be there if they asked you.''

''No,'' Wes said. ''You're wrong about that. It'll never work, Jess.''

''But it already has worked.'' She smiled again. ''Everyone I've talked to promised to come.''

Wes frowned. ''They did?''

''Mmm-hmm. The women are bringing food enough for an army, and the men are dusting off their tool belts. It's going to be incredible, Wes. And before the weekend is over, that barn of yours won't be a barn at all. It'll be the Taj Mahal of stables.''

Wes looked at Ben, who nodded once more. ''It's true,'' he said. ''She's been like a bumblebee on a caffeine high putting this thing together.''

He just shook his head. ''I can't believe it.'' Then

he looked at Taylor, who was very quiet and wide-eyed. "Hey, Doc, what's wrong?"

She lowered her eyes, shook her head. "I was just thinking...how lucky you are, Wes."

"Heck, they aren't always this nice," he said. But he said it softly, and touched her face so she'd look at him again. Damned if there wasn't moisture in her eyes. "Most of the time they're a royal pain in the backside."

She smiled, but it was shaky. "I'd give an awful lot for a handful of pains like these two."

"Well, now, that's good to know," Wes said softly. And her eyes met his, widened a little, maybe in alarm, he wasn't sure. He'd dropped a pretty heavy-duty hint there. Was it too soon? Would he scare her off?

Jessi cleared her throat, and Taylor looked away. "You know," Jess said, "I've never seen the upstairs. Would you show me, Taylor?"

Taylor nodded and turned toward the stairs. As she led Jessi up, Wes sent his sister a warning glance. She read it, nodded to tell him she wasn't going to push or pry or meddle. But he figured he knew her well enough to know she would anyway.

When they were out of sight, Ben clamped a hand down on Wes's shoulder. "So? You gonna tell me what's going on between you two?"

Wes sighed. "Not much to tell. I'm nuts about her."

"But?"

He looked at his older brother whose shaggy blond mane made him look more rock star than cowboy. Oversize bulk concealing his grace. Unless you caught him at dawn, doing those tai chi moves out on the front lawn, facing the sunrise.

"She doesn't trust me, Ben. I lied to her once and I'm not sure she can get past it now."

Ben pursed his lips in thought. "A person can get past just about anything," he said.

"Not this."

"I know it might seem that way now, but..." His head came up. "Do you trust *her?*"

"Sure, I do."

"No. I mean, really trust her. Implicitly. Wes, the best way to win her trust is to show her that she has yours. All of it. You can't hold anything back, nothing at all, because as wary as she is, she's bound to sense it if you do. And if she senses you're keeping something inside, how's she gonna be able to trust you?"

Wes frowned as he thought about the things he'd shared with Taylor. And then about the things he hadn't told her. The site of Little Sparrow's grave. The things Turtle had told him today. What he planned to do tonight. He blinked at his brother. "Maybe you're right."

Ben nodded.

"What about you, brother?"

"What *about* me?"

Wes sighed. "I've been thinking about you a lot the last couple of days." He lowered his head. "I don't think I knew just how bad you must be hurting until..."

"Until you fell in love," Ben said.

Wes nodded. "Yeah. Before now I was just thinking you ought to be getting over...losing Penny. Now...I have to wonder if it's even possible."

Ben's head tipped upward, and he stared at some spot beyond the windows at Wes's back. "I don't think you ever get over losing the woman you love," he said. "You know, Penny and I knew she was dying when we fell in love. We both knew our time together was going to be short, so we filled it with…joy. Just sheer joy. It was the most incredible time of my life."

"But now?" Wes prompted.

Ben met his eyes. "The joy died with her." He drew a deep breath. "She made me promise that I would find someone else, eventually. She said she wouldn't be at peace if I went through the rest of my life alone, mourning her. So I said I would, but you know, I'm sore afraid that's one promise I won't be able to keep. And it's the only promise I ever made to Penny that I broke." He looked at the floor. "I've never told anyone about that before."

Wes nodded, understanding more than he ever had, how his brother must be feeling. "It's only been two years," he said. "Give yourself time, Ben. Don't feel guilty for loving your wife. She wouldn't have wanted that, either."

Ben's lips curved very slightly in a sad half smile. "I hadn't thought of it that way."

"There's plenty of time to keep that promise. Penny would understand."

"Yeah," Ben said. "I guess she would." Then he seemed to shake the deep sadness from his eyes, though Wes was sure it lingered in his heart. "Let's take a walk, have a look at that barn. I'm under orders to organize the volunteers into teams and assign each team to a project."

"Jessi again?"

"You really need to ask?"

"You're good for my brother," Jessi said.

Taylor paused in perusing what would have to be the master bedroom, and looked at Jessi quickly.

"He's always been such a loner," Jessi said. "But he's opening up. I can see it in his eyes. And I think it has a lot to do with you."

"I don't think—" Taylor began.

"He's in love with you. You know that, right?"

Taylor blinked and averted her face. "I think you're jumping to conclusions."

"No way. I know my brother. He's nuts about you. Gosh, Taylor, you mean he hasn't told you yet?"

Taylor licked her lips. "No."

"He will. You give him time, and he will."

"I'm not sure I…want him to."

Jessi touched Taylor's arm, drawing her gaze again. "You mean, you aren't sure how you feel about him?"

Taylor nodded. Then bit her lip, not wanting to insult Jessi by implying her brother wasn't up to her standards. "He's the most incredible man I've ever met," she said slowly, thinking her words through. "I mean…my…uncertainty—it has to do with me, not with Wes."

"It's his job to *make* you certain," Jessi said, nodding hard. "Apparently he hasn't done it very well, though." She frowned hard. "If he lets you slip through his fingers, I'll never forgive him."

That made Taylor smile. "I guess that's a compliment."

Jessi grinned at her, and ran a soothing hand over Taylor's hair. "You're beautiful, Taylor. And smart. You've touched Wes's heart when nobody else could…well, nobody besides the kids, at least. He's just mush when it comes to Bubba and little Maria. But with everyone else there's always this wall…I don't even think it's intentional on his part, but it's there."

Taylor nodded, listening intently.

"Besides," Jessi said. "You fit."

"I *fit?*"

"The family," Jessi told her. "You're like a missing puzzle piece. You come to that barn raising on Saturday and you'll see what I mean. You just fit. Trust me, I always know when someone belongs in our family."

Taylor tilted her head. "And you've never been wrong?"

Jessi made an exaggerated pout. "Well...once. About my brother Adam."

"Adam," Taylor said. "I haven't met him, have I?"

"Not yet," Jessi said. "A few years back Adam was engaged to his high-school sweetheart, Kirsten Armstrong. And I was so sure they were perfect for each other..." She shook her head.

"And what happened?"

Jessi sighed. "She didn't show up for the wedding. Left him standing at the altar and just didn't show. We found out later she'd eloped with the richest jerk in the county, a fellow old enough to be her father."

"God, how horrible for Adam," Taylor said.

"It was. Crushed him. Not long after that he headed to the East Coast. Works for a bank there and says he loves being a big-shot executive city slicker. But I know better. He only left so he'd never have to face her again. If he'd stayed, he might have run into her. Not that it's likely. She's like a hermit now. No one ever sees her."

"Still," Taylor said softly, "you were wrong once. Could be you're wrong this time, too."

"Nah," Jessi said. "I know better. Besides, who says I was wrong about Adam and Kirsten? I still feel like I had the right idea with those two, and I get the feeling there's going to be a sequel to that little episode in my brother's life.''

Taylor laughed. ''You really don't give up easily, do you?''

''I don't give up *at all.*''

Chapter 14

By the time Jessi and Ben finally finished inspecting the place, and—Wes thought—satisfying their curiosity about his relationship with Taylor, it was well after eleven. And he'd promised Turtle he'd come tonight for...

Well, hell, it sounded too far-fetched to think about, so he let the thought die. Taylor sat on the lowest step of the front porch, watching Ben's taillights fade in the darkness. Wes sat down beside her.

"So..."

She stiffened a little. It was awkward as hell. She was probably thinking he expected a little more of what she'd given him last night. But he knew better. He just didn't know how to tell her that.

She glanced at her watch.

"It's getting late," Wes said. "You want me to take you back?"

She blinked up at him. "You want to take me back?"

He smiled and decided to be honest with her. "Hell, no, Doc, I *want* to take you to bed. But it's too soon for that. Last night...last night happened, and I'll never stop bein' grateful it did. But the next time we make love, I'm hoping it will be with no walls still standing between us. No doubt in your pretty eyes."

As he spoke, she stared hard at him, first in confusion and then in some kind of wonder. "You're one special man, you know that? I must be nuts to be dragging my feet this way. Any other woman would—"

"I don't want any other woman," Wes said, and he ran the backs of his fingers down her cheek, as soft as down. "And I don't want you feeling pushed and unsure of me. Take your time, Taylor. Just don't write me off and walk away, okay?"

She lowered her head, swallowed hard. "The funding for this dig runs out on Sunday."

An icy fist gripped Wes's heart. He closed his eyes slowly. Took deep breaths. Counted to ten. Resisted the urge to grab her by the shoulders and tell her not to go. Shake her until she realized that his feelings were real. Beg her to listen to him for once. Instead he grated his teeth. "And you haven't decided what you're going to do about that yet," he said softly, but there was an edge to his words. Patience had never been his strong suit.

"No. I mean...I just don't know, Wes. There's another job waiting. I could call it off...to stay..."

"If you were sure there was something worth staying for," he finished for her.

She met his gaze, saying nothing. And she was feeling the stress; he could see it building in her eyes.

Telling herself to make up her mind, to either trust him or not trust him and just get it the hell over with. Scorning her own insecurities, when they were no more than the results of past heartbreak and his own foolish mistakes.

He didn't want her feeling all that pressure because of him. He drew a deep breath, let it out slowly, relaxed his muscles. "Then I guess I'd best work fast to convince you, hadn't I, Doc?"

She blinked up at him. "This isn't your problem, Wes. I keep telling you that."

"I disagree with you there. Hell, any Don Juan worth his salt would have swept you right off your feet by now. I'm obviously not going about this the right way."

She shook her head, but Wes leaned forward and kissed her mouth very gently. "You stop worrying and leave it to me, Doc. I got connections now. I'll figure things out."

Frowning, she tilted her head to one side. "What kind of connections are you talking about?"

He pursed his lips. Remembered what Ben had said about trusting her first. Nodded his decision. "Turtle says that wolf last night was really a spirit guide. He says it came to let me know I'm…er…a shaman."

Her eyes widened.

"He told me," Wes said slowly, "that what that means is up to me, but that above all, it means I can get in touch with…" He shook his head slowly. "I'm trying to be open about all this, but it feels a little silly."

"It's not silly," she said quickly. And she impulsively pushed his hair away from his face. "It's almost…holy."

"Yeah. And almost insane."

She smiled at him. "You're a little bit scared, aren't you?"

"Scared? Of course I'm not scared. For crying out loud, why would I be—?"

She met his eyes, lifting her brows.

Wes licked his lips. "Yeah, I guess I am."

"I would be, too. Actually I already am. I feel... wrapped up in all of this somehow."

He nodded, understanding why she felt that way. She was wrapped up in it all. "Turtle wants me to come over tonight. I told you he buckled and went back to the trailer, didn't I?"

She nodded. "It's awfully late. Will he still be up?"

"Yeah. Probably already knows exactly when I'll show." Wes shivered a little. Then started in surprise when Taylor slid her hand into his and squeezed, moving herself closer to his side.

"I shouldn't keep you, then. It sounds important."

"Sounds downright creepy."

"I'd offer to come along," she said softly, "but I have a feeling this is something you need to do alone."

He turned her head up with one hand on her chin. "You getting to be as perceptive as Turtle is?"

"As long as you don't start thinking *I'm* creepy." He touched her nose with his, and her eyes fell closed.

"If...if it gets too intense, and you want to talk," she said.

"I know where to find you, Doc." He kissed her then, lingeringly, and he thought maybe he was making some progress after all.

Because he'd told some of his secrets. But not all of them. There was one secret that simply wasn't his to tell.

* * *

When he arrived at Turtle's place, the old man had set up the tepee in the front lawn, and was sitting patiently outside it, waiting as if he'd never had any doubt Wes would show.

"What happened?" Wes asked when he approached the old man. "You get so attached to that thing you decided to keep sleeping in it?"

Turtle shook his head. "You are late."

"I was with Taylor. Sorry about that."

The old man only shrugged. "The night is good. Clear. There is still time." He got to his feet and looked at Wes as if waiting for him to do something.

Wes looked back, lifted his hands. "What?"

"The sweat lodge is ready for you, Raven Eyes. But you are not ready for it."

"I..."

"Take off your clothing." When Wes gaped, Turtle grinned and shook his head in silent amusement. "If you wish, I will turn my back, Raven Eyes, though if you are that painfully shy, this is the first time you've shown it."

"Very funny," Wes said, and he stripped right there on Turtle's front lawn, thanking his stars the trailer was on a deserted bit of back road. Turtle gave him a towel to anchor around his hips, and then held the tepee's flap open. And Wes felt the heat hit him in the face hard enough to knock him to his knees when he peeked inside. He saw the pit of glowing coals in the center of the tepee. Saw the woven mat where he was to sit, and ducked inside, feeling as if he'd just been shoved into an oven.

Turtle came in behind him, wearing no more than Wes was, and carrying a pail of water. As Wes sat silently, Turtle used a wooden ladle of some sort to spoon water over the red-hot coals, sending wafts of steam into the air. And Turtle kept this up until the steam became too thick to see through.

"This purifies the body," he explained, and he was a voice in the mists now. Invisible. Like a spirit. "You must prepare yourself before attempting to communicate with the spirits. Sit in silence. Empty your mind. Release every thought."

Wes tried to do that. It was hot as hell, but within a short time he forgot about that. His brain got hazy. He smelled something pungent and sweet, and wondered what sorts of mystical—quite possibly illegal—herbs Turtle had sprinkled over the coals to add their scents to the mix. He felt his hair growing damp, then clinging to him. His skin was soaked in the steam and his own sweat. The temperature was soaring in here, and still getting hotter. And time seemed to stop moving. He could no longer tell if he'd been in the tepee for a half hour or a half a day. And since he couldn't see in the mists, he closed his eyes and opened his mind. And the scent of the herbs got stronger and made him cough.

"Speak to the spirit of the wolf when he shows himself to you, Raven Eyes. Ask him your questions."

Wes moved his mouth to say he would, but no sound emerged. His head was swimming, and he thought it might be heat exhaustion. How long had he been in here, anyway? He opened his eyes, but couldn't see anything. Not Turtle or the tepee's sides or even those glowing coals. There was only the steam. Thick, swirling clouds of it, encompassing him. And as he strained to see through the stuff, it formed itself into a shape. The shape…of a wolf.

Wes blinked and looked again. Tried to breathe

deeply and calmly. But the apparition was still there, a wolf-shaped cloud with glowing red eyes that might have been embers…or might not.

"W-wolf spirit?" Wes asked slowly, uncertainly. A distant, ghostly howl was his answer. And the eyes glowed a little brighter.

Wes cleared his throat. Okay, he was here, he was hallucinating, he might as well run with it. "H-how can I win Taylor's trust without betraying the secrets of…of my people?" he asked. Because more than anything else, this was what he wanted to know.

The mist faded and blended into the rest, and the wolf was gone, and for a minute Wes thought he'd failed, and he closed his eyes in misery. But when he did, he saw a vision, just as clear as if he were watching a movie. He saw Wolf Shadow standing a long distance away, facing a woman who had to be Little Sparrow. They were surrounded by rocks and boulders, like that place where she rested. And as he watched, the camera of his mind seemed to zoom in closer and closer, until he could see the loincloth and bear-claw necklace Wolf Shadow wore, and Little Sparrow's beaded white dress of doe hide. And still closer his viewfinder moved, focusing in on Wolf Shadow's hands. They were moving, lifting something. A pendant on a thong, lowering it slowly around Little Sparrow's neck.

The turquoise heart! That was what it was. That was what he was seeing! But why? What did it mean?

Then, as if to answer his question, his point of view backed away from the hands, widening the angle until he could see only the two faces. But instead of those long-dead lovers, he was seeing his own face. And he was seeing Taylor's. And as the view broadened still further, he saw the clothing change to their own modern dress.

And then the vision faded until it was gone. He saw only darkness. He opened his eyes to see the steam thinning. And light coming through the sides and top of the tepee. And Turtle sitting silently on the opposite side of the pit of cooling stones.

He drew a deep breath, let it out and then started to get up, but the kinks in his back and legs almost put him back on the ground again. He stumbled to the flap, pushed it open and stepped outside.

Turtle was right behind him. "The wolf came to you. He spoke to you."

"Yeah," Wes said, eyeing the sun's alarming height in the sky. "I'm just not sure what he was telling me."

"Come. Clarity of mind is what you need now. You'll understand. If you let the understanding come on its own, rather than trying to force it." He clutched Wes's forearm and tugged him around behind the trailer to where the small stream ran shallow and fast.

Wes barely clung to his towel as he hurried along. His bare feet were not used to walking over pebbles and stones. But Turtle was ruthlessly dragging him along, and he stopped only when he reached a spot where the stream's flow had been partially blocked, resulting in a small pool of swirling, deeper water.

"Jump into the pool," Turtle instructed.

Wes slanted him a glance. "You're kidding, right? Turtle, do you have any idea how cold that water must be? It's still morning. And it's a fast-running stream, probably bubbling right out of some underground all but icy spring." Turtle crossed his arms over his chest and stared at him. "Turtle, I just spent half the night in hundred-degree heat. Now you want me to—hey!"

Too late. Turtle shoved Wes with one had, and snatched his towel away with the other. Wes hit the icy water hard, and went under. It felt as if his skin were being flash frozen. When he emerged again, Turtle was laughing out loud, but a second later the old man was splashing down beside him.

Wes shook his head and clambered out, reaching for his towel and wondering what sort of torture the old goat had in store for him next. Turtle came out, too. "Now your mind is clear," he said to Wes.

"Clear as ice water," he snapped. "Are we done with this little sadistic ritual of yours yet, pal?"

Turtle grinned, knotted his towel and nodded once. "For now," he said. "Now you must contemplate your vision. If you listen to the wolf, you will know what to do."

Wes shook his head, rubbed his arms and made his way around to the front lawn again to retrieve his clothes from the ground beside the tepee. "It'll take some thinking," he said.

"Then go and think," Turtle told him. "Time is short, you know."

Wes nodded. It was short, though he hadn't told Turtle that. He pulled on his clothes and headed to his truck. But the ideas were coming to him before he got a mile down the road.

When Taylor claimed to have seen Little Sparrow, she said it was like looking into a mirror. When Wes saw Little Sparrow, her image slowly changed into Taylor's beautiful face. Turtle said that Little Sparrow was Taylor's ancestor.

Now, following the same line of thinking, when Wes had seen what he thought was the ghost of Wolf Shadow, it had been…like looking into a mirror. He shivered, but continued following his train of thought. When he saw Wolf Shadow in the vision, that face had slowly changed into his own. Turtle said Taylor was to marry Wolf Shadow's descendant, and he refused to tell Wes who that man was. He'd even said it was something Wes had to learn for himself.

He jammed the brake pedal and came to a dusty stop in the middle of the dirt road.

For crying out loud. Was it *him?* Was *Wes himself* the last living relative of Wolf Shadow? Was *he* the one Turtle was so determined would marry Taylor?

He blinked in shock.

One way to find out. He gently eased up on the brake and drove, and decided that tomorrow he'd head into the town and the hall of records. They'd have something there. They must have. Why hadn't he ever checked this out sooner? It just hadn't occurred to him.

What if he was Wolf Shadow's descendant? What the hell would it mean?

Wes showed up at the site just as Taylor and the students were cleaning up the breakfast mess. And he looked…haunted. Pale and tired. Dark shadows ringed his eyes.

She stopped what she was doing and just looked at him. He'd stopped walking and stood there looking at her a little oddly. Taylor dropped the tin plate in her hands and went to him, touched his face. "You look exhausted."

"Haven't slept."

She narrowed her eyes, scanning his face. "Something happened last night…with Turtle."

He seemed to blink out of the state he was in then. "I can't…I can't talk about it, Doc. Not yet."

A prickle of suspicion danced up her spine and into her nape, but she shook it away. ''Is Turtle all right?''

He nodded.

''Are you?'' she asked him, because he really didn't look as if he was.

''Yeah. I just need some rest, is all.''

So she nodded. ''You should go home.''

''I'll tell you all of it, Taylor. As soon as I—'' he shook his head ''—figure out what it means.'' He touched her hair, searched her face and seemed to sense her doubts. ''I'm not keeping secrets from you, Taylor. I just...I'm not really sure what the hell happened. I need some time...I have to—''

''It's okay. I understand. You'll tell me when you're ready.'' She hoped her words carried more conviction than she was feeling. But all she could think was that he was keeping something from her...again.

His eyes blinked slowly closed. He forced them open again.

''Go home,'' she told him. ''Get some sleep.''

''I'll get some sleep,'' he said. ''But not at home.'' His tired eyes roamed her face for a moment. ''I need to be near you.''

She felt herself smile, and warmth pooled in the pit of her stomach. ''My tent, then?''

He nodded, stroked her hair slowly, then turned and walked toward the tents. He ducked into her tent and let the flap fall closed behind him. She stared at the tent after he'd disappeared inside, and then she walked quietly closer and peered in at him.

He'd crawled into her bed, and was hugging her pillow to him with his face nestled in its folds.

I need to be near you.

Taylor backed away in silence, and blinked at the sudden burning in her eyes.

Wes still hadn't talked to her about his late-night ritual with Turtle. That bothered Taylor. And it shouldn't. She told herself that over and over as they drove together to Wes's ranch for the barn raising his sister had arranged. It had been a personal thing; something deep had happened to him. She could sense that. But his reluctance to discuss it still gnawed at her gut. Another secret between them. God, how she hated them.

But why? Why was she letting this come between them this way? He'd been as attentive as ever. Helping out at the site, taking her to dinner at the ranch each night as they worked side by side to put the house in some kind of order. He'd gone out and bought the exact light fixture she'd described to him, and installed it in the living-room ceiling, then took her over there to show her.

She glanced up at the wagon-wheel chandelier and felt herself get soft inside again. So many things he did made her feel that way. She should love this man. She should get past her stupid mistrust and let herself love him. He was almost perfect.

Almost. It was that damned *almost* that kept getting in the way. If only he'd open up, tell her the things he was keeping from her.

And if only he'd do it before she finished up on the site and had to make a decision. One more day. That was all she had left. One more day. And she hadn't found anything at all on that entire chunk of Comanche land that indicated it was some kind of sacred ground. Nor anything that would make the tribe prosperous as the legend had foretold. No reason in the world they shouldn't sell it to Hawthorne and collect the money they so desperately needed. Nothing.

Nothing except a niggling feeling in her gut. And the Comanche elders couldn't take that to the bank, or use it to repair their children's schools or send them to college. Or fix up their homes or…or anything at all.

One more day.

Wes pulled the truck to a stop and killed the engine. Then he just sat there blinking at what he saw. Taylor pulled herself out of her thoughts and looked ahead, and saw people. So many people there didn't seem room for two more. Milling around like ants, each seemingly intent on doing his or her part. Men and women worked with crowbars to pry bad lumber from the barn walls. Two men in hard hats were on a ladder, stringing an electrical cable to the barn. Five or six were way up on that roof replacing the shingles. And a half dozen more were removing boards from inside the barn, carrying in fresh new lumber.

Taylor shook her head in wonder.

"I can't believe…" She looked at Wes when he stopped speaking, and saw his throat move as he swallowed hard.

"You're more well liked than you thought you were, I guess," Taylor told him.

Shaking his head, Wes opened the door and got out, and Taylor did likewise. The noise hit her at once, not unpleasant. But beautiful. The whir of circular saws, the steady thud of hammers, the loud grinding sound of the generator that provided electricity for the power tools, the ebb and flow of voices raised above the ruckus. One raised louder than the rest. One she recognized. She searched the crowd and spotted Jessi, hurrying from one group of workers to another, pointing and shouting directions above the din.

"That sister of yours should have been a drill sergeant."

Wes looked at Taylor, and she nodded toward Jessi. He spotted his sister and smiled. "I'll be..."

Elliot was up on the roof nailing shingles down. Garrett manned a saw, steadily cutting lumber on a pair of sawhorses. Lash took each cut board away, carrying it into the barn, while Ben was on Garrett's other side, hefting new lumber onto the horses to be sawed each time they were empty.

And there were others she recognized. The man from the little general store in town, manning several huge coffee urns on a picnic table. The bartender from that place with the funny name—La Cucaracha, wasn't it?—wielding a hammer. Three young men she thought must be brothers, tying bundles of shingles to a rope to be hauled up to the roof. Chelsea and several other women alternated between watching the children who played a few yards from the hub of activity, and working with the men.

Jessi spotted them standing there, and came rushing over. "Isn't this great?" she shouted above the noise. "Everyone in town is here. Paul Loomis dropped the boys off and headed back home. Said he had a vat of his special chili brewing to bring over later."

She was grinning ear to ear.

Wes just shook his head. Jessi tugged his arm. "Well, come on, brother, don't just stand there. They need you inside. Want to know how many stalls you want and how big the tack room should be and..." She dragged him a few steps, then turned. "You have some say in this, too, Taylor. Shake a leg, willya?"

Taylor met Wes's bemused gaze. And then he smiled at her, and she went to join him.

Trouble lights dangled from every possible appendage inside the barn, and the place smelled of sawdust. One man pulled Wes aside, and they leaned over a makeshift table made up of a stack of lumber, while the man pointed to some drawings on a large sheet of graph paper, and shouted questions.

Wes frowned at the designs, took the pencil, made a few scratches on the sheet, then turned and waved at her to come over. "What do you think?" he asked her. "These stalls could be smaller. We could get more in."

She blinked at him, and then saw in his eyes that he *wanted* her opinion. *Valued* it. That he felt she had a stake in this, just as his sister did. And she closed her eyes slowly, because he was assuming so much. Moving so fast. Acting as if this would be her place, as well as his, when she wasn't even sure…

"C'mon, Doc. I need you with me on this."

She met his eyes, went warm all over. Damn, he had that effect on her every time he glanced her way. Then he pushed the pencil into her hand, and she couldn't refuse him. She'd worry about later—later. She leaned over the drawings, pushing her hair behind her ear. "I think the bigger stalls are better," she said. Then she glanced up at the barn. "We can always add on later. Build a whole new section if we…"

She bit her lip. She'd said *we.* As if…as if…she'd already made up her mind.

But Wes was nodding hard. "She's right," he told the other man. "Forty stalls is plenty to start. It'll be years before we fill 'em all and need more."

Years. We.

She swallowed hard and tried to stop her heart from racing. He hadn't told her so, but Wes was making it pretty obvious he wanted her to be a part of his life…for a long time to come.

And yet…he was still keeping something from her. And she'd sensed he was even before his mysterious night with Turtle, so it had to be more than that. Would it always be this way? Her wondering what he had to hide? Her mistrusting him constantly? God, she couldn't live that way.

He smiled at her, and her heart tripped. "I'm going outside," she said. "The dust…" And she dropped the pencil atop the page and turned to leave him.

Since Wes was everywhere from the roof to the sawhorses, hopping from one project to another like a Mexican jumping bean, Taylor headed over to the area where Chelsea supervised the children. She couldn't be near him, couldn't listen to him asking how she wanted things in the barn, as if it were hers, too. Not yet. She wasn't ready for all this.

Chelsea sat on a blanket spread on the ground, where Jessi's little baby sat propped with pillows, gnawing a toy she held in her chubby hands. Little Ethan—Bubba to the Brands—ran and played with several other children, trying to catch grasshoppers. Chelsea patted a spot on the blanket beside her, and Taylor sat down.

Maria dimpled, crawled closer and climbed right into Taylor's lap.

"You look worried," Chelsea said. "Everything okay?"

Taylor stroked the baby's reddish hair, so like her mother's. It felt like corn silk against her palm. Maria leaned her head on Taylor's chest.

"I don't know," Taylor said. "I just..."

"He's moving too fast," Chelsea said.

Taylor lifted her head in surprise. How could she know...?

"He's my brother-in-law. I know him. He doesn't have a patient bone in his body, Taylor."

Taylor shook her head. "He's trying. Told me to take my time, that he wouldn't rush me. But then he keeps talking about this place in terms of 'we' and 'us' and it—"

"It's just a Freudian slip," Chelsea told her. "It's how he hopes it will be. It's on his mind, so it comes out in what he says, especially when he's not thinking. It's normal. Don't take it as pressure."

Taylor lowered her head. "How can I not? Chelsea, I don't want to hurt him, but—"

"But you're scared. And you're uncertain. And you're not ready to make a commitment to a man you still aren't sure you can trust."

Sighing, relieved to have it said so plainly for her, Taylor nodded. "Exactly."

"Wes is a big boy, Taylor. He can handle being hurt. It's yourself you have to think about now."

"That feels so selfish."

"Then be selfish. Look, you can't love Wes the way he wants you to until you take care of those old hurts you're still nursing inside. So by thinking of yourself, you're doing what's best for both of you."

That made perfect sense. So why did it feel so wrong? "I want to love him," she whispered.

"I have a news flash for you," Chelsea said softly. And Taylor looked up, met her eyes. "You already do."

"I—"

''I've seen the way you look at him, the way you two are together. God, to look at the two of you, I'd think you'd already been together for a hundred years.''

Taylor licked her lips. ''Sometimes…it feels like we have.''

''Take it slow, Taylor. Take your time. Wait until you're sure, and then—''

''But I don't have time.'' Taylor blurted it, and saw the alarm in Chelsea's eyes. She closed her own. ''I have to pack up and leave the site tomorrow. Time's up, Chelsea, and I have to decide what to do. I can't just hang around here waiting for the clouds to part and tell me. And I can't just leave Wes with the vague promise that I might come back someday. I can't do that to him.''

Chelsea's soft hand closed around Taylor's and squeezed. ''Then maybe it's time you stopped thinking, and let yourself feel. I think your answer is in your heart, Taylor. Maybe you should listen to what it's telling you.''

Trust herself, in other words. And trust Wes.

She bit her lip and wished to God that was as easy to do as it was to think.

Chapter 15

Wes's frustration ate at him all day. Even through the thrill he felt at seeing his barn being converted into the stable of his dreams. And the even bigger rush of seeing nearly everyone in town pitching in to help him the way they were.

There had been nothing to find in the hall of records. And then he'd checked with the tribal elders, but they'd had no information for him, either.

He barely saw Taylor through the morning. The work kept him so busy he couldn't get away to search for her. But at noon, when people started hauling coolers full of food out of their vehicles, and Paul Loomis arrived with a kettle of chili that outdid the sawdust for aroma, he found her.

And she smiled and put on a very nice show for him, but he saw through it. She was thinking about leaving him. And he couldn't lose her. He couldn't lose her now.

He started toward her, when a heavy hand fell on his shoulder. And he turned to see his brother Ben, looking as worried as Wes felt.

"Did you do what I told you?"

Wes blinked and drew a blank. "What did you tell me?"

"Little brother, you can be dense as solid granite. What did I tell you?" He shook his shaggy head. "That if you want her to trust you, you have to show her that you trust her. Completely. Implicitly. Prove it to her beyond any doubt. Now, dammit, it doesn't look to me like you've done that, have you?"

Wes lowered his head, shook it slowly. "No. I guess I haven't."

"And why the hell not?"

"Look, Ben, if I thought it was that simple, I'd—"

"It *is* that simple. Damn, Wes, you gonna let her walk away? She's the best thing that ever happened to you, and you know it."

Glancing at Taylor again, Wes nodded. "I know it."

"Something's eating at her, Wes. You gotta chase those shadows of doubt out of her eyes once and for all. No matter what it takes, you have to do it."

"But—"

"No buts."

"Ben, it's not that easy. If I tell her—"

"Then you *are* keeping something from her." Ben shook his head. "And here I thought she was wrong about that."

"It's not my secret to tell," Wes said, and he felt his heart breaking with every word.

"Then you're gonna lose her," Ben told him. He sighed heavily. "Wes, I'm telling you, it's not worth it. I lost the only woman I ever loved, so you can take my word on that. Hell, I'd shout government secrets from the rooftops if I thought it could bring Penny back to me.''

His voice broke a little, and Wes's heart broke with it for his brother's pain.

''No stupid secret is worth losing her, Wes. I guarantee it. And I'll tell you something else. If you really did love her, you'd trust her. And if you really trusted her, you'd know your deep dark secret would be safe in her hands.'' He nodded toward where Taylor was standing. ''Safe as little Maria is there.''

Wes followed Ben's gaze and saw Taylor snuggling Maria in her arms, sitting down at the picnic table with the baby on her lap, lifting a spoon to eager lips.

''Damn,'' he whispered.

''Looks awful good with the baby in her arms, doesn't she, little brother?''

Wes had to avert his face. Hot moisture burned his eyes, and he blinked it away.

''Don't do it, Wes. Don't lose her. You'll never forgive yourself if you do.'' Ben clapped Wes on the shoulder one last time, then wandered over to the picnic area to join the others.

And Wes knew his brother was right. If he lost Taylor, he'd never forgive himself. Maybe it was time he took Turtle's advice, and listened to the visions. Let his gut or his guide or whatever the hell you wanted to call it, tell him what to do, and stop thinking so much. He'd seen that vision or hallucination or whatever it was. And instead of believing in it, he'd gone out looking for proof of what it had shown him. Well, it was too late for proof, and maybe he didn't need any. Maybe he should just believe. Just trust. Trust the vision.

Trust Taylor.

He swallowed hard. Okay. Then he'd trust her.

Wes sat with her as they ate lunch, but it was all too brief an interlude. Within minutes the men were swarming over that barn like bees on a honeycomb, and the women were collecting the dishes and putting away the food.

Wes got up to leave, but then he leaned down over her, his lips brushing her ear, and he whispered, "You don't have to worry about this anymore, Doc. I think I finally have it figured out."

She turned quickly, frowning up at him. He only planted a kiss on her mouth, and then smiled, and turned to join the workers.

Taylor frowned after him, wondering what on earth he could mean. He'd said he couldn't talk about what had happened that night with Turtle until he'd figured it out. Was that it, then? He was ready to talk to her about it?

And was that going to make the difference? Would she get past this stupid suspicion that he was still hiding things from her then? Would it be enough?

She was a fool. The biggest fool in Texas if it wasn't. But she also knew in her heart that Chelsea was right. She had to be sure. They'd both be miserable unless she was.

By the time the sun went down, the wiring work on the barn was complete, and the men who'd done it had headed into the house to check out the wiring in there. The stalls were in place, the tack room half-finished, the roof brand-new and leak free. People were beginning to pack up and head home.

''Tomorrow we can slap a coat of paint on this baby,'' one man announced loudly.

''Plumbing still needs doing. An all-day job,'' someone else said.

The three men came out of the house nodding and talking among themselves, and one called out to Wes. ''Wiring in the house isn't bad at all. Couple of places need repairing, but it shouldn't take long. And you need a new pump. It's shot, but once you get one, and a hot-water heater, that place'll be darned near perfect.''

Jessi sniffed. ''Won't be perfect till we get some paint and wallpaper in there, and patch those holes in the plaster.''

Wes made a face at his sister. ''Women. I suppose it won't be livable until we hang lace curtains and line the shelves with knickknacks, either.''

''That's right, brother.'' Jessi winked at Taylor. ''But I think we girls can handle that end of things, when your budget allows.'' Then she came closer. ''How is the money holding up, Wes? All this lumber and stuff must've cost a fortune.''

''There's still enough left for that pump and water heater,'' he told her. ''You saved me a bundle, setting this up. You know what it would have cost me to hire someone to get all this done?''

She smiled and lifted her chin. ''That's what baby sisters are for.'' And she smiled at Taylor. ''My brothers hate to admit it, but they couldn't get along without me if their lives depended on it.''

Lash came forward and slipped an arm around her shoulders. ''Neither could I,'' he said, and dropped a kiss on top of her head.

But Wes was frowning. ''I think we'll be a little

short of funds for lace curtains and wallpaper, though. Whatever's left has to go for breeding stock." He smiled softly. "Mares," he said. "Lots of mares."

Taylor opened her mouth...then she snapped it shut again. She'd very nearly blurted that she had savings enough to decorate the entire house. Damn. She was falling into Wes's fantasy again. Thinking as if the place were her home, as well as his.

Instead she said, "You could board a few head, bring in some cash that way. You'll have empty stalls for a while. And you could always give riding lessons on the side."

Garrett came forward then, and the big man was holding Bubba's tiny hand in his, and taking small steps so the little guy could keep up. That toddler looked up at Garrett with sheer worship in his eyes. "Wes, you know you still own a share of the Texas Brand. One-sixth of the place is yours."

"And if you're thinking I'll keep taking one-sixth of the profits when I'm not working full-time on the ranch, you're nuts, big brother."

Garrett shrugged. "You could let me buy your share of the place."

Wes blinked, and Taylor could see he hadn't even considered it before. "I don't know—"

Garrett nodded toward the house. "Place needs paint," he said. "Roofing. And those front steps need replacing, and the porch rail." He met Wes's eyes. "You think it over, and we'll talk, okay?"

Cars were pulling away now, engines purring or growling, headlights flashing over their faces. Only the Brands remained here now. The real Brands. Taylor felt like an outsider.

Then Wes slipped an arm around her shoulders, and

she got the overwhelming feeling that she belonged right here, at his side, surrounded by this huge family.

"I'll think about it," Wes said. "Thanks, Garrett." Then he squeezed Taylor closer. "We'd best go now, though. I got something needs doing."

He met Ben's eyes. Ben nodded encouragement, told him without a word to do whatever it took. And Wes swallowed hard and prayed his trust in Taylor would be well placed.

Wes took Taylor back to the Texas Brand, instead of the site. As they pulled in beneath the giant arch, she asked him why, but he only shook his head and kept driving.

He pulled the truck to a stop near the stables, and when she got out, he drew her into the musty dimness, flicking on lights as he went. He released her hand and hurried to the back, disappearing into what must be the tack room and returning with two saddles, and a pair of bridles over his arm.

"Feel like a moonlight ride?" he asked her. But the way he said it, the way he looked, she got the feeling he was asking for a lot more. That her answer was vital.

"Wes, what's this about?"

"It's about everything, Doc. Just come with me. Trust me." He dropped the saddles to the floor and came closer, taking one of her hands in both of his. "Trust me, Taylor. Just this once."

And she trembled. But she nodded. "All right."

Wes seemed to sag in relief, but only for a moment. Then he was drawing a horse from a stall, saddling it and moving on to ready a second mount for her. Side by side they led the horses from the stable, and Taylor kept searching Wes's face for some hint of what he was up to. But he showed nothing. So good at hiding things. Damn.

He held her horse while she mounted, and then climbed aboard his own. "This way," he said. And he dug in his heels, setting off at a fast pace. Breaking into a gallop across the fields. Taylor kicked her horse into action, falling into the familiar rhythm of horse and rider, and they raced through the night, her hair flying behind her. It was exhilarating, and for a while she forgot to worry about her feelings for Wes, her inability to trust him, his secrets, and just lost herself in the heady thrill of racing heedlessly through the darkness.

She rode up to his side and together they ran, and she wished they could be like this, this carefree and wonderful together, for always. But then she realized where they were heading, and all the old questions and doubts crept in again. Gnawing at her brain like hungry rodents.

They skirted the site, and ended up in the cool desert, and Wes drew his horse in a bit, slowed to a walk.

"Is it Turtle?" Taylor asked, her horse close beside Wes's. "Is he back out here with that raggedy tepee again?"

"No. Turtle's safe in his trailer. It's just you and me tonight, Doc."

"Wes, this is really throwing me. Can't you tell me what—?"

"I have a present for you." He fumbled with something at his waist for a moment. It was too dark to see what. But seconds later he reached out and handed her a rawhide thong, and she recognized it. He'd taken it from that medicine pouch he always wore tied either to a belt loop or around his neck. As she took it from him, he stuffed the pouch into a pocket.

Taylor held the thong, looked at it and shook her head. "I don't understand."

"You will," he said. And then he fell into silence. There was only the gentle night wind blowing, rippling the horses' manes, and the steady soft sound of hooves on arid ground. And then the rocky hill rose up in the darkness just ahead, and Wes pulled in front of her. Single file was the only way to pick through the boulders. He was moving up higher, not down toward the spot where Turtle had set up his deathwatch such a short time ago. It seemed as if it had been much longer since that night. The night she'd spent wrapped in Wes's strong arms. Making love to him.

His horse's tail twitched, and pebbles clattered underfoot. And then Wes stopped, and he climbed down, twining the reins around the limb of a scraggly tree. He came to her, and helped her down, as well, leading her horse up beside his, tying it there. He took her hand.

"I figured something out today," he said. "Took a lot of help. Turtle's been trying to tell me, I think, but he wanted me to see it for myself. Ben…well, Ben's a little more blunt about these things."

Taylor drew a breath. Let it out slowly. Waited. He was going to tell her something. Something important. Please, she thought, let me be right. Let him open up to me, finally.

Wes turned, drawing her close to his side, and walked a few steps farther. "You told me once, Doc, that your career means everything to you."

"It has," she said. *Until now.* But she didn't say that last part aloud.

''The sacred ground on this site isn't meant to be invaded,'' he told her. ''If it is, its magic will die. But if it's treated with the respect it should be...then The People will prosper because of it. That's the way the legend goes, anyway.''

She nodded. ''I know all that, Wes. But there is no sacred ground. I haven't found anything to indicate—''

''There is.''

She frowned and tilted her head, searching his face.

''There are only two people alive who know where, Doc, but there is a magical place here. Turtle knows. But as shaman he was sworn to keep the secret, to keep the ground from being desecrated by outsiders. But he was torn, because unless the spot was discovered, the elders were determined to sell this property. That was why he wanted me to play the Wolf Shadow game with you. To convince you there was magic here without letting you get close enough to actually find it. But I'm taking that decision out of his hands, because... because I can't lose you now.''

The breath was knocked from her lungs. She didn't know what to say. And then something occurred to her that hadn't before. ''I'm Comanche,'' she said softly. ''Why would it desecrate the ground if I discovered the site?''

''Because your career is your life. And a find like this one could make your career more than it ever was. You could get backing, dig it all up, put the artifacts on display in some white man's museum.''

She lowered her head very slowly. Did Turtle really believe she would do that? And then she blinked. Maybe he was right. Because maybe she would have, a few short weeks ago. But she wasn't the same person she had been. She was Comanche now.

Her head came up quickly as she replayed all Wes had said. ''You said there were two people who knew where this sacred place was.'' And Wes nodded. She licked her lips. ''Are you the other one?''

He stared hard into her eyes, and she knew he was opening his soul to her at this moment. ''I found it that night Turtle was out here. I was looking for firewood, and...''

''And that's what you've been keeping from me.'' And why did it hurt so much? Why did it sting to know he didn't trust her any more than Turtle did?

''Give me the thong,'' he said softly. And she did, not looking up or meeting his eyes.

But then he knelt on the ground and pulled some stones away from the base of a boulder. And he reached inside. Taylor stood riveted as he fumbled in the darkness. Then he rose and turned to face her. And he lifted the thong, and she saw the turquoise heart, roughly hewn, but all the more beautiful for its crudeness. As she sucked in a breath, Wes draped the pendant around her neck.

''Wes...?''

''That night I spent with Turtle, I had a vision, Taylor. And this is what I saw. I'm not keeping anything from you anymore. Because I trust you. And everything inside me is telling me that this is the only way to make you see that. I trust you, Taylor. This is the site you've been looking for. It can make you famous, if you want it to.''

''My God,'' she whispered. ''Then it's all true. This is...this is where Little Sparrow is buried. This is her necklace.''

''It's your necklace. I think...I think that's what the vision was trying to tell me.''

"But…but this…this ground…the legend…"

Wes shrugged. "What you choose to do with this spot is up to you now, Taylor. The elders gave you permission to dig here, and you can excavate most of this spot before your time runs out tomorrow. Or you can leave it, as the legend says it should be left."

Taylor looked at the ground, shook her head slowly.

"I can only tell you one thing for sure," Wes said, and he reached out to trace the shape of the heart where it rested on her chest with a forefinger. "No matter which choice you make, right or wrong, Doc, I'm gonna be right here. Because I'm in love with you." He paused, touched her face and shook his head in wonder. "I love you, Sky Dancer." He bent closer, kissed her gently and then he straightened and turned, began walking back toward the horses.

"Wes."

He stopped, his back to her, and stood motionless, waiting.

"I feel like I know her," she said softly. "It's like she's with me, like she's been with me all my life. I just…never let myself feel it. Didn't even know how to let myself feel it."

Wes turned, and she knew he could probably see the tears in her eyes. But she didn't care. She could trust Wes with her tears.

"No one is going to be digging on this site. I'll make the elders understand that they can't sell it to Hawthorne. But I won't betray Little Sparrow for the sake of my career." She touched the necklace, felt it warming in her palm. "And I won't betray you."

As he stood, maybe shocked motionless, maybe unsure, she sniffed. She hadn't told him how she felt for him. Not yet. But first…

She lifted the necklace over her head, and bent to lovingly tuck it back into the place where it had been. Bracing one hand on the boulder to steady herself, she looked for the hole. But then she paused, because something slick and wet was coating her palm. She straightened fast, turning her hand, trying to see what it was.

"Taylor?" Wes came to her. "What is it?"

Taylor drew her hand to her face and sniffed at the substance. She shook her head, and took Wes's hand in her clean one, drawing it forward until his fingertip touched the wetness on the stone.

"What the…?"

Wes rubbed his forefinger with his thumb, and then he sniffed, as well.

And then his eyes widened. "It…it smells like…"

"Oil." They said it together. And then they turned, bending nearly double to trace the trickle of black gold back to its source. And they found it, uphill, nearly three hundred yards from the site of Little Sparrow's grave, a tiny chasm between the boulders where the small stream of liquid seemed to disappear into the earth.

Taylor looked up at Wes. "Thank God it's not too late," she said, beaming. "The People still own this land. If this is what we think it is, they…" She shook her head slowly.

"Hawthorne must have known about this," Wes said slowly. "It's bugged me all along that he'd make such a generous offer on this hunk of ground." He looked at Taylor and smiled. "Do you know what this is going to mean to the Comanche people here?"

And a voice came from behind Wes, an aged, wise

voice. ''It means, Raven Eyes, that the prophecy is being fulfilled.''

Wes turned fast, and Taylor went forward to stand close beside him. His arm came around her shoulders as Turtle stood smiling at them.

''How the heck did you get up here, Turtle?'' Wes asked. ''What are you doing here?''

''By preserving Little Sparrow's resting place, you two have ensured the fulfillment of Wolf Shadow's promise. The People will know prosperity now.'' He nodded slowly. ''You did well to listen to the visions, Raven Eyes. I knew you would.''

''I'm glad someone did,'' Wes said. ''But, Turtle, you could have saved us all a lot of grief if you'd just told us about this from the start.''

Turtle blinked slowly. ''That I could not do. Sky Dancer had to come here. She had to find herself in the spirits of her ancestors, and to know who she is. And you, Raven Eyes, you needed to find your own way. To tell you would have accomplished nothing. And now there is only one part of the prophecy left unfulfilled. The spirits of Wolf Shadow and Little Sparrow are still not at peace. Not until they are united. And, Sky Dancer, this part of the prophecy, only you can fulfill.''

Taylor's stomach clenched. She closed her eyes, lowered her head. ''You mean, you want me to marry this man you have chosen for me...the last descendant of Wolf Shadow. That's what you're saying, isn't it, Turtle?''

When she dared open her eyes and look at him, Turtle was nodding slowly.

''I'm so sorry,'' she whispered. ''But I can't.''

Wes started to say something, but Turtle held up a hand. "Tell me why," Turtle said.

Taylor drew a deep breath. She turned and looked into Wes's eyes, and whispered, "Because I'm in love with someone else. There's only one man I want, Turtle. Only one man...and for the life of me I can't imagine why it's taken me so long to realize that."

Wes's hands came to rest in her hair, stroking it slowly as he searched her face, unashamed tears brimming in his eyes. "Taylor?"

"I love you, Wes," she whispered. "Tell me I didn't wait too long. Tell me it's not too late."

His lips trembled as he lowered his head to kiss her. And when he lifted his head again, he whispered, "I'd have waited a lifetime, if that's what it took."

Turtle came closer. She hadn't heard him approach, so it startled her when his powder-soft hand closed on hers, and gently took the pendant away. Holding her to his side, Wes turned to face Turtle.

The old man held the pendant up before him, looking at it, eyes gleaming. "There is no need to put the pendant back into the ground, Sky Dancer. Because it is yours to wear. As your ancestor, Little Sparrow, wore it before you."

But he didn't hand it to her. Instead he pushed the heart into Wes's hands. "And yours to give to the woman you love, Raven Eyes. Just as your ancestor, Wolf Shadow, gave it before you."

Taylor blinked twice, and then sucked in a breath. "You mean...?"

Turtle nodded in a very turtlelike way. And then he simply vanished. Before her eyes. She emitted a startled cry, and scanned the place where he'd been standing only a second ago. But he was gone. And when she met Wes's eyes, she saw that they were wide…but accepting.

He put the pendant to his lips, kissed it reverently and then lowered it over her head as he had before. "Marry me, Sky Dancer," he whispered. "Share that ranch with me. Share everything with me—our lives, our children…*everything*."

"Yes," she told him. "Yes."

Epilogue

Wes stood on a rocky hilltop, holding Taylor's hands in his. Beyond them a wrought-iron-filigree rail surrounded the sacred resting place of Little Sparrow. And in the distance the beginnings of an oil rig loomed like a shadow. But the work on that had stopped for today.

His family surrounded him, smiling, crying some. He'd cried once or twice himself today, and maybe would again before it was over. He'd never dreamed he could be this happy, love this deeply, feel this much.

Taylor wore a doeskin dress, bleached white and lined with fringe and beads. And the turquoise heart hung around her neck. And Turtle recited words in his native tongue above them, and they both answered in the same language, which he'd been teaching to them, along with so many other things.

And then Wes held Taylor close in his arms, and he kissed her as if he would never stop. And she kissed him back just as deeply. And when Wes lifted his head away, he saw something, far off in the distance. And he touched her face and pointed, and she looked and saw it, too.

The two lovers, twined in one another's arms, as thin and transparent as mist, and as real as the ground under their feet. From somewhere beyond them a wolf yipped and then howled in a long, joyous wail. And then the phantom shapes vanished, and a warmth like nothing he'd ever known settled over Wes's heart.

"They're together," Taylor whispered. "They've finally found each other."

"And so have we, Sky Dancer," Wes whispered. "So have we."

* * * * *